GALACTIC HOT DOGS™

COSMOE'S WIENER GETAWAY

BY MAX BRALLIER
ILLUSTRATED BY RACHEL MAGUIRE
& NICHOLE KELLEY

CREATED BY MAX BRALLIER

ALADDIN
New York   London   Toronto   Sydney   New Delhi

ALADDIN

An imprint of Simon & Schuster Children's Publishing Division

1230 Avenue of the Americas, New York, NY 10020

First Aladdin paper-over-board edition May 2015

Copyright © 2015 by Pearson Education, Inc.

All rights reserved, including the right of reproduction in whole or in part in any form.

ALADDIN is a trademark of Simon & Schuster, Inc., and related logo is a registered trademark of Simon & Schuster, Inc.

For information about special discounts for bulk purchases, please contact Simon & Schuster Special Sales at 1-866-506-1949 or business@simonandschuster.com.

The Simon & Schuster Speakers Bureau can bring authors to your live event. For more information or to book an event contact the Simon & Schuster Speakers Bureau at 1-866-248-3049 or visit our website at www.simonspeakers.com.

Designed by Rachel Maguire and Dan Potash

The text of this book was set in Good Dog.

Manufactured in the United States of America 0315 FFG

10 9 8 7 6 5 4 3 2 1

Library of Congress Control Number 2014946268

ISBN 978-1-4814-2494-3 (POB)

ISBN 978-1-4814-2495-0 (eBook)

For Alyse—endlessly supportive, endlessly encouraging, endlessly loving, endlessly cute. Also Luke, Leia, Han, and the rest of the gang—where would I be without you?!

—M. B.

To the trifecta. Nichole—this book couldn't have been completed without her. She totally doesn't want this kind of attention, but she deserves it. My cat, Becky—she isn't much of a reader, but I'll show her this page so she can sleep on it. Jon—this will be the first time when reading a dedication that it wasn't for someone else. Exciting! ^_^

—R. M.

MEGA-DOG IN THE BUN!

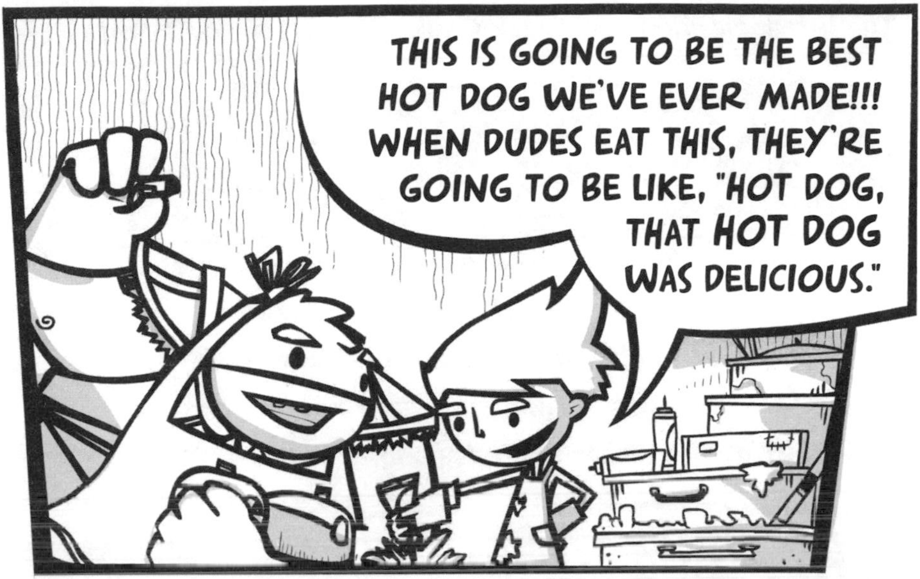
THIS IS GOING TO BE THE BEST HOT DOG WE'VE EVER MADE!!! WHEN DUDES EAT THIS, THEY'RE GOING TO BE LIKE, "HOT DOG, THAT HOT DOG WAS DELICIOUS."

"Two more dashes of Jupiter Jolt sauce," my buddy Humphree says as he piles on the ingredients.

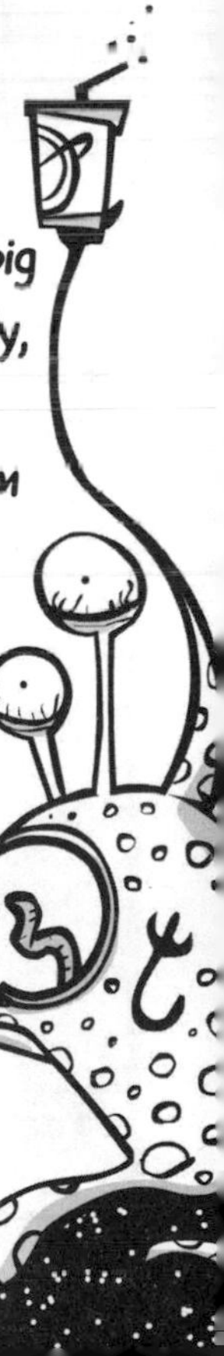

That's me, Cosmoe, the little human from Earth with the big funky hair. I own a flying hot dog truck with my best buddy, Humphree (he's the big, alien-looking guy). Why am I here, in space? Well, that's a story for another time . . . Why am I here *today*? We're on Space Port Funketoun, cooking up a Mega-Dog for the Intragalactic Food Truck Cook-Off.

"Dude! This dog is the size of a Jeep!" I exclaim.

"What's a Jeep?" Humphree asks.

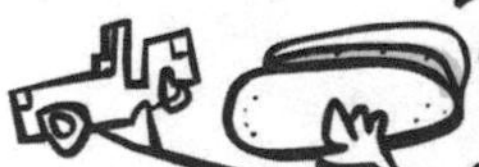

Ugh. Sometimes I forget I'm the only one around here from Planet Earth. "Never mind! C'mon, let's get this thing to the cook-off!"

The Intragalactic Food Truck Cook-Off is a major event.

FLYING FOOD TRUCKS COME FROM ALL ACROSS THE GALAXY TO SERVE UP CRAZY TREATS FOR THE QUEEN.

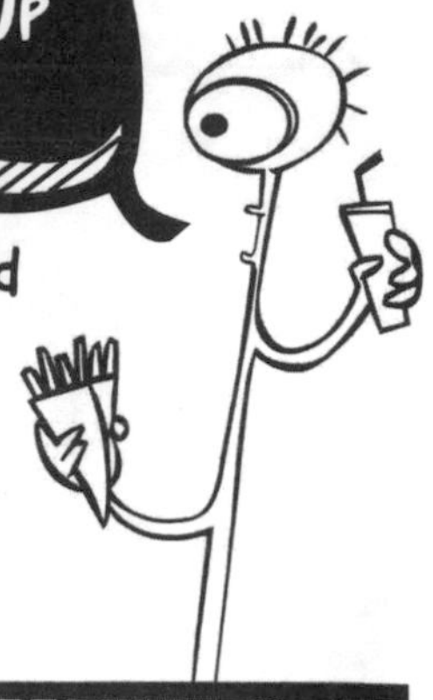

Our truck is the *Neon Wiener*, and it's docked close to the market where the contest goes down. Sweet scents from a thousand different exotic dishes waft through the air.

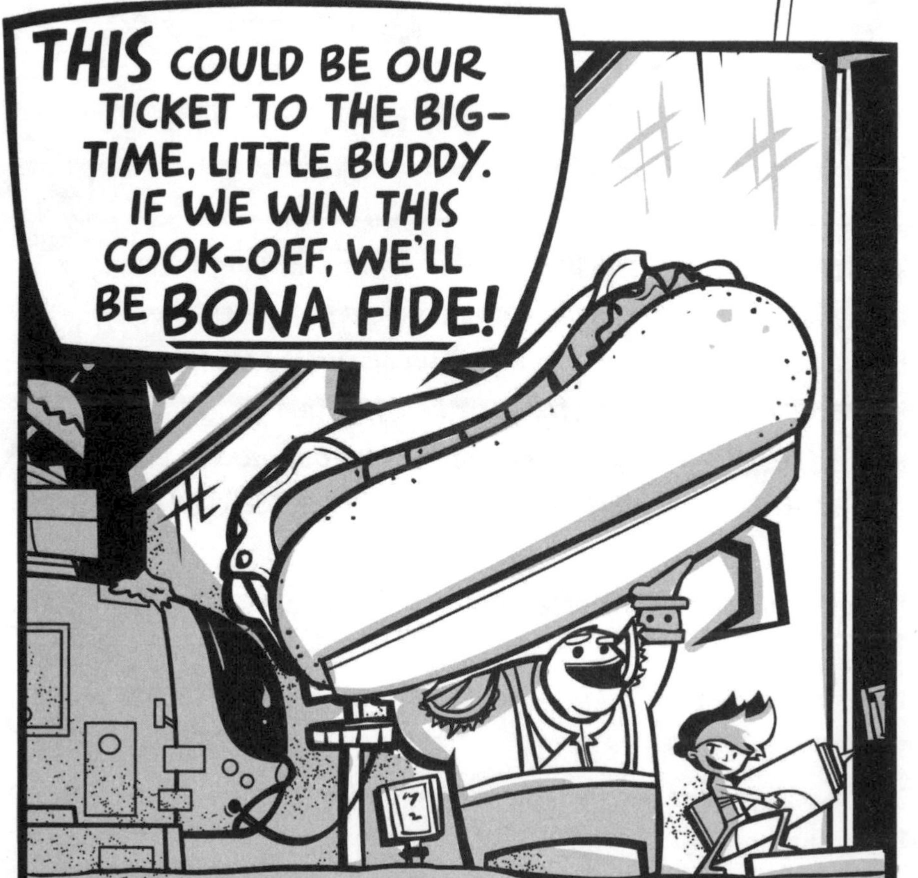
THIS COULD BE OUR TICKET TO THE BIG-TIME, LITTLE BUDDY. IF WE WIN THIS COOK-OFF, WE'LL BE BONA FIDE!

Evil Queen Dagger judges the cook-off. She's royalty and she's mega-rich, so she has, like, **37 MILLION** soldiers and spies working for her. And if she doesn't like your food, she just might disintegrate you . . .

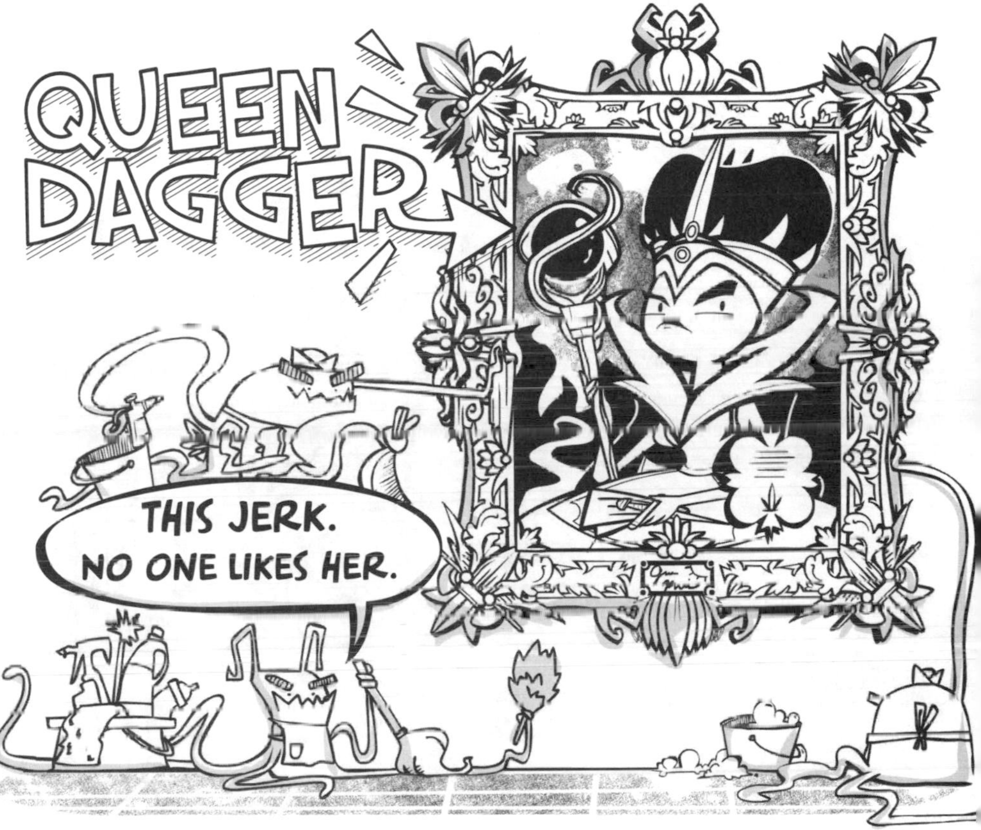
QUEEN DAGGER
THIS JERK. NO ONE LIKES HER.

"You think Evil Queen Dagger will like the Mega-Dog?" I ask Humphree.

Humphree can tell I'm nervous. He's observant like that. "Of course she'll like it," he says. "No one's going to have anything nearly as good as this. I doubt there will be any competition at all—"

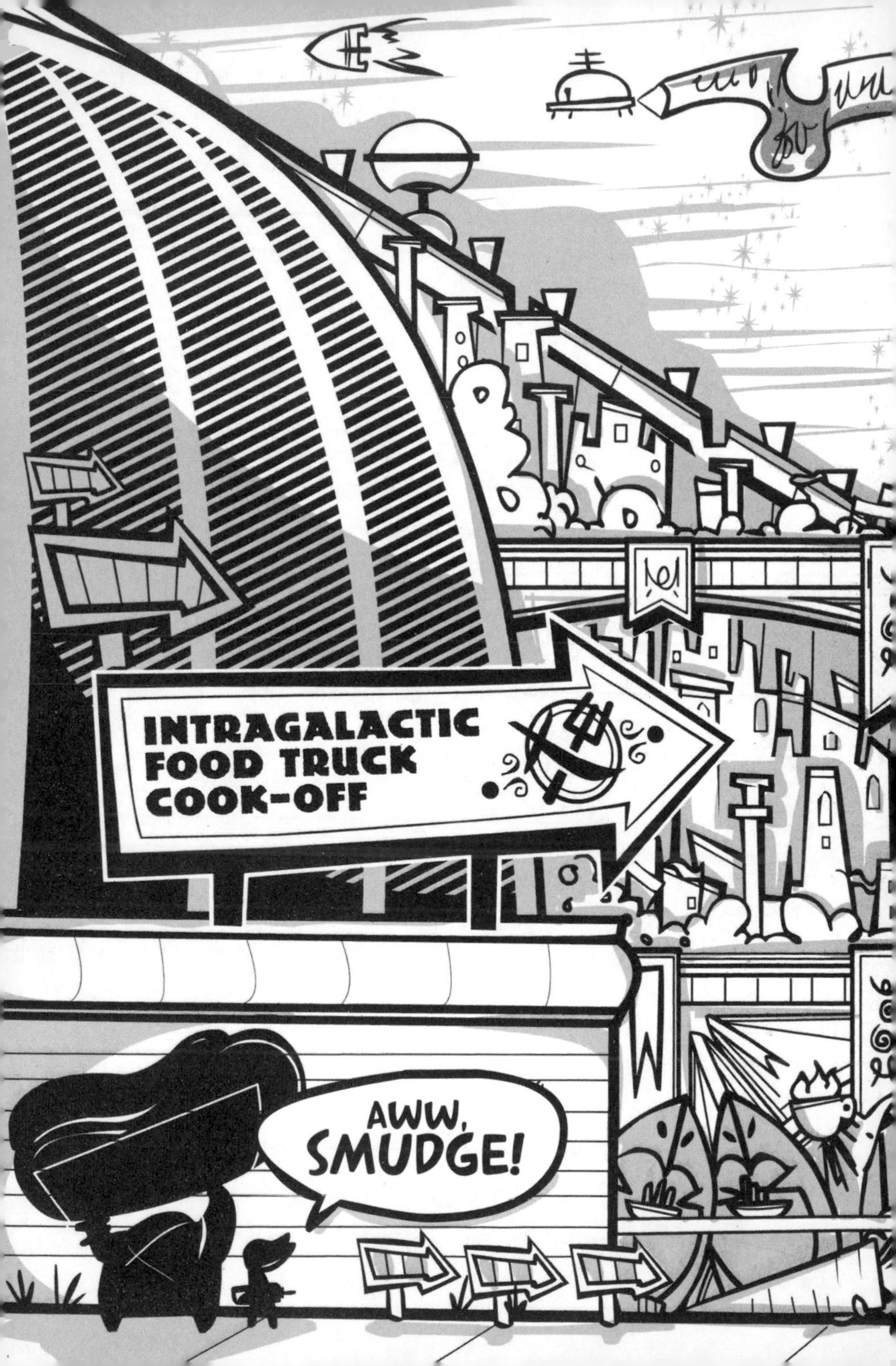
INTRAGALACTIC
FOOD TRUCK
COOK-OFF
AWW, SMUDGE!

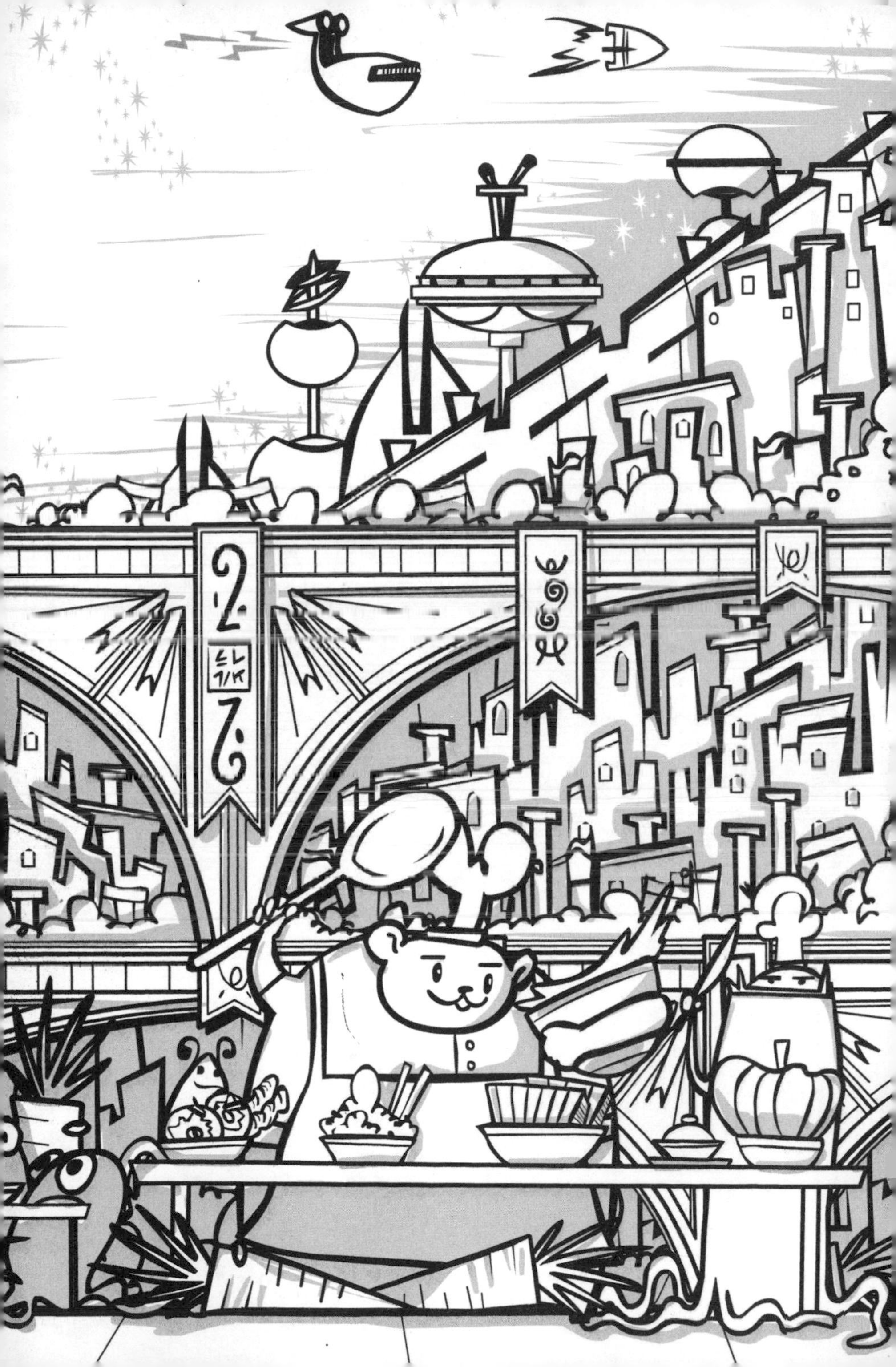

"Dude, don't stress it," Humphree says. "As long as we have the Mega-Dog, we can't lose. And the Mega-Dog isn't going anywhere, right?"

WRONG!

JUST THEN—

"That hooded fiend nabbed our Mega-Dog!" I shout.

Humphree doesn't say anything. He just makes his ol' rumbling noise.

Ever since Humphree retired from the pirate life, he's been a pretty mellow, chilled-out guy. But when he gets really mad, he starts making this rumbling noise and— whoo boy, watch out—you don't want to mess with him. I mean, look at his stats:

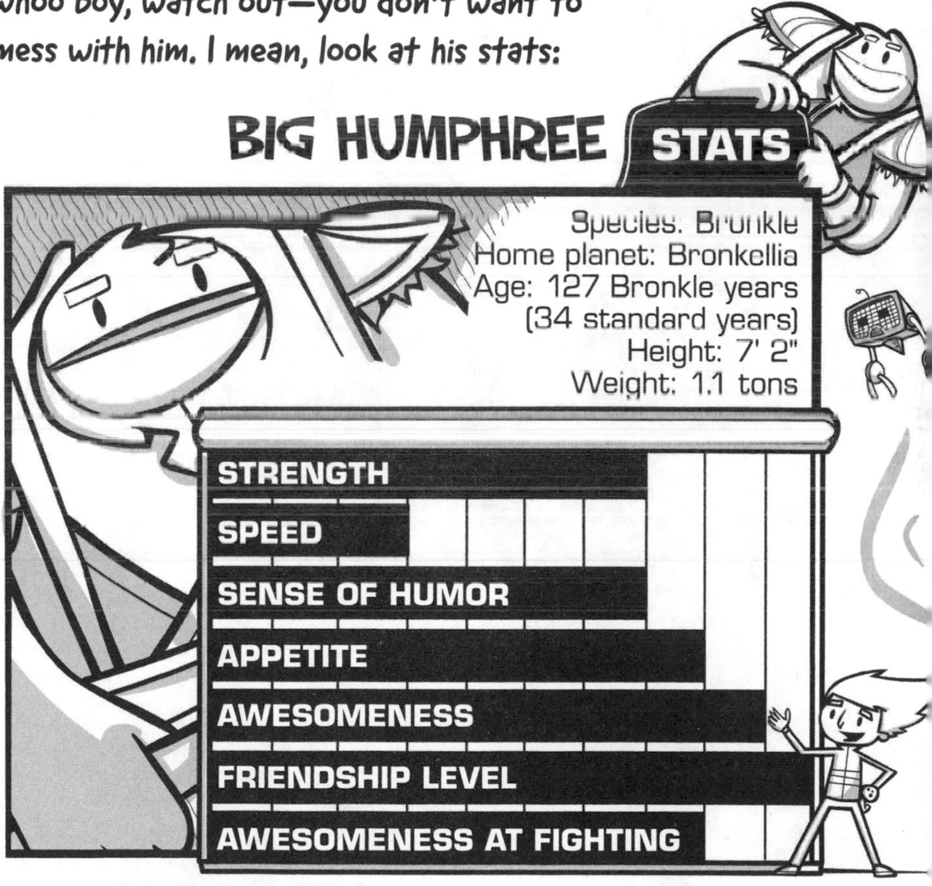

BIG HUMPHREE STATS

Species: Bronkle
Home planet: Bronkellia
Age: 127 Bronkle years
(34 standard years)
Height: 7' 2"
Weight: 1.1 tons

STRENGTH						
SPEED						
SENSE OF HUMOR						
APPETITE						
AWESOMENESS						
FRIENDSHIP LEVEL						
AWESOMENESS AT FIGHTING						

"Humphree . . ." I say, trying to remain cool and calm. "Just relax. Don't get all crazy on me. This is a job for—"

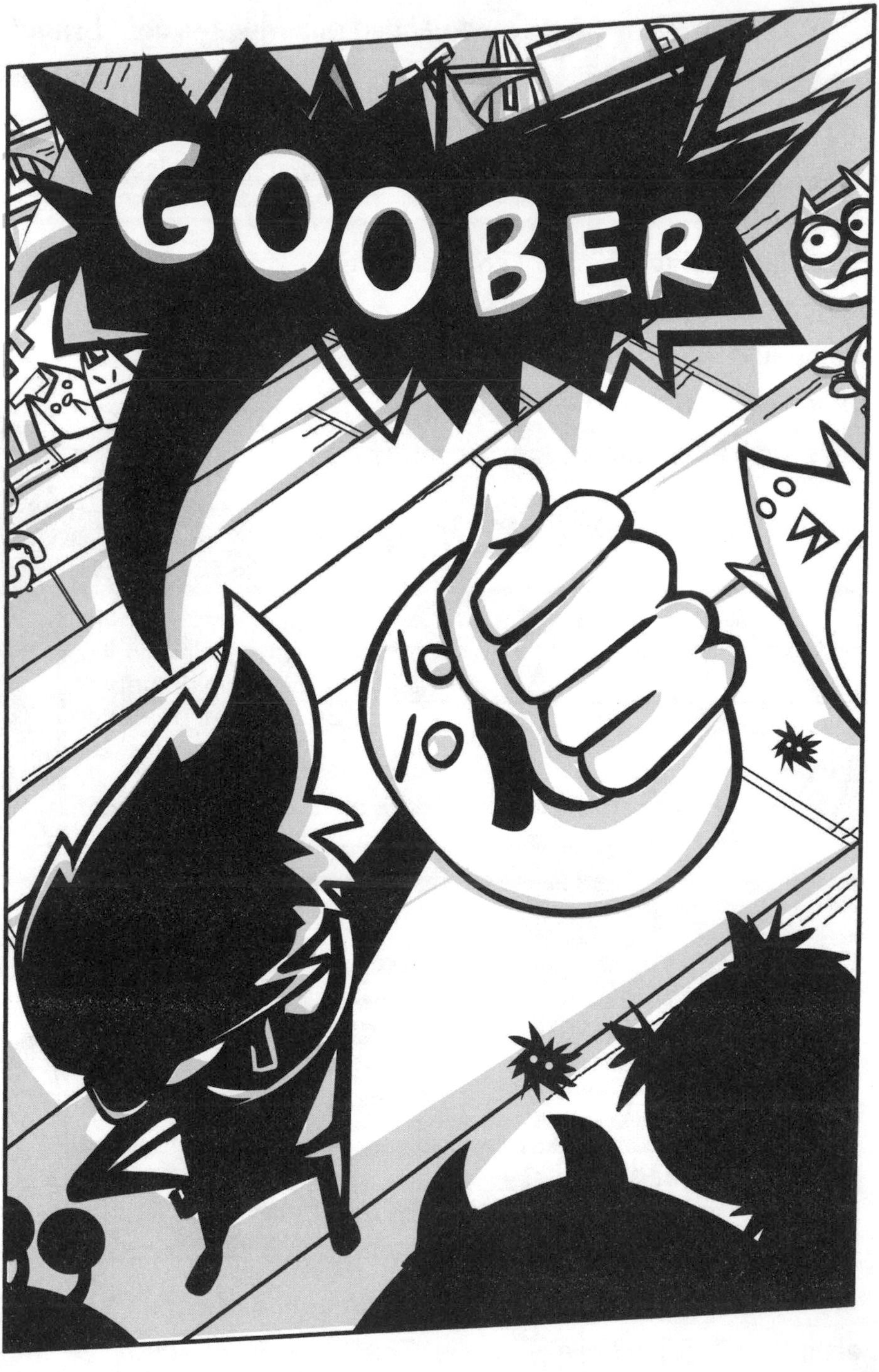
GOOBER

MEET MY BUDDY GOOBER

FACT: Goober is the rubbery, elastic blob that is forever wrapped around my wrist. Goober is symbiotic and lives off my adrenaline—that means he can't leave my side or he'll die! But it's worth it, 'cause Goober is frappin' rad and can turn into all sorts of awesome junk, like . . .

GOOBER THE HAMMER!

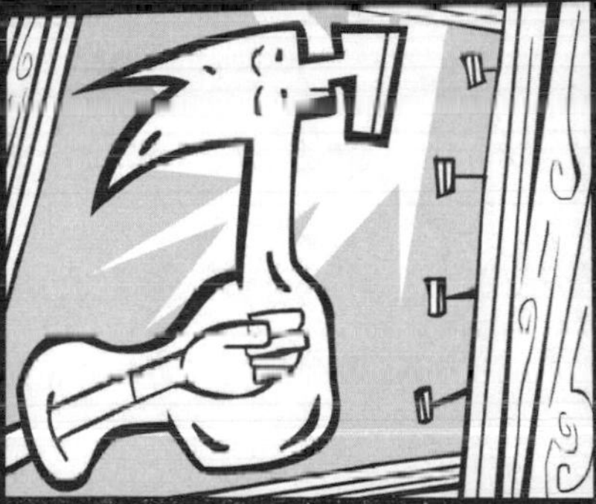

GOOBER THE FIST!

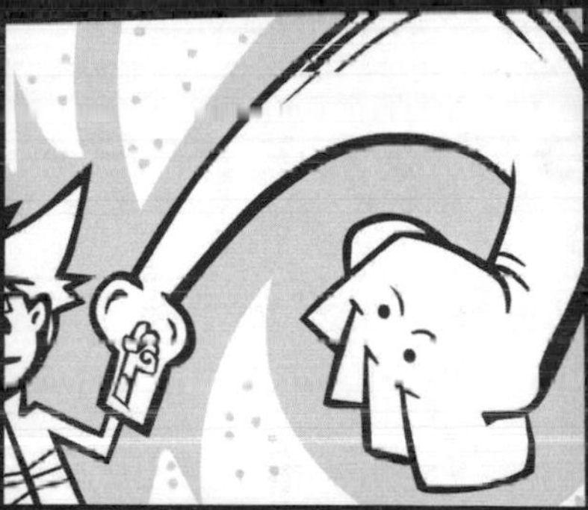

GOOBER THE ANNOYING PAL WHO NEVER, EVER LEAVES

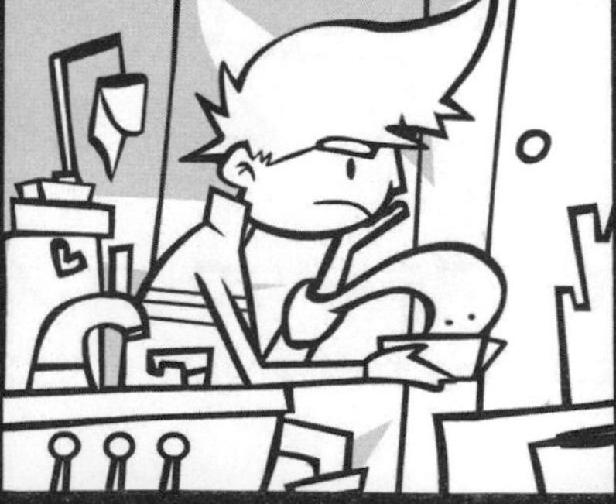

GOOBER THE FART DAMPENER!

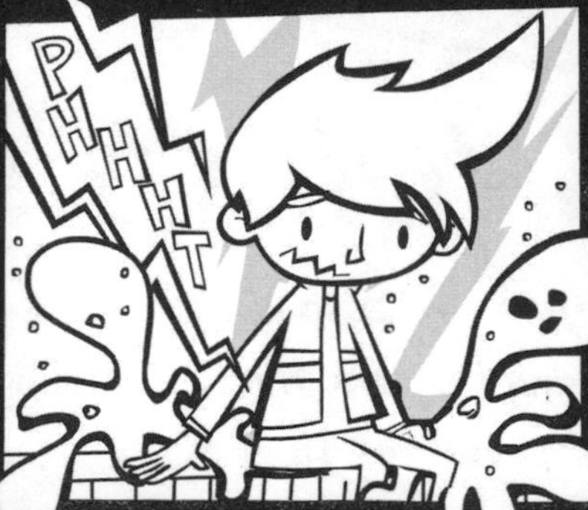
PHHHHT

BACK TO THE ACTION!

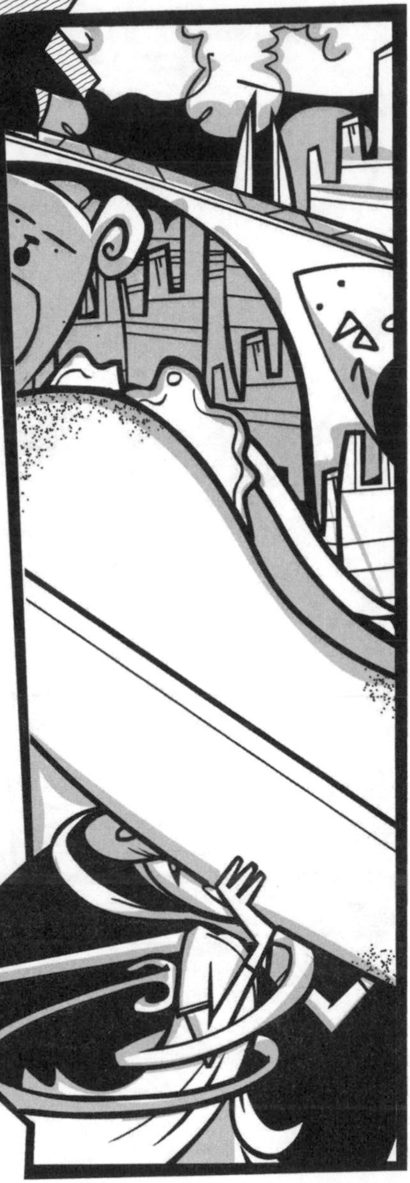

I'm darting through the market trying to find the thief. I catch a glimpse of the Mega-Dog, bobbing above the crowd.

THERE!

The crowd clears and goofy aliens step to the side.

PERFECT!

I flex my wrist, letting Goober know it's about to be action time. "Goober, go!" I shout, and then . . .

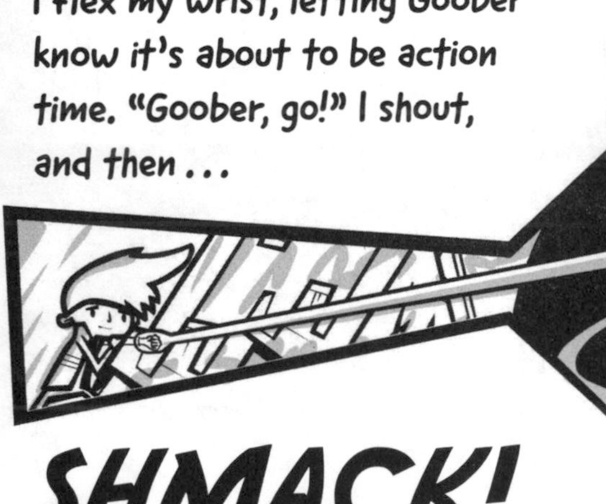

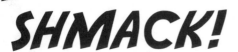

SHMACK!

I yank on Lasso-Goober and—***SUPERB LASSO MOVE***—bring the jerk thief stumbling back. And that's when I discover the thief is . . .

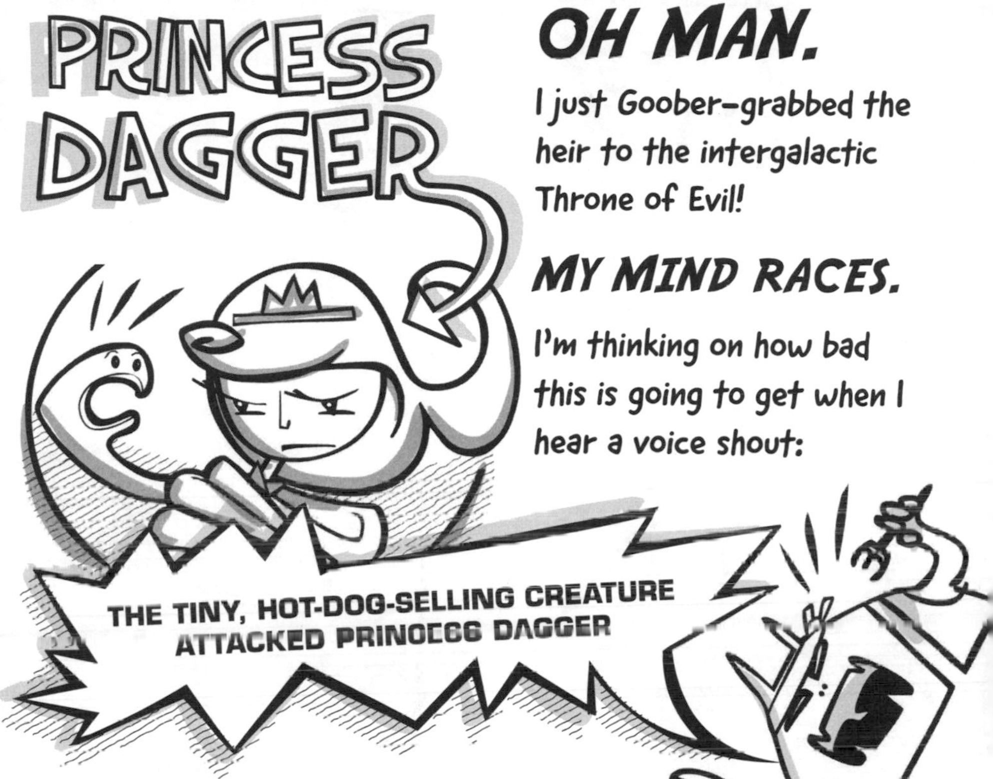
PRINCESS DAGGER
THE TINY, HOT-DOG-SELLING CREATURE ATTACKED PRINCESS DAGGER

OH MAN.

I just Goober-grabbed the heir to the intergalactic Throne of Evil!

MY MIND RACES.

I'm thinking on how bad this is going to get when I hear a voice shout:

Hang on, folks. This is about to get uglier than a butt convention.

"Whoa, whoa, whoa!" I shout. "Little misunderstanding here. I didn't attack anyone. And I'm not a 'tiny, hot-dog-selling creature'— ***I AM COSMOE THE EARTH-BOY!***"

Humphree grabs me by the shoulder. "We need to split!"

I yank the Mega-Dog out of the thief's hands. "Not without this!"

And then it's off to the races . . .

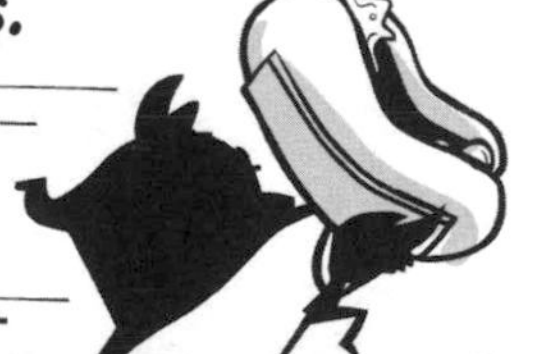

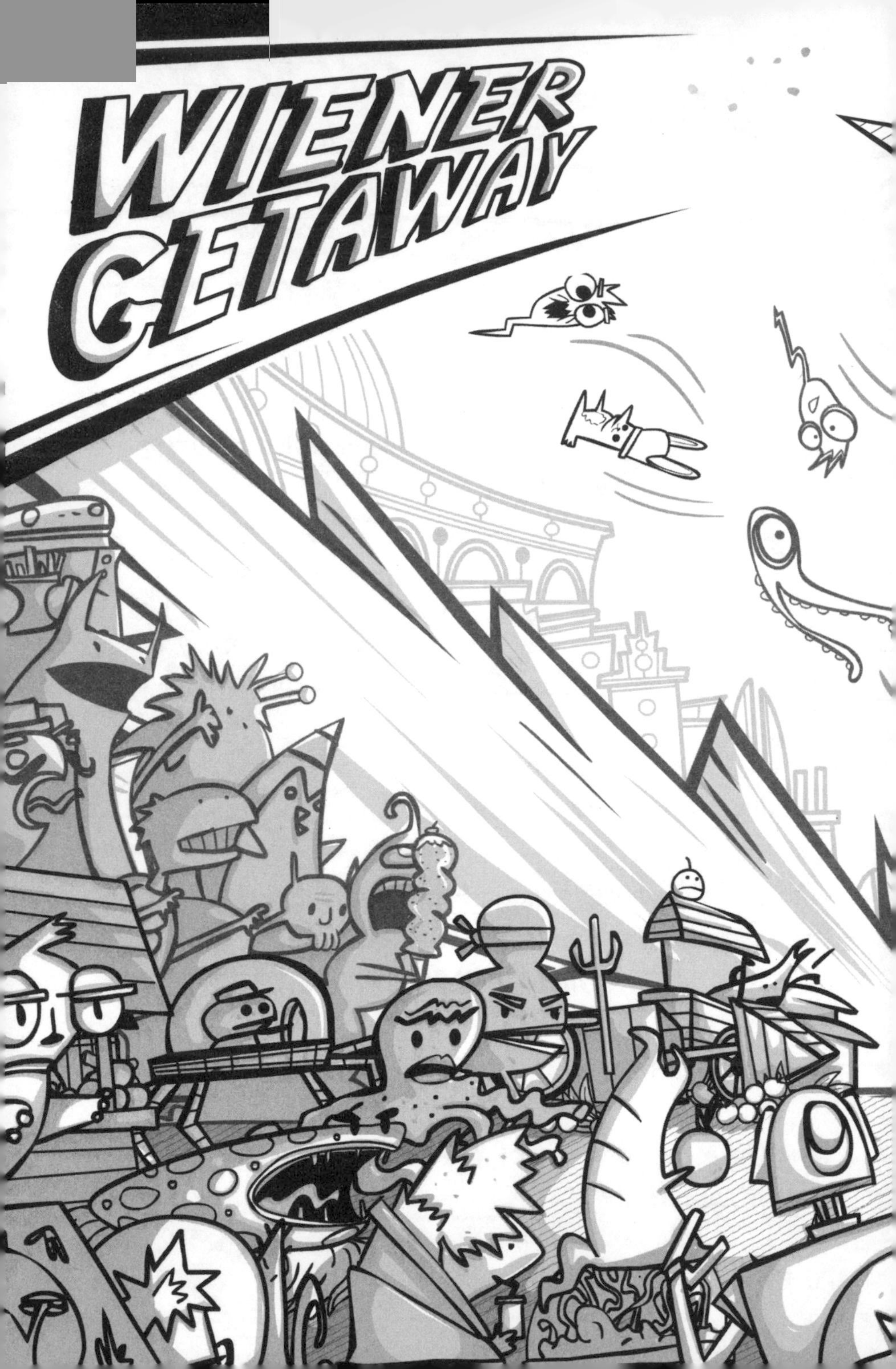
WIENER GETAWAY

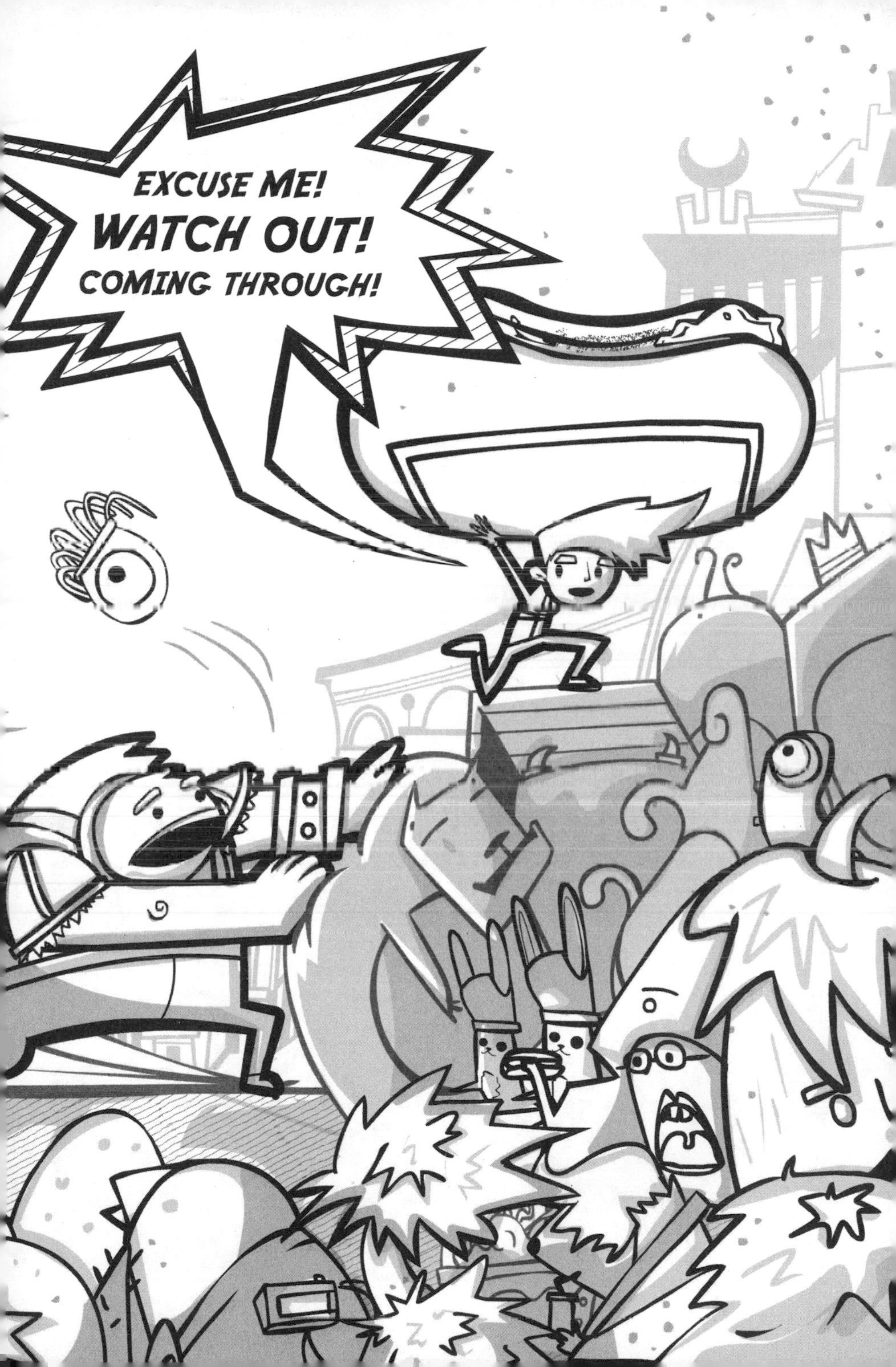
EXCUSE ME!
WATCH OUT!
COMING THROUGH!

We come out of the crowd, and I see our ship in the distance! I fish inside my pocket, grab the *Neon Wiener* keys, and hit the **UNLOCK DOOR** button.

Behind us, energy cannons are blasting away. Lucky for me, Humphree is both heavily armored and heavily protective. Humphree holds up the angry mob while I try to squeeze the Mega-Dog through the door.

"***GET INSIDE!***" Humphree barks.

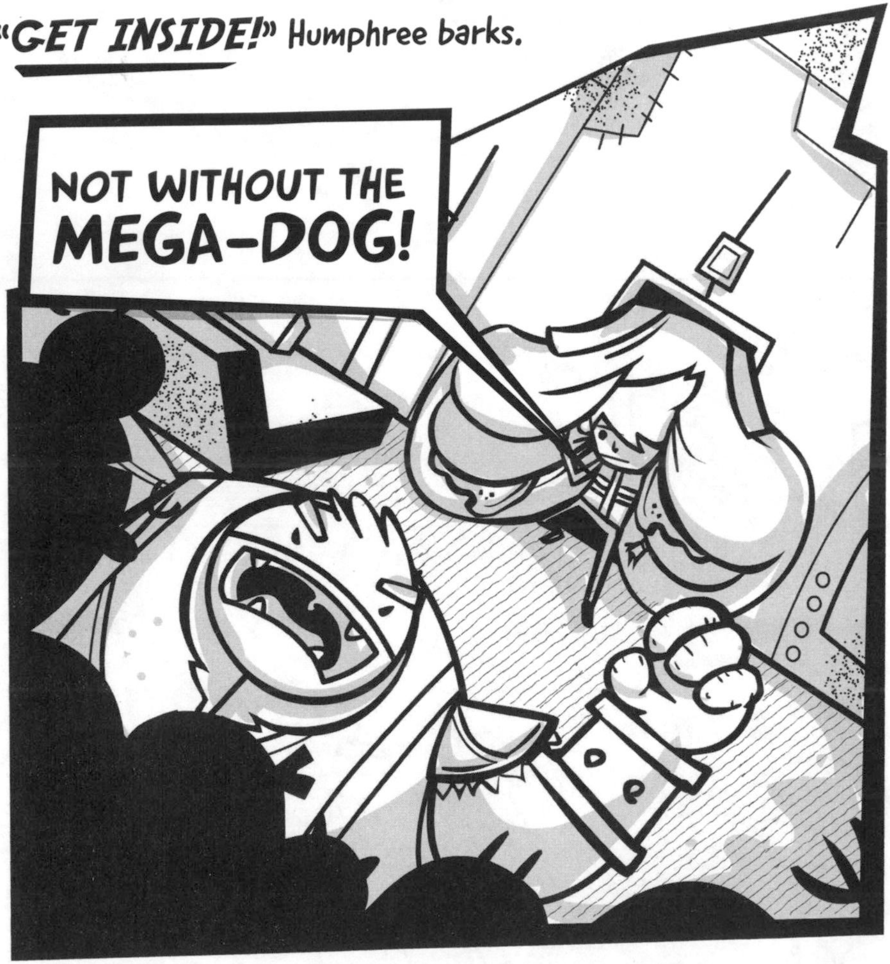
NOT WITHOUT THE MEGA-DOG!

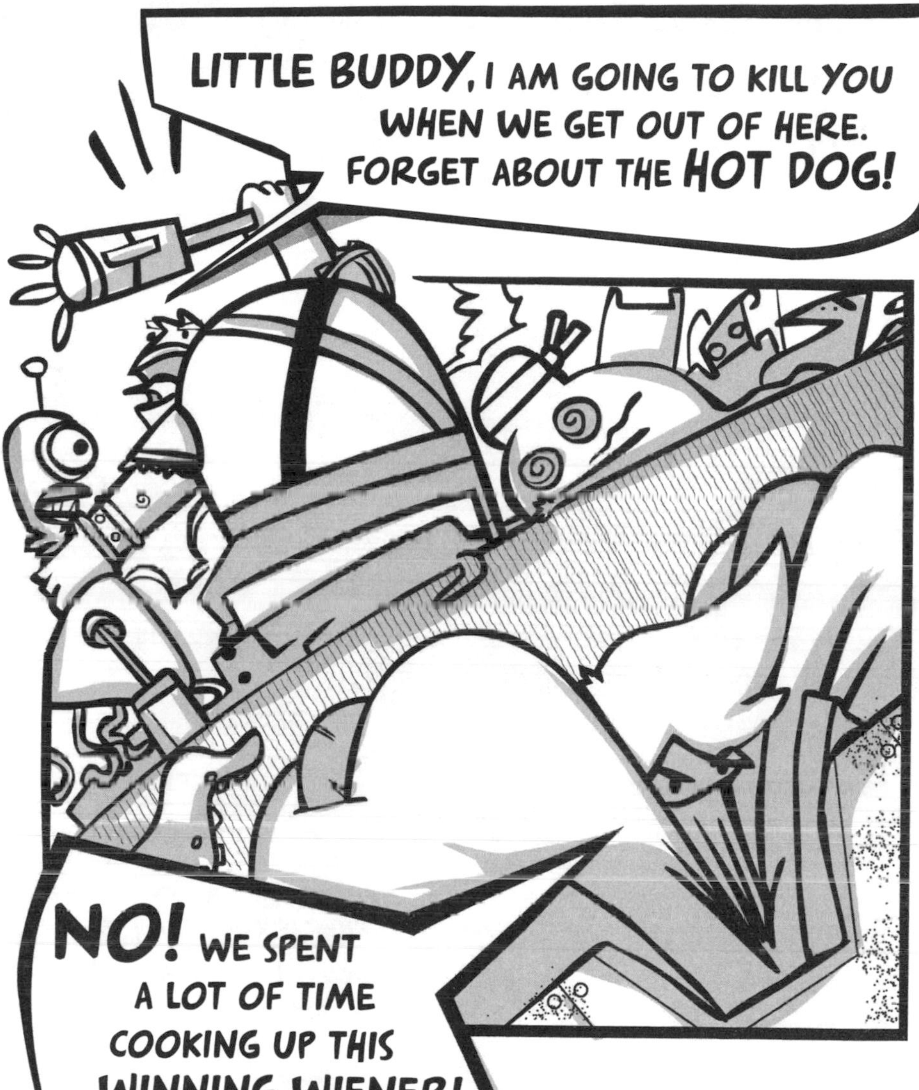
LITTLE BUDDY, I AM GOING TO KILL YOU WHEN WE GET OUT OF HERE. FORGET ABOUT THE HOT DOG!
NO! WE SPENT A LOT OF TIME COOKING UP THIS WINNING WIENER!

I push and push and push.

Arghhh! I'm totally scuffing up the Mega-Dog.

Finally, it squeezes through.

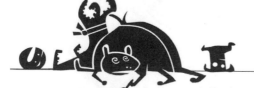

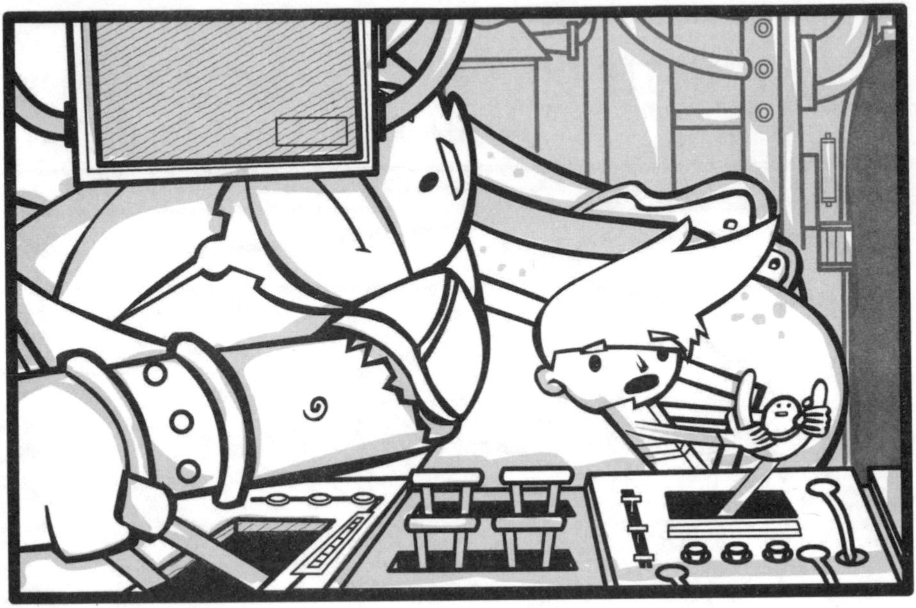

Inside the cockpit, I'm flipping switches, and pressing buttons, and spinning knobs like crazy.

Humphree makes it inside, and about **5** space seconds later, the engines are heating up and the ship is undocking.

Another **7** seconds and the *Neon Wiener* is rocketing into interstellar space, leaving behind Princess Dagger and the angry Port Funketoun mob.

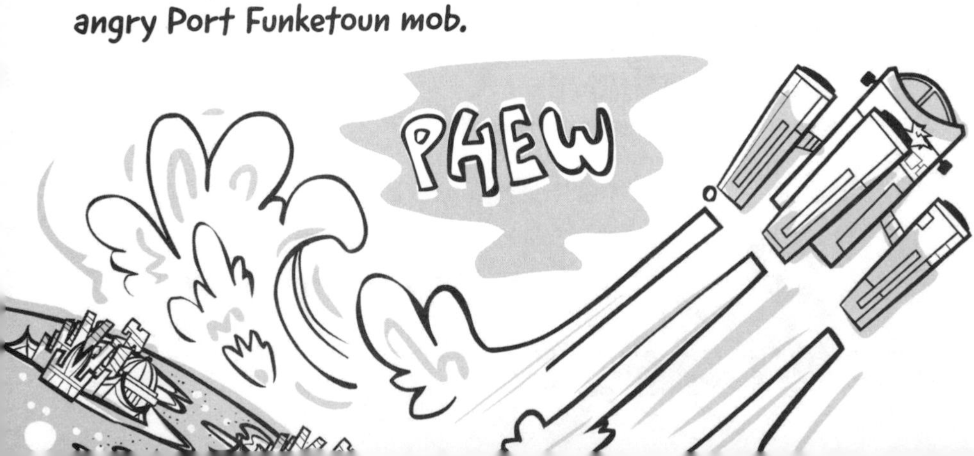
PHEW

But now Big Humps wants to talk . . .

He places one of his massive paws on my shoulder.

"COSMOE—HEART-TO-HEART TIME. YOU CAN'T JUST BE WHIPPING GOOBER AROUND AND LASSOING EVIL PRINCESSES. IT'S BAD FOR BUSINESS!"

I hang my head. "I'm sorry, Humps. But she was stealing the Mega-Dog!"

Humps scratches his chin. "Good point, but still—"

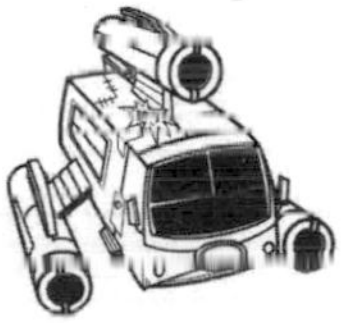

We're interrupted by a silky smooth voice saying . . .

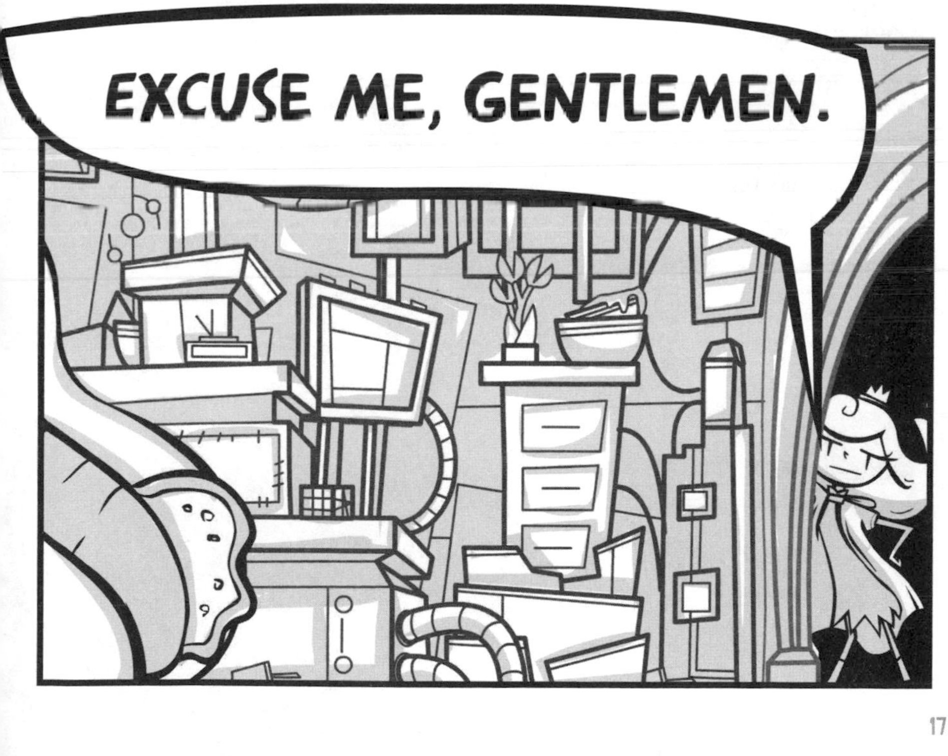
EXCUSE ME, GENTLEMEN.

My throat goes "gulp."

IT'S EVIL PRINCESS DAGGER.

And she is aboard our ship! "What the butt?! What are you doing here?!"

"Stealing your ship, silly. I'm an evil princess. Y'know?"

I start stuttering, **"NO-NO. NO-NO. NO.** You can't be here! Your evil mom is gonna think we kidnapped you. She'll **KILL** us!"

Princess Dagger is about to respond, when—

BLEEP BLEEP BLEEP

"Brace for impact," our pet robot, F.R.E.D., says.

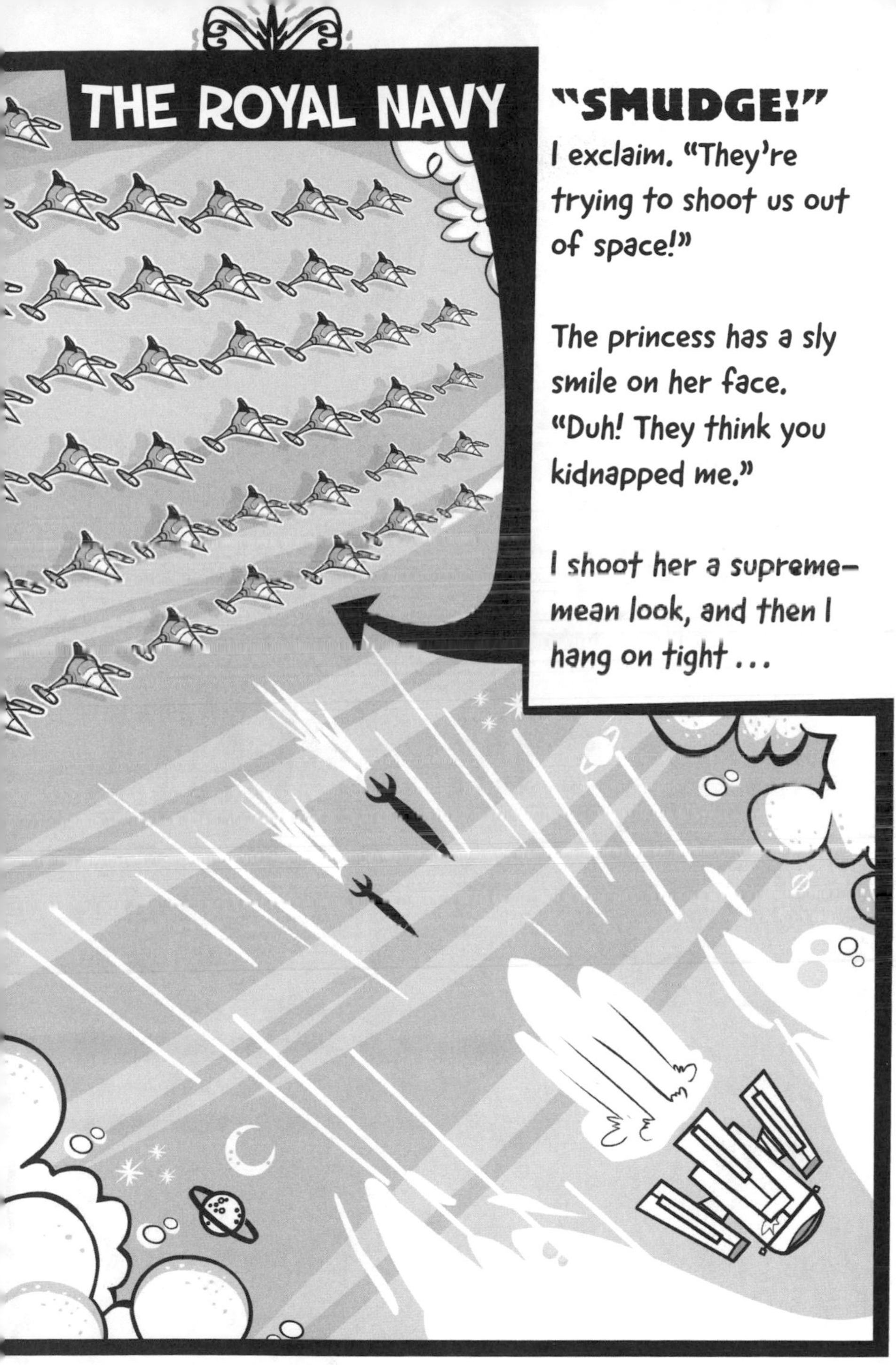
THE ROYAL NAVY

"SMUDGE!" I exclaim. "They're trying to shoot us out of space!"

The princess has a sly smile on her face. "Duh! They think you kidnapped me."

I shoot her a supreme-mean look, and then I hang on tight . . .

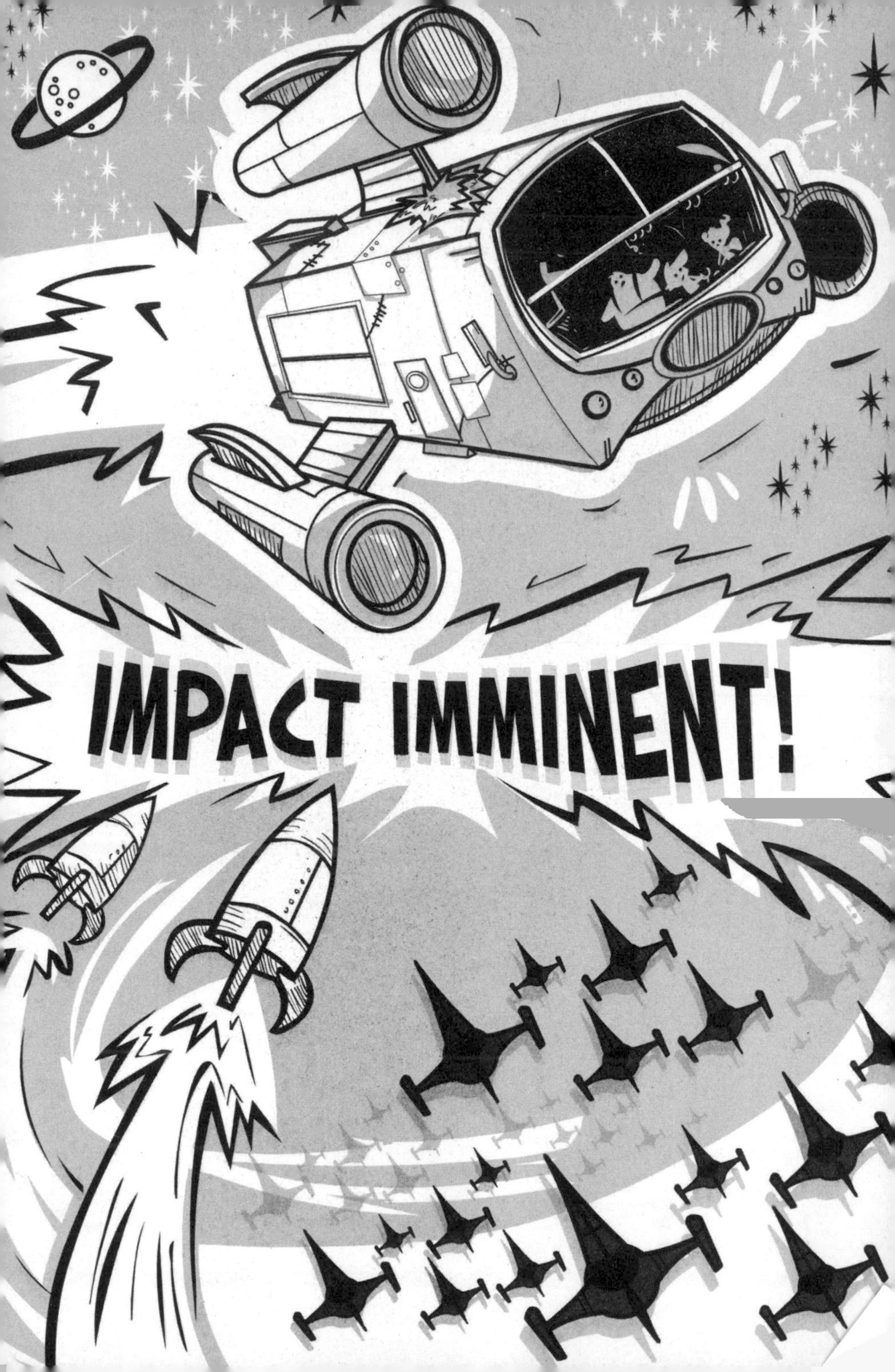
IMPACT IMMINENT!

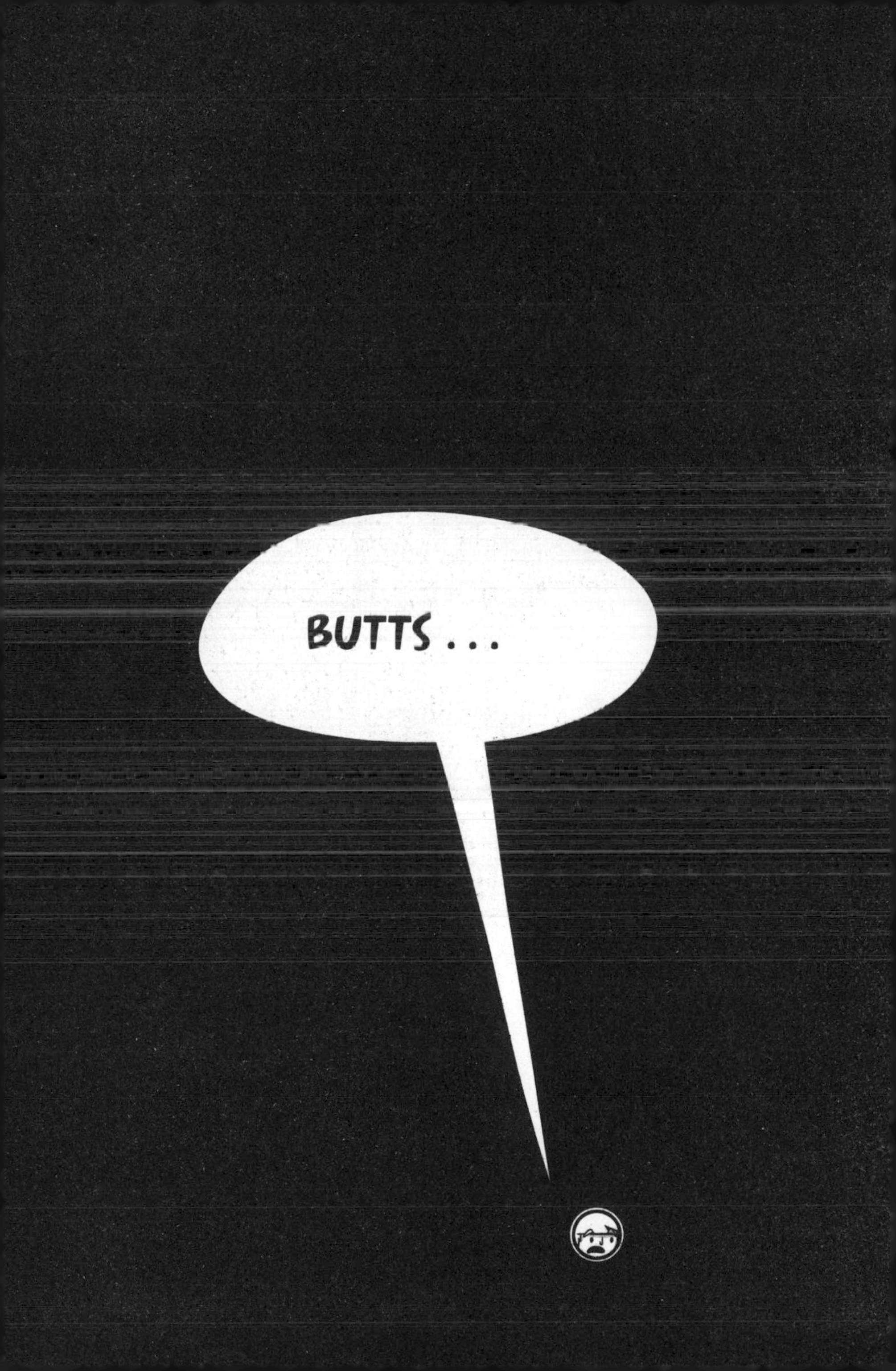
BUTTS . . .

PRINCESSES ARE A PAIN

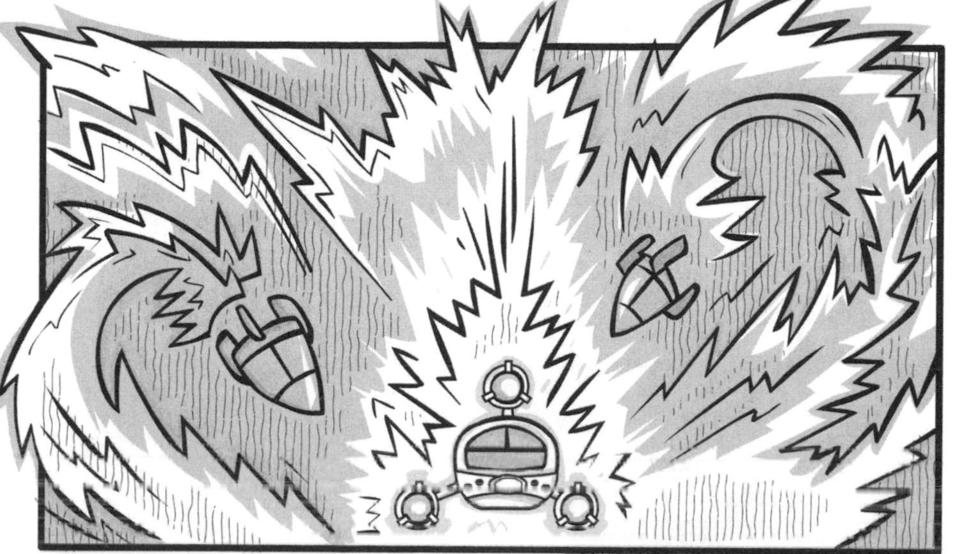

I'm scared. Not going to lie—big-time nervous. These two royal rockets are closing in

FAST.

I'm at the cockpit, hands on the wheel, squeezing it so tightly my knuckles are fleshy white. I'm pretty definitely positive I'm about to get blown up.

Suddenly, Princess Dagger yells out, "***HEY, WEIRD HAIR. WATCH OUT!***" and lunges at the

BRAKES—

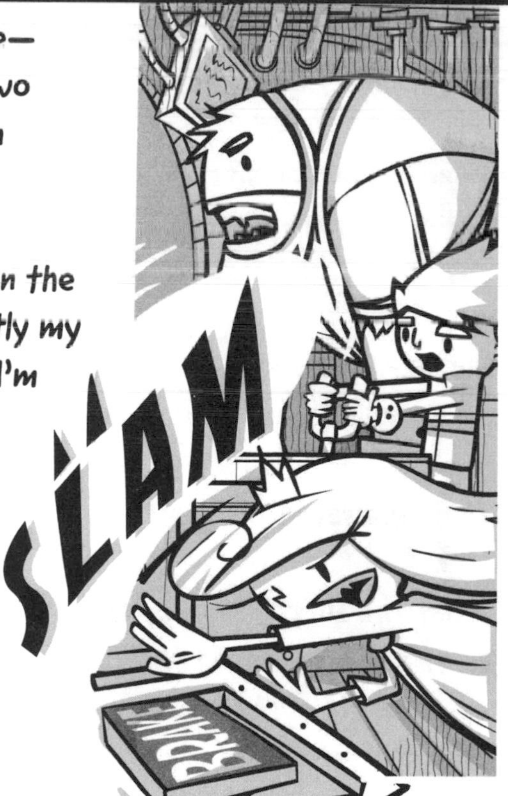
SLAM
BRAKE

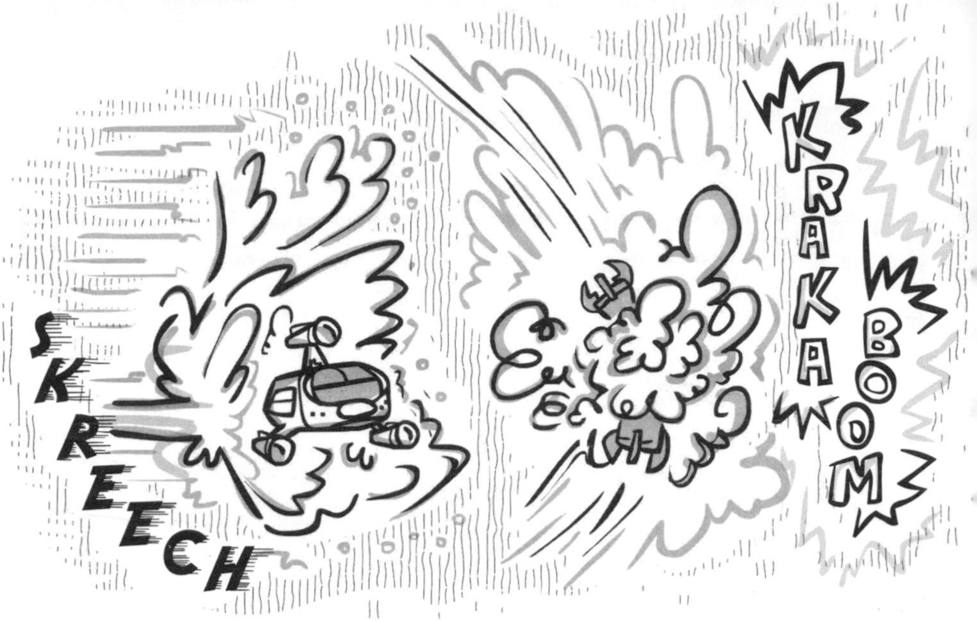
SKREEECH
KRAKA
BOOM

The explosion is massively, monstrously King Kong–sized and white-chocolate hot. We all tumble back onto our butts.

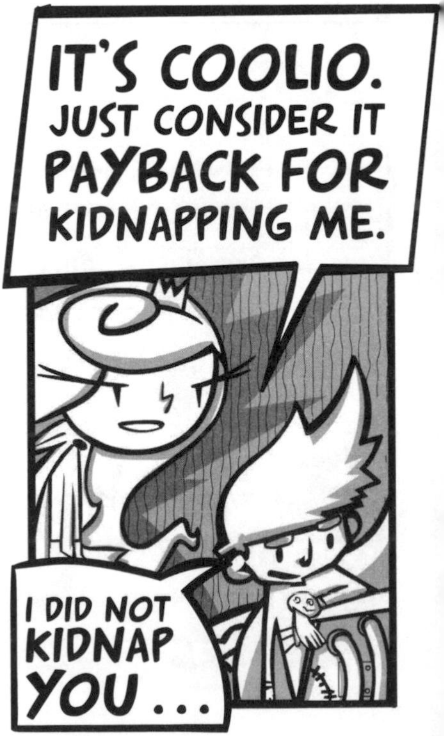
IT'S COOLIO. JUST CONSIDER IT PAYBACK FOR KIDNAPPING ME.
I DID NOT KIDNAP YOU . . .

Princess Dagger sits up, scratches her head, and whispers, "Wow, that was heart-nukingly crazy."

Humphree chuckles as he gets to his feet and says, "The princess is good, Cosmoe. I'll give her that. She saved our butts."

What the fuzz?! I'm supposed to be the hero, doing all the saving and everything! Where does this princess get off?!

Humphree says, in his deep, ***DEEEEEP*** voice, "We need to skedaddle, bud. We're lucky we're not applesauce right now. Soon the whole Royal Armada will be after us."

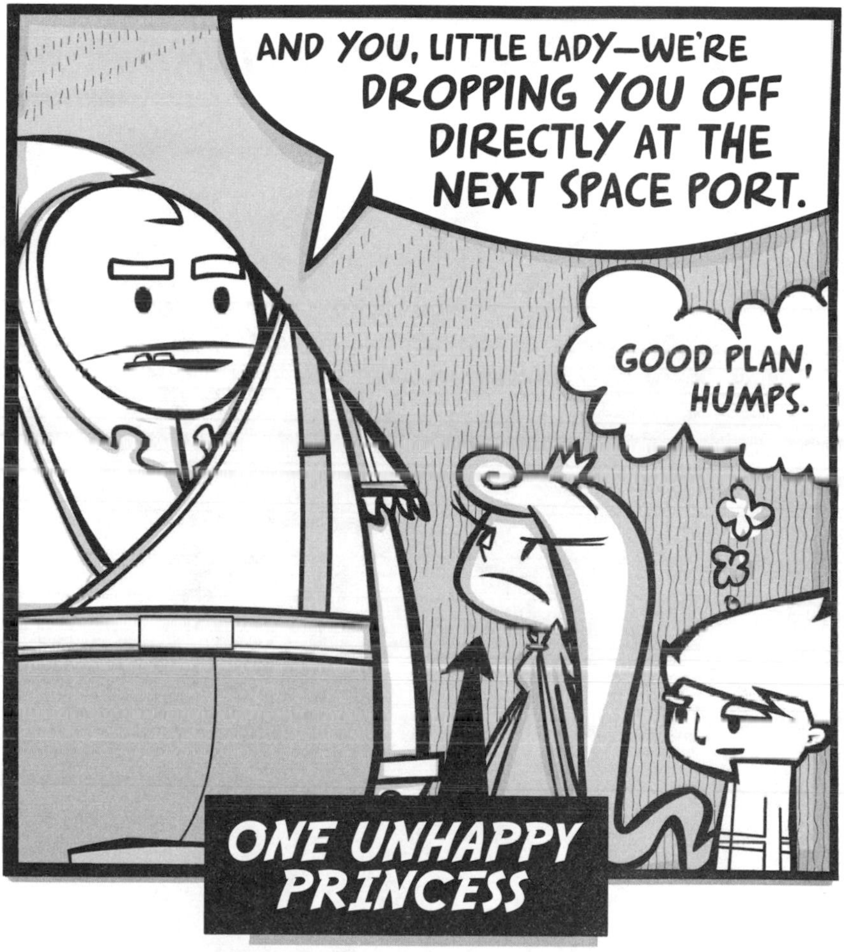
AND YOU, LITTLE LADY—WE'RE DROPPING YOU OFF DIRECTLY AT THE NEXT SPACE PORT.
GOOD PLAN, HUMPS.
ONE UNHAPPY PRINCESS

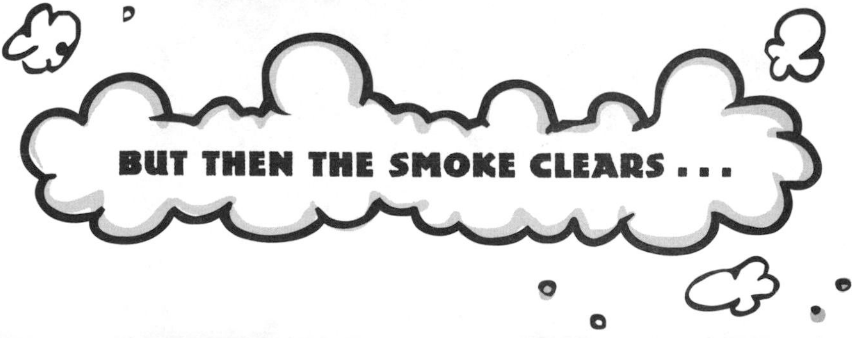
BUT THEN THE SMOKE CLEARS . . .

We are most definitely not out of trouble yet. My eyes are as wide as flying saucers. That Royal Armada that Humps mentioned . . . ?

I THINK IT'S ALREADY HERE . . .

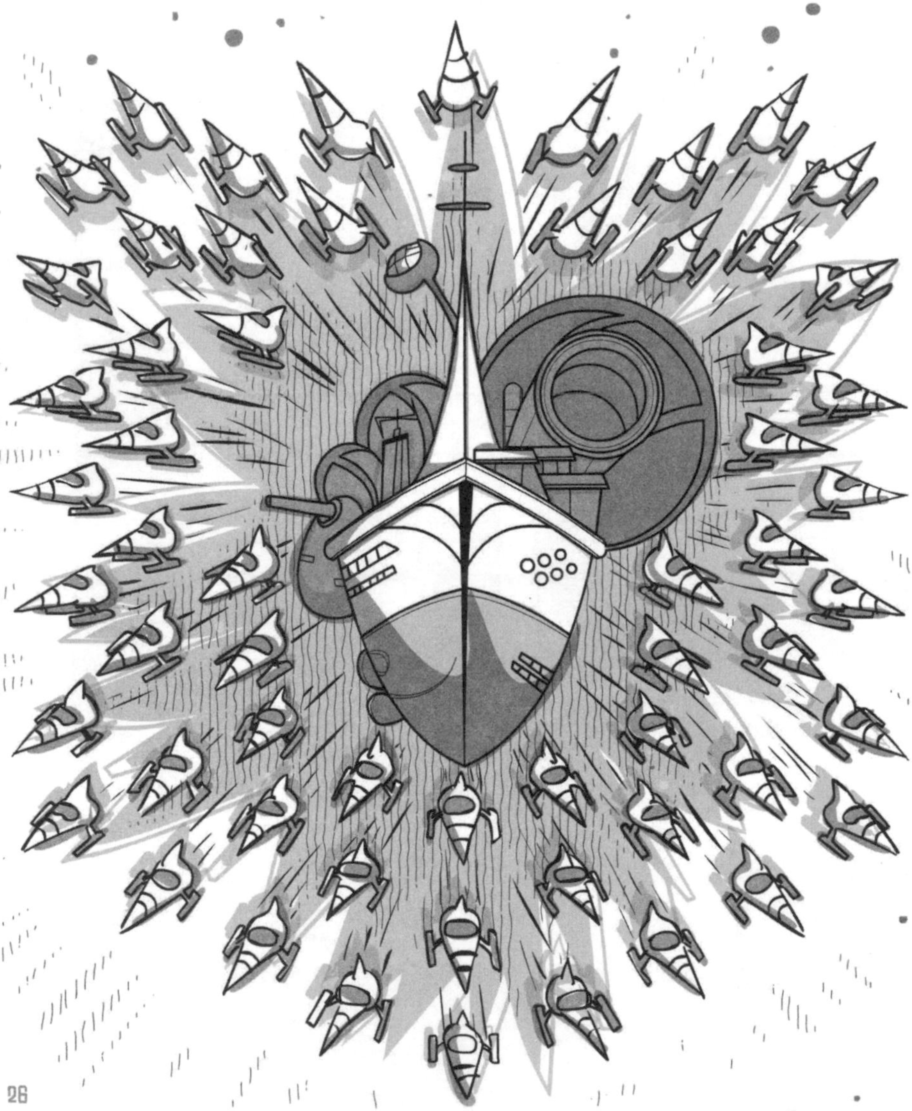

F.R.E.D. makes a frazzly noise. The robot's screen–face flashes, and my ***HEART ABOUT STOPS.*** I'm staring right into the gray, soulless eyes of Evil Queen Dagger. She's hijacked the radio!

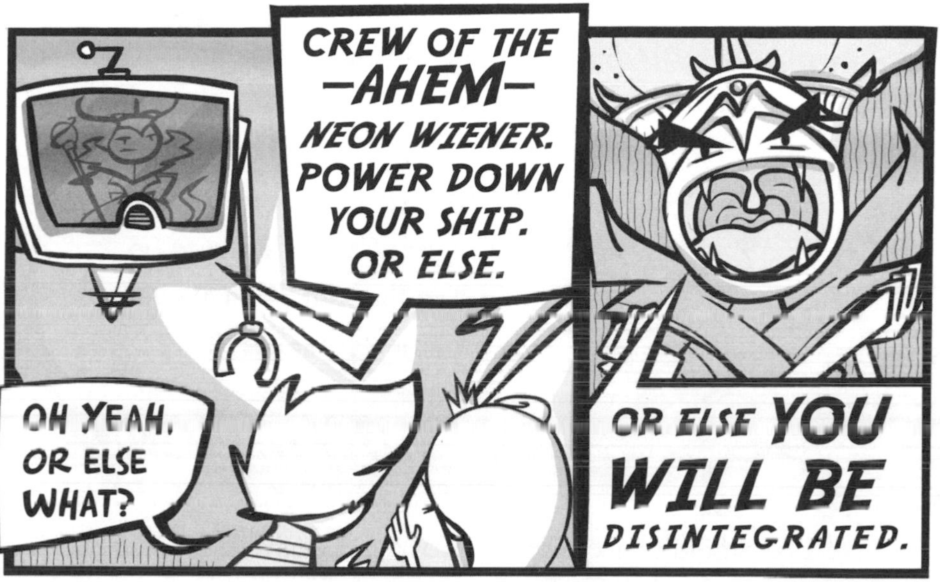
CREW OF THE —AHEM— NEON WIENER. POWER DOWN YOUR SHIP. OR ELSE.
OH YEAH, OR ELSE WHAT?
OR ELSE YOU WILL BE DISINTEGRATED.

Okay, I'm convinced. Aaaand powering down . . .

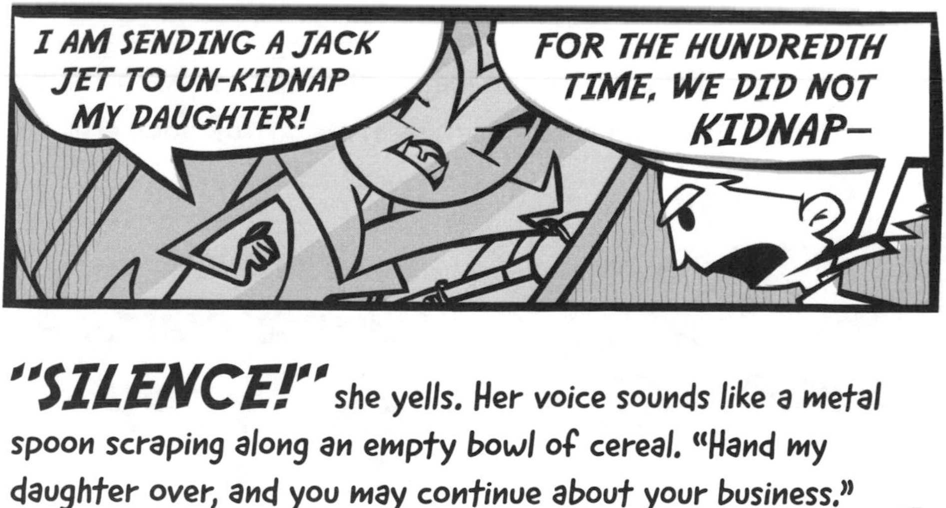
I AM SENDING A JACK JET TO UN-KIDNAP MY DAUGHTER!
FOR THE HUNDREDTH TIME, WE DID NOT KIDNAP—

"SILENCE!" she yells. Her voice sounds like a metal spoon scraping along an empty bowl of cereal. "Hand my daughter over, and you may continue about your business."

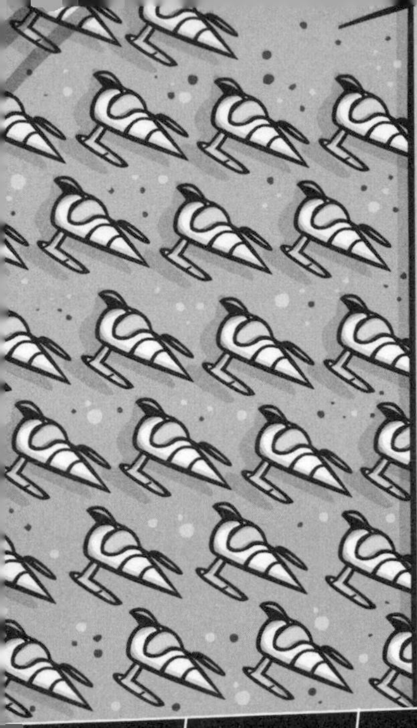

A single Jack Jet departs the massive wall of ships, leaving a gap in the perfect arrangement.

"They're coming to take me away," Princess Dagger says quietly.

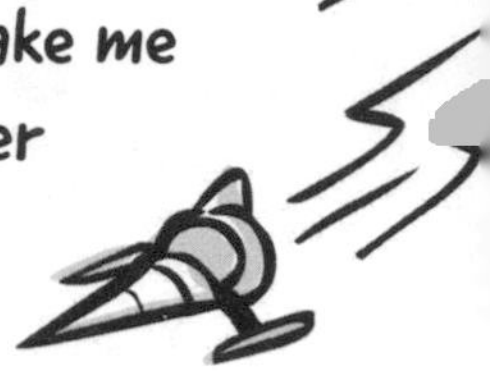

Good, I think. I want the princess gone, now. She's fuzzing up me and Humphree's relaxing life of awesomeness!

BUT THEN

I feel something weird and sort of cold and clammy on my hand. I look down. It's Princess Dagger.

HER TINY HAND IS NESTLED INSIDE MINE.

I swallow, thinking maybe she really doesn't want to go home. And then, from out of nowhere, Princess Dagger reveals . . .

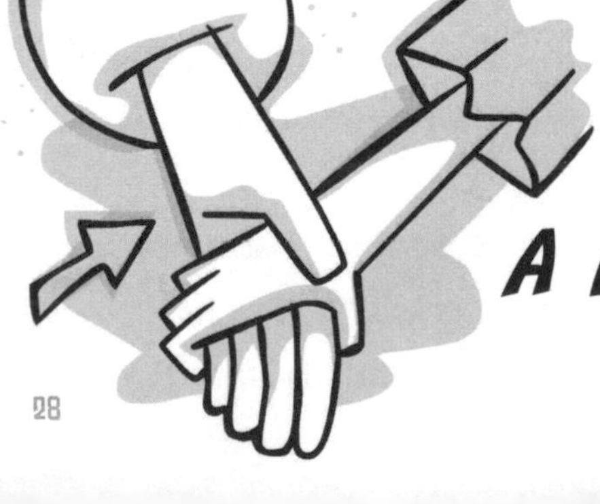

A SWORD?

AN ENERGY BLASTER??

A LASER AX???

NO . . . A—

RANGE OF DRAMATIC EMOTION!

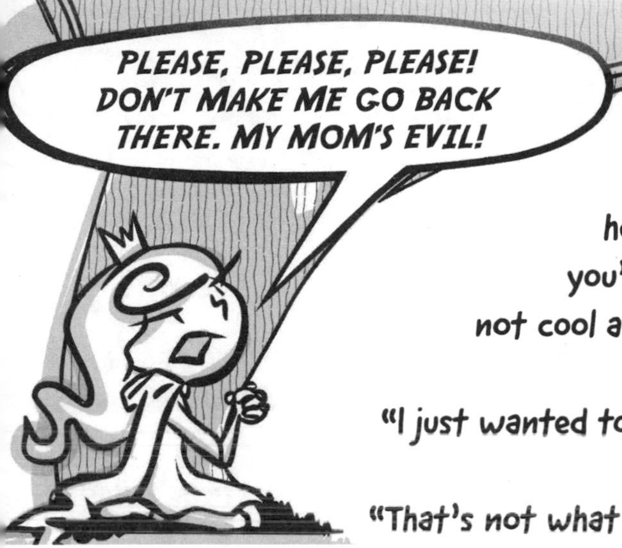
PLEASE, PLEASE, PLEASE! DON'T MAKE ME GO BACK THERE. MY MOM'S EVIL!

I yank my hand away from hers and yell, "Princess, you're evil! You acted way not cool and you stole from us."

"I just wanted to be friends," she says.

"That's not what friends do!" I exclaim.

The princess hangs her head. "I don't really know how to be friends, I guess. I've always been evil. But I don't want to be! It's just I—I—***HAVE*** to be. It's in my genes . . ."

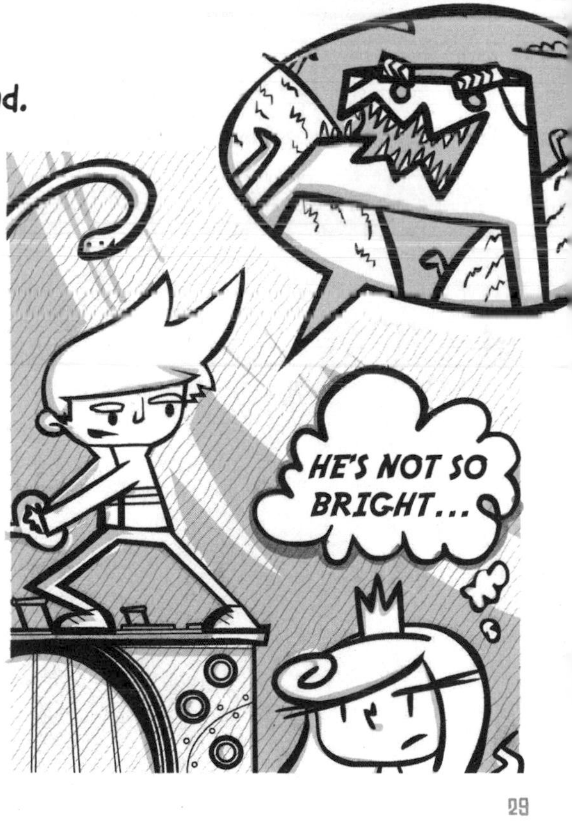
HE'S NOT SO BRIGHT...

"Your jeans?!" I scream. "Evil jeans?! Why didn't you say so earlier?? I'll handle this—I dealt with a pair of evil jeans one time on the Moon of Leevye."

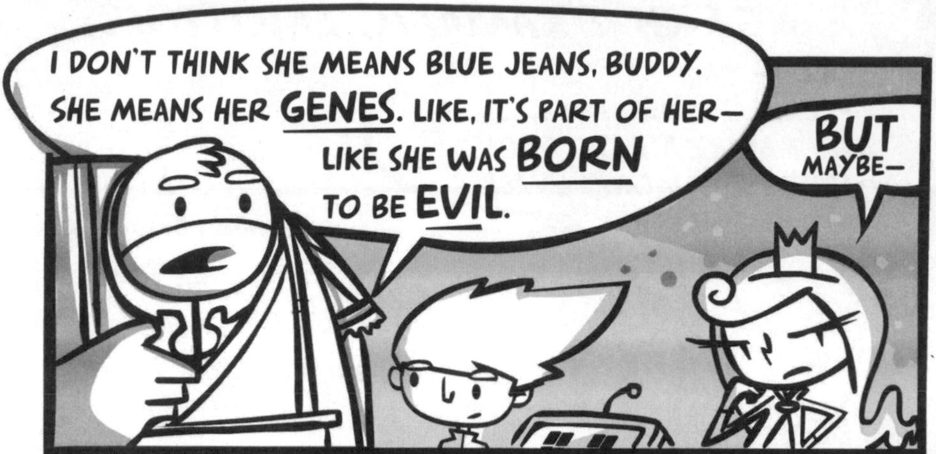
I DON'T THINK SHE MEANS BLUE JEANS, BUDDY. SHE MEANS HER GENES. LIKE, IT'S PART OF HER— LIKE SHE WAS BORN TO BE EVIL.
BUT MAYBE—

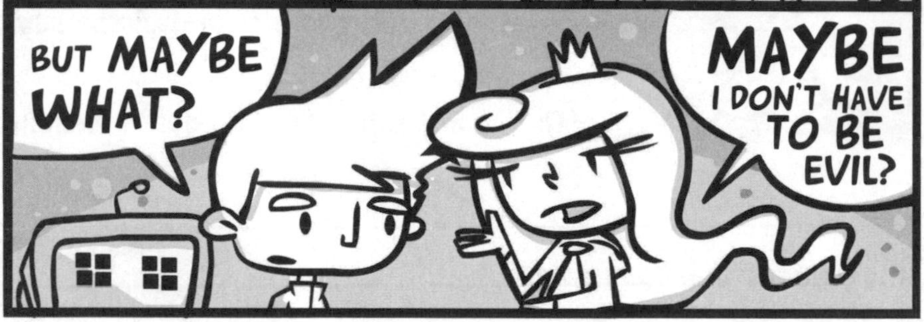
BUT MAYBE WHAT?
MAYBE I DON'T HAVE TO BE EVIL?

But there's no more time to talk. The ship shudders and shakes as the Jack Jet docks alongside the *Neon Wiener*.

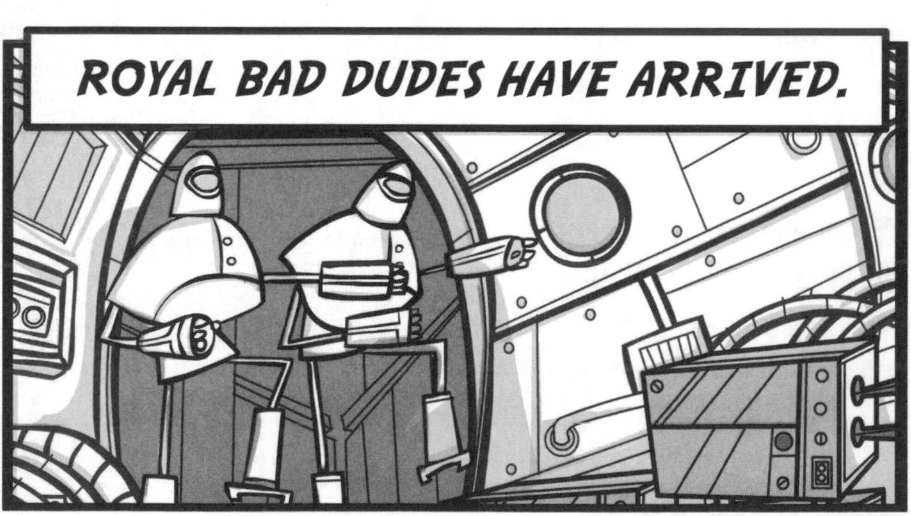
ROYAL BAD DUDES HAVE ARRIVED.

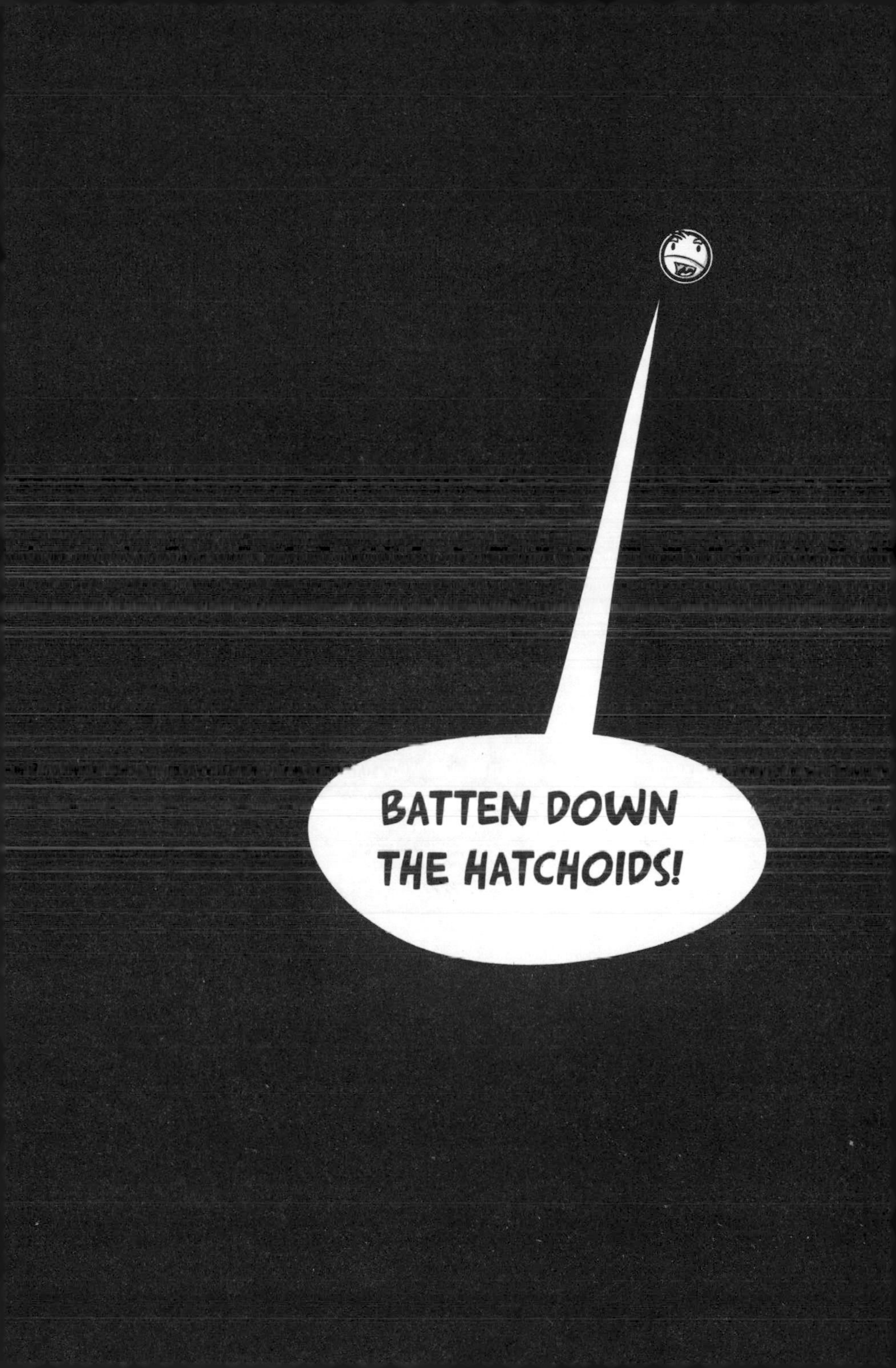
BATTEN DOWN THE HATCHOIDS!

NEVER TELL ME THE ODDS!

I inch closer to my buddy Humphree as the air lock rumbles. There's a loud ***CLANG, CLANG, CLANG.*** The door slides open with a ***VOOSH,*** revealing—

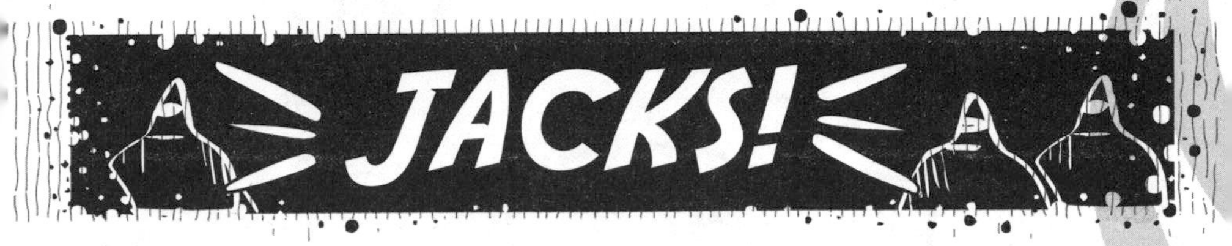
JACKS!

Oh boy.

Jacks are Evil Queen Dagger's royal robot soldiers. I hate these guys!

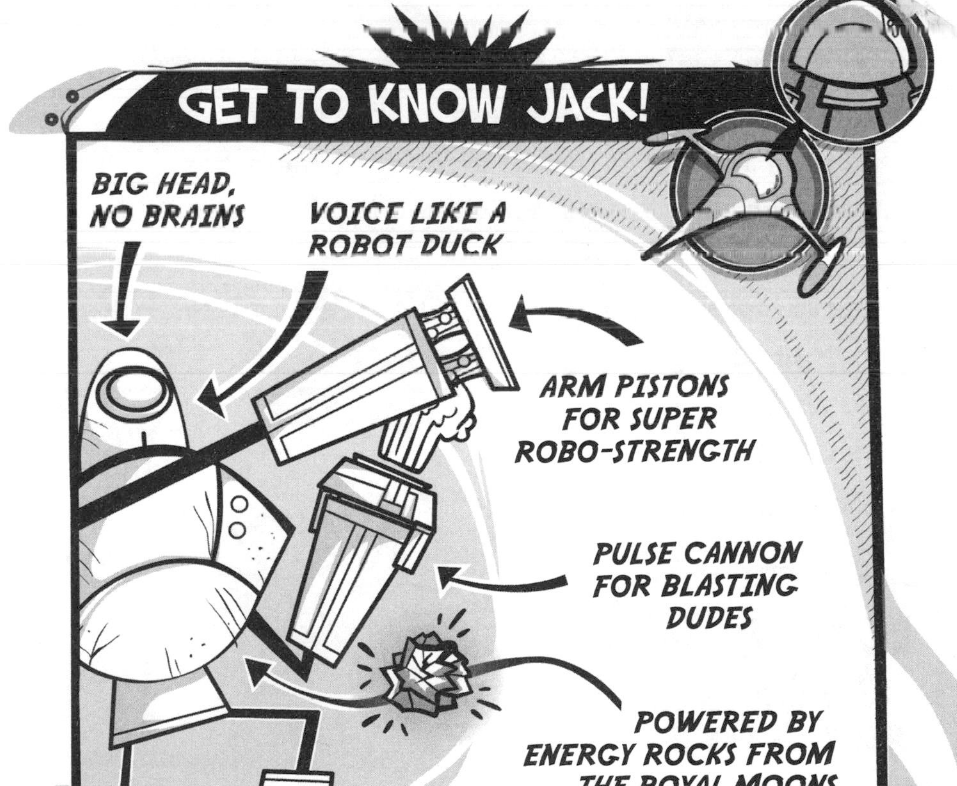
GET TO KNOW JACK!
BIG HEAD, NO BRAINS
VOICE LIKE A ROBOT DUCK
ARM PISTONS FOR SUPER ROBO-STRENGTH
PULSE CANNON FOR BLASTING DUDES
POWERED BY ENERGY ROCKS FROM THE ROYAL MOONS

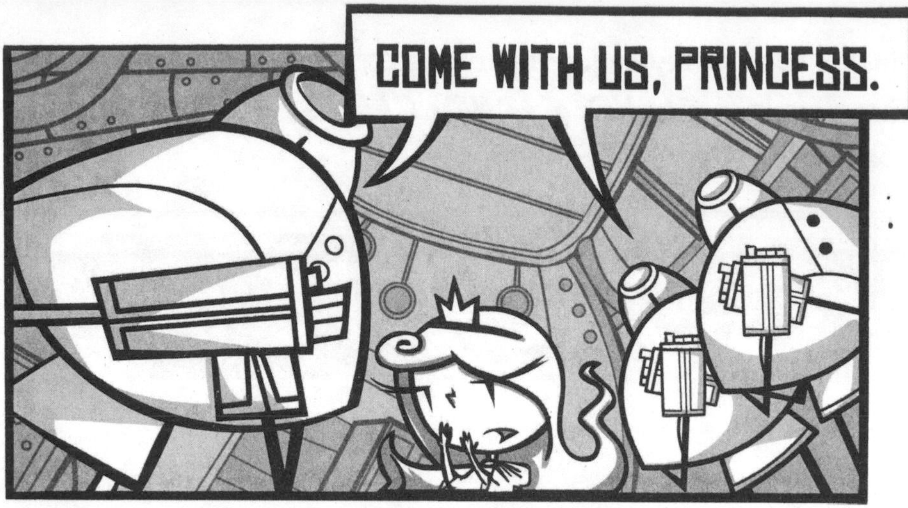
COME WITH US, PRINCESS.

My head is confused. I really don't think we should let those Jack jerks take her!

I mean, I know we're in big trouble the minute we start stealing princesses. But we're not really stealing her! She doesn't want to go home! Right now, there are tears welling up in her big, evil eyes!

Humphree looks down at me and shakes his head. He knows what I'm thinking.

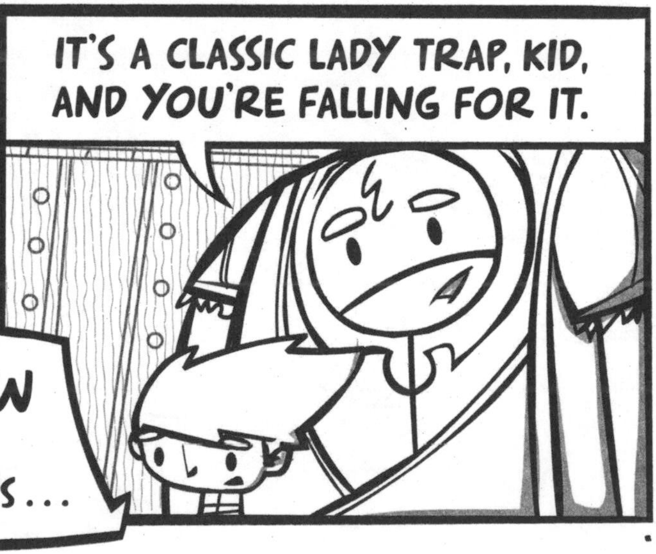
IT'S A CLASSIC LADY TRAP, KID, AND YOU'RE FALLING FOR IT.
LOOK HOW CUTE AND HELPLESS SHE IS . . .

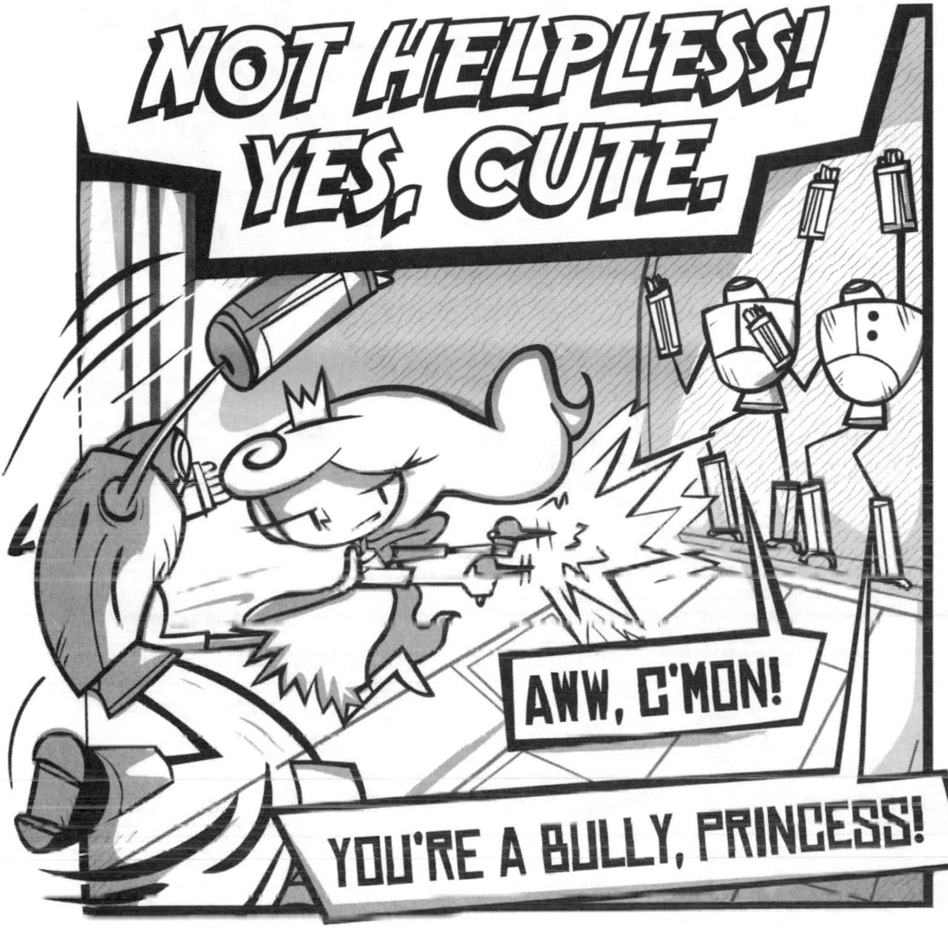
NOT HELPLESS! YES, CUTE.
AWW, C'MON!
YOU'RE A BULLY, PRINCESS!

WHOA! I can't believe what I'm seeing! The princess is slugging it out with those brainless Jacks!

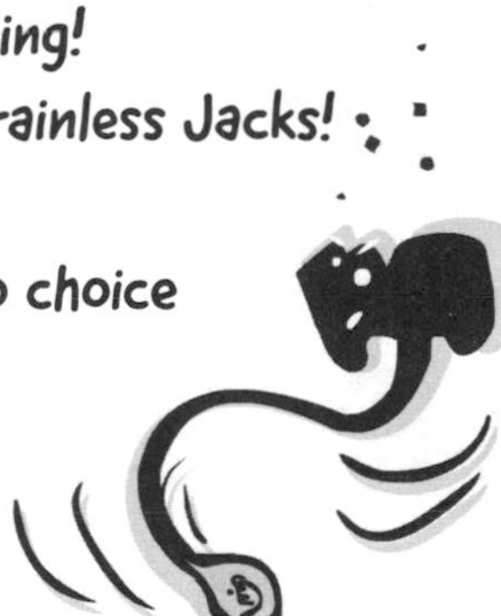

Humphree bellows out, "Guess we've got no choice but to **CRACK SOME METAL SKULLS!**"

I flex my wrist, letting Goober know it's time for a royal robot rumble . . .

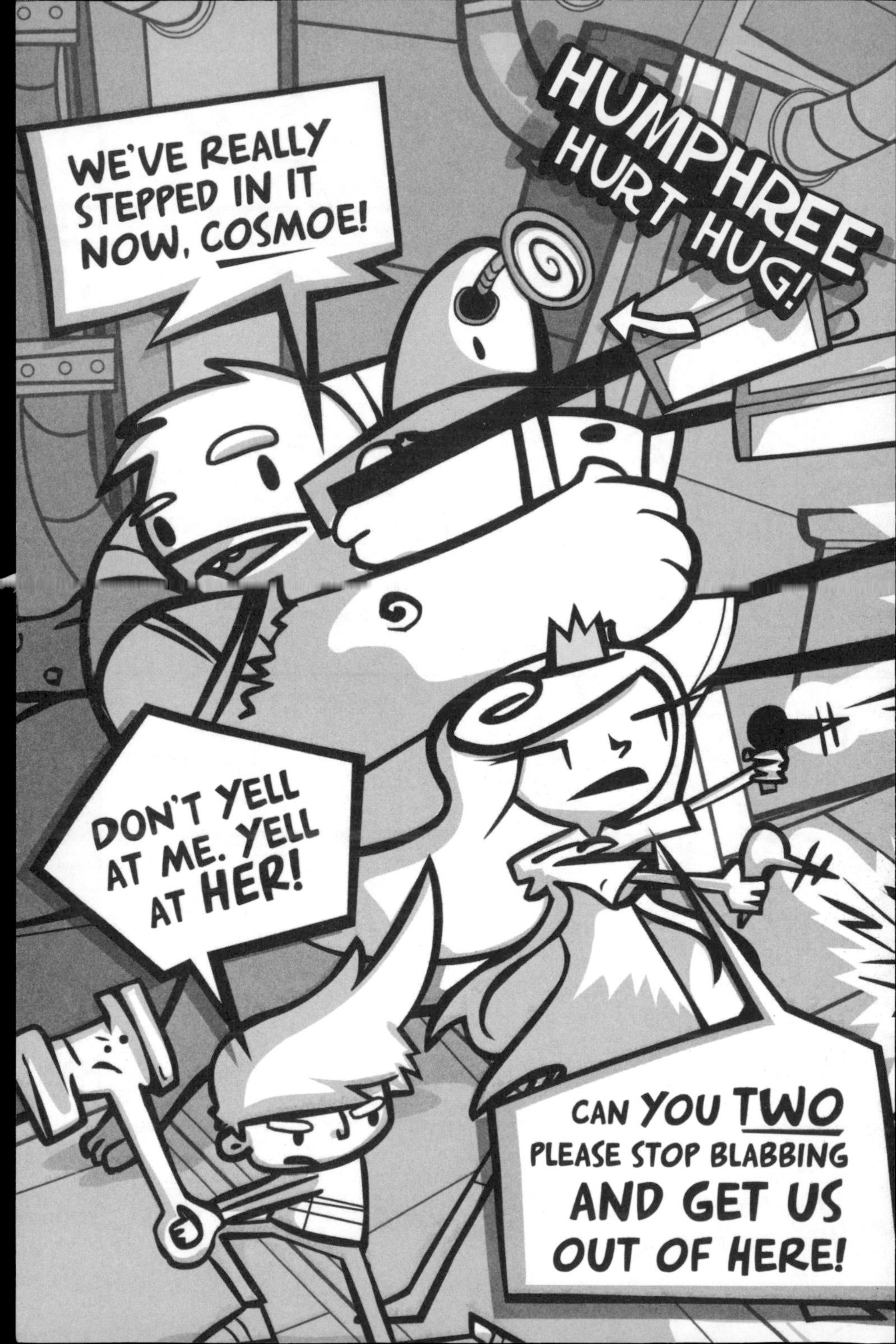
HUMPHREE HURT HUG!
WE'VE REALLY STEPPED IN IT NOW, COSMOE!
DON'T YELL AT ME. YELL AT HER!
CAN YOU TWO PLEASE STOP BLABBING AND GET US OUT OF HERE!

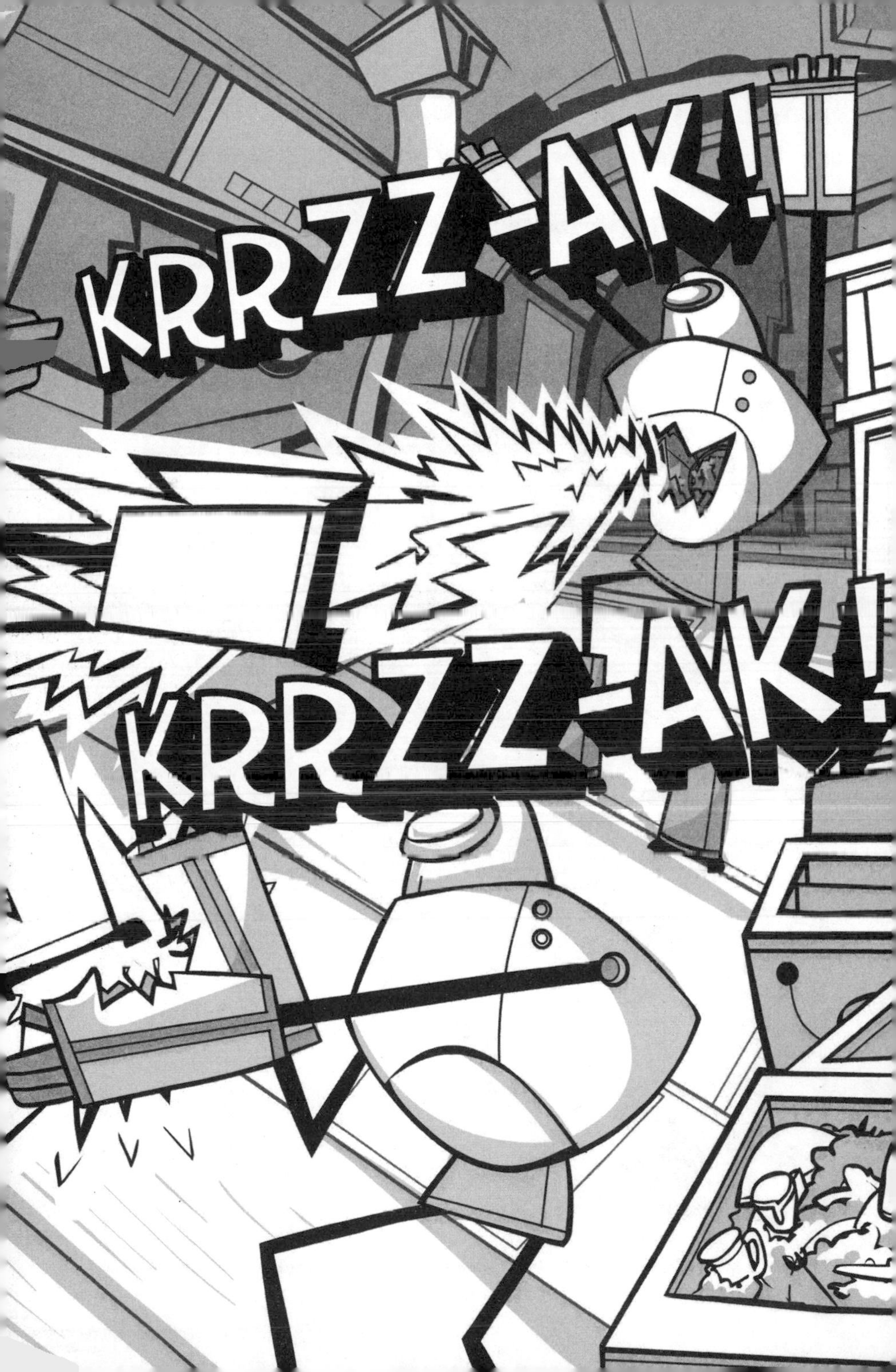
KRRZZ-AK!
KRRZZ-AK!

I sprint into the cockpit—Humphree can handle the fighting. I need to lose that Jack Jet hanging off the side of my ship.

I ***SLAM*** my fist down on the **EMERGENCY DISENGAGE** button.

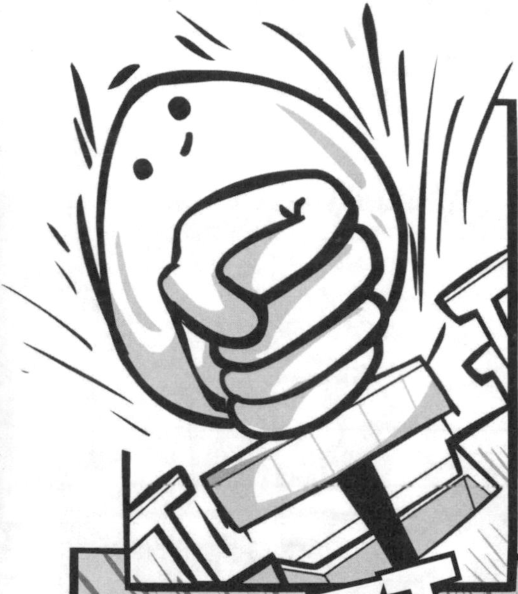

There's a

SHATTERING

mechanical tearing noise, and then, just like that, the *Neon Wiener* is ripping away from the Jack Jet. It's all like—

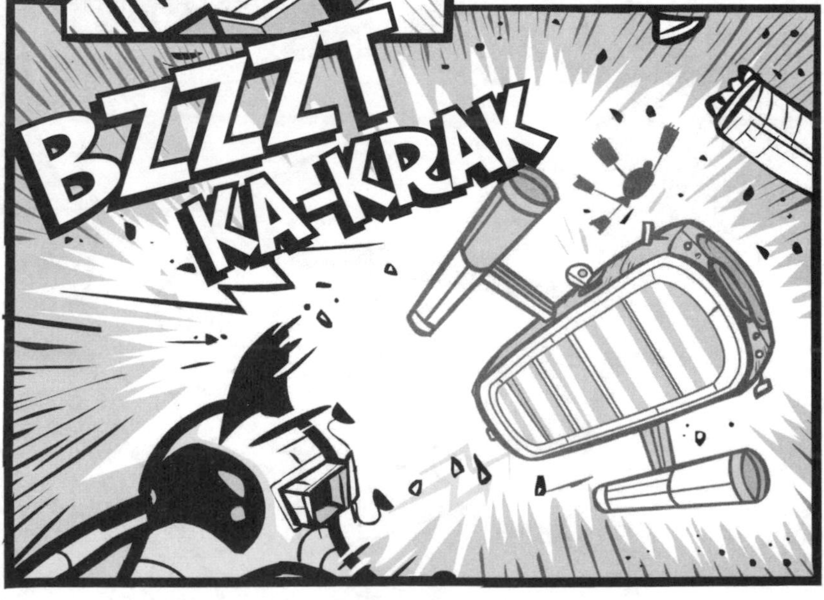
BZZZT
KA-KRAK

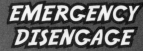

Princess Dagger bursts through the door and points to the wall of ships ahead of us. "So now we gotta try to outrun the Royal Armada?!"

I turn to the princess and narrow my eyes. I'm looking way concentrated and super pilot-like. "We're not outrunning 'em. We're going right at them—right for the gap left by that Jack Jet."

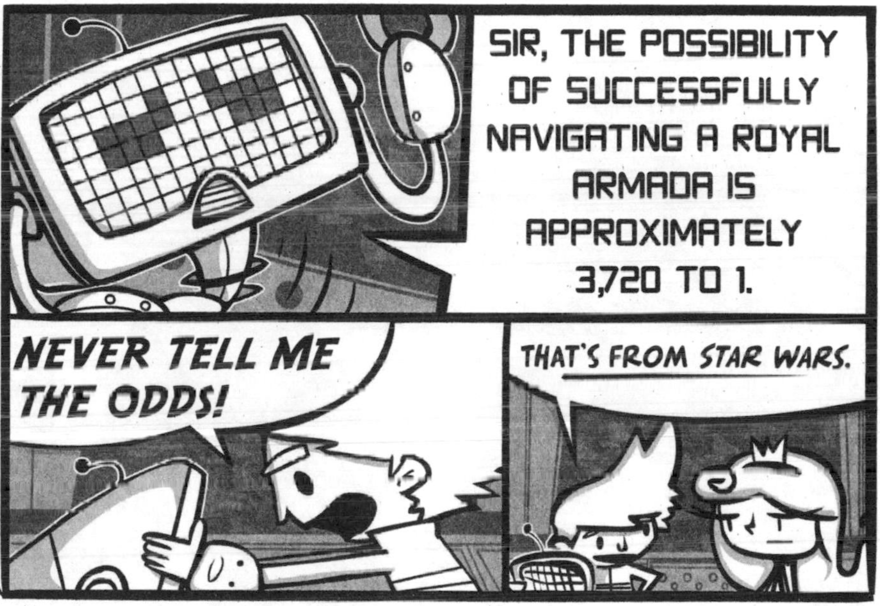
SIR, THE POSSIBILITY OF SUCCESSFULLY NAVIGATING A ROYAL ARMADA IS APPROXIMATELY 3,720 TO 1.
NEVER TELL ME THE ODDS!
THAT'S FROM STAR WARS.

"*Star Wars?*" Princess Dagger asks.

"Y'know, the movie," I say.

"What's a movie?"

I sigh. "Sometimes I really, really miss Earth . . .

NOW HANG ON. HERE GOES—"

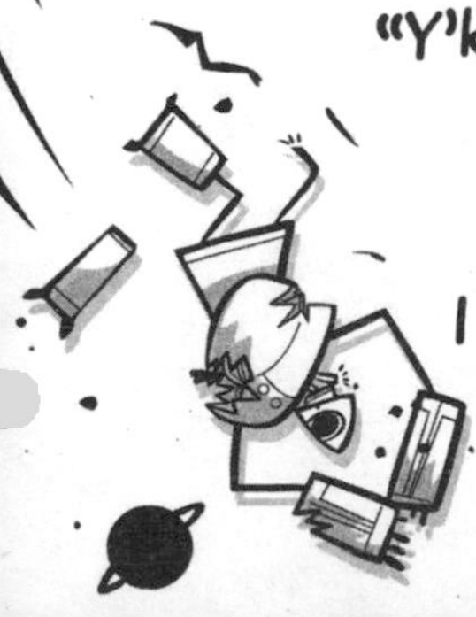

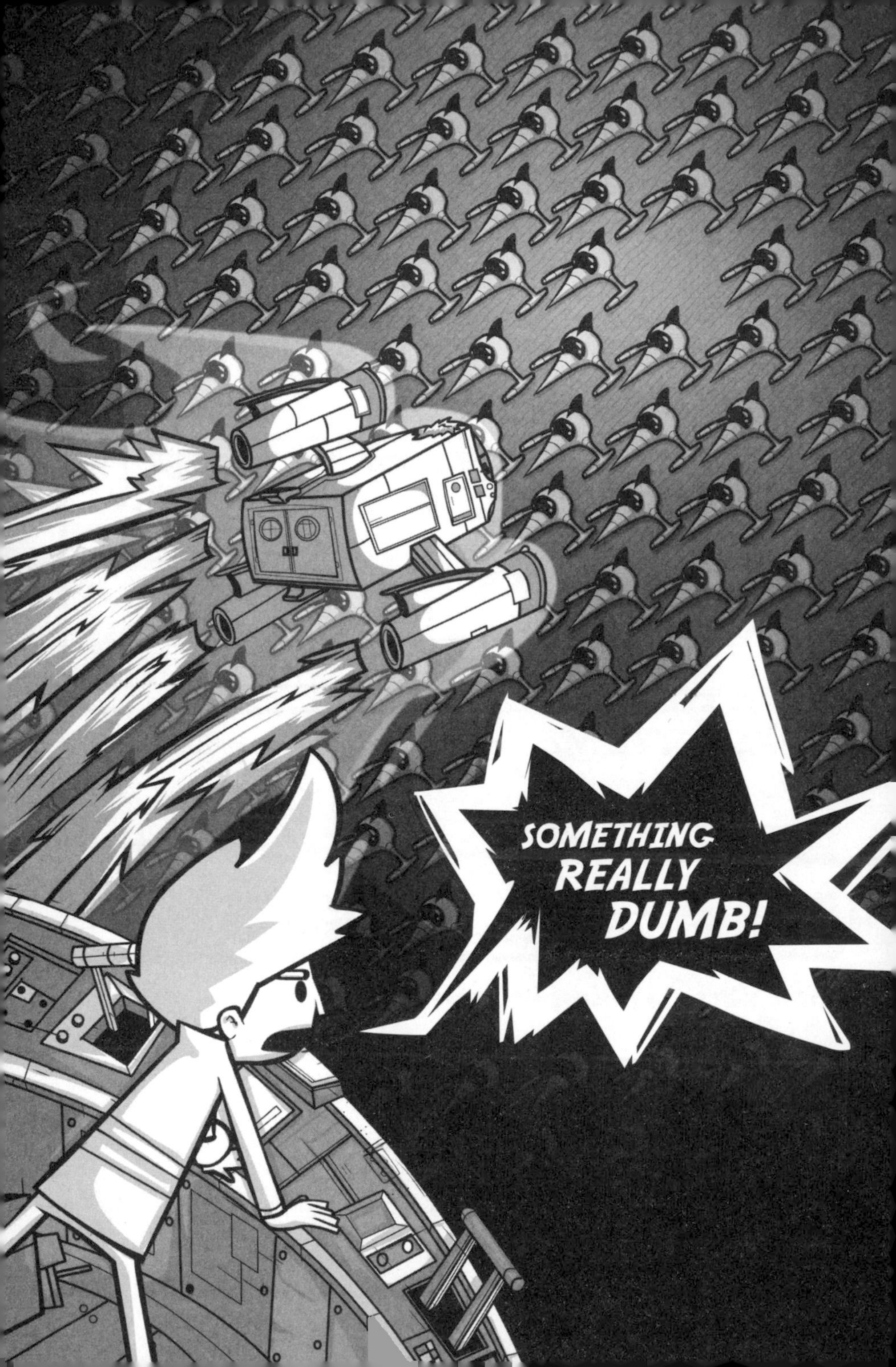
SOMETHING REALLY DUMB!

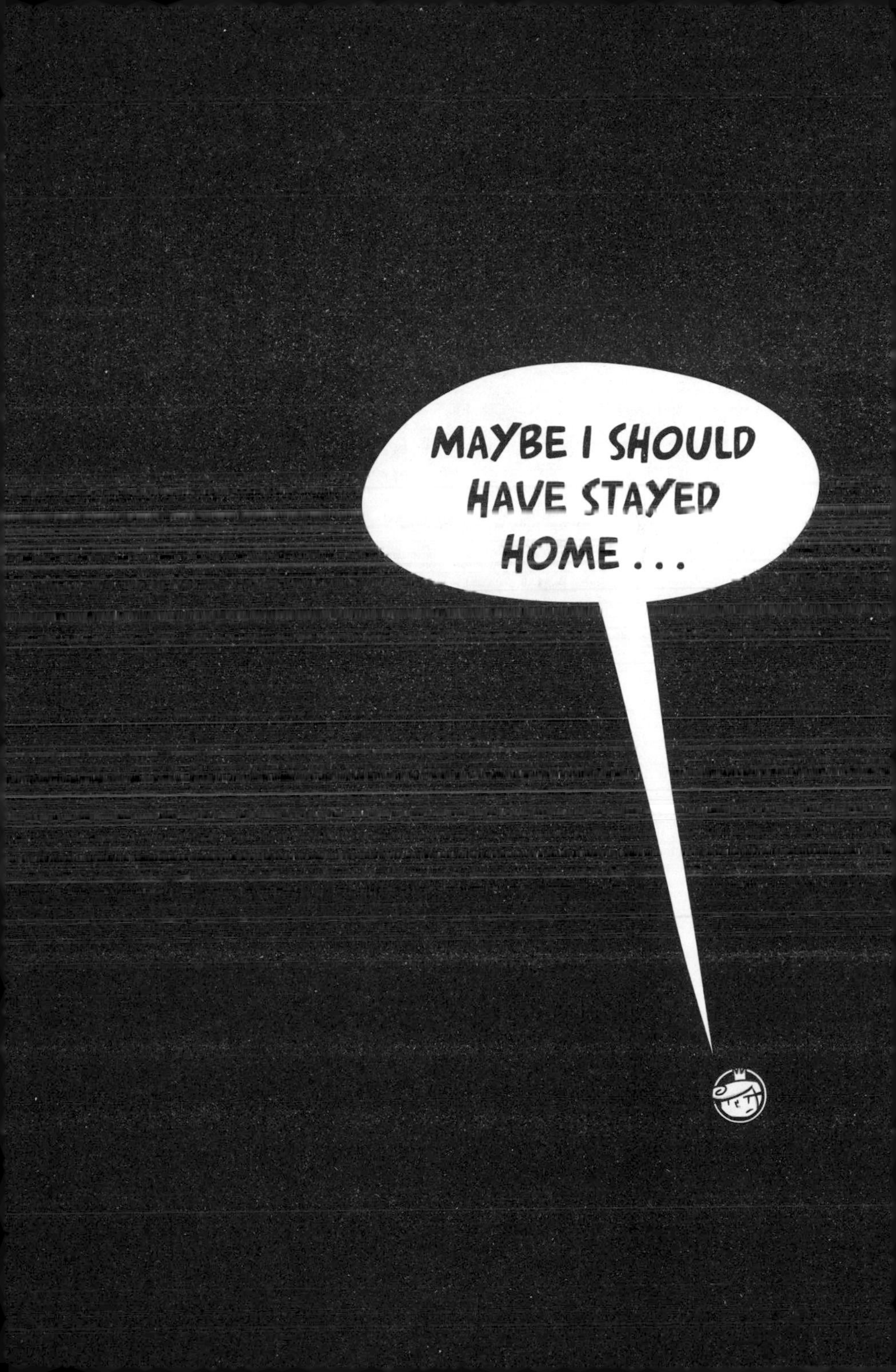
MAYBE I SHOULD HAVE STAYED HOME . . .

GUYS, I HATE TO INTERRUPT THE LOVEFEST, BUT—

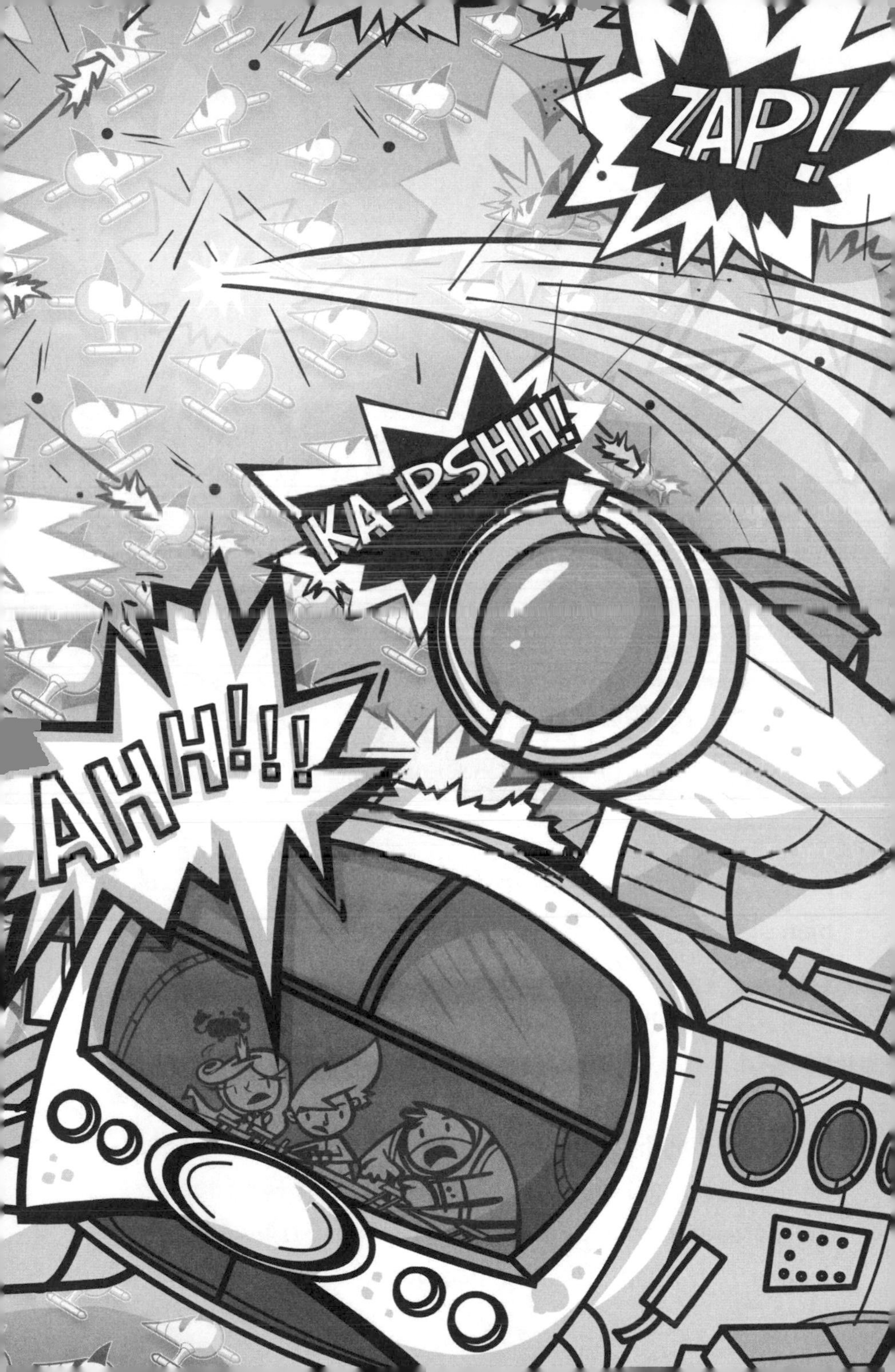
ZAP!
KA-PSHH!
AHH!!!

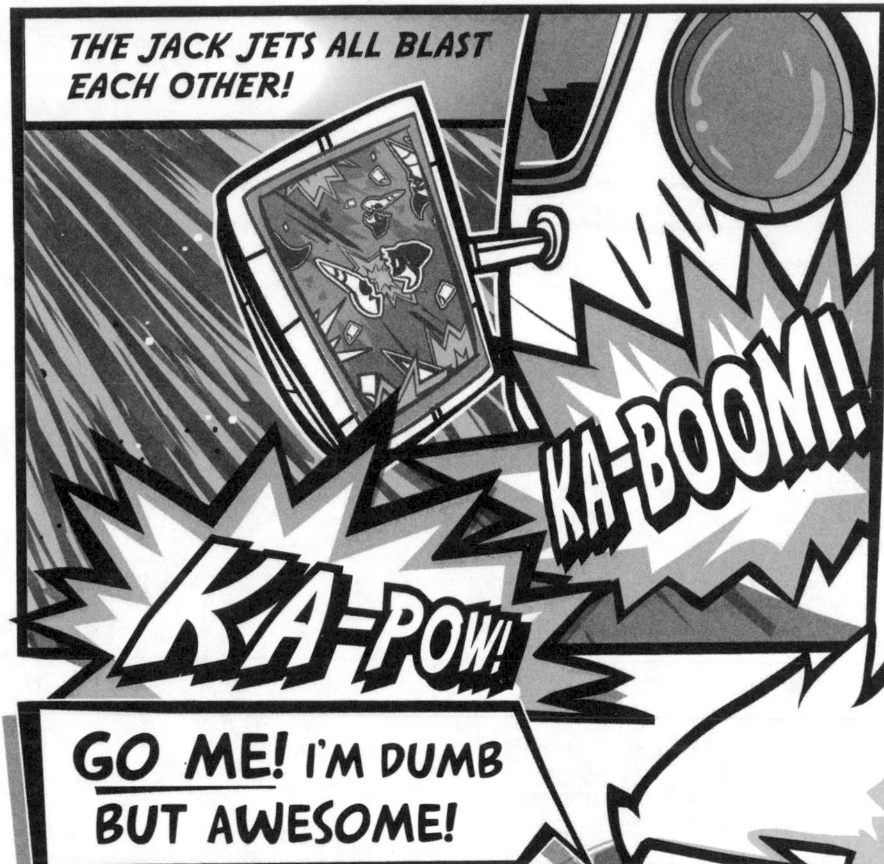
THE JACK JETS ALL BLAST EACH OTHER!
KA-BOOM!
KA-POW!
GO ME! I'M DUMB BUT AWESOME!

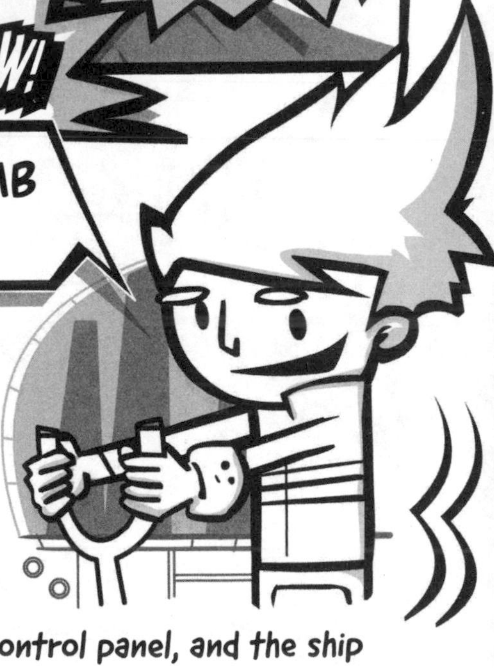

I can't believe it! My dumb plan actually worked! I think that's the first time a dumb plan of mine has ***EVER*** worked.

I punch a tiny button on the control panel, and the ship adjusts course. I announce, "Now we head for the interstellar highway. Time to put some distance between us and that flying flock of bad guys."

As the ship turns, Princess Dagger plops down next to me. I grind my teeth. Just make yourself at home, Princess . . .

The royal brat turns to me and says, "So, dude. Cool escape and all. But now I'm sort of hungry. Do you have any of that Space Paste stuff?"

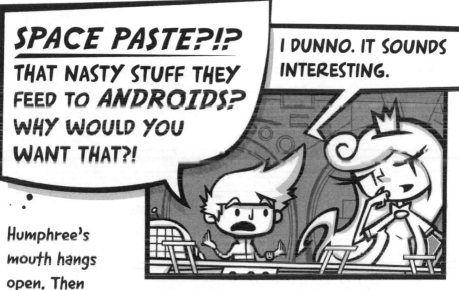

SPACE PASTE?!? THAT NASTY STUFF THEY FEED TO ANDROIDS? WHY WOULD YOU WANT THAT?!
I DUNNO. IT SOUNDS INTERESTING.

Humphree's mouth hangs open. Then he exclaims, "You want to eat space paste because it

SOUNDS INTERESTING?

Lady, when I was a space pirate, we ***HAD*** to eat space paste—it was all we had!"

GUYS, I HATE TO INTERRUPT THE LOVEFEST, BUT—

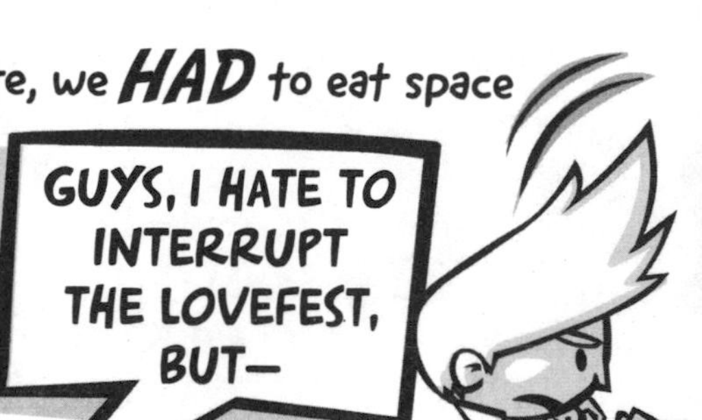

"Well, it sounds like you were a pretty crummy space pirate," Princess Dagger says.

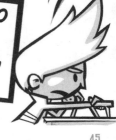

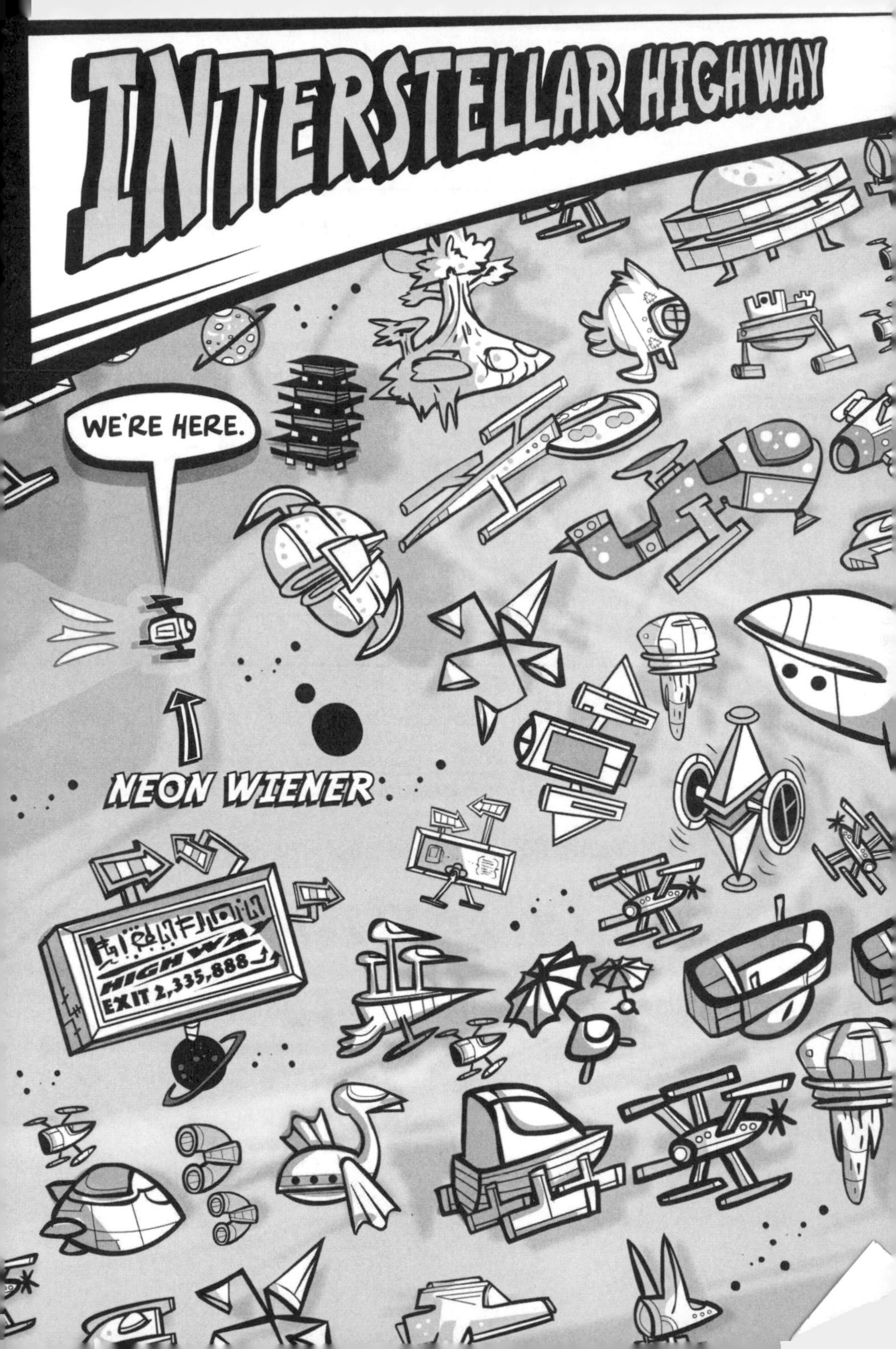
INTERSTELLAR HIGHWAY
WE'RE HERE.
NEON WIENER
EXIT 2,335,888

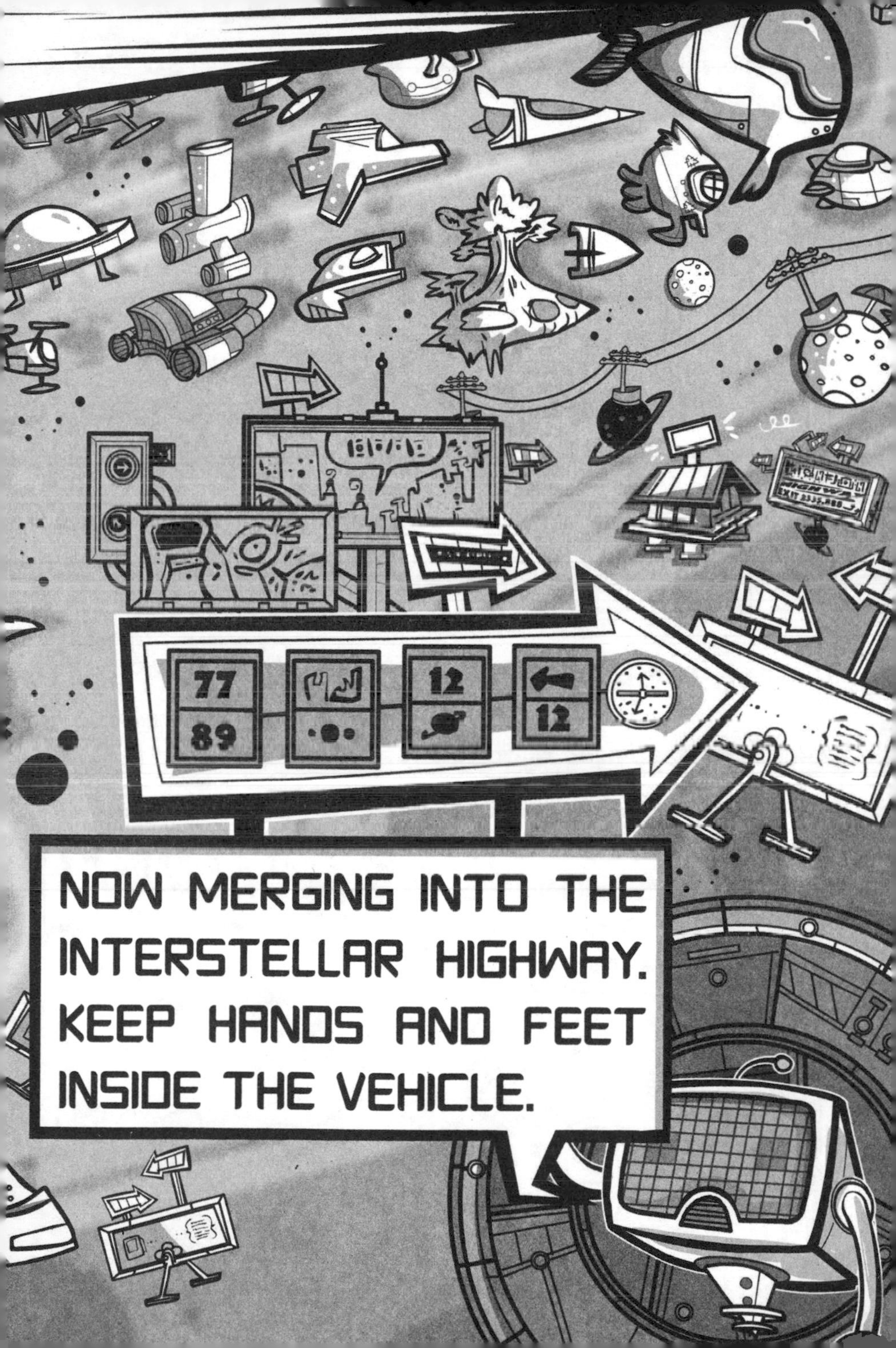
NOW MERGING INTO THE INTERSTELLAR HIGHWAY. KEEP HANDS AND FEET INSIDE THE VEHICLE.

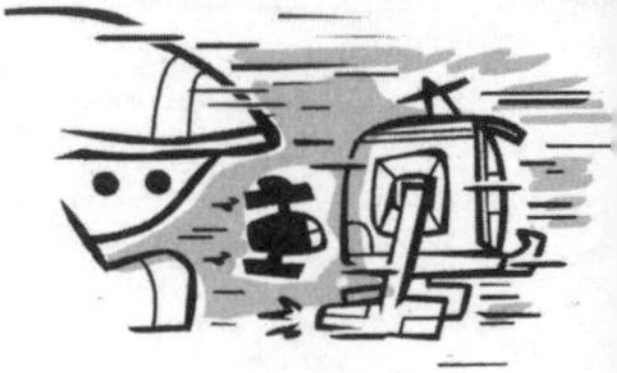

I breathe a massive sigh of relief. We're on the highway. **WE ARE SAFE!**

I'm feeling pretty good. I mean, in the past hour I've had my giant hot dog stolen, escaped a space port, dodged a bunch of rockets, and outrun a Royal Armada!

And me and my buddy and this bratty princess are still alive! I don't want to brag, but I think I've handled all this junk pretty well. Honestly? I'm kind of an awesome space guy today.

But here's the thing about life among the stars.

It can go from good to bad like ***THAT***—light speed quick!

And that's happening right now . . .

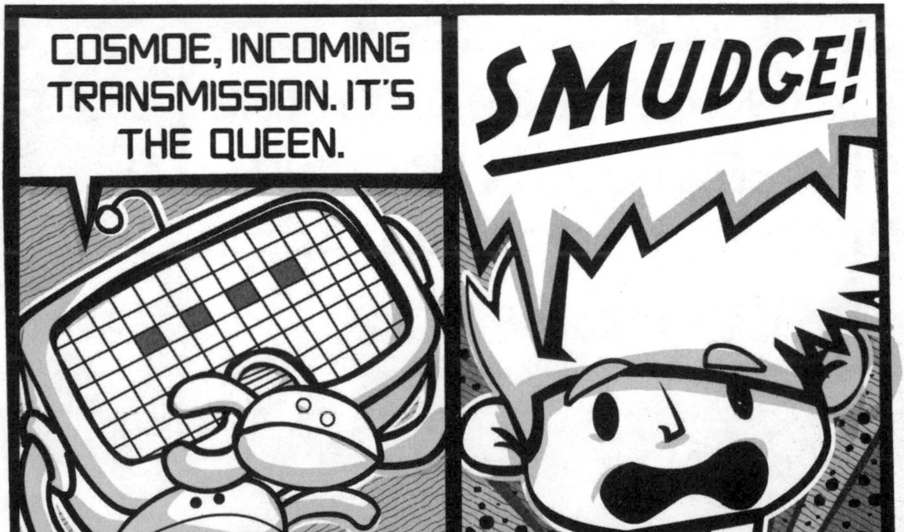
COSMOE, INCOMING TRANSMISSION. IT'S THE QUEEN.
SMUDGE!

F.R.E.D.'s speakers crackle and the queen's voice comes on. Uh-oh. It's an intergalactic transmission. These are big deals—they go out to every ship in the galaxy.

NOT GOOD!

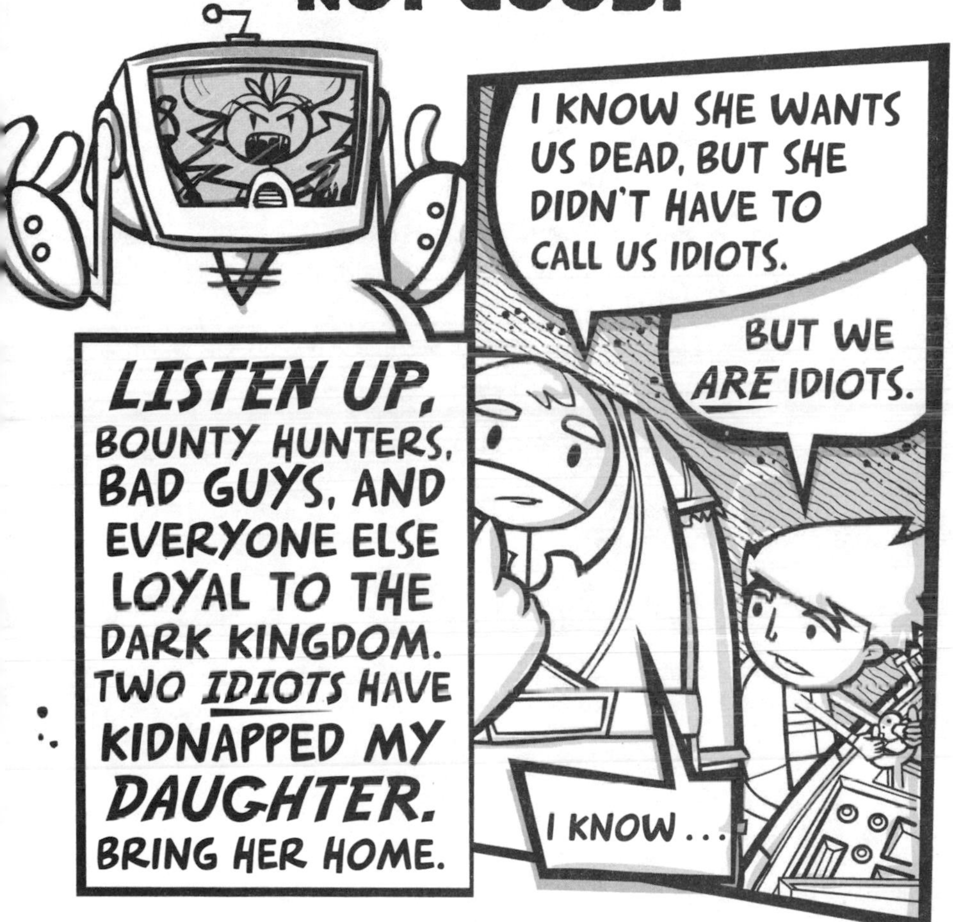
LISTEN UP, BOUNTY HUNTERS, BAD GUYS, AND EVERYONE ELSE LOYAL TO THE DARK KINGDOM. TWO IDIOTS HAVE KIDNAPPED MY DAUGHTER. BRING HER HOME.
I KNOW SHE WANTS US DEAD, BUT SHE DIDN'T HAVE TO CALL US IDIOTS.
BUT WE ARE IDIOTS.
I KNOW . . .

So like I said, things can go from good to bad with light speed quickness.

And this, right now, is ***BAD.*** Because the interstellar highway is jam-packed full of—

BOUNTY HUNTERS, BAD GUYS, AND EVERYONE ELSE LOYAL TO THE QUEEN!

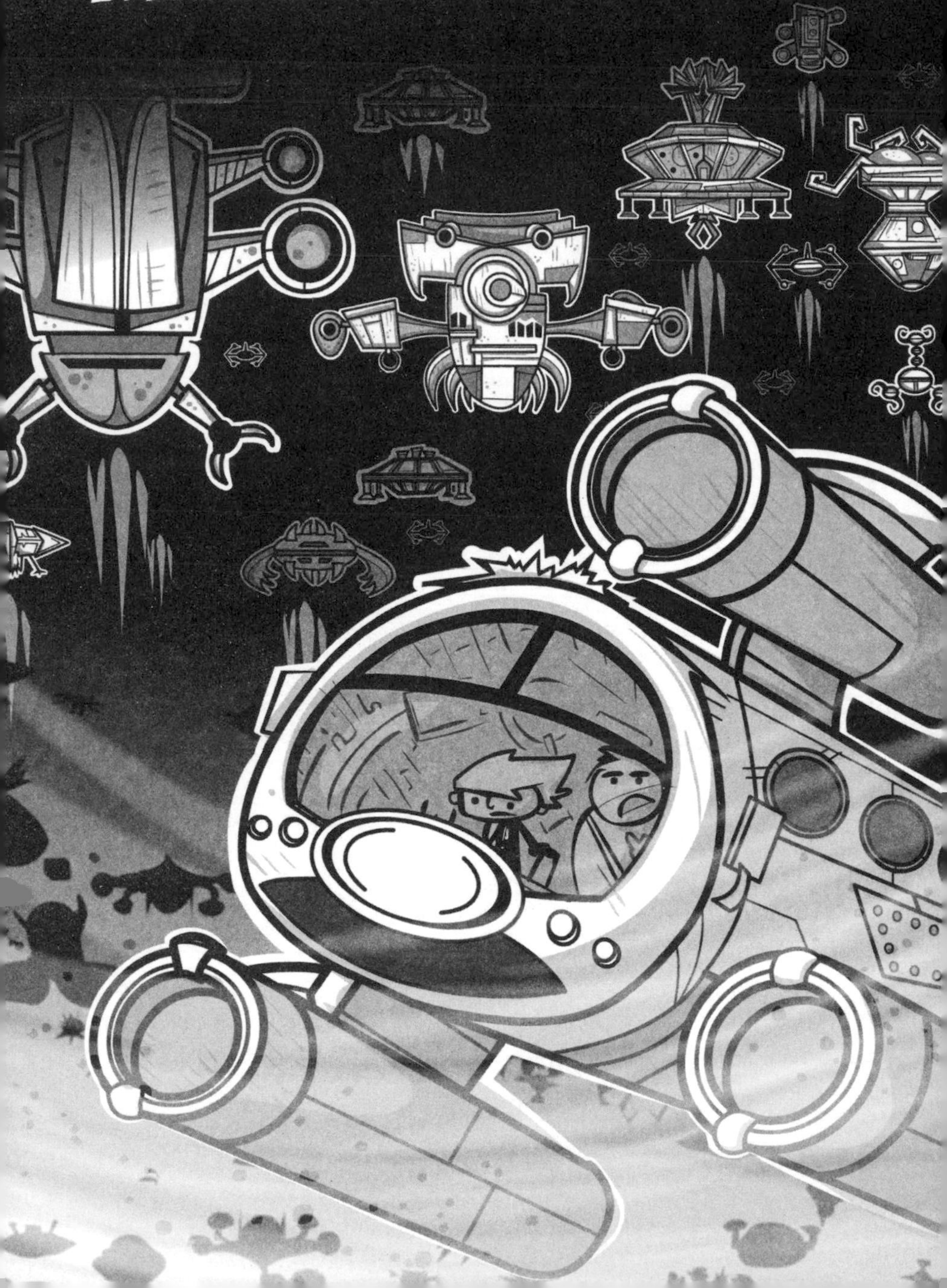

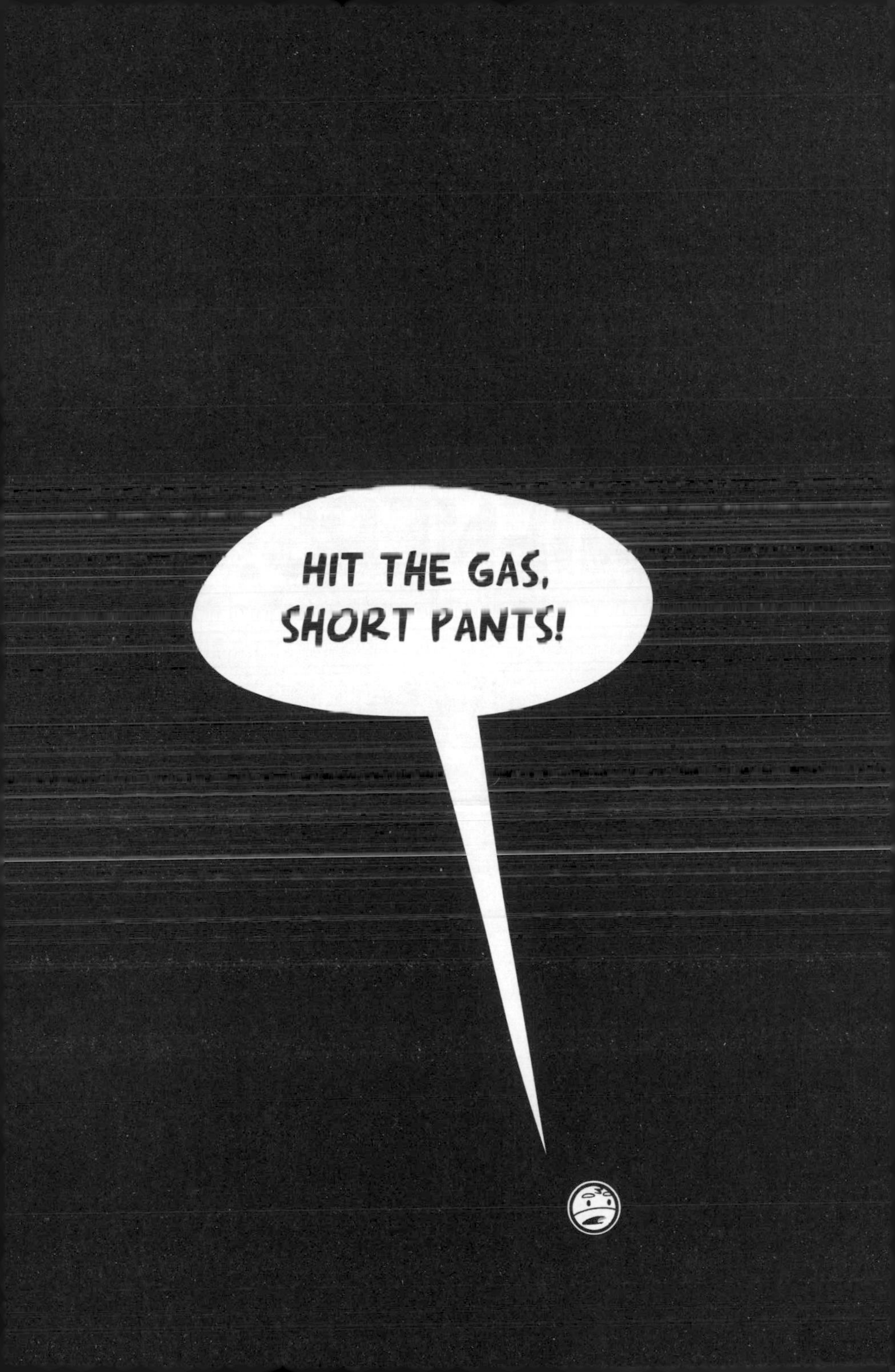
HIT THE GAS, SHORT PANTS!

KRACK
-A-
LACKING
WIENERS!

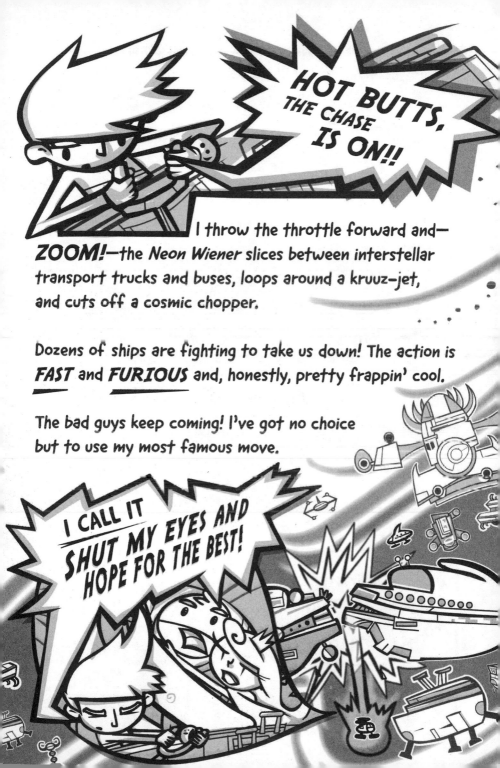

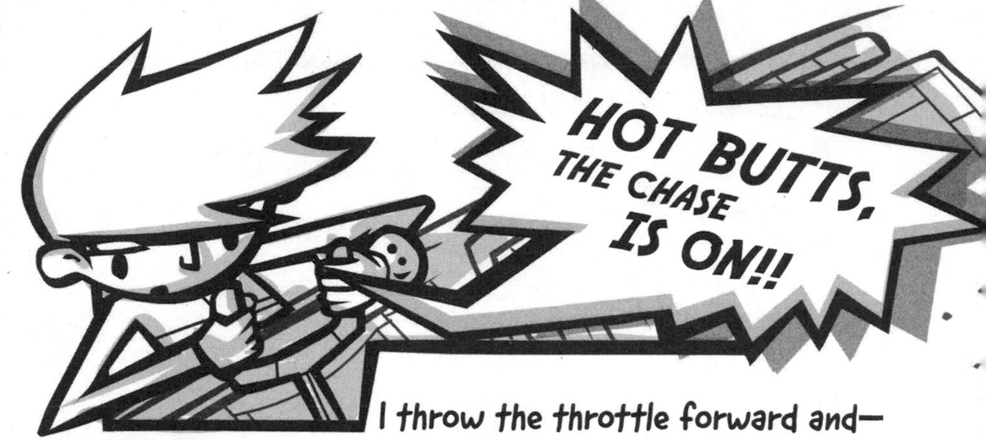
HOT BUTTS, THE CHASE IS ON!!

I throw the throttle forward and—***ZOOM!***—the *Neon Wiener* slices between interstellar transport trucks and buses, loops around a kruuz-jet, and cuts off a cosmic chopper.

Dozens of ships are fighting to take us down! The action is ***FAST*** and ***FURIOUS*** and, honestly, pretty frappin' cool.

The bad guys keep coming! I've got no choice but to use my most famous move.

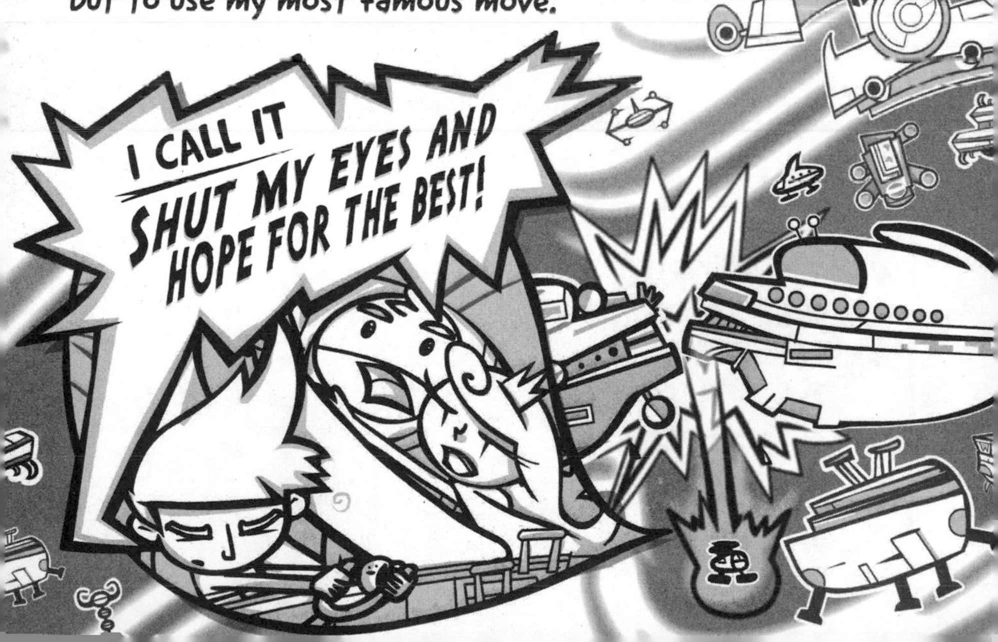
I CALL IT SHUT MY EYES AND HOPE FOR THE BEST!

And now, of course, Princess Dagger picks a horrible time to start a conversation! She clears her throat and says:

"WE SHOULD PROBABLY—"

KA-BAM! A cruiser **SLAMS** into the side of the Neon Wiener. My hands shake.

Princess Dagger keeps yapping. **"TALK ABOUT—"**

BA-BANG! A shark-shaped ship **RAMS** us from below. I'm nearly tossed from my seat.

Princess Dagger is shouting now.

"OUR FUTURE TOGETHER!"

I wheel around. "What future?! We have no future together!"

"WELL . . . WHAT DO YOU GUYS DO?" Princess Dagger asks. **"Y'KNOW, FOR FUN?"**

MOSTLY WE FLY AROUND AND **SELL** HOT DOGS AND GET INTO ADVENTURES.

THAT! I WANT TO DO THAT!

I'm so annoyed I'm about to explode. "Princess, you ever think that we don't want you joining us? You just jumped on board and now the whole galaxy—starting with your mom—is trying to kill us."

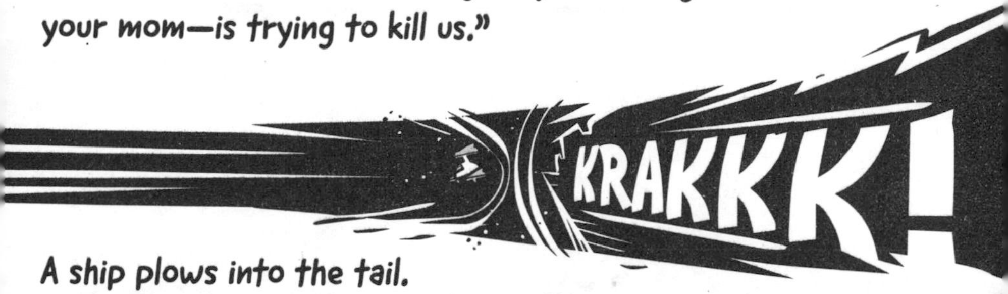
KRAKKK!

A ship plows into the tail.

Everything shakes. But Princess Dagger isn't giving up . . .

She puts her hands on her hips and shouts,

BUT I COULD HELP OUT!
WITH THE HOT-DOG-SELLING THING!

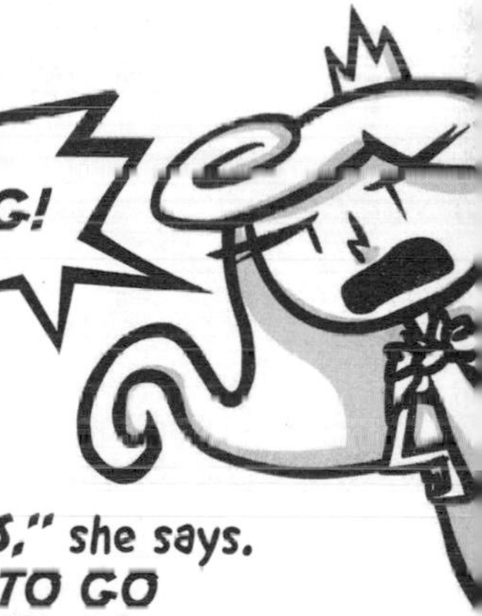

"Why do you want to sell hot dogs?! You're a princess!" I scream.

"BUT I DON'T WANT TO BE A PRINCESS," she says. ***"I WANT TO SEE THE GALAXY! I WANT TO GO VOLCANO DIVING AND I WANT TO WATCH MUTANT WORM WRESTLING AND I WANT TO PUNCH A RHUNO GATOR IN THE NOSE AND I WANT TO—WELL—LIVE!"***

Humphree roars, "If you two don't pipe down, <u>**NONE**</u> of us are going to live!"

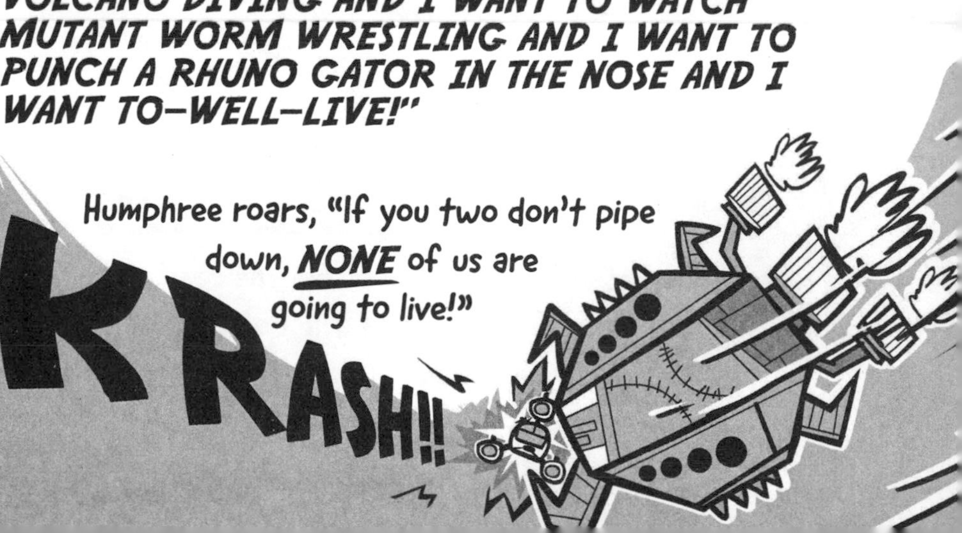
KRASH!!

"What if I arrange a super-smooth getaway for us?" the princess asks hopefully. "Then can we be a team?"

"Don't worry!" the princess exclaims. "I have a kickin' plan!"

"Is the plan evil?" I ask.

"Um. No . . ." she says.

"Be honest," I say.

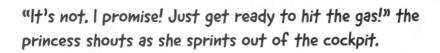

"It's not. I promise! Just get ready to hit the gas!" the princess shouts as she sprints out of the cockpit.

I'm pretty sure this plan is going to be evil . . .

"You're cool with this, buddy?" Humphree asks.

I feel my forehead scrunch up real tight. My brain wheels are turning. Am I cool with this? I don't know! The princess is big trouble for me and Humphree! But deep down in my hot-dog-filled gut, I think everyone has the right to choose not to be evil and to choose to chill out with buddies!

So I say, "Yes, Humps. I'm cool with this."

"The three of us will be on the run ***FOREVER,*** " Humphree says. "You know what we're gonna be then? Hobos."

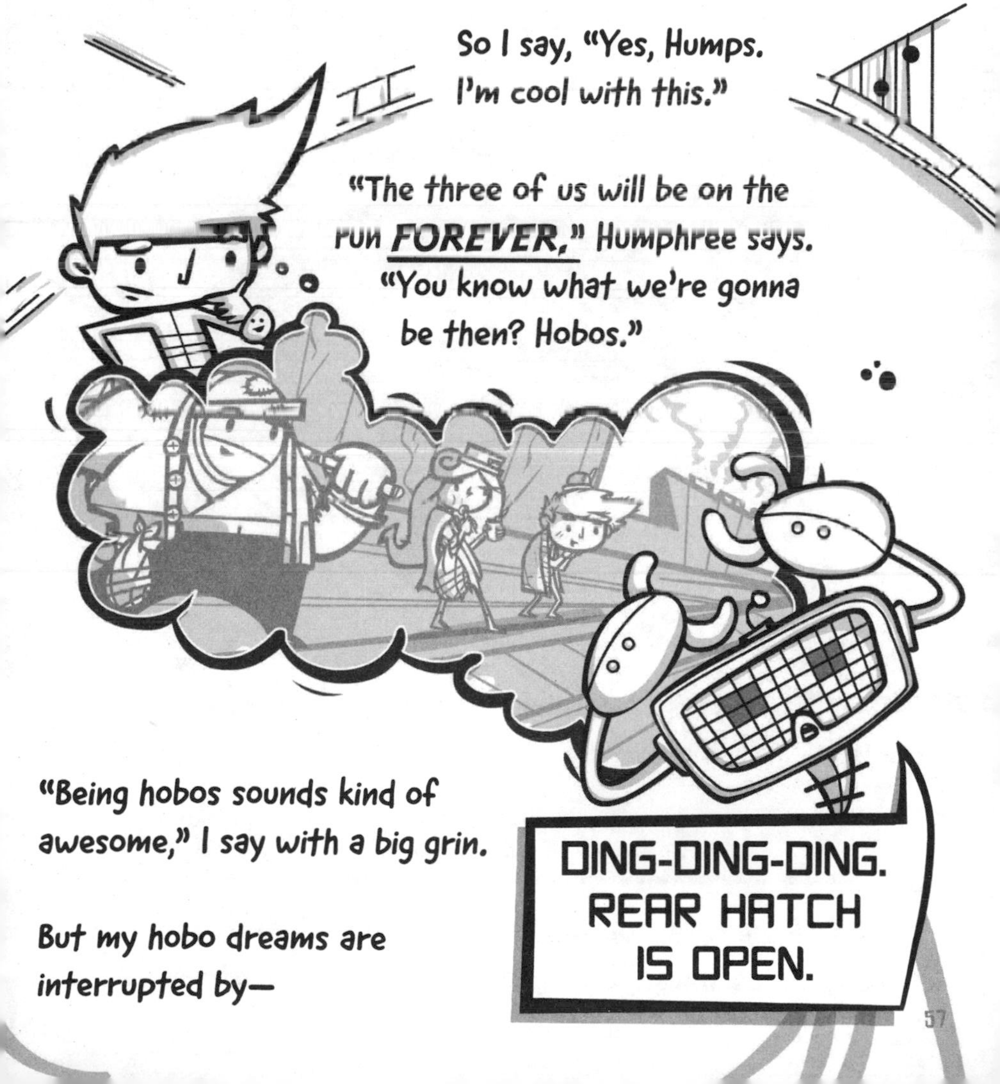

"Being hobos sounds kind of awesome," I say with a big grin.

But my hobo dreams are interrupted by—

DING-DING-DING. REAR HATCH IS OPEN.

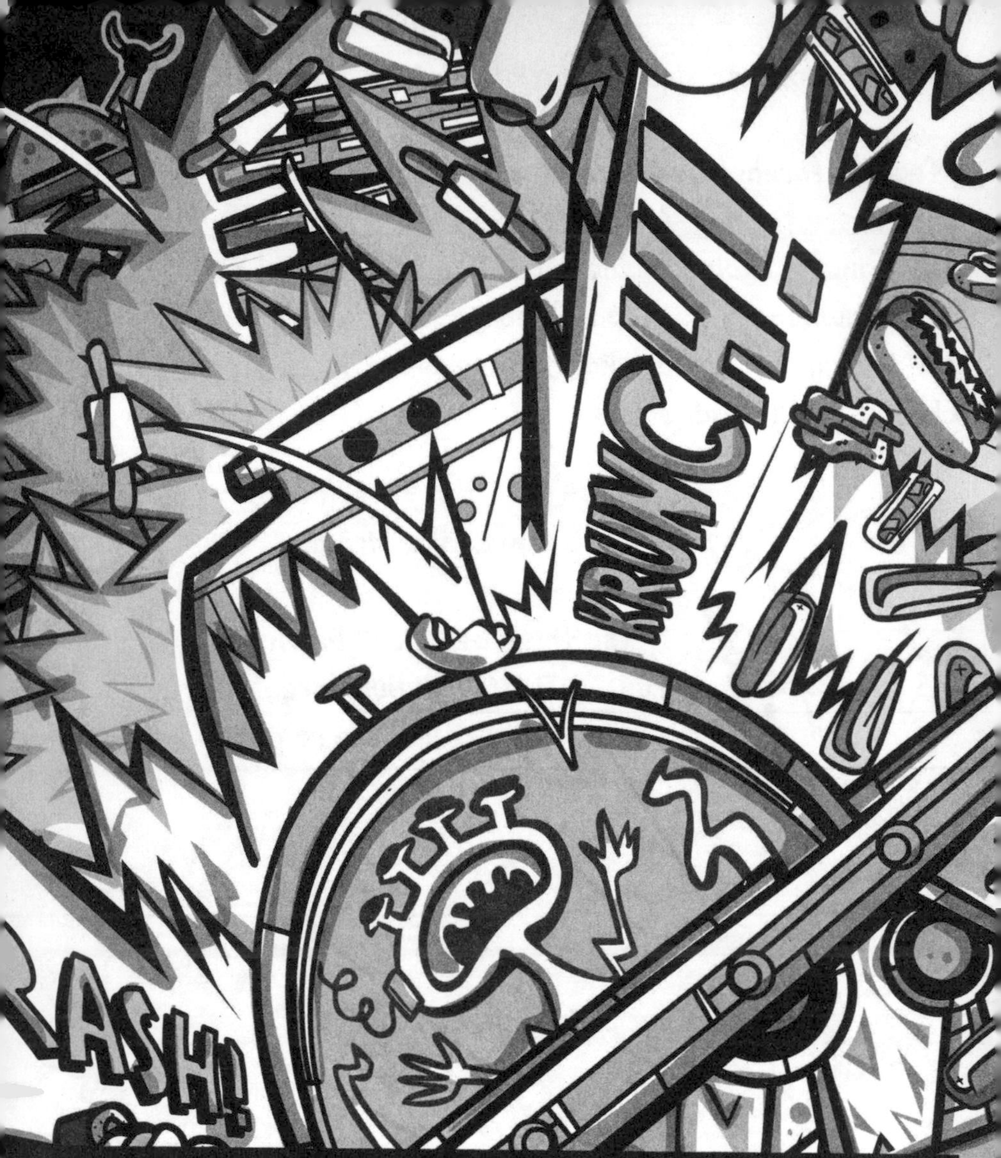
KRUNCH!!
ASH!!

I'm looking at the mirror,

AND I CAN'T BELIEVE IT!

It's a full-fledged, top-notch wiener parade! Hot dogs fill the sky! Ships smash, crash, and bash into each other.

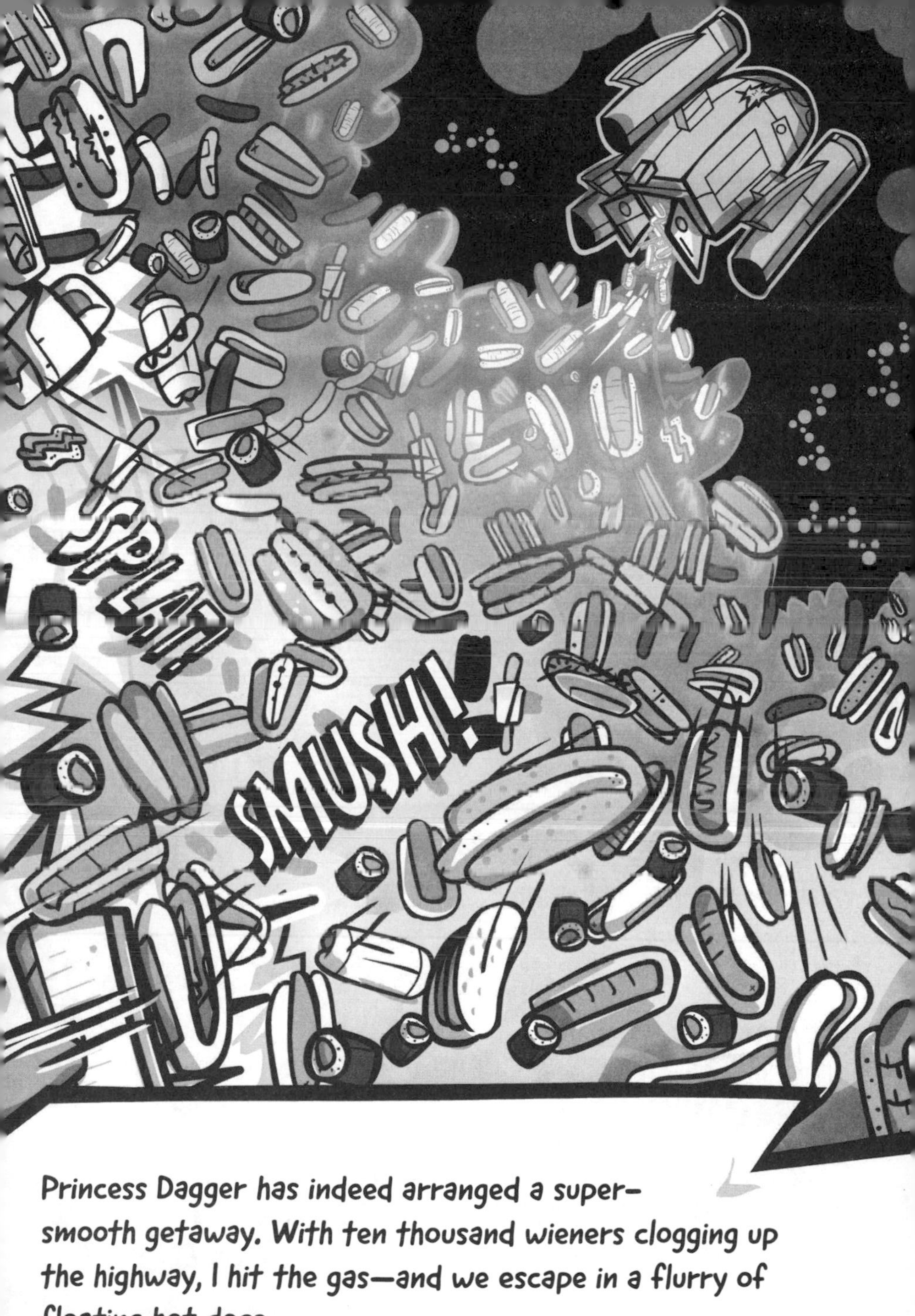
SPLAT!
SMUSH!

Princess Dagger has indeed arranged a super-smooth getaway. With ten thousand wieners clogging up the highway, I hit the gas—and we escape in a flurry of floating hot dogs.

LATER . . .

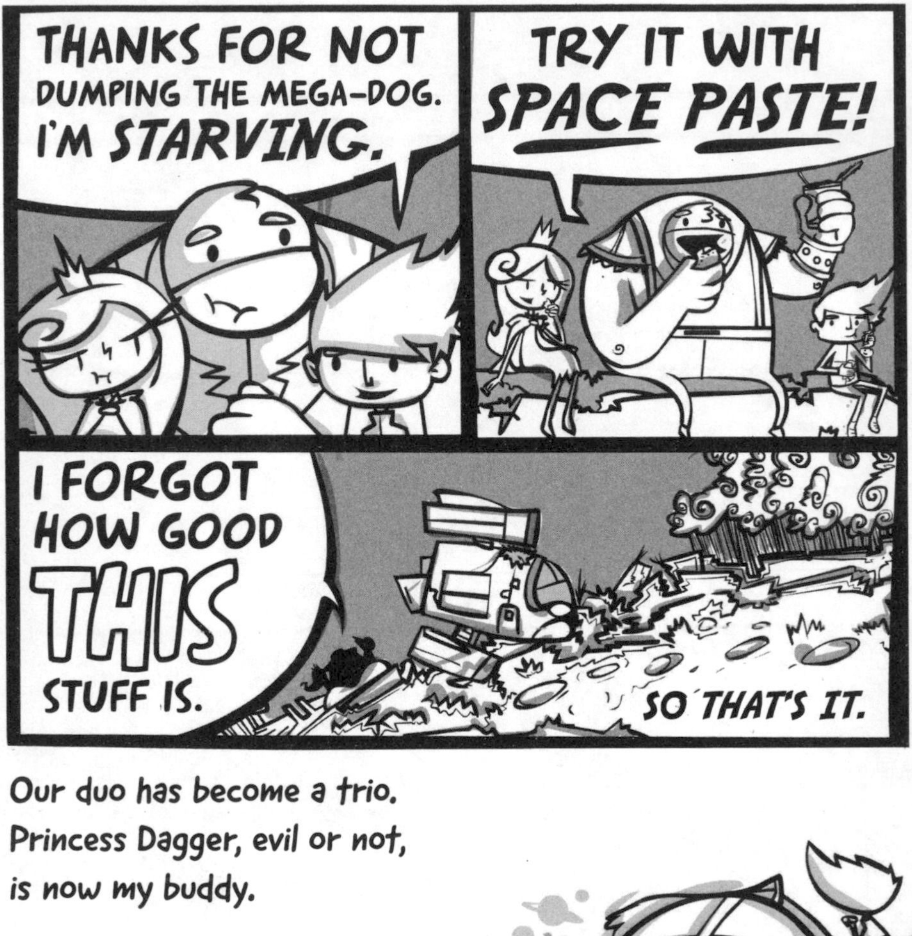
THANKS FOR NOT DUMPING THE MEGA-DOG. I'M STARVING.
TRY IT WITH SPACE PASTE!
I FORGOT HOW GOOD THIS STUFF IS.
SO THAT'S IT.

Our duo has become a trio. Princess Dagger, evil or not, is now my buddy.

But that does not mean all is well. The evil queen is **ANGRY!**

And I'm pretty sure she will not rest until she has her daughter back . . .

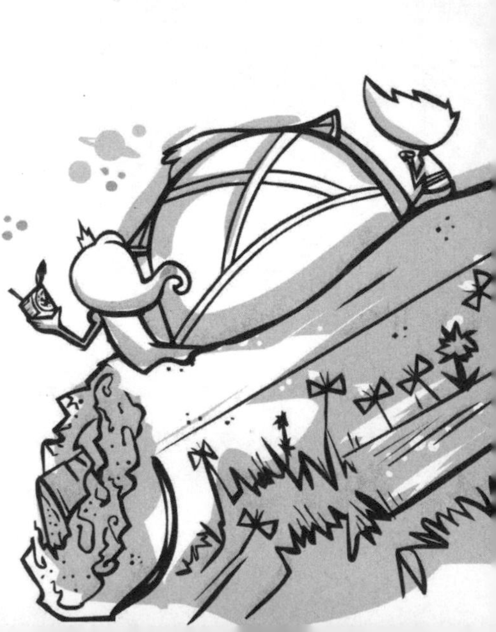

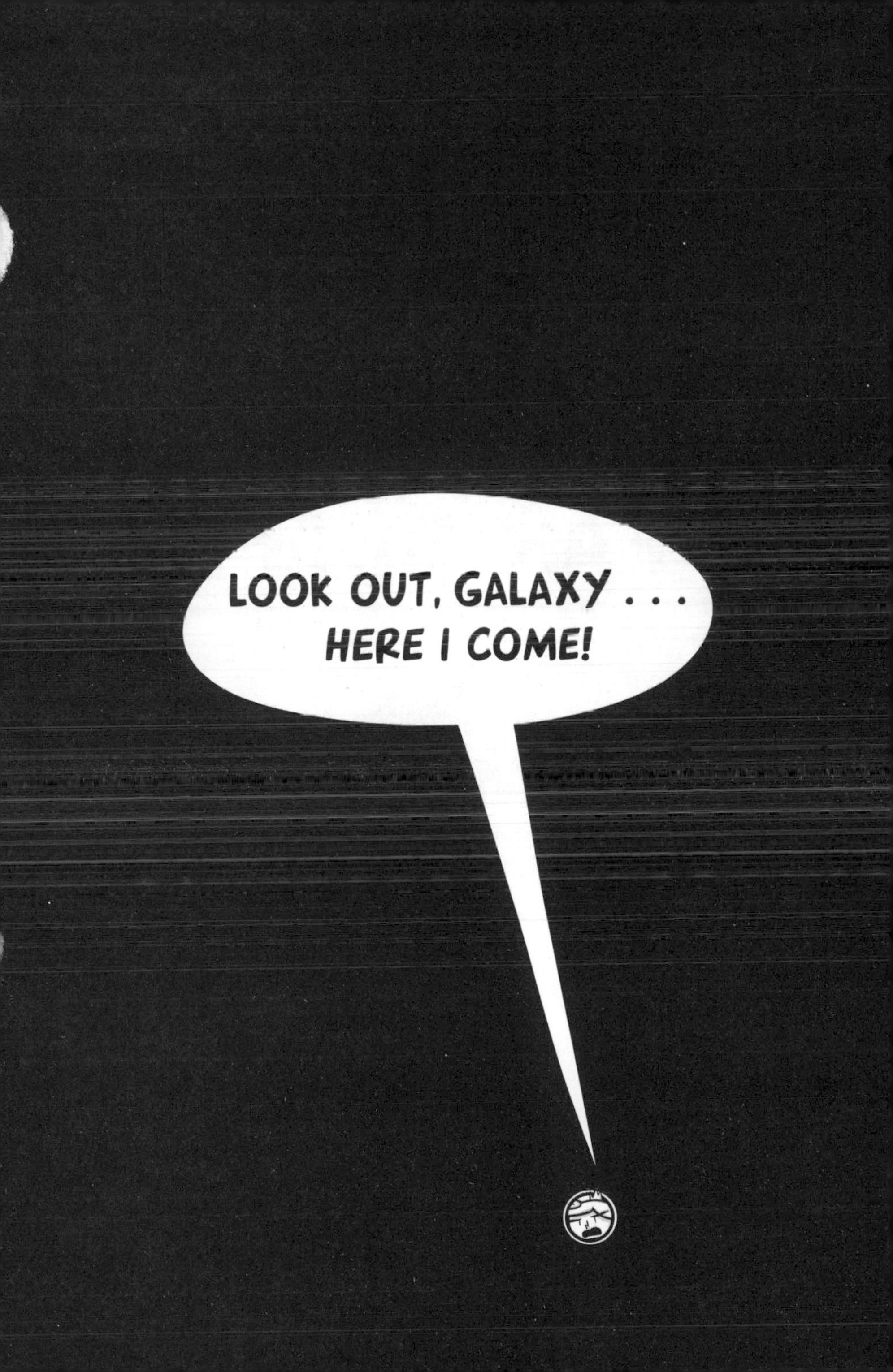
LOOK OUT, GALAXY . . . HERE I COME!

TURBO EAR SLAP!

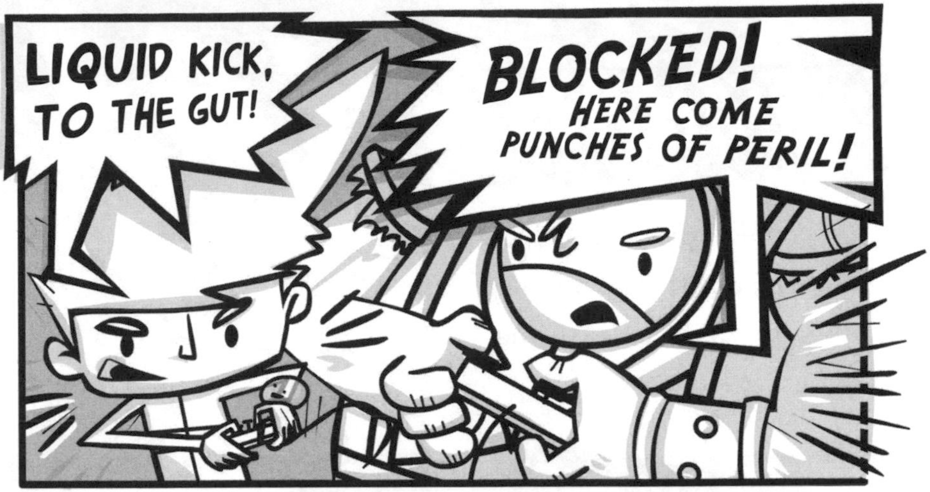
LIQUID KICK, TO THE GUT!
BLOCKED! HERE COME PUNCHES OF PERIL!

Humphree and I are battling it out at the most kick-butt videogame ever—

SUPER MOON NINJA DEATH JAB.

Usually, I win at videogames. See, back on Earth, all I did was play video games. But right now, things are not going my way.

"BOOM! GOTCHA!" Humphree yells.

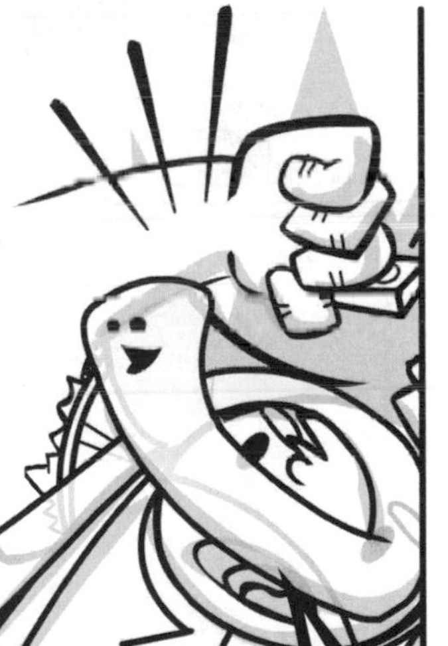

Aw man! He just nailed my ninja with a **9,000**-point Extreme Elbow Bite!

I need Goober help—

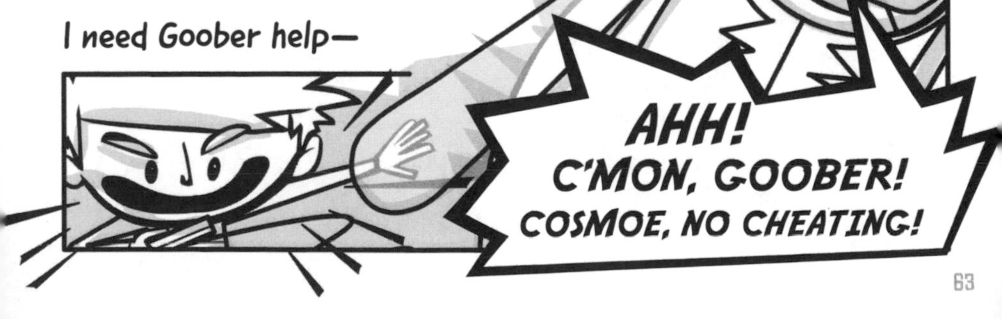
AHH!
C'MON, GOOBER!
COSMOE, NO CHEATING!

MUAHAHAHA!

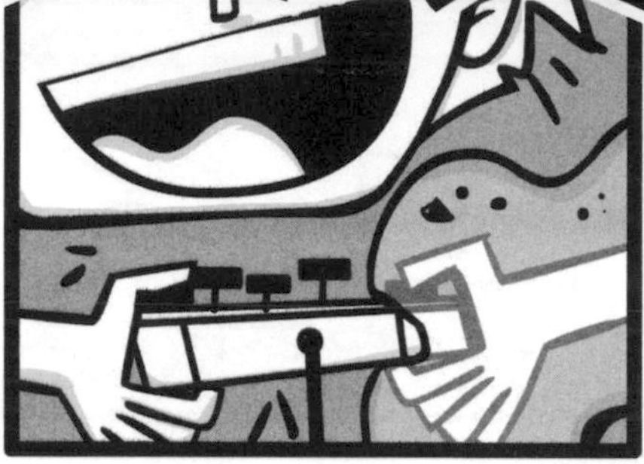

Now I got Humphree! My thumbs pound the controller and my ninja is about to unleash the mightiest of moves—

THE

TURBO EAR SLAP!

But then—

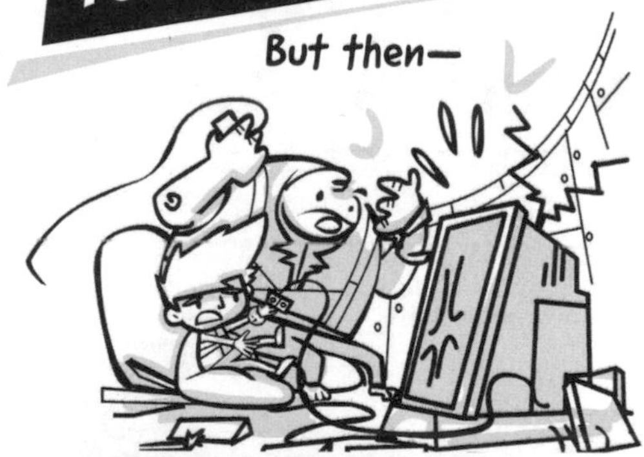

"Hey! What the smudge?!" I shout. "Who shut off the game?!"

"I was about to break Cosmoe in two!" Humphree moans.

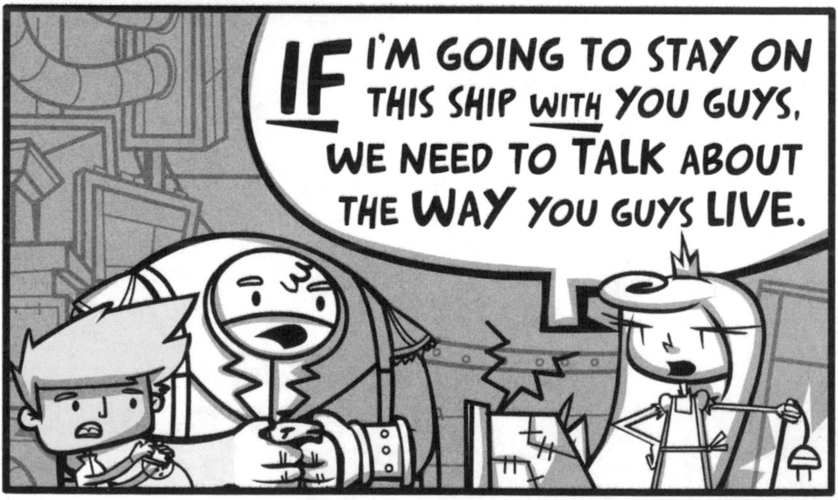
IF I'M GOING TO STAY ON THIS SHIP WITH YOU GUYS, WE NEED TO TALK ABOUT THE WAY YOU GUYS LIVE.

Oh great. Mom's here. Wonderful. "What's wrong with the way we live? There's nothing wrong with the way we live!" I exclaim.

"The ship is a total mess!" the princess says. "There's junk everywhere! And where there's not JUNK, there's GUNK! We need a chore chart. You guys need to clean. You're slobs!"

"Hey!" I say, jumping to my feet, all offended. "We're not slobs! Right, Humps?"

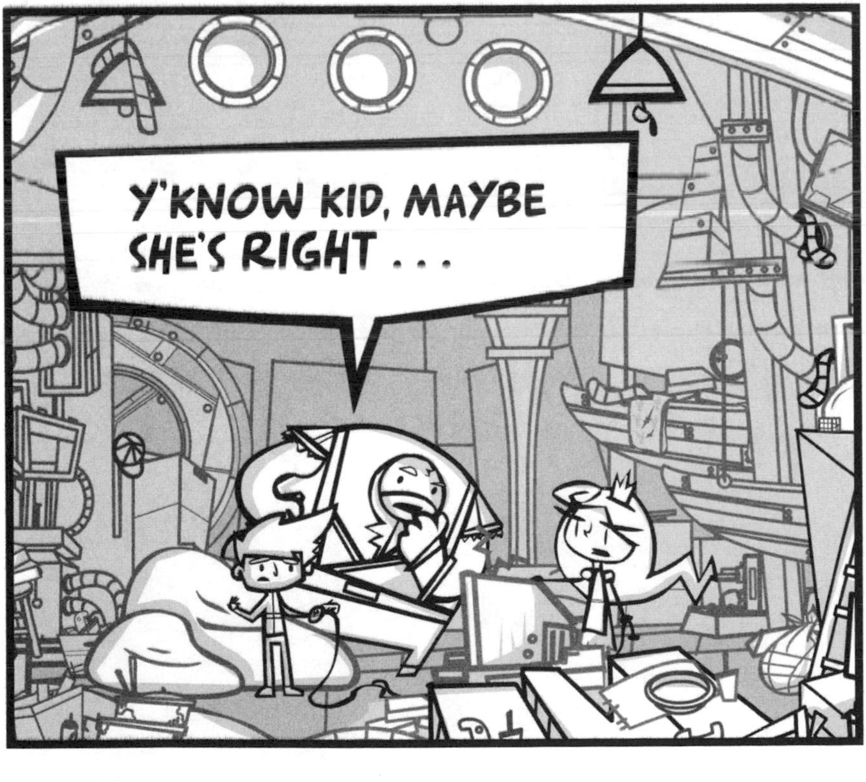
Y'KNOW KID, MAYBE SHE'S RIGHT . . .

LATER . . .

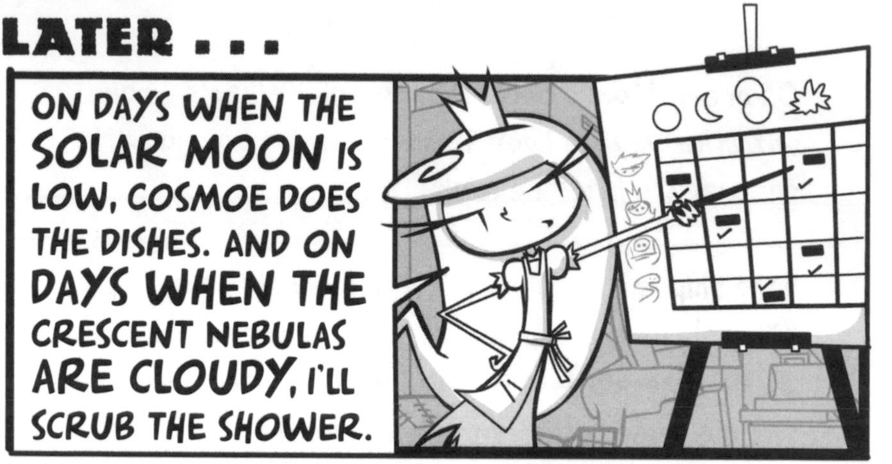
ON DAYS WHEN THE SOLAR MOON IS LOW, COSMOE DOES THE DISHES. AND ON DAYS WHEN THE CRESCENT NEBULAS ARE CLOUDY, I'LL SCRUB THE SHOWER.

WHAT. THE. SMUDGE.

Before Princess Dagger showed up, all Humphree and I did was goof around and get into adventures. And now we're talking chore charts?!?!

"The sooner you finish the chores," the princess says, "the sooner you can get back to video dork hour."

"It's not video dork hour!" I shout.

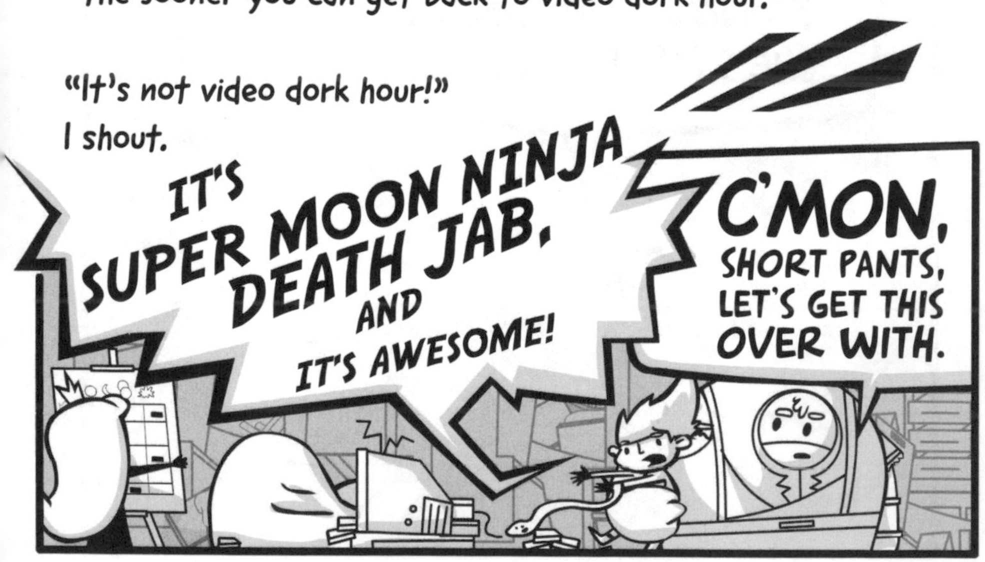
IT'S SUPER MOON NINJA DEATH JAB, AND IT'S AWESOME!
C'MON, SHORT PANTS, LET'S GET THIS OVER WITH.

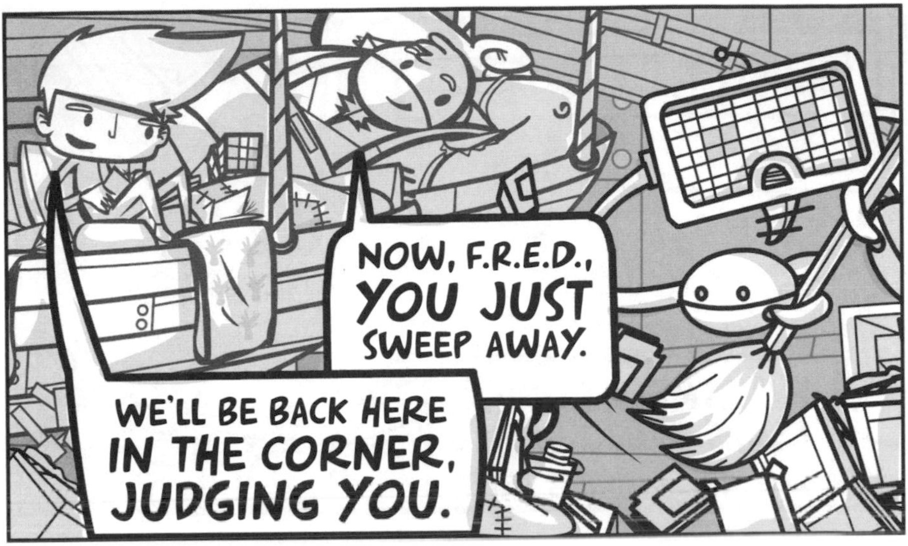
NOW, F.R.E.D., YOU JUST SWEEP AWAY.
WE'LL BE BACK HERE IN THE CORNER, JUDGING YOU.

Because I'm mentally awesome and crazy creative, I figure out how we avoid cleaning:

WE GET F.R.E.D. TO DO IT!

Turns out, though, F.R.E.D. is a pretty crummy butler. He's jabbing the broom everywhere.

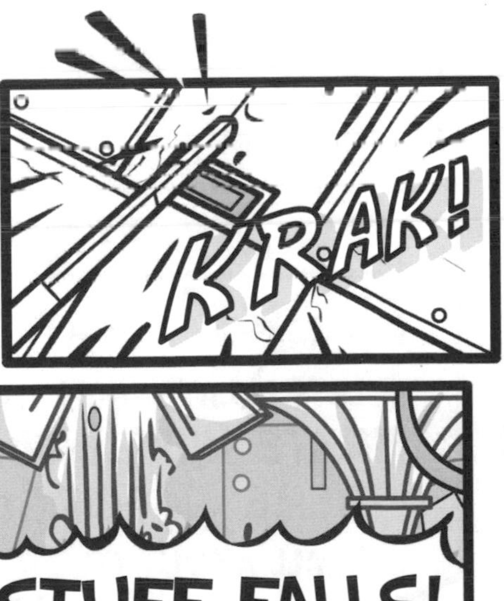
KRAK!

I know all about sweeping from my days on Earth. I'm about to show him how it's done when—

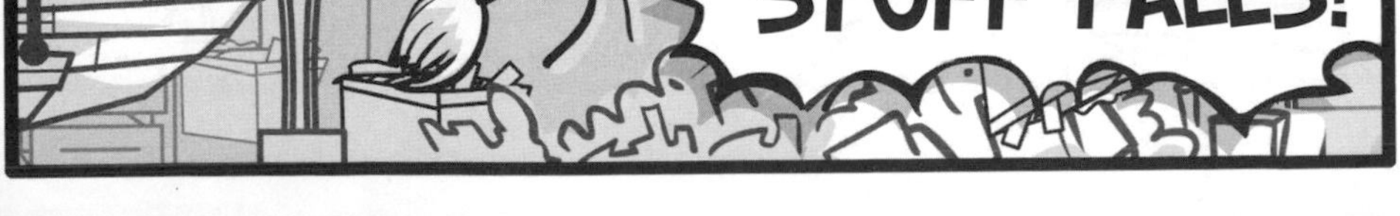
STUFF FALLS!

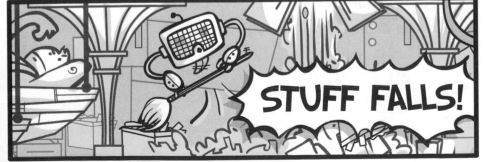

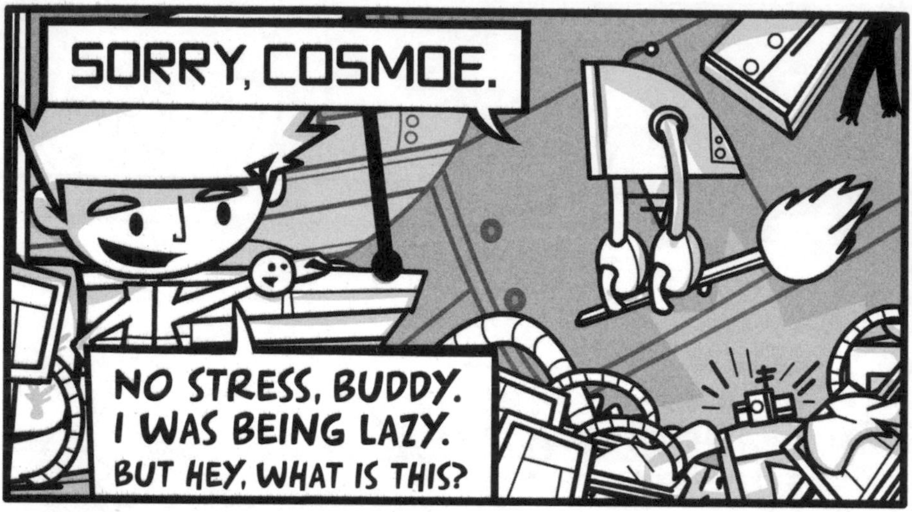
SORRY, COSMOE.
NO STRESS, BUDDY. I WAS BEING LAZY. BUT HEY, WHAT IS THIS?

Something strange just fell from the crack in the ceiling. It's like some sort of fancy electronic bracelet. Lights are flashing on it and it's making a beeping sound.

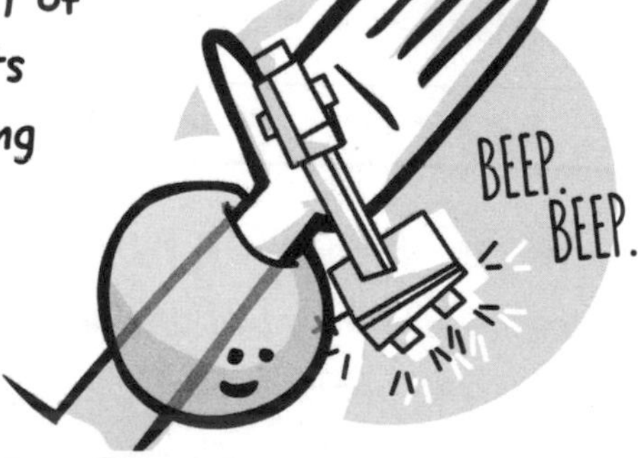
BEEP. BEEP.

Humphree's eyes go wide and he rushes over.

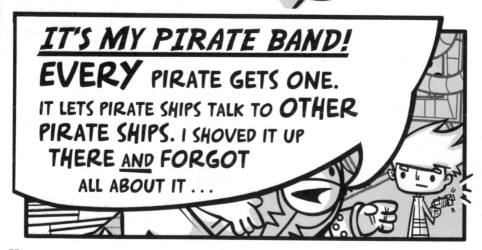

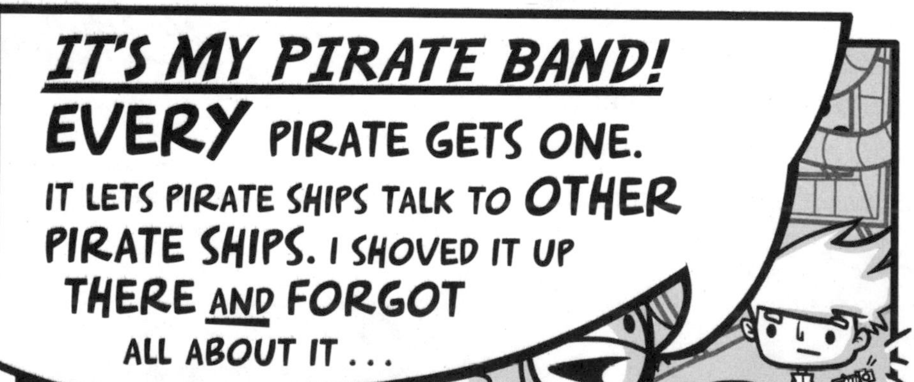
IT'S MY PIRATE BAND! EVERY PIRATE GETS ONE. IT LETS PIRATE SHIPS TALK TO OTHER PIRATE SHIPS. I SHOVED IT UP THERE AND FORGOT ALL ABOUT IT . . .

Princess Dagger comes through the door, all set to yell and scream at us for being lazy. But she just says,

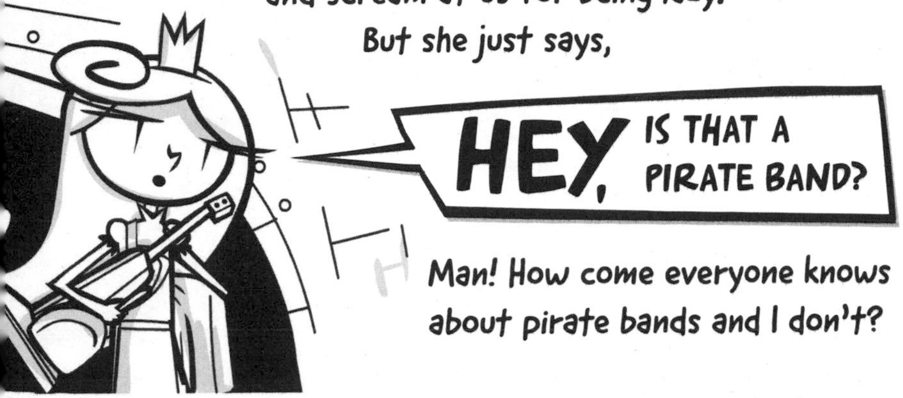
HEY, IS THAT A PIRATE BAND?

Man! How come everyone knows about pirate bands and I don't?

"My mom used to collect those. From pirates she, y'know, got rid of . . ." Princess Dagger says, sort of sadly.

"So why's it all blinking and beeping?" I ask.

Humphree looks at me very seriously. "It's a distress signal. It means, somewhere, a pirate ship is in trouble."

"How long has it been doing that?" I ask.

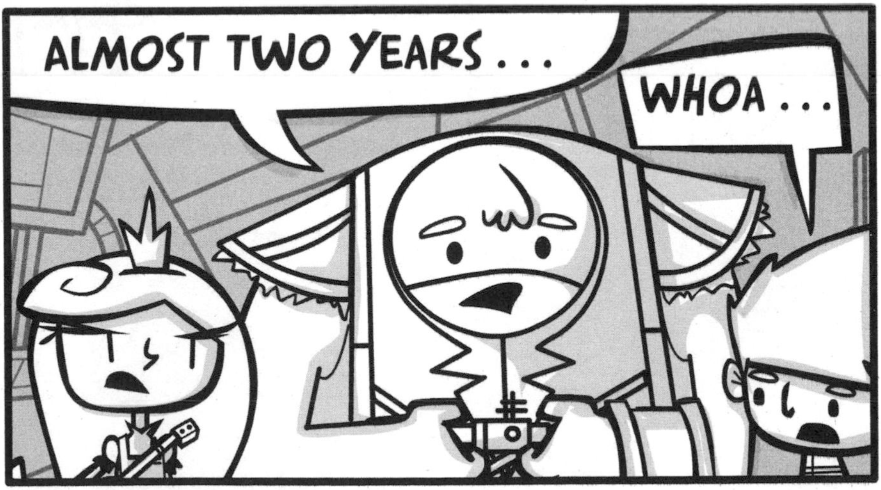
ALMOST TWO YEARS . . .
WHOA . . .

Humphree hands the band to F.R.E.D. and asks, "Is there a message attached to the distress signal?"

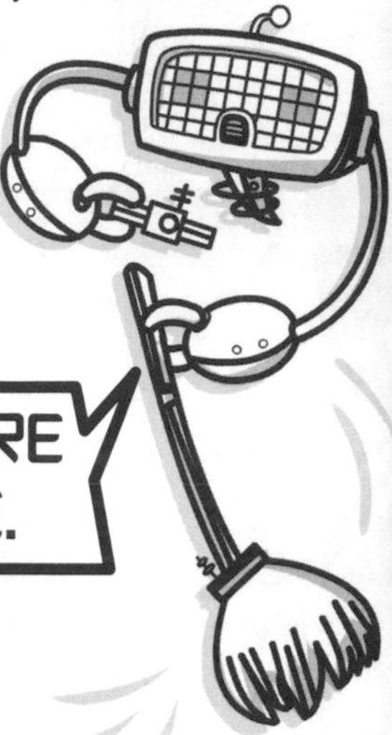

We all wait. Holding our breath. F.R.E.D. buzzes and whirs as he analyzes the band, then says . . .

MESSAGE CONFIRMED: WE ARE INSIDE THE LOST TRIANGLE.

Humphree gulps—a thunderous gulp from his thunderous throat that echoes in the room. Humps says, "So it's real. The Lost Triangle is real. And someone found it . . ."

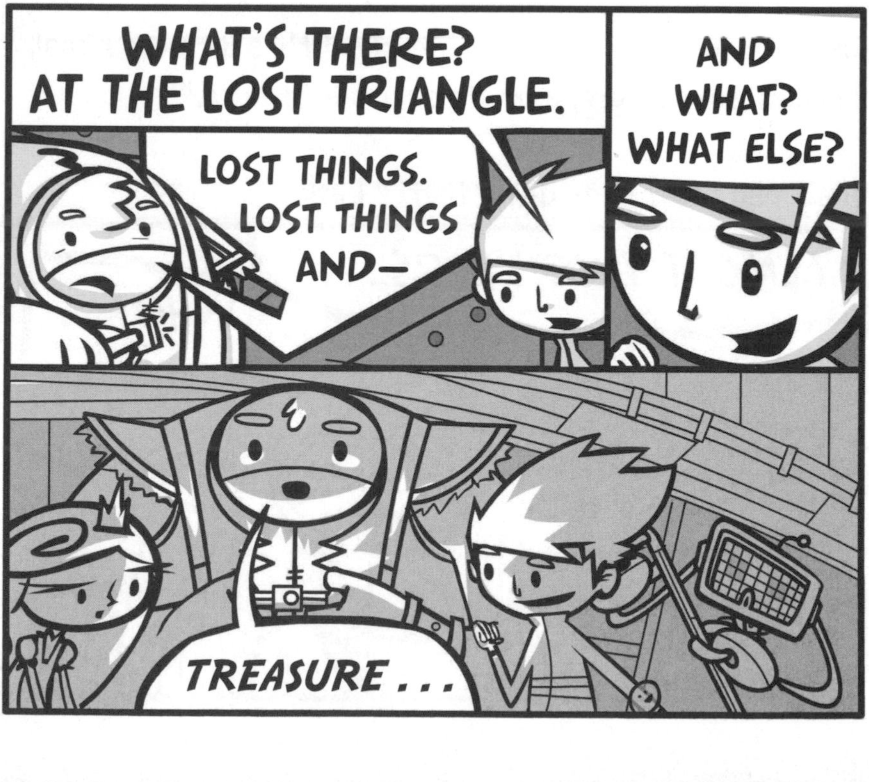
WHAT'S THERE? AT THE LOST TRIANGLE.
LOST THINGS. LOST THINGS AND—
AND WHAT? WHAT ELSE?
TREASURE . . .

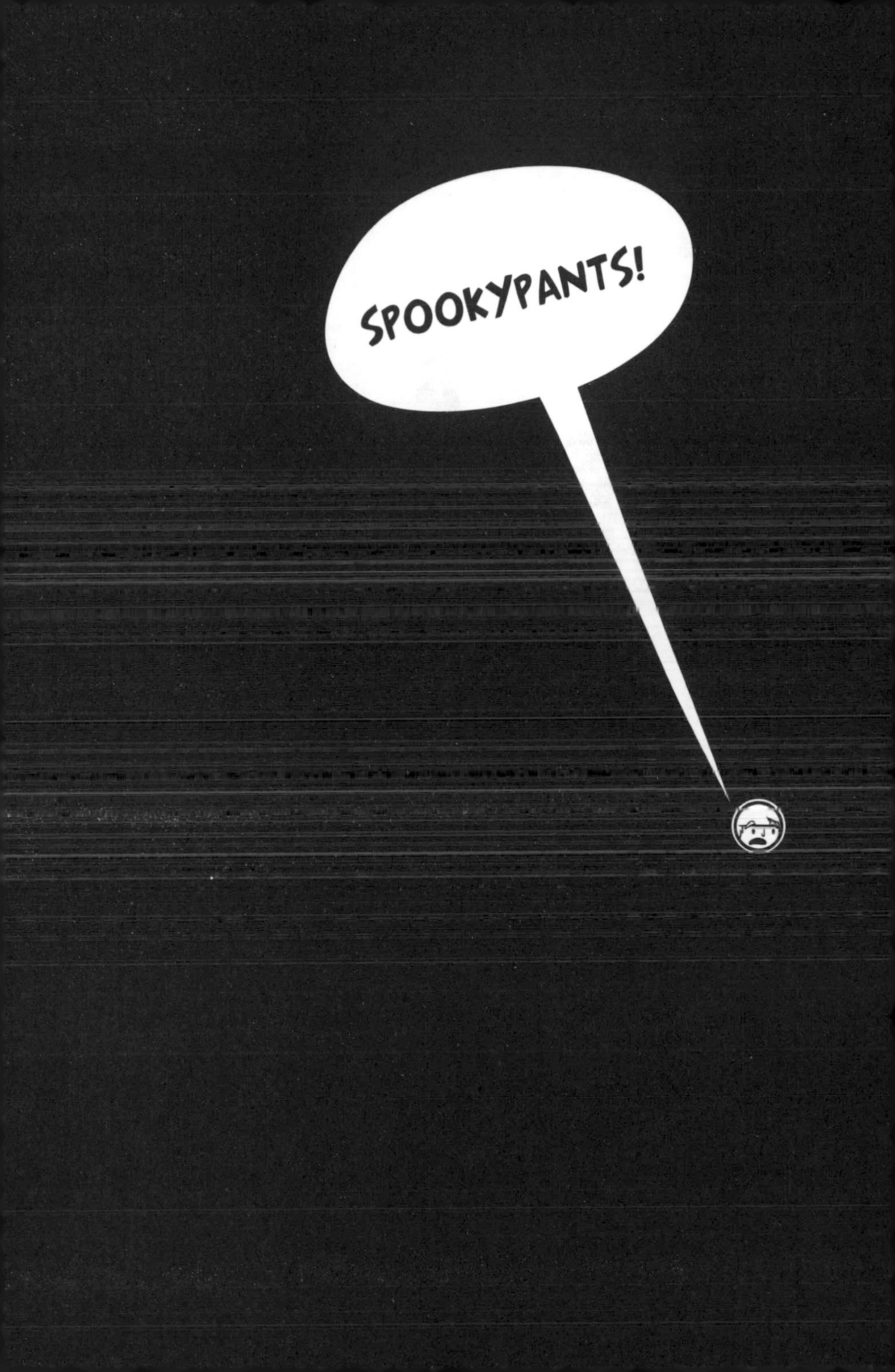
SPOOKYPANTS!

A SPACESHIP GRAVEYARD?

7

As we race toward the Lost Triangle—the source of this distress signal—I'm starting to feel pretty nervous. I've got that stomach-cavern feeling, like I'm real hungry, but I can't eat. I know a little bit about Humphree's old life as a pirate, and none of it is good. Pirates are bad dudes. And let's be honest—

THE LOST TRIANGLE?

A place full of lost stuff? That sounds creepy.

Princess Dagger interrupts my runaway train of worry. "So what exactly is the Lost Triangle?" she asks. "I've never heard of it."

Humphree says, "Every pirate captain I ever knew was obsessed with finding it. But most of us buccaneers just thought it was a legend."

SO SPILL IT!

YEAH! WHAT'S THE LEGEND?

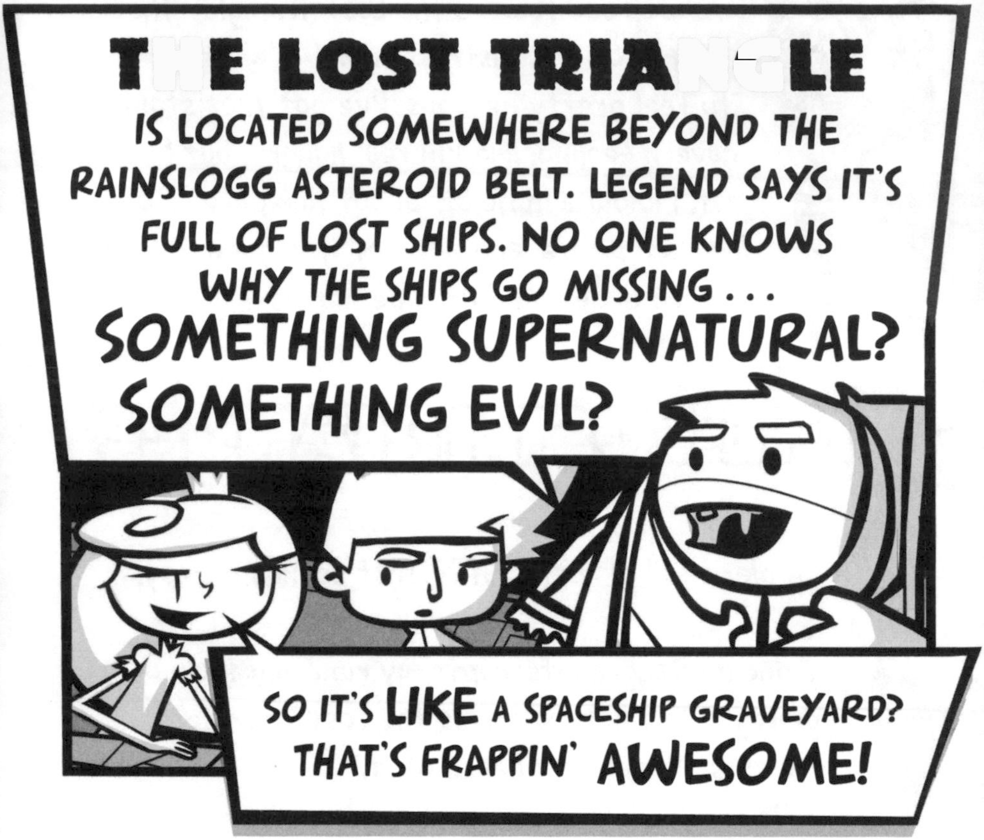
T E LOST TRIA LE
IS LOCATED SOMEWHERE BEYOND THE RAINSLOGG ASTEROID BELT. LEGEND SAYS IT'S FULL OF LOST SHIPS. NO ONE KNOWS WHY THE SHIPS GO MISSING . . . SOMETHING SUPERNATURAL? SOMETHING EVIL?
SO IT'S LIKE A SPACESHIP GRAVEYARD? THAT'S FRAPPIN' AWESOME!

"WAIT, WAIT, WAIT," I say. "If every ship that goes there ends up missing, how come people keep going? Sounds pretty dumb to me. And wait again . . .

HOW COME WE'RE GOING???"

Humps leans close and whispers, "It's treasure fever, short pants. ***TREASURE FEVER . . .*** It makes people do crazy things. Back in my pirate days, I would have done anything to find the Lost Triangle . . ."

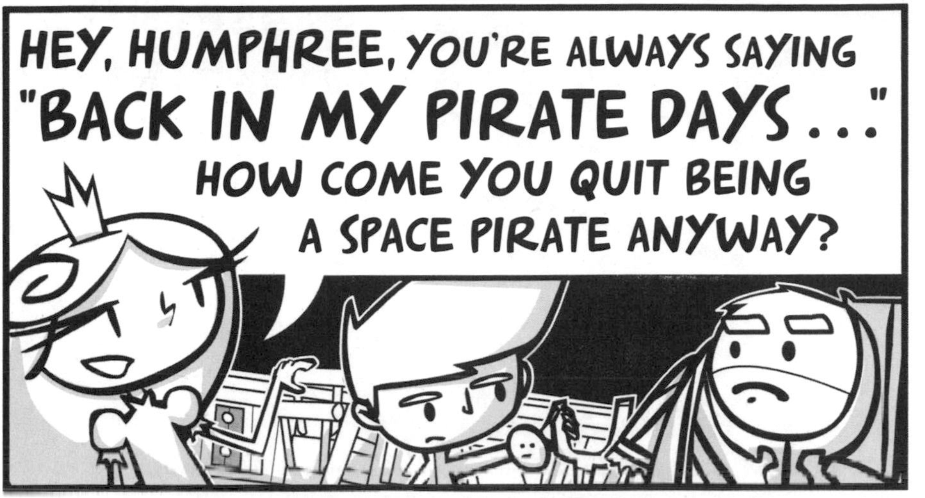
HEY, HUMPHREE, YOU'RE ALWAYS SAYING
"BACK IN MY PIRATE DAYS . . ."
HOW COME YOU QUIT BEING
A SPACE PIRATE ANYWAY?

Humphree gives me a look—***AN <u>UNCOMFY</u> FROWN.***

I know the reason he quit. It's long and complicated—and it involves me. Humphree doesn't like talking about it.

"Well, Humphree—how come?" the princess asks, pushing him. But before he has time to answer, we're saved by—

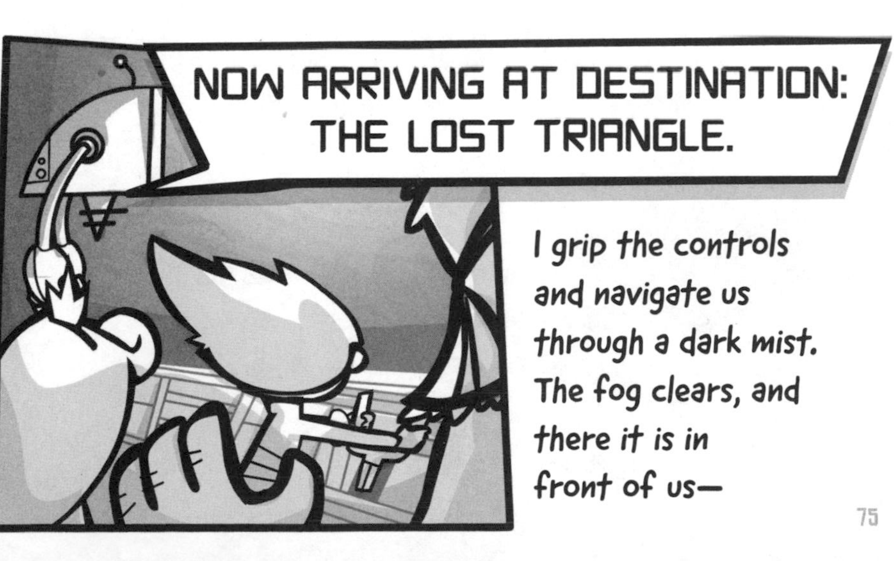
NOW ARRIVING AT DESTINATION:
THE LOST TRIANGLE.

I grip the controls and navigate us through a dark mist. The fog clears, and there it is in front of us—

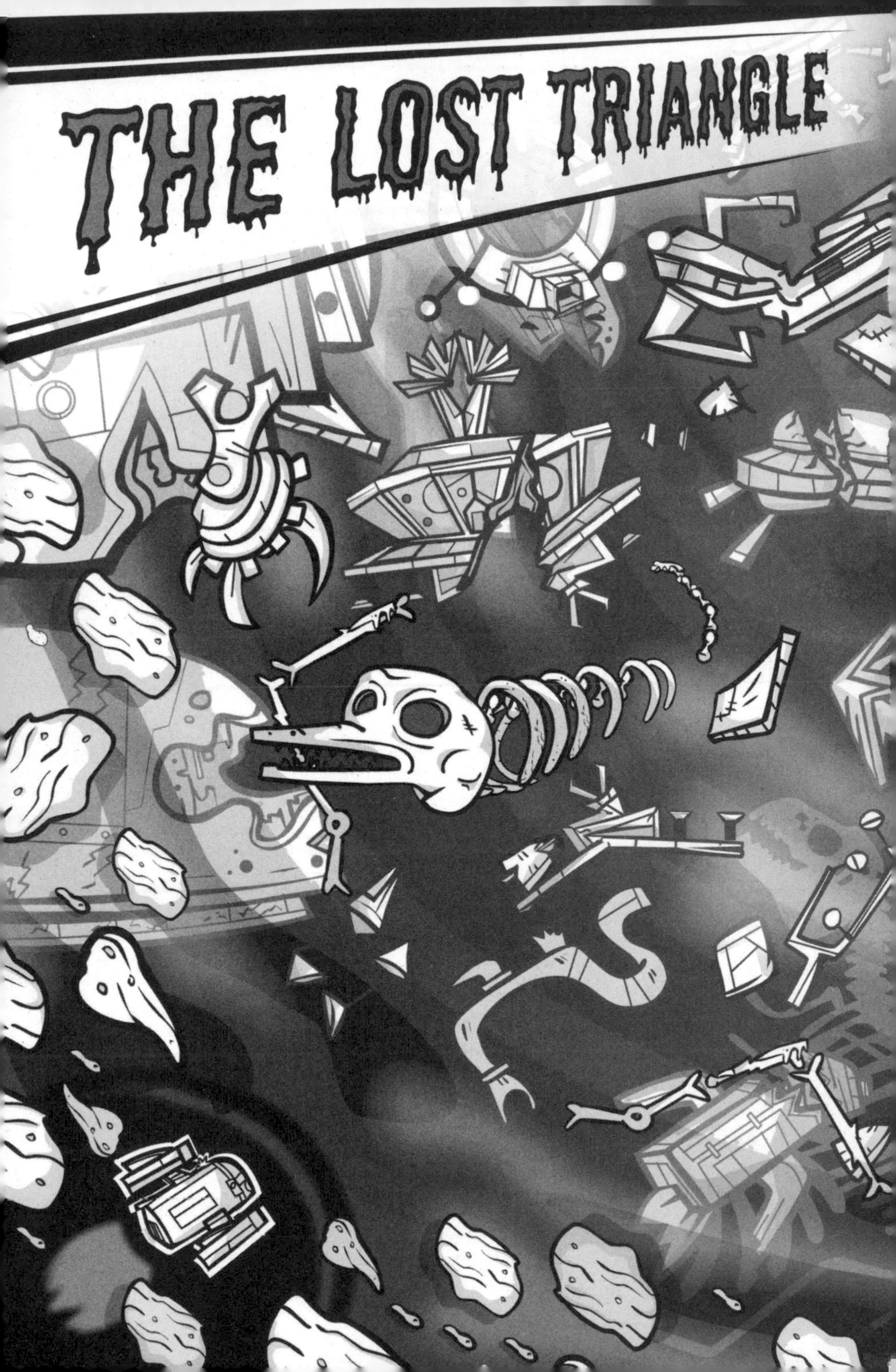
THE LOST TRIANGLE

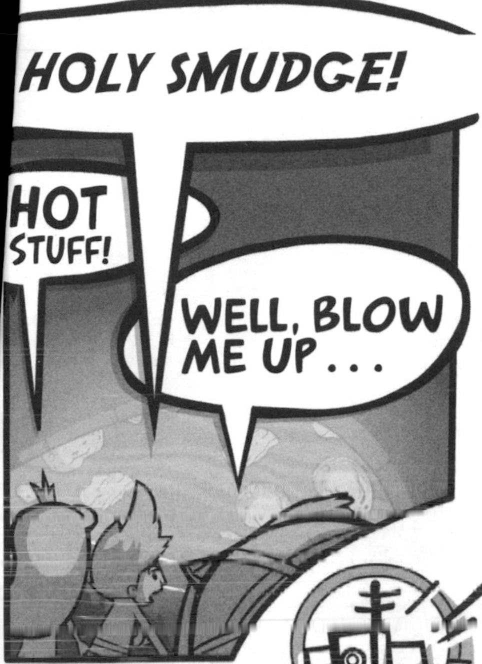
HOLY SMUDGE!
HOT STUFF!
WELL, BLOW ME UP . . .

I cut the power and the *Neon Wiener* goes silent. We drift past giant ships: some as big as the Empire State Building! Bigger even—***AS BIG AS THE SAND PALACE ON OFTAR 12!***

The beeping on the pirate band gets louder.

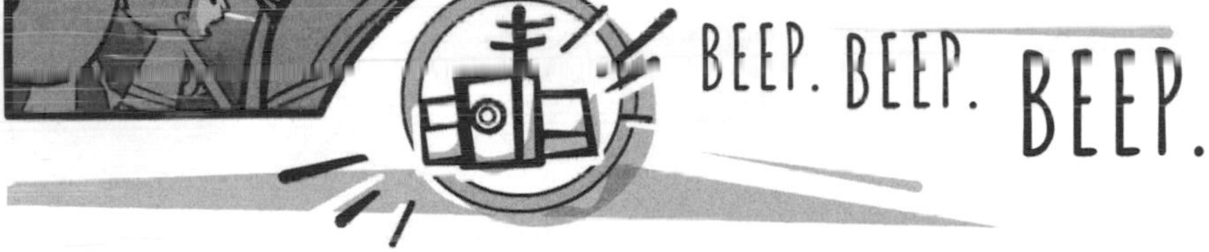
BEEP. BEEP. BEEP.

And then we spot it—the pirate ship sending out the distress signal. The ship is hurt bad. That's no surprise—it's been floating there for two years, being assaulted by asteroids and slammed by other ships.

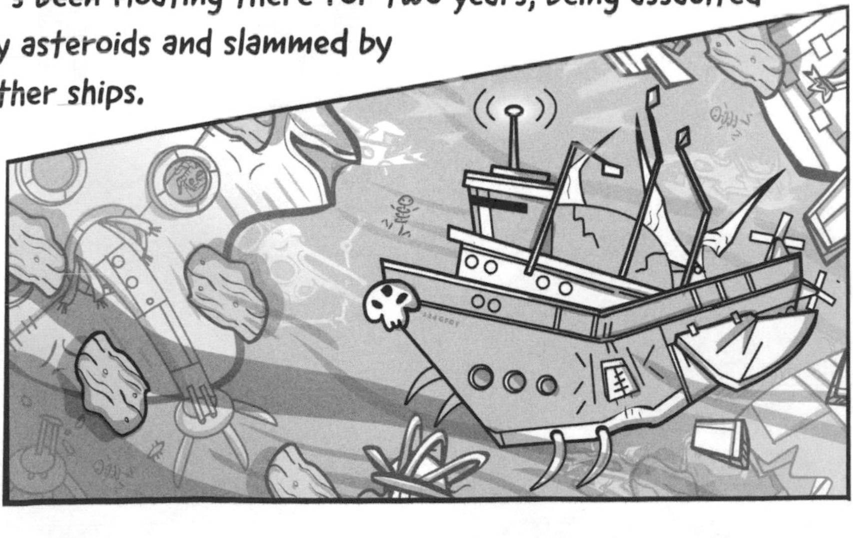

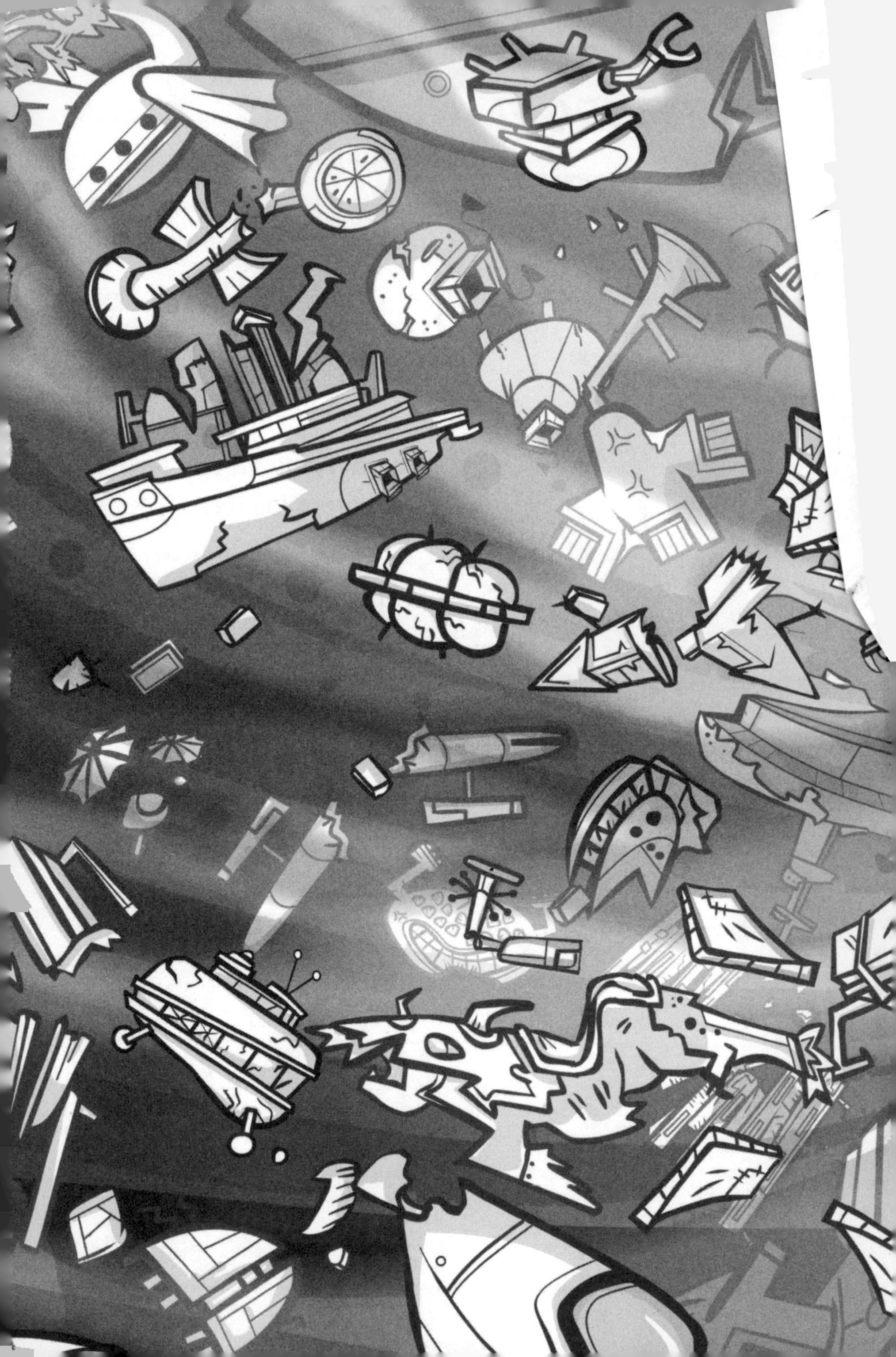

"There's the ship's air dock," Humphree says, pointing. "But it's too beaten up for the *Neon Wiener* to attach to. One of us needs to go over there . . ."

I want to go! I'm real nervous about this whole thing, but I can feel my old adventure bones rattling. There's action over on that ship. There's something mysterious over there. And I want to see it!

"We'll shoot for it!" I say. "Odds or evens! I'm odds!"

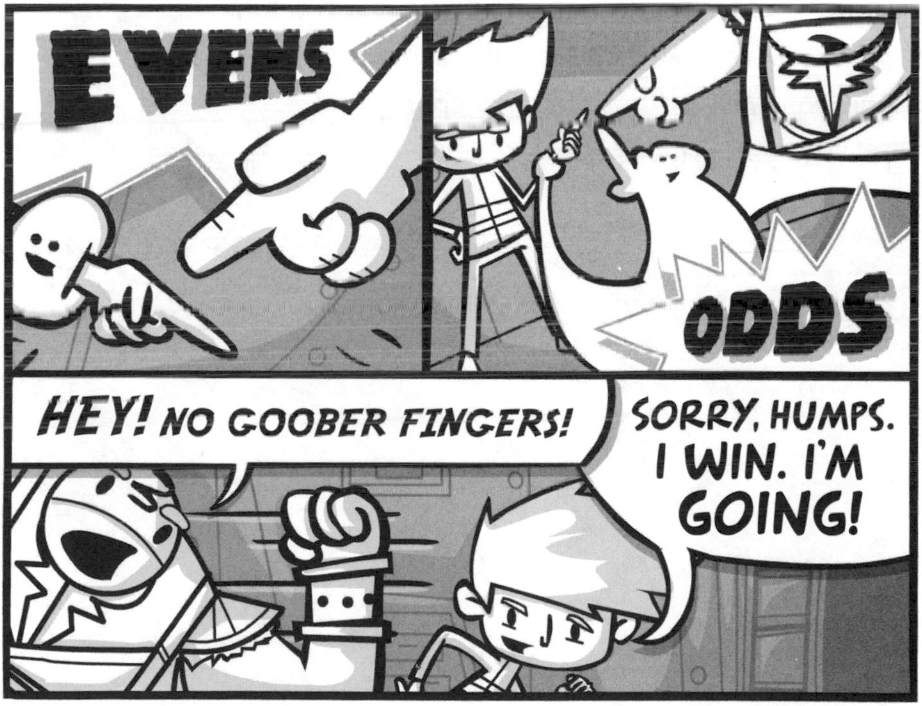
EVENS
ODDS
HEY! NO GOOBER FINGERS!
SORRY, HUMPS. I WIN. I'M GOING!

Woo-hoo! Before Humphree can protest, I race into the bedroom to suit up. Three minutes later, I step into the air lock, ready to go. But Humphree stops me—

I can tell Humphree is worried about me going over to that ship alone. "Relax your head, Humps," I say. "I'll be careful! Besides, **SOMEONE** has to stay with the *Wiener* . . ."

Princess Dagger pipes up. "I'll stay with the ship!"

Humphree looks at the princess and lets out an annoyed sigh. "Fine, Cosmoe. Go."

The princess starts moaning and groaning, but I don't have time to listen. I'm stepping through the air lock, out into space, and jet-packing toward danger . . .

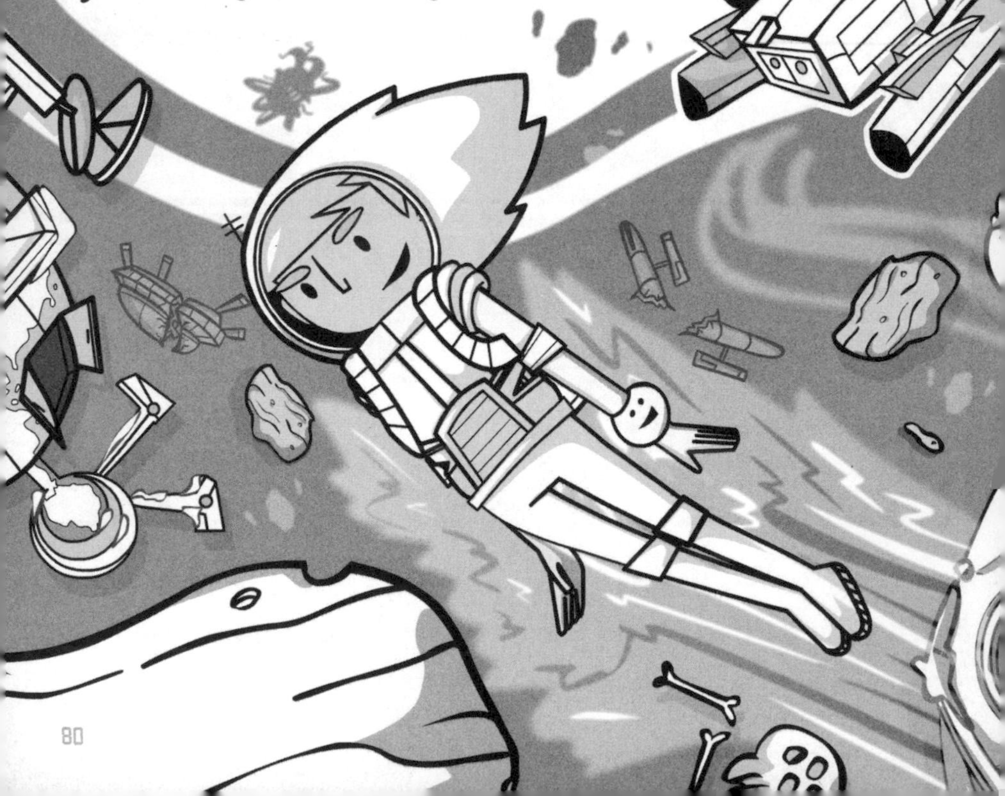

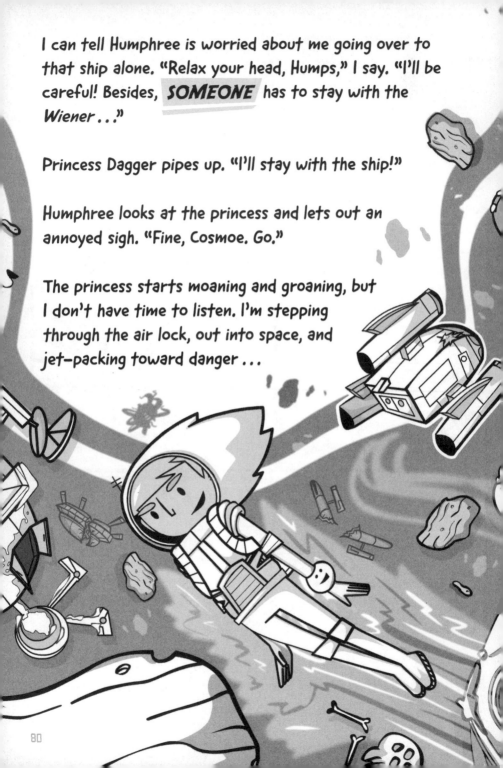

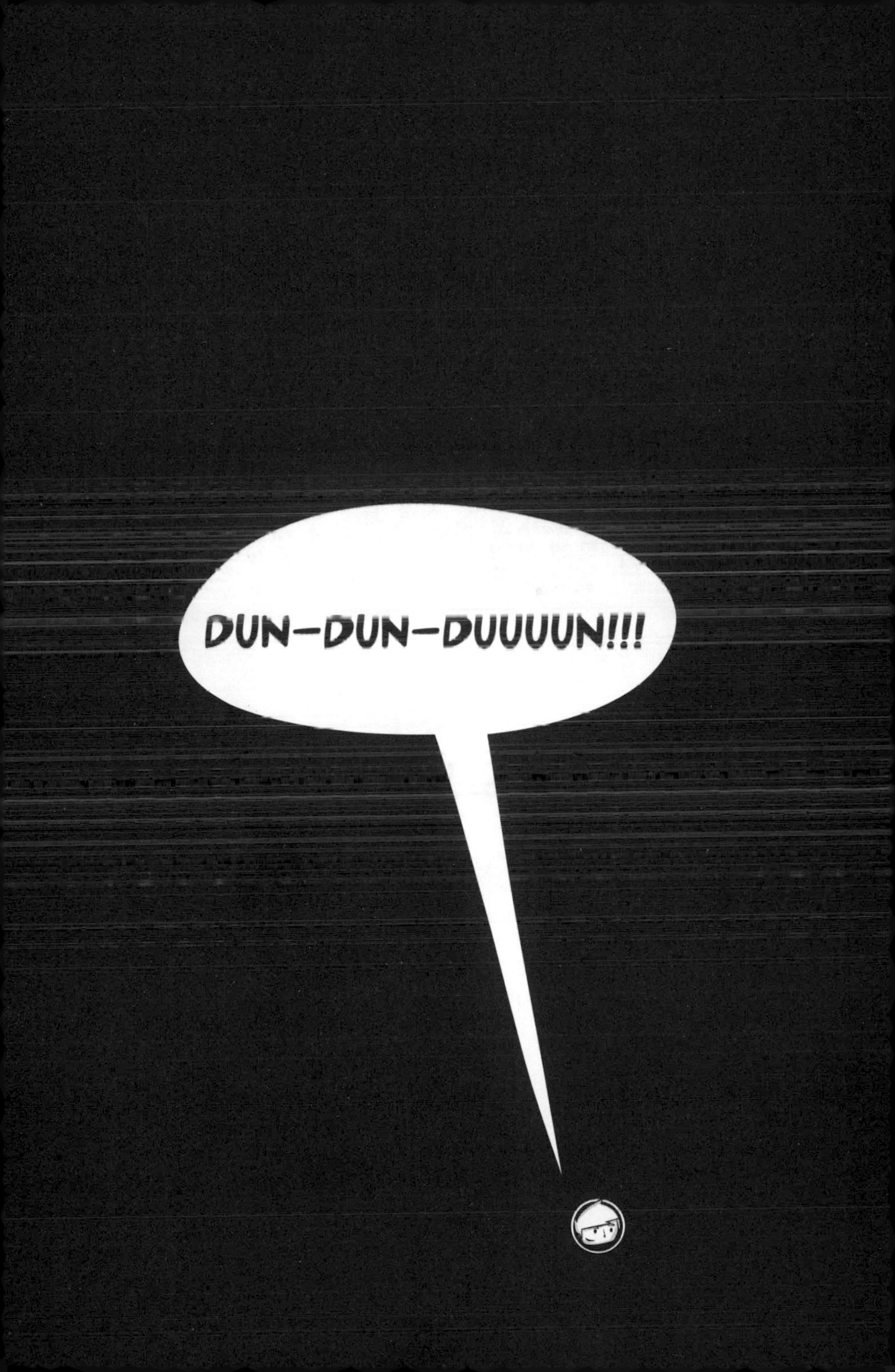
DUN-DUN-DUUUUN!!!

EXTREME HORRIBLE HORROR!

The pirate ship's air dock is all busted up, so I need to find another way inside. I hit the jets and cruise toward one of the ship's many porthole windows.

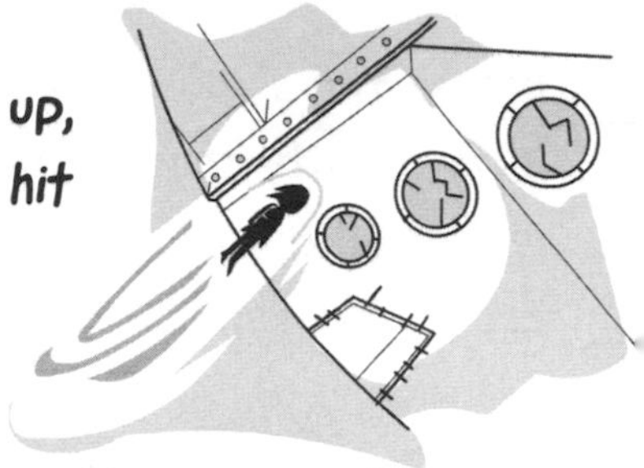

For a kid who spends all his time cruising the cosmos, I don't love being out in space all alone. It reminds me of being in the ocean, back on Earth. And I hate the ocean. I mean, I only went to the beach once, but it gave me the big-time willies. **IT'S JUST SO ENDLESS . . .**

SO YEAH, I'M EAGER TO GET INSIDE THAT SHIP.

Time for the ol' ***GOOBER HAMMER . . .***

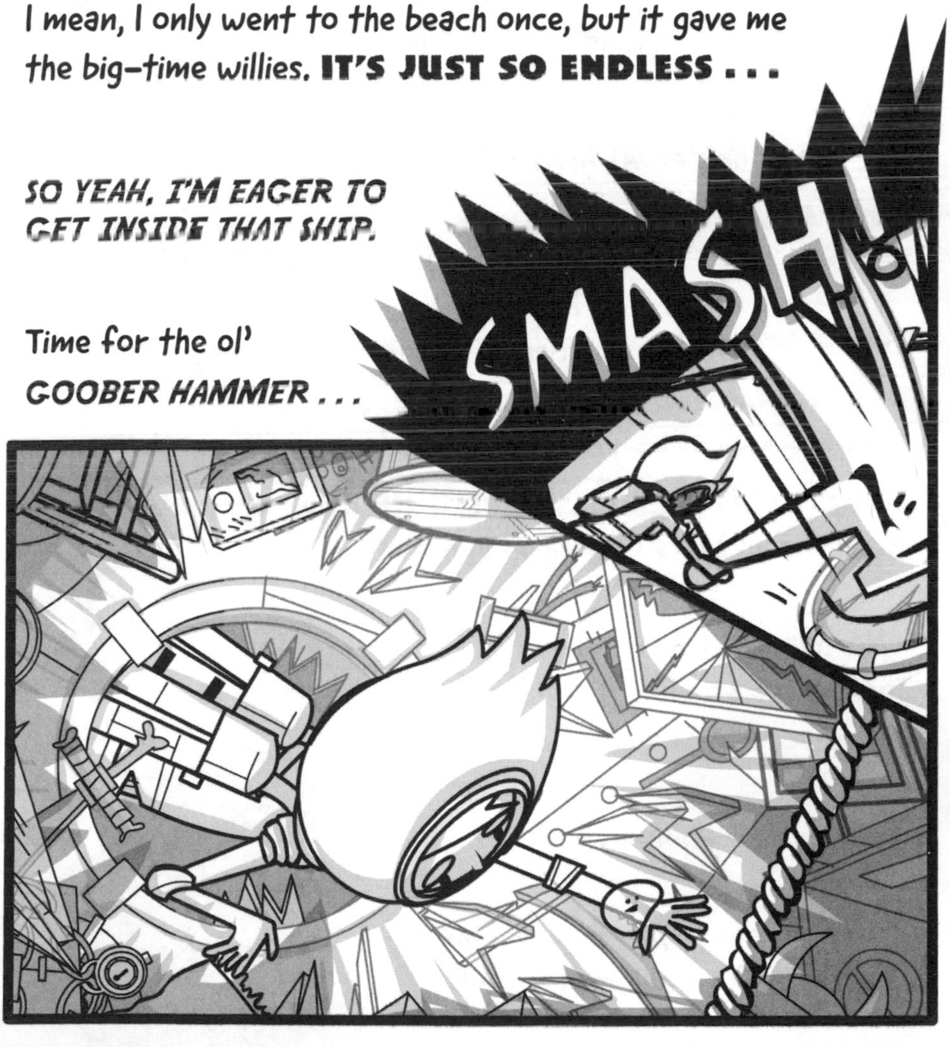
SMASH!

Inside, the ship is **EERIE.** There are no lights. I guess the anti-gravity thingamajig broke, because everything that isn't tied down is drifting through the air: pirate swords, crusty old sandwiches, and me.

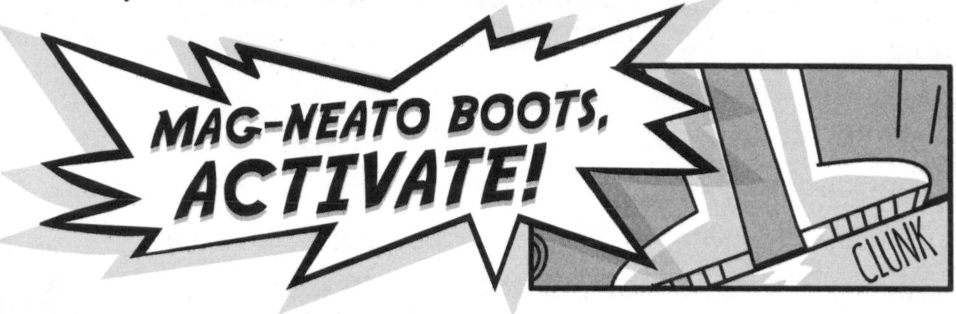
MAG-NEATO BOOTS,
ACTIVATE!
CLUNK

OK, that's better. At least I'm not drifting around.

KRRTTTCHHH! It's Humphree, on the walkie. He says, "Hey, Cosmoe. Keep an eye out for Helio Jalapeños! I need them for my hot sauce."

Humphree is working on this new hot sauce recipe. He's going to call it HUMPHREE'S ORIGINAL HOT HOT SAUCE. He needs all sorts of weird ingredients.

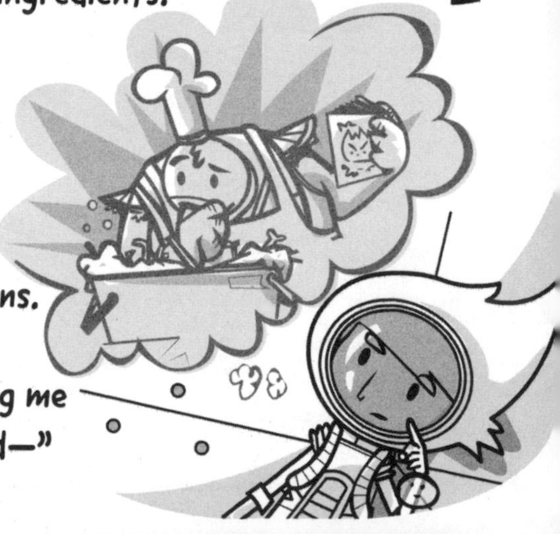

"No, Humps," I say. "I'm not looking for stuff for your hot sauce right now!"

"Why not?!" Humphree moans.

"Because this ship is freaking me out and it feels haunted and—"

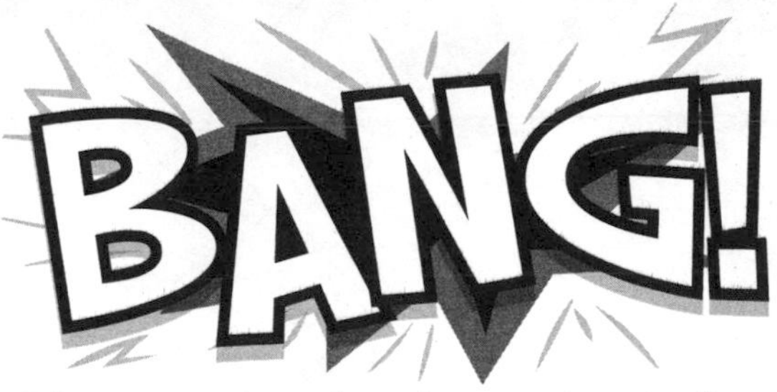
BANG!

"What was that?
Humphree whispers.

I gulp. "I'm not sure."

There are two big doors ahead of me. And coming from beyond those doors are strange noises.

I hear Princess Dagger say, "Maybe we should forget about the treasure . . ."

There's a slam.
And then a heavy banging
and a moaning sound.

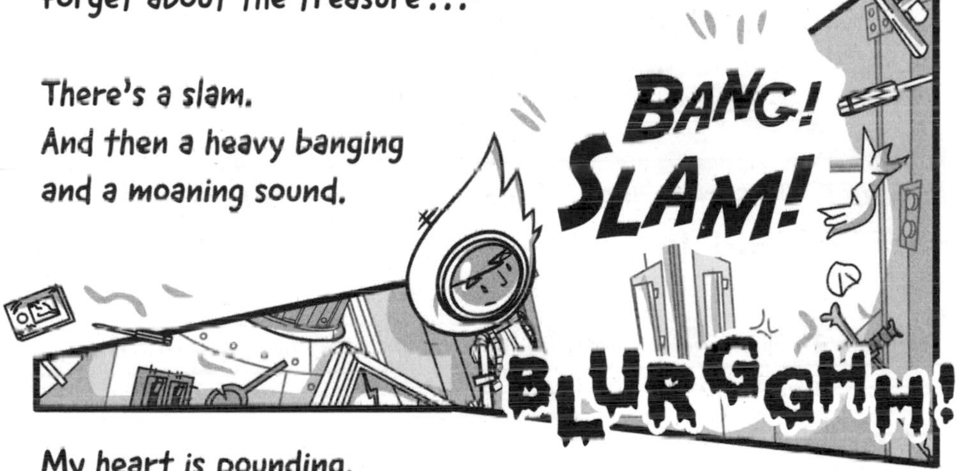
BANG!
SLAM!
BLURGGHH!

My heart is pounding.
What's beyond those doors?

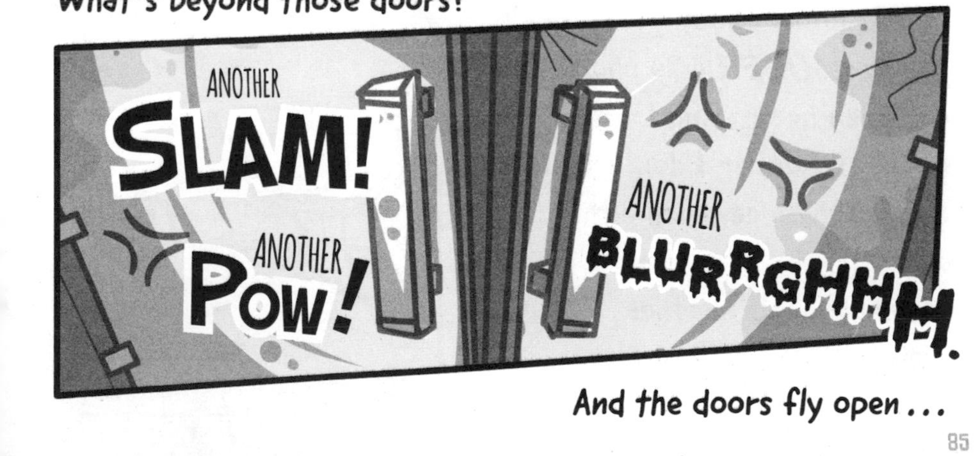
ANOTHER
SLAM!
ANOTHER
POW!
ANOTHER
BLURRGHHHH.

And the doors fly open . . .

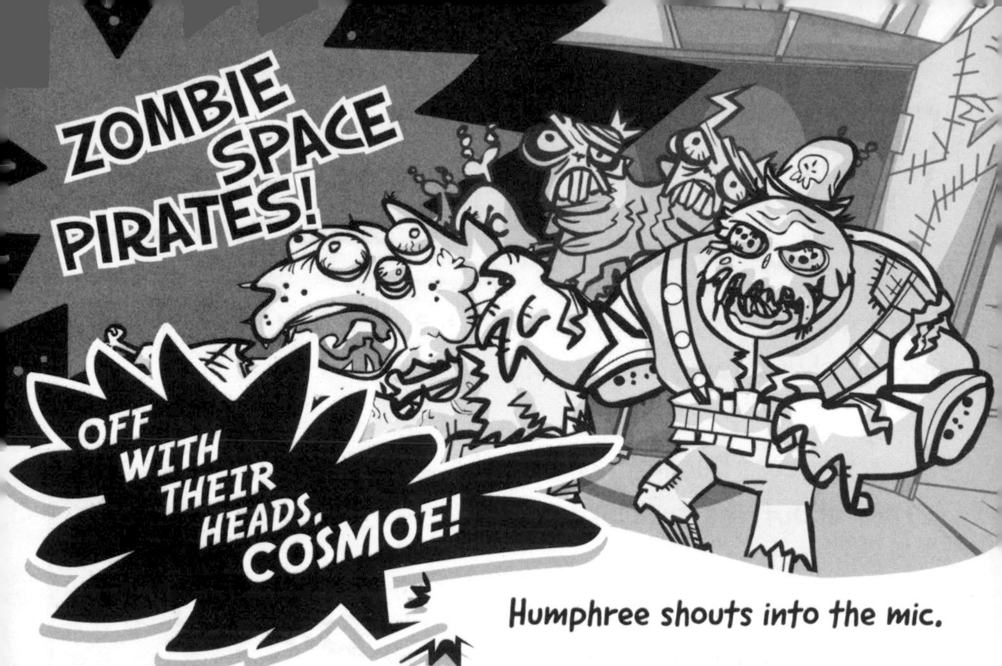
ZOMBIE SPACE PIRATES!
OFF WITH THEIR HEADS, COSMOE!

Humphree shouts into the mic.

"WHAT?" I shriek. "I don't want to do an ***'OFF WITH THEIR HEADS'*** thing!!"

"Kiddo, they're **ZOMBIES**. They're already **DEAD!** If they sink their pirate fangs into you, ***YOU'LL*** be a zombie too!"

I don't know about you—but I'm just not ***SUPER*** into chopping off alien heads. And looking down at Goober, I don't think he's digging the idea much either . . .

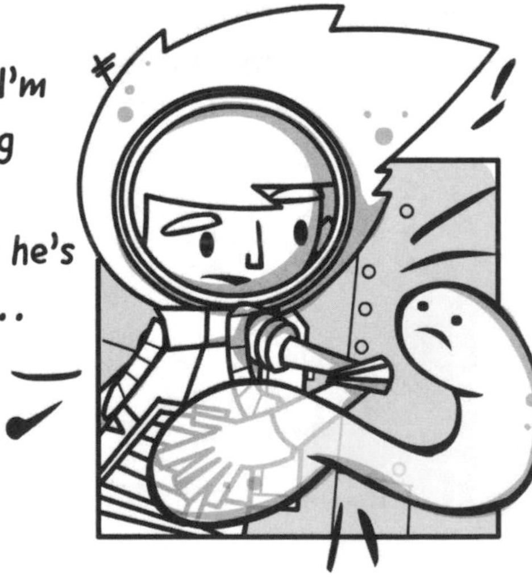

Maybe there's another way to deal with these undead bozos . . .

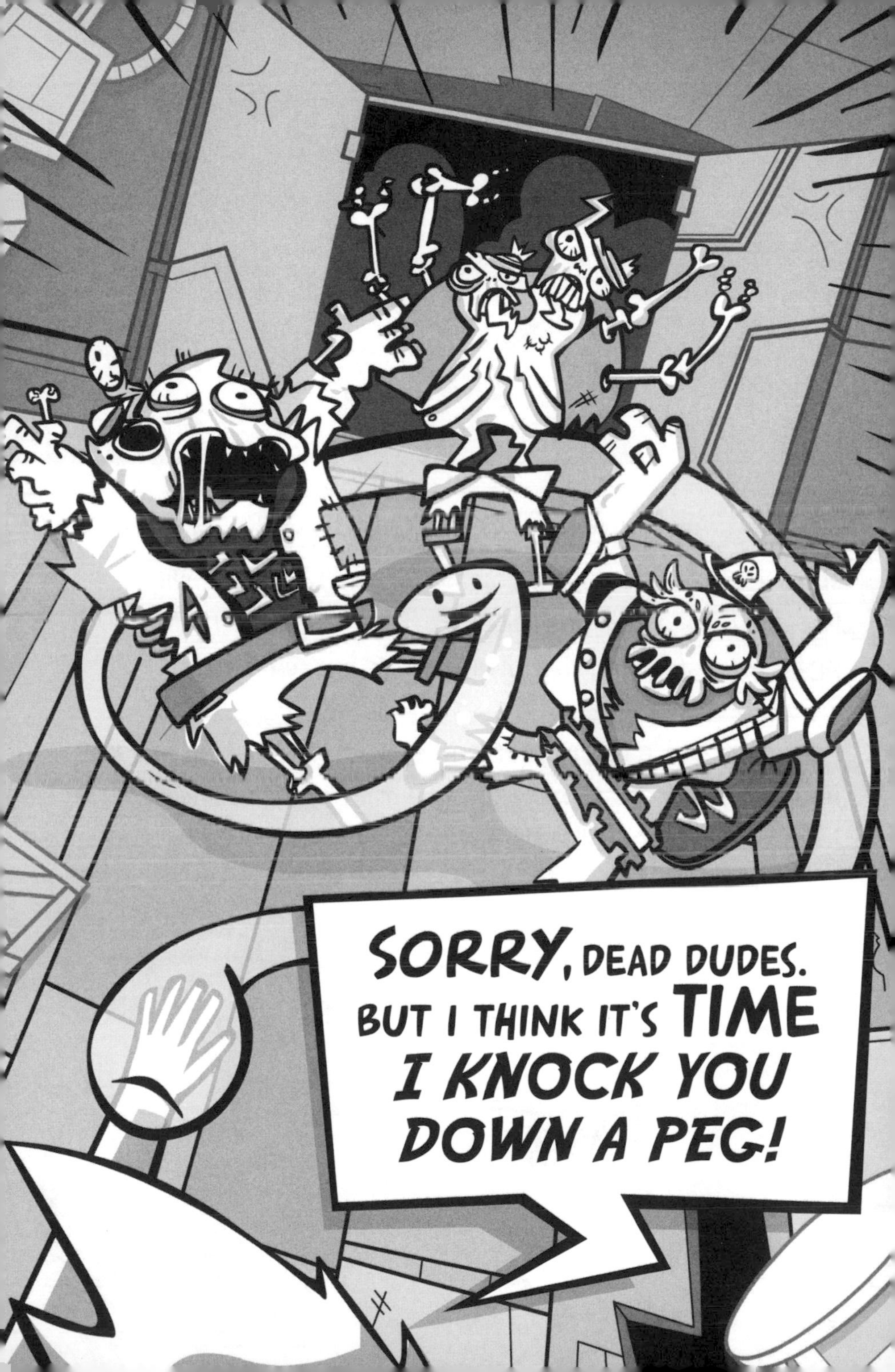
SORRY, DEAD DUDES. BUT I THINK IT'S TIME I KNOCK YOU DOWN A PEG!

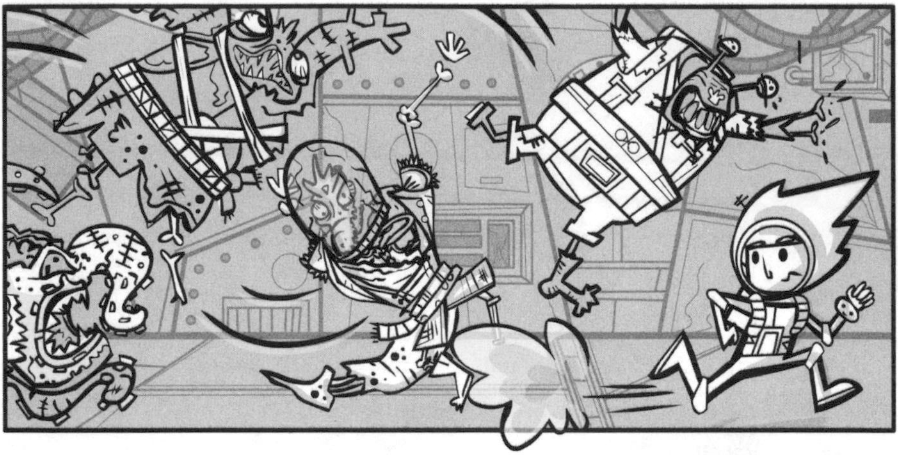

I race past the floating zombie space pirates. Strange, super-spooky moans are coming from all over the ship. Probably more zombie space pirates, trapped in their pirate-y bedrooms with their zombie space parrots.

I step through a metal door and slam it shut behind me. I'm now in what looks like the bridge—that's where the captain hangs out. Y'know, like that big room in ***STAR TREK.***

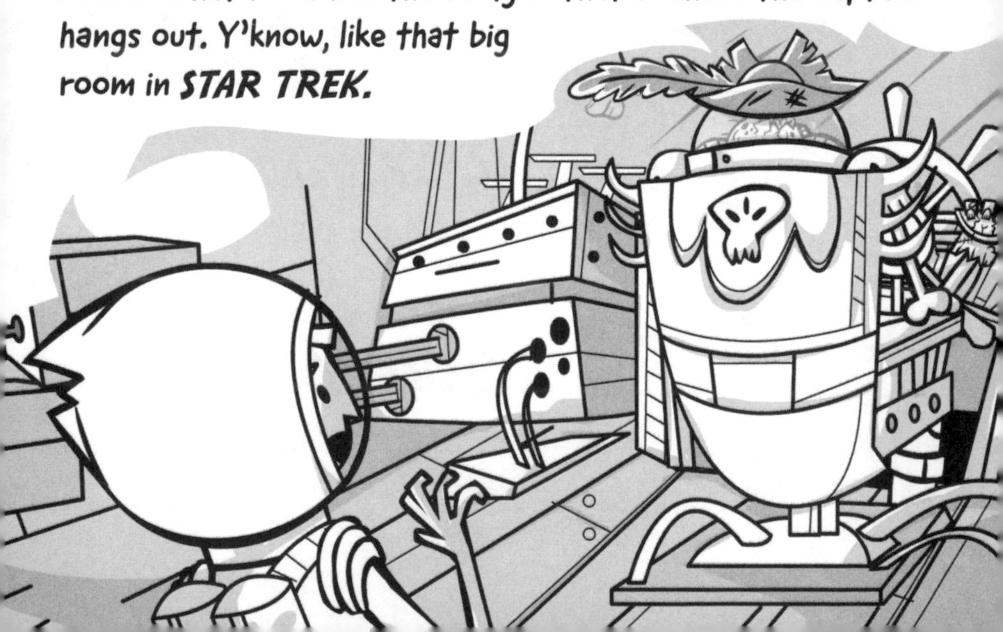

I carefully step around to the front of this captain's chair, and—

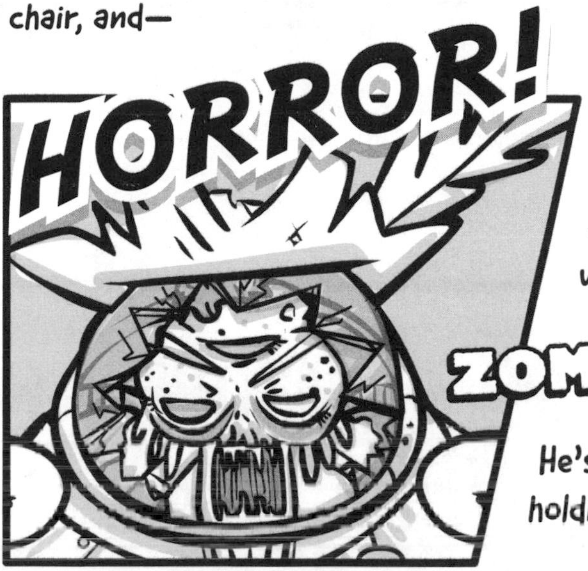
HORROR!

I swallow and whisper into the mic, "I'm looking at a space captain with a frappin'

ZOMBIE FACE!

He's not moving. He's holding something . . ."

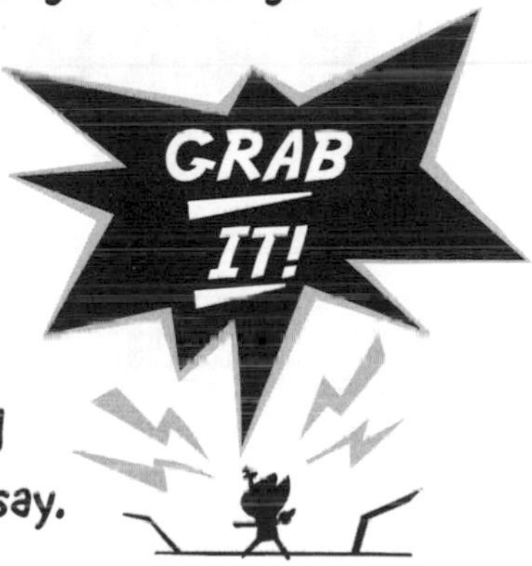
GRAB IT!

"Whatever he's holding could have something to do with the treasure!" the princess shouts into the mic.

"I don't wanna touch it! It's got undead hands on it! I'm icked out right now!" I say.

"Don't be a ***BABY,***" Princess Dagger says.

ARGH! The princess really knows how to push my buttons. I reach down and pry the thing from the dude's creepy undead fingers.

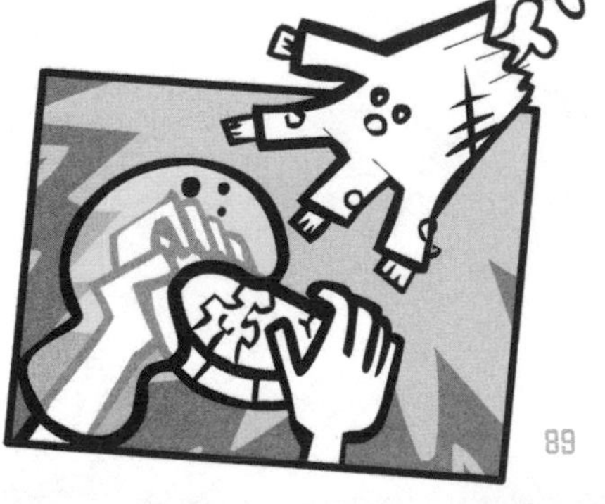

And that's when things go from bad to worse. The zombie space captain's eyes flash open like ***WHOA!***

He's coming at me, half-stepping, half-floating, and reaching for my face!

And he is saying crazy-scary-weirdo junk!

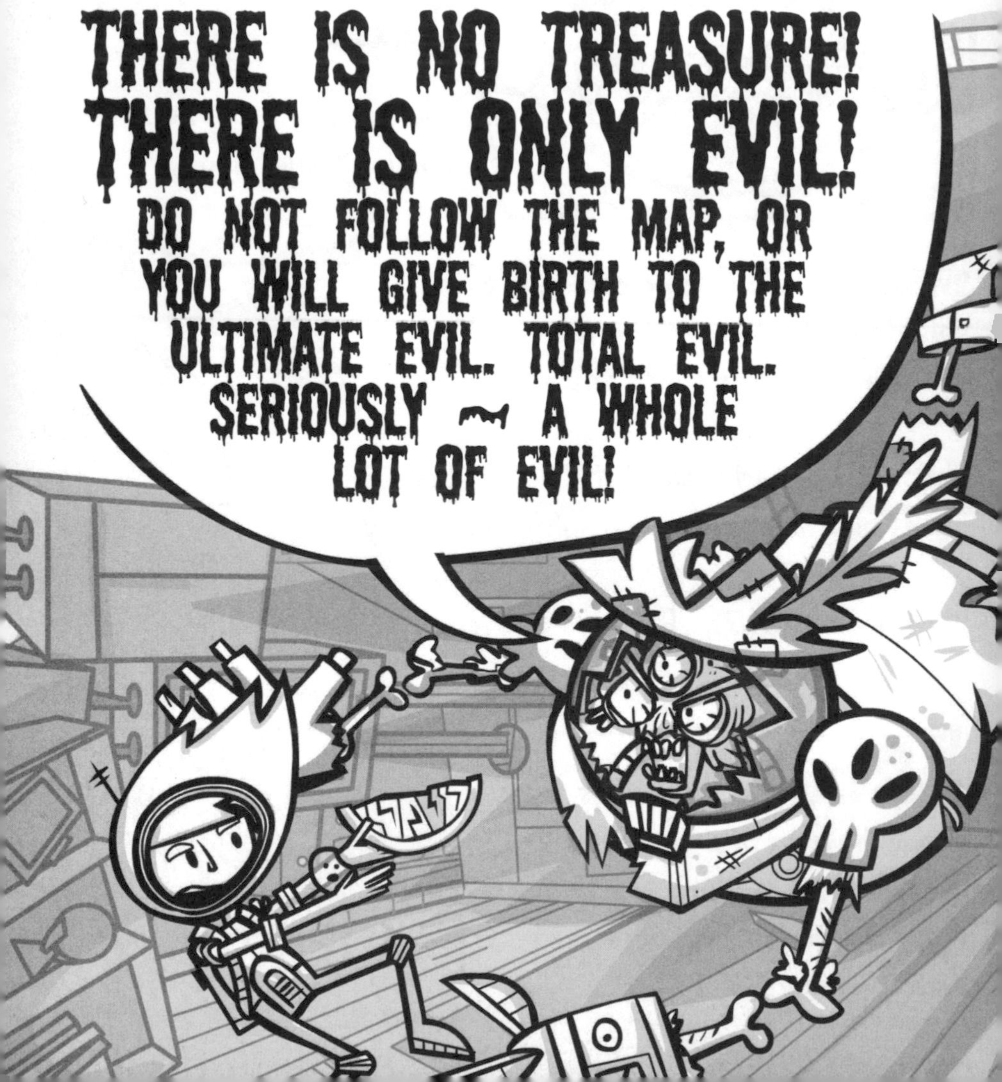
THERE IS NO TREASURE!
THERE IS ONLY EVIL!
DO NOT FOLLOW THE MAP, OR YOU WILL GIVE BIRTH TO THE ULTIMATE EVIL. TOTAL EVIL. SERIOUSLY ~ A WHOLE LOT OF EVIL!

ZOMBIFICATION IS QUITE COMMON IN THE MILKY WAY GALAXY. IT IS GENERALLY ACCEPTED THAT THE MOST GRUESOME ZOMBIES IN GALACTIC HISTORY WERE:

1. NEVIL'S ARMY OF NINE-ARMED NEOMITES
2. JULIE THE ORGAN-JUGGLER
3. STEVE

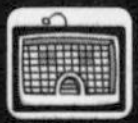

WHAT'S A WATERMELON?

THE ZOMBIE SPACE PIRATE IS UPON ME!

THIS REANIMATED RAIDER IS ABOUT TO DIG HIS ZOMBIE FANGS INTO MY SOFT, WARM, AND PROBABLY

DELICIOUS NECK FLESH!

I go for a Goober attack, but Goober doesn't even **MOVE**. The little guy's eyes are wide. *HE'S PETRIFIED.* I guess Goober doesn't much like zombies...

WHICH MAKES SENSE BECAUSE **NO ONE** WHO **ISN'T** A ZOMBIE **LIKES** ZOMBIES.

The undead captain grabs my collar with his gnarly fingers. My suit tightens around my throat. He's about to bite!

IS THIS IT? AM I DONE FOR?

Is this the end of Cosmoe the Earth-Boy?

ROOR GHH!!!

OT THE EN!

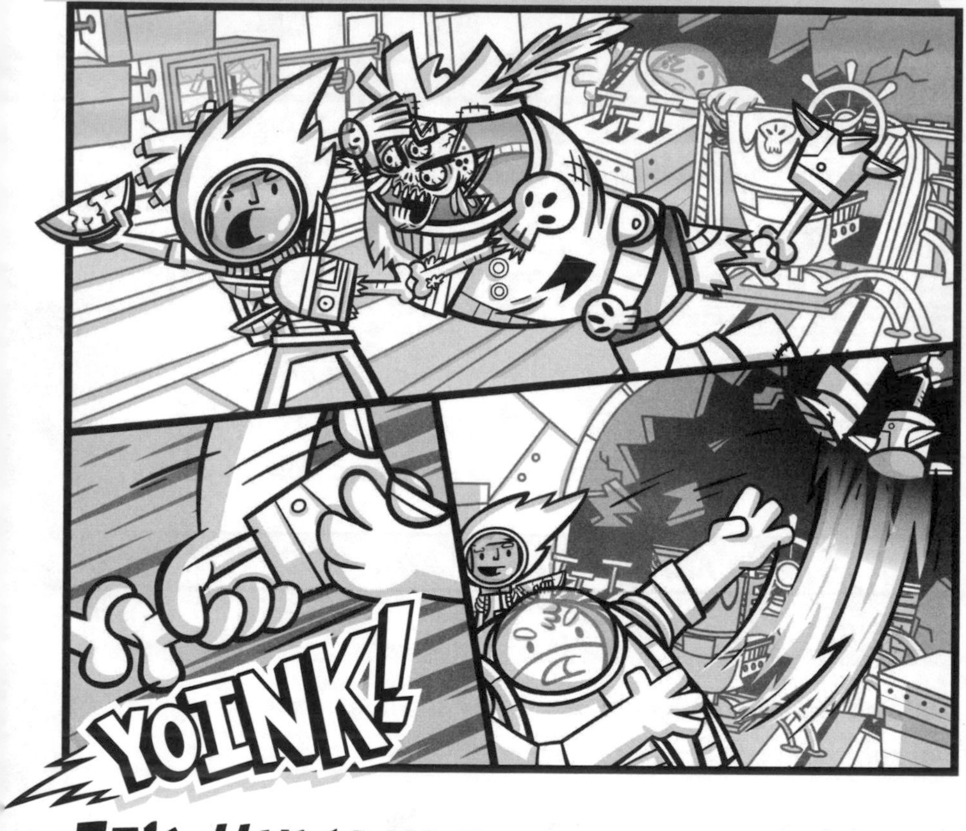
YOINK!

IT'S HUMPHREE TO THE RESCUE!

It pays to have friends who are really big, really strong, and have jet-pack-equipped space suits.

"THANKS FOR THE RESCUE, HUMPS," I manage to say.

"Anytime, short pants!" he says, slapping me on the shoulder.

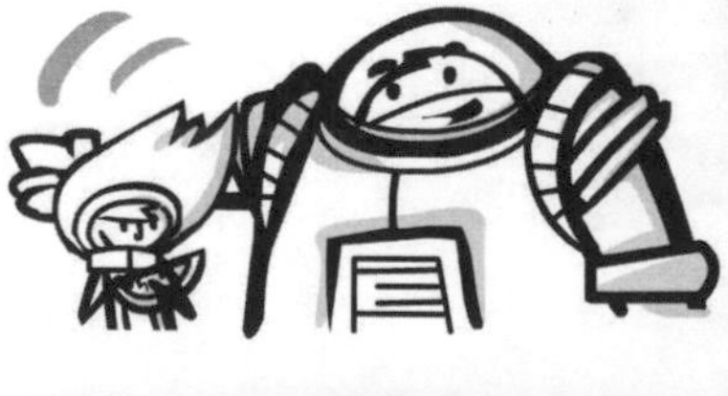

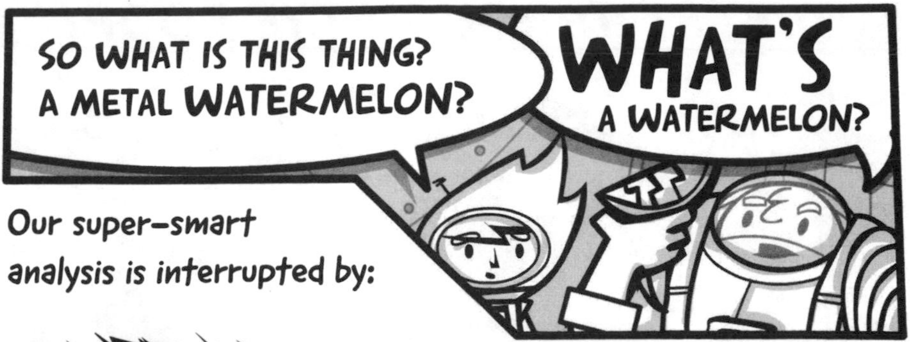
SO WHAT IS THIS THING? A METAL WATERMELON?
WHAT'S A WATERMELON?

Our super-smart analysis is interrupted by:

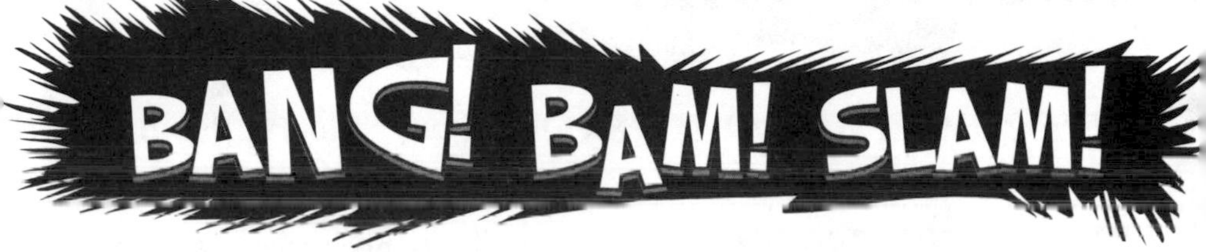
BANG! BAM! SLAM!

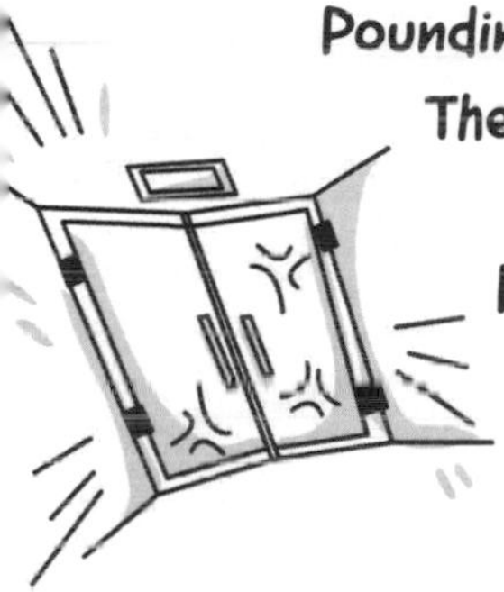

Pounding and moaning at the door to the bridge! These zombie space pirates are starving!

I'm trying to look for a way out, but Humphree is looking at something else: *A CABINET LABELED "SNACKS"!*

It's true: sometimes space captains—even pirate space captains—like to munch while they're flying.

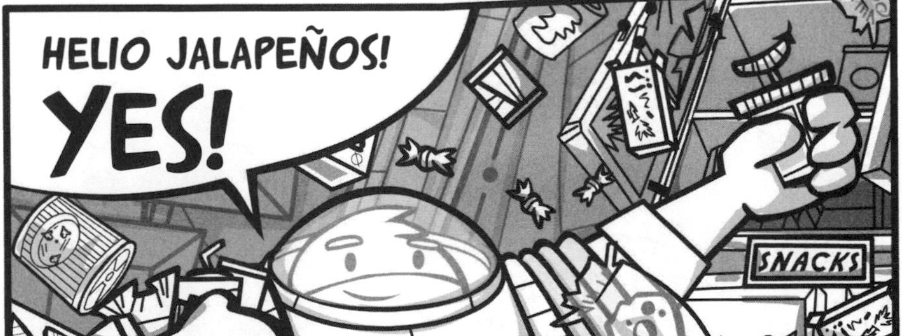
HELIO JALAPEÑOS! YES!
SNACKS

THEY'RE THROUGH THE DOOR!

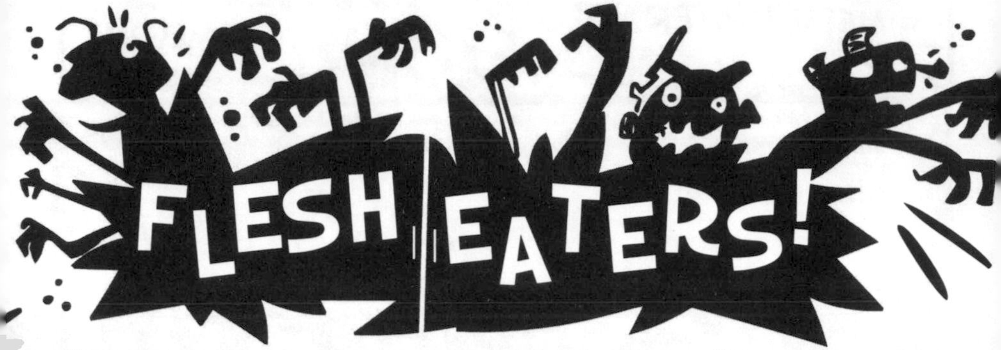
FLESH EATERS!

"***THE ZOMBIE SQUAD IS HERE!***" I shout. "Hurry, Humps!"

"***I GOT THE JALAPEÑOS!!***" he yells as he barrels across the bridge, cradling the jar of hot hots.

"And I got the weird slice-thing!"

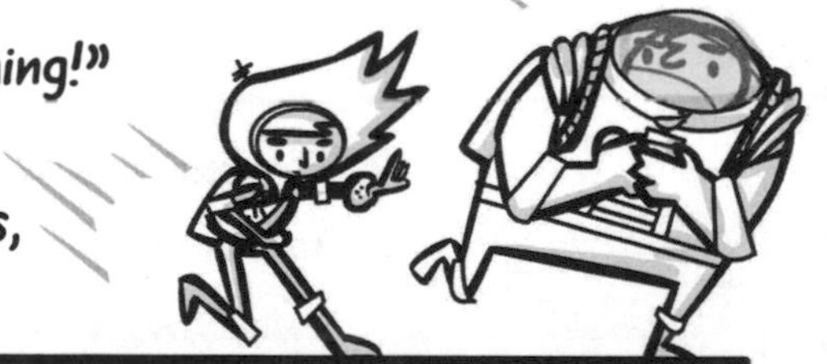

"Then, kiddo," Humphree says,
"***LET'S SPLIT!***"

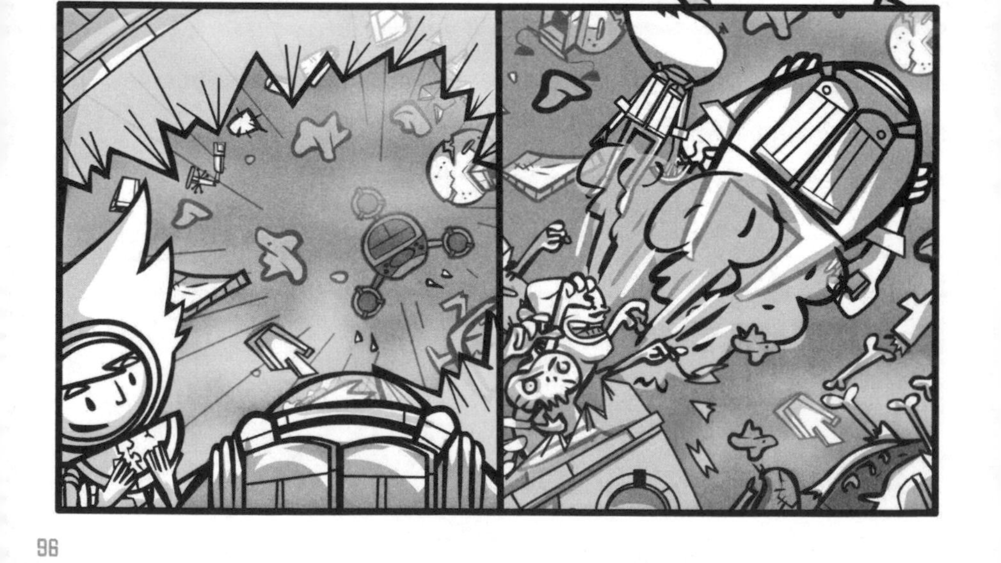

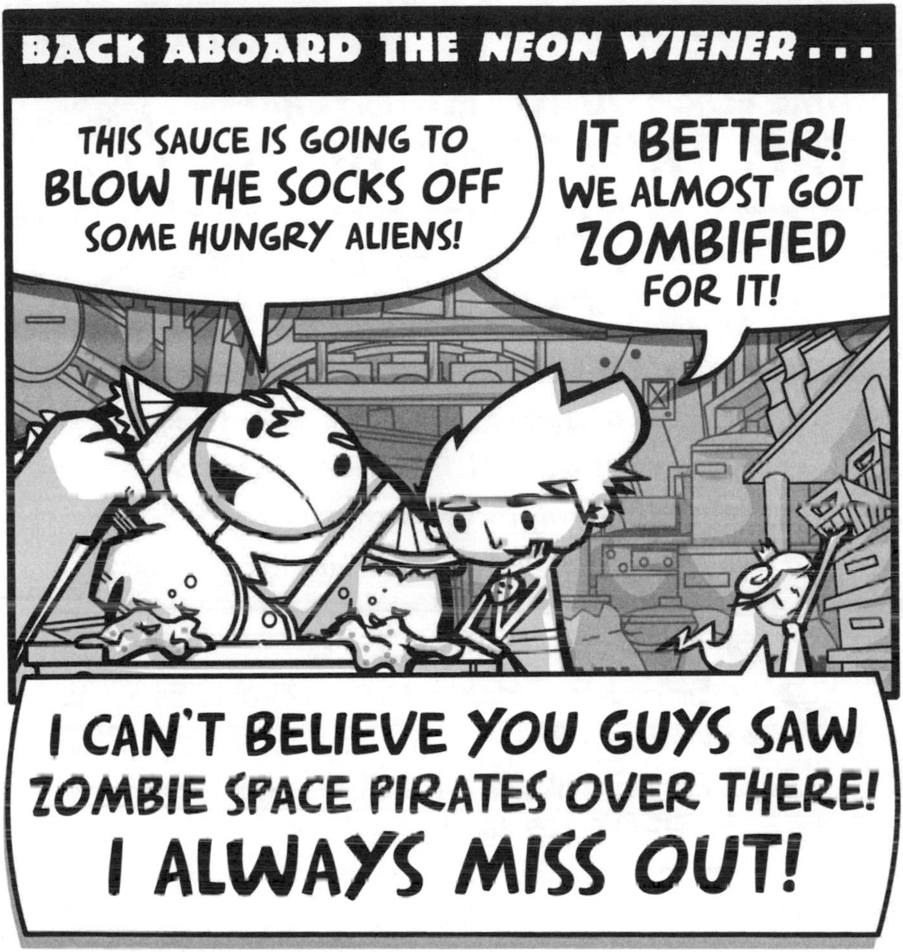
BACK ABOARD THE NEON WIENER . . .
THIS SAUCE IS GOING TO BLOW THE SOCKS OFF SOME HUNGRY ALIENS!
IT BETTER! WE ALMOST GOT ZOMBIFIED FOR IT!
I CAN'T BELIEVE YOU GUYS SAW ZOMBIE SPACE PIRATES OVER THERE! I ALWAYS MISS OUT!

"Whatever the next dangerous–scary thing we do is, you can join," I tell the princess.

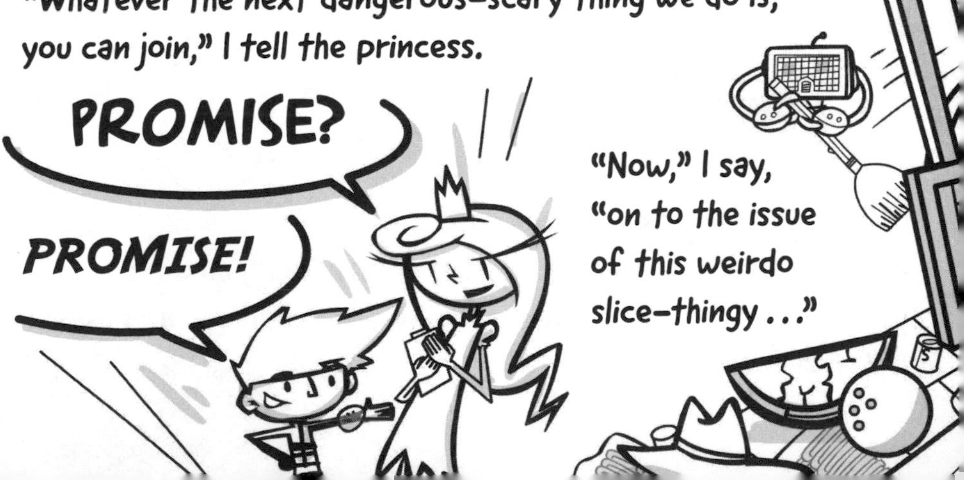
PROMISE?
PROMISE!

"Now," I say, "on to the issue of this weirdo slice–thingy . . ."

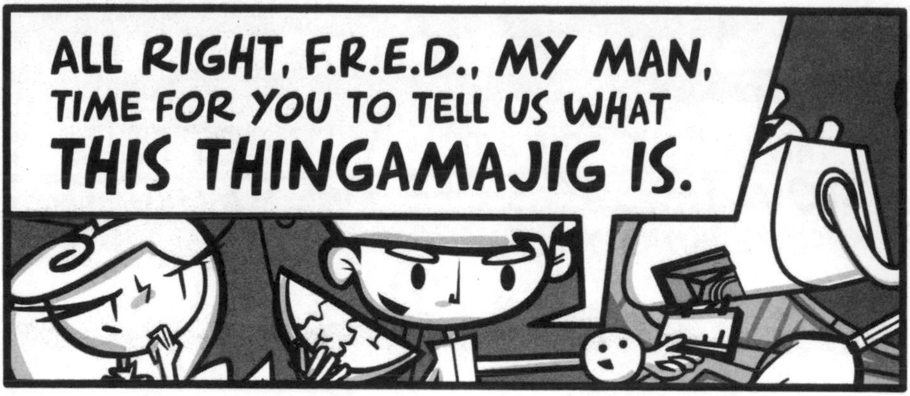
ALL RIGHT, F.R.E.D., MY MAN, TIME FOR YOU TO TELL US WHAT THIS THINGAMAJIG IS.

I open up F.R.E.D.'s back, and I shove the slice–thing inside like it's a bag of Pop Secret. And just like Pop Secret, three minutes later F.R.E.D. starts beeping. He's finished examining it.

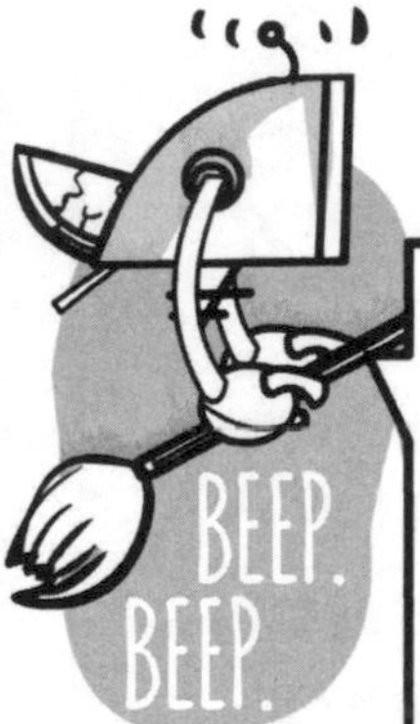
BEEP. BEEP.
THIS IS A SLICE OF A MAP-O-SPHERE. THERE ARE THREE SLICES. WHEN ALL THREE SLICES ARE ASSEMBLED, IT WILL LEAD TO THE GREAT SPHERE.

"So it **IS** a map, like that zombie said?" I ask. "Like, each piece shows you how to get to the next piece?"

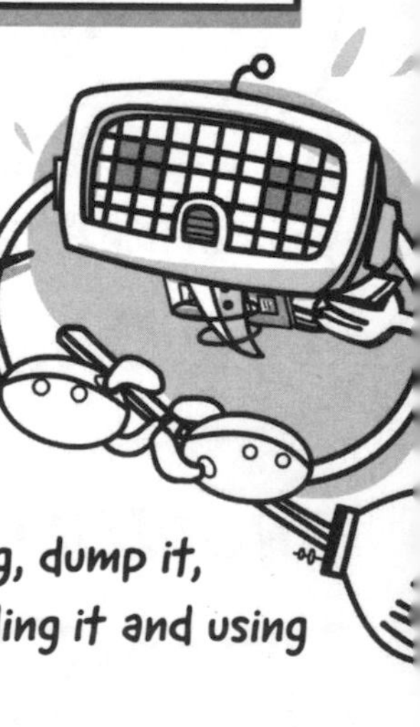
AFFIRMATIVE.

I sigh. "Too bad it only leads to evil stuff, not treasure . . . We have to destroy the thing, dump it, get rid of it. We don't want anyone else finding it and using it for evilness."

Princess Dagger's eyes are sort of fogged over as she stares at the Map-O-Sphere slice. She looks like she just fell head over heels in love or something. I bet I know what she's thinking . . .

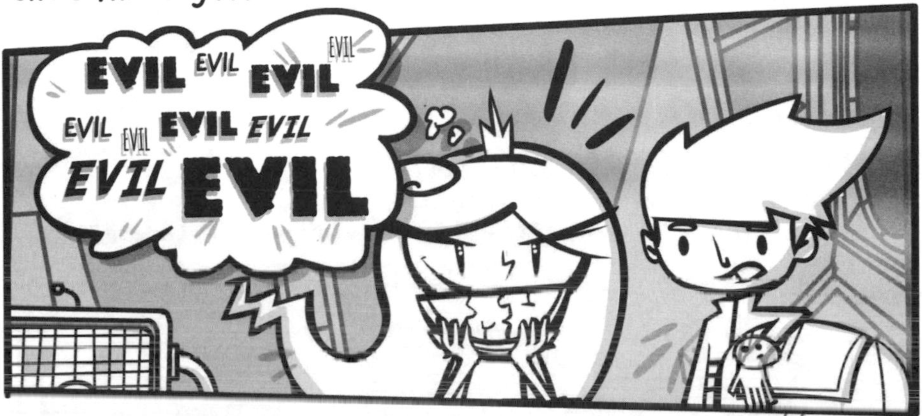
EVIL EVIL EVIL EVIL
EVIL EVIL EVIL EVIL
EVIL EVIL

"Hey, Princess!" I say, snapping my fingers in her face. "Wake up!"

She blinks twice.

Softly, she says, "It leads to the Ultimate Evil? Don't you think we should see what that is?"

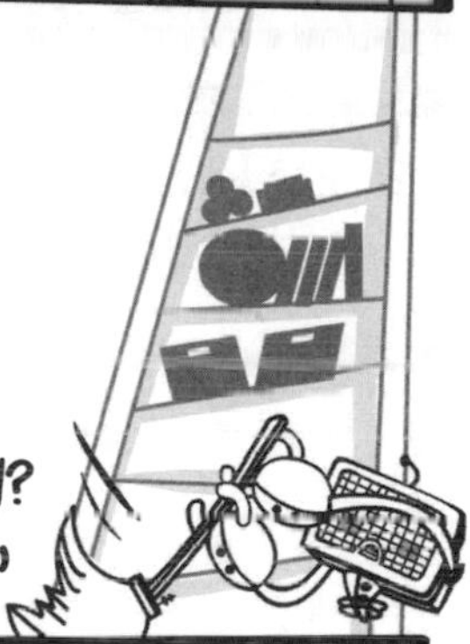

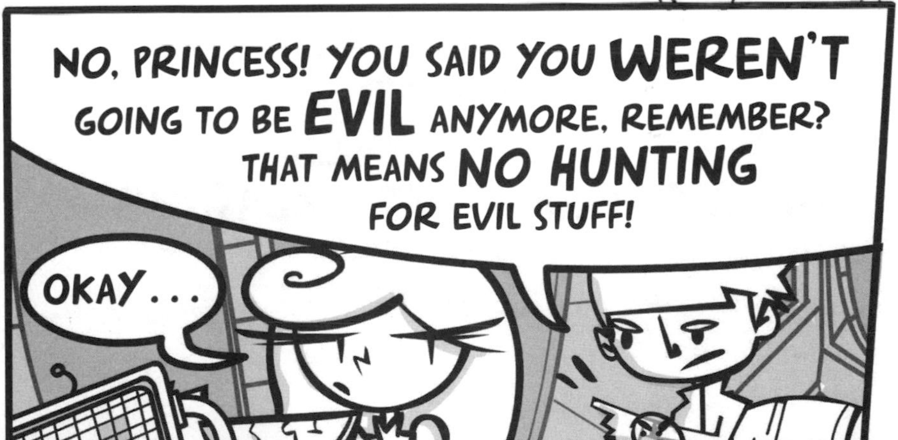
NO, PRINCESS! YOU SAID YOU WEREN'T GOING TO BE EVIL ANYMORE, REMEMBER? THAT MEANS NO HUNTING FOR EVIL STUFF!
OKAY . . .

But now, this—this is where I mess up **BIG TIME.** Pay attention, because everything is about to change . . .

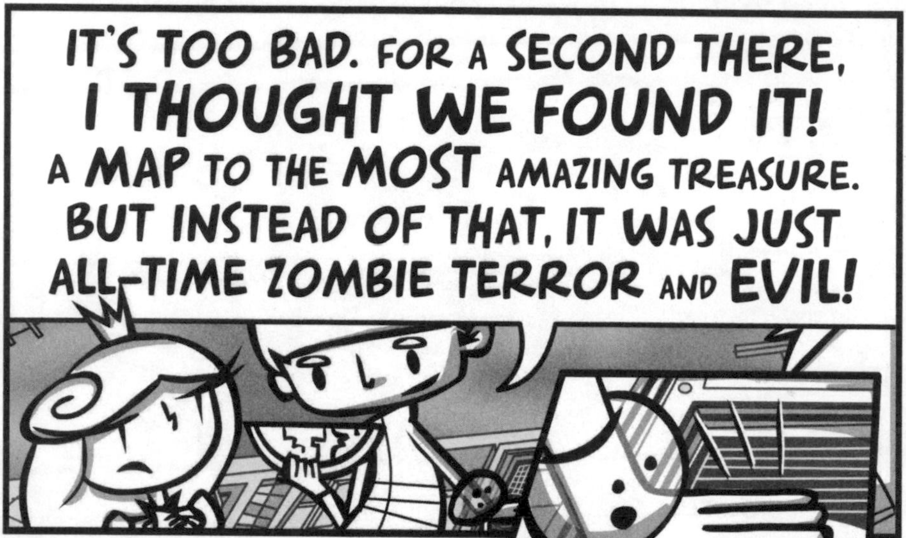
IT'S TOO BAD. FOR A SECOND THERE, I THOUGHT WE FOUND IT! A MAP TO THE MOST AMAZING TREASURE. BUT INSTEAD OF THAT, IT WAS JUST ALL-TIME ZOMBIE TERROR AND EVIL!

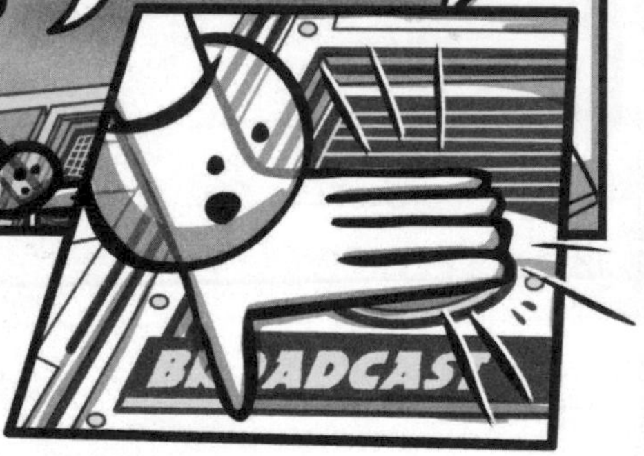
BROADCAST

I don't know it, but my hand is on the **BROADCAST** button—and that blasts out a big mass message! And most broadcasts out of the Lost Triangle are *really* cruddy. F.R.E.D. repeats the message back to me, and it sounds like—

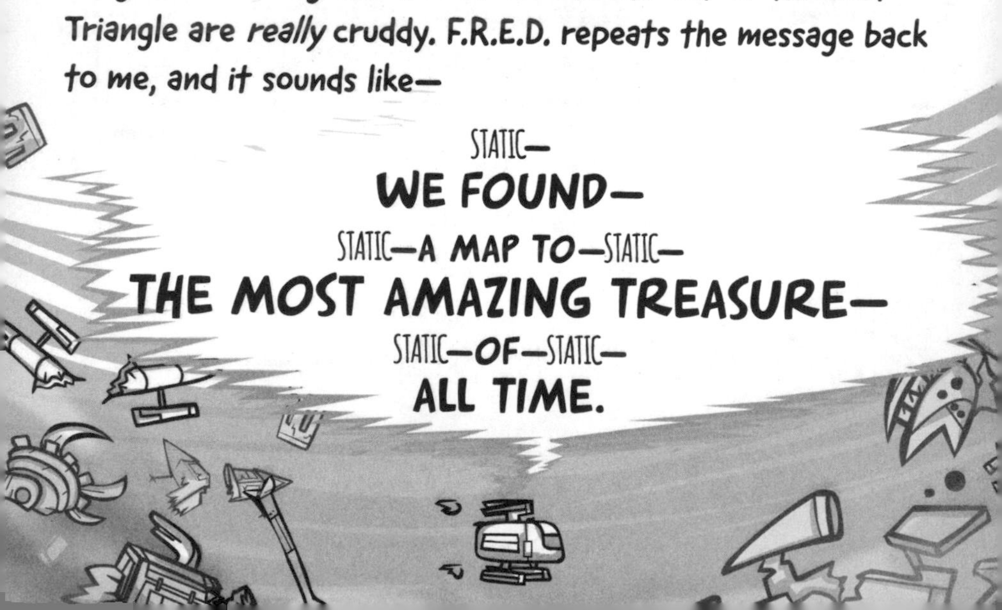
STATIC—
WE FOUND—
STATIC—A MAP TO—STATIC—
THE MOST AMAZING TREASURE—
STATIC—OF—STATIC—
ALL TIME.

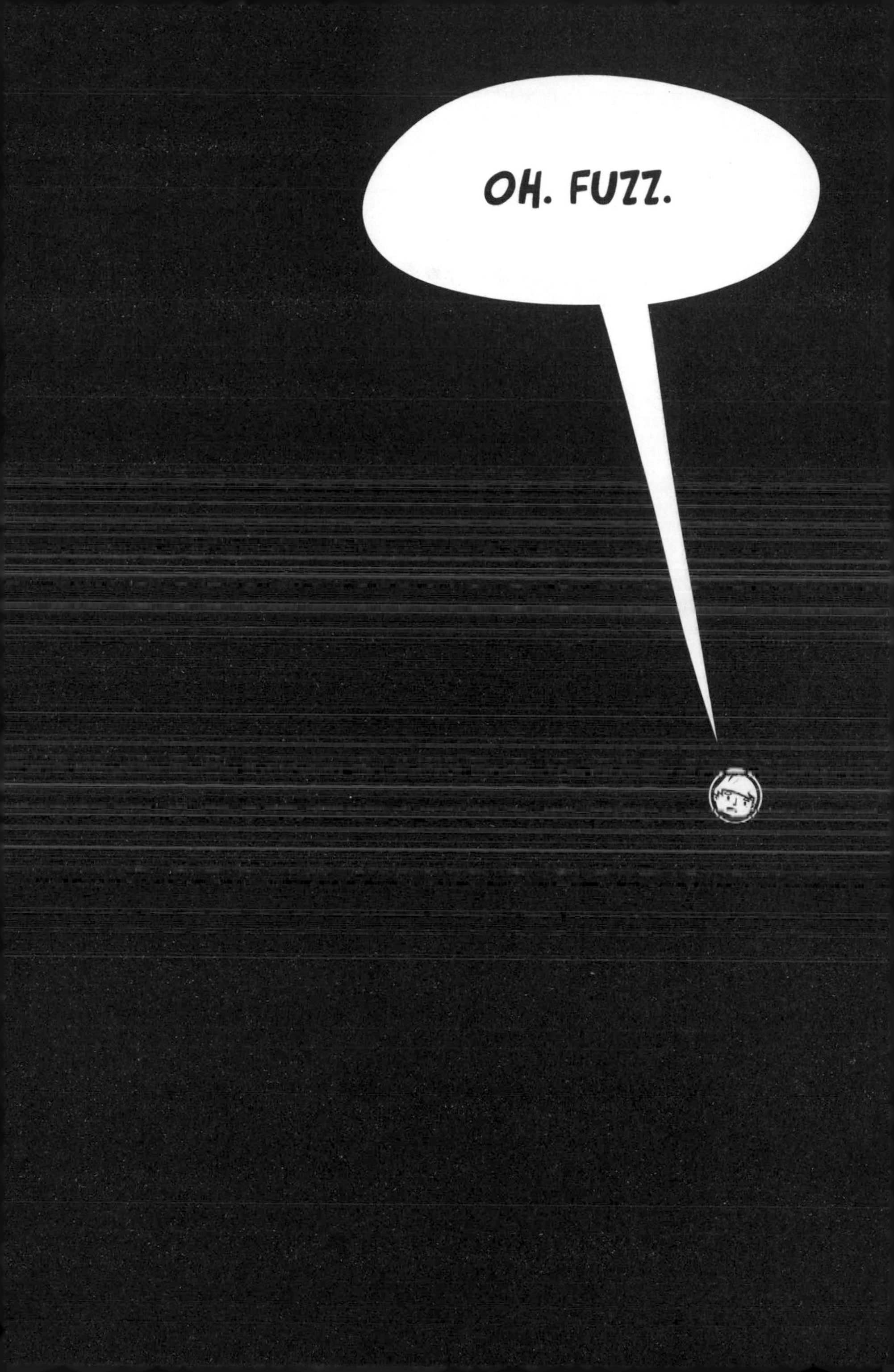
OH. FUZZ.

I STINK LIKE YARLAK ARMPITZ

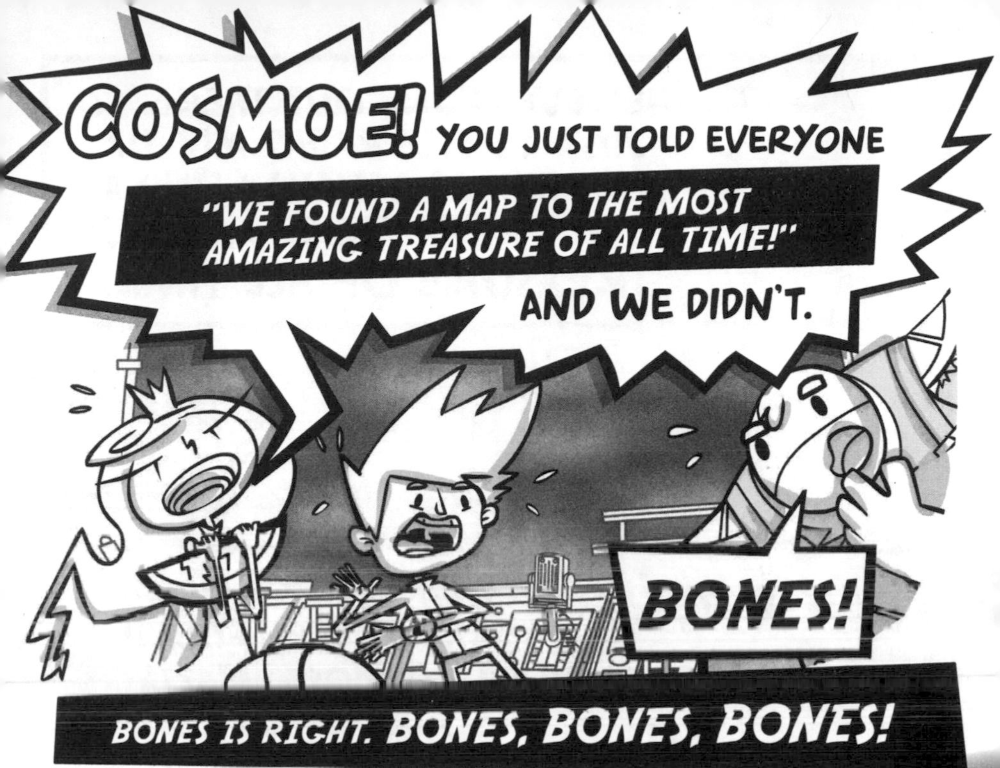
COSMOE! YOU JUST TOLD EVERYONE
"WE FOUND A MAP TO THE MOST AMAZING TREASURE OF ALL TIME!"
AND WE DIDN'T.
BONES!
BONES IS RIGHT. BONES, BONES, BONES!

But I got this. I totally got this. Just a small miscommunication. Fixable. Entirely **100%** fixable.

"Dagger, Humps—just relax your faces," I say. "I'll handle this."

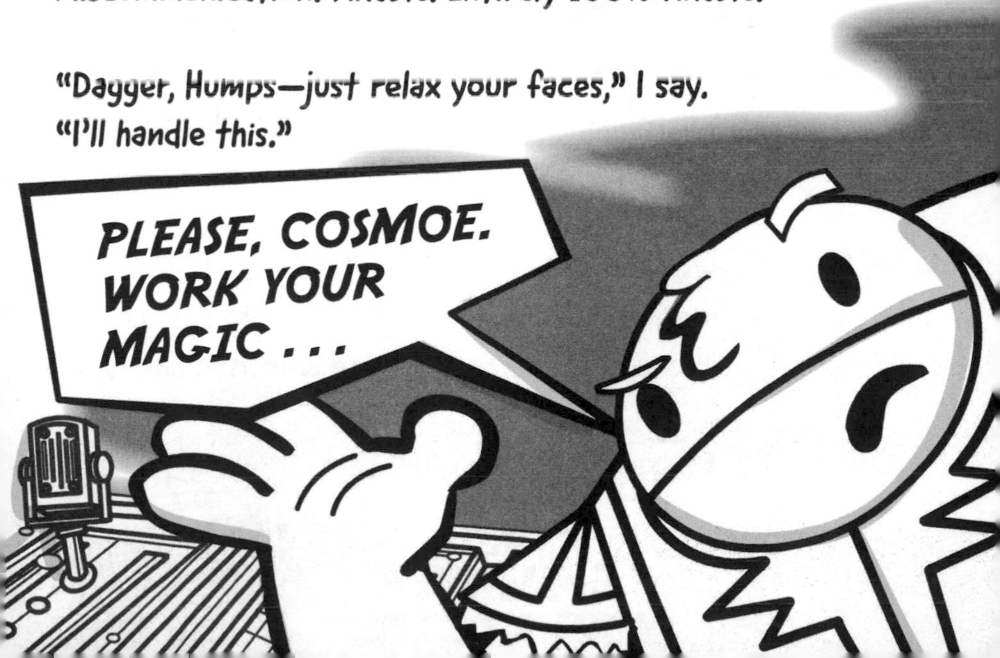
PLEASE, COSMOE. WORK YOUR MAGIC . . .

HEY, EVERYONE OUT THERE. SO, JUST A LITTLE RADIO MIX-UP. WE DID NOT ACTUALLY FIND A MAP TO THE MOST AMAZING TREASURE OF ALL TIME.

YEAH RIGHT!

THAT'S EXACTLY WHAT SOMEONE WHO FOUND A MAP TO THE MOST AMAZING TREASURE OF ALL TIME WOULD SAY! WE'RE ALL COMING FOR YOU!

OK—so this is maybe not a totally easy fix. Time to find out exactly how much trouble we're in. "Um, F.R.E.D., how many ships were listening when I said that stuff about the map?" I ask.

While F.R.E.D. runs the numbers, Humps stares at me like he wants to give me the ol' Bronkle strangle. I try to reassure him. "Humps, I'm sure, like, basically no one was listening..."

2,297,187 SHIPS WERE LISTENING.

SMUDGE.

AND IT GETS WORSE.

JUDGING BY THE ACTIVITY ON THE INTER-GALACTIC SOCIAL SPACE. THE GALAXY IS BUZZING WITH NEWS OF YOUR MAP TO THE MOST AMAZING TREASURE OF ALL TIME.

"Oh, c'mon!" I say, grabbing F.R.E.D. "Let me see!"

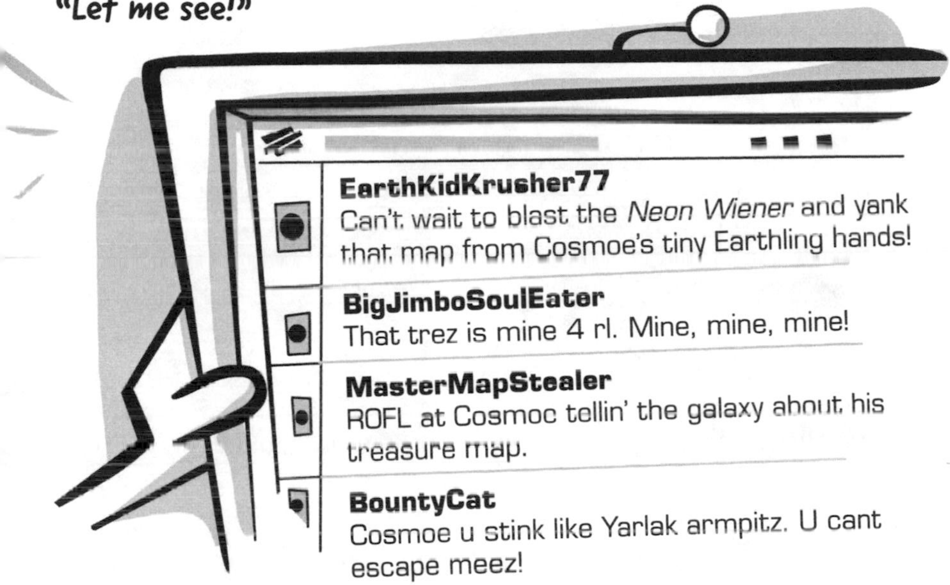

EarthKidKrusher77
Can't wait to blast the *Neon Wiener* and yank that map from Cosmoe's tiny Earthling hands!
BigJimboSoulEater
That trez is mine 4 rl. Mine, mine, mine!
MasterMapStealer
ROFL at Cosmoe tellin' the galaxy about his treasure map.
BountyCat
Cosmoe u stink like Yarlak armpitz. U cant escape meez!

I collapse into the captain's chair. BountyCat is right. I do stink like Yarlak armpitz. Only a captain that stinks like Yarlak armpitz would mess up this majorly . . .

"Humphree," I say, "you know all about these bad dudes—who are the absolute most bad-news fortune hunters out there?"

Humphree tells us . . .

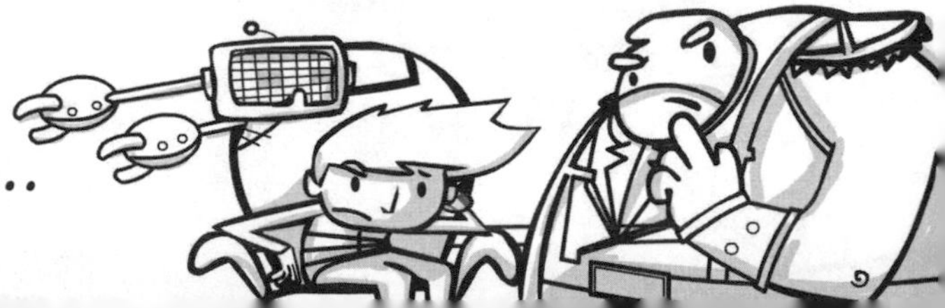

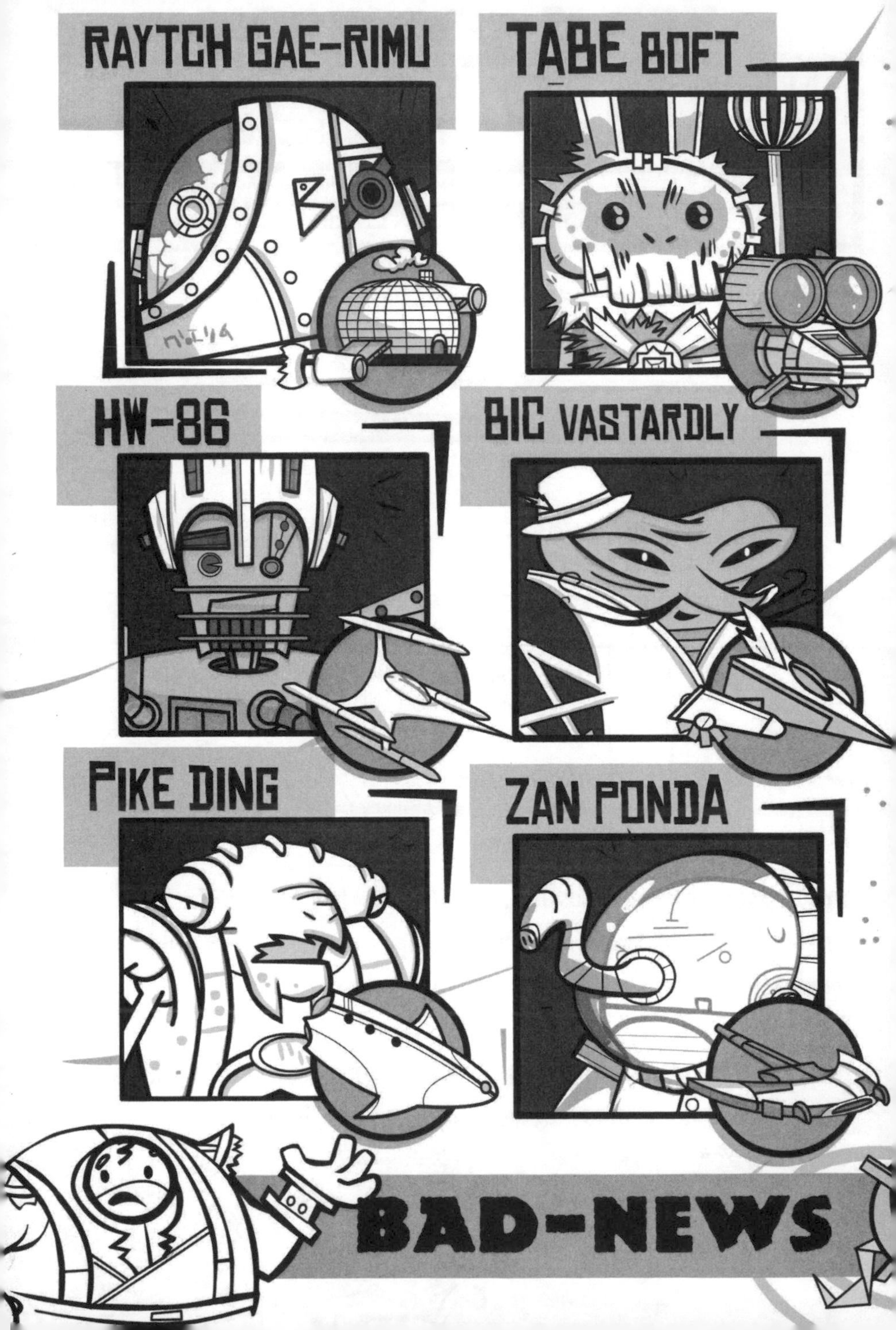
RAYTCH GAE-RIMU
TABE BOFT
HW-86
BIC VASTARDLY
PIKE DING
ZAN PONDA
BAD-NEWS

JAE FALCON

OGRE ED

GENERAL KRAX von GRUMBLE

KAFF FIEND

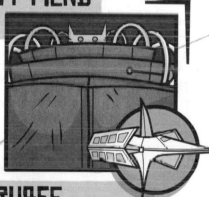

NAYTHAN "KNIVES" PO-TASH

RUBEE "RICOCHET" PO-TASH

FORTUNE HUNTERS

All those dudes will be hunting for us! All those dudes will be trying to blast us out of the sky and get their hands on the Map-O-Sphere! And that's when I realize we only have one choice . . .

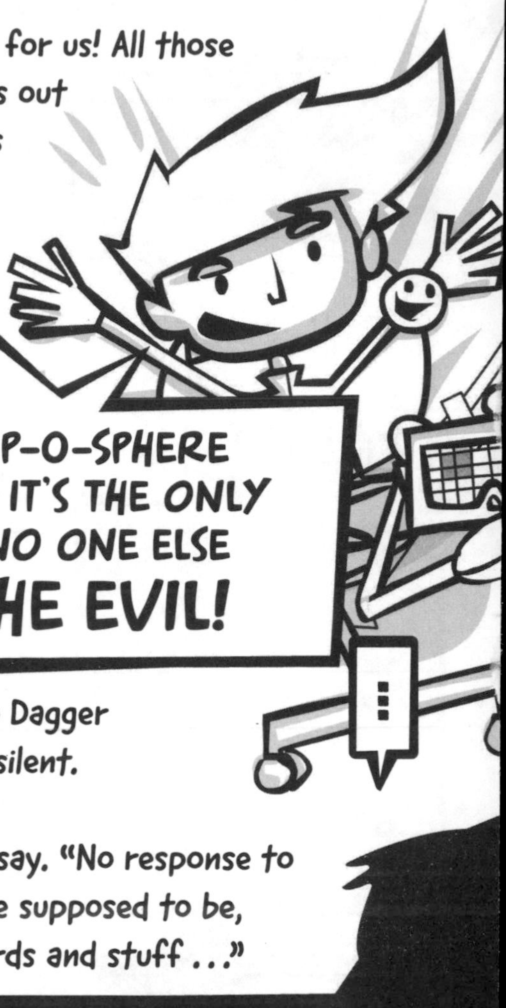

WE MUST FIND ALL THE SLICES OF THE MAP-O-SPHERE AND THEN DESTROY IT! IT'S THE ONLY WAY TO MAKE SURE NO ONE ELSE **UNLEASHES THE EVIL!**

I look from Humphree to Dagger and back again. They're silent.

"Really, guys?" I say. "No response to that? Those were supposed to be, like, inspiring words and stuff . . ."

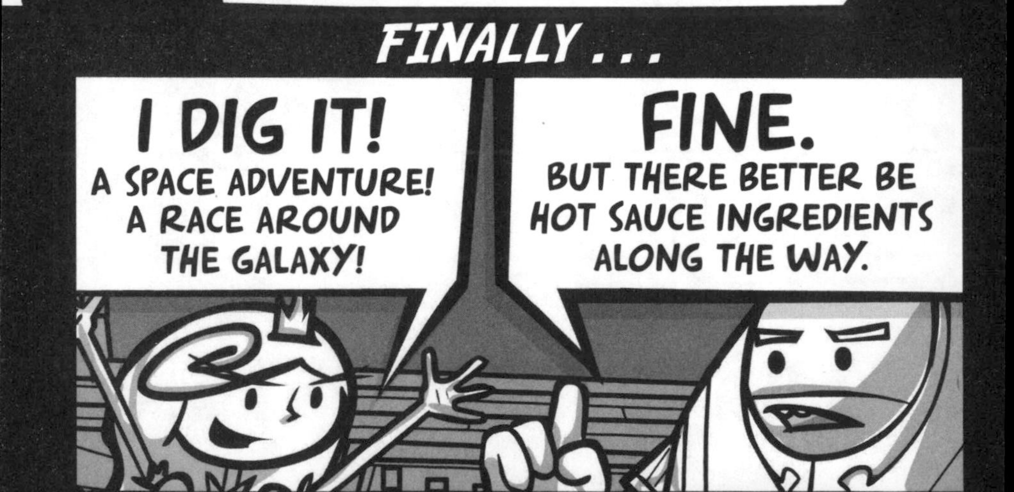
FINALLY . . .
I DIG IT! A SPACE ADVENTURE! A RACE AROUND THE GALAXY!
FINE. BUT THERE BETTER BE HOT SAUCE INGREDIENTS ALONG THE WAY.

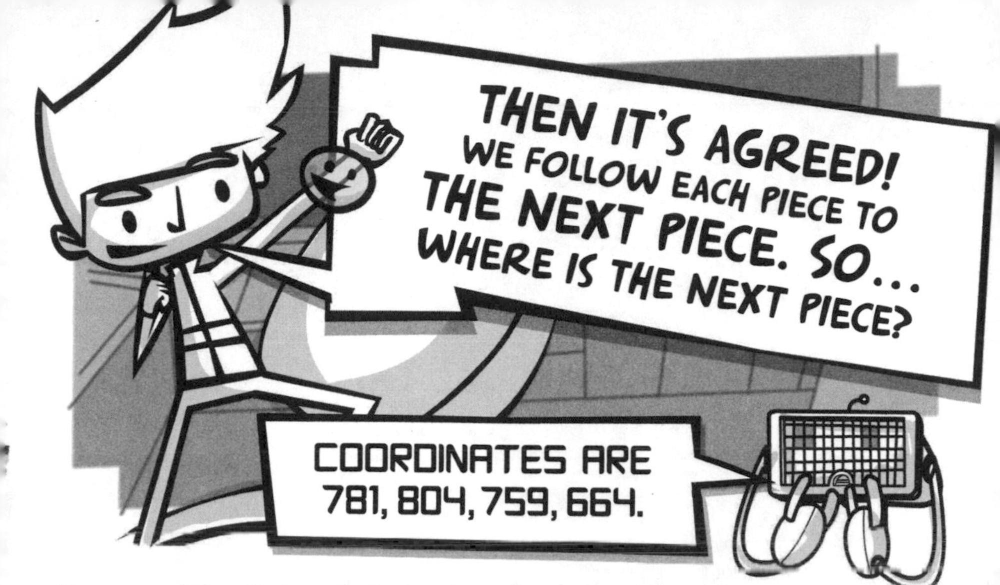
THEN IT'S AGREED! WE FOLLOW EACH PIECE TO THE NEXT PIECE. SO... WHERE IS THE NEXT PIECE?
COORDINATES ARE 781, 804, 759, 664.

Hmm . . . 781, 804, 759, 664. That sounds familiar . . .
"Hey, F.R.E.D., what's at those coordinates?" I ask.

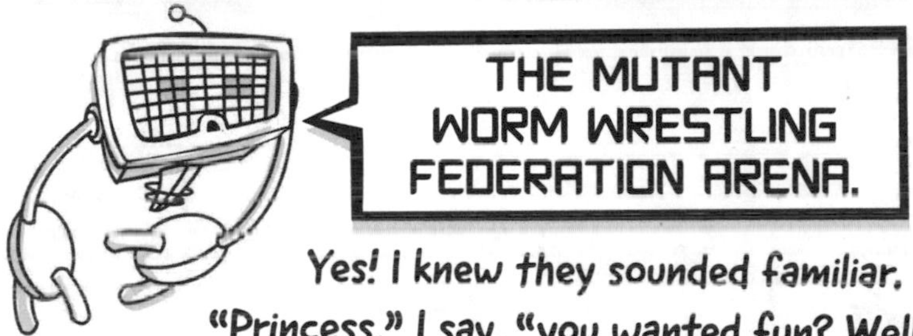
THE MUTANT WORM WRESTLING FEDERATION ARENA.

Yes! I knew they sounded familiar.
"Princess," I say, "you wanted fun? Well, we got fun. We're going to a mutant worm wrestling match!"

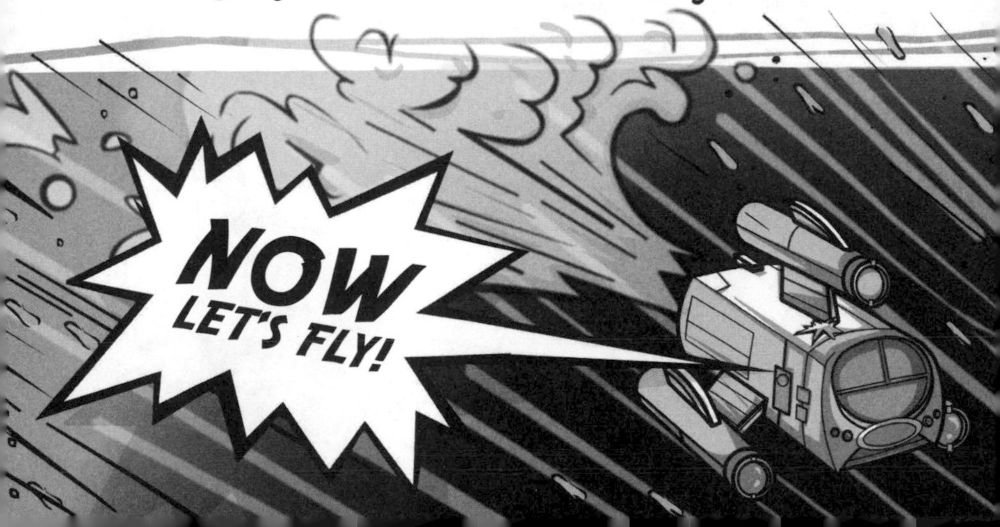
NOW LET'S FLY!

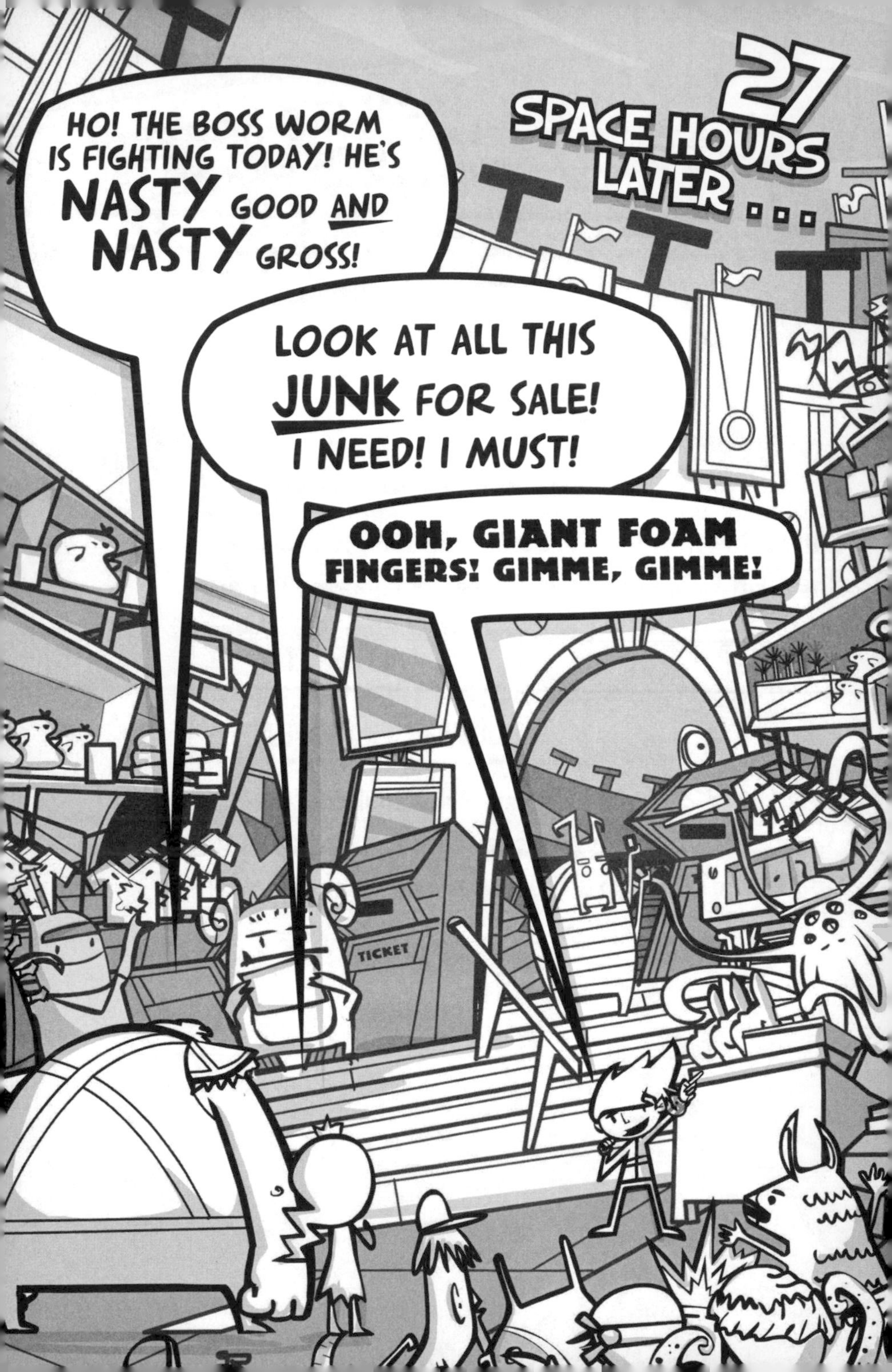
27 SPACE HOURS LATER...
HO! THE BOSS WORM IS FIGHTING TODAY! HE'S NASTY GOOD AND NASTY GROSS!
LOOK AT ALL THIS JUNK FOR SALE! I NEED! I MUST!
OOH, GIANT FOAM FINGERS! GIMME, GIMME!
TICKET

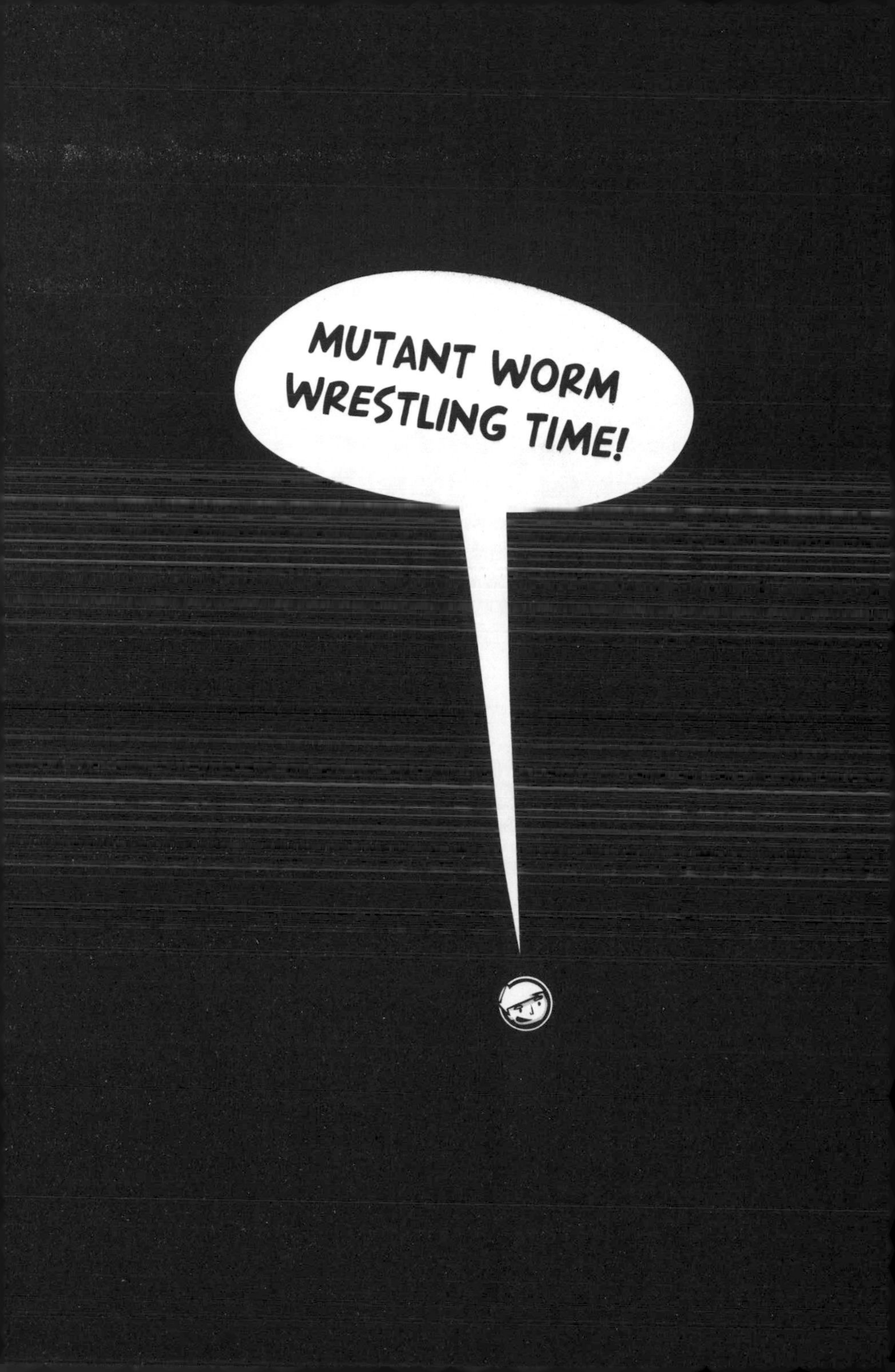
MUTANT WORM WRESTLING TIME!

ADIOS,
LAMES-VILLE!

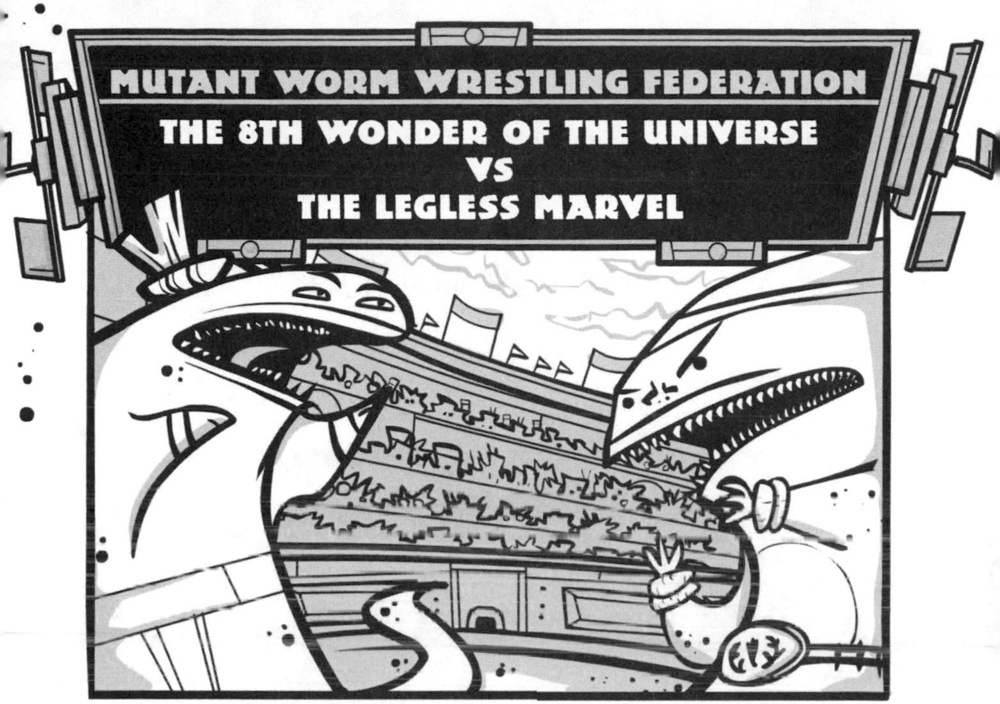
MUTANT WORM WRESTLING FEDERATION
THE 8TH WONDER OF THE UNIVERSE
VS
THE LEGLESS MARVEL

We settle in for the match. F.R.E.D. can't pinpoint the exact location of the next slice—we just know it's somewhere around here. I'm trying to keep my eye out, but it's tough with all the killer action onstage.

And the action **IS** killer. Let me be clear—

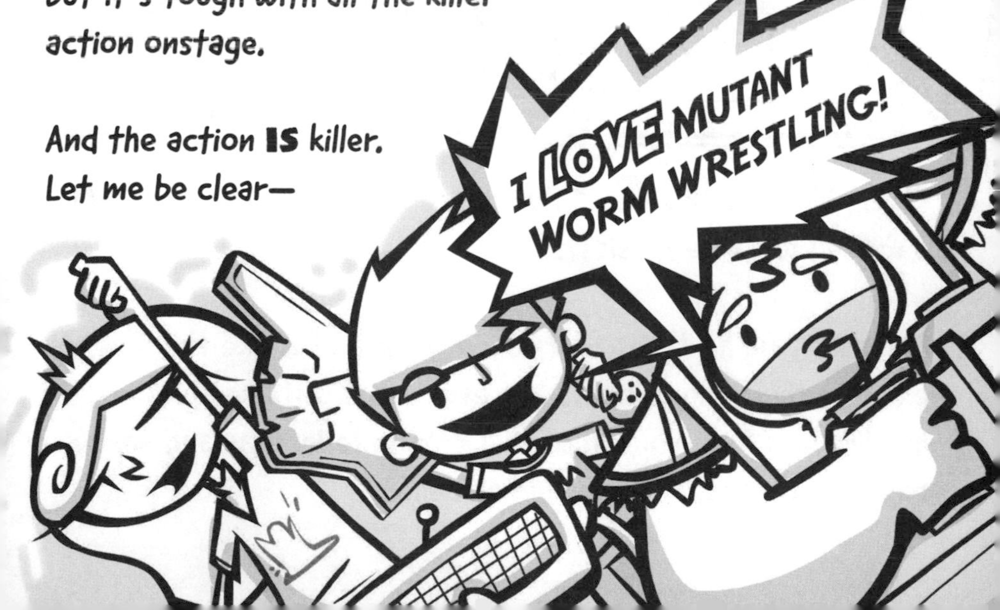
I LOVE MUTANT WORM WRESTLING!

But today, it's not about enjoying the action in the ring—it's about finding the Map-O-Sphere! But still, it's fun watching Princess Dagger. I even gave her the F.R.E.D. seat, since it's her first time at a mutant worm wrestling match.

And from the sound of it, she's enjoying herself . . .

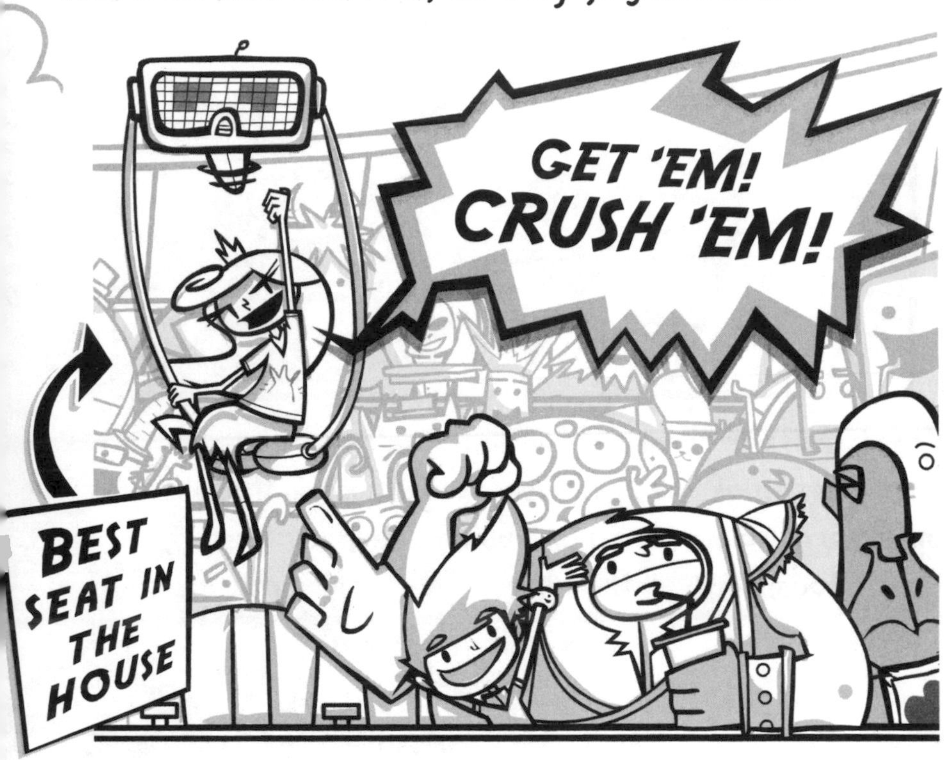
GET 'EM!
CRUSH 'EM!
BEST SEAT IN THE HOUSE

"Well, blow me down . . ." Humphree says. "The royal rascal is a wicked worm enthusiast!"

I don't blame her! Two worms duking it out is like the most exciting thing the princess has ever seen! Until she met us, her life was just a bunch of evil etiquette lessons and fancy ballroom dances. Basically, lames-ville.

Now, I know I'm supposed to be looking for the Map-O-Sphere. But I mean, I should get to have some fun, right?

Right!

That's why I'm using Goober to perfect my own twist on the classic "Tap the other shoulder, made you look!" move . . .

But bad-news butts for me: my "Tap the other shoulder, made you look!" move is about to get me in big trouble. Because right now there is a big-time bad dude tripping over my rubbery buddy, Goober!

A big-time bad dude by the name of—

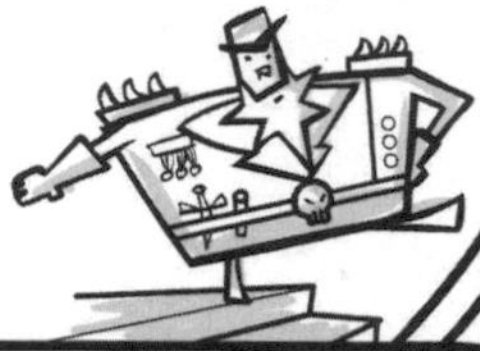

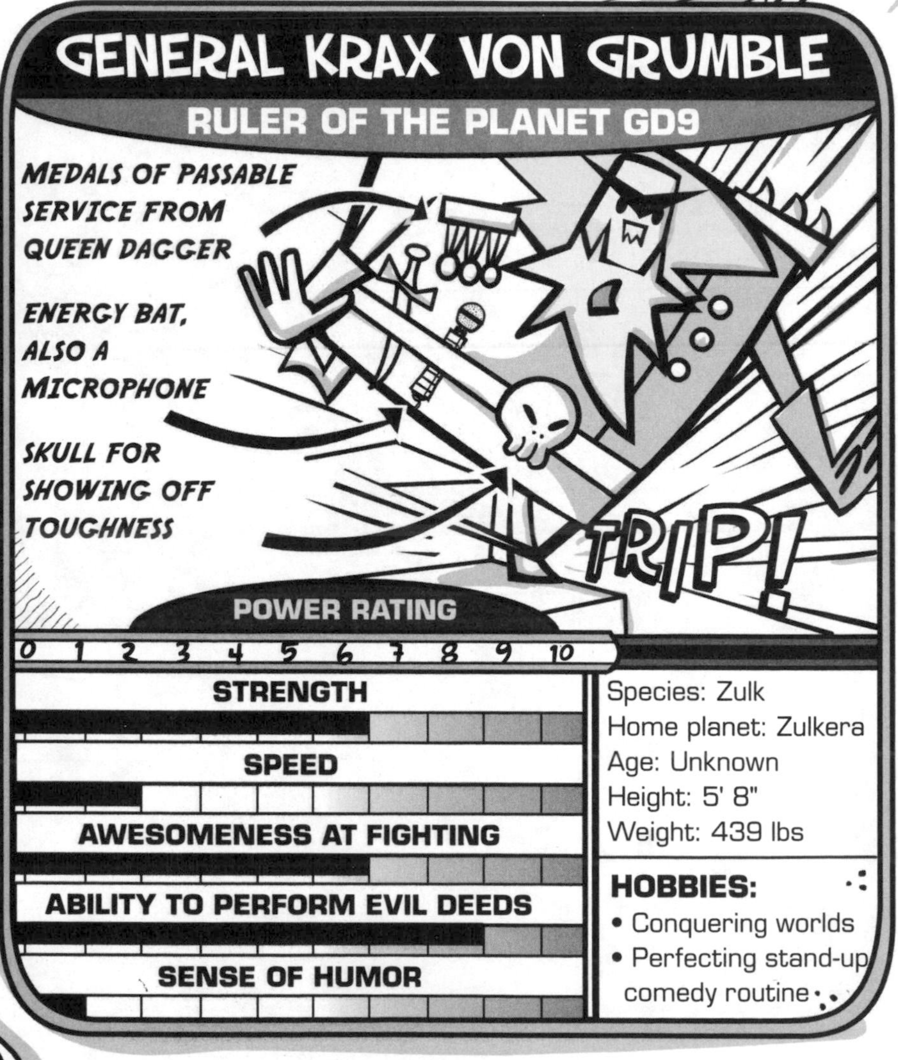

GENERAL KRAX VON GRUMBLE
RULER OF THE PLANET GD9
MEDALS OF PASSABLE SERVICE FROM QUEEN DAGGER
ENERGY BAT, ALSO A MICROPHONE
SKULL FOR SHOWING OFF TOUGHNESS
TRIP!
POWER RATING
0 1 2 3 4 5 6 7 8 9 10
STRENGTH
SPEED
AWESOMENESS AT FIGHTING
ABILITY TO PERFORM EVIL DEEDS
SENSE OF HUMOR
Species: Zulk
Home planet: Zulkera
Age: Unknown
Height: 5' 8"
Weight: 439 lbs
HOBBIES:
• Conquering worlds
• Perfecting stand-up comedy routine

There's a colossal commotion as General Krax von Grumble tumbles, head over heels, down the stairs. For a moment, no one can believe it!

But then the entire arena erupts into laughter!

"He fell! He fell right on his fat face!" an Eef named Trachsup shouts.

"What a dummy!" a very insecure Elppa named Axie shouts.

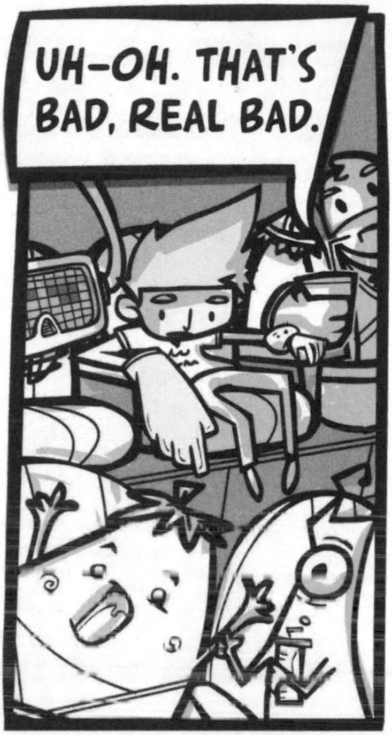
UH-OH. THAT'S BAD, REAL BAD.

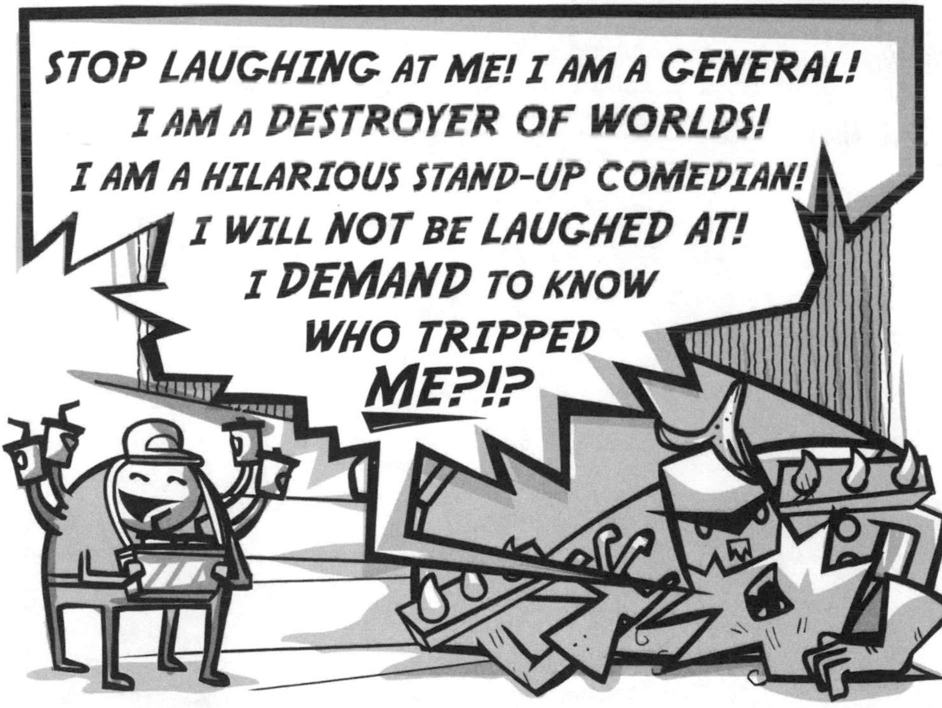
STOP LAUGHING AT ME! I AM A GENERAL! I AM A DESTROYER OF WORLDS! I AM A HILARIOUS STAND-UP COMEDIAN! I WILL NOT BE LAUGHED AT! I DEMAND TO KNOW WHO TRIPPED ME?!?

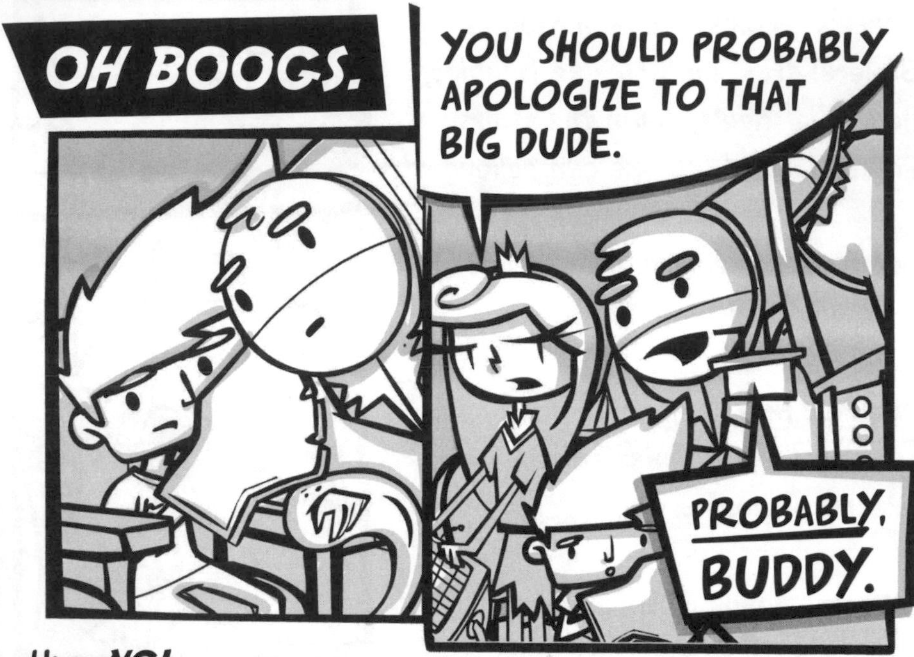
OH BOOGS.
YOU SHOULD PROBABLY APOLOGIZE TO THAT BIG DUDE.
PROBABLY, BUDDY.

Um—NO!

Sometimes—***AND IT STINKS***—you have to take responsibility. I totally know that. But now is not one of those times.

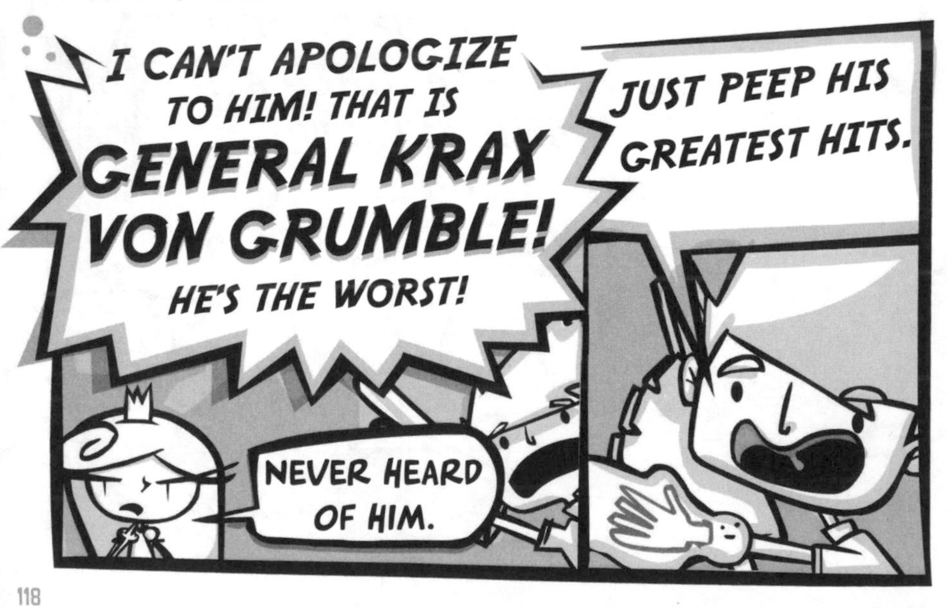
I CAN'T APOLOGIZE TO HIM! THAT IS GENERAL KRAX VON GRUMBLE! HE'S THE WORST!
NEVER HEARD OF HIM.
JUST PEEP HIS GREATEST HITS.

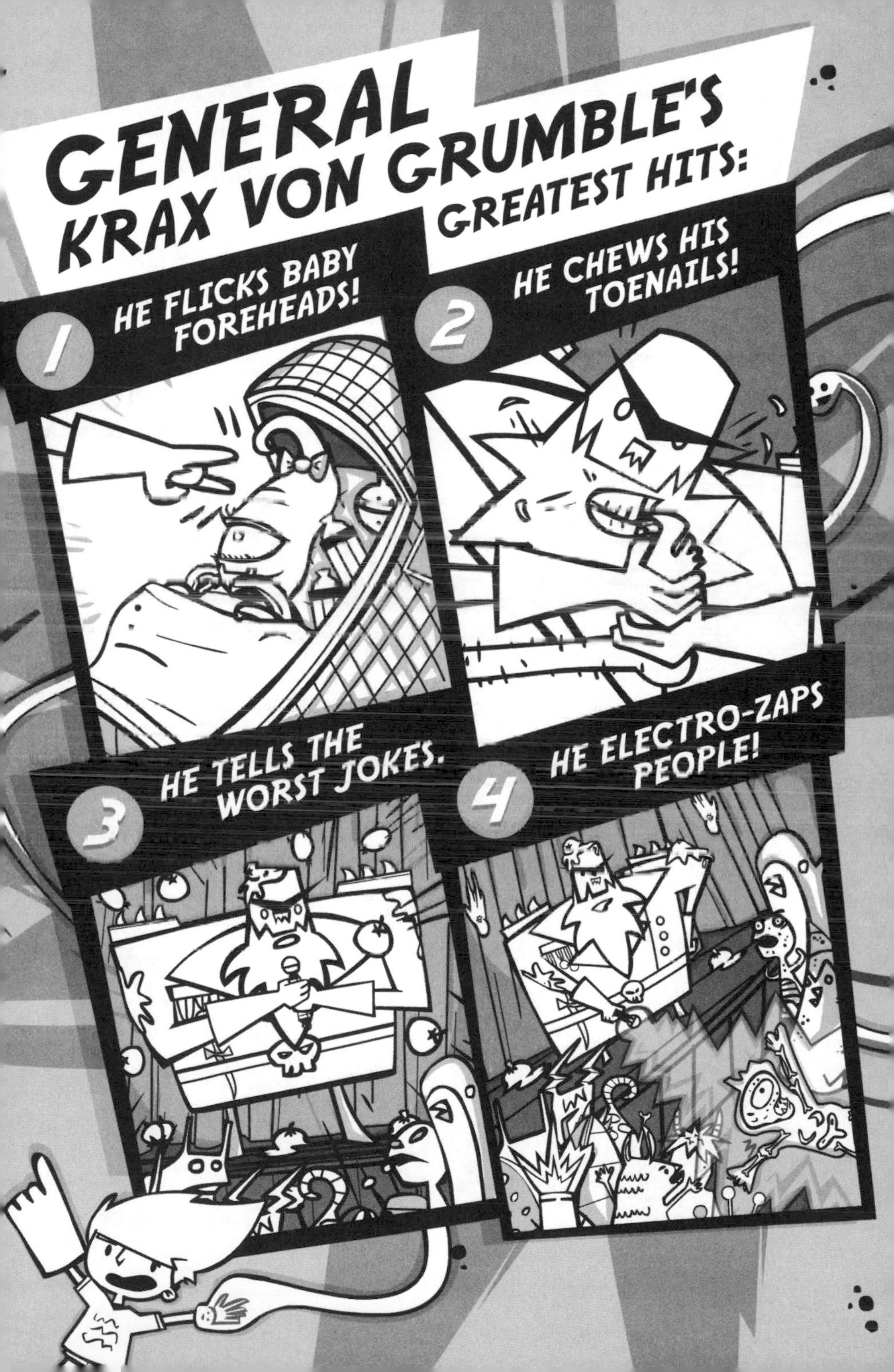
GENERAL KRAX VON GRUMBLE'S GREATEST HITS:
1
HE FLICKS BABY FOREHEADS!
2
HE CHEWS HIS TOENAILS!
3
HE TELLS THE WORST JOKES.
4
HE ELECTRO-ZAPS PEOPLE!

"ELECTRO-ZAP?" Princess Dagger says. ***"YIKES . . .*** Maybe you should just lay low and play it cool. Then we can find the slice of the Map-O-Sphere and split."

But laying low and playing it cool is ***NOT*** an option! One of the general's soldiers saw ***THE WHOLE THING*** go down.

TATTLETALE

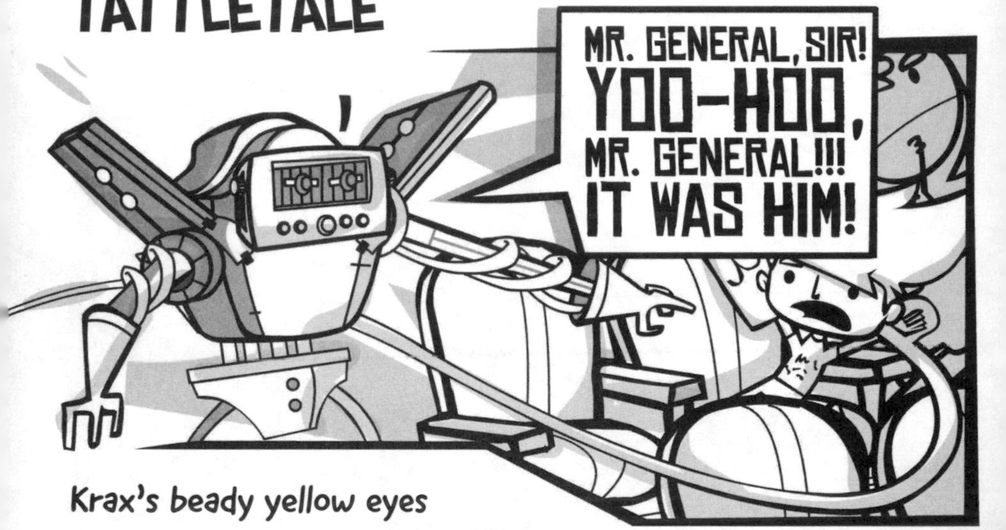
MR. GENERAL, SIR! YOO-HOO, MR. GENERAL!!! IT WAS HIM!

Krax's beady yellow eyes dart across the arena and lock in on me. His mouth curls into a gruesome smile as he raises his energy bat and—

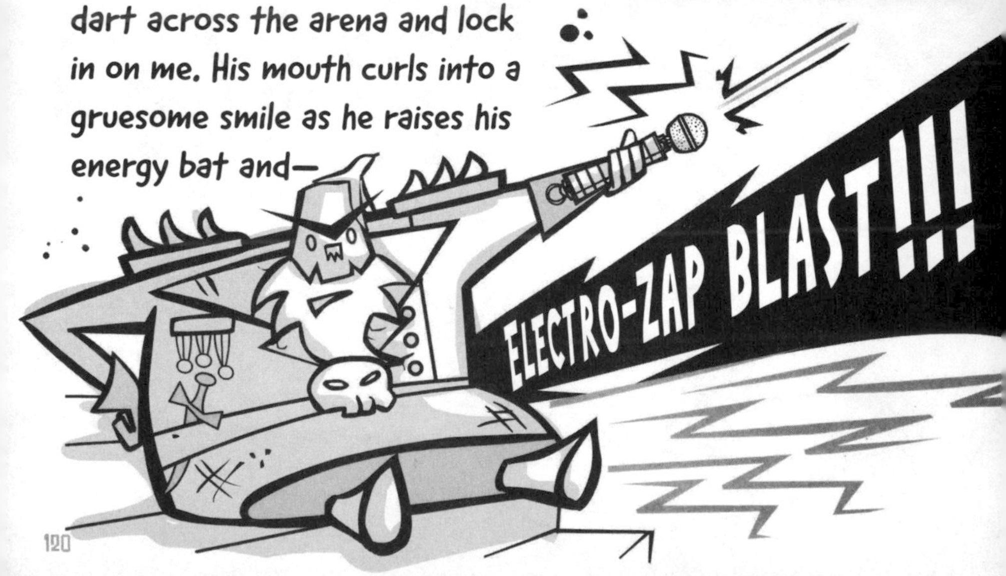
ELECTRO-ZAP BLAST!!!

GENERAL KRAX'S INFAMOUS WEAPON IS PART MICROPHONE AND PART ENERGY BLASTER. IT ALSO HAS SLOTS FOR STORING HANDY ITEMS LIKE:

1. KRAX'S FAVORITE SNACK: CHOCOLATE-COVERED ZIK-BUGS.

2. A SPARE TONGUE. [KRAX'S TONGUE FALLS OUT A LOT. IT'S A LONG STORY . . .]

3. NOSE HAIR TRIMMERS.

MY BUTT'S PRESSING AGAINST MY RIBS

12

My brain feels like a scrambled egg.

WHAT HAPPENED?

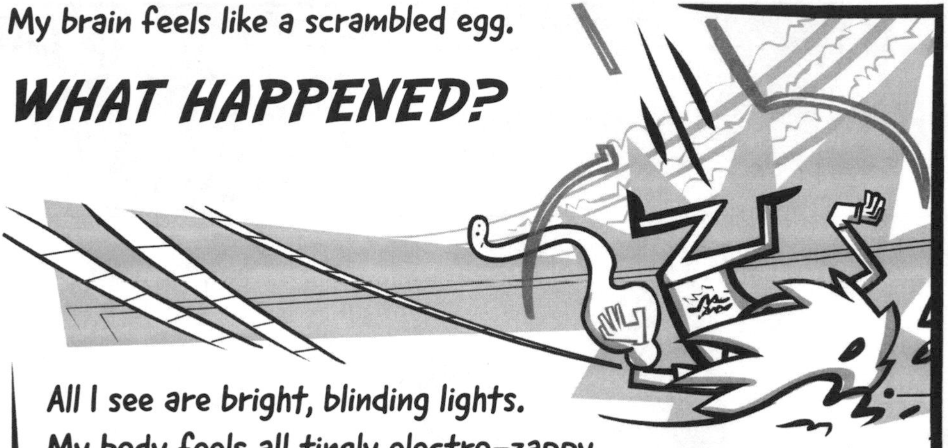

All I see are bright, blinding lights.
My body feels all tingly electro-zappy.

I hear the crackle of a microphone, then a TAP-TAP noise.

Oh smudge. Now I remember. General Krax von Grumble.
He zapped me.

And now he's going to make me fight . . .

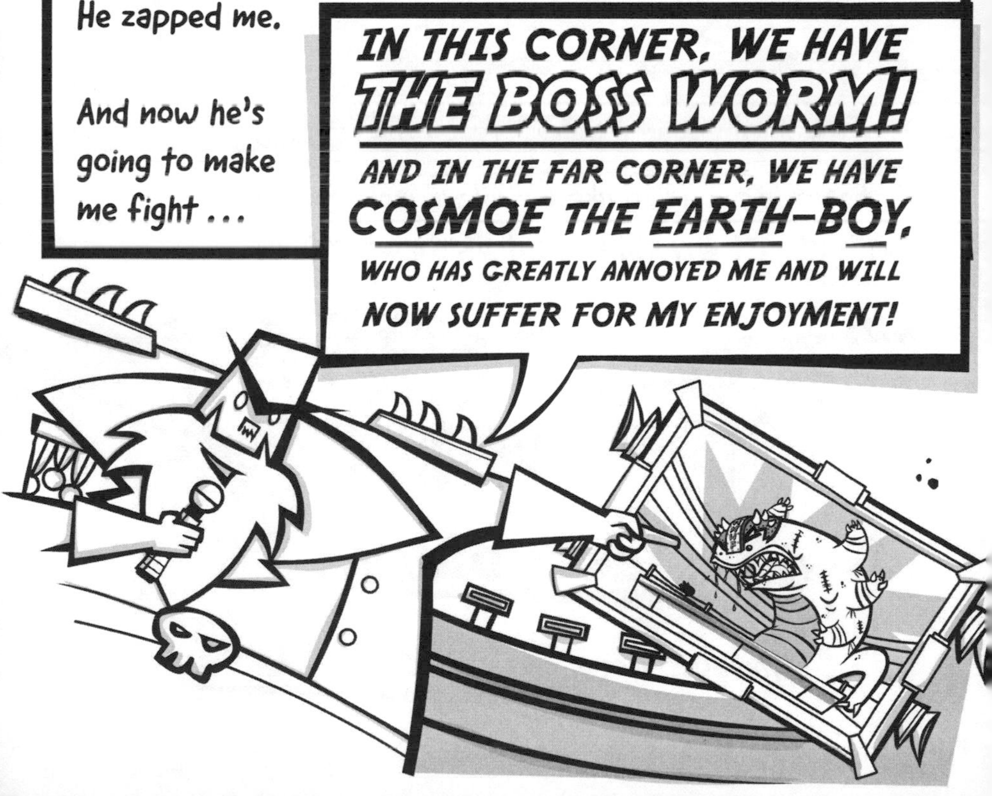
IN THIS CORNER, WE HAVE
THE BOSS WORM!
AND IN THE FAR CORNER, WE HAVE
COSMOE THE EARTH-BOY,
WHO HAS GREATLY ANNOYED ME AND WILL
NOW SUFFER FOR MY ENJOYMENT!

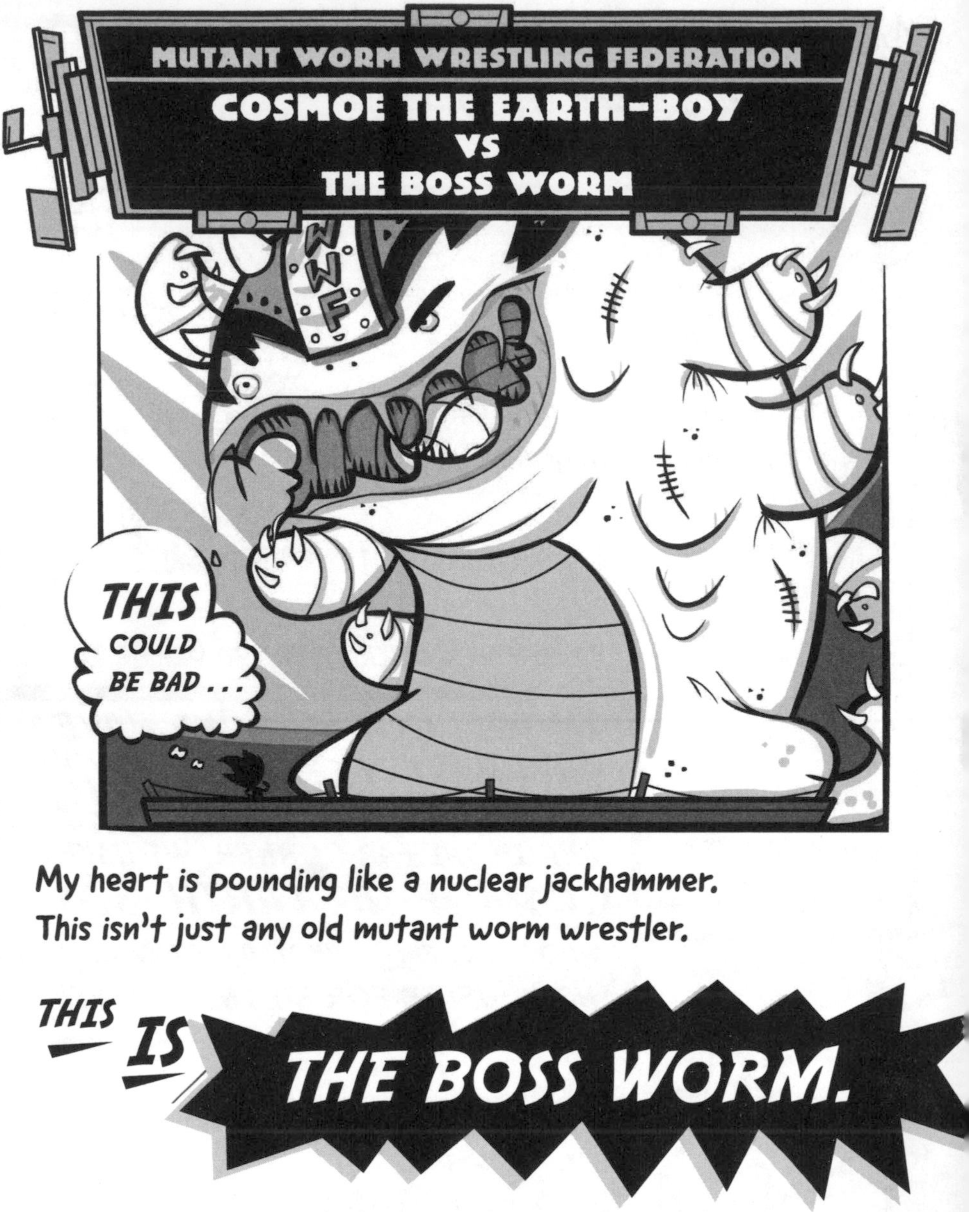
MUTANT WORM WRESTLING FEDERATION
COSMOE THE EARTH-BOY
VS
THE BOSS WORM
WWF
THIS COULD BE BAD . . .

My heart is pounding like a nuclear jackhammer. This isn't just any old mutant worm wrestler.

THIS IS THE BOSS WORM.

The Boss Worm is **LEGENDARY.**

The Boss Worm **DOESN'T LOSE.**

I try to block out the lights as I scan the crowd, looking for my friends.

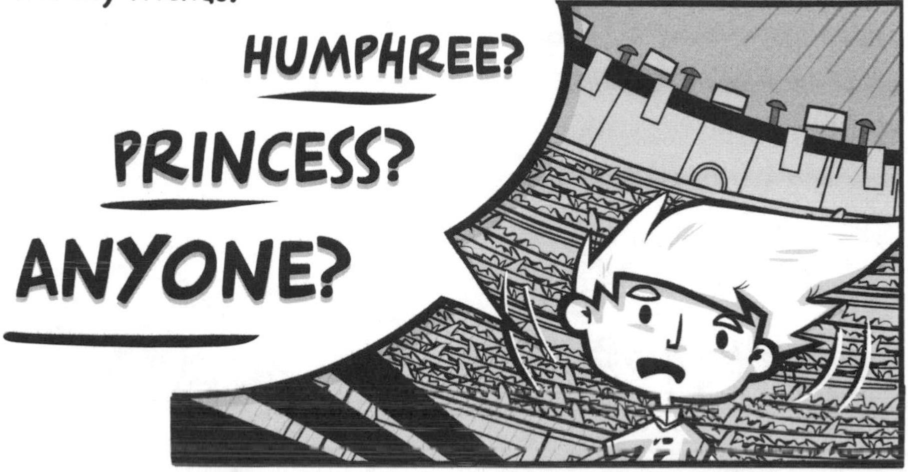
HUMPHREE?
PRINCESS?
ANYONE?

Looks like I'm all alone in this. Crazy stuff went down while I was knocked out. Princess Dagger is tied up and Humphree is wearing . . . THE

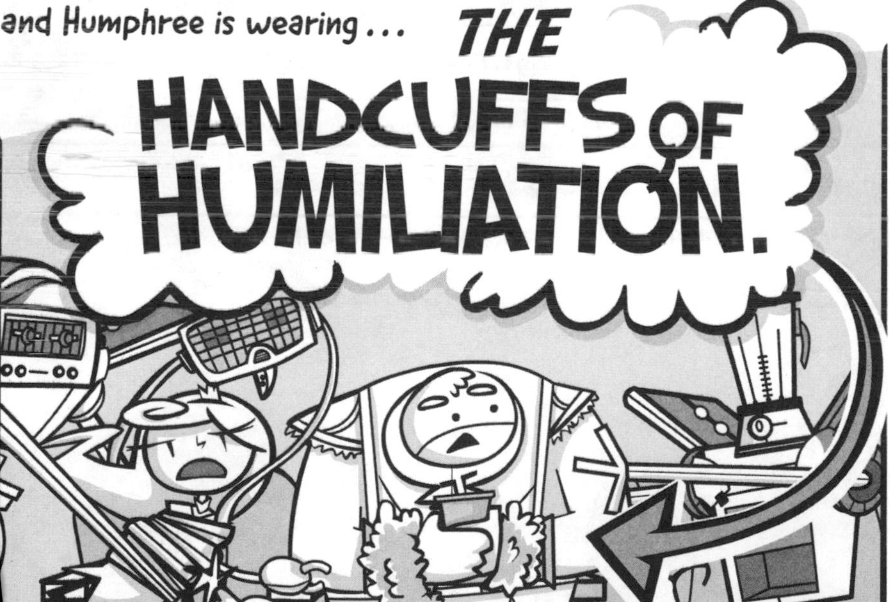
HANDCUFFS OF HUMILIATION.

Worst of all, after the Boss Worm beats you, he eats you. That's his tagline! It's sold on T-shirts and alarm clocks and stuffed animals all over the galaxy. I even bought one of the stupid shirts!

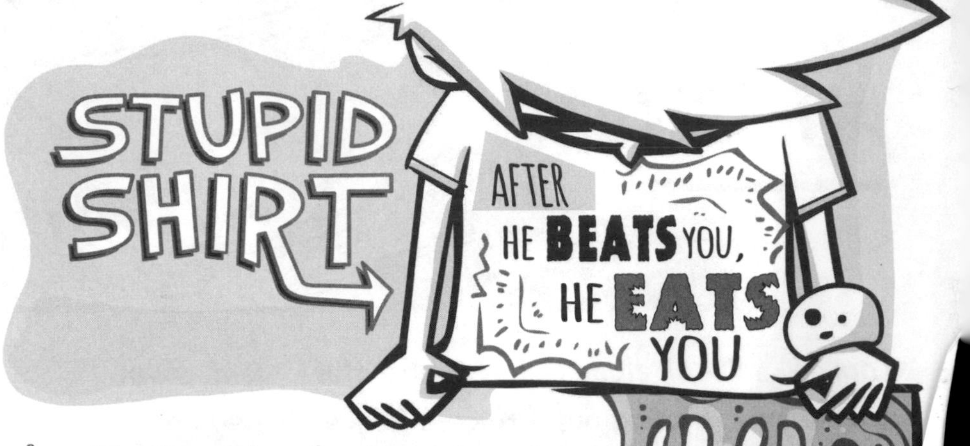
STUPID SHIRT
AFTER HE BEATS YOU, HE EATS YOU

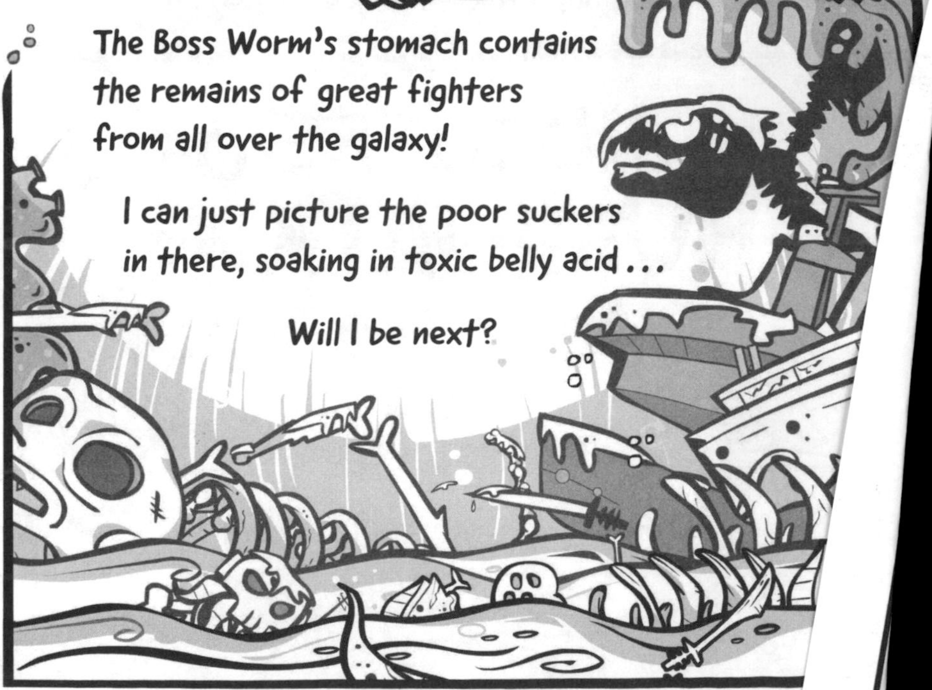
The Boss Worm's stomach contains the remains of great fighters from all over the galaxy!
I can just picture the poor suckers in there, soaking in toxic belly acid . . .
Will I be next?

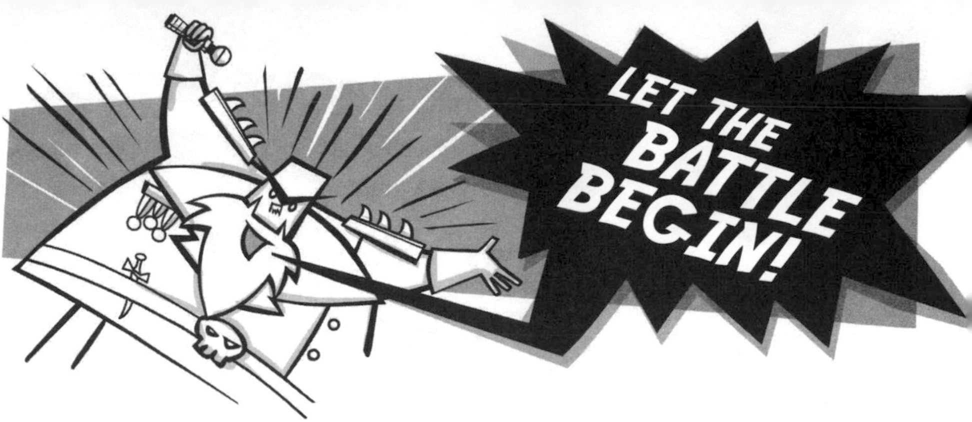
LET THE BATTLE BEGIN!

The crowd freaks! But I hear something over the roars and the screams. It's Princess Dagger, cheering me on! She has two guards by her side, but she doesn't ***GIVE A WHAT!***

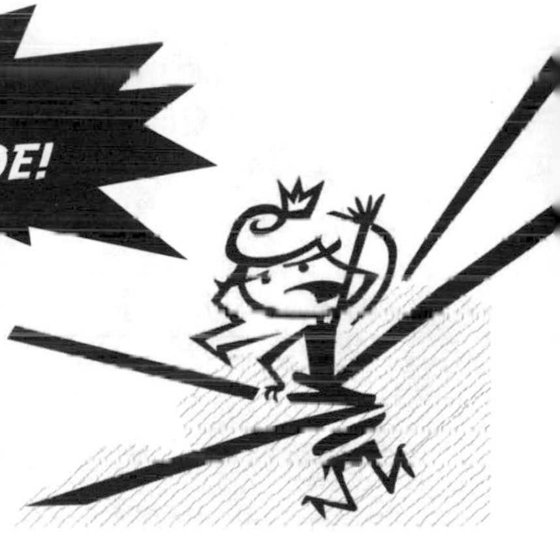
DESTROY THAT BIG
DUMB WORM, COSMOE!

My confidence blows up.
I can do it. I'm gonna wipe the ring with his stinky worm carcass!

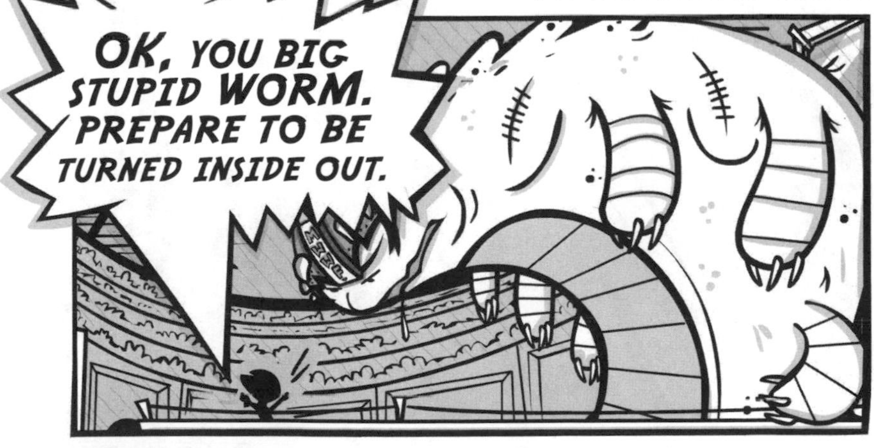
OK, YOU BIG STUPID WORM. PREPARE TO BE TURNED INSIDE OUT.

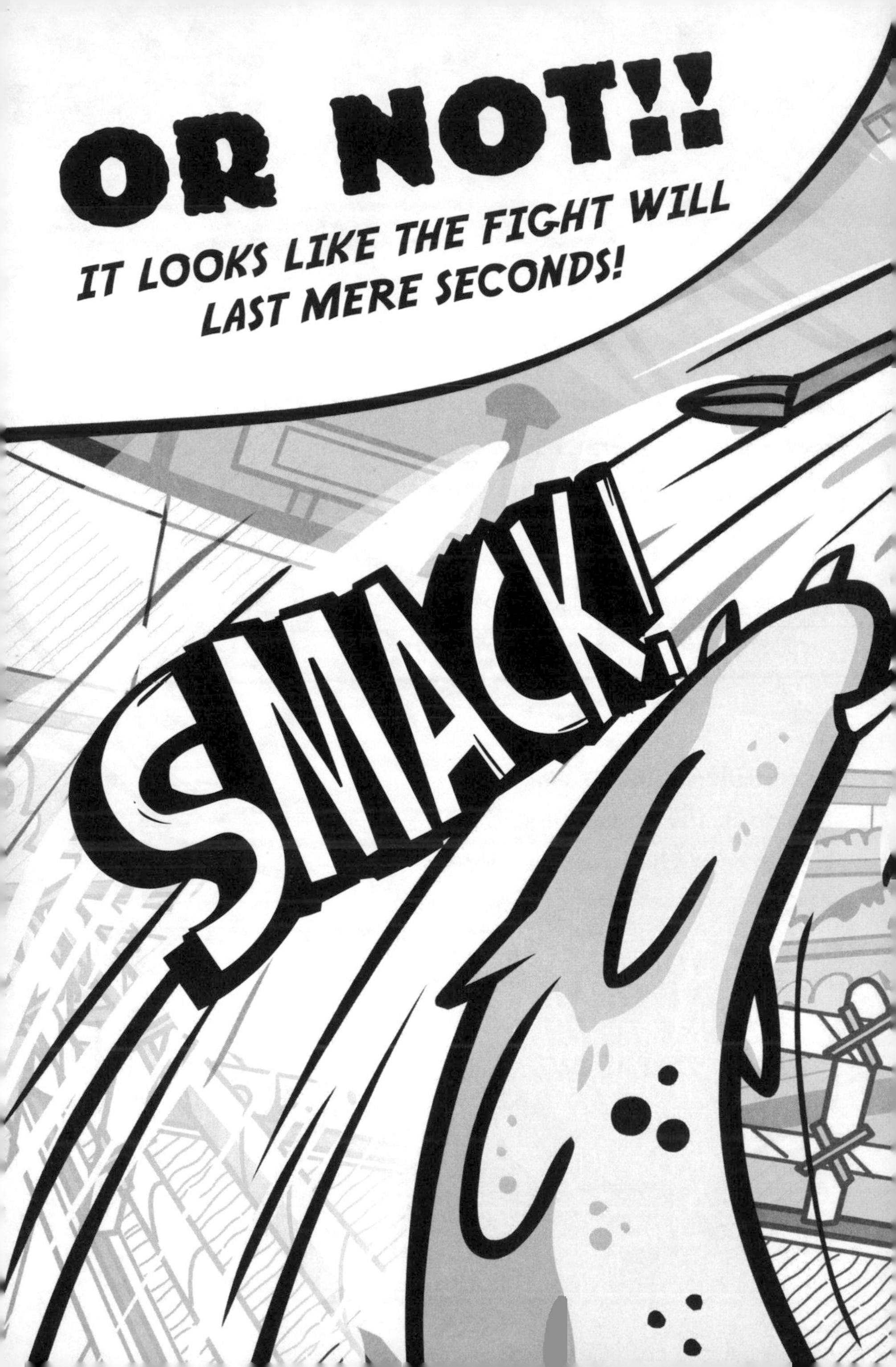
OR NOT!!
IT LOOKS LIKE THE FIGHT WILL LAST MERE SECONDS!
SMACK!

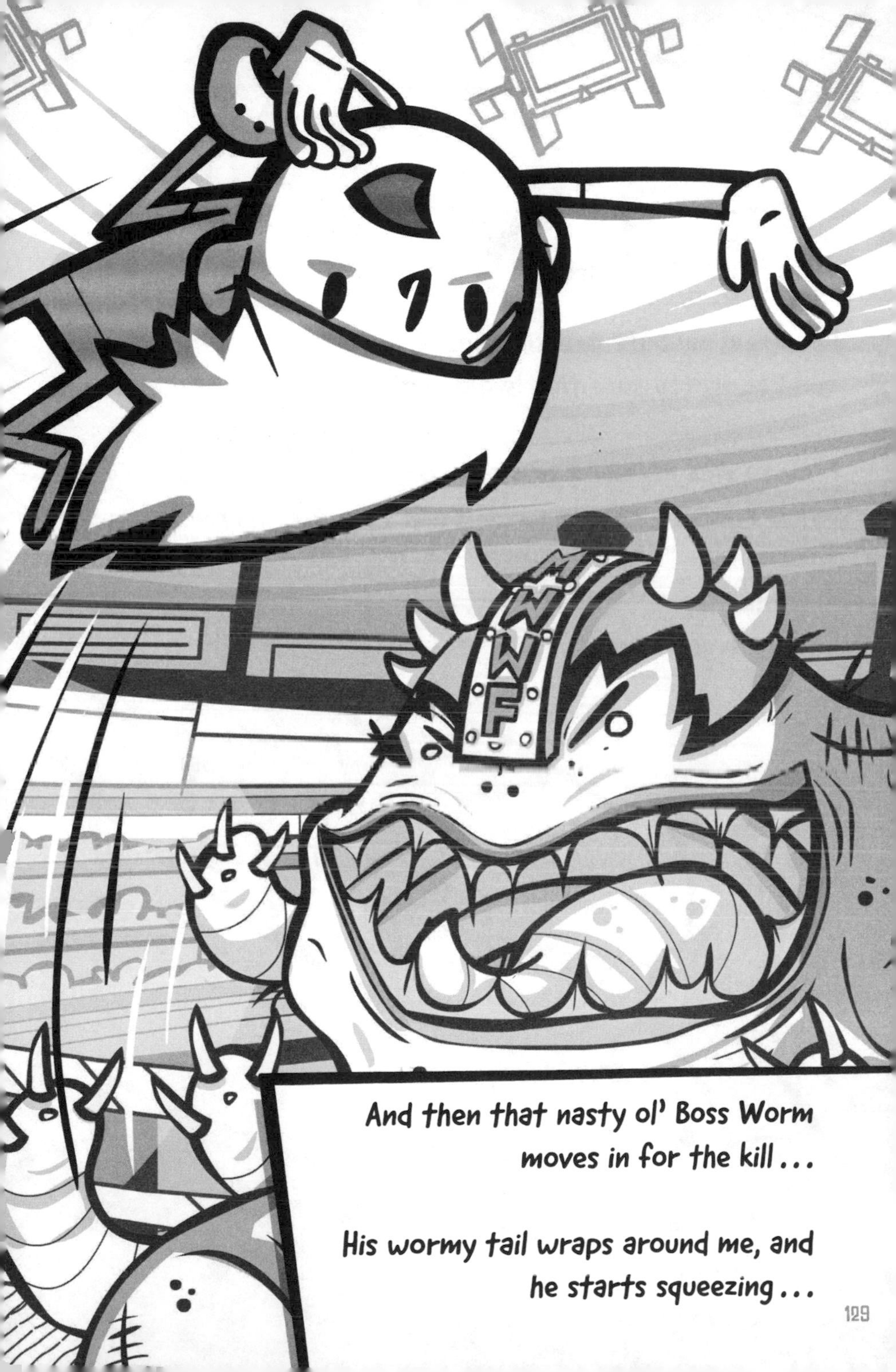
M
W
W
F

And then that nasty ol' Boss Worm
moves in for the kill . . .

His wormy tail wraps around me, and
he starts squeezing . . .

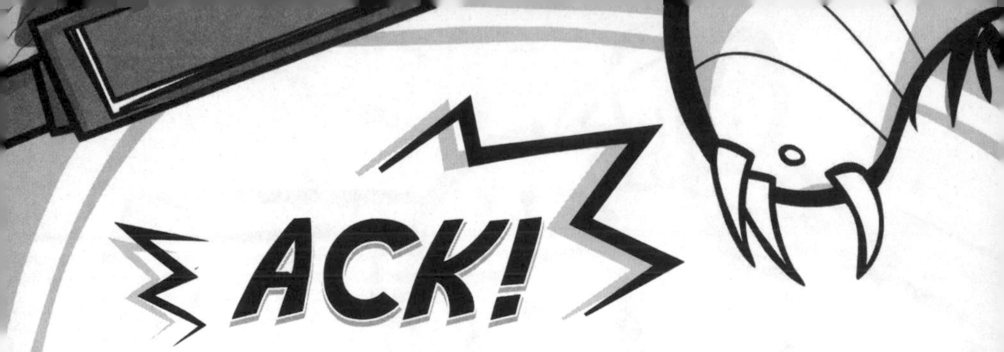
ACK!

I can feel my butt pressing against my ribs—
and I'm pretty sure that's a bad thing.

I try to flex my wrist and get some help from Goober,
but it's no use. I can't move. I can't do ***ANYTHING.***

And the Map-O-Sphere slice.
I never even found it . . .

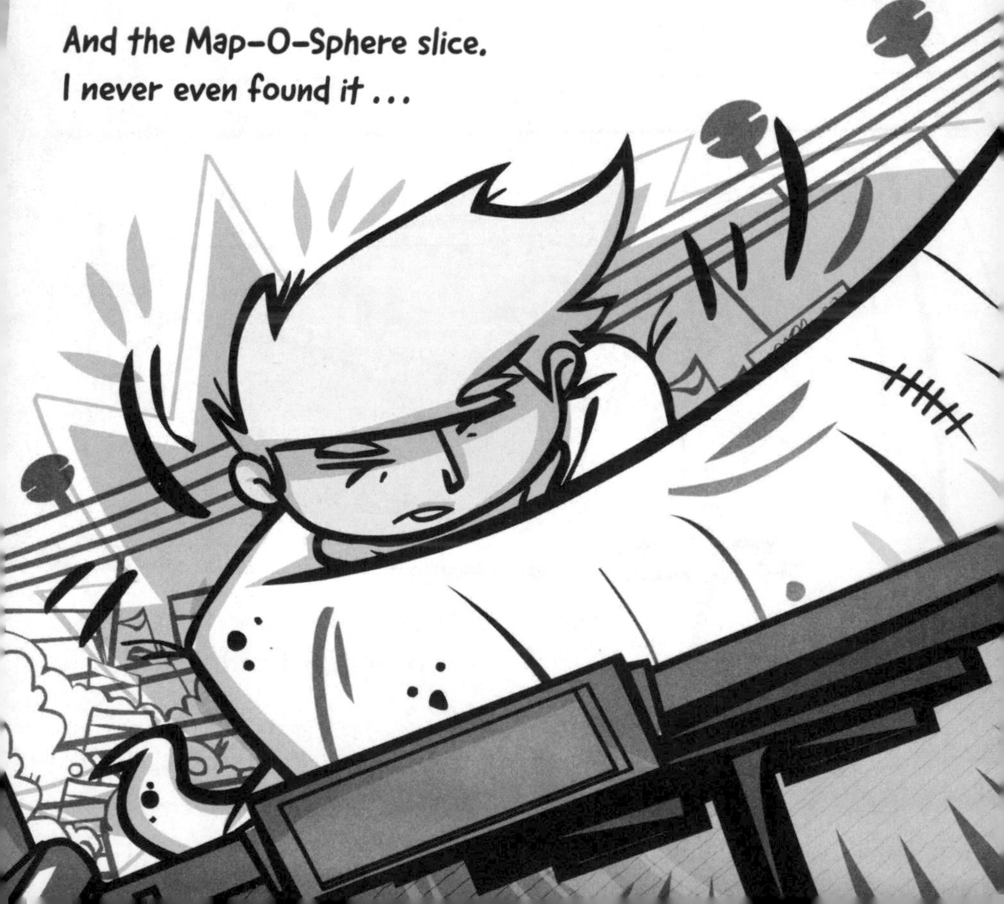

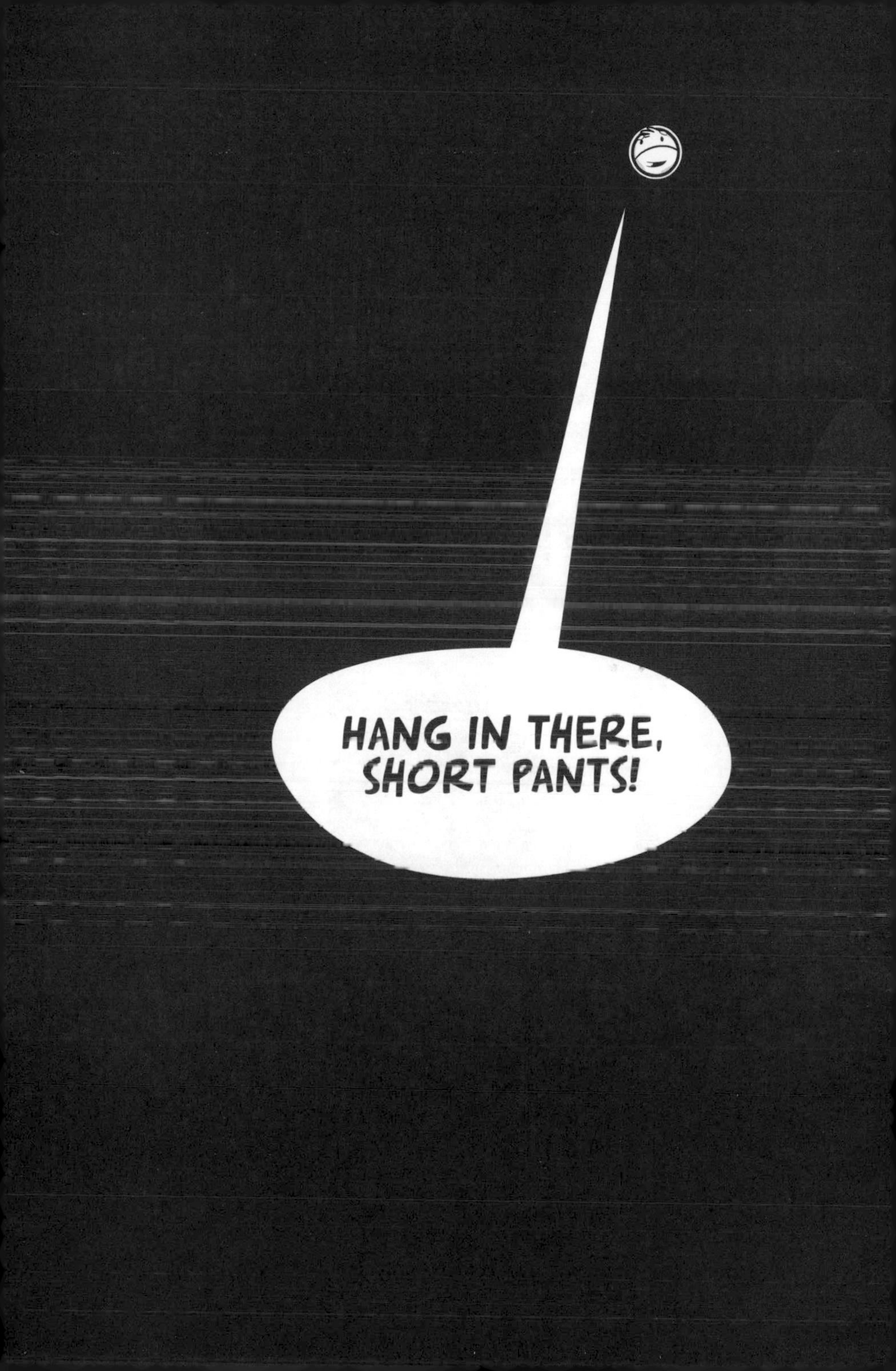
HANG IN THERE, SHORT PANTS!

HE SMELLS LIKE TOE JAM!

13

The Boss Worm is

SQUEEZING ME,

CRUSHING ME,

DESTROYING ME!

WHEN—

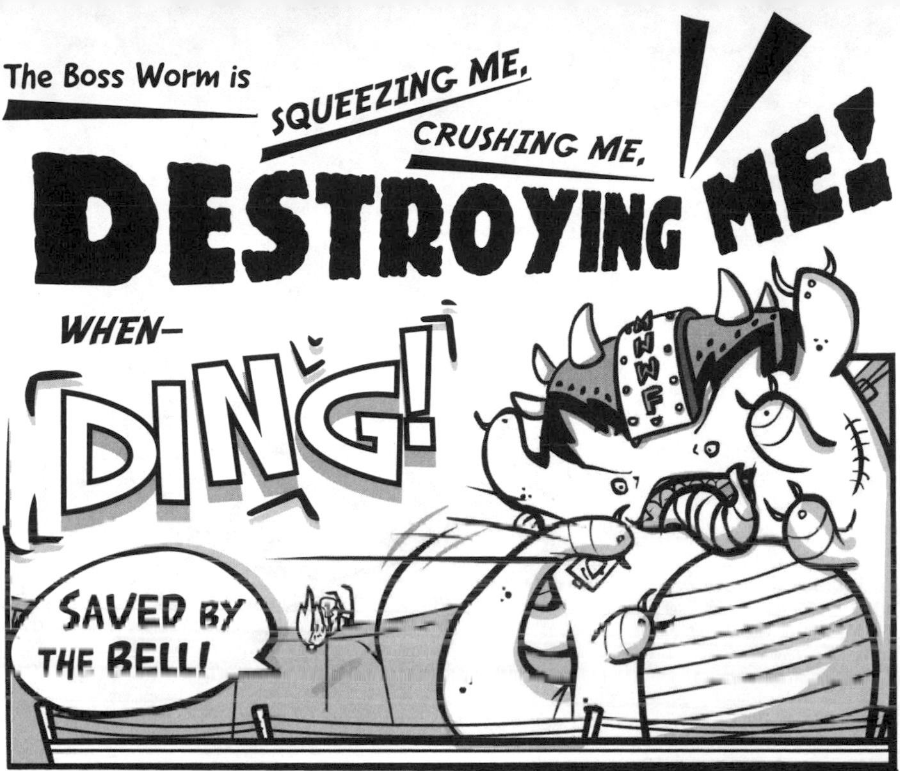
DING!
SAVED BY THE BELL!

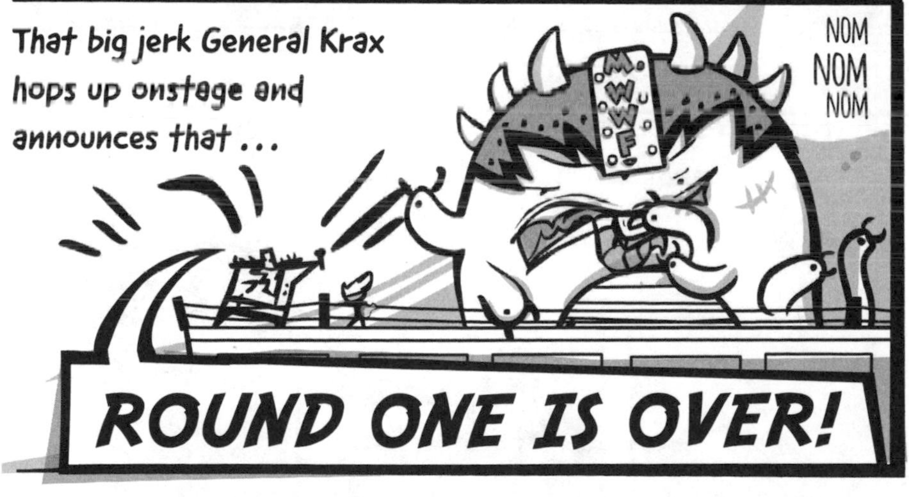
That big jerk General Krax hops up onstage and announces that . . .
NOM NOM NOM
ROUND ONE IS OVER!

I stagger to the edge of the ring and pretty much tumble into the ropes. My noggin is pounding from that Boss Worm beating. It's then, trying to catch my breath, that I spot it. ***THE BOSS WORM'S CROWN . . .***

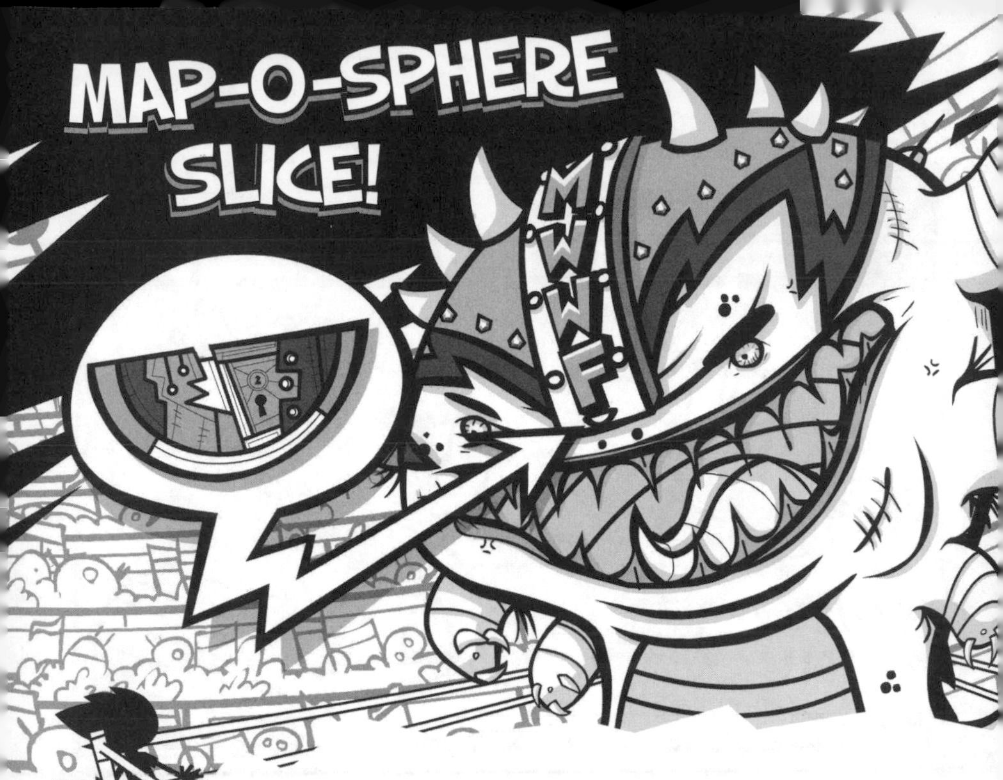
MAP-O-SPHERE SLICE!

That's where the Map-O-Sphere slice is hidden! It's part of the Boss Worm's crown! And that means I must defeat the Boss Worm! It's the only way I can get my hands on the second slice!

BUT HOW?

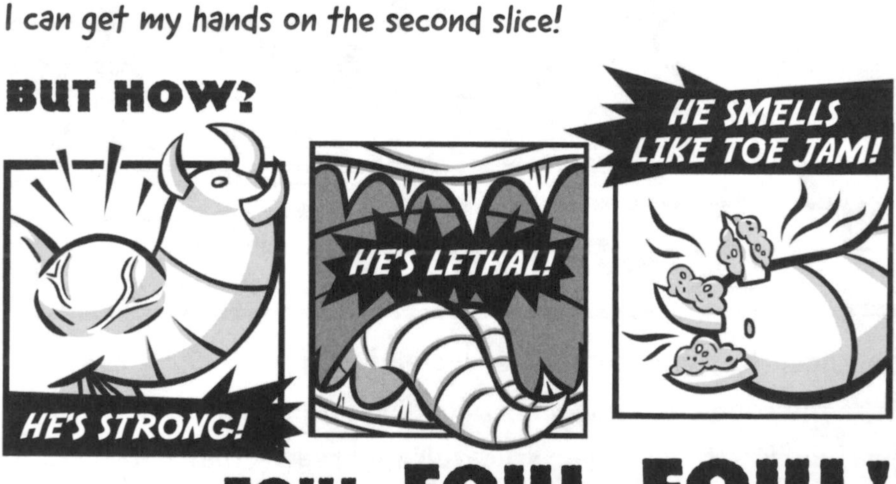
HE'S STRONG!
HE'S LETHAL!
HE SMELLS LIKE TOE JAM!

HE'S FOUL, FOUL, FOUL!

IF I have any chance of beating this beastie, I need help. But Humphree and Princess are both prisoners. It's time to call on—

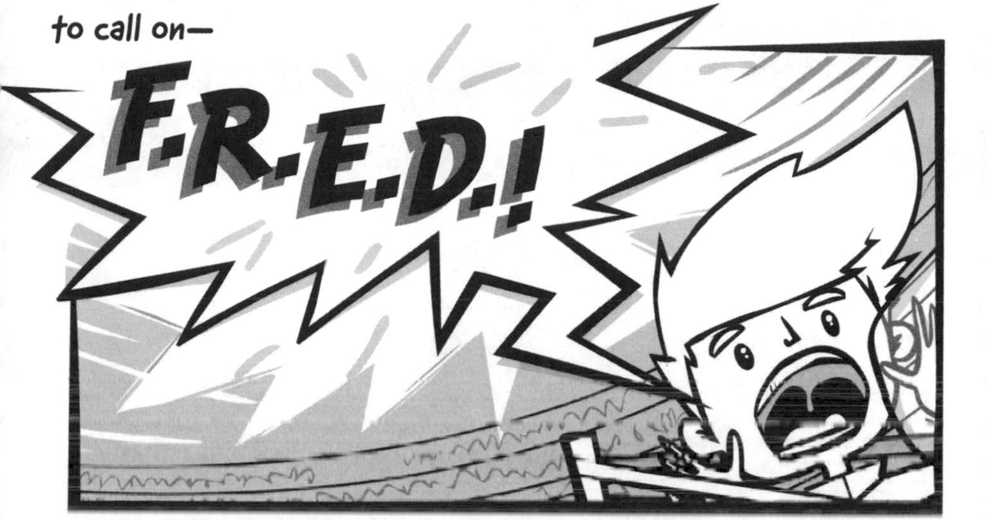
F.R.E.D.!

F.R.E.D. is programmed to respond to the sound of my voice, which is great because it's as loud as an earthquake toot in this joint.

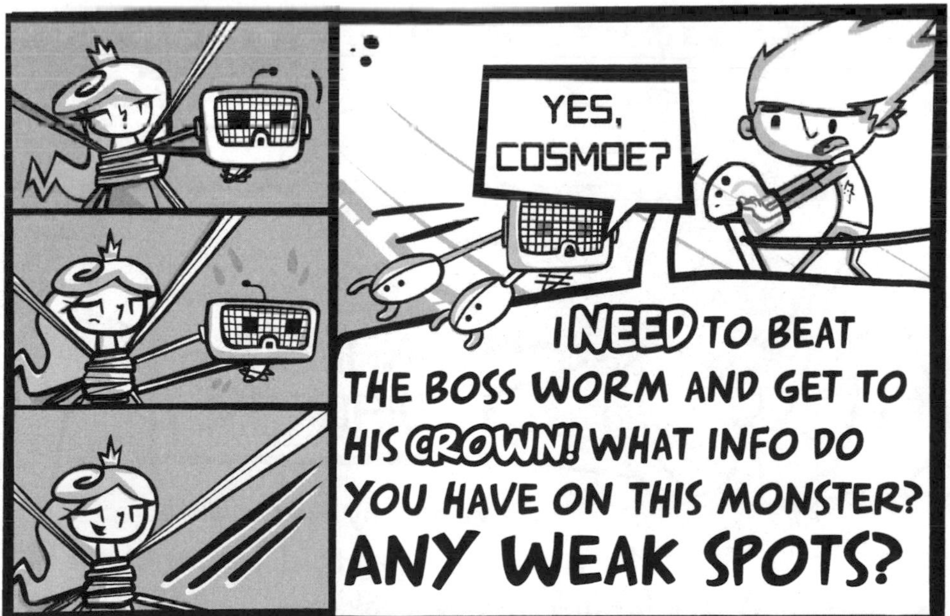
YES, COSMOE?
I NEED TO BEAT THE BOSS WORM AND GET TO HIS CROWN! WHAT INFO DO YOU HAVE ON THIS MONSTER? ANY WEAK SPOTS?

See, this is why I love F.R.E.D. He's like a giant-sized encyclopedia, with ill hologram skills. In a jam, he can tell you just about anything about everything.

AND I AM IN A **JELLY** OF A **JAM**.

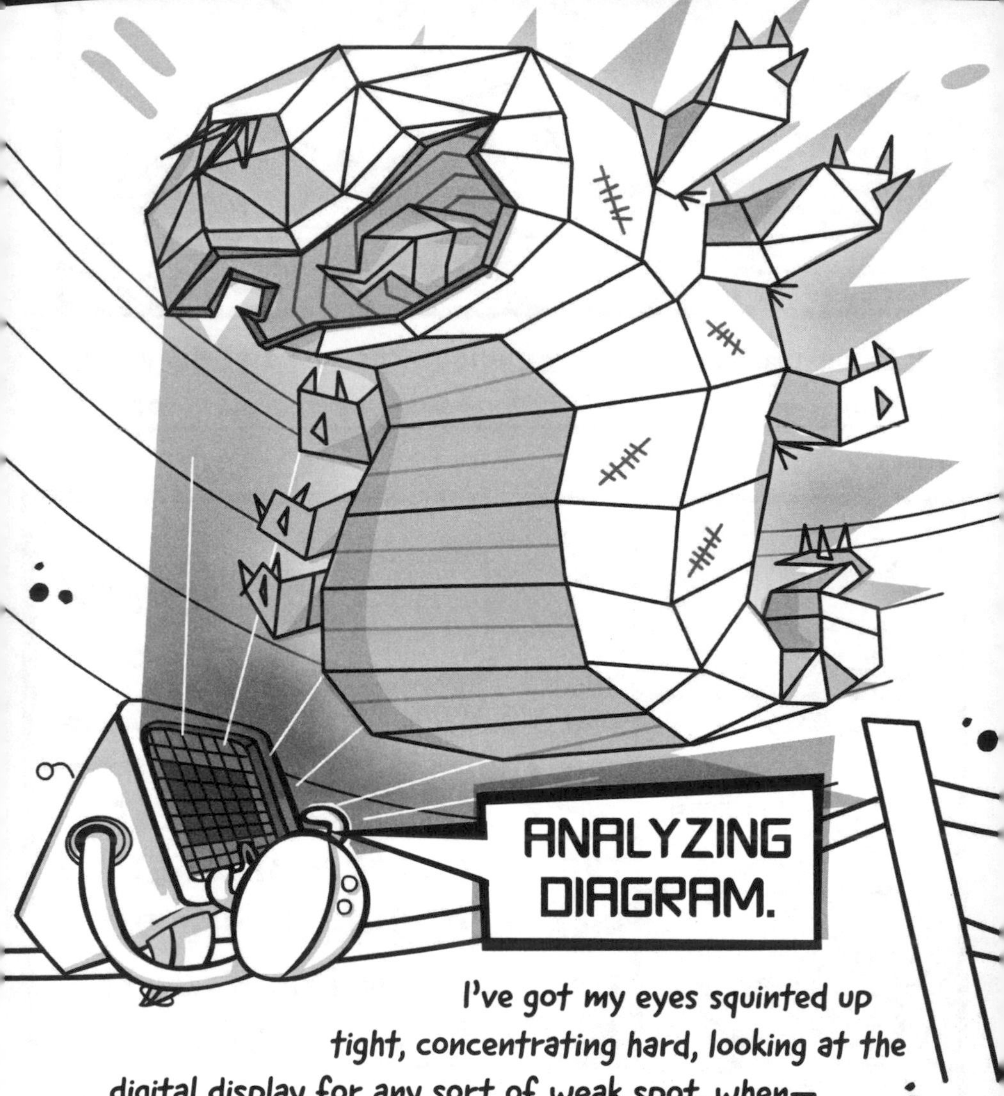
ANALYZING DIAGRAM.

I've got my eyes squinted up tight, concentrating hard, looking at the digital display for any sort of weak spot, when—

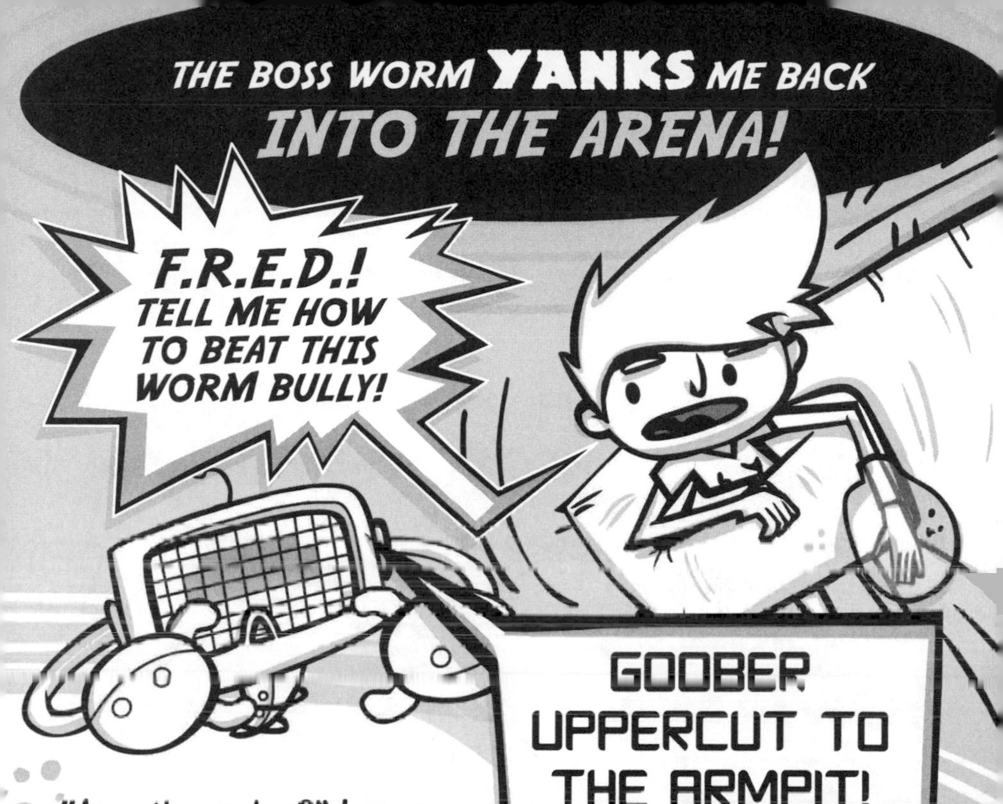
THE BOSS WORM YANKS ME BACK INTO THE ARENA!
F.R.E.D.! TELL ME HOW TO BEAT THIS WORM BULLY!
GOOBER UPPERCUT TO THE ARMPIT!

"Armpit punches?" I groan. "Ugh. Really? It's all bushy in there!"

"Target the armpit!" F.R.E.D. repeats.

Argh. Fine! You know what they say:

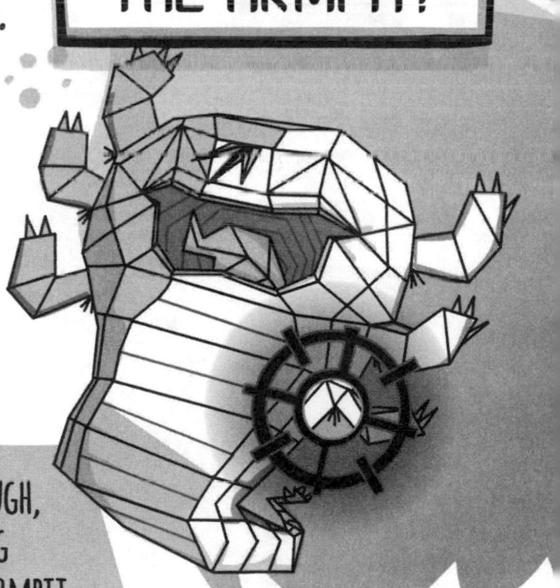

WHEN THE GOING GETS TOUGH, THE TOUGH START PUNCHING MUTANT WORMS IN THE ARMPIT.

I slip from the Boss Worm's grip and do a double backward somersault across the ring. Phew! I flex my wrist, letting Goober know it's super-action-punching time.

The Boss Worm comes at me, slithering back and forth. He swings! I duck

AND

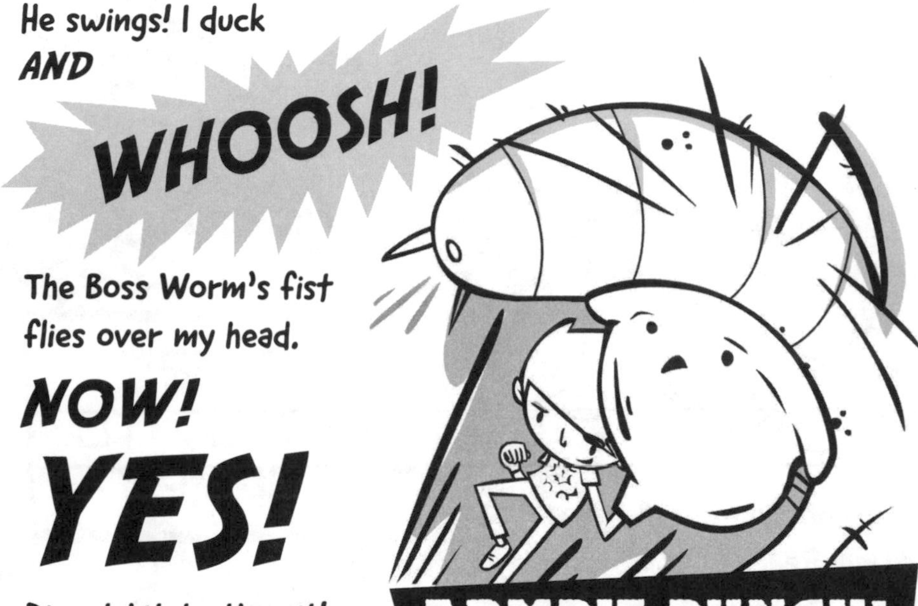
WHOOSH!

The Boss Worm's fist flies over my head.

NOW!

YES!

Direct hit to the pit!

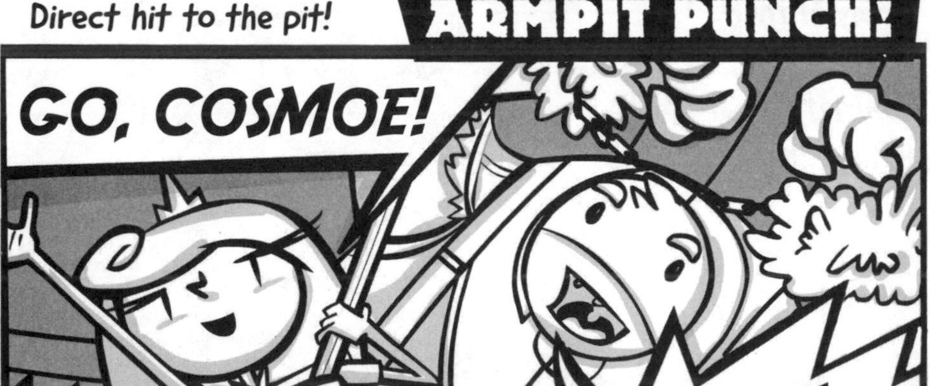
ARMPIT PUNCH!
GO, COSMOE!
GET 'EM, SHORT PANTS!

The Boss Worm shrieks! His eyes are wide and foggy. Slimy spit bubbles from his lips. He's stunned!

Now to finish him off!

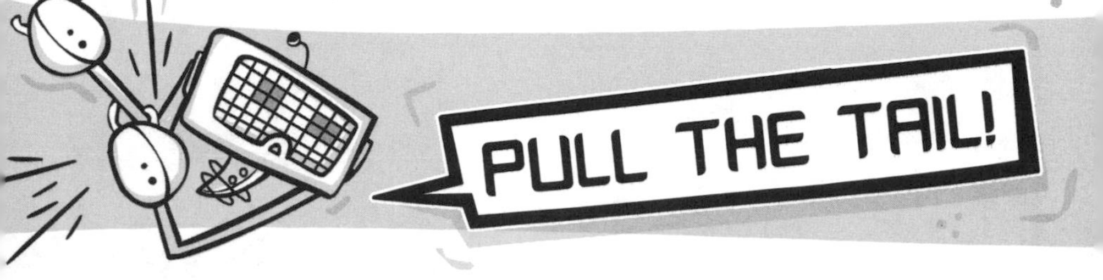
PULL THE TAIL!

But before I can go for the tail, the Boss Worm's mammoth mouth opens and his thick tongue lashes out. He's trying to eat me whole!

That leaves me with just one move . . .
And it's an ***AWESOME*** move.

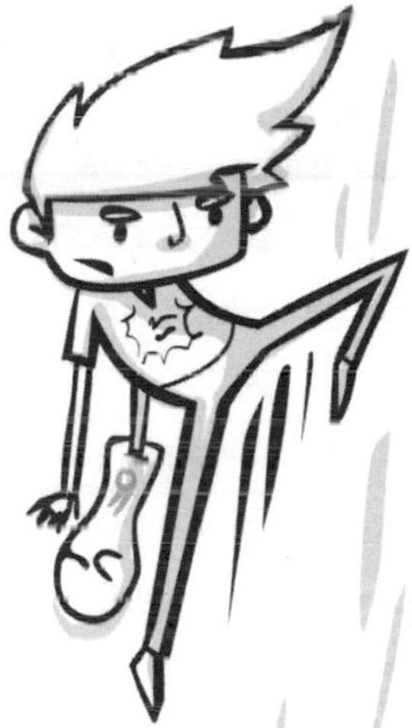

I charge up the Boss Worm's tongue! My sneakers splish-splash up the fleshy strip.

Just as the Boss Worm's jaws are about to clamp shut and devour me, ***I LEAP!***

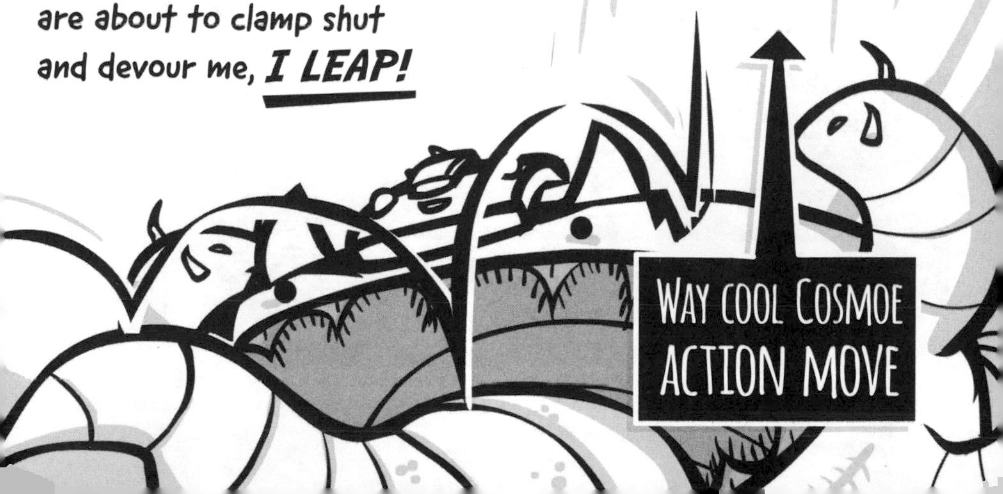
WAY COOL COSMOE
ACTION MOVE

I land on the mat,

BEHIND THE BOSS WORM,

and tug on his fat tail!

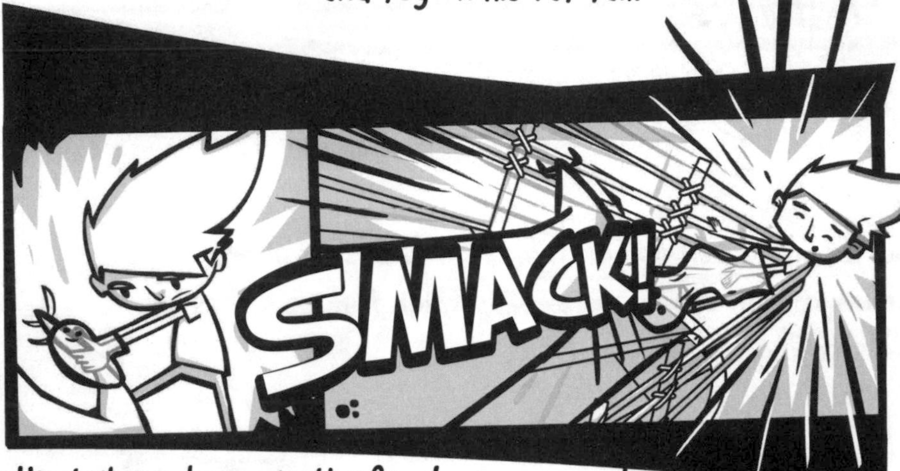
SMACK!

His tail cracks me in the face!
The crowd gasps as he closes in . . .

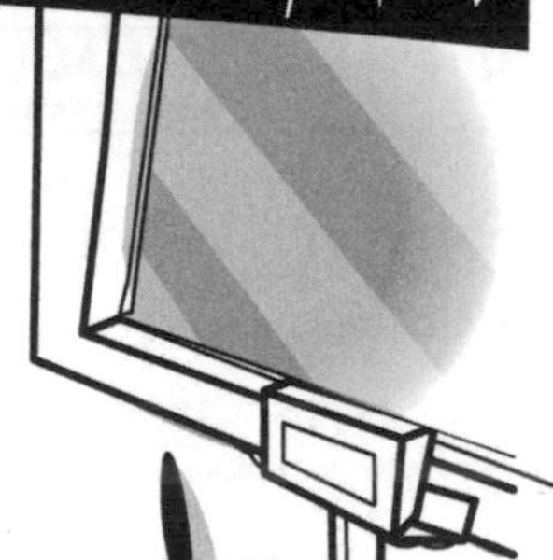

As I'm hanging from the ropes, I spot the giant screen above the ring. My funky brain wheels start turning.

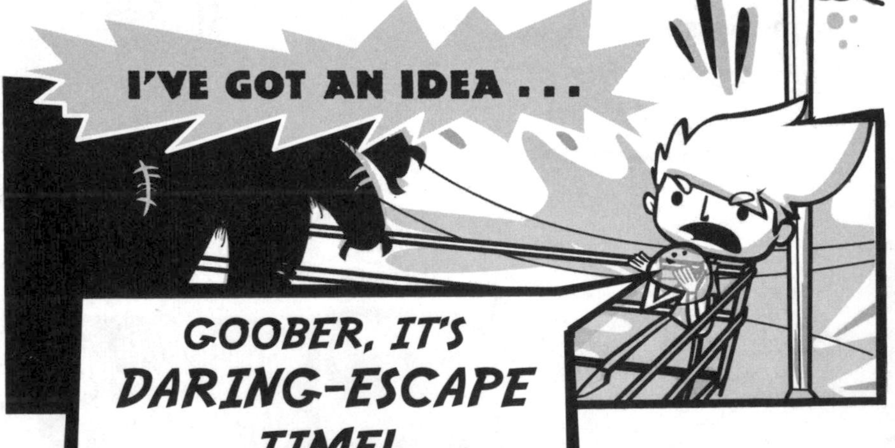
I'VE GOT AN IDEA . . .
GOOBER, IT'S DARING-ESCAPE TIME!

FREE THE DUMB PRISONERS!

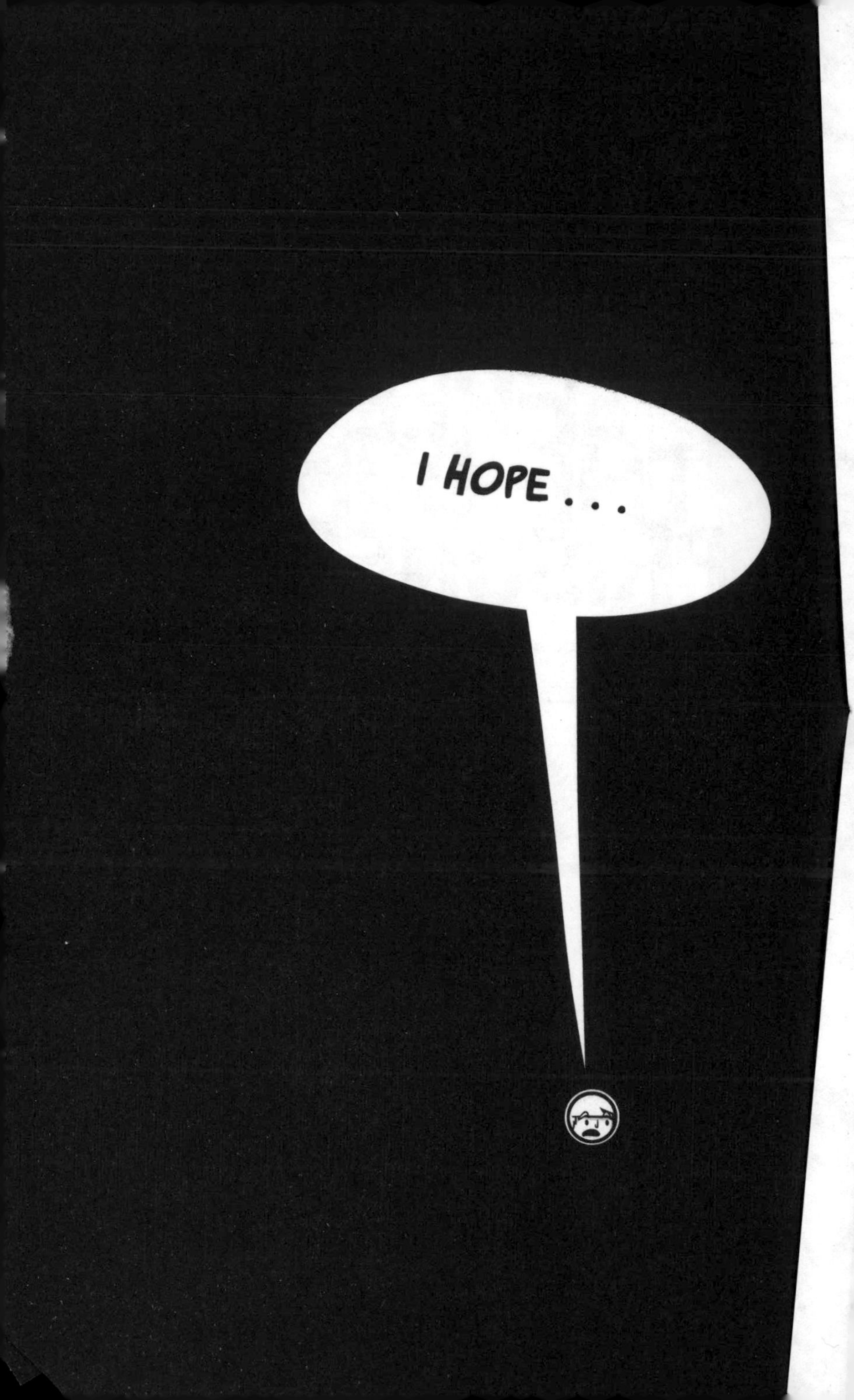
I HOPE . . .

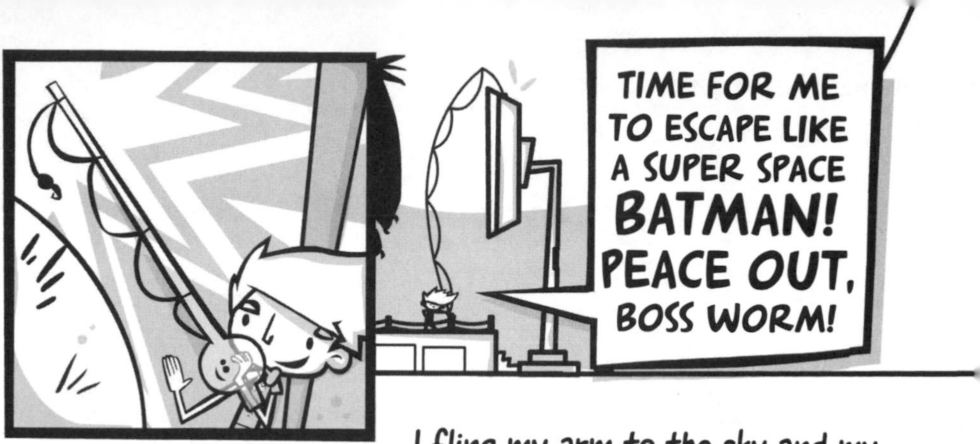
TIME FOR ME TO ESCAPE LIKE A SUPER SPACE BATMAN! PEACE OUT, BOSS WORM!

I fling my arm to the sky and my rubbery buddy flies up through the air. With a ***SHMACK,*** Goober latches on to the giant screen above the ring.

I tug on Goober, and—

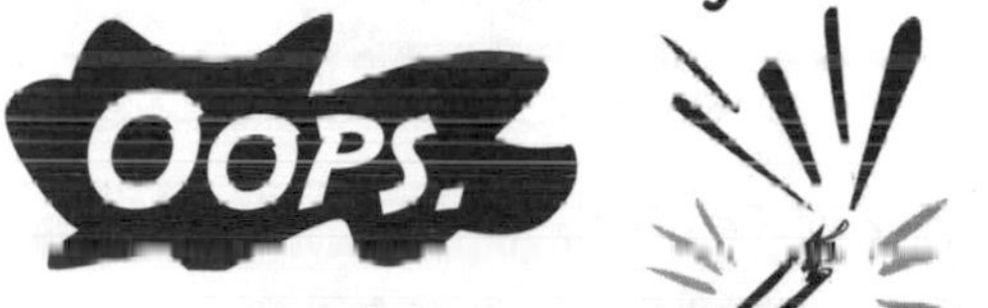
OOPS.

We are not pulled to safety. Instead, the huge screen breaks free and plummets down, toward the ring, until—

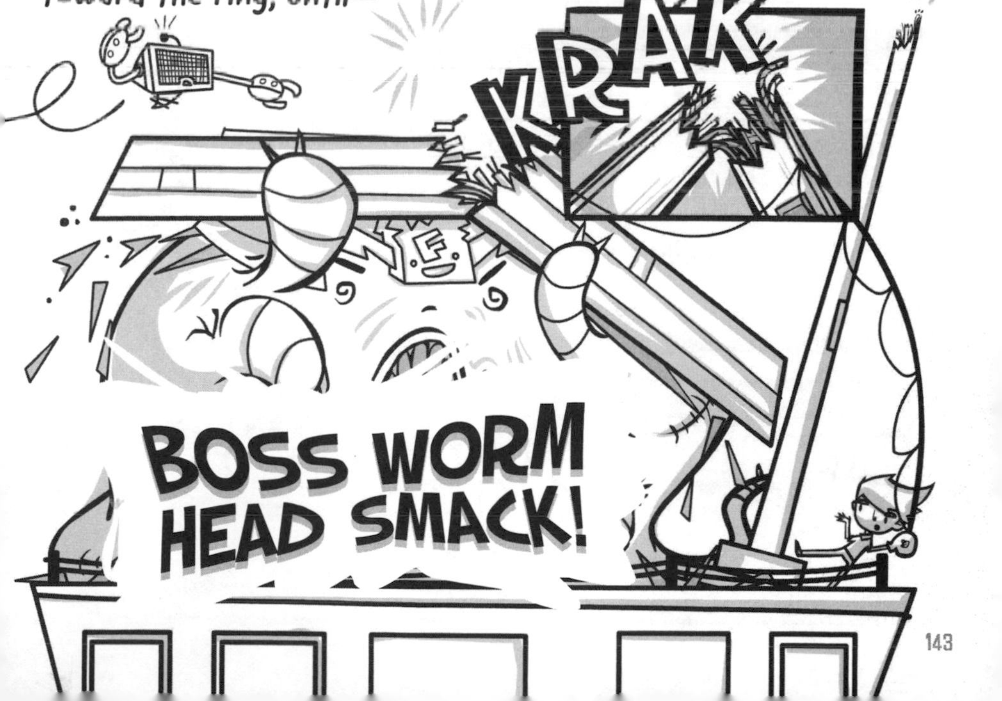
KRAK
BOSS WORM HEAD SMACK!

Hmm. That didn't go exactly as planned, but it did work . . .

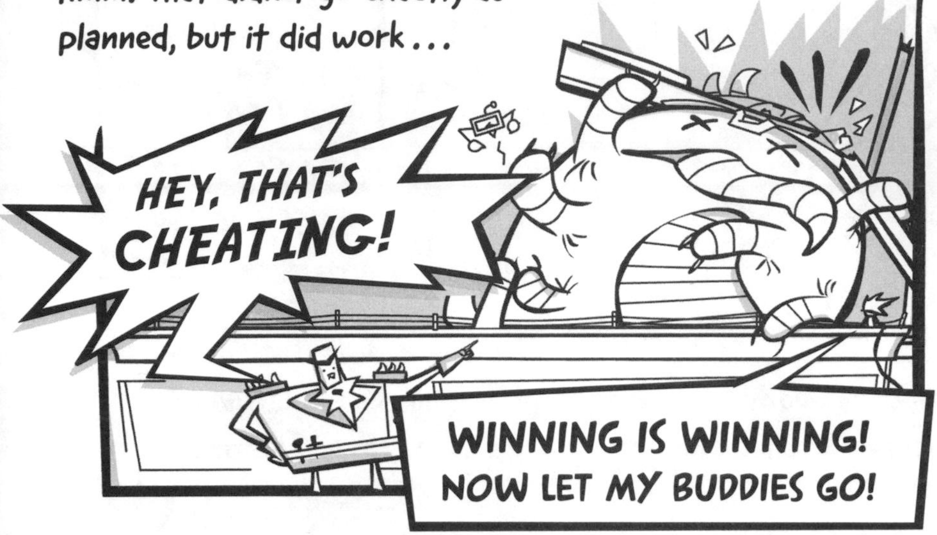
HEY, THAT'S CHEATING!
WINNING IS WINNING! NOW LET MY BUDDIES GO!

Now I need to pull the Map-O-Sphere from that crown on top of the Boss Worm's head. But I can't grab it. Not until Krax lets my buddies go. As soon as I mess with that crown, things are going to go a little bit space bananas . . .

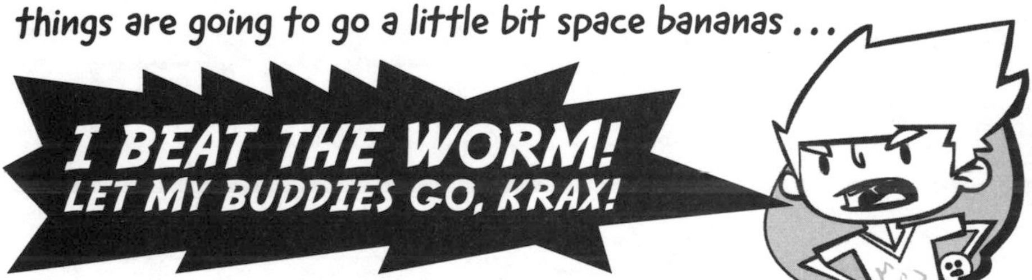
I BEAT THE WORM! LET MY BUDDIES GO, KRAX!

General Krax finally calls out—

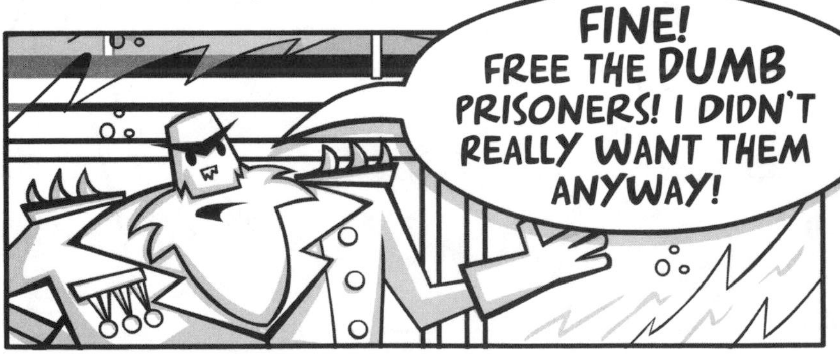
FINE! FREE THE DUMB PRISONERS! I DIDN'T REALLY WANT THEM ANYWAY!

Krax's Rumblers do as they're told. As soon as Humphree and Dagger are free, I make my move. I charge up the side of the Boss Worm's mushy body, scrambling up to the top, and then—

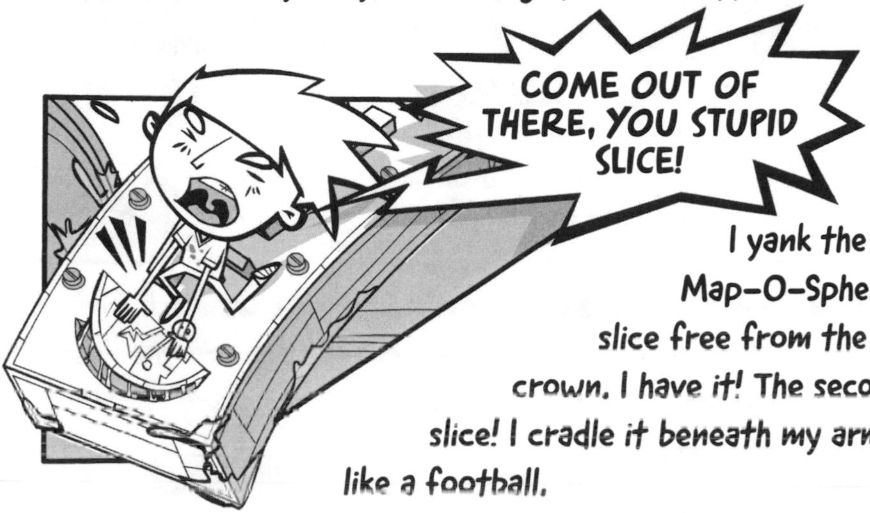
COME OUT OF THERE, YOU STUPID SLICE!

I yank the Map-O-Sphere slice free from the crown. I have it! The second slice! I cradle it beneath my arm like a football.

"C'mon, Cosmoe!" Princess Dagger shouts. "Let's get back to the *Neon Wiener!*"

OH. NO. *PRINCESS. MESSED. UP.* BIG. TIME.

The entire arena goes silent. You could hear a pin drop. Or anything else that's, like, small—you could probably hear that drop too.

Princess Dagger whispers, "Whoops . . ." as she realizes what she did.

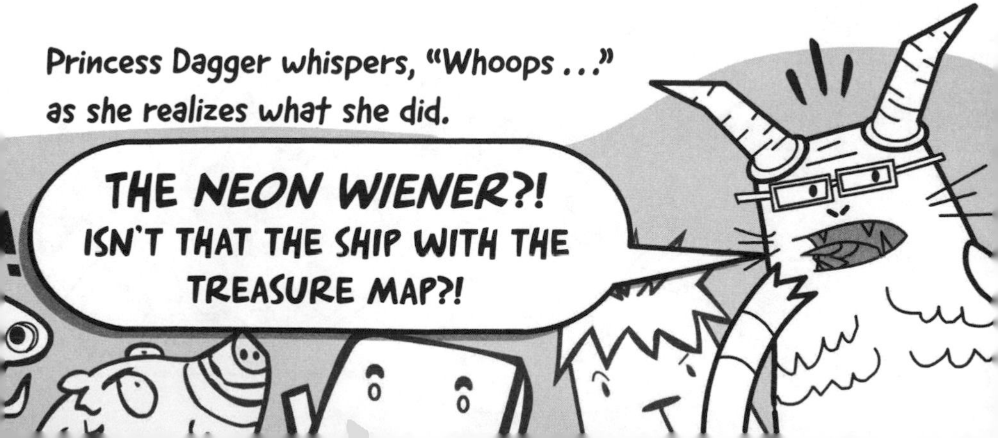
THE *NEON WIENER*?! ISN'T THAT THE SHIP WITH THE TREASURE MAP?!

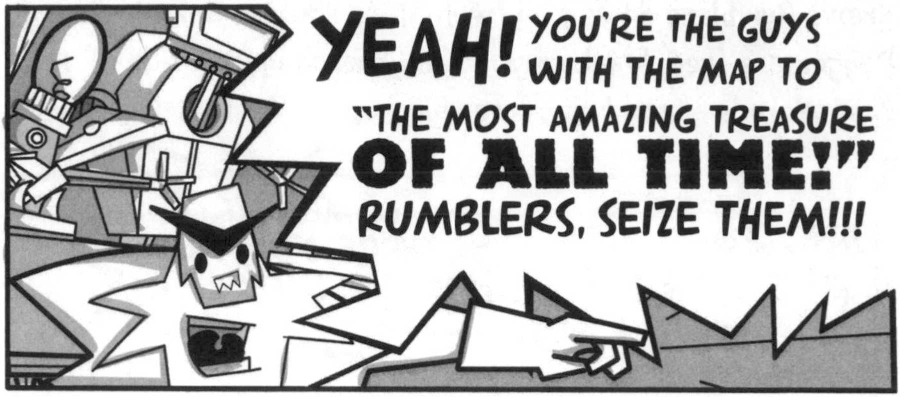
YEAH! YOU'RE THE GUYS WITH THE MAP TO "THE MOST AMAZING TREASURE OF ALL TIME!" RUMBLERS, SEIZE THEM!!!

Every alien in the arena goes crazy! Everyone wants the treasure! They want us! Greedy aliens race toward the Boss Worm and start climbing up the side! They're going to tear me limb from limb!

Grumble's Rumblers try to grab hold of Humphree and Dagger, but my buddies aren't going down without a fight . . .

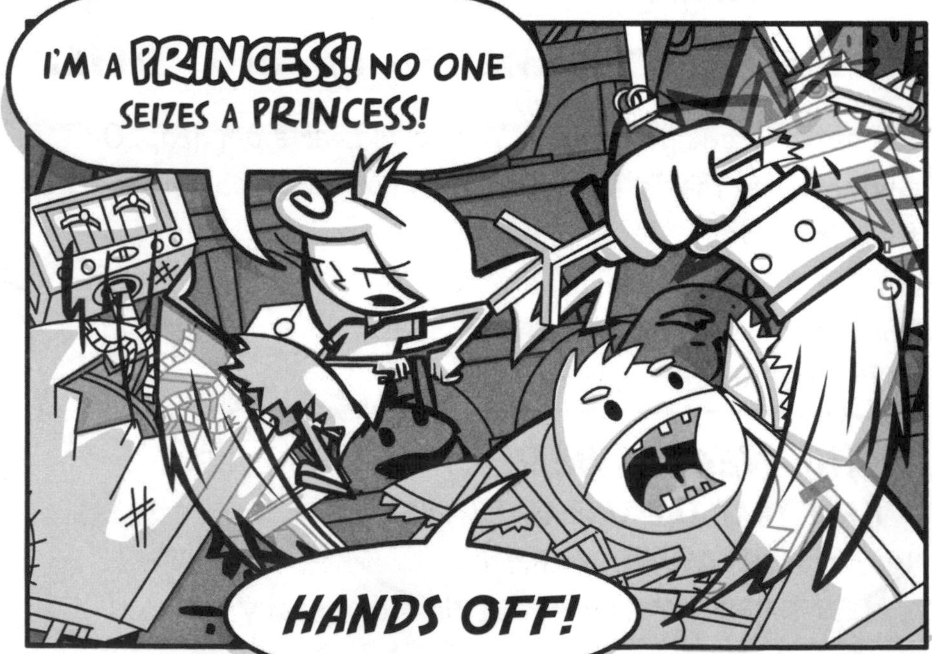
I'M A PRINCESS! NO ONE SEIZES A PRINCESS!
HANDS OFF!

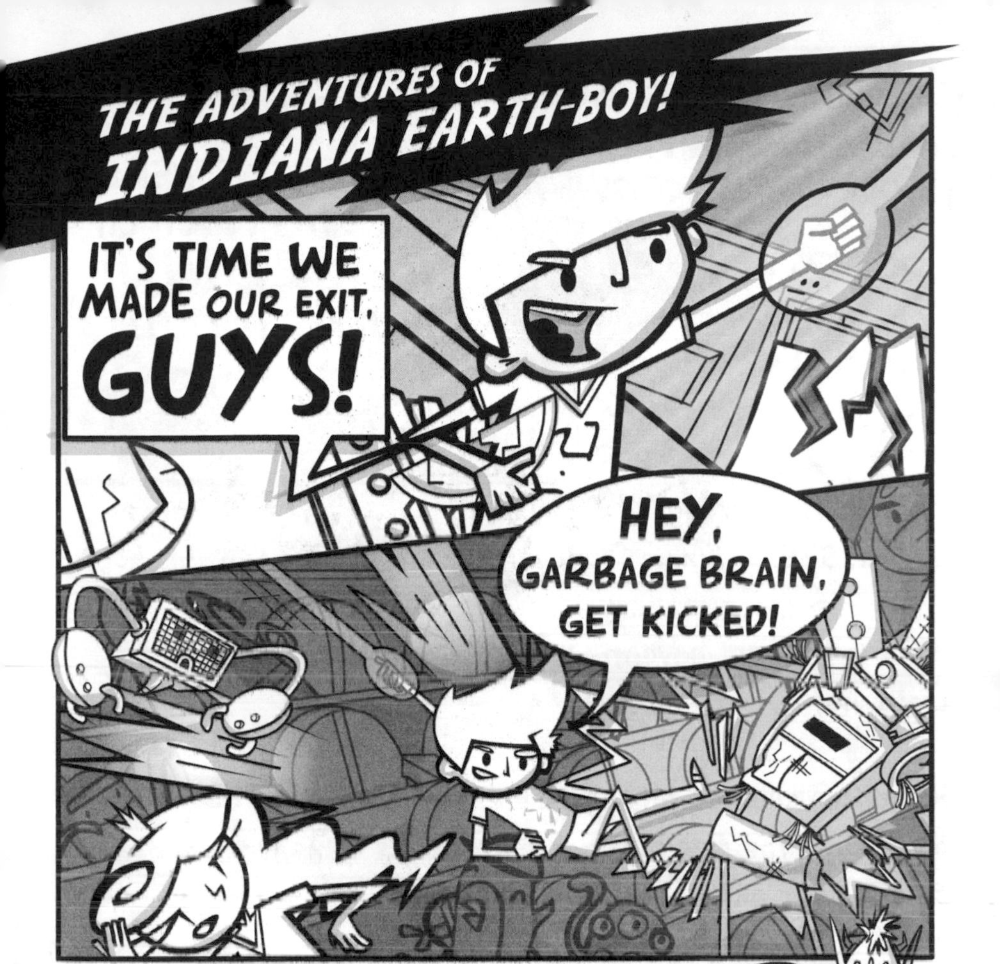
THE ADVENTURES OF INDIANA EARTH-BOY!
IT'S TIME WE MADE OUR EXIT, GUYS!
HEY, GARBAGE BRAIN, GET KICKED!

The crowd is going more and more nutso! They've all got treasure fever! Thousands of aliens, climbing over seats, climbing over each other, trying to get their grubby extraterrestrial paws on us!

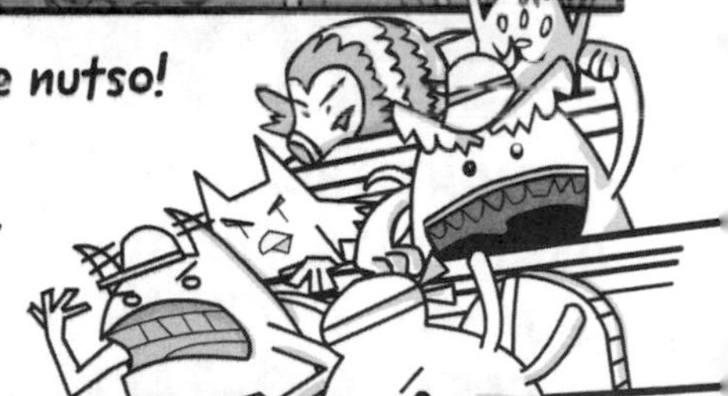

"All right, friends," Humphree bellows. **"ESCAPE TIME!"** With that, Humphree reaches down, throws the princess and me over his shoulders, and charges toward the exit.

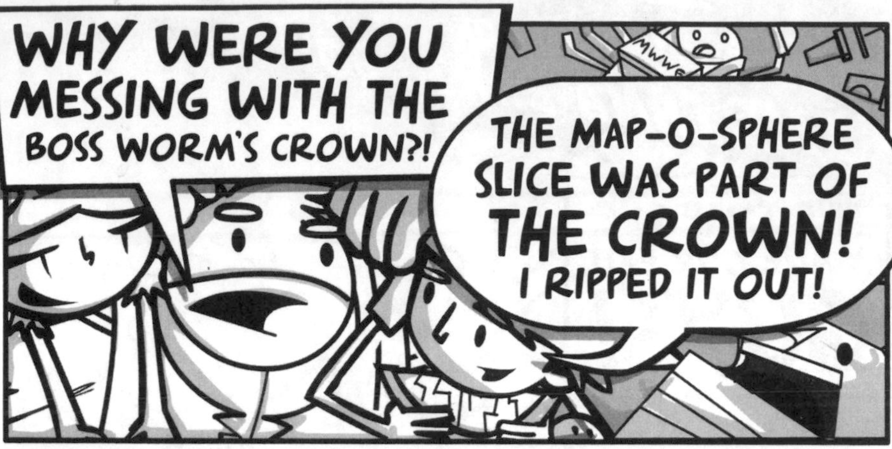
WHY WERE YOU MESSING WITH THE BOSS WORM'S CROWN?!
THE MAP-O-SPHERE SLICE WAS PART OF THE CROWN! I RIPPED IT OUT!

As we barrel through the crowd, I steal a glance at Princess Dagger. She's grinning from ear to ear. "Having fun?" I shout.

"This is the best adventure ever!" Dagger exclaims. "And we're not even being evil!"

Humphree charges through the exit and onto the docking bay. I spot the *Neon Wiener*. But there's some jerk blocking our path . . .

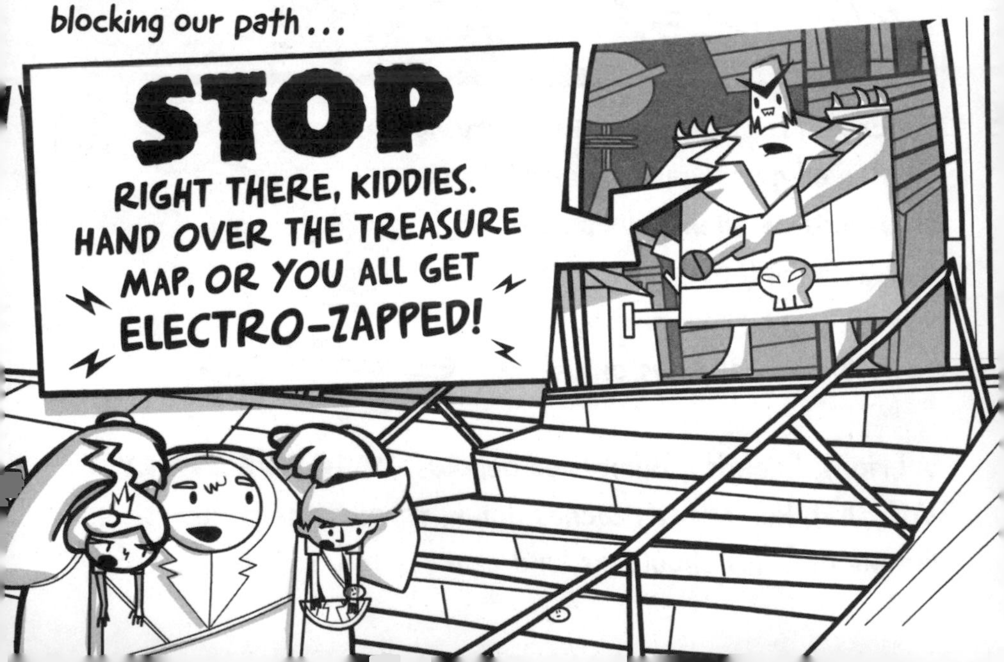
STOP RIGHT THERE, KIDDIES. HAND OVER THE TREASURE MAP, OR YOU ALL GET ELECTRO-ZAPPED!

UH-OH. I was electro-zapped earlier. It's not fun. It's basically the opposite of fun. It's pain. Much pain.

Just then Princess Dagger slips out of Humphree's grip. She stands on the platform. Next, she takes a cool, confident step toward Krax. What's she doing? I wonder.

"Hey, Krax," Princess Dagger says, all swagger-like. "Fire? Or ice?"

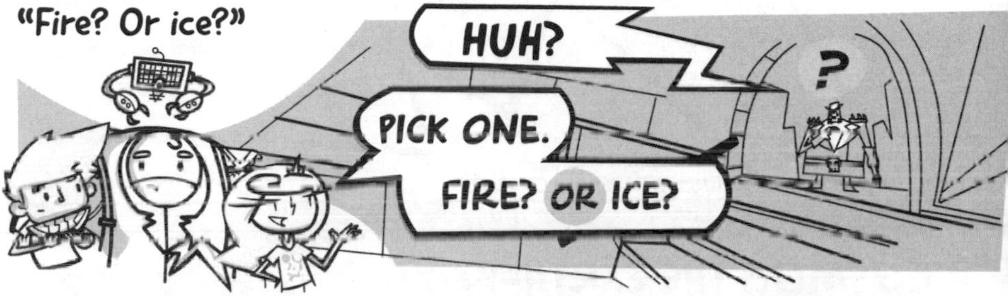
HUH?
?
PICK ONE.
FIRE? OR ICE?

Krax scratches at his head. "Hmm. Why do you ask? Fire can be fun. It's destructive. But I do enjoy a nice, tall, cool drink. So, hmm, I guess—yeah—I'll go with **ICE.**"

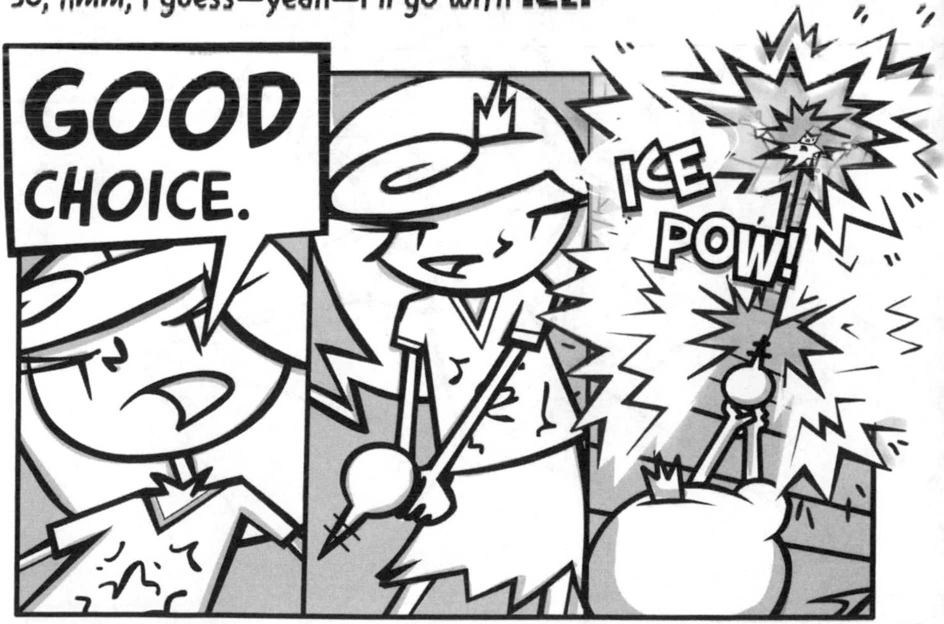
GOOD CHOICE.
ICE POW!

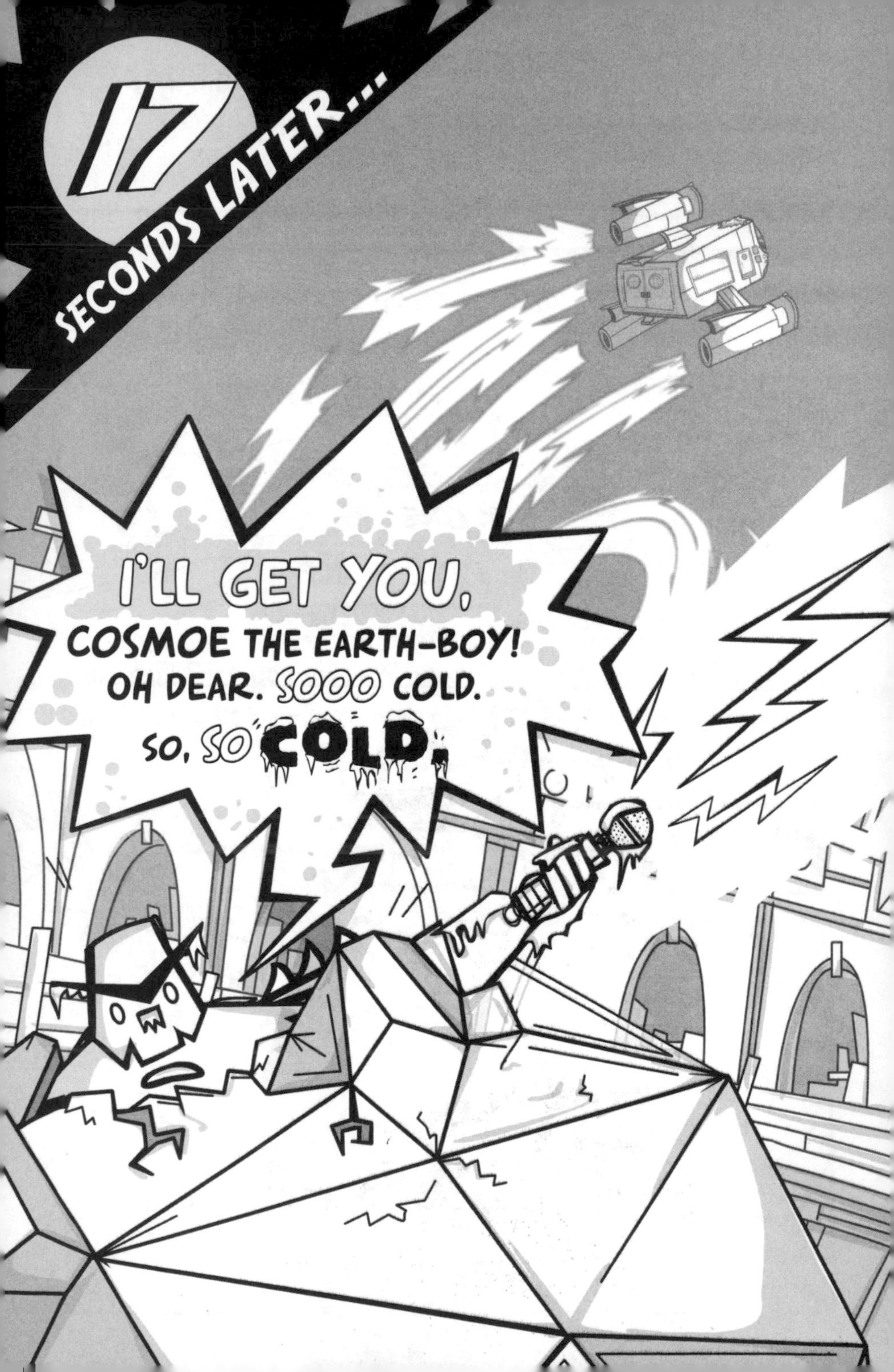
17 SECONDS LATER...
I'LL GET YOU, COSMOE THE EARTH-BOY! OH DEAR. SOOO COLD. SO, SO COLD.

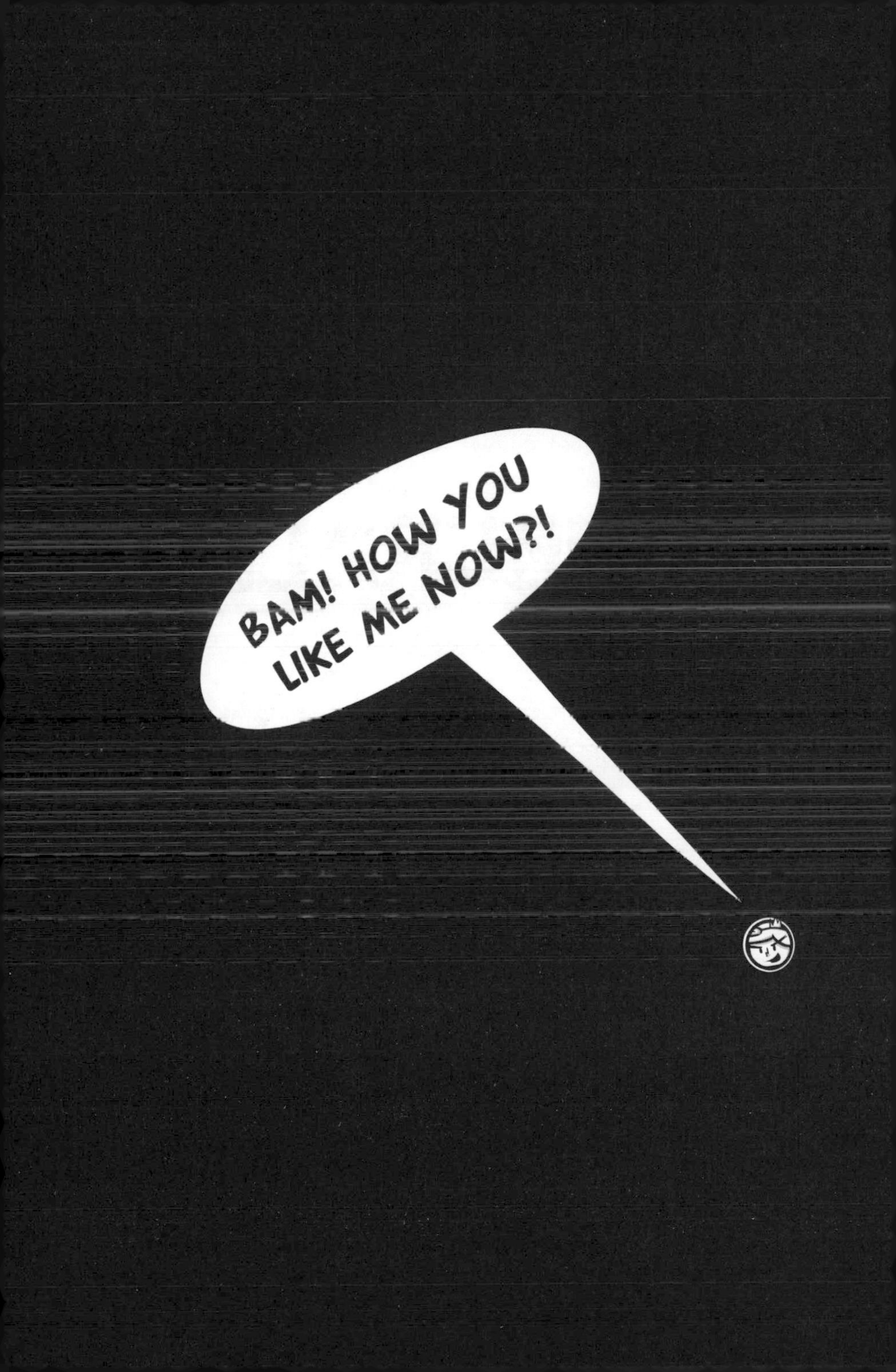
BAM! HOW YOU LIKE ME NOW?!

HAMBURZLES!!

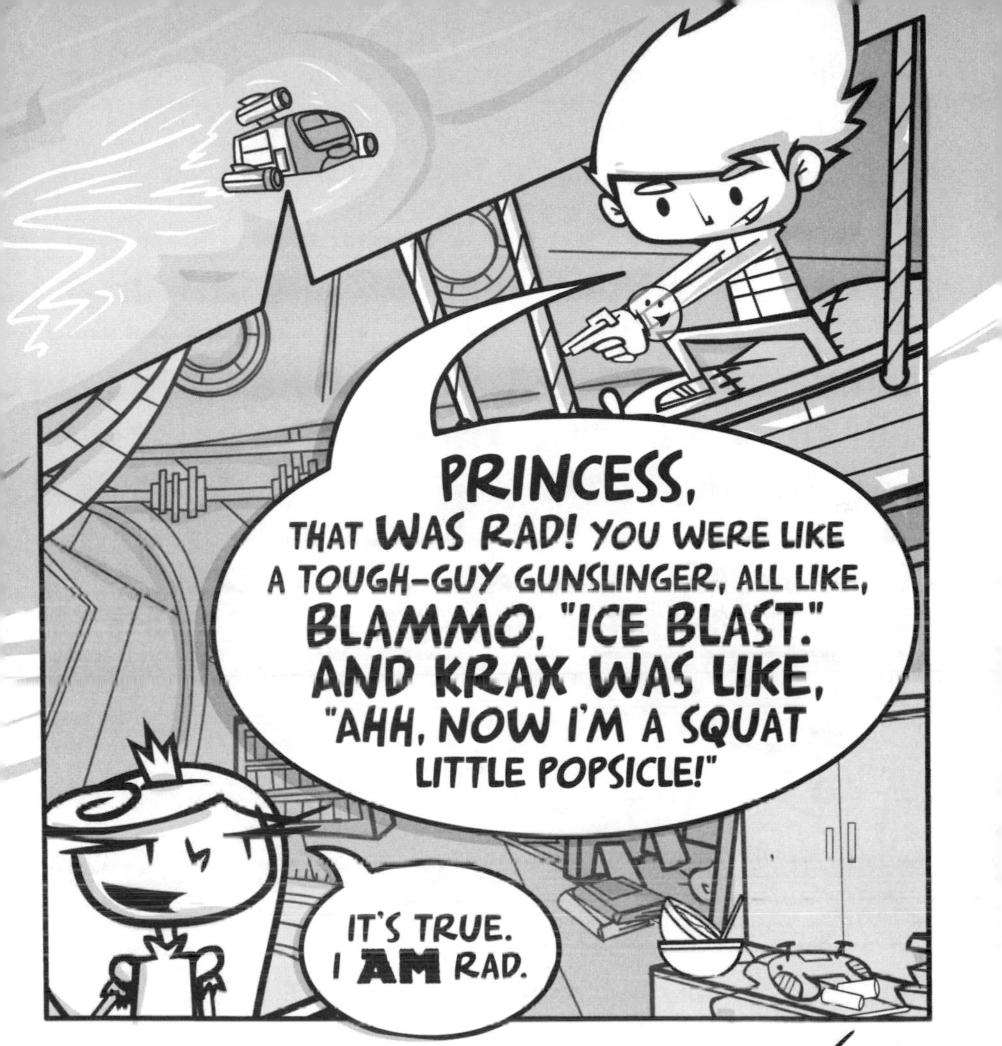
PRINCESS,
THAT WAS RAD! YOU WERE LIKE A TOUGH-GUY GUNSLINGER, ALL LIKE, BLAMMO, "ICE BLAST." AND KRAX WAS LIKE, "AHH, NOW I'M A SQUAT LITTLE POPSICLE!"
IT'S TRUE. I AM RAD.

"And not only did we escape," I say happily, "we escaped with the next slice of the

MAP-O-SPHERE!"

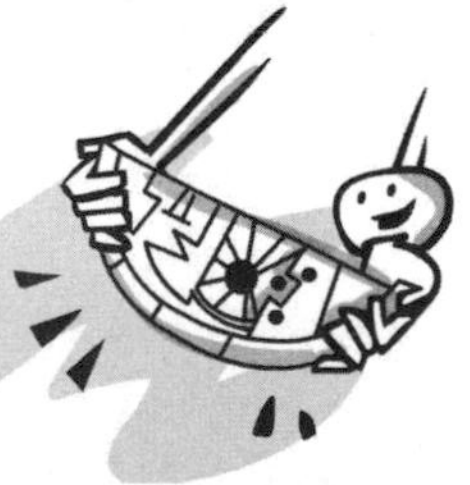

The second slice is the same size as the first. It seems like the two should fit together like LEGOs or something.

Time to figure this out . . .

I'm up in the hammock bed, futzing with the Map-O-Sphere while Humphree and Dags watch TV. They're watching the Eat Network—All Food, All the Time. And we get some **BAD NEWS . . .**

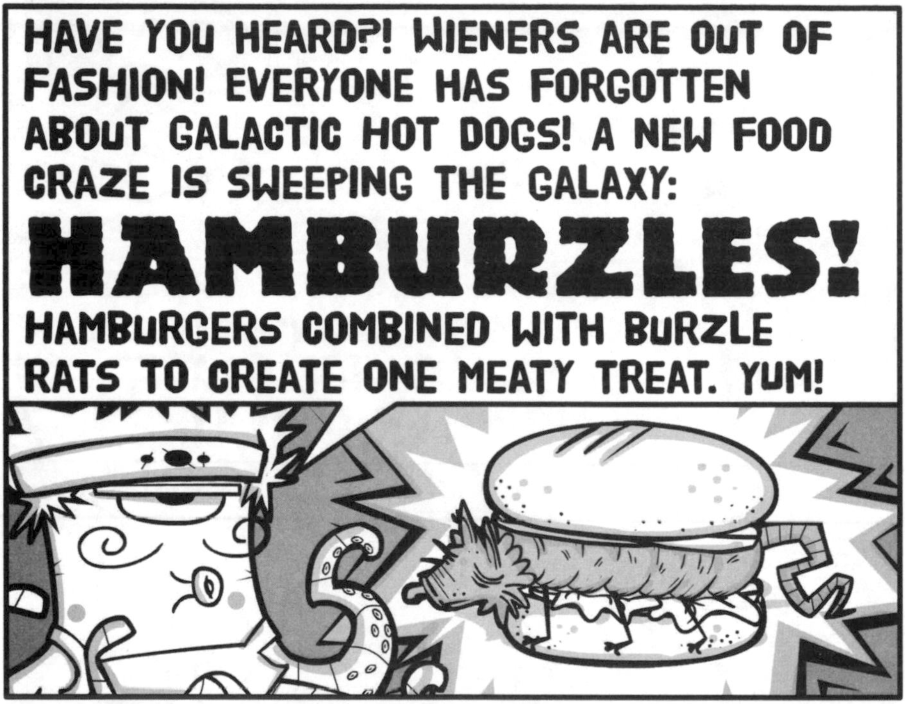
HAVE YOU HEARD?! WIENERS ARE OUT OF FASHION! EVERYONE HAS FORGOTTEN ABOUT GALACTIC HOT DOGS! A NEW FOOD CRAZE IS SWEEPING THE GALAXY:
HAMBURZLES!
HAMBURGERS COMBINED WITH BURZLE RATS TO CREATE ONE MEATY TREAT. YUM!

"***BONES!***" Humphree screams. "***BIG-TIME BONES!*** Cosmoe, all our space racing is messing up our business! People are forgetting about Galactic Hot Dogs!"

"Humps, we're saving the galaxy. More important."

"***NO!*** When we finish this adventure, we need to come back ***STRONG***. I picked up bolide beans at the M.W.W.F. arena—time to work on my HOT HOT SAUCE recipe!" Humphree says as he dashes off toward the kitchen.

I spend hours trying to make the two Map-O-Sphere slices fit together. Twisting, jiggering, forcing, squeezing.

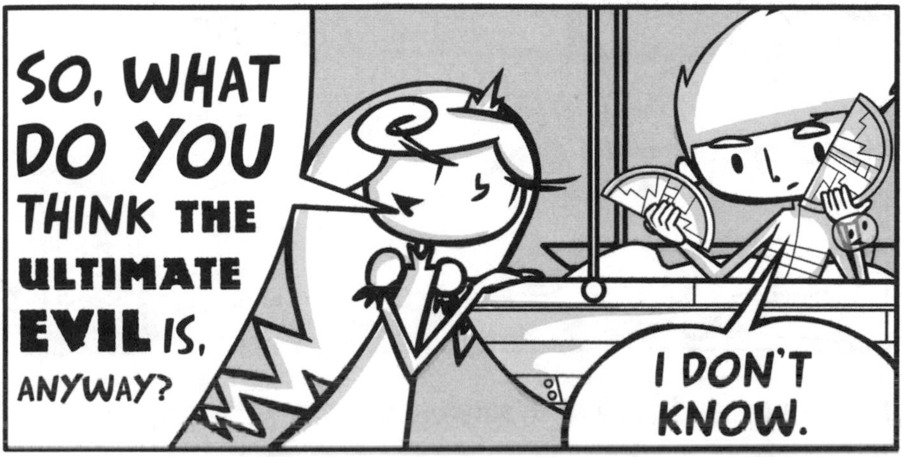
SO, WHAT DO YOU THINK THE ULTIMATE EVIL IS, ANYWAY?
I DON'T KNOW.

"Do you think it's like an ancient demon with a whole bunch of heads?"

"Could be," I say.

"Or maybe it's a planet with big fangs that eats other planets! Or a giant soul-sucking fog beast! Oh man, I'm so curious. I can't wait to see the Ultimate Evil!"

"Princess!" I shout. "As soon as we complete the sphere, I'm destroying it! **NO ONE** gets to see the Ultimate Evil!"

Softly, the princess says, "Oh yeah. I forgot . . ."

She slinks across the room and plops down on the floor. But a second later, she's back up, excited, as Humphree comes charging into the room . . .

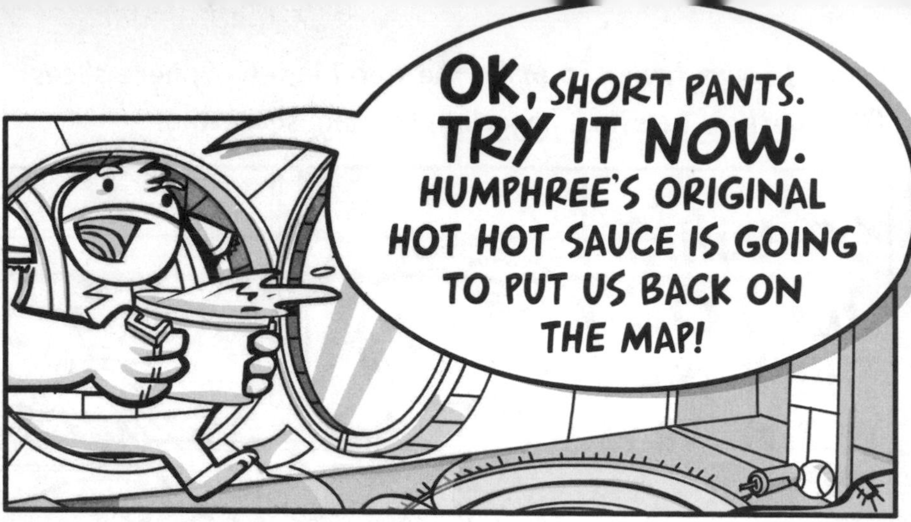
OK, SHORT PANTS. TRY IT NOW. HUMPHREE'S ORIGINAL HOT HOT SAUCE IS GOING TO PUT US BACK ON THE MAP!

I wave my hand at Humps, shooing him away. "Not now, dude. I'm trying to put the sphere slices together. I'm so close!"

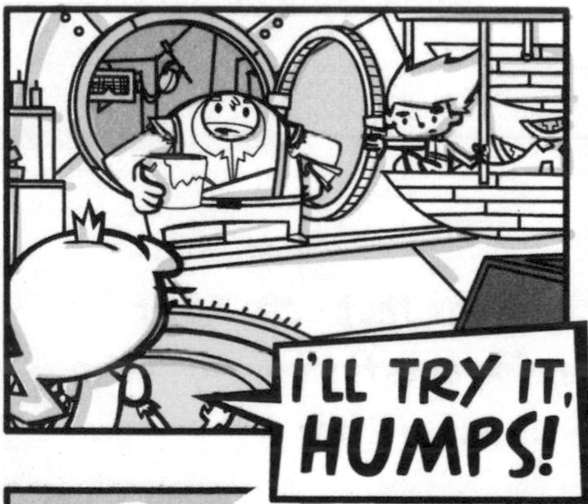
I'LL TRY IT, HUMPS!

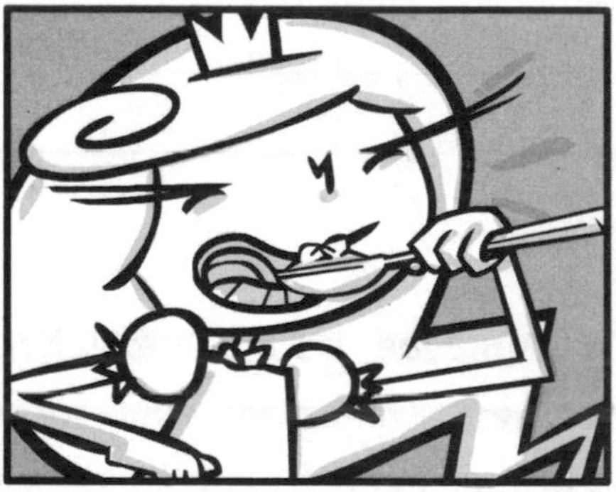

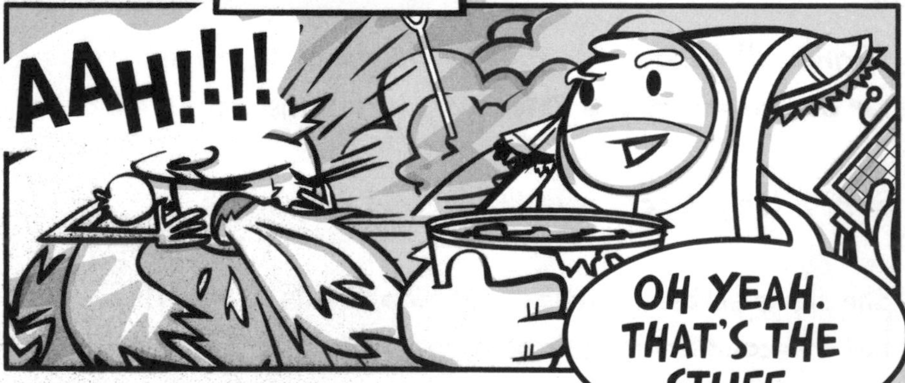
AAH!!!!
OH YEAH. THAT'S THE STUFF.

.R.E.D. brings up an image of the flyer for this videogame tournament. My eyes just about pop out of my head.

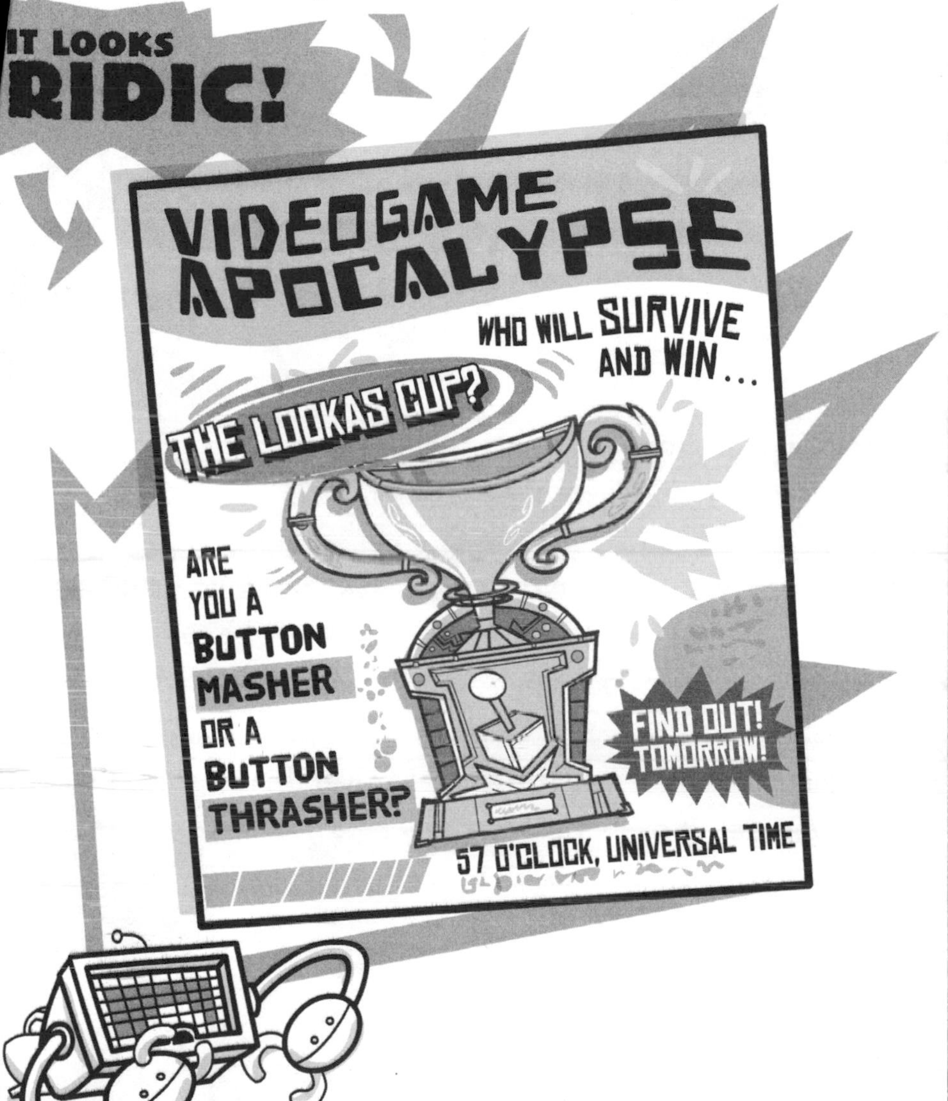
IT LOOKS RIDIC!
VIDEOGAME APOCALYPSE
WHO WILL SURVIVE AND WIN...
THE LOOKAS CUP?
ARE YOU A BUTTON MASHER OR A BUTTON THRASHER?
FIND OUT! TOMORROW!
57 O'CLOCK, UNIVERSAL TIME

"Look at the trophy," I say, pointing. "There, on the side, it's the final slice of the Map-O-Sphere! I just need to win the contest, and then we can complete the sphere! I totally got this!"

I twist the pieces with super concentration. Then, sudde[n]
finally, there's a **CLICK** and—

ENERGY GLOW!

I GOT IT!

"Yes!" Dagger exclaims. "Just one
more slice to go! Where do we find it?"

F.R.E.D.'s arms extend out and he yanks the Map-O-Sphere
from my hands. "I'll do it myself this time," he says as he
inserts it into his back opening and begins examining.

We all wait with bated breath, whatever that means. I heard
someone say it once. I don't know how you bate breath,
but mine is definitely super bated right now.
And then—

THE THIRD AND
FINAL SLICE IS
LOCATED AT
THE VIDEOGAME
APOCALYPSE
TOURNAMENT.

WAIT.
FOR REAL?
YES!!!!

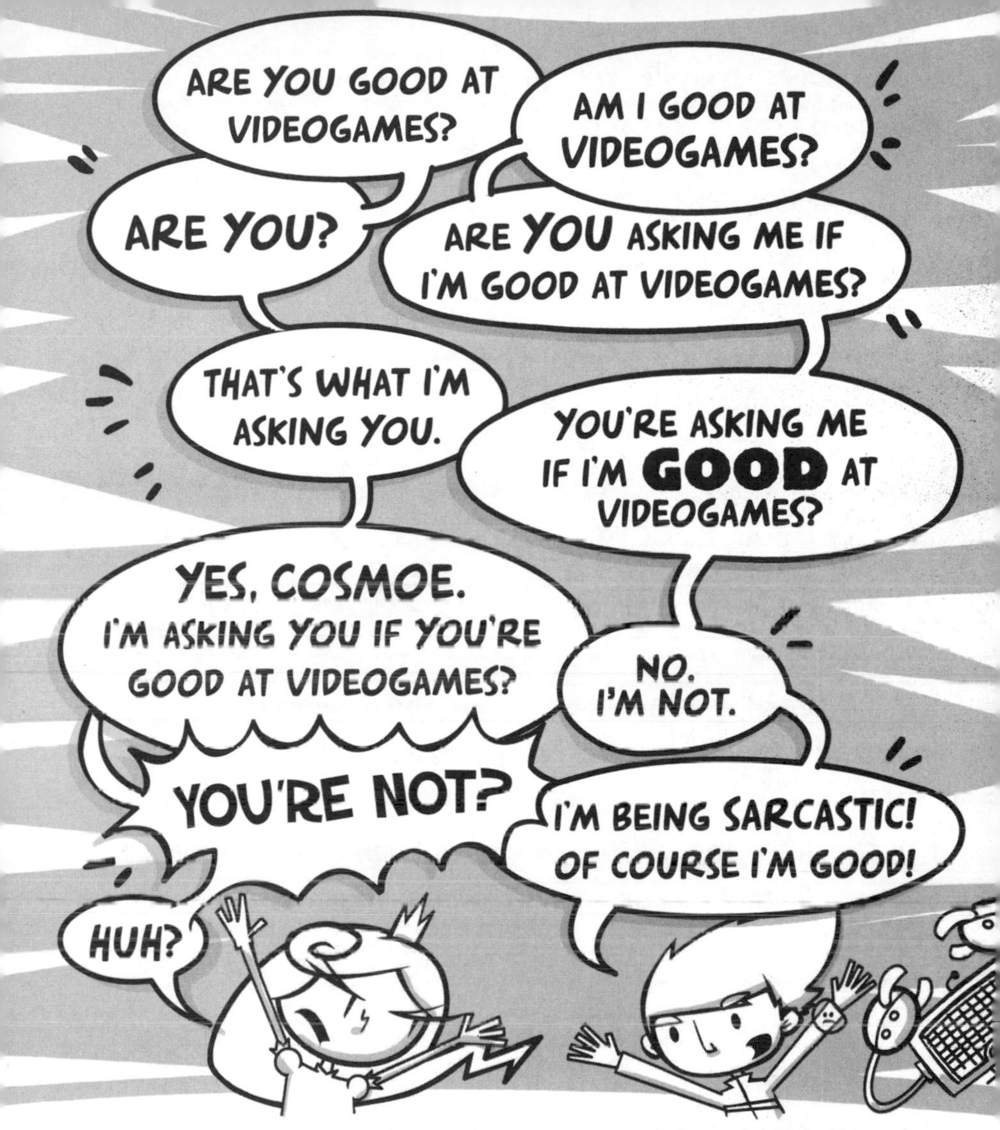
ARE YOU GOOD AT VIDEOGAMES?
AM I GOOD AT VIDEOGAMES?
ARE YOU?
ARE YOU ASKING ME IF I'M GOOD AT VIDEOGAMES?
THAT'S WHAT I'M ASKING YOU.
YOU'RE ASKING ME IF I'M GOOD AT VIDEOGAMES?
YES, COSMOE. I'M ASKING YOU IF YOU'RE GOOD AT VIDEOGAMES?
NO. I'M NOT.
YOU'RE NOT?
I'M BEING SARCASTIC! OF COURSE I'M GOOD!
HUH?

"Argh! Never mind! Look, back on Earth, all I ever did was play videogames. So yes, I'm good at videogames. I mean, I'm not just good—**I'M REAL GOOD. I'M A WIZARD.**"

And with that, I trot off to the bedroom, feeling stupendous. This whole crazy plan is going to work. But I need my rest if I'm going to win this tournament . . .

A few hours later, I'm snoozing away in my hammock, having standard Cosmoe dreams—

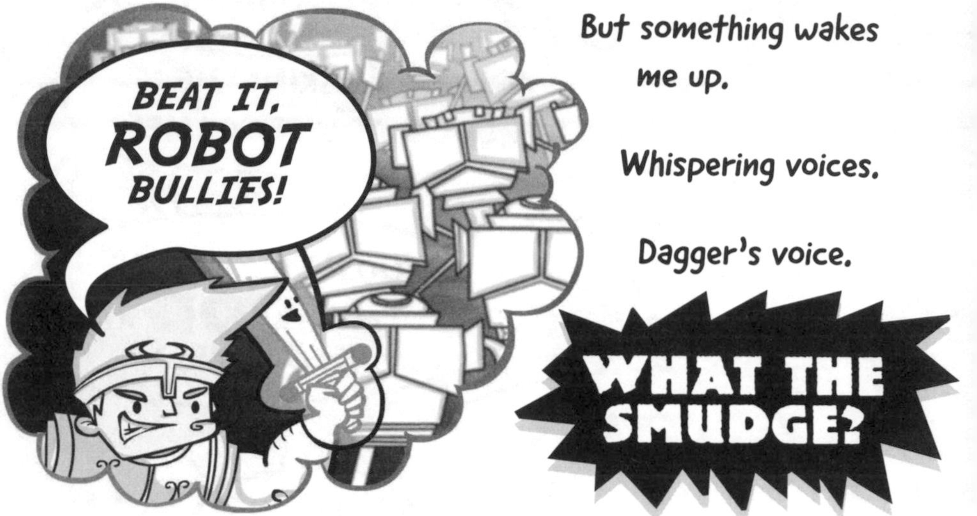
BEAT IT, ROBOT BULLIES!

But something wakes me up.

Whispering voices.

Dagger's voice.

WHAT THE SMUDGE?

I crawl out of my hammock. Humphree is snoring away, as loud as a fusion-powered freight train.

I tiptoe down the hall to the engine room, which is where Princess Dagger sleeps now. Peeking my head around the corner, I see—

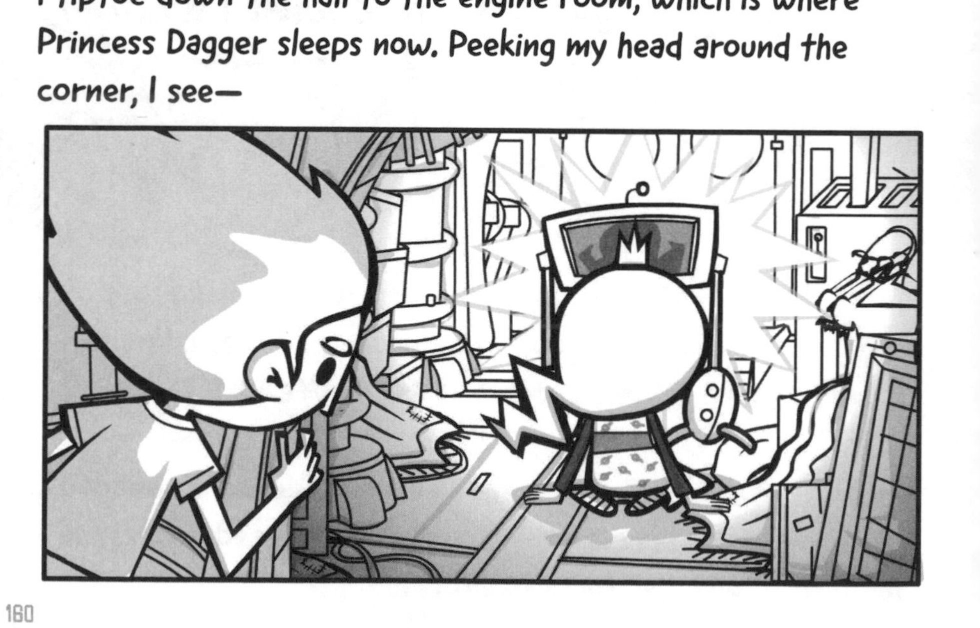

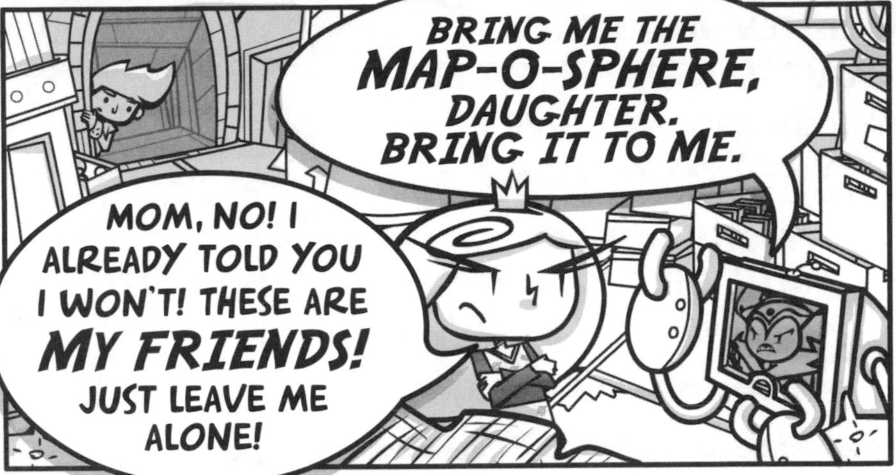
BRING ME THE MAP-O-SPHERE, DAUGHTER. BRING IT TO ME.
MOM, NO! I ALREADY TOLD YOU I WON'T! THESE ARE MY FRIENDS! JUST LEAVE ME ALONE!

Not cool, Queen, not cool . . .

I watch the princess and her jerky jerk mom argue back and forth . . .

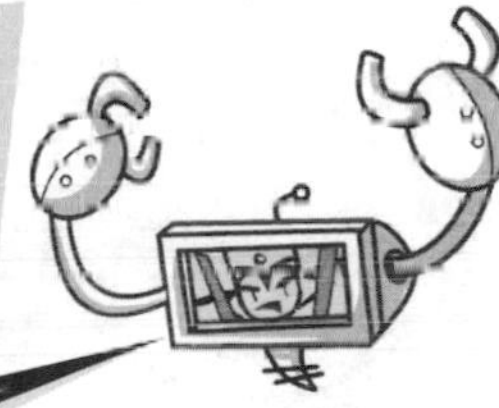

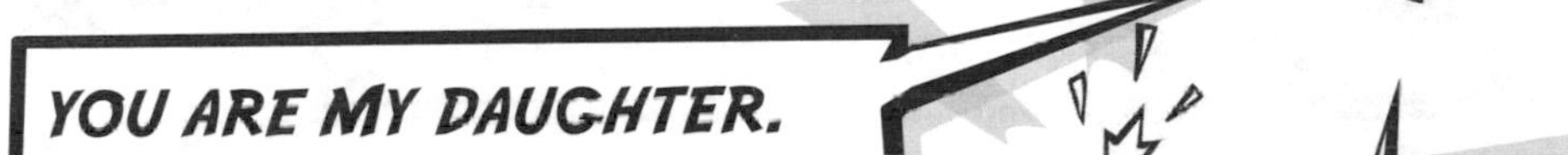
YOU ARE MY DAUGHTER. FIGHT IT ALL YOU WANT, BUT YOU ARE EVIL.
MAYBE I AM EVIL. BUT I'M LEARNING HOW NOT TO BE.
YOU ARE MY DAUGHTER. YOU WILL ALWAYS BE EVIL!

Princess Dagger goes silent. She hangs her head. I'm about to explode with dinosaur-strength anger . . . I've had enough! I jump from around the corner and stomp toward them.

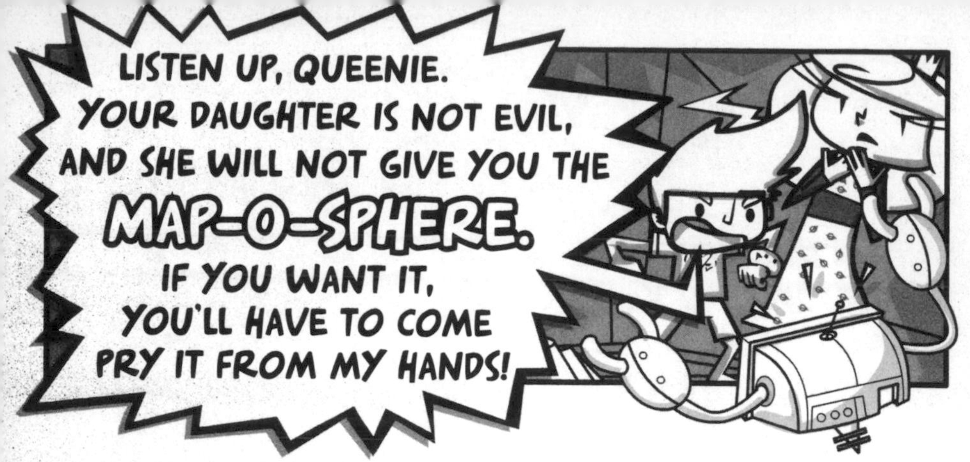
LISTEN UP, QUEENIE. YOUR DAUGHTER IS NOT EVIL, AND SHE WILL NOT GIVE YOU THE MAP-O-SPHERE. IF YOU WANT IT, YOU'LL HAVE TO COME PRY IT FROM MY HANDS!

"I would do just that," Evil Queen Dagger says, "if only I knew where you were . . . But I don't think you'll tell me."

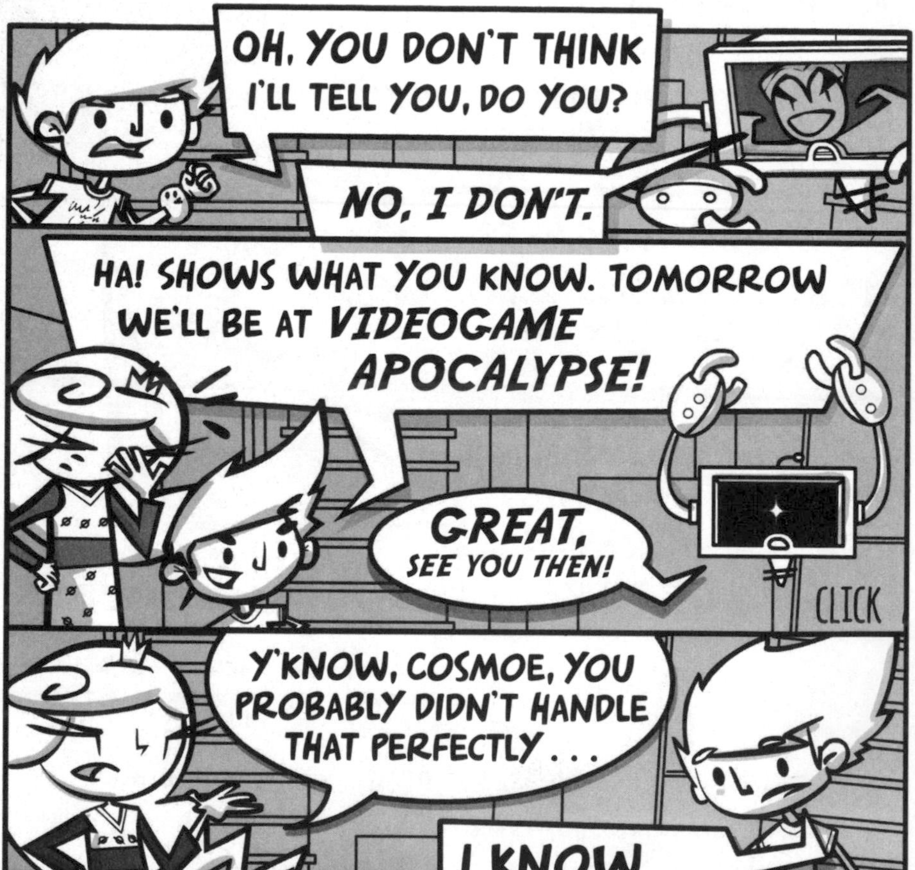
OH, YOU DON'T THINK I'LL TELL YOU, DO YOU?
NO, I DON'T.
HA! SHOWS WHAT YOU KNOW. TOMORROW WE'LL BE AT VIDEOGAME APOCALYPSE!
GREAT, SEE YOU THEN!
CLICK
Y'KNOW, COSMOE, YOU PROBABLY DIDN'T HANDLE THAT PERFECTLY . . .
I KNOW . . .

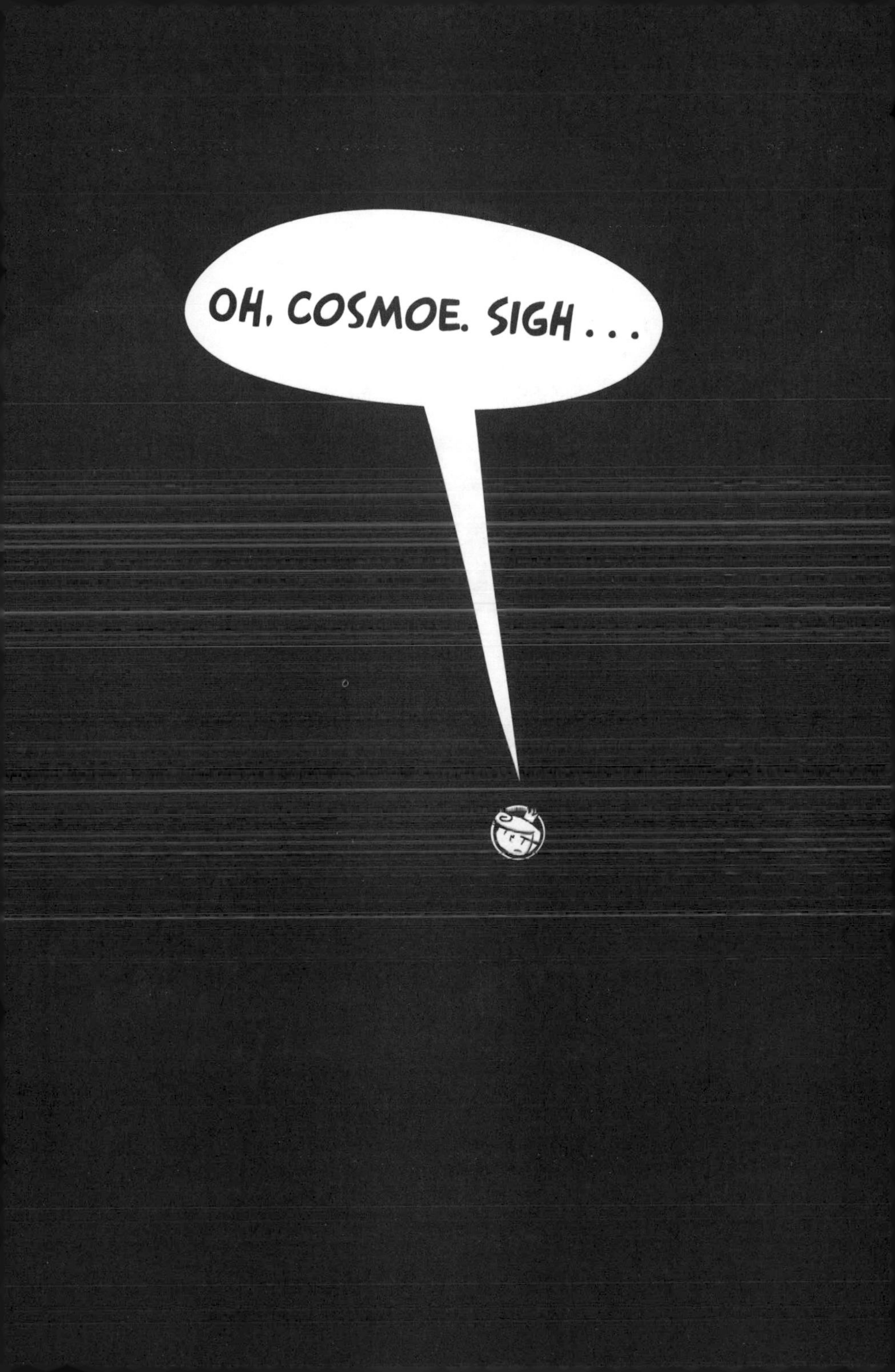
OH, COSMOE. SIGH . . .

COSMOE THE EARTH-TURD

16

We're rocketing toward the big event:

VIDEOGAME APOCALYPSE.

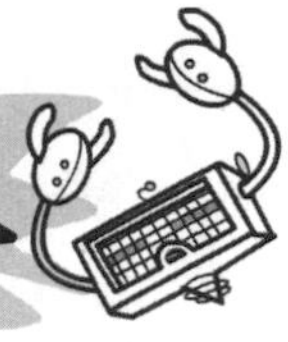

A radio blast just informed us that two bad-news fortune hunters have dropped from the chase. Space pirate Pike Ding was sucked into a thermal vortex and Kaff Fiend was swallowed by space sharks. So that's rad! But maybe not rad enough. . . .

I know I was ***ALL CRAZY-CONFIDENT*** before, but now the doubts are creeping in. Since I left Earth, I've only played videogames aboard the *Neon Wiener* with Humphree!

But at Videogame Apocalypse? I'm gonna be battling moon warlords and android assassins and—

DUNG TONGUE! We're here . . .

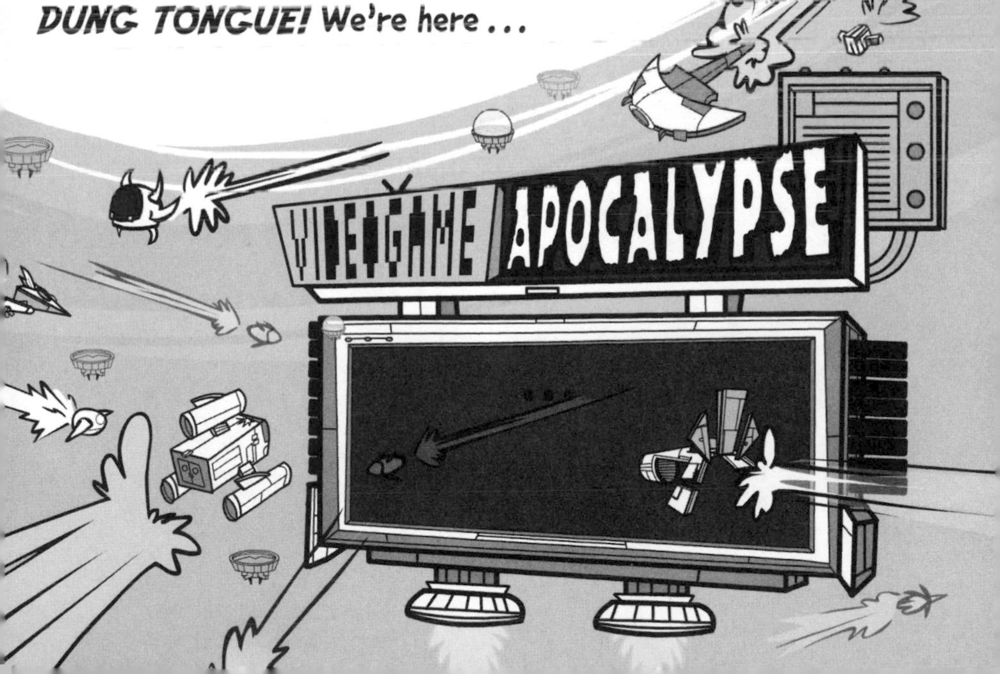
VIDEOGAME APOCALYPSE

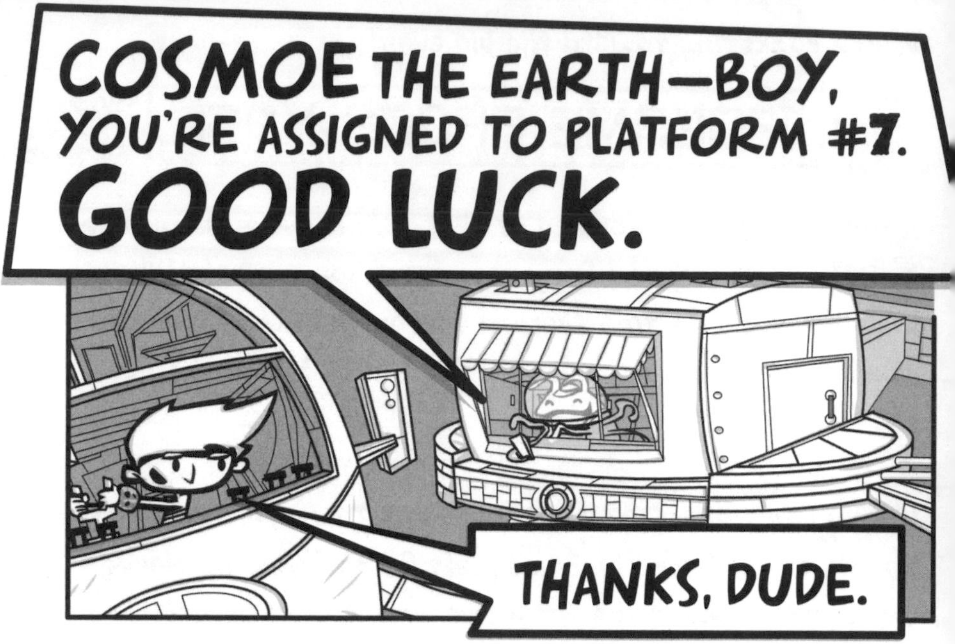
COSMOE THE EARTH—BOY, YOU'RE ASSIGNED TO PLATFORM #7. GOOD LUCK.
THANKS, DUDE.

After the alien directs us to our platform, we slowly cruise through the crowd. I recognize some of the other contestants: bad, bad dudes like robo-thief HW-86 and bounty hunter Tabe Boft. This one alien, Bic Vastardly, has six arms! I mean, c'mon, that seems really unfair . . .

And—oh smudge—I see

THESE TWO FAT HEADS

touching down.

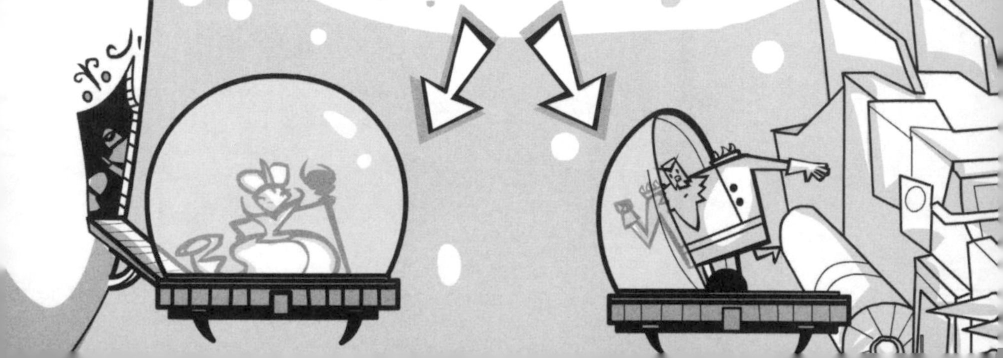

After landing the *Neon Wiener*, I step out onto Platform #7's smooth, shiny surface. An energy sphere covers the contraption, allowing me to breathe without my space suit.

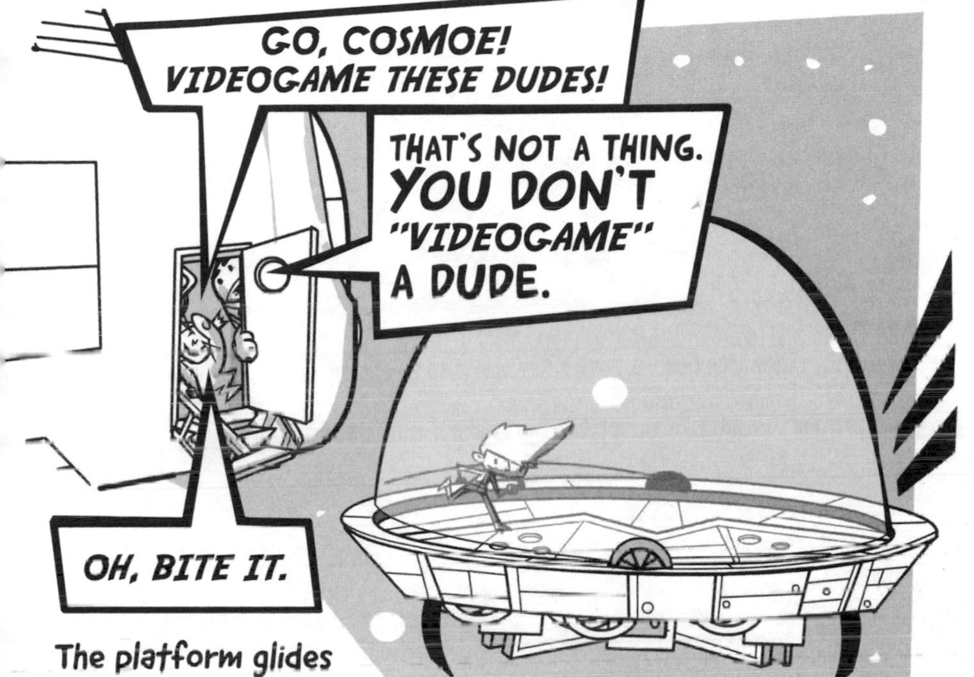
GO, COSMOE! VIDEOGAME THESE DUDES!
THAT'S NOT A THING. YOU DON'T "VIDEOGAME" A DUDE.
OH, BITE IT.

The platform glides away from the *Wiener*, toward the screen.

I'm all confuzzled. There's no controller! Just a metallic circle on the ground.

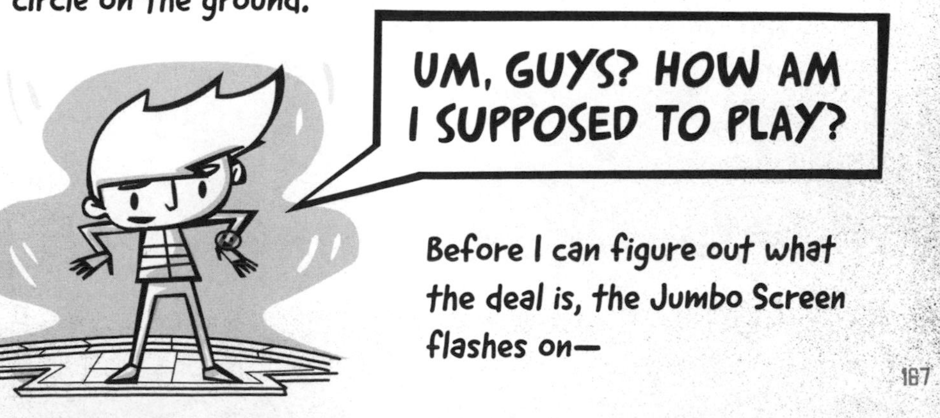
UM, GUYS? HOW AM I SUPPOSED TO PLAY?

Before I can figure out what the deal is, the Jumbo Screen flashes on—

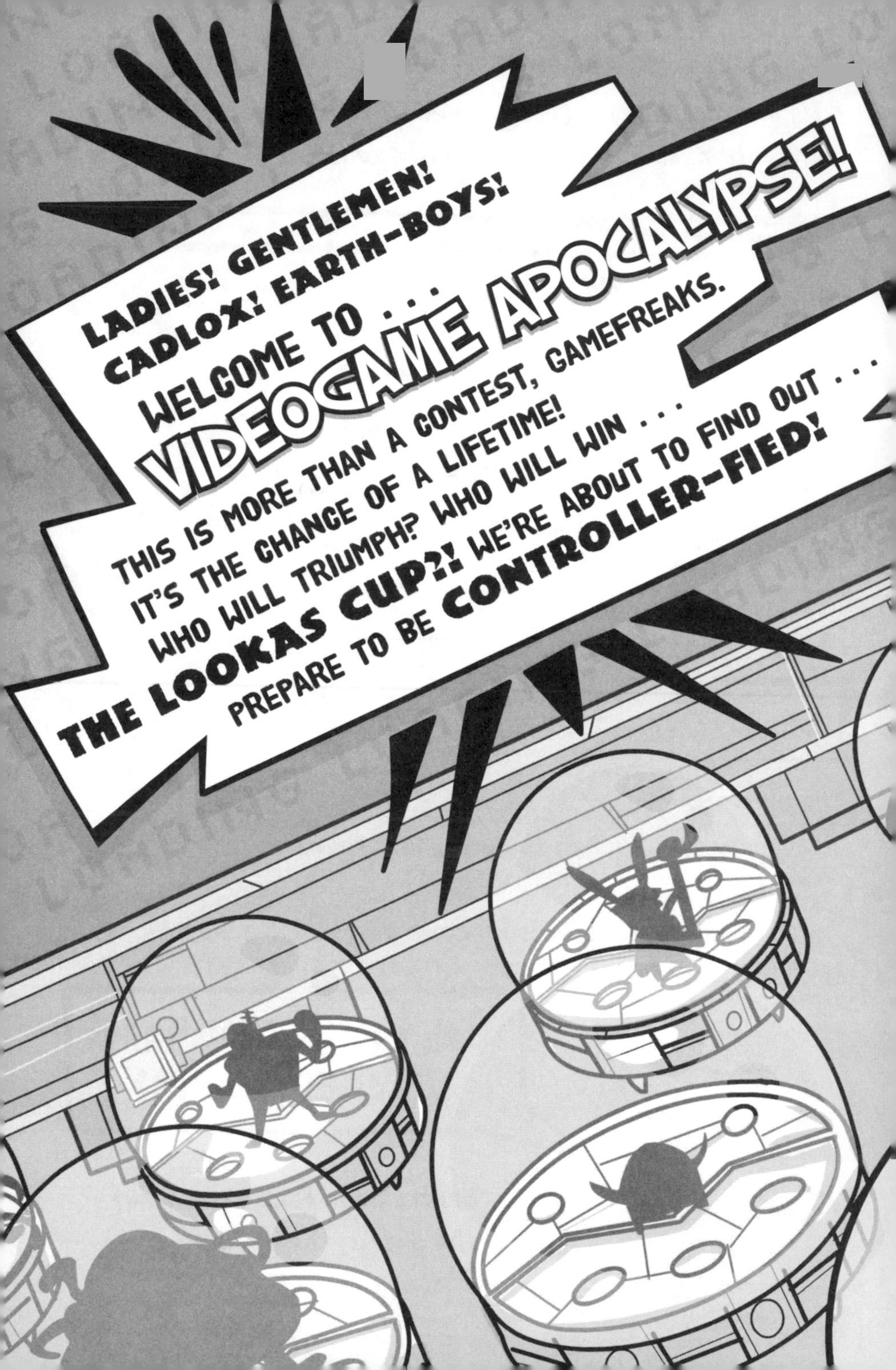
LADIES! GENTLEMEN!
CADLOX! EARTH-BOYS!
WELCOME TO . . .
VIDEOGAME APOCALYPSE!
THIS IS MORE THAN A CONTEST, GAMEFREAKS.
IT'S THE CHANCE OF A LIFETIME!
WHO WILL TRIUMPH? WHO WILL WIN . . .
THE LOOKAS CUP?! WE'RE ABOUT TO FIND OUT . . .
PREPARE TO BE CONTROLLER-FIED!

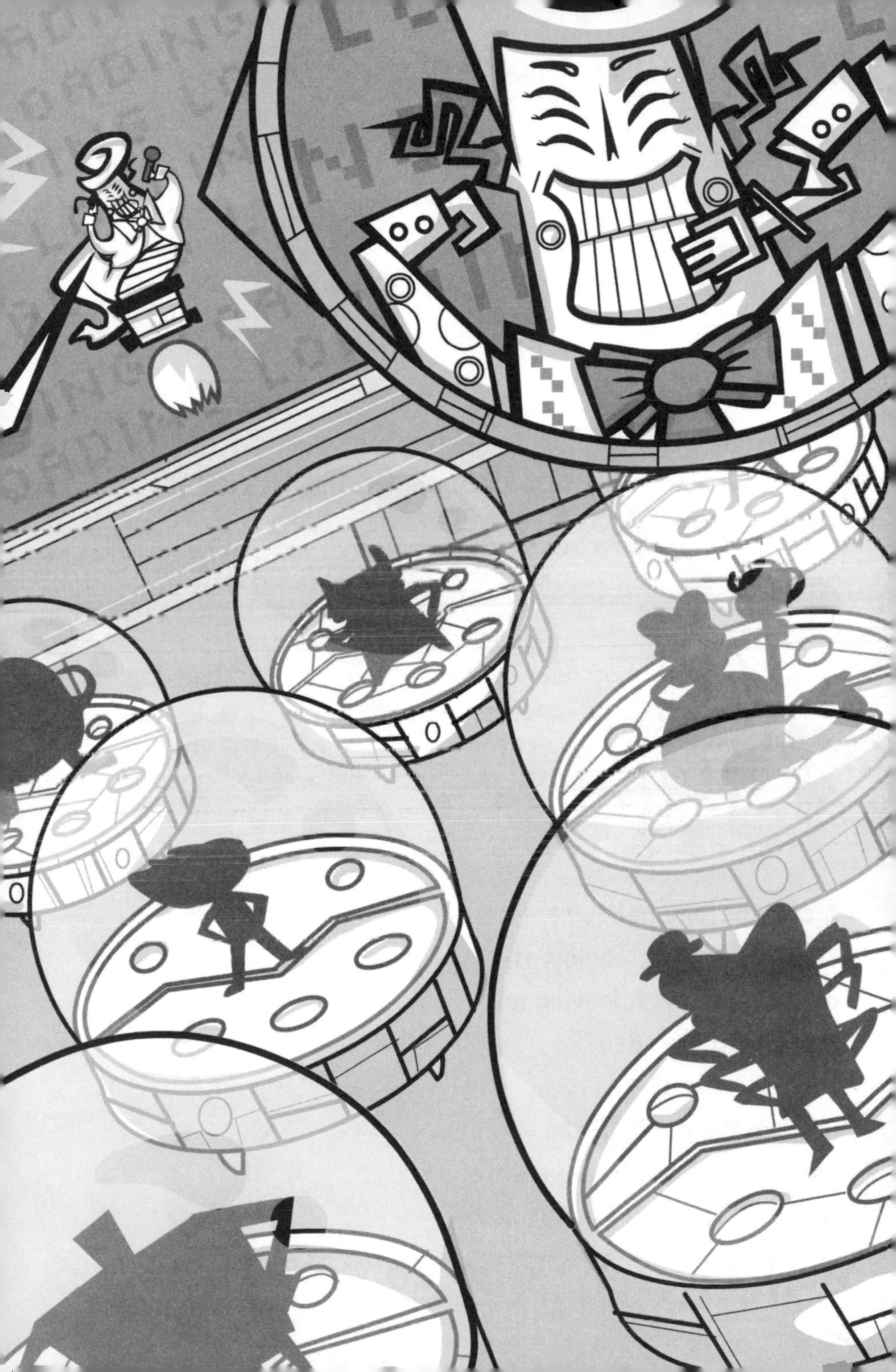

UM . . . What does "***CONTROLLER-FIED***" mean?!?!?

And then I find out—

The ring at my feet begins rising up off the platform! Strange metal grabbers take hold of my legs! Others grasp my arms!

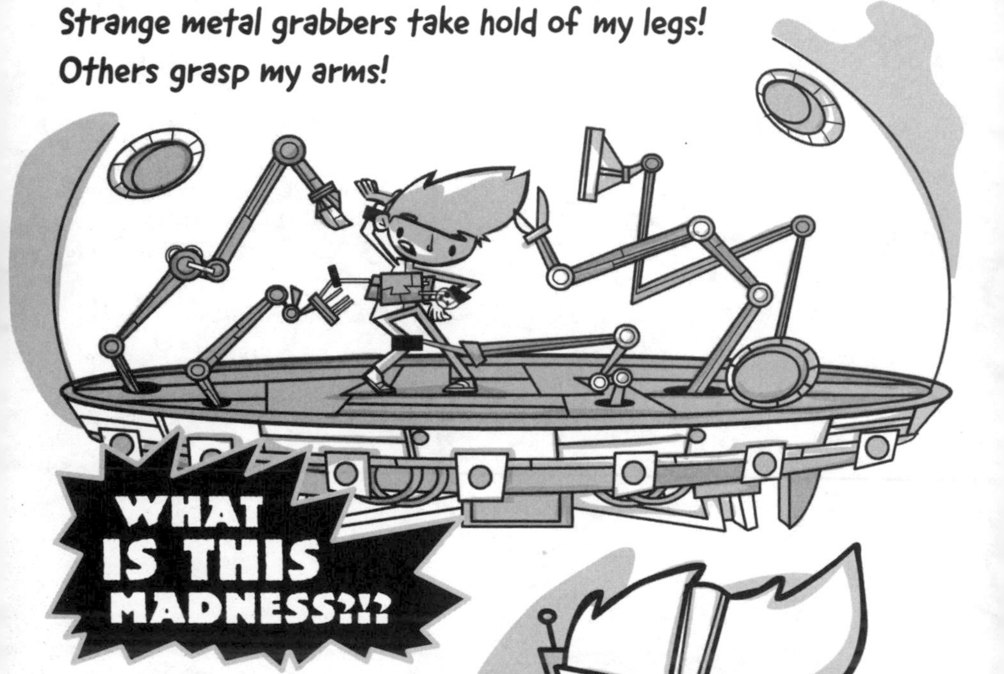
WHAT IS THIS MADNESS?!?

A cold metally belt wraps around my belly. Finally, the platform lowers, leaving me suspended in midair!

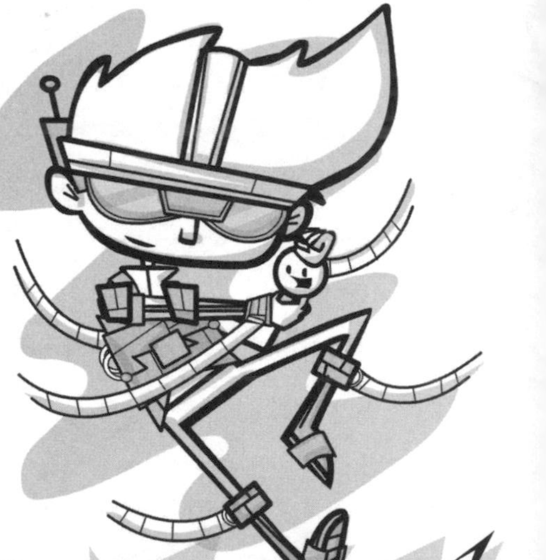

It's like I'm part of the controller. No, it's even more ridonc than that! I have become—

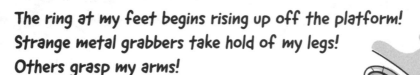

ONE WITH THE CONTROLLER!

General Krax shouts at me, "You better win, Cosmoe the Earth-Turd, or the final Map-O-Sphere slice is mine!

"It won't only be the Map-O-Sphere you lose," Queen Dagger yells. "I'll be taking back my daughter, too!"

Gulp. No fooling around here. I **MUST** win! If I fail, I won't just cause that crazy evil to be unleashed, I'll lose my new friend . . .

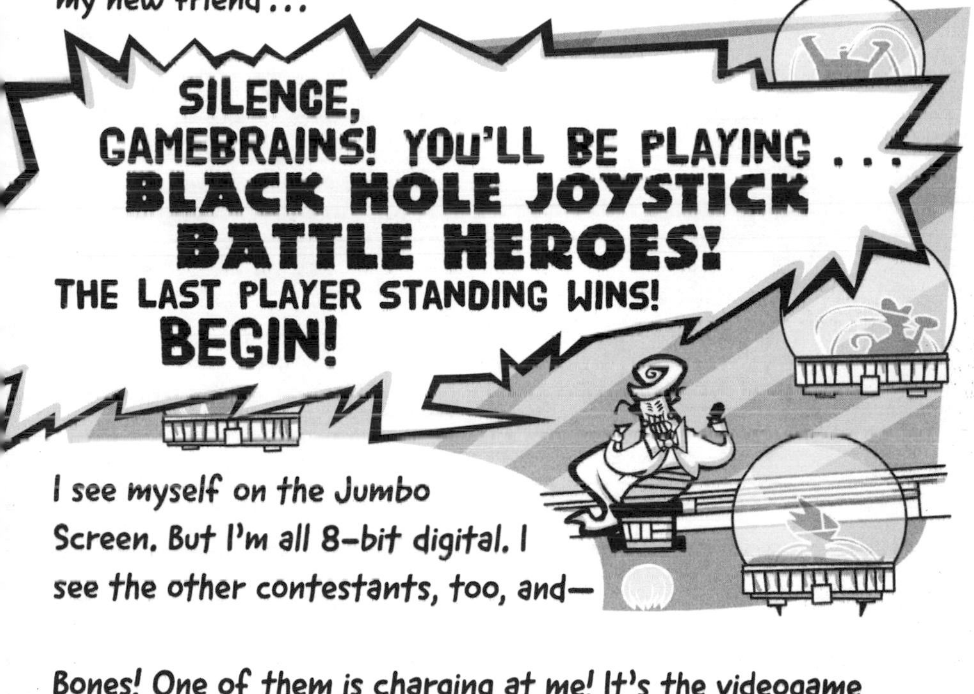
SILENCE, GAMEBRAINS! YOU'LL BE PLAYING . . .
BLACK HOLE JOYSTICK BATTLE HEROES!
THE LAST PLAYER STANDING WINS!
BEGIN!

I see myself on the Jumbo Screen. But I'm all 8-bit digital. I see the other contestants, too, and—

Bones! One of them is charging at me! It's the videogame version of General Krax, and he's swinging his Micro-Blast Bat!

I shout, "Goober! Mace to the face!" and I swing!

It works! My character on the Jumbo Screen does exactly what I do—

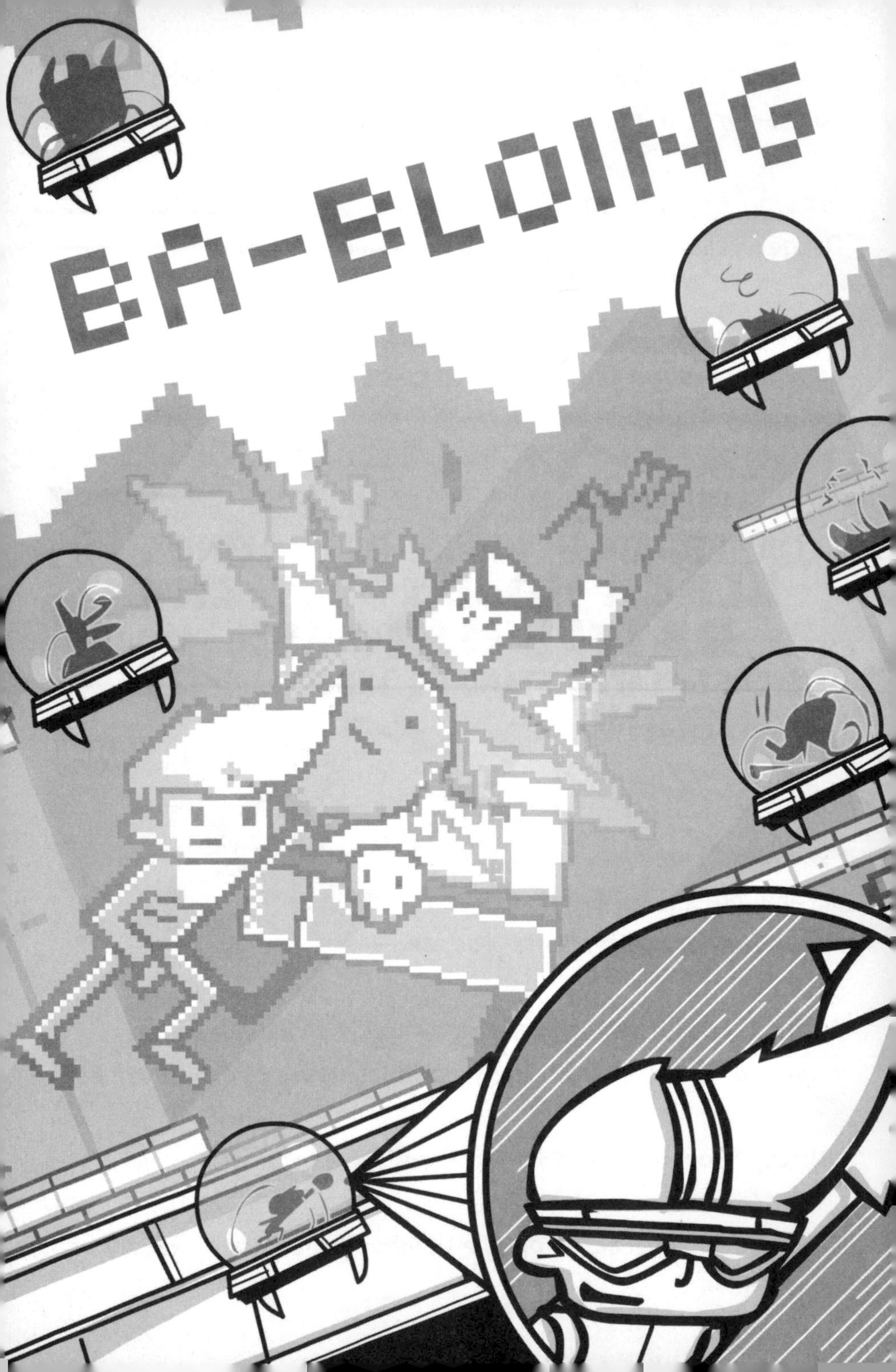
BA-BLOING

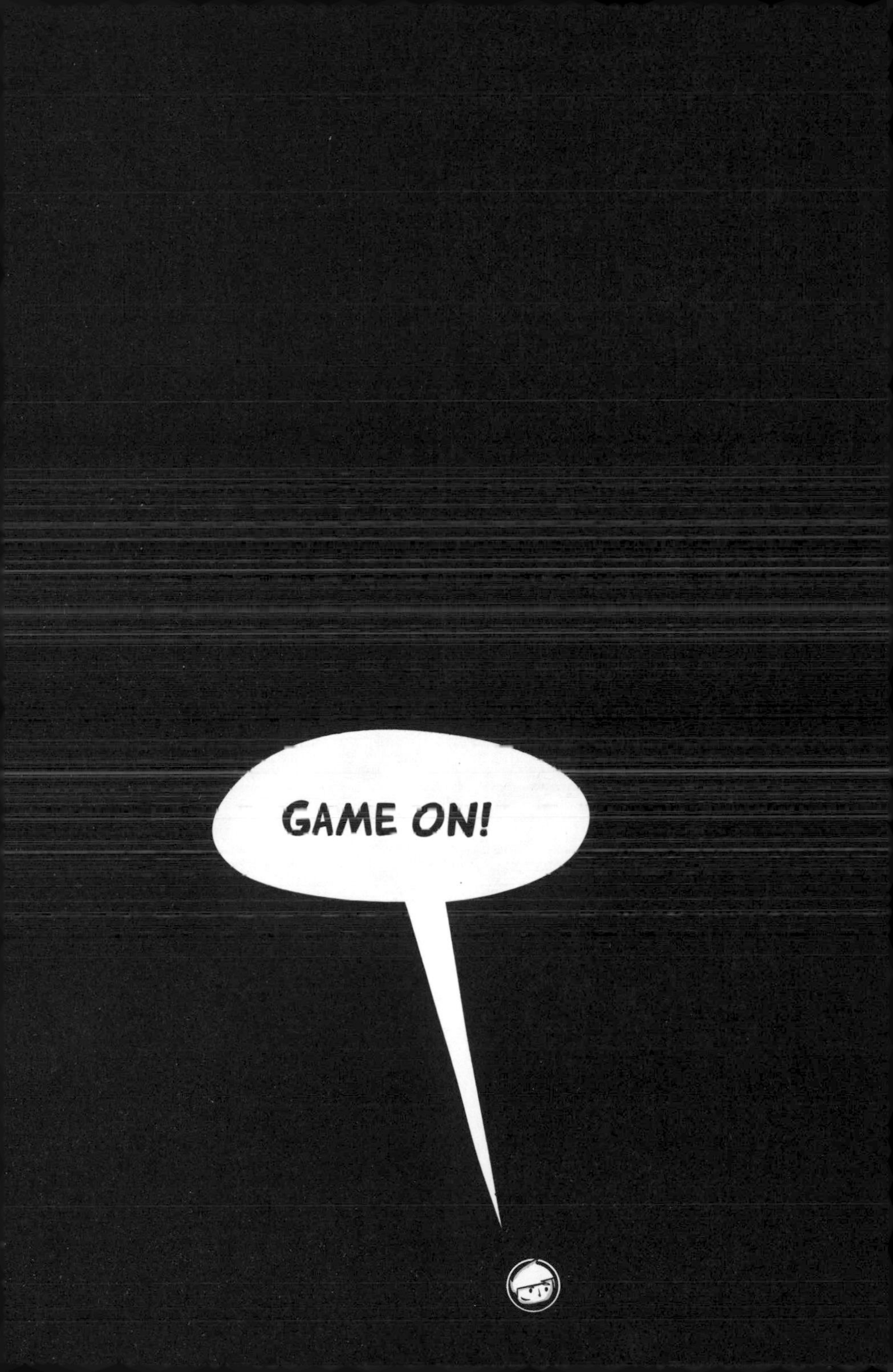
GAME ON!

BLACK HOLE JOYSTICK BATTLE HEROES

17

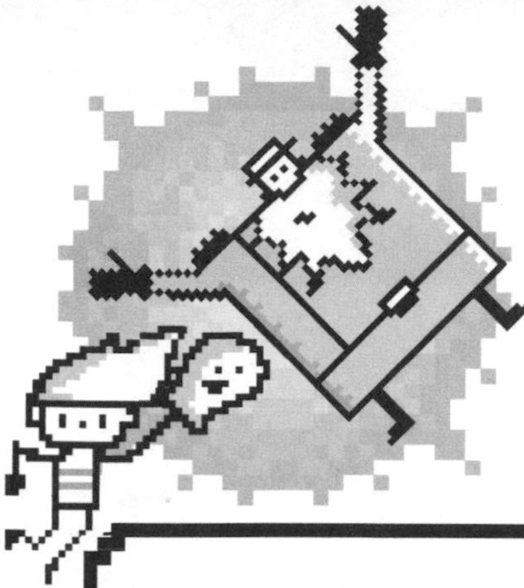

I just Goober-maced General Krax in a videogame! And that is high-level ***BONKERS!*** But there's no time to think about the ***BONKERS*** level, because—

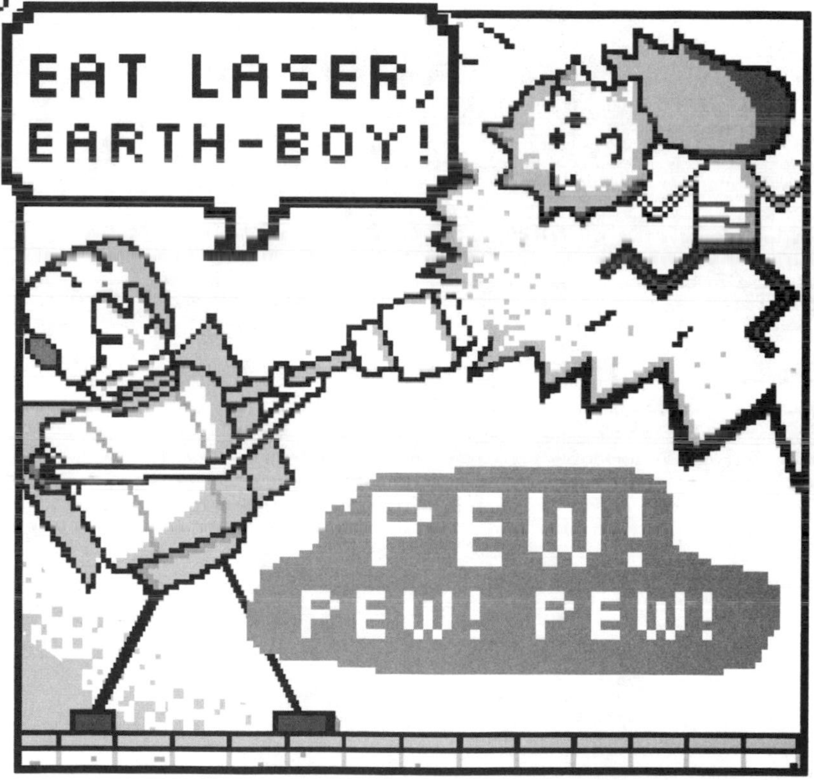
EAT LASER, EARTH-BOY!
PEW!
PEW! PEW!

HW-86 just blasted me! My controller unit reacts to the hit, twirling the real me around.

When the spinning stops, I glimpse the screen. And I can't believe what I see—

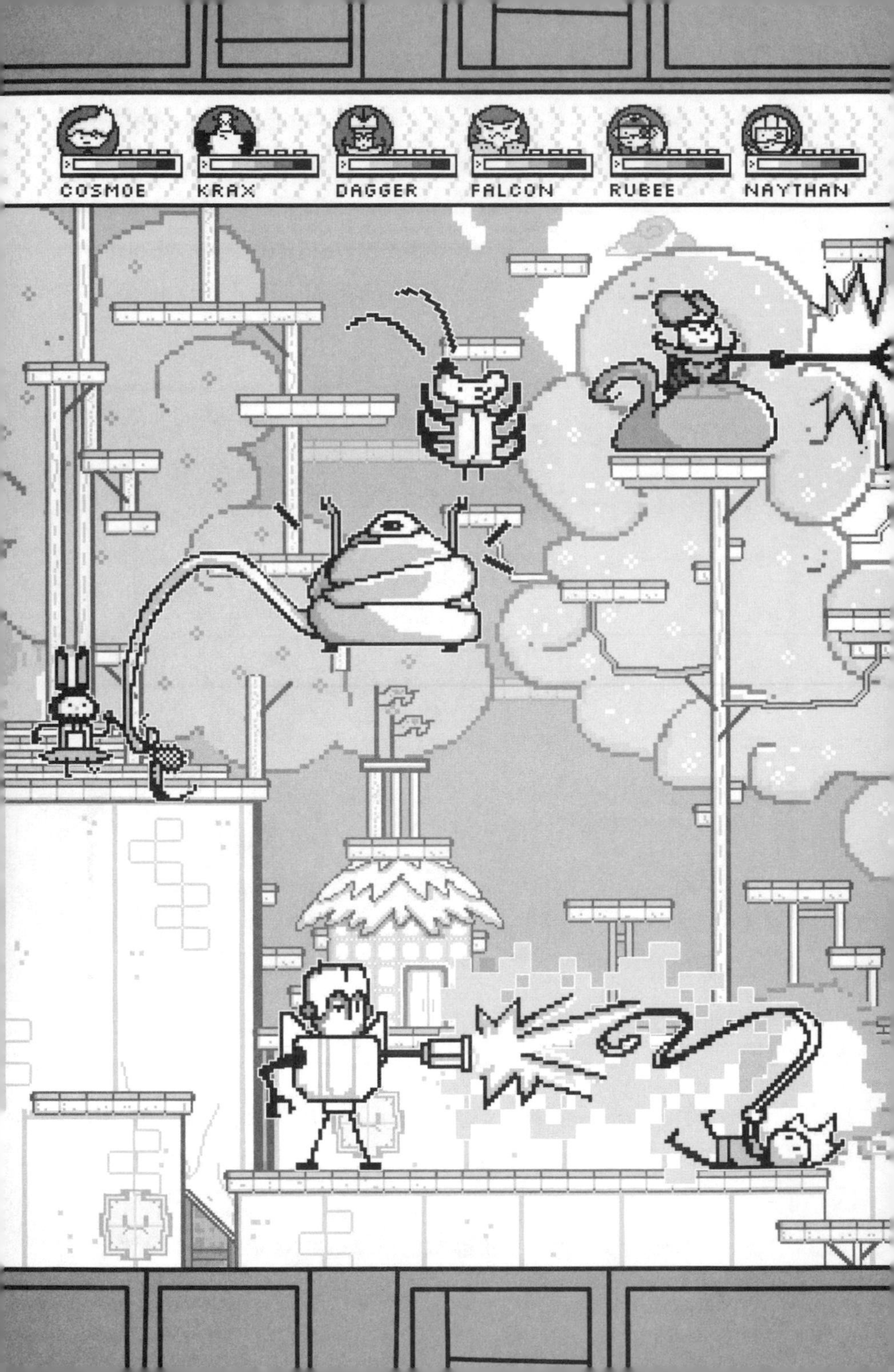
COSMOE
KRAX
DAGGER
FALCON
RUBEE
NAYTHAN

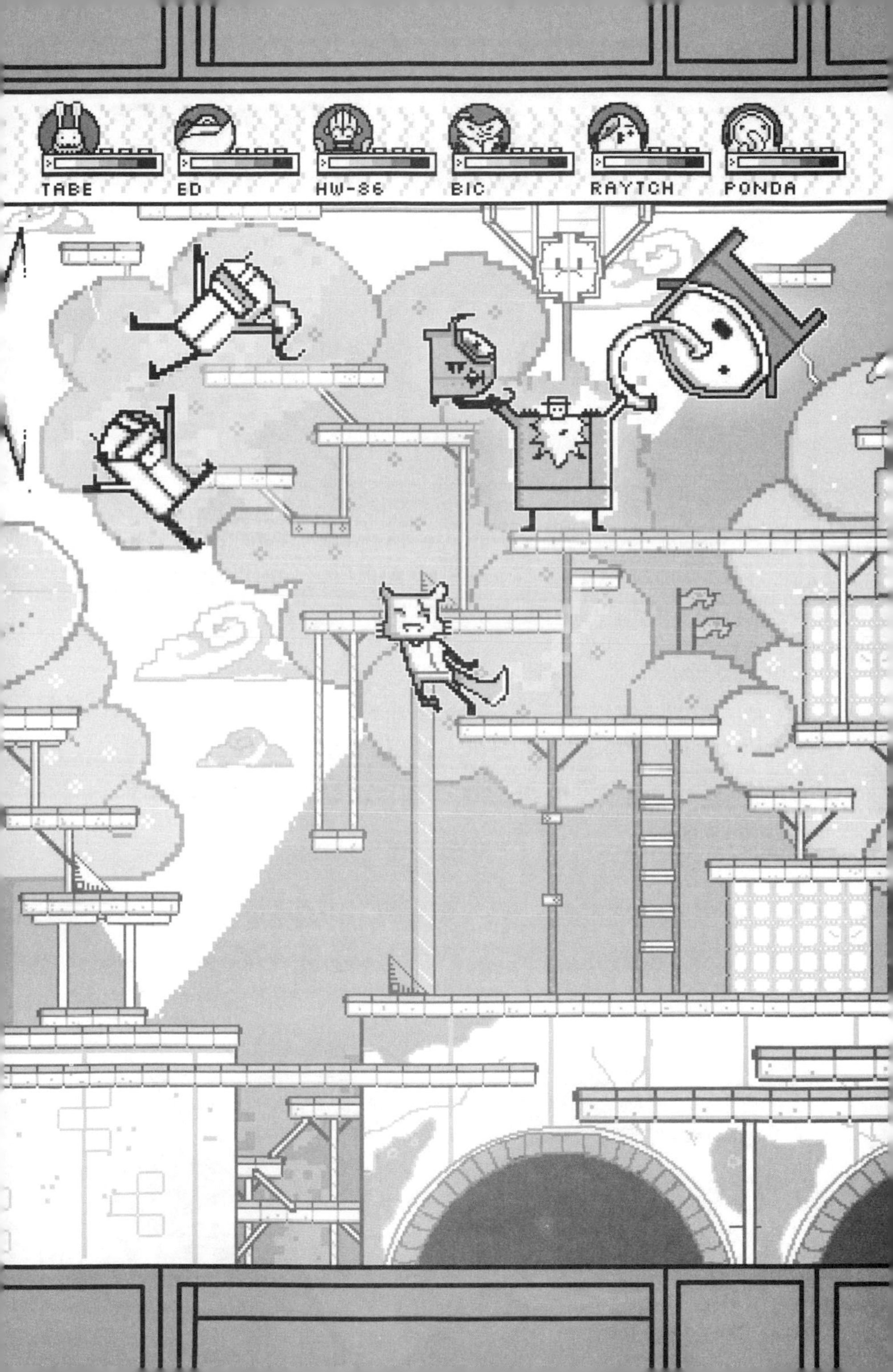
TABE
ED
HW-86
BIC
RAYTCH
PONDA

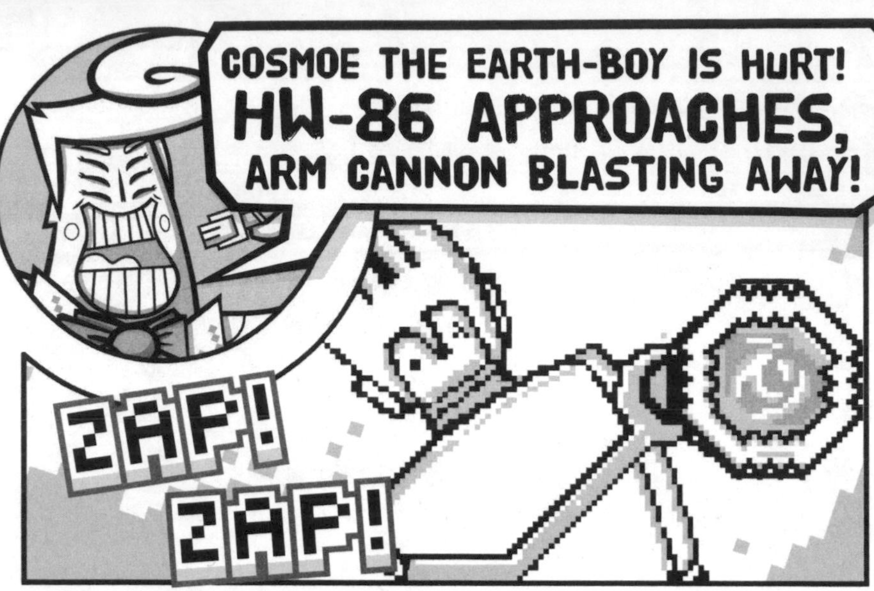
COSMOE THE EARTH-BOY IS HURT! HW-86 APPROACHES, ARM CANNON BLASTING AWAY!
ZAP!
ZAP!

Laser fire peppers the ground at my feet and whizzes past my head! Am I done for? Headed for the big starship in the sky . . . ?

NO! I'm killer good at videogames! I can't forget that! Just 'cause I'm playing in this crazy space place, I don't suddenly stink!

If I were gaming back on Earth, on my tiny old TV, what would I do? How would I react if I were getting thumped by laser blasts?!

JINGO! I know! ***PLAY DEFENSE!***

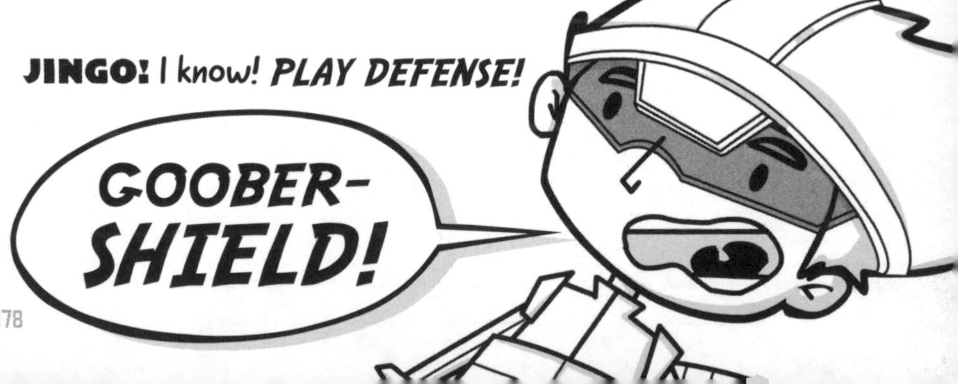
GOOBER-SHIELD!

A milli-micro-second after I speak, a digital Goober-shield appears. I set my feet, grip the shield tight, and prepare for another HW-86 laser-blast blitz.

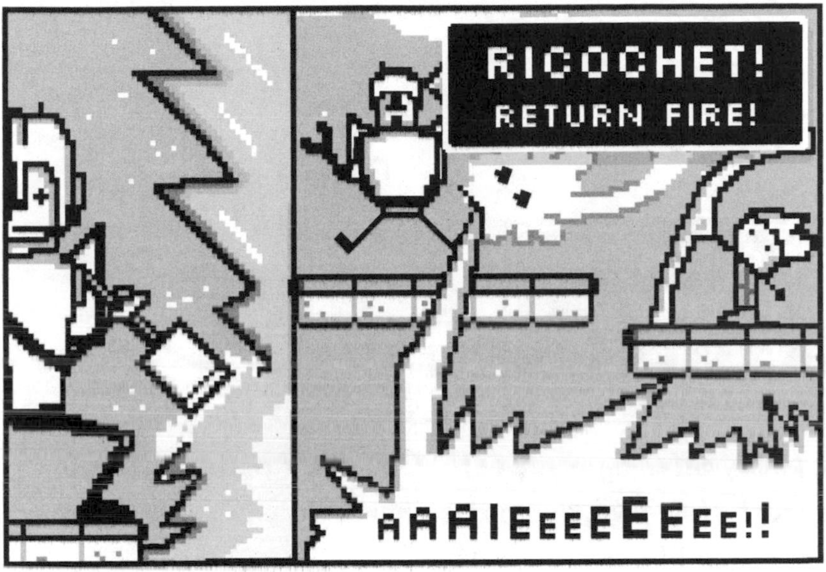
RICOCHET!
RETURN FIRE!
AAAIEEEEEEEEE!!

This is my one shot to knock the robo-villain out of the game! My legs move like crazy in the controller unit, and on the screen, my character dashes toward HW-86. "Batter up, Goober!" I shout.

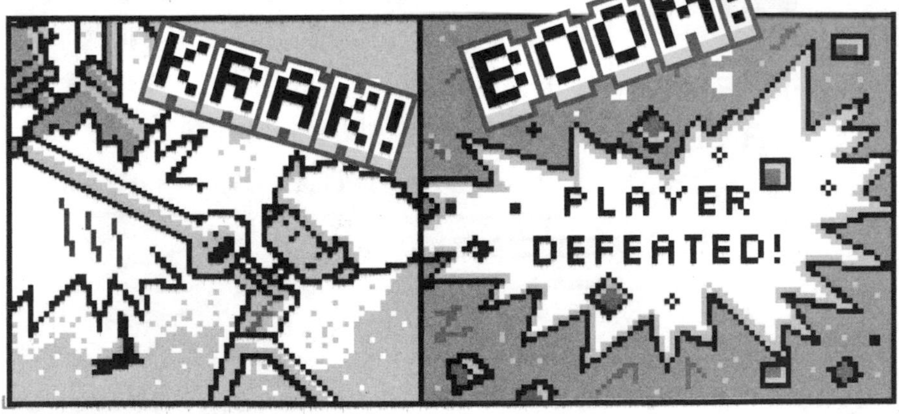
KRAK!
BOOM!
PLAYER DEFEATED!

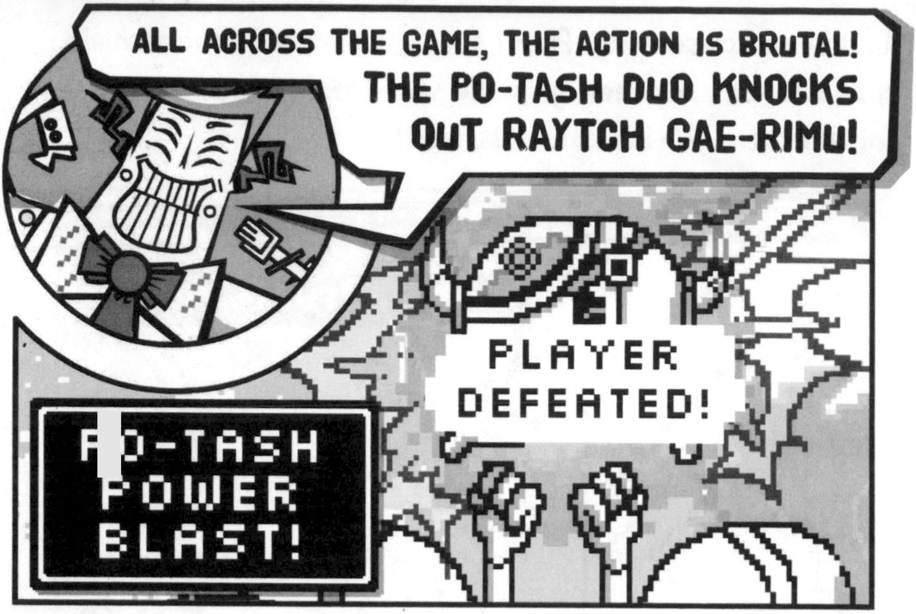
ALL ACROSS THE GAME, THE ACTION IS BRUTAL! THE PO-TASH DUO KNOCKS OUT RAYTCH GAE-RIMU!
PLAYER DEFEATED!
PO-TASH POWER BLAST!

OK, phew, catching my breath. One more player down! If I can just stay alive, I've got a chance to win this thing. But that's when I hear—

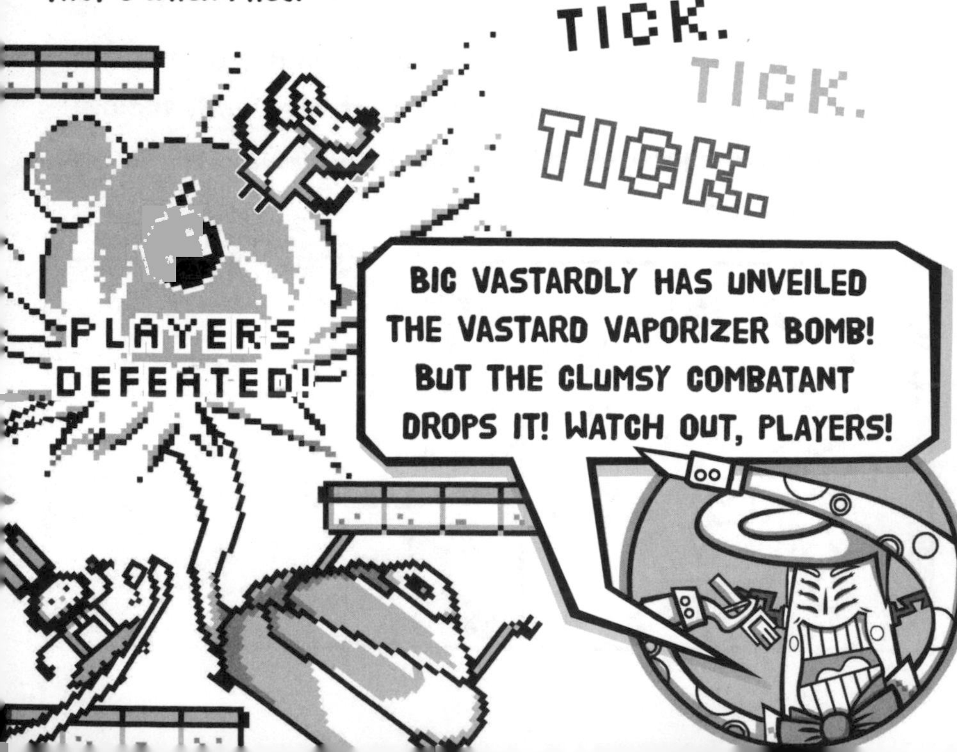
TICK.
TICK.
TICK.
PLAYERS DEFEATED!
BIG VASTARDLY HAS UNVEILED THE VASTARD VAPORIZER BOMB! BUT THE CLUMSY COMBATANT DROPS IT! WATCH OUT, PLAYERS!

The Vastard Vaporizer detonation knocks videogame me halfway across the level. My character hits the ground and the real me is tossed around the controller unit. Now I know what underwear in a dryer feels like . . .

I'm trying to get myself back up for battle, when I hear—

BEHIND YOU, COSMOE!

I spin around. Fuzz! Zan Ponda is flying at me! The big brute is about to kick me in the ear!

"Goober-whip!" I shout as I lash out with my rubbery buddy. Goober wraps around Zan Ponda's meaty leg, and then—

PLAYER DEFEATED!

TREE THUMP!

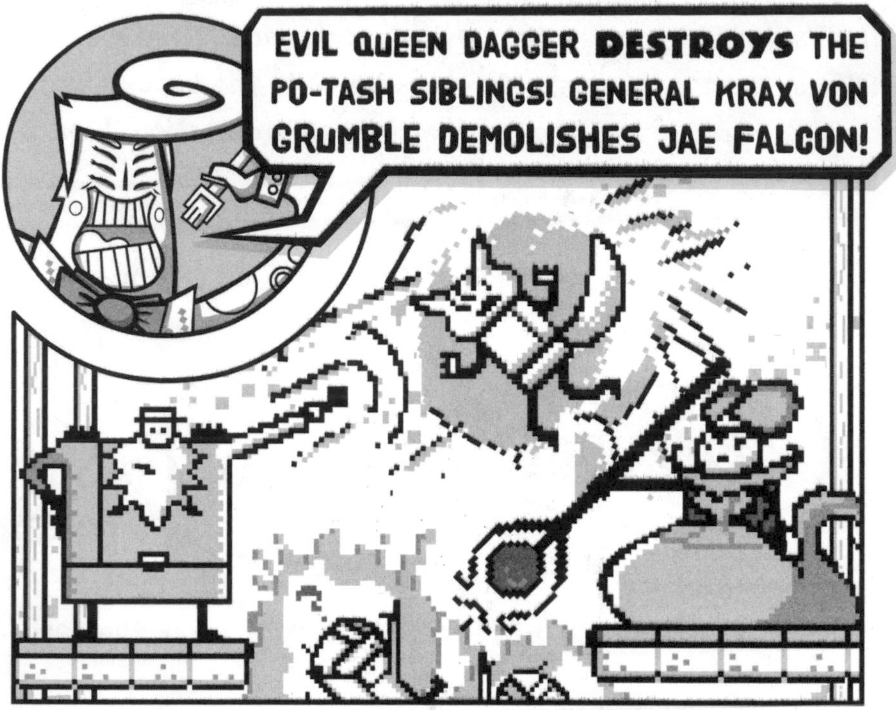
EVIL QUEEN DAGGER **DESTROYS** THE PO-TASH SIBLINGS! GENERAL KRAX VON GRUMBLE DEMOLISHES JAE FALCON!

My eyes dart across the screen. Nine players defeated. Only three remain: Evil Queen Dagger, General Krax, and me.

But I'm in a titanically tight spot . . .

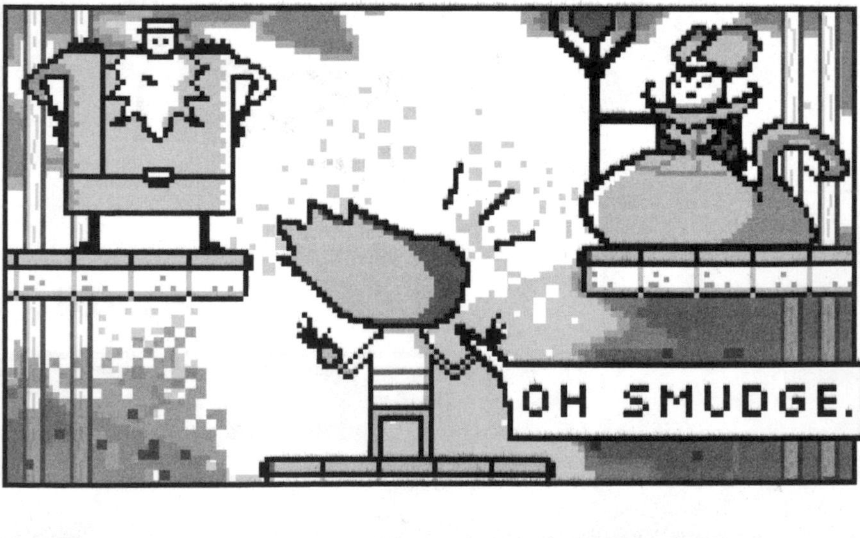
OH SMUDGE.

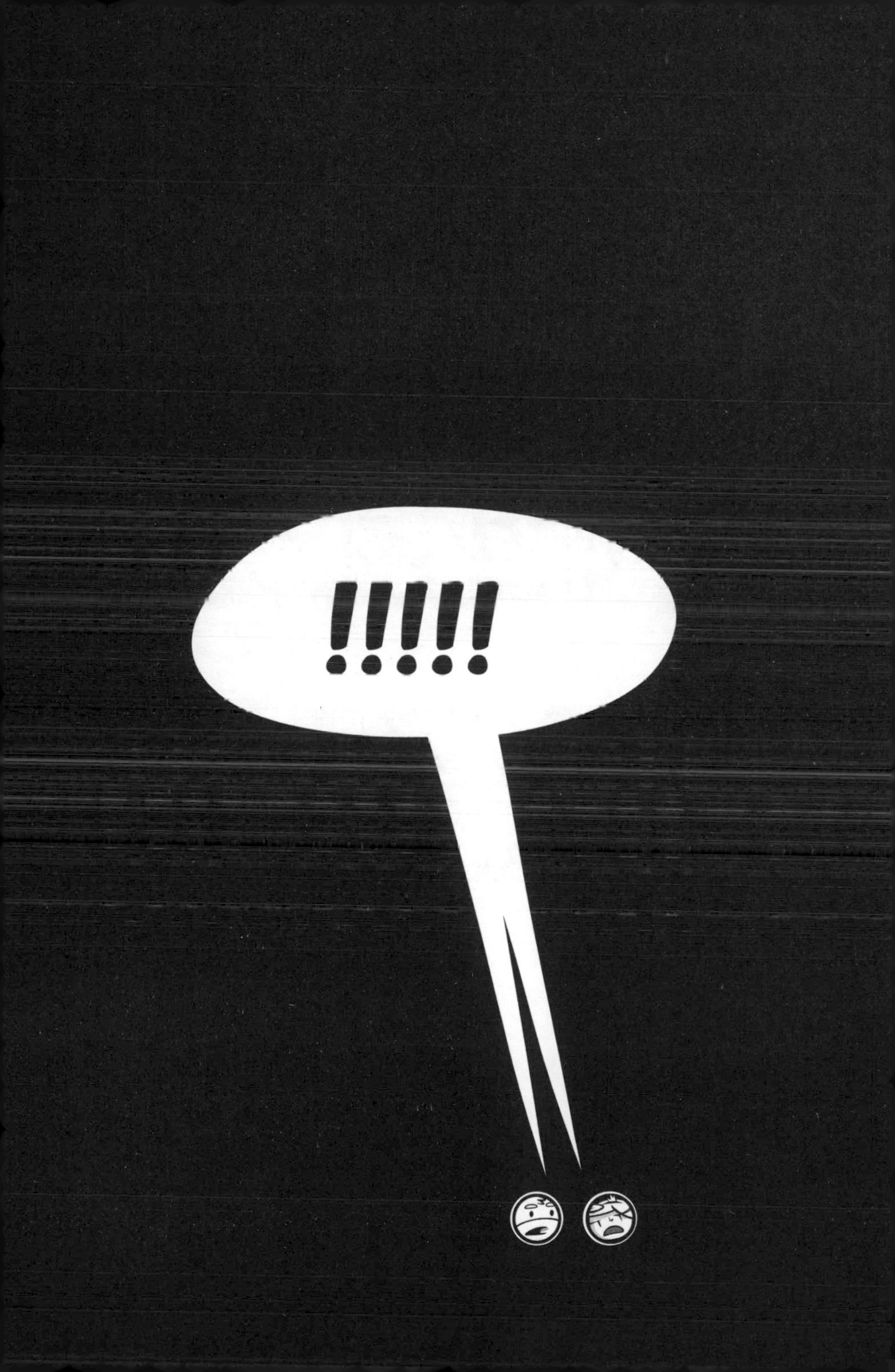
!!!!!

ELEVEN BAD-DUDE VESSELS

My eyes flick back and forth, left to right, right to left, as my archenemies barrel toward me.

With every heavy step, the controller unit shakes. My feet jump.

I notice something: the platform my character is standing on is made of blocks. And wait—this is *A LOT* like that Mario game I used to play back on Earth! And in Mario games, blocks can break. I wonder ...

COSMOE, IF THEY GET *YOU*, IT'S **GAME OVER!** THIS IS **NOT** A DRILL, BUDDY!

That's true ...
But **THIS IS** a drill ...

DIG IT, GOOBER!

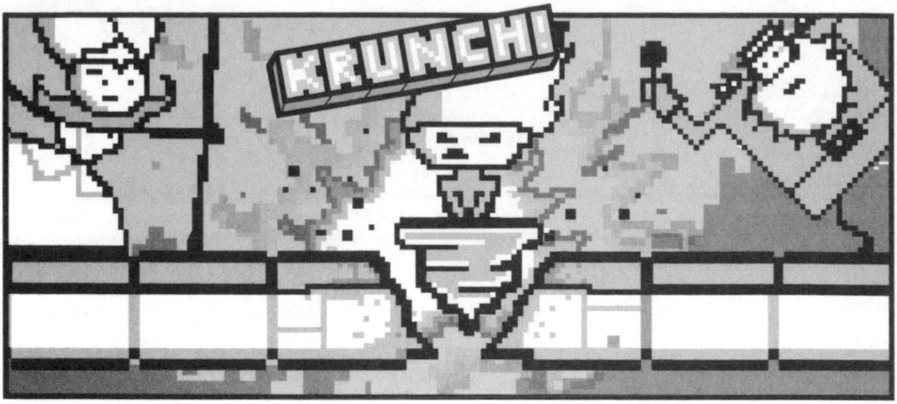
KRUNCH!

BLOCK BREAK ESCAPE!

My character drops down to the lower platform. The queen and General Krax are now on a ***COLLISION COURSE!***

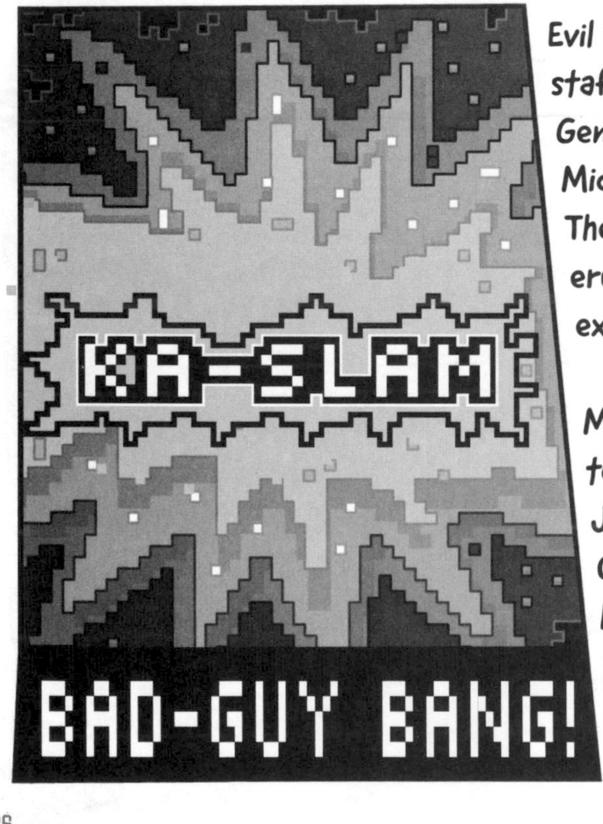
KA-SLAM
BAD-GUY BANG!

Evil Queen Dagger's staff crashes against General Krax's Micro-Blast Bat. There's a sudden eruption of explosive energy!

My eyes flash up to the top of the Jumbo Screen. Evil Queen Dagger's health is draining. So is General Krax's! Oh man, this could be ***IT . . .***

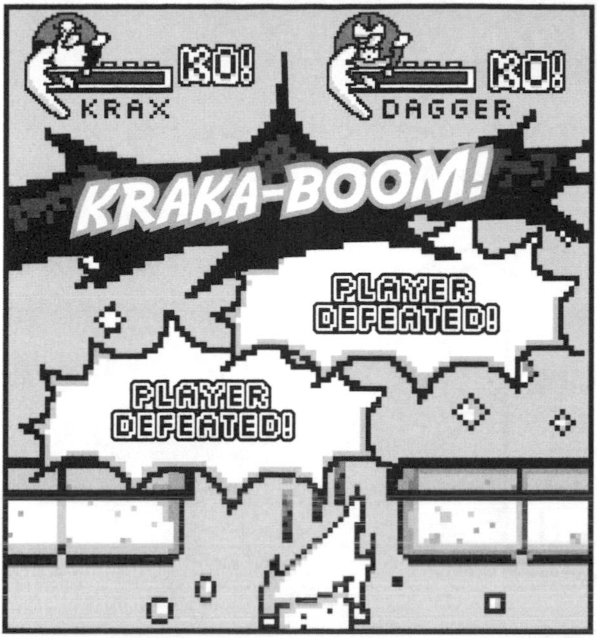
KO!
KRAX
KO!
DAGGER
KRAKA-BOOM!
PLAYER DEFEATED!
PLAYER DEFEATED!

HOT SMUDGE, I DID IT!

But it doesn't feel great, like it does when I beat Humphree at a game of Super Moon Ninja Death Jab.

Really, I just feel relieved . . .

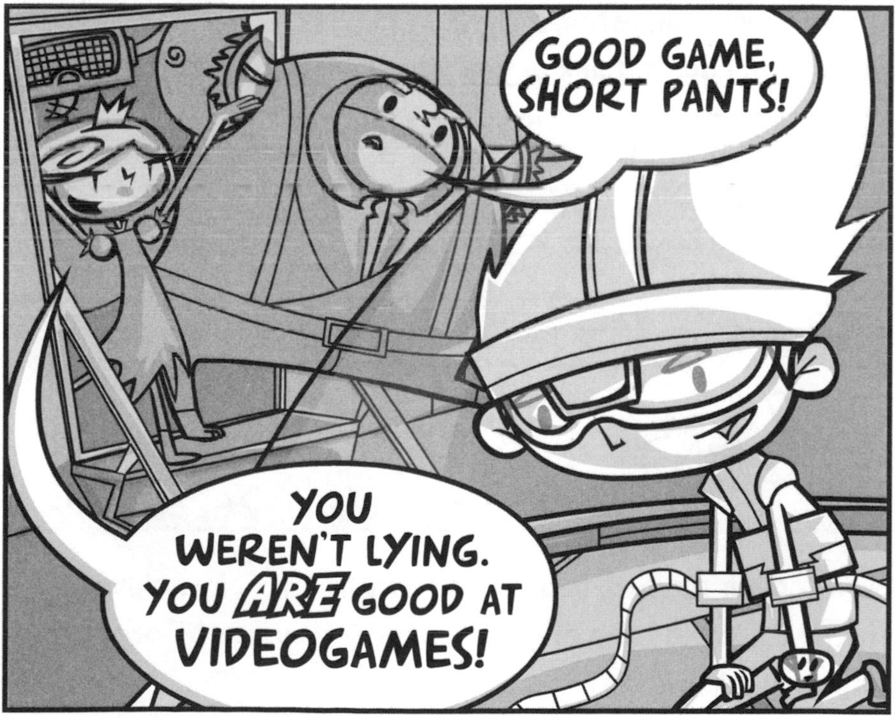
GOOD GAME, SHORT PANTS!
YOU WEREN'T LYING. YOU ARE GOOD AT VIDEOGAMES!

17 SPACE MINUTES LATER . . .

All the player platforms have come together, creating one giant bubble for the award ceremony.

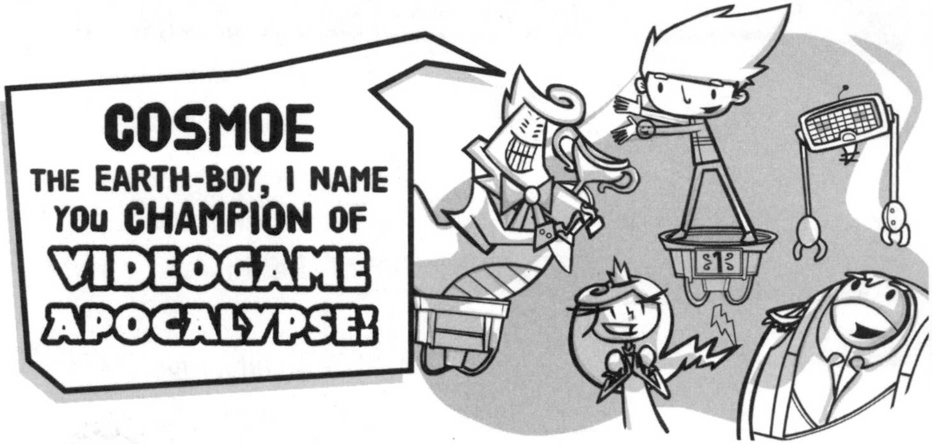
COSMOE THE EARTH-BOY, I NAME YOU CHAMPION OF VIDEOGAME APOCALYPSE!

All the other contestants (*THE LOSERS!*) are looking super ticked off. I don't think any of them are happy that they lost to a dorky kid from lame-o Planet Earth . . .

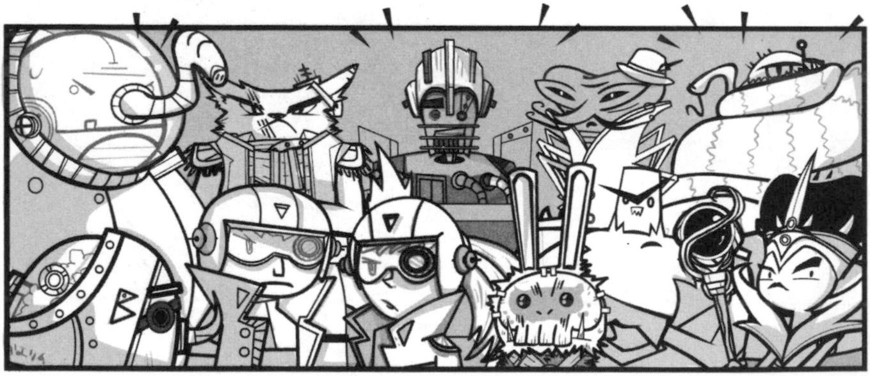

Even though the bad, bad dudes know the trophy holds the final piece of the Map-O-Sphere, they're still pretty surprised when—

HEE-
YAH!

SMASH!

Shattered pieces of the trophy lay in a pile at my feet.
I reach down and pull out the Map-O-Sphere slice.

"Here you go, buddy,"
Humphree says, handing
me the rest of the
Map-O-Sphere.

I take a deep breath.
This is it. I finally hold
every piece of the
Map-O-Sphere in my
hands. I slowly slip
the last piece in . . .

MAP-O-SPHERE
COMPLETE!

Humphree and the princess are grinning. I can tell they're pretty super-proud of me. Looking at my buddies, my whole body feels good and warm, like I've got hot chocolate pumping through my veins.

But that's not the only reason I feel warm. Holding the full Map-O-Sphere, I feel its power. It's hot. It begins shaking. Numbers begin appearing on it: coordinates to the ultimate evil . . .

OK. No more delaying. It's time to end this . . .

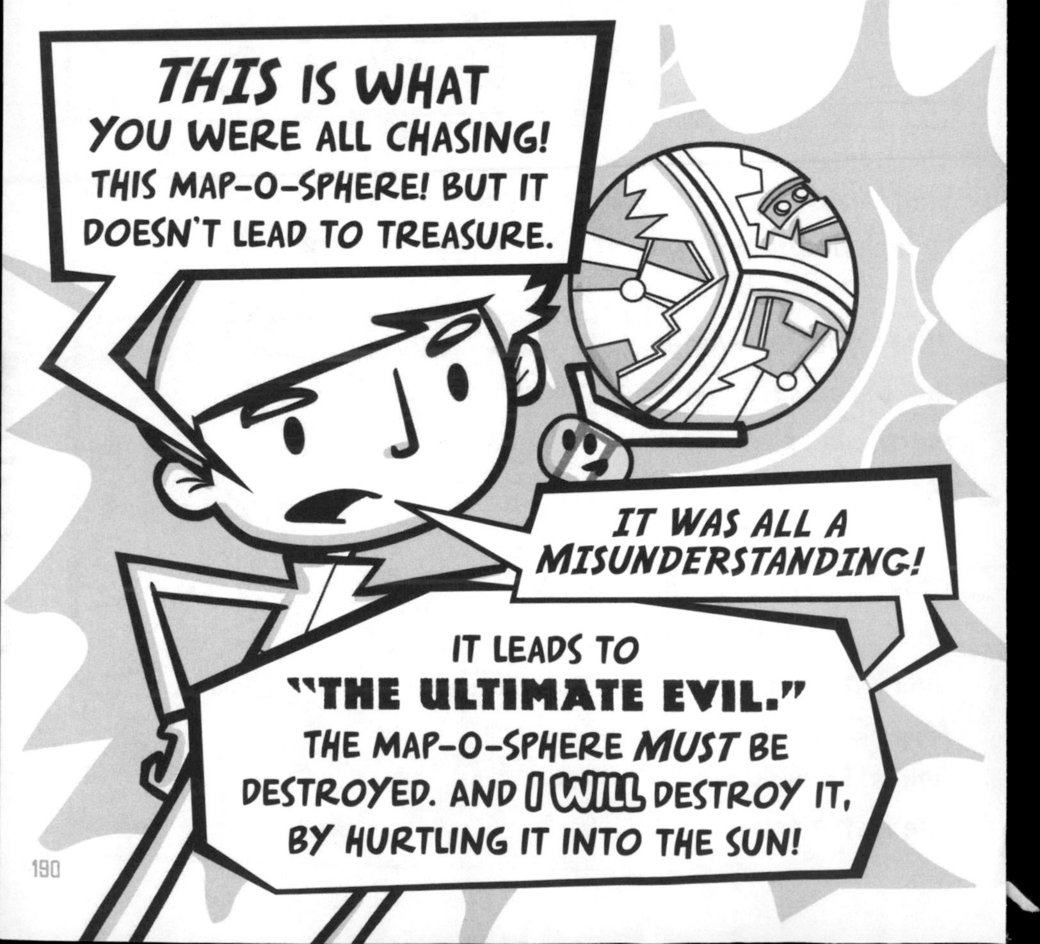
THIS IS WHAT YOU WERE ALL CHASING! THIS MAP-O-SPHERE! BUT IT DOESN'T LEAD TO TREASURE.
IT WAS ALL A MISUNDERSTANDING!
IT LEADS TO **"THE ULTIMATE EVIL."** THE MAP-O-SPHERE *MUST* BE DESTROYED. AND **I WILL** DESTROY IT, BY HURTLING IT INTO THE SUN!

I thought that would be it.

I thought they would all understand that Ultimate Evil is bad. I really did.

But I'm stupid. I'm wrong. I'm very, ***VERY*** wrong . . .

Evil Queen Dagger snarls, raises her energy staff, and points it directly at me and my friends! The globe on her staff begins to glow spooky green as she prepares a mighty, evil blast . . .

"Princess, get down!" I shout, pushing her out of the way.

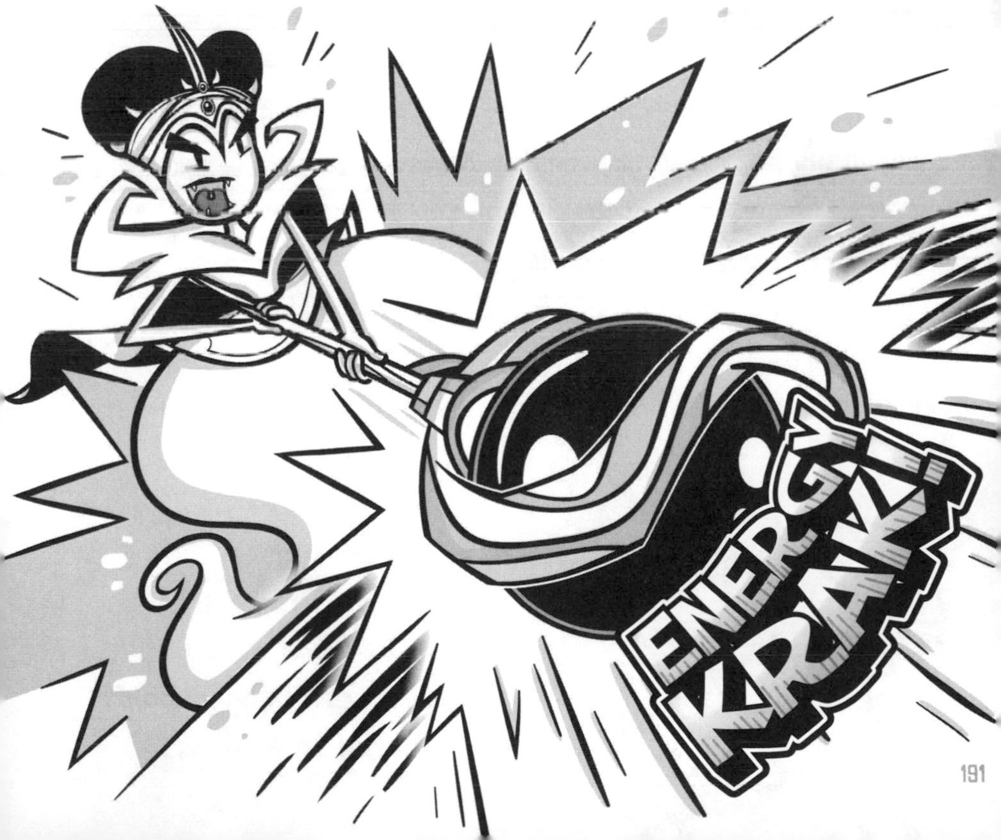
ENERGY KRAK!

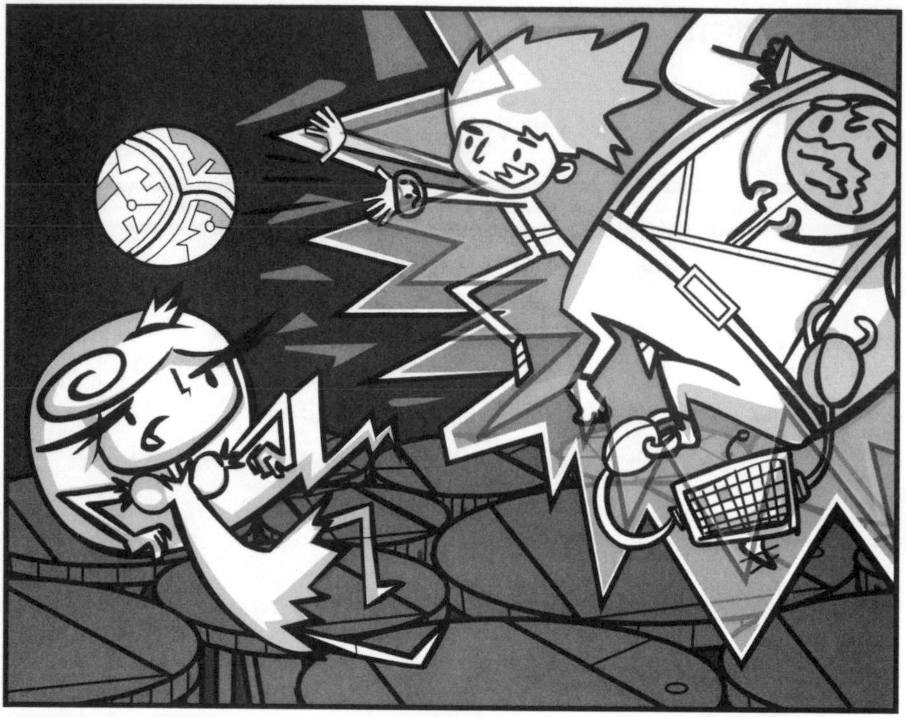

I'm hurtled backward. My fingers loosen as **ENERGY** rips through my body. My grip on the Map-O-Sphere weakens . . .

And then it's out of my hands. The Map-O-Sphere is soaring through the air. ***SPINNING.*** **TUMBLING.**

Everyone's eyes are wide, mouths hanging open, watching it. And then—

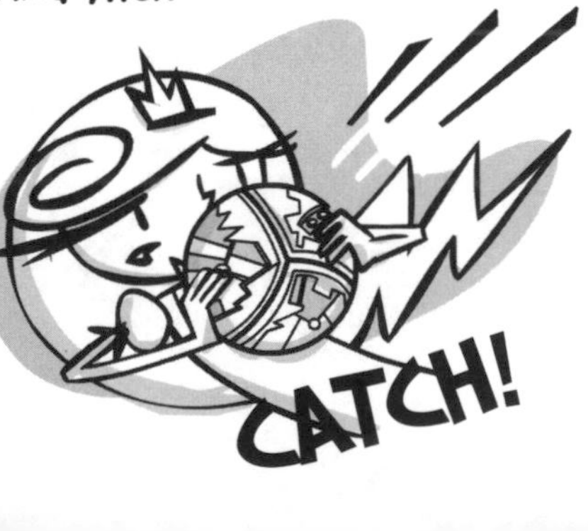
CATCH!

"YES!" I cry out. "Great save, Princess!"

But Evil Queen Dagger won't be defeated so easily . . .

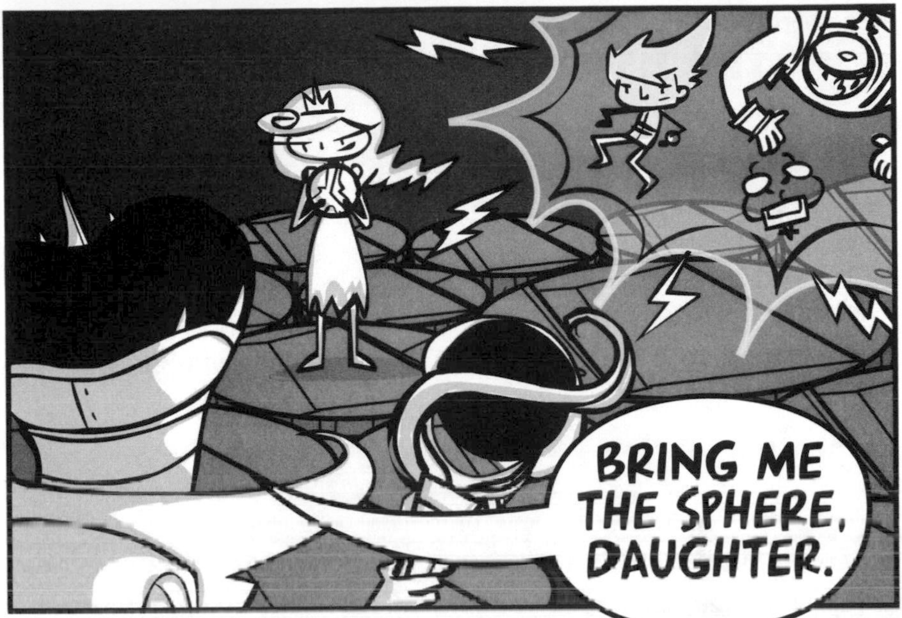
BRING ME THE SPHERE, DAUGHTER.

"No," Princess Dagger says. "We need to destroy it."

The queen laughs, and waves her hand toward me. "So go ahead. Give the sphere to your tiny friend with the goofy hair. Give it to him so he can destroy it."

But the princess doesn't move.

The queen smiles cruelly. "Well, daughter? Why are you hesitating?"

"I'm not," the princess says quietly.

"Yes, you are," the queen says. "Why?"

The princess is trembling now. "I . . . I . . . I don't know . . ."

"Because you are **EVIL!**" the queen roars. "And that sphere leads to **THE ULTIMATE EVIL!** You want to know what it is just as badly as I do."

The princess says nothing.

"Admit it!" the queen says. "Your evil heart longs to know what wicked, malevolent forces that sphere will unleash."

I GULP.

This should be an easy choice for the princess. On one side, yeah, her mother is tugging at her with evil motherly power. But on the other side it's us! Her two best buddies!

Easy breezy, should barely be a choice! I hope . . .

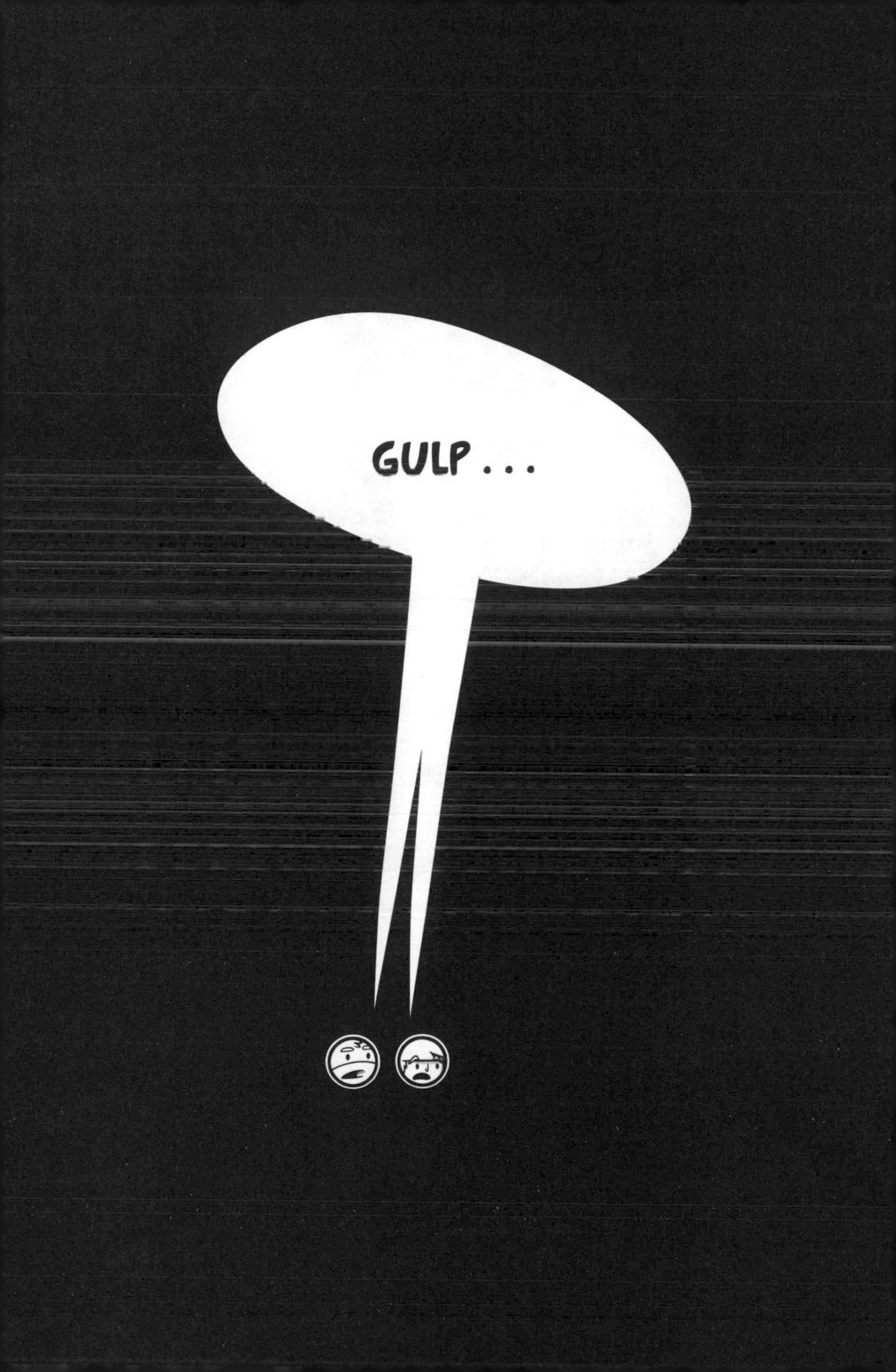
GULP . . .

ONLY COOL GUYS (LIKE US) ALLOWED!

19

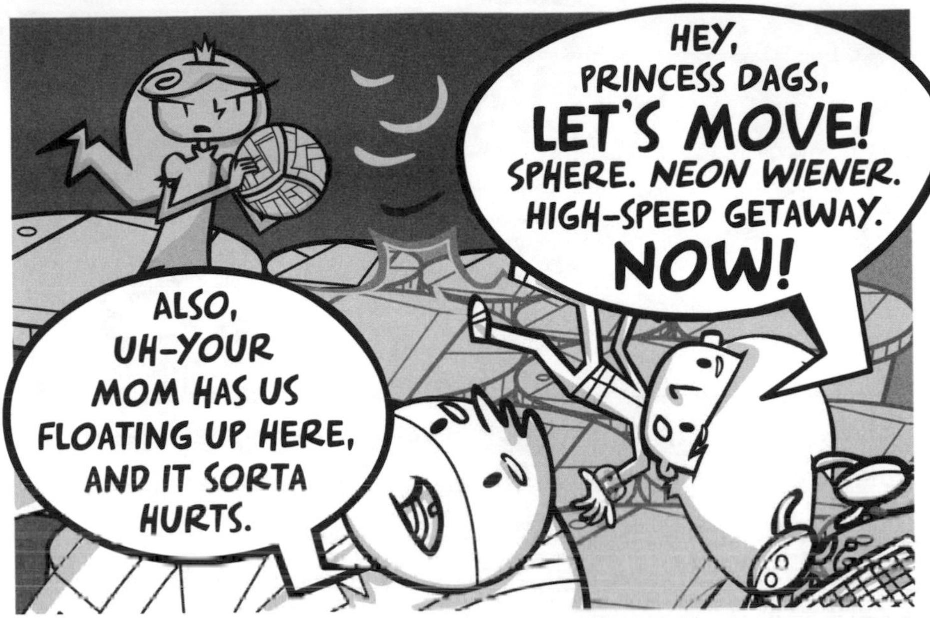
HEY, PRINCESS DAGS, LET'S MOVE! SPHERE. NEON WIENER. HIGH-SPEED GETAWAY. NOW!
ALSO, UH—YOUR MOM HAS US FLOATING UP HERE, AND IT SORTA HURTS.

Princess Dagger turns and shoots me a look so icy cold that I feel a chill creep all the way down my spine and back up again. There's a squeezing feeling in my gut—a feeling that says we might not be out of trouble yet . . .

A feeling that says I've underestimated the strength of the evil inside my friend. That the evil blood pumping through Princess Dagger's veins is more powerful than my tiny human brain ever imagined.

And then she says it.

Two words.

Two words that feel like a double spinning roundhouse kick to my emotion box.

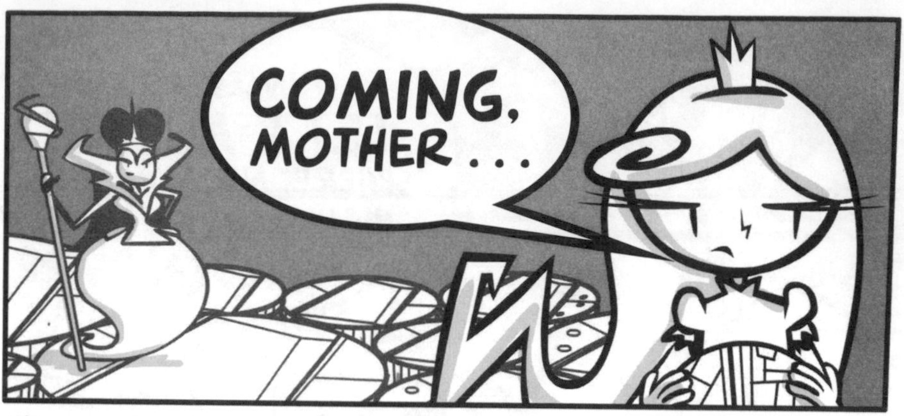
COMING, MOTHER . . .

"Hurry, daughter," the evil queen says, lowering her staff. Humphree and I tumble to the floor of the contest dome.

Rubbing my head, I mutter, "This isn't going down like I hoped . . ."

Humphree yanks me to my feet and pulls me, stumbling, running, toward the *Wiener.* "Knowing the evil queen," he says, "it's about to get a lot **WORSE . . .**"

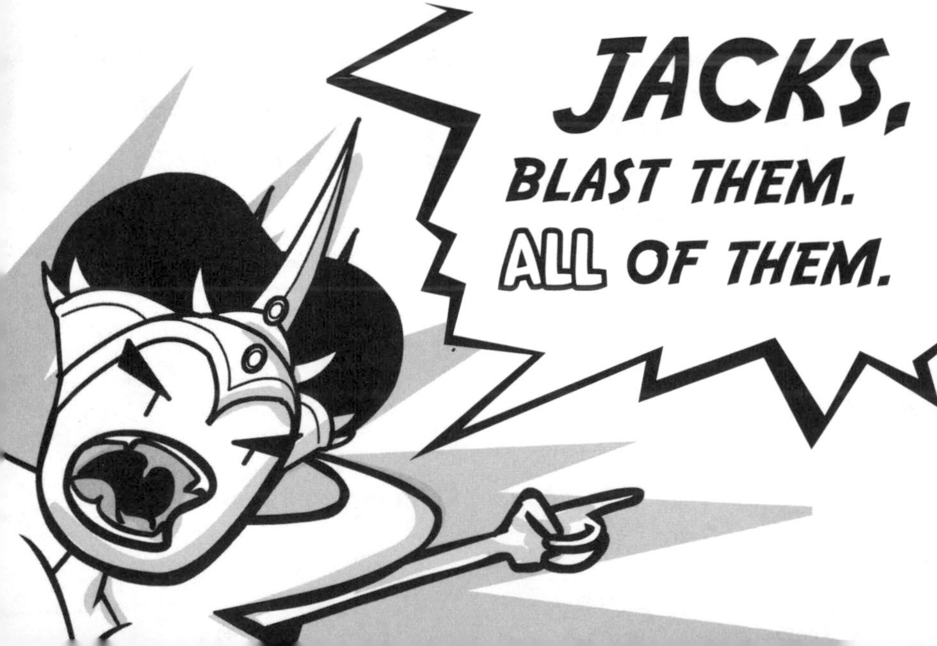
JACKS,
BLAST THEM.
ALL OF THEM.

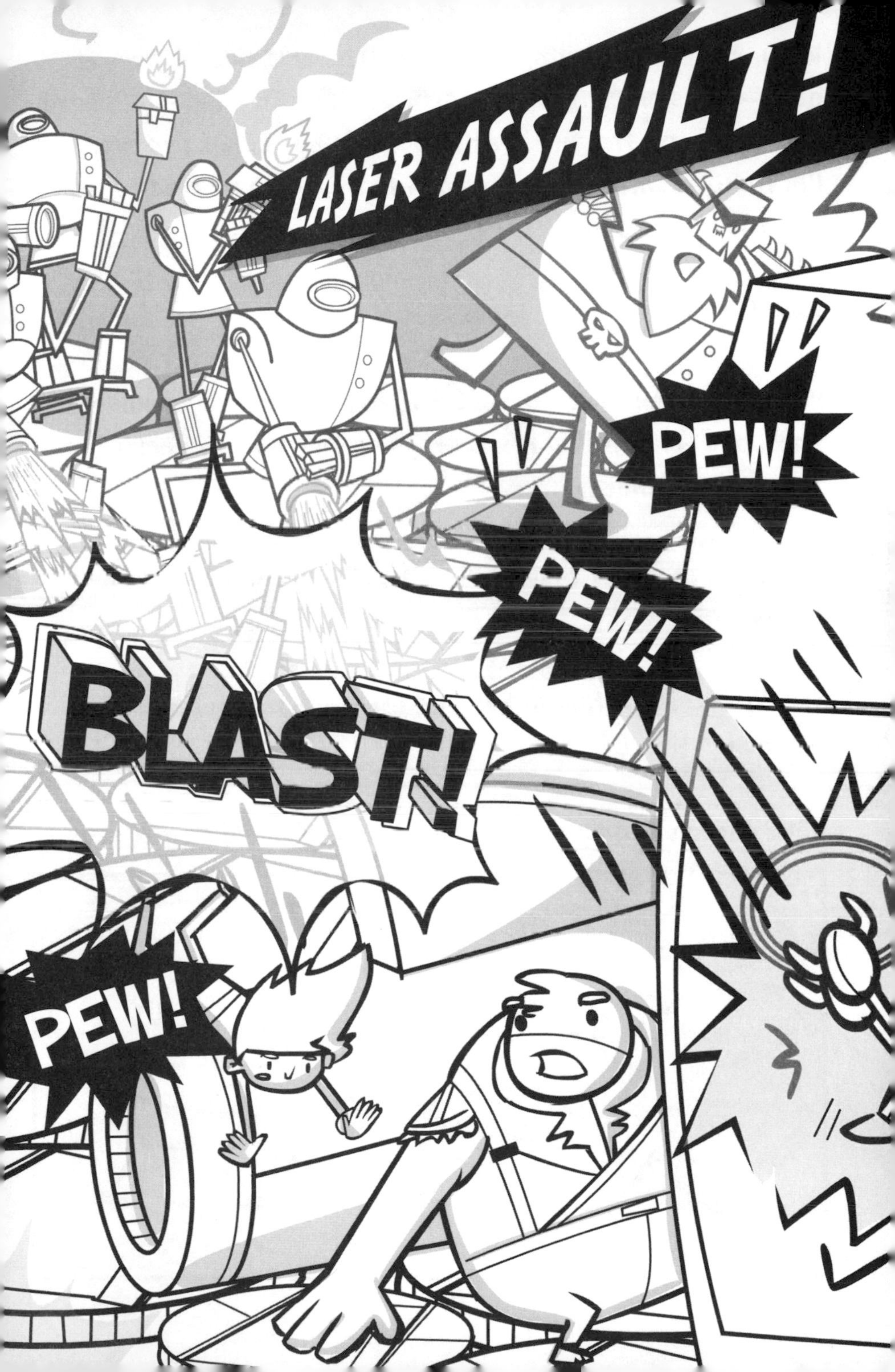
LASER ASSAULT!
PEW!
PEW!
BLAST!
PEW!

When the smoke clears, Evil Queen Dagger's ship, *Biggun*, is gone—and along with it, the princess and the Map-O-Sphere. I'm trying to catch my breath, but it's not coming to me. I'm too overwhelmed: too mega-angry, too betrayed, and too—just—***SMUDGE!***

And it appears I'm not the only one . . .

"The evil queen tried to blast me! ***ME!*** I'm her loyal minion! She'll pay for this!!!" Krax roars, sounding a little angry and a lot offended.

"Yeah!" Zan Ponda shouts. "Let's chase her down and blow her out of the sky!"

"We'll find the Ultimate Evil and create our own Dark Kingdom!" HW-86 declares.

"And there will only be cool guys like us allowed!" Krax says.

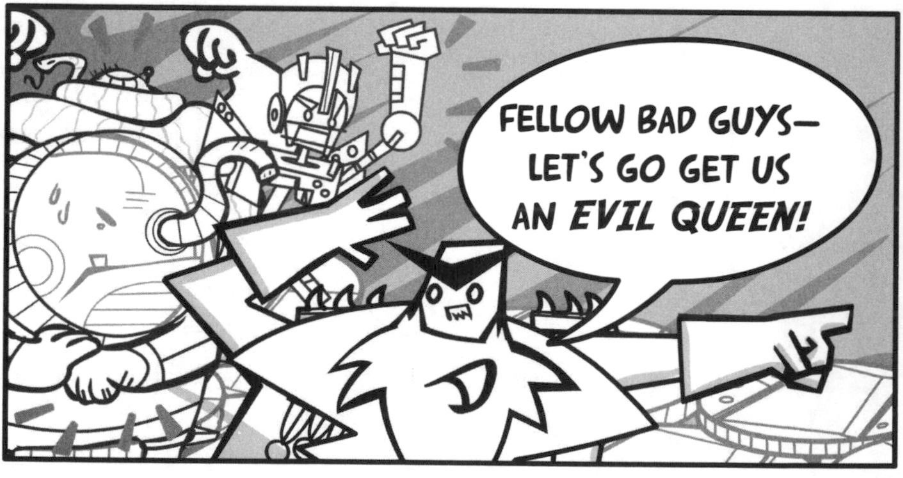
FELLOW BAD GUYS—LET'S GO GET US AN *EVIL QUEEN!*

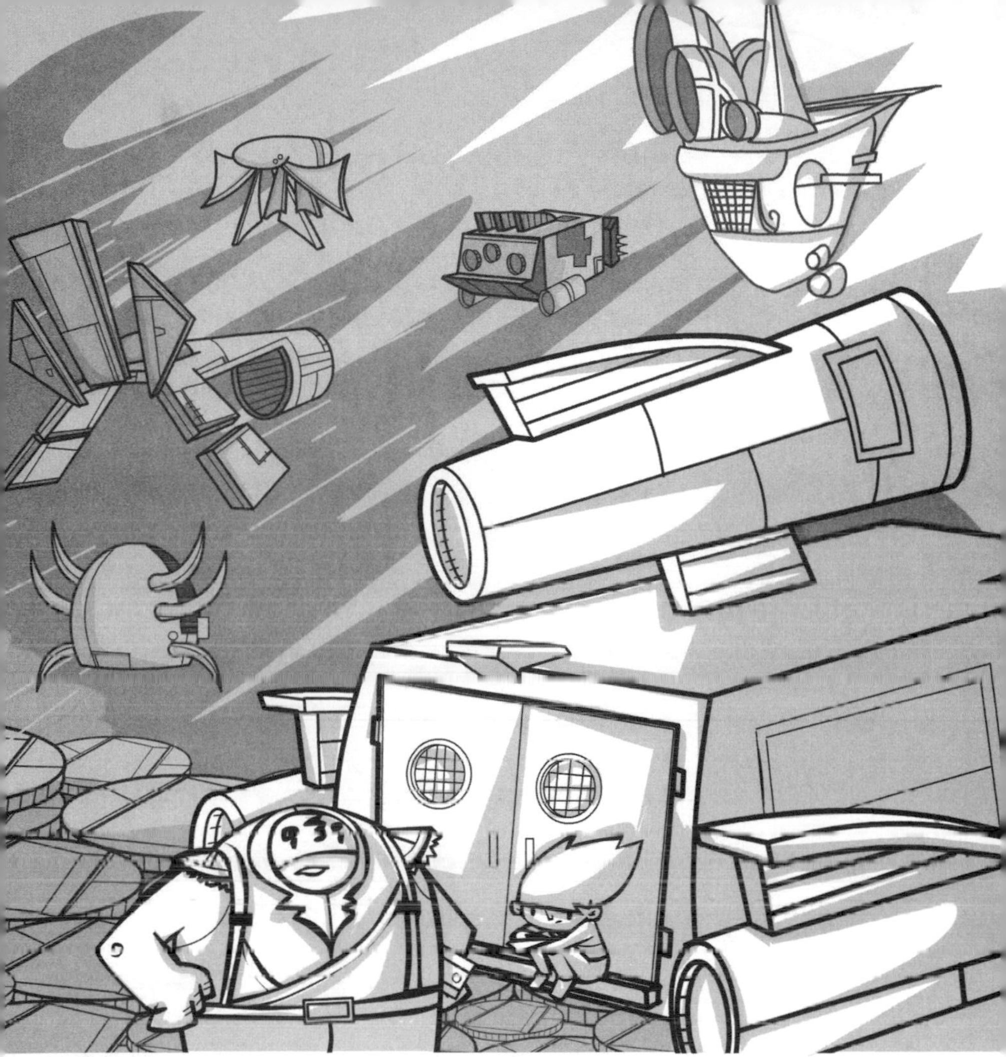

The entire videogame contest dome shakes, and there's a tremendous, deafening roar as bad-guy ships blast off in chase of Evil Queen Dagger.

Only one ship remains. ***MY SHIP.***

There's only one word to describe how I feel right now.

Actually, three words: **BIG-TIME BETRAYED.**

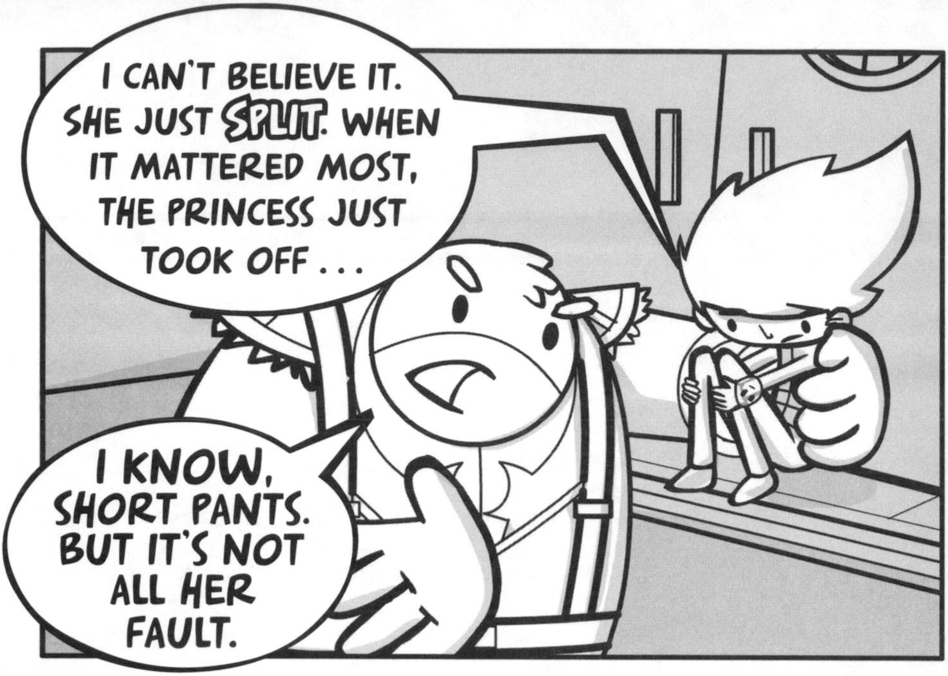
I CAN'T BELIEVE IT. SHE JUST SPLIT. WHEN IT MATTERED MOST, THE PRINCESS JUST TOOK OFF . . .
I KNOW, SHORT PANTS. BUT IT'S NOT ALL HER FAULT.

Humphree continues, "That poor princess has **EVILNESS** in her system . . . Remember, her evil genes?"

"That's no excuse!" I shout. "I wouldn't just ditch you or Goober or F.R.E.D. because my genes told me to!"

"Picture it like this, bud. In her heart, the princess knows what's good:

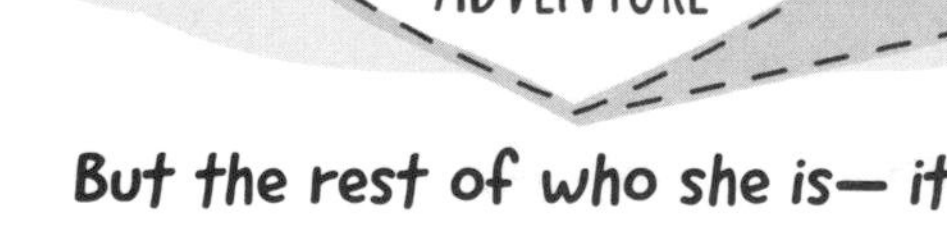
• STOMPING OUT BULLIES
• BEING RIGHT-ON
• ADVENTURE

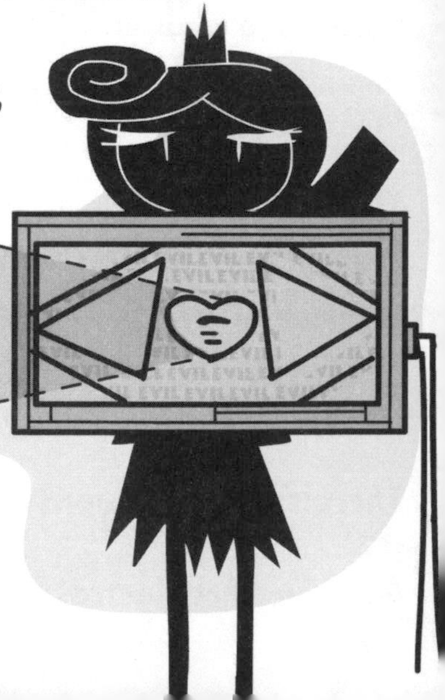

But the rest of who she is— it's just **EVIL** pumping through her."

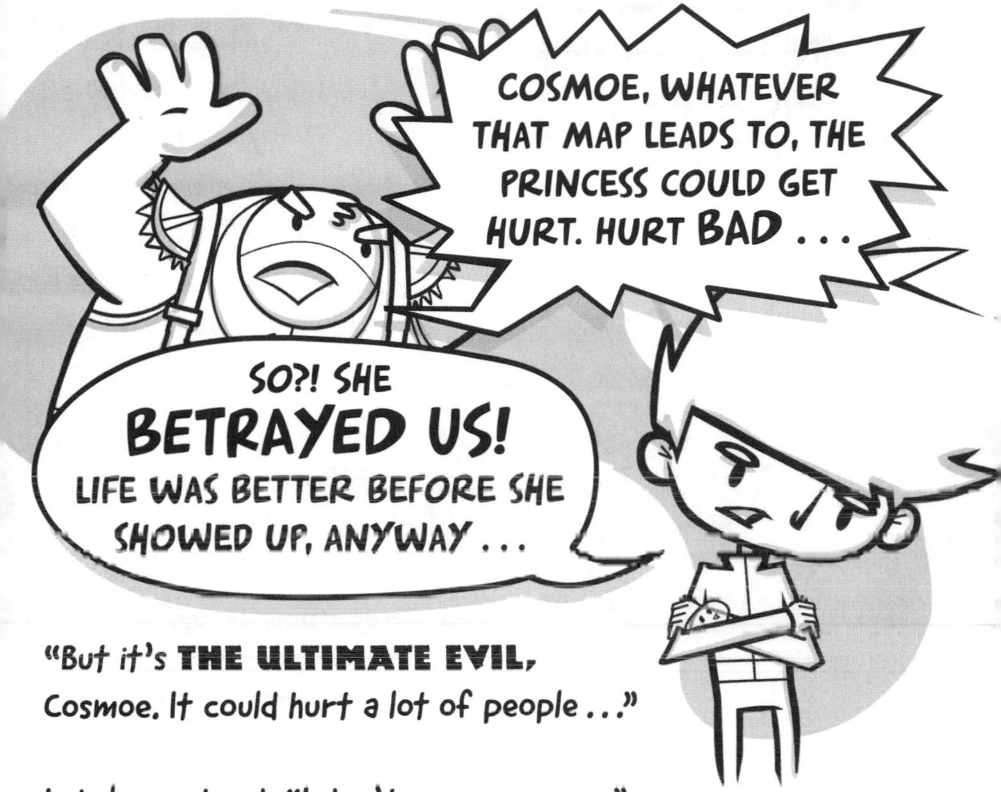
COSMOE, WHATEVER THAT MAP LEADS TO, THE PRINCESS COULD GET HURT. HURT BAD . . .
SO?! SHE BETRAYED US! LIFE WAS BETTER BEFORE SHE SHOWED UP, ANYWAY . . .

"But it's **THE ULTIMATE EVIL,** Cosmoe. It could hurt a lot of people . . ."

I shake my head. "I don't care anymore."

"Bud, you once swore an oath to fight space jerks in all their many forms. And the Ultimate Evil is gonna be ***REALLY*** jerky. So you need to decide: Are you going to fight it, or are you going to give up on your oath?"

I swallow. There's a big lump in my throat. It's like suddenly, all this stuff is too much for me. Too much for my tiny Earth hands to handle.

But before I can think on it any more, there's a crackling sound, like a broken stereo. A busted-sounding buzzing . . .

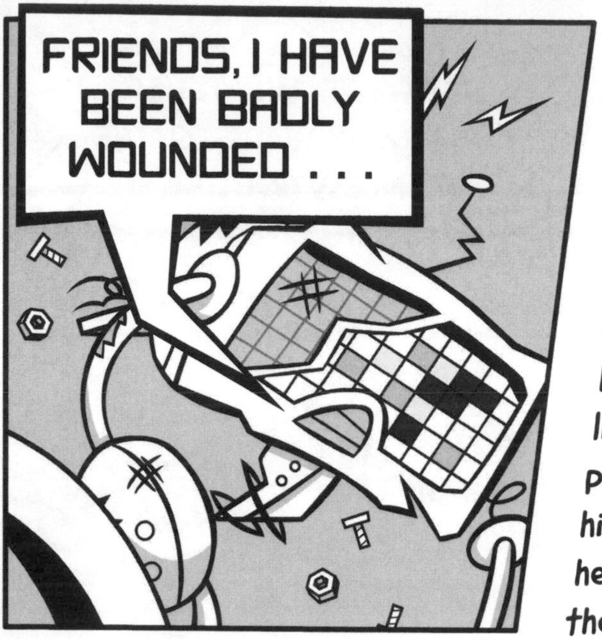
FRIENDS, I HAVE BEEN BADLY WOUNDED . . .

"F.R.E.D.!!!" I cry out, leaping to my feet.

Sparks are shooting out of his side. He's flying all weird, like he's hovering with a limp, if that's even possible. I run toward him, but before I can help him, he crashes to the dome floor.

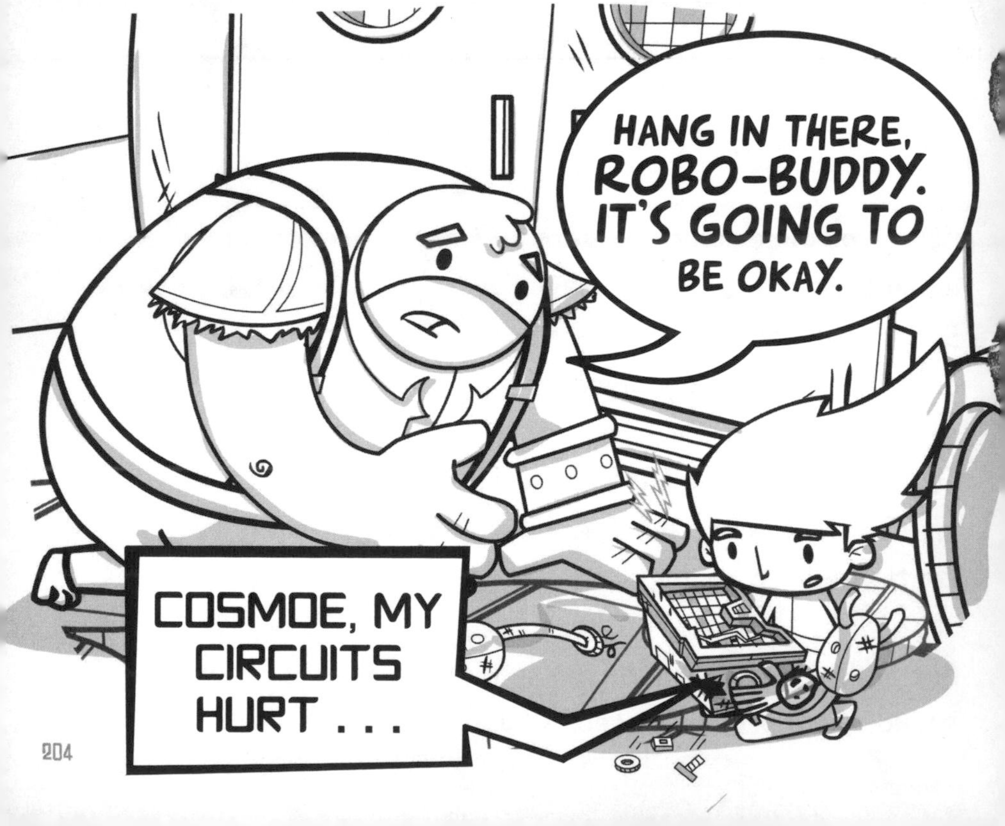
HANG IN THERE, ROBO-BUDDY. IT'S GOING TO BE OKAY.
COSMOE, MY CIRCUITS HURT . . .

GREAT. I'M TALKING TO MYSELF.

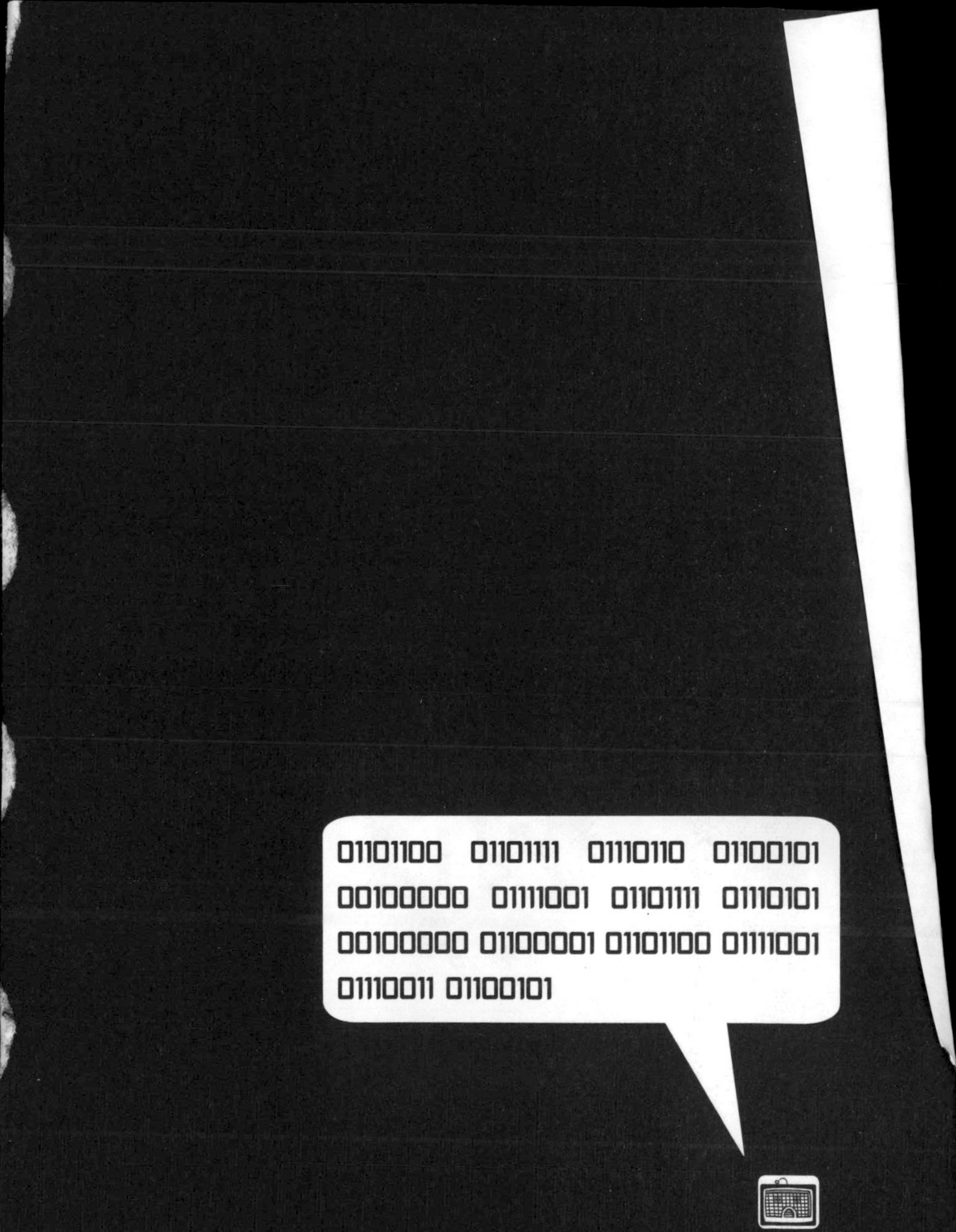
01101100 01101111 01110110 01100101 00100000 01111001 01101111 01110101 00100000 01100001 01101100 01111001 01110011 01100101

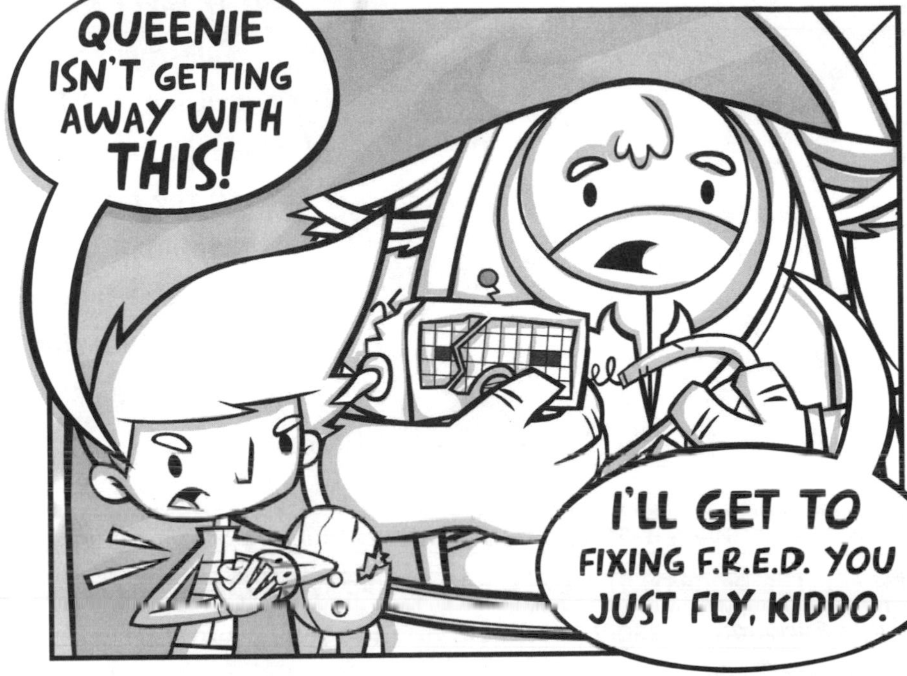
QUEENIE ISN'T GETTING AWAY WITH THIS!
I'LL GET TO FIXING F.R.E.D. YOU JUST FLY, KIDDO.

I slide into the captain's chair and take a deep breath. Big Humphree and I have been in some double-blaster-barreled adventures, but nothing like this . . .

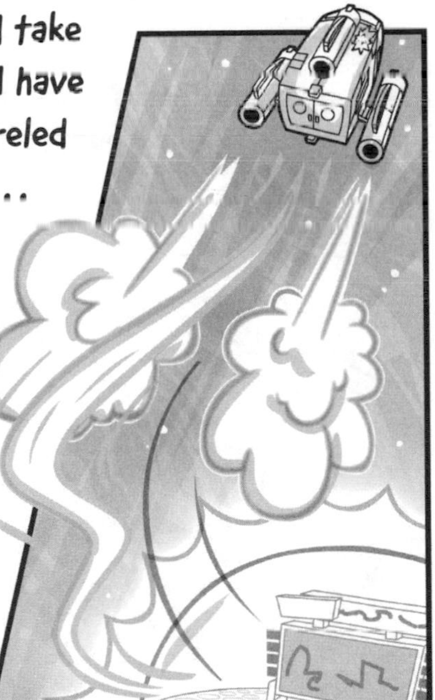

I ask myself, "Can you do this, Cosmoe? Really, can you?"

I nod. "Yes, Cosmoe. I can."

Great. I'm talking to myself. That means this is heavyweight business. That means it's time to fly.

It takes some full-throttle cruising, but I manage to catch up to the posse of bad dudes. I lay off the gas a smidge, hanging back, keeping my eye on the ships' taillights.

I can see all eleven of the bad-dude vessels—but *Biggun* is by far the biggest. The evil queen's ship is **_ENORMOUS._** A dreadnought: deadly powerful and loaded up with an arsenal of evil weapons.

I flip on the windshield's binoc-u-zoom feature, bringing up a digital view screen. I zoom in on Evil Queen Dagger's ship. I spot her, standing at the stern of the ship. And— **_UNBELIEVABLE_**—she's staring right at me . . .

Looking into her evil eyes, I can't believe I was feeling sorry for myself.

Not anymore.

Now I'm mad. Not just mad. Ticked off to the trillionth power. Blood boiling hotter than the Sixth Sun of Solune.

Princess Dagger betrayed us? OK, that I can handle. I've been burned before.

But her evil mom, stealing our map? Her mom's robo-minions just flat-out **SHOOTING** F.R.E.D.? And now she's just watching me with a cold-bloodedly cruel grin!

We're going to have words over that.
Tough words. Fightin' words . . .

It's a long flight to the farthest reaches of the galaxy. I'm sort of zoning out, thinking about my revenge, when brake lights begin dotting the starry horizon. The convoy is slowing down. I pull back on the throttle, drifting behind the group.

And then I see it . . .

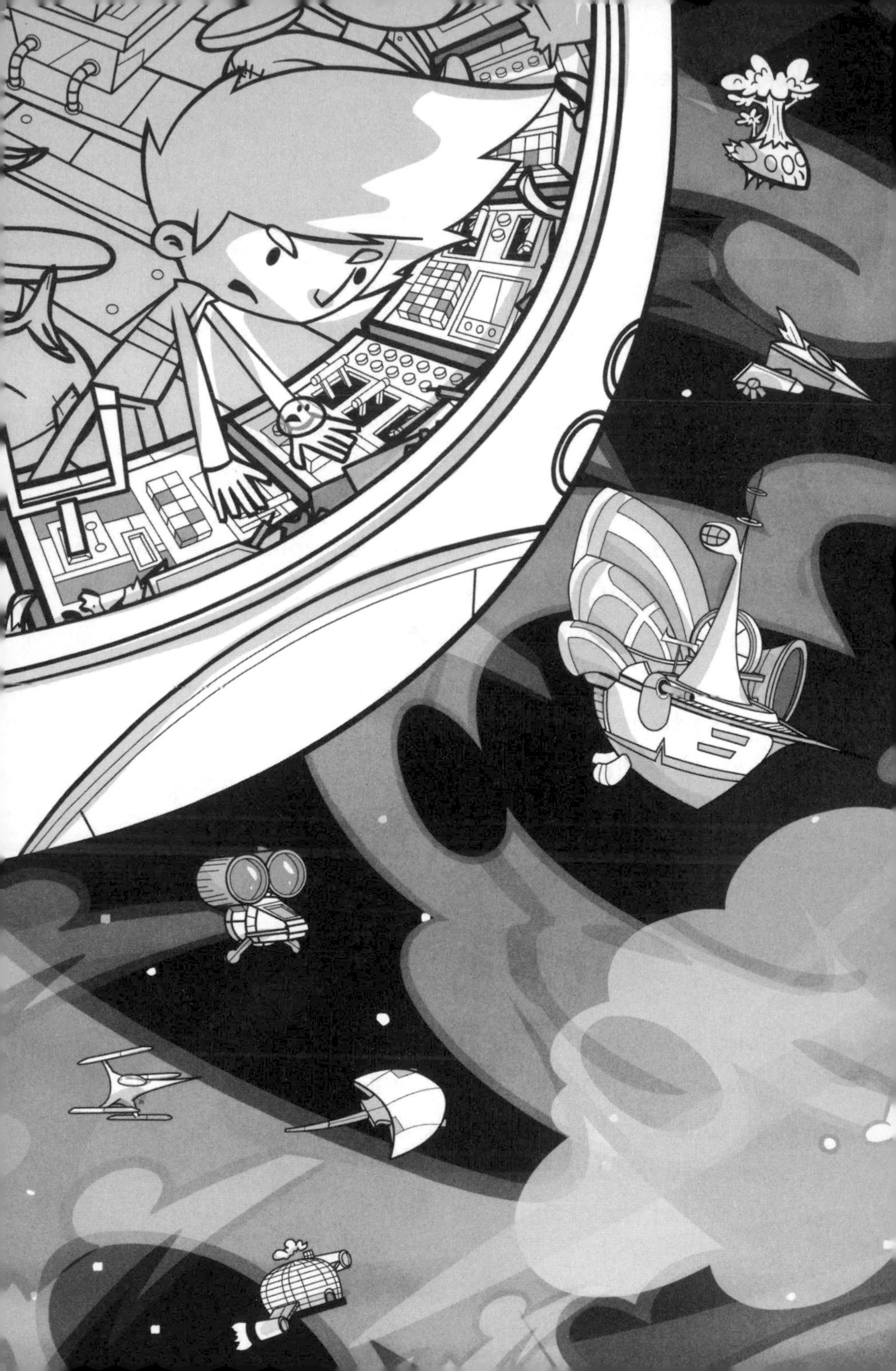

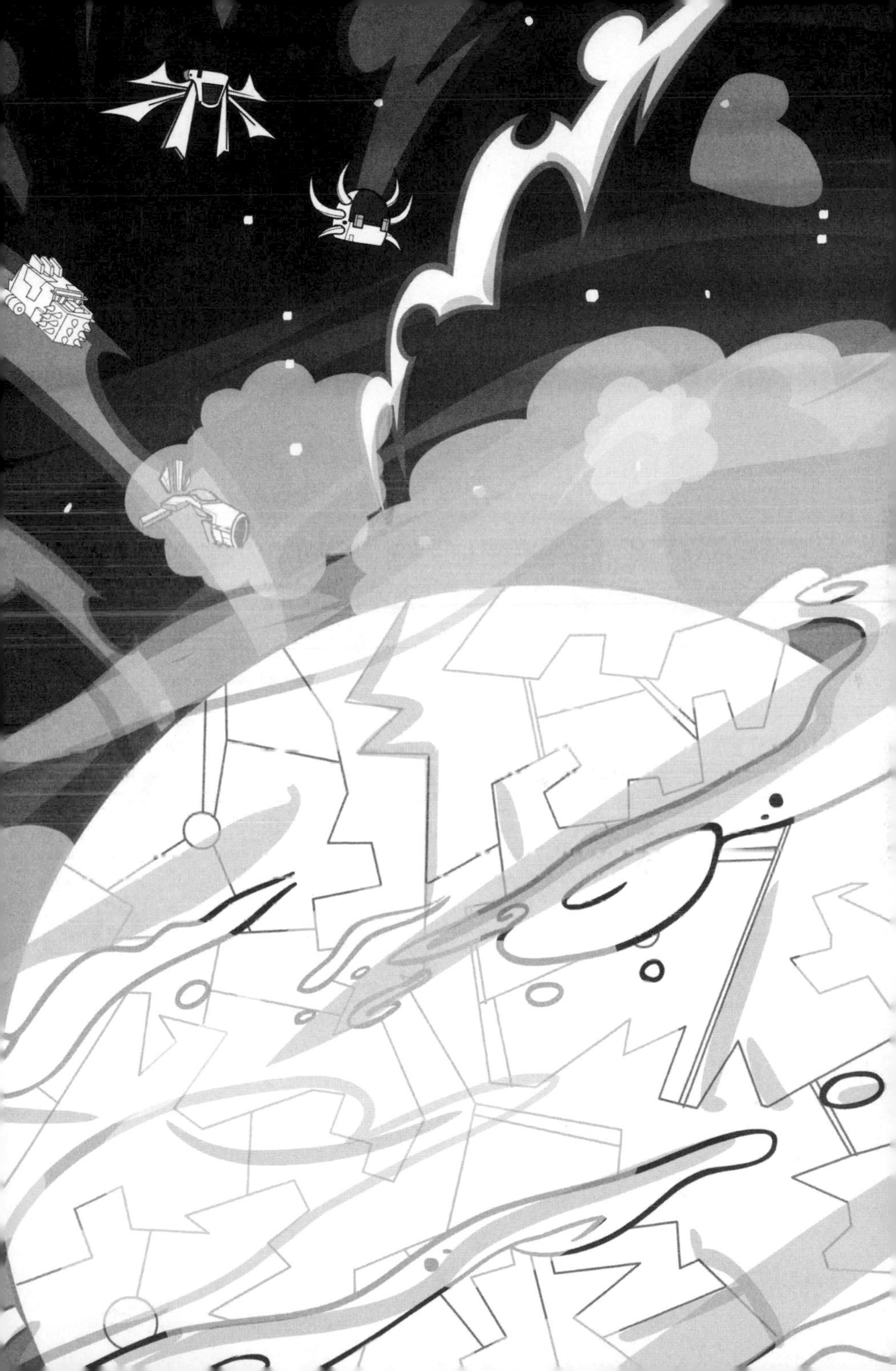

I switch off the main engines and put the *Wiener* in hover-park. Dashing into the hangout room, I say, "Humphree, we're here." I'm trying not to sound nervous, but I hear my voice crack.

F.R.E.D. is on the floor, with his side panel open and wires sticking out. Humphree's thick fingers are turning a screw-twister. "One second," Humphree says.

"How is he?" I ask. "How's F.R.E.D.?"

MEGA-DOG! WORM WRESTLING! BEST SEAT IN THE HOUSE! GET 'EM WHILE THEY'RE HOT!

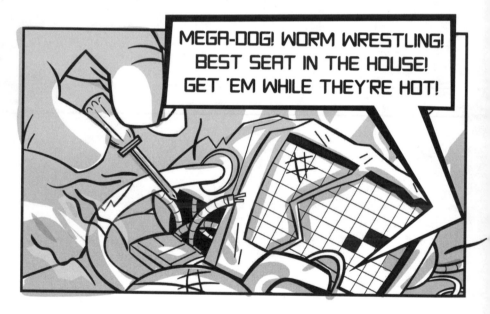

"He's pretty fried," Humphree says, standing up. "He's spewing nonsense. But I'll fix him."

Humphree wipes off some grease and oil and follows me through the ship. Coming into the cockpit, I hear him softly say, "Oh boy . . ."

HOW COME NOBODY'S GOING DOWN THERE, YOU THINK?

PROBABLY ALL **SPOOKED.**

I turn to my Bronkle friend. "Are **YOU** spooked?"

Humphree shrugs. "I don't spook easy. But unexplored planets? Never know what you'll find. Especially when you follow a map to one because it's supposed to be evil. Also, it **IS** surrounded in mist."

"Just that word 'mist,'" I say. "It's creepy, right?"

Humphree shakes his head slowly. "It sure isn't 'not-creepy.'" He stands up. "I need to keep working on F.R.E.D. Buzz me if any of these bozos—"

"Look!" I say, cutting him off. "A ship is going down there!"

We both lean closer to the windshield, squinting.

Of course . . .

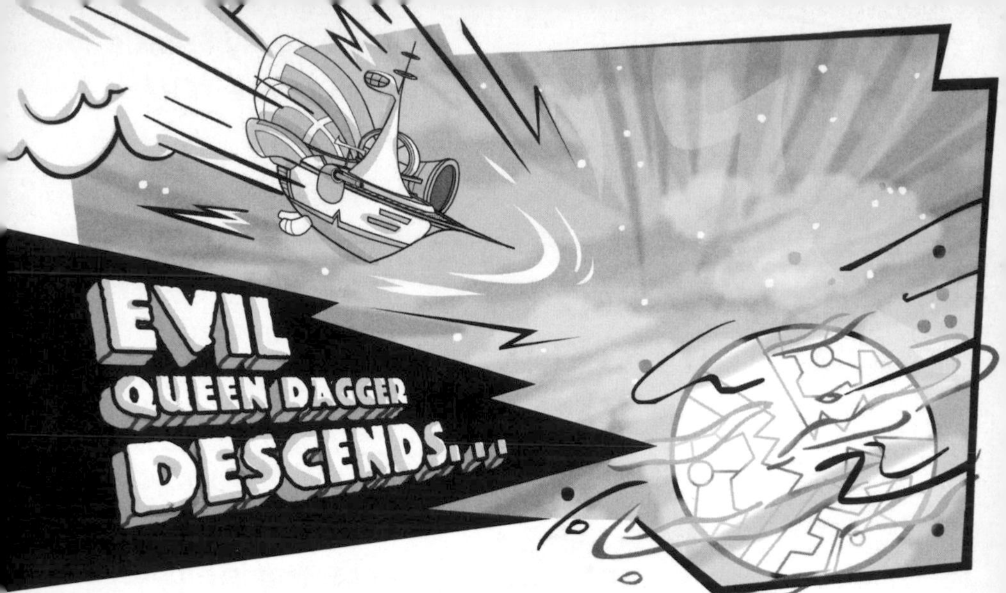
EVIL
QUEEN DAGGER
DESCENDS...

I clench my jaw. "I'm going after them."

"You don't have to play tough, Cosmoe," Humphree says as he turns to go retrieve F.R.E.D. "I know you're spooked . . ."

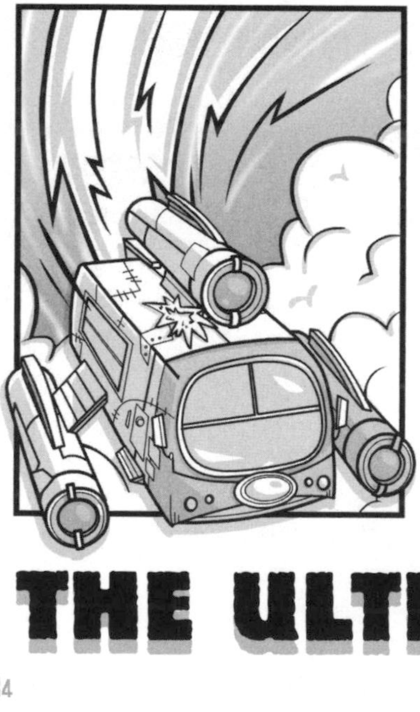

"I'm too heated to be spooked," I say. With that, I throw the throttle forward, the thrusters kick in, and the *Neon Wiener* begins speeding toward the strange planet's surface.

It's time to find out what all the fuzz is about—time to learn the truth about . . .

THE ULTIMATE EVIL.

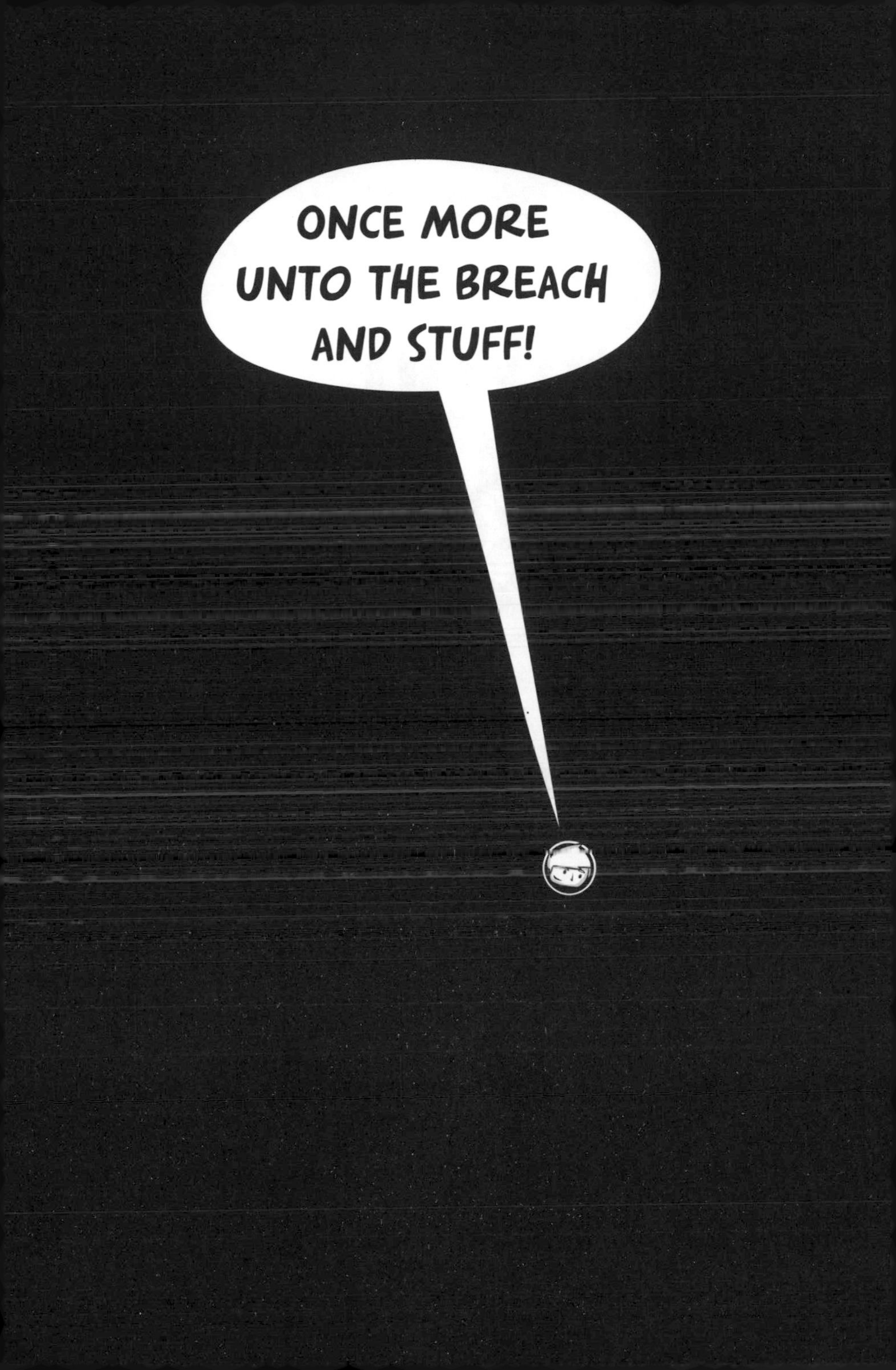
ONCE MORE UNTO THE BREACH AND STUFF!

YOU COULD BE AWESOME!

21

I flip on the big headlights as the ship touches down, allowing me a full view of the planet's surface. It looks smooth. Like, ***REALLY*** smooth: no mountains, no canyons, no rocks, no dirt, no nothing. It's like a marble . . .

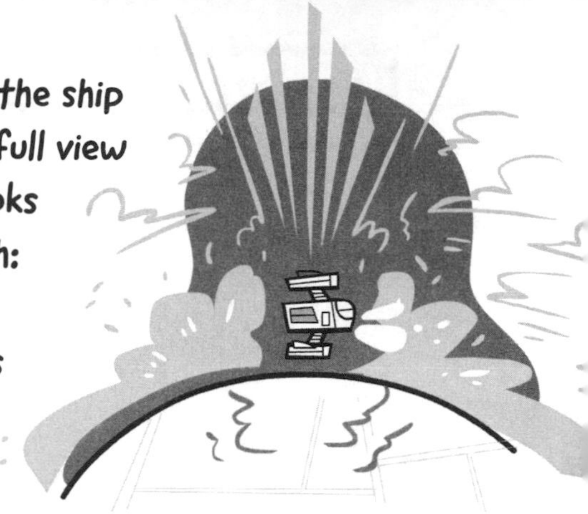

A moment later, Humphree steps back into the cockpit, now carrying F.R.E.D. "So what are we looking at?"

"Not sure. Any chance F.R.E.D. can clue us in?"

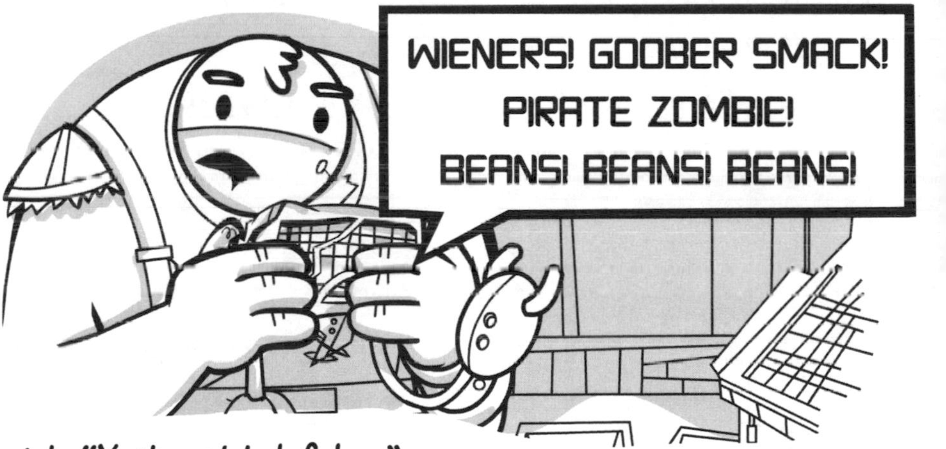
WIENERS! GOOBER SMACK! PIRATE ZOMBIE! BEANS! BEANS! BEANS!

I sigh. "Yeah, not helpful . . ."

Humphree checks the ship's instruments. "Doesn't say anything about life on the planet, but it looks like the air is breathable."

That's all I needed to hear. Time to do this thing . . .

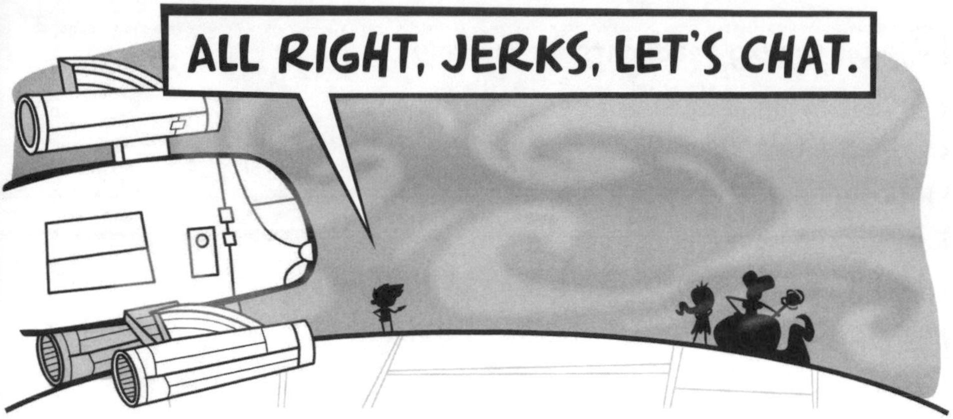
ALL RIGHT, JERKS, LET'S CHAT.

The princess hangs her head. She looks like a kid in school who got caught shooting spitballs at the teacher.

I can feel Humphree watching me from the *Wiener.* He probably wants to tell me I'm putting us in serious danger, like get-your-head-chopped-off-by-the-evil-queen-type danger. But I don't give a smudge. I'm handling this . . .

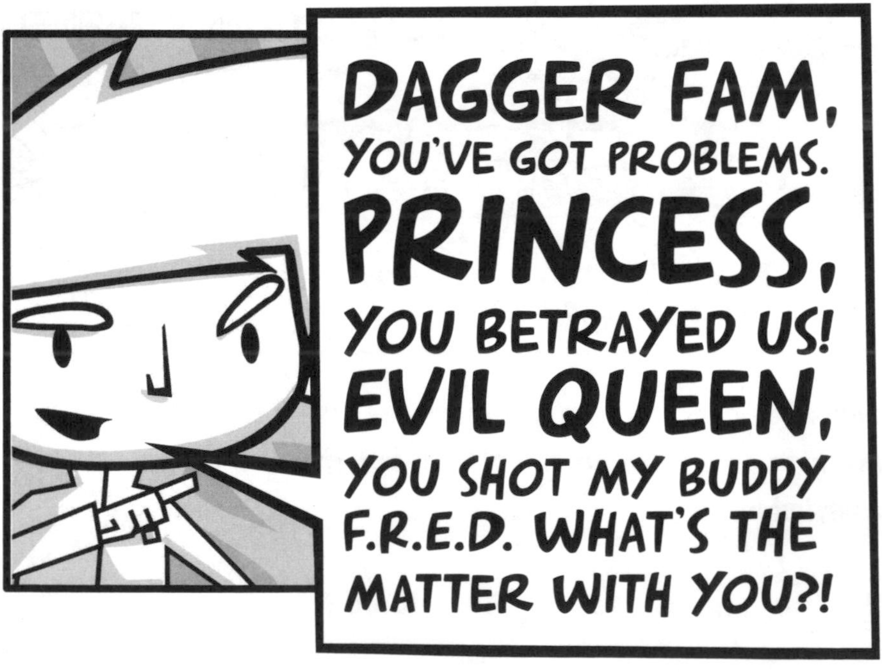
DAGGER FAM, YOU'VE GOT PROBLEMS. PRINCESS, YOU BETRAYED US! EVIL QUEEN, YOU SHOT MY BUDDY F.R.E.D. WHAT'S THE MATTER WITH YOU?!

MY MOM TOLD ME I WOULD **ALWAYS BE EVIL.** I WAS TRYING NOT TO BE, **BUT SHE'S RIGHT . . .**

YOU'RE NOT EVIL! YOU'VE GOT A HEART FULL OF ADVENTURE! YOU COULD BE AWESOME!

"Listen," I continue. "Would someone *EVIL* care about keeping the ship clean and making Humphree and me be responsible non-slobs?!"

The princess sort of shrugs, still hanging her head.

"Would someone *EVIL* cheer me on when I was freaking out and tell me I could beat the Boss Worm?!"

Again, the princess sort of shrugs.

"Would someone *EVIL* blast General Krax and save us when he had us cornered?!"

Before the princess can shrug again, I say, "**NO!** Because you're **NOT** evil, Princess. You're a good friend! You don't have to be like your family! No one does!"

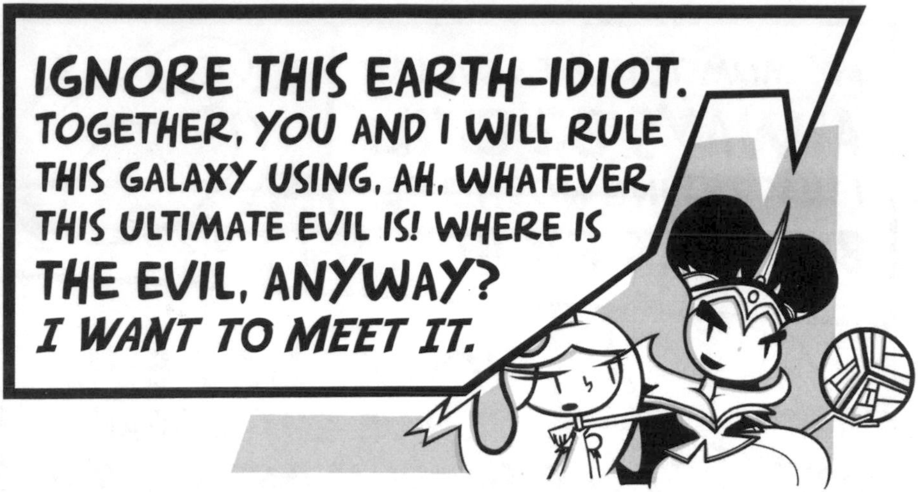
IGNORE THIS EARTH-IDIOT. TOGETHER, YOU AND I WILL RULE THIS GALAXY USING, AH, WHATEVER THIS ULTIMATE EVIL IS! WHERE IS THE EVIL, ANYWAY? I WANT TO MEET IT.

Oh yeah. Where **IS** the evil? All we have here is a big empty, smooth planet. We followed the map, so . . . what's the deal?!

There's a sound then, like a soft cracking. My eyes look up at the Map-O-Sphere in Evil Queen Dagger's hand. Something is happening . . .

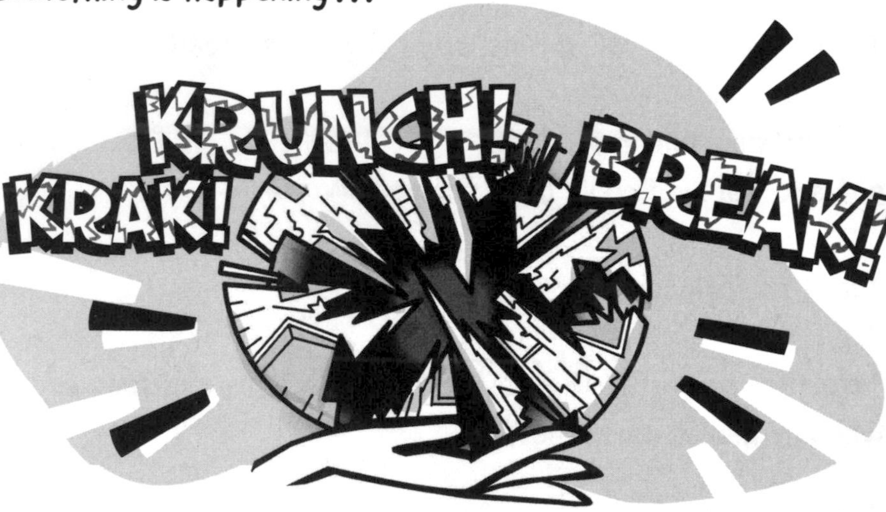
KRUNCH!
KRAK!
BREAK!

As the sphere breaks, the whole planet begins to shake. Small cracks slice across the planet's surface.

SHORT PANTS, THINK IT'S TIME WE MADE OUR EXIT!

"Yeah, Humphree," I say. "Yeah, I think you're right . . ."

But as I watch the queen tugging on her daughter, pulling her away, I realize . . .

NO!

Betrayal or not, Princess Dagger is still my friend, and I can't let her mom take her. I have to—

KRUNCH!

Oh smudge. The ground shakes harder and faster, and the cracks become bigger, everything quaking, and then there's a thunderous shattering—

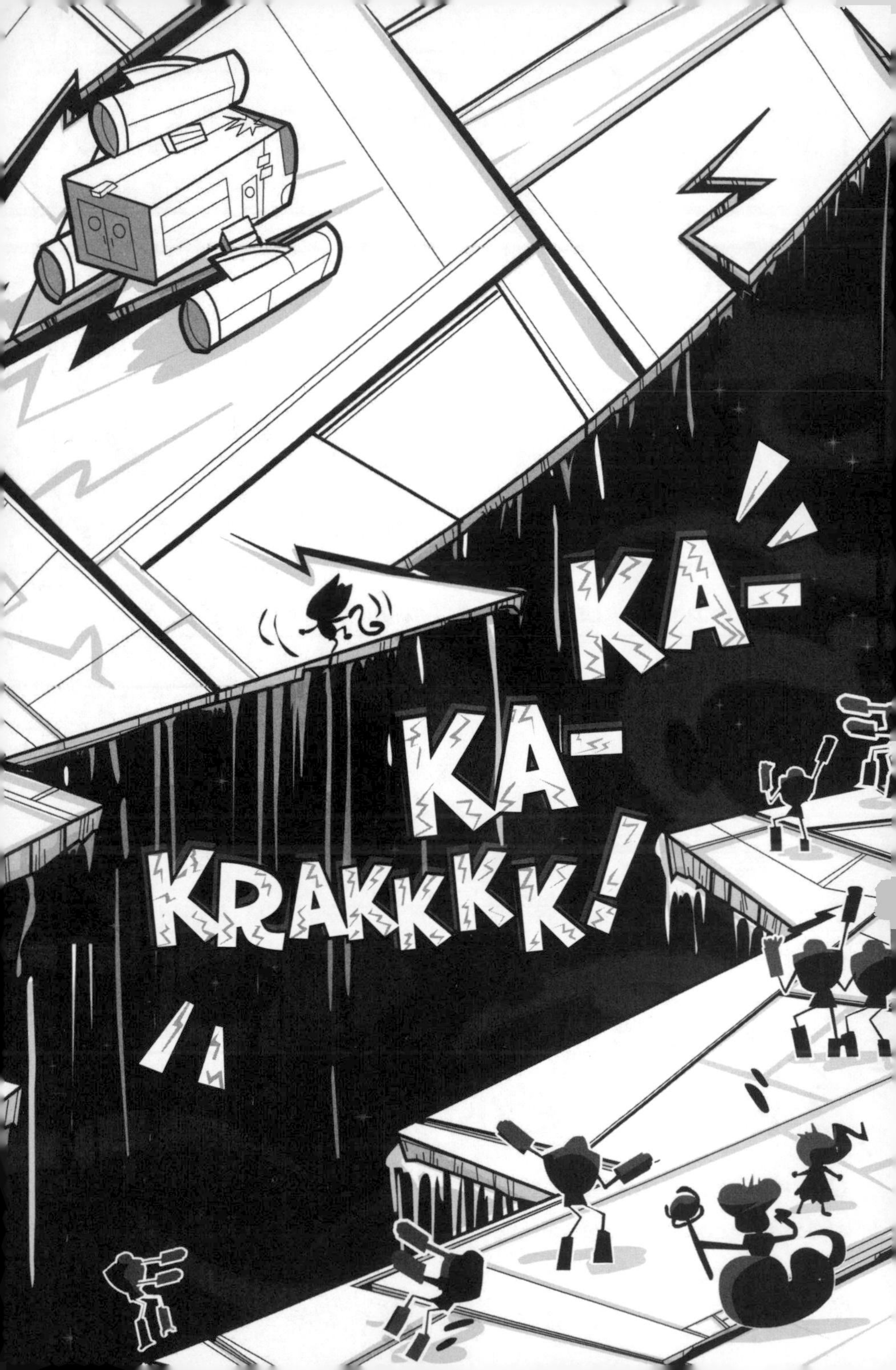
KA-KA-KRAKKKK!

"Get me out of here!" the evil queen shouts, dragging the princess toward *Biggun.* "Jacks, fire on those fools!"

One Jack raises his arm cannon at me, about to shoot. But the planet splits wider, and the robot lets out a mechanical shriek as he plummets into the cracking, cavernous hole.

Now's my chance . . .

The first time I met Princess Dagger, I Goober-lassoed her. Now it's time to do it again: a Goober-lasso grab across a giant chasm. But first—

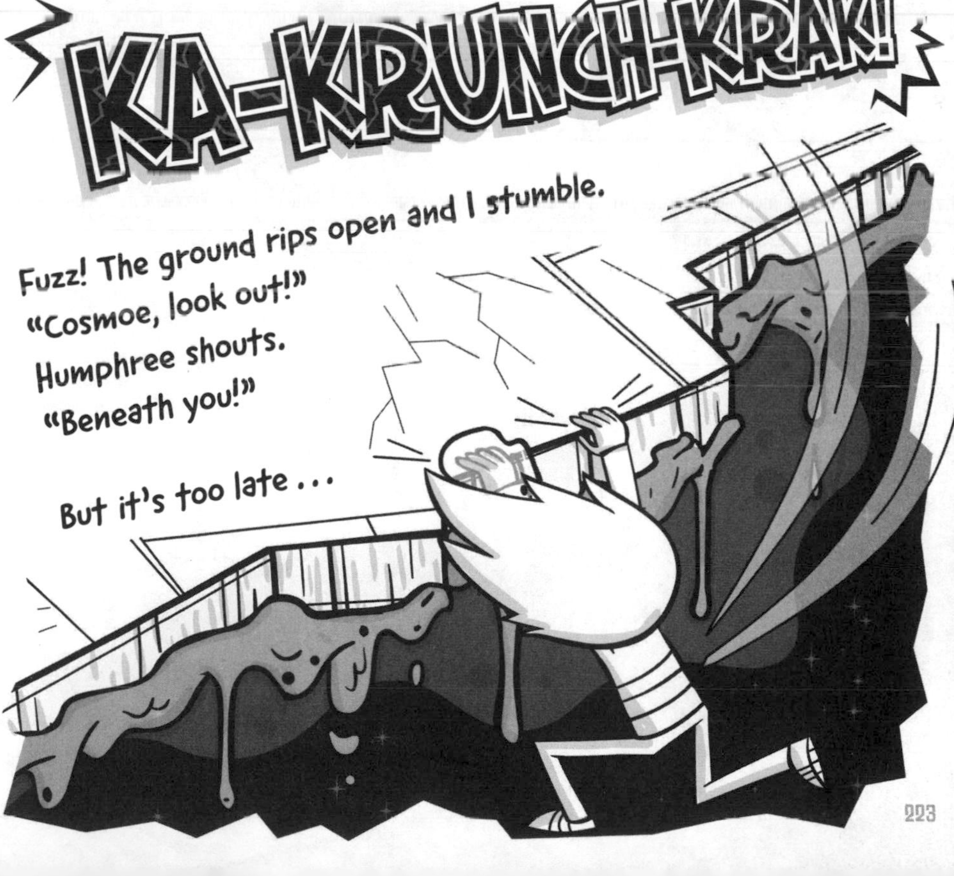
KA-KRUNCH-KRAK!
Fuzz! The ground rips open and I stumble.
"Cosmoe, look out!" Humphree shouts. "Beneath you!"
But it's too late . . .

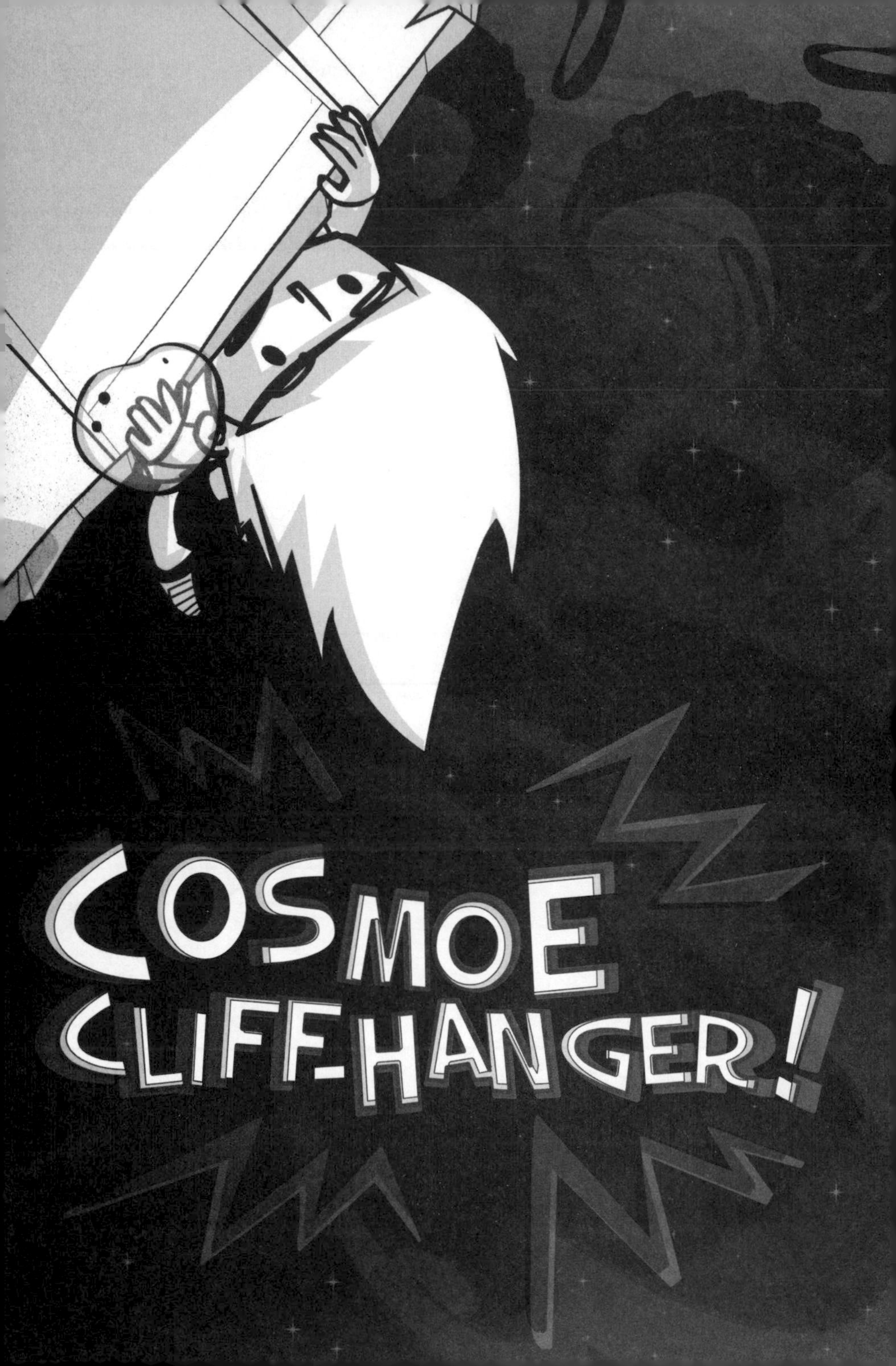
COSMOE CLIFF-HANGER!

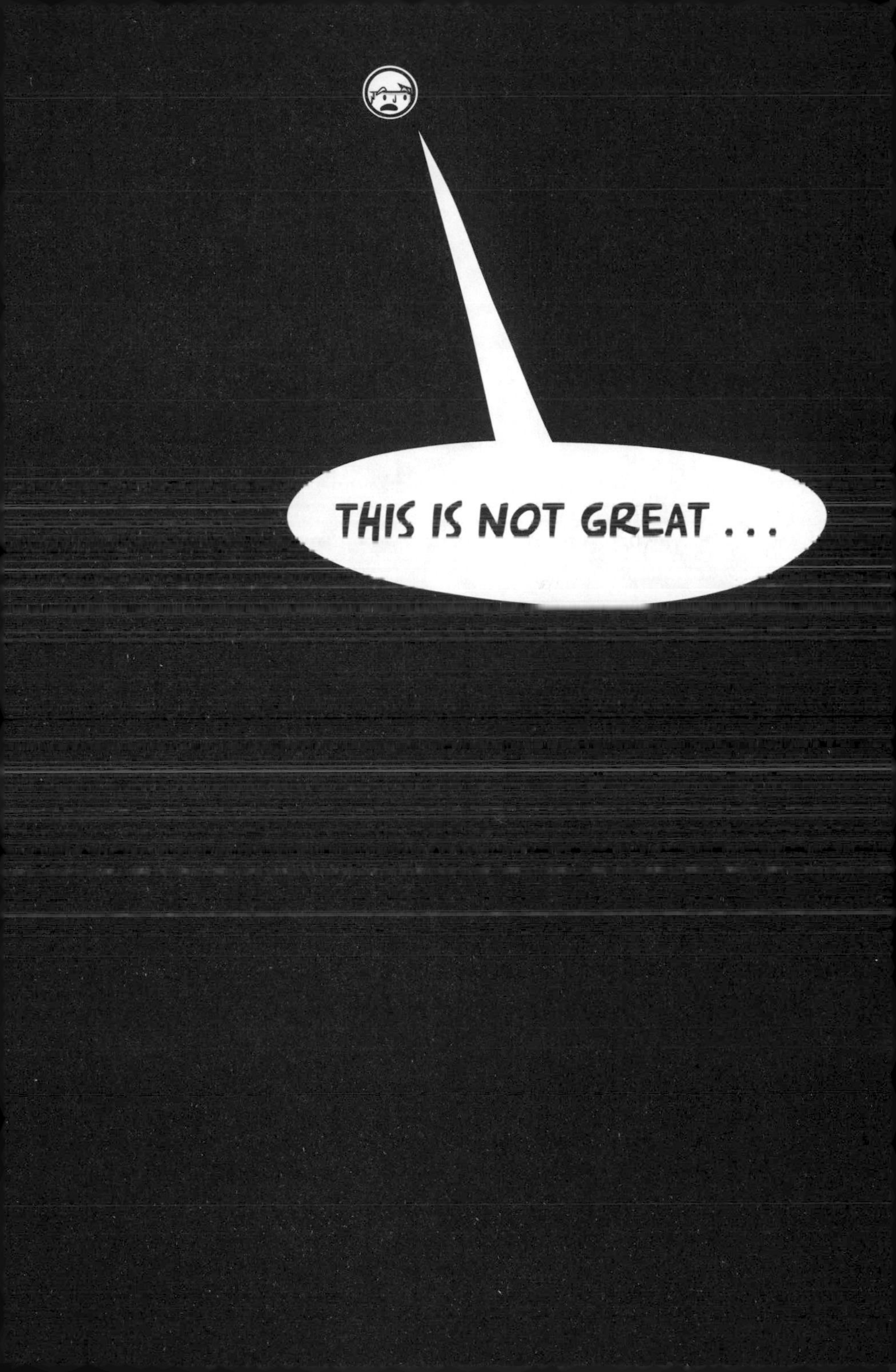
THIS IS NOT GREAT . . .

ASTEROID-SIZED EGGSHELL, DEAD AHEAD!

22

I'm kicking wildly,
trying to find a hold to
stick my feet into, but
there's nothing there. It's like
this whole thing is hollow.
But this is a planet, and yeah,
I failed 6th grade science—but
I'm still pretty sure planets
aren't hollow ...

Time to do something dumb—look
down into the darkness ...

It's nearly pitch-black. Squinting,
I see what looks like the inside of a
jack-o'-lantern. Gunky mucus-type
stuff drips down from the underside
of the planet's surface.

A hot wind blows up toward me. And
then—*gulp*—I think I see something
moving.

My grip is loosening. The
mucus-gunk completely coats
my fingers. I'm slipping ...

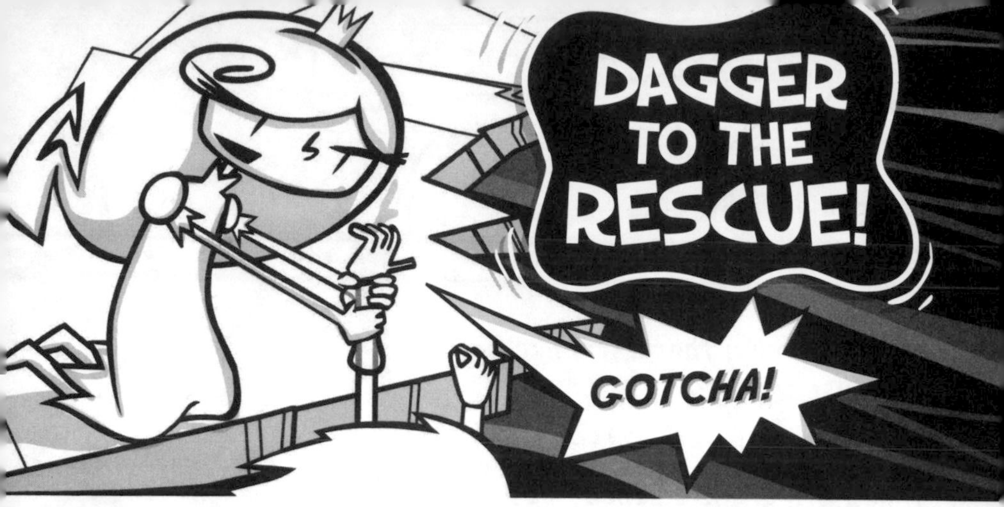
DAGGER TO THE RESCUE!
GOTCHA!

Dagger yanks me up over the side. "Princess?!" I gasp. "How'd you get over here?!"

Princess Dagger grins proudly. "I'm a really good jumper. Didn't you know? Kind of like my evil power."

My mind is racing. Trying to figure out just what the smudge is happening here. Map-O-Sphere. Glowing energy. Ultimate evil. Quaking ground. Hollow planet.

No time to put the pieces together—there's an evil lady's evil voice calling from across the canyon.

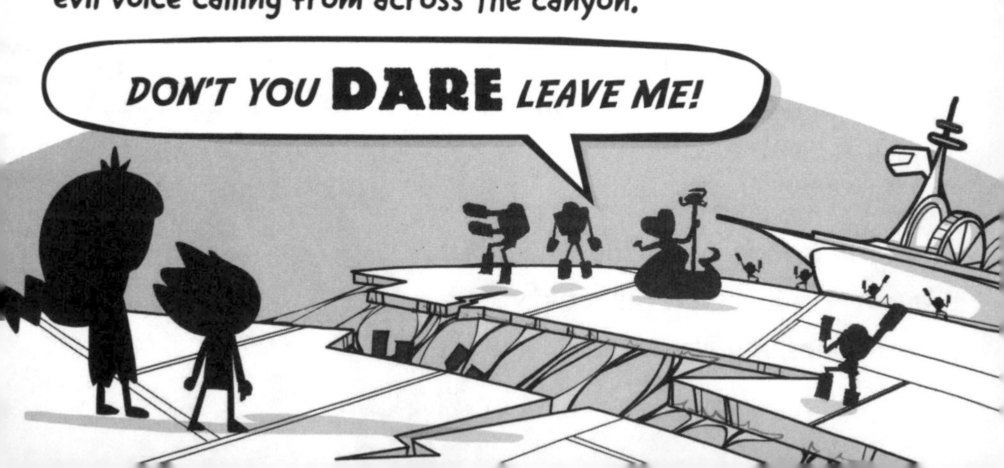
DON'T YOU DARE LEAVE ME!

LOOK AT WHAT YOUR EVIL NEED FOR EVIL TREASURE HAS DONE! COSMOE WAS RIGHT. I'M NOT LIKE YOU! GOODBYE, MOTHER!

Humphree shouts from the *Neon Wiener*, roaring so he's heard over the planet's rumbling.

"YOU TWO! NOW! IT'S SPLITTIN' TIME!"

I grab the princess by the hand, and we take off for the ship, leaving the evil queen to ponder her evilness, minus one daughter.

A volley of Jack fire erupts behind us. A laser blast nearly takes off a piece of my perfect hair. Not cool. "Humps!" I shout. "Could use some cover here!"

Humphree hooks us up . . .

The *Neon Wiener* opens fire. Laser blasts fly over our heads. Behind us, I hear a series of mechanical explosions as the *Wiener*'s cannons tear apart the Jacks.

Just a few steps from the *Neon Wiener*, and I stumble. My hand punches through the planet's surface. As I lie there, with my head pressed against the ground, I hear something. It sounds a little like Humphree when I wake him up from a hyper-snooze. Like something was asleep for a long time, and is finally stirring.

And all of a sudden, it clicks inside my brain.

Scrambling to my feet, I urge the princess forward. "Faster! We need to leave **NOW!** This is about to get a whole lot weirder."

"I don't think it can get any weirder!"

"Trust me!"

Racing into the *Neon Wiener*, I see Humphree jabbing at the controls. "We're blowing this joint," he says. "This whole planet is about to cave in."

That's when I tell them. "Guys, this is no planet . . ."

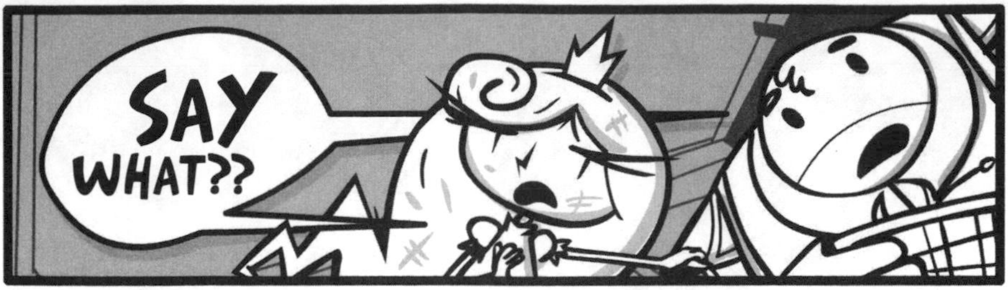
SAY WHAT??

Rapid-quick, I say, "I was thinking about everything, and then I remembered what that zombie space pirate said when we found the first piece of the map. He said we'd

"GIVE BIRTH TO THE ULTIMATE EVIL."

"So?"

"BIRTH!" I say.

"Cosmoe, talk sense, huh?" Humphree says.

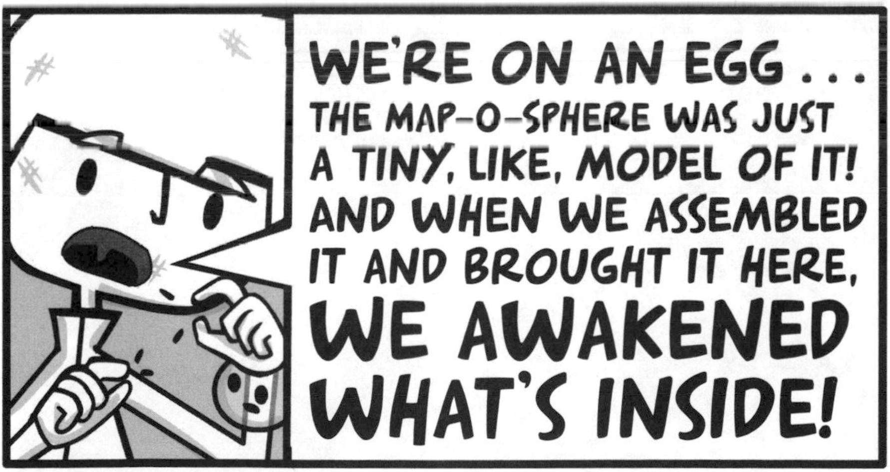
WE'RE ON AN EGG . . .
THE MAP-O-SPHERE WAS JUST A TINY, LIKE, MODEL OF IT! AND WHEN WE ASSEMBLED IT AND BROUGHT IT HERE, WE AWAKENED WHAT'S INSIDE!

The princess gasps. Humphree curses in Bronklese. And as the *Neon Wiener* blasts away, the egg erupts, exploding into trillions of pieces, revealing at last—

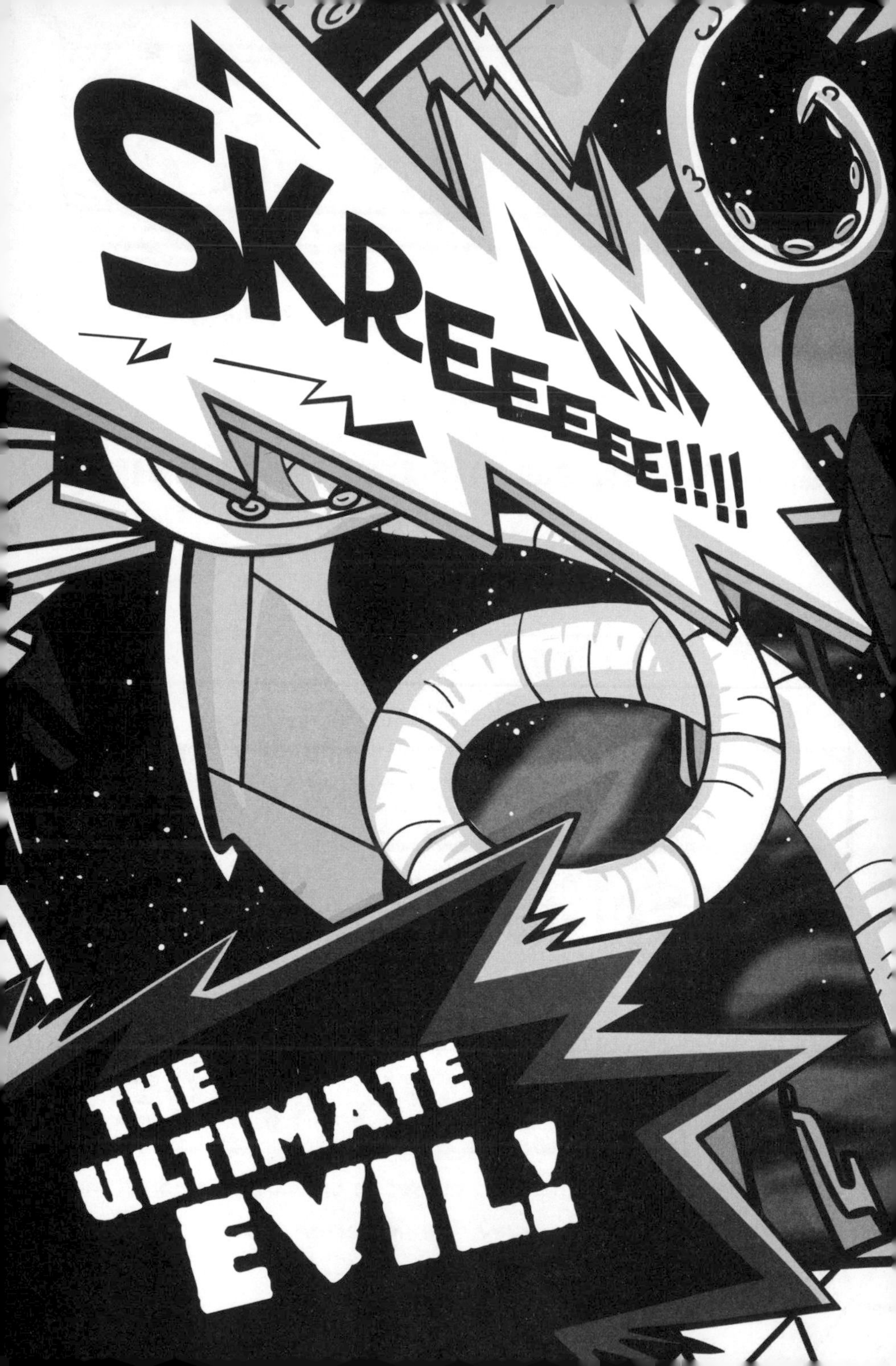
SKREEEEEEM!!!!!
THE ULTIMATE EVIL!

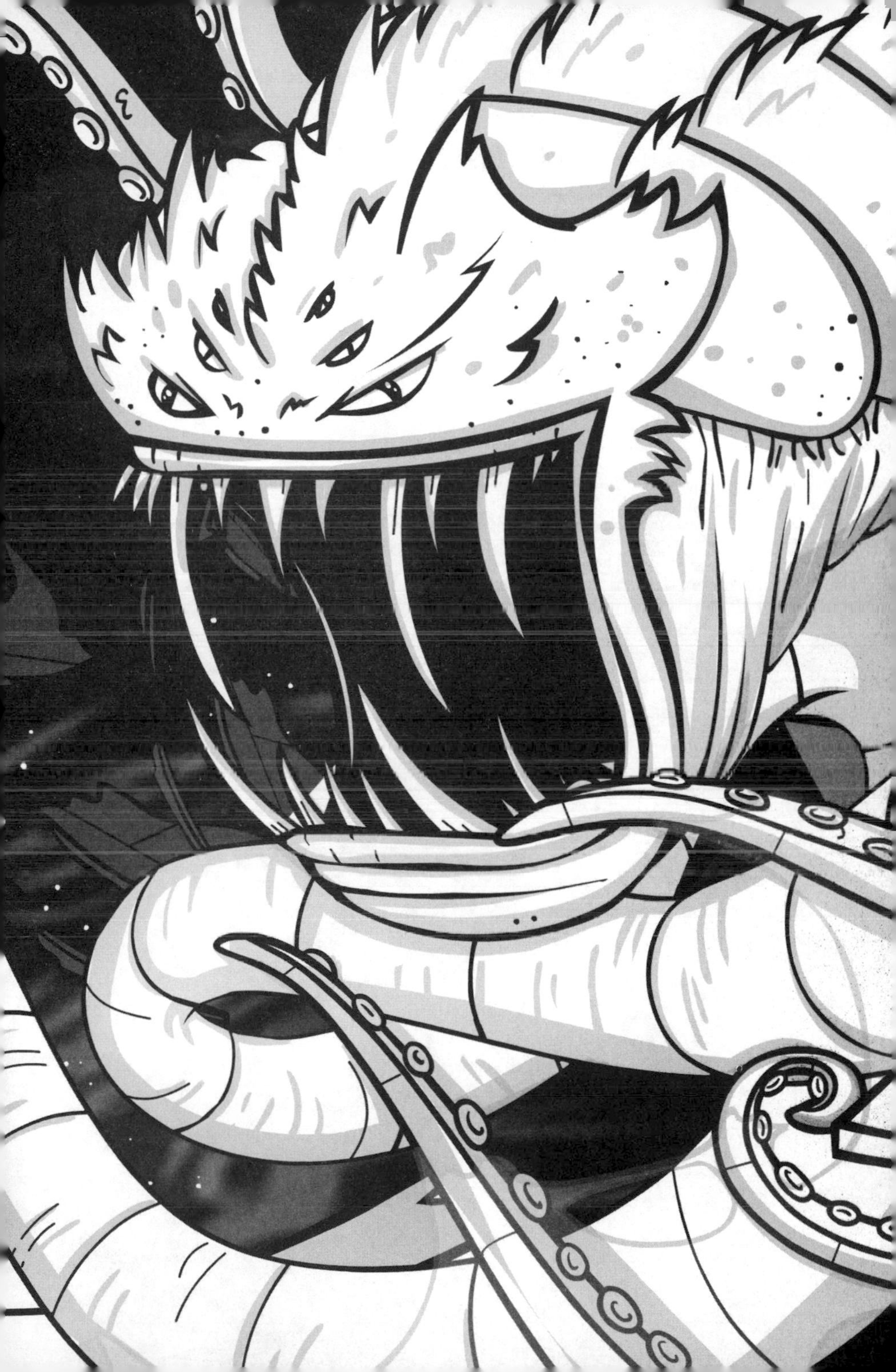

The enormous eruption rocks the *Neon Wiener.* The ship is spiraling helplessly through space. Chunks of eggshell surround us, pounding the ship.

Suddenly, Princess Dagger screams and points, "Asteroid-sized eggshell, dead ahead!"

"I see it," Humphree growls, wrestling with the controls. "I see it."

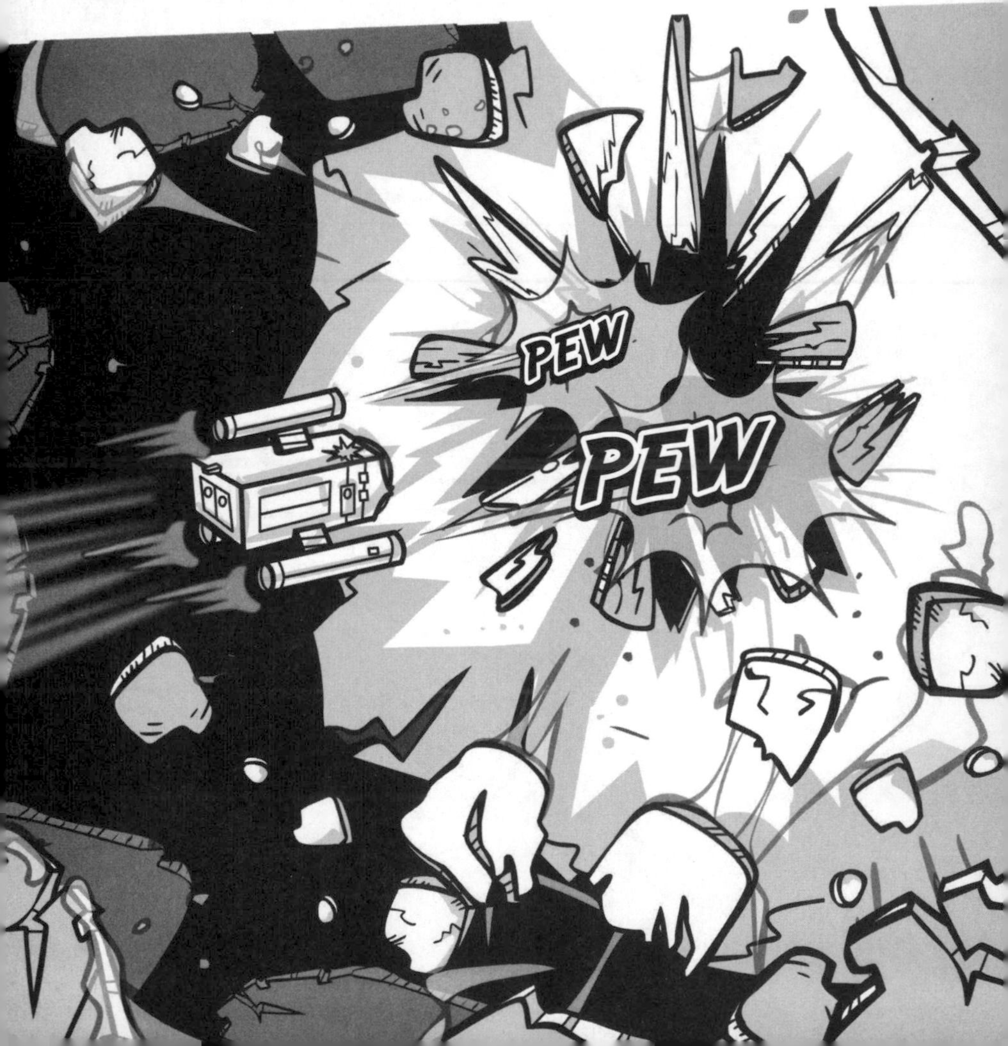
PEW
PEW

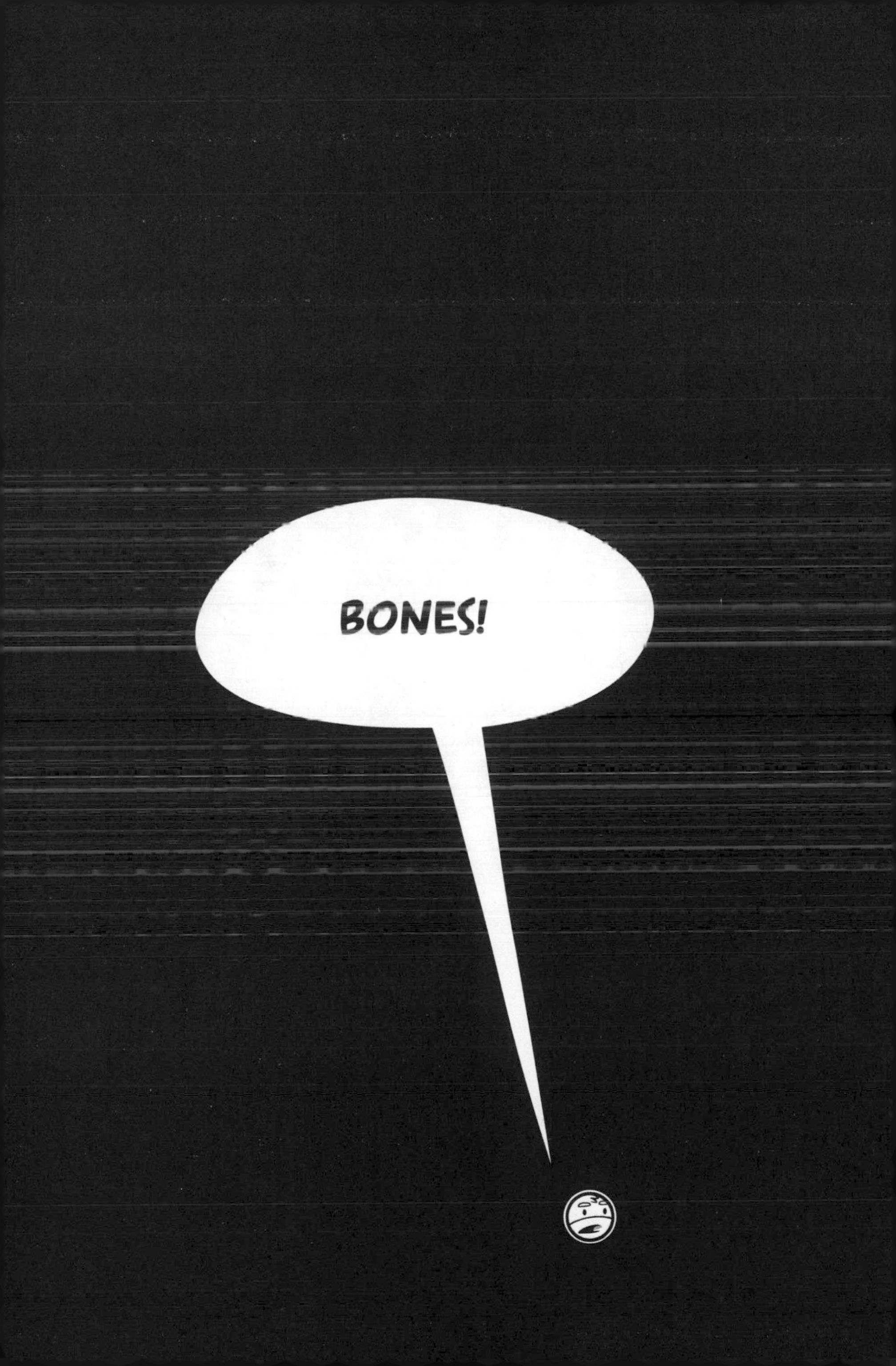
BONES!

INEFFECTIVE EYEBALL ATTACK!!

We blast through the shattered eggshell, but we're not out of trouble yet. Not by a long shot. A thunderous, angry roar echoes through space—the roar of the

ULTIMATE EVIL MONSTER.

"I think that thing is chasing us!" the princess calls out.

Humphree narrows his eyes. "It's not the only one . . ."

The *Neon Wiener* rocks suddenly, and one thruster begins sparking while the lights and buttons and gizmos inside the cockpit flash. We're hit!

I glance up, checking the mirror. "It's Krax! Watch out!"

"Trying!" Humphree shouts as he spins the wheel and the *Neon Wiener* cuts hard to the right.

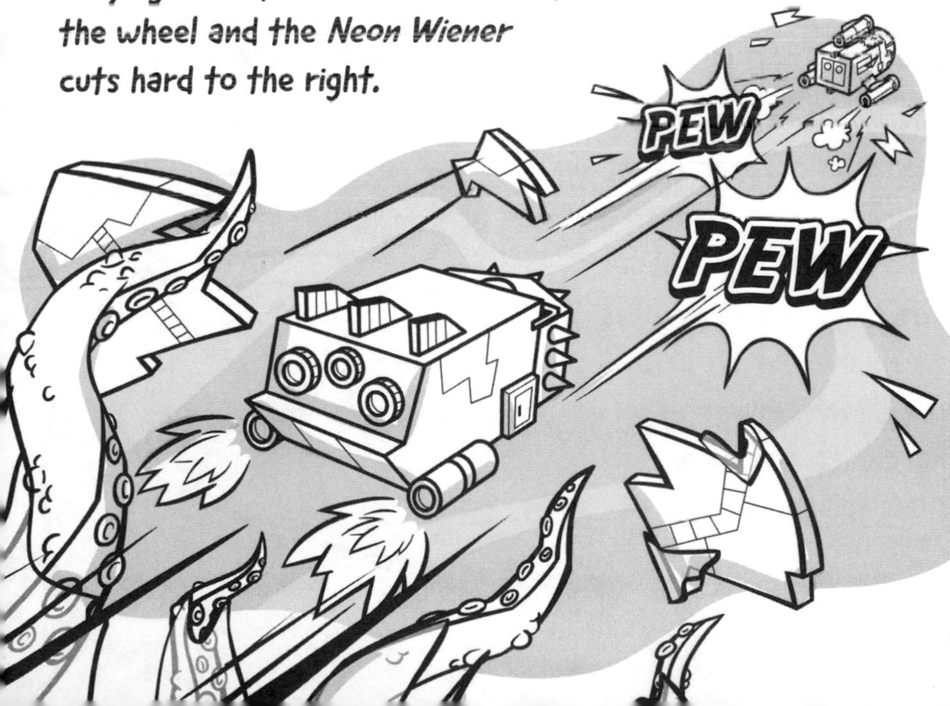
PEW
PEW

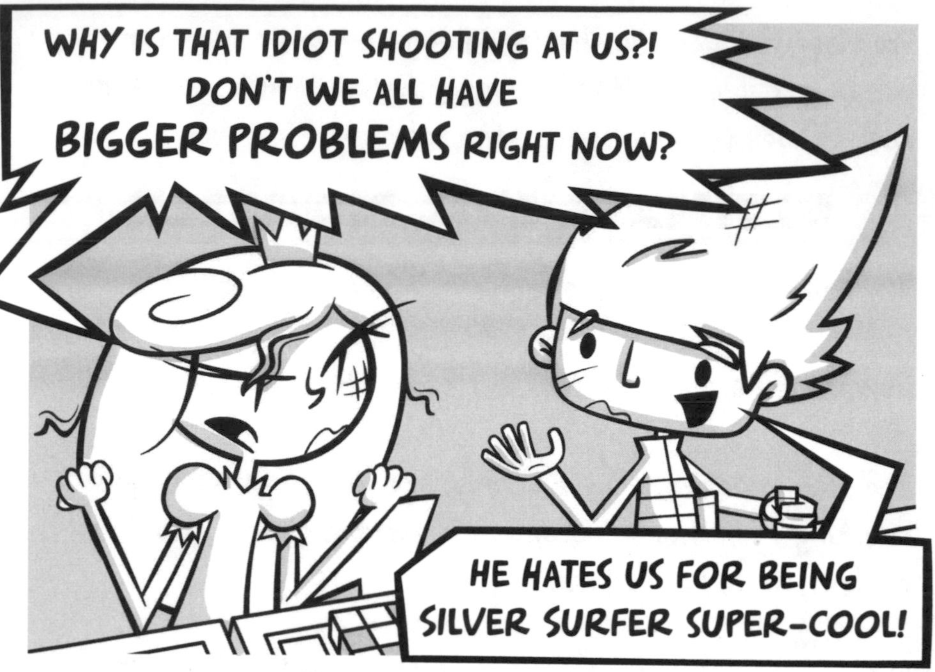
WHY IS THAT IDIOT SHOOTING AT US?! DON'T WE ALL HAVE BIGGER PROBLEMS RIGHT NOW?
HE HATES US FOR BEING SILVER SURFER SUPER-COOL!

Ahead of us, the monster's long tentacles protrude from his body, like a living forest. "We can lose Krax in there!" I say.

"Strap in, you two," Humphree barks as he pushes the *Wiener* closer to the monster's tentacle-covered flesh. He banks the ship, turning it on its side, zigzagging around the tentacles. Krax tries to follow, but his ship is fatter than ours—harder to maneuver. Also, he's lame.

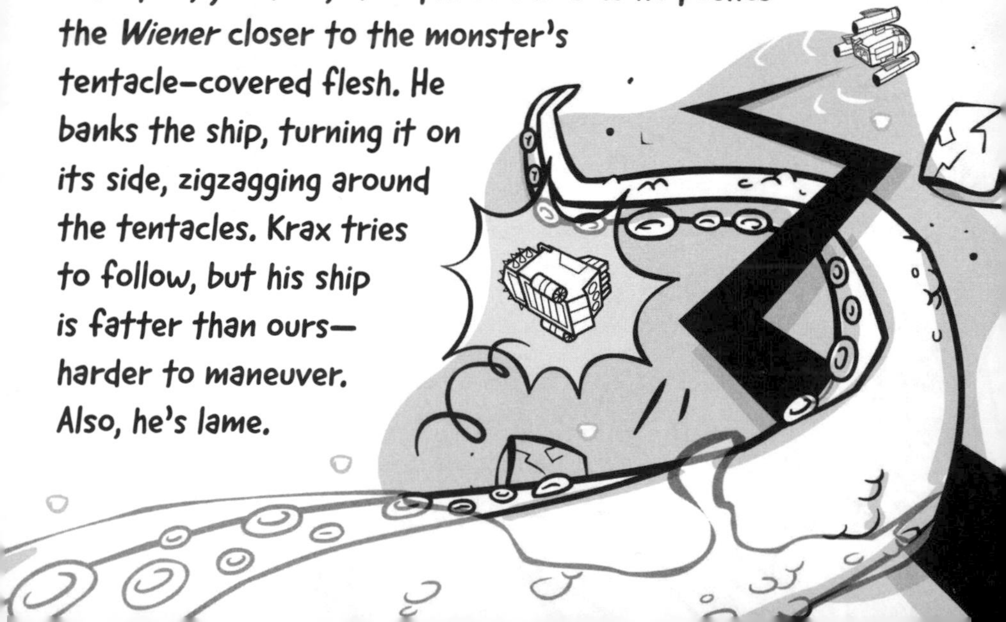

"Enough of this!" Humphree says, reaching for the turbo-speed toggle. "We're getting *FAR, FAR* away from this mess."

"No!" Princess Dagger exclaims. "We *CAN'T* let this monster eat all these treasure hunters. That would be **EVIL!**"

I grin happily. The princess is back! And she's not-so-evil!

Suddenly, F.R.E.D. starts buzzing and an image flashes on his cracked screen.

A BILLION—SPACEO REWARD TO THE SHIP THAT DEFEATS THIS MONSTER! NO QUESTIONS ASKED!

I look at Humphree, eyes wide, excited. Humphree whistles softly and says, "A billion spaceos, huh ... ? Well, I'll stick my big neck out for *THAT MUCH* loot."

And with that, he throws the throttle forward, plunging us into the raging battle.

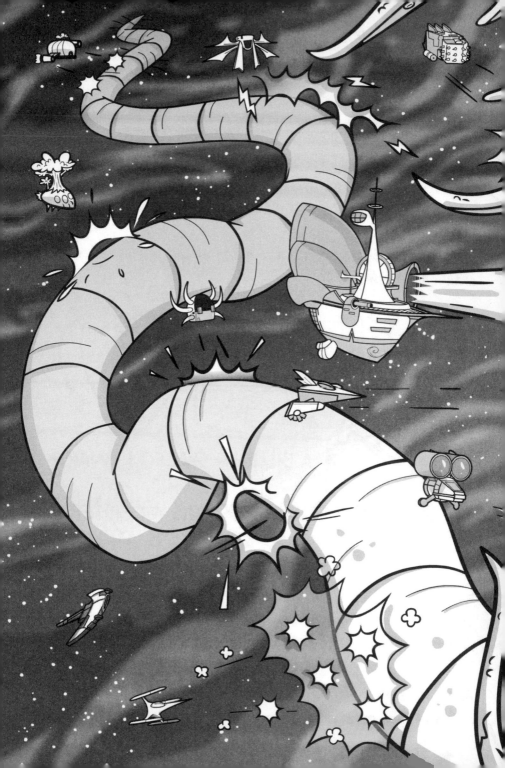

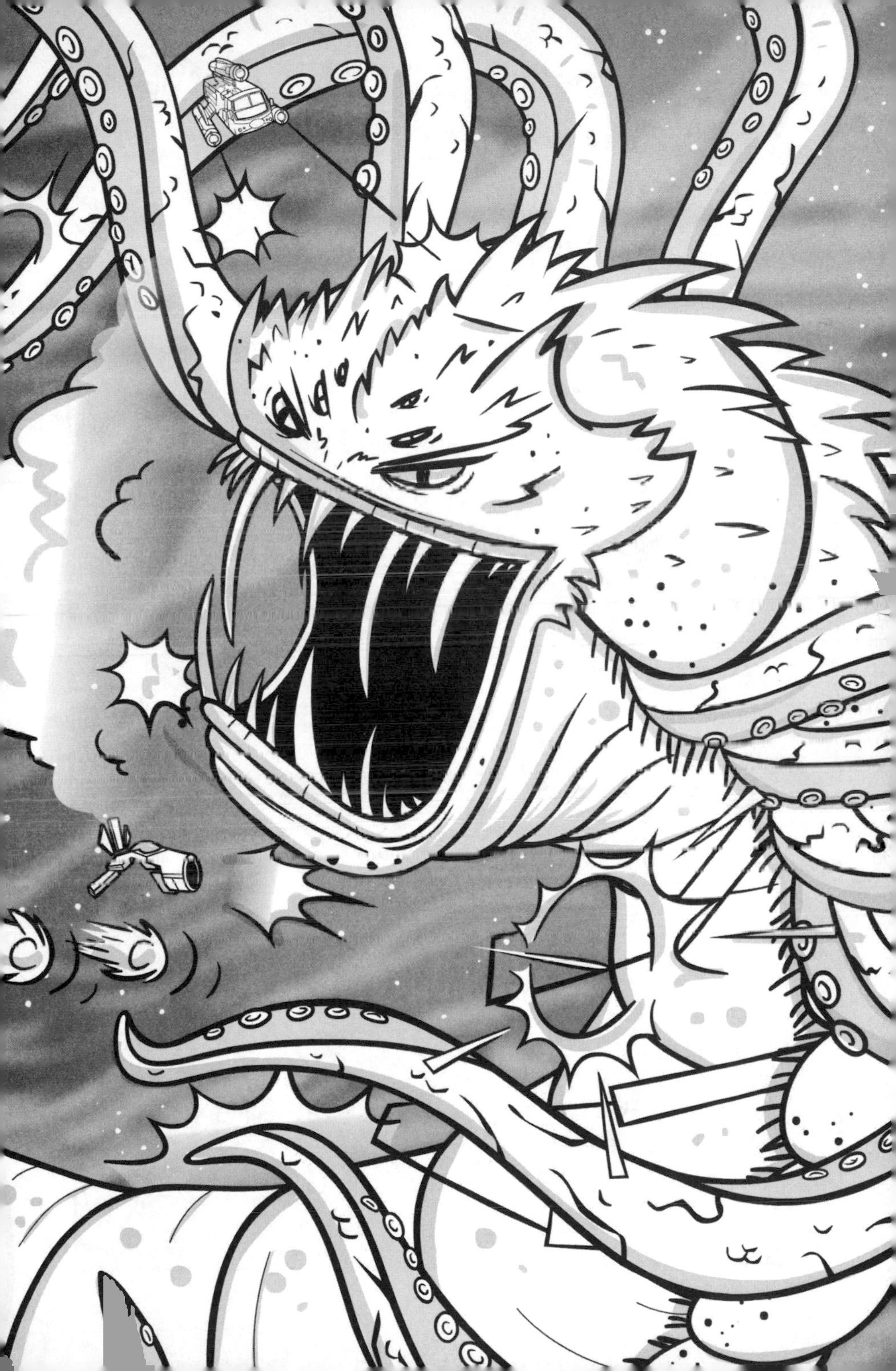

A FUTILE ASSAULT!

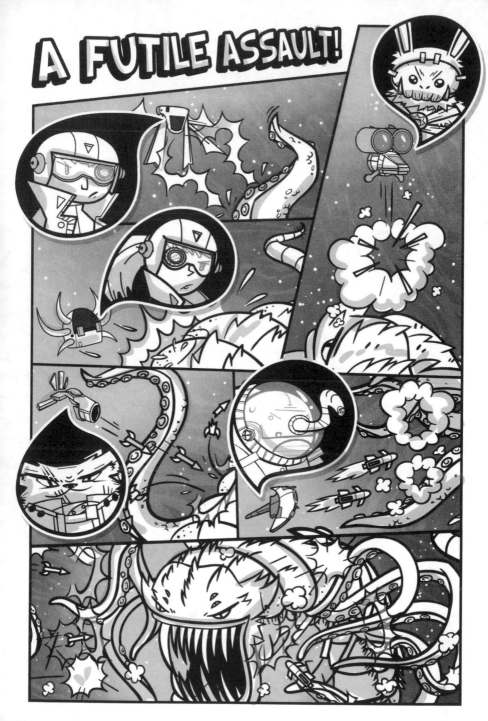

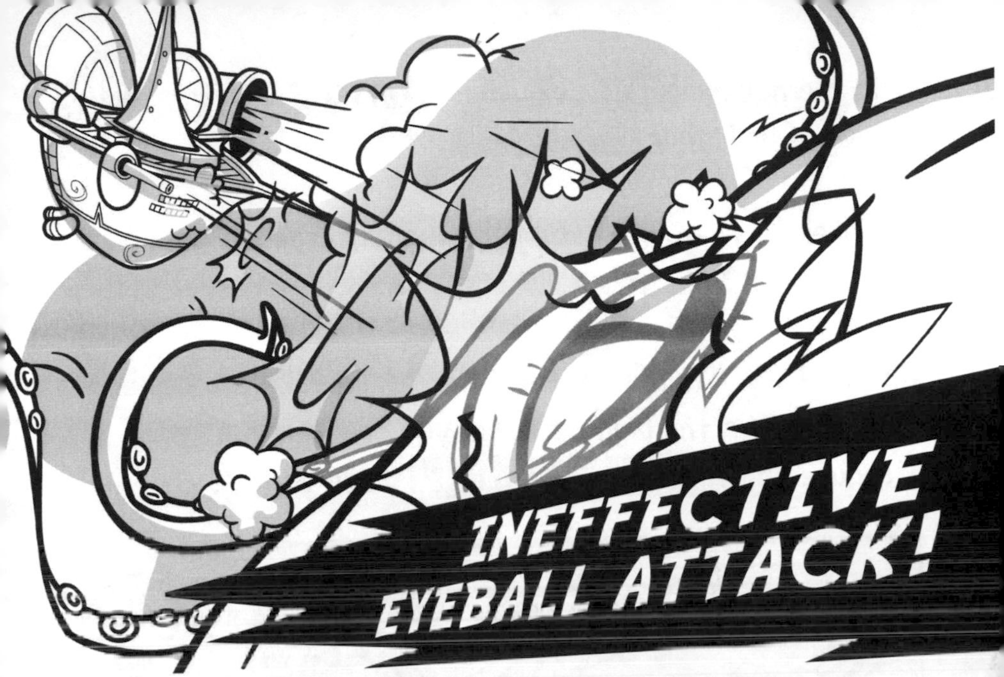
INEFFECTIVE
EYEBALL ATTACK!

"Not even your mom's ship can hurt it," I say to the princess. "The monster's got armor like a frappin' tank!"

Stray laser fire skims the side of our ship. "We need a plan, Cosmoe!" Humphree barks. **"NOW!"**

"Doesn't F.R.E.D. have any ideas?" Princess asks.

I shake my head. "Your mom blasted F.R.E.D. and now his electro-brain is all fuzzed up. See?"

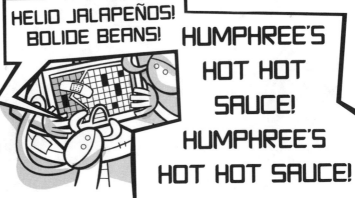

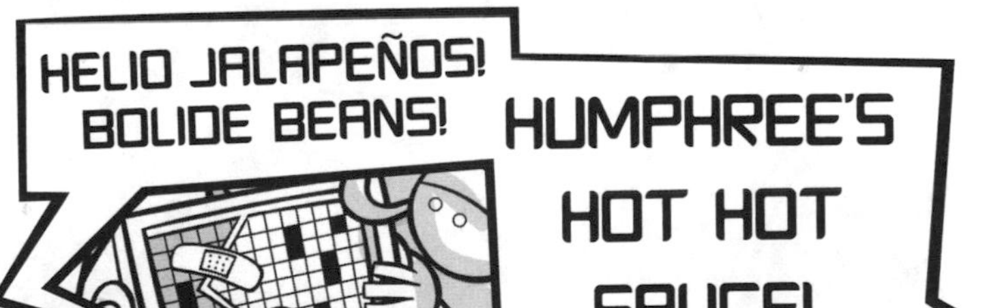
HELIO JALAPEÑOS!
BOLIDE BEANS!
HUMPHREE'S HOT HOT SAUCE! HUMPHREE'S HOT HOT SAUCE!

"Hold the hamburgers!" I exclaim. "***THAT'S IT!*** Humps, did you ever finish your HOT HOT SAUCE?"

He shakes his head. "I'm still jiggering with the recipe. I think I made it ***TOO*** hot. It's **EXPLOSIVE.**"

"Jingo!" I say. "That's perfect! Humps, I'll take the wheel. You go cook up the biggest batch you can. It's time to introduce HUMPHREE'S HOT HOT SAUCE to the galaxy . . ."

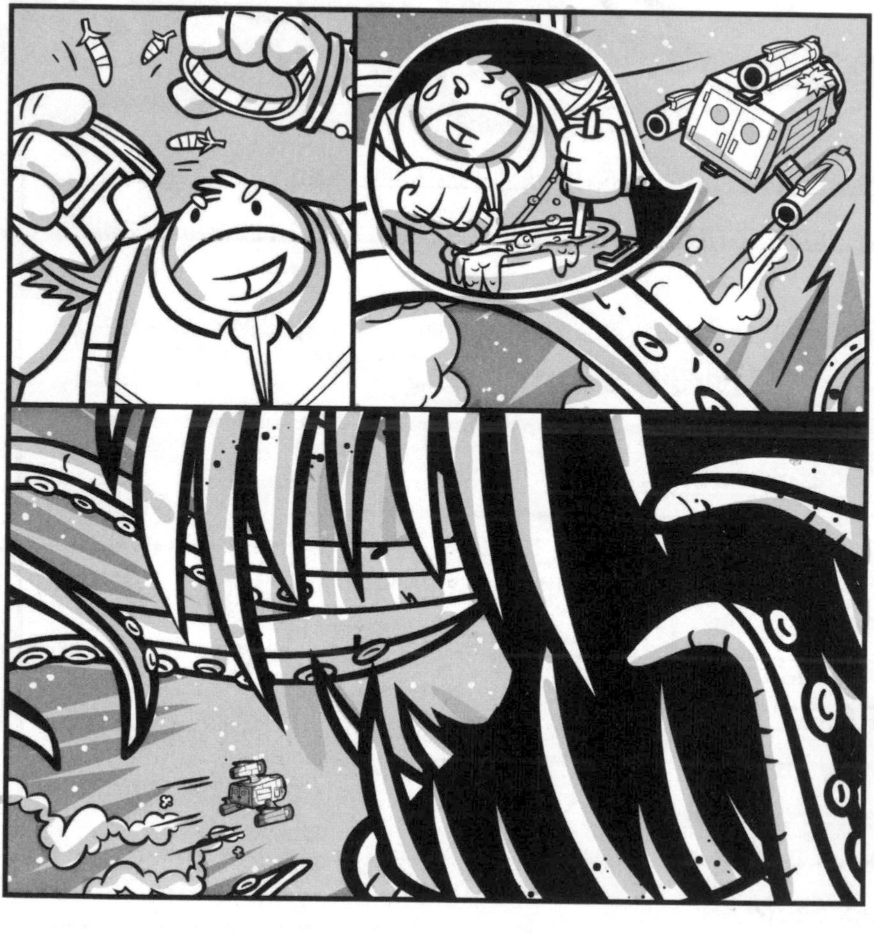

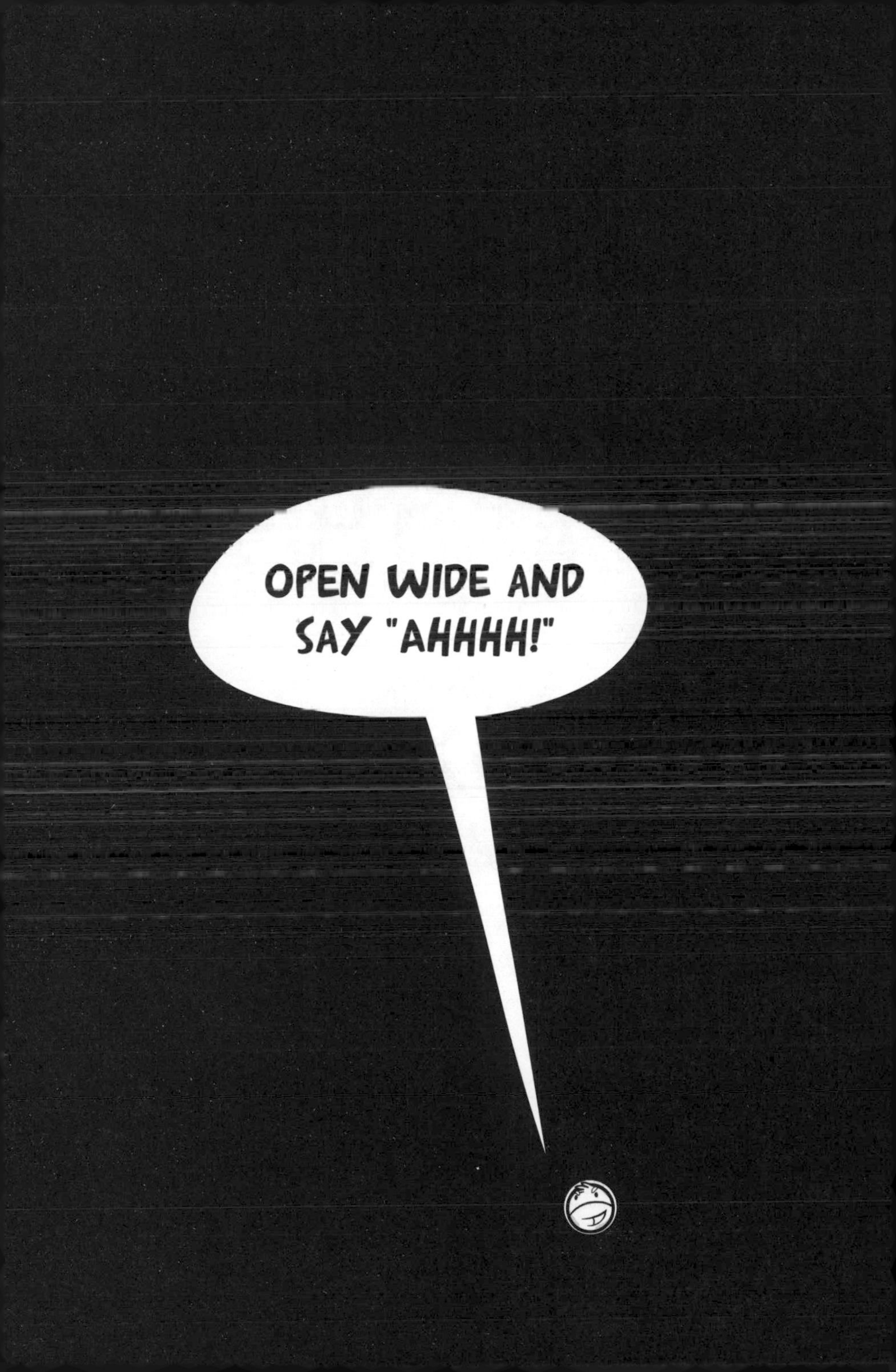
OPEN WIDE AND SAY "AHHHH!"

EAT THIS!

I fly the *Neon Wiener*
directly into the monster's wide-open
mouth and steer us down his gnarly esophagus.

"Um, Cosmoe?" the princess says nervously.
"You just flew inside the Ultimate Evil Monster . . ."

I nod. "Yep. I am aware, Princess."

"OK," she says. Then a moment later she asks,
"Was there a reason for that, or . . . ?"

I nod again. "I'm blowing up this beast from the inside."

Before the princess can whack me on the head, a blast
rocks the ship. Cannons erupt behind us. Krax is
back, and he's not alone . . . A dozen ships are
rocketing behind us, firing away!

"WHAT THE SMUDGE?" I shout.

"Don't these jerks realize we're trying to **SAVE** them?!"

The princess shrugs. "They must **REALLY** want that billion spaceos . . ."

A laser blast hits the rear engine stabilizer, and the *Neon Wiener* spins wildly. Smudge! I'm never going to make it all the way to the center of this beast with all those jerks on my tail . . .

"Princess!" I shout. "Run to your bedroom! Clear away all my old junk and man the rear energy cannon!"

I DON'T KNOW HOW TO DO THAT! I'VE NEVER FIRED A REAR ENERGY CANNON!

YOU'RE PART EVIL! YOU CAN DEFINITELY FIGURE OUT HOW TO USE A BIG BLASTER!

"Fine!" she says. I get a glimpse of her face as she takes off running. She's grinning. I figured.

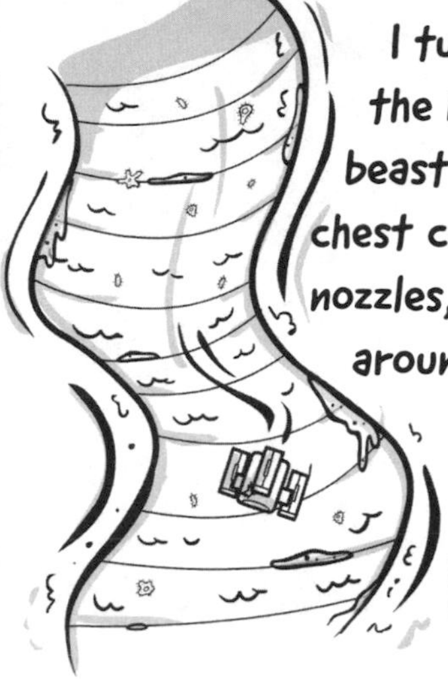

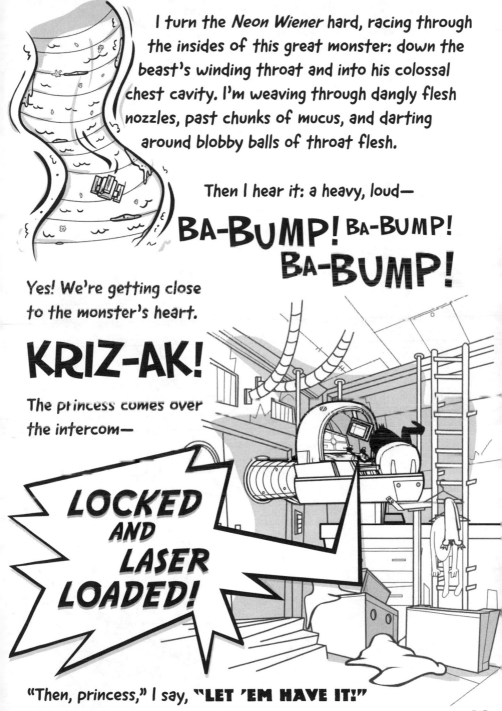

I turn the *Neon Wiener* hard, racing through the insides of this great monster: down the beast's winding throat and into his colossal chest cavity. I'm weaving through dangly flesh nozzles, past chunks of mucus, and darting around blobby balls of throat flesh.

Then I hear it: a heavy, loud—

BA-BUMP! BA-BUMP! BA-BUMP!

Yes! We're getting close to the monster's heart.

KRIZ-AK!

The princess comes over the intercom—

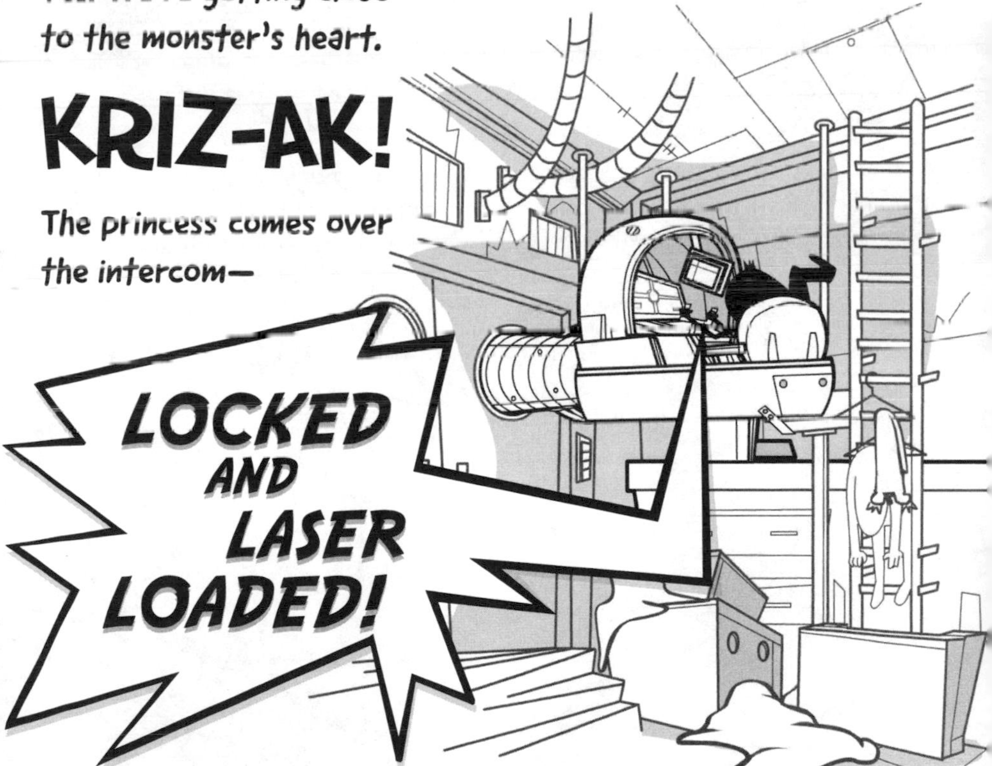
LOCKED AND LASER LOADED!

"Then, princess," I say, **"LET 'EM HAVE IT!"**

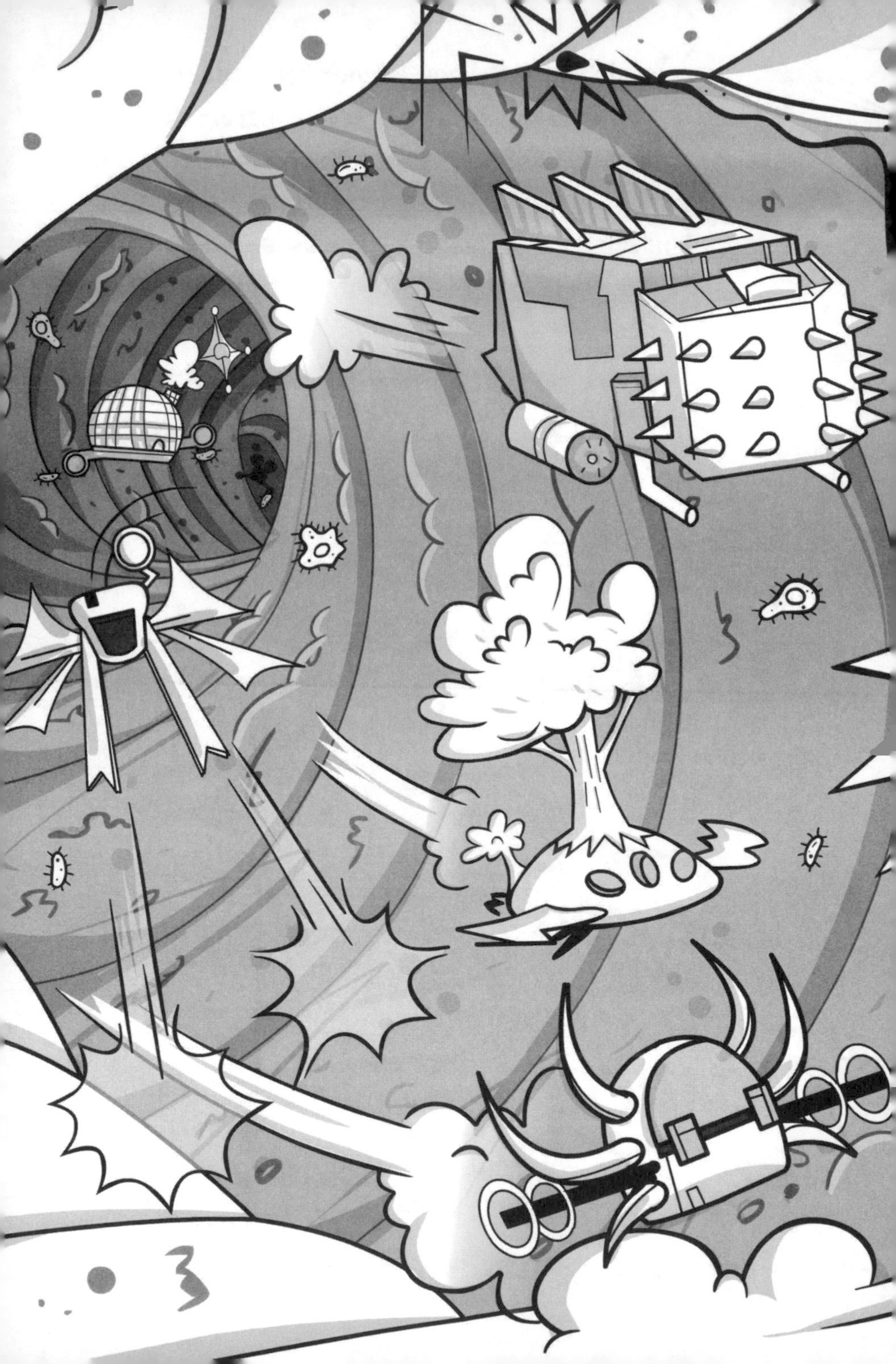

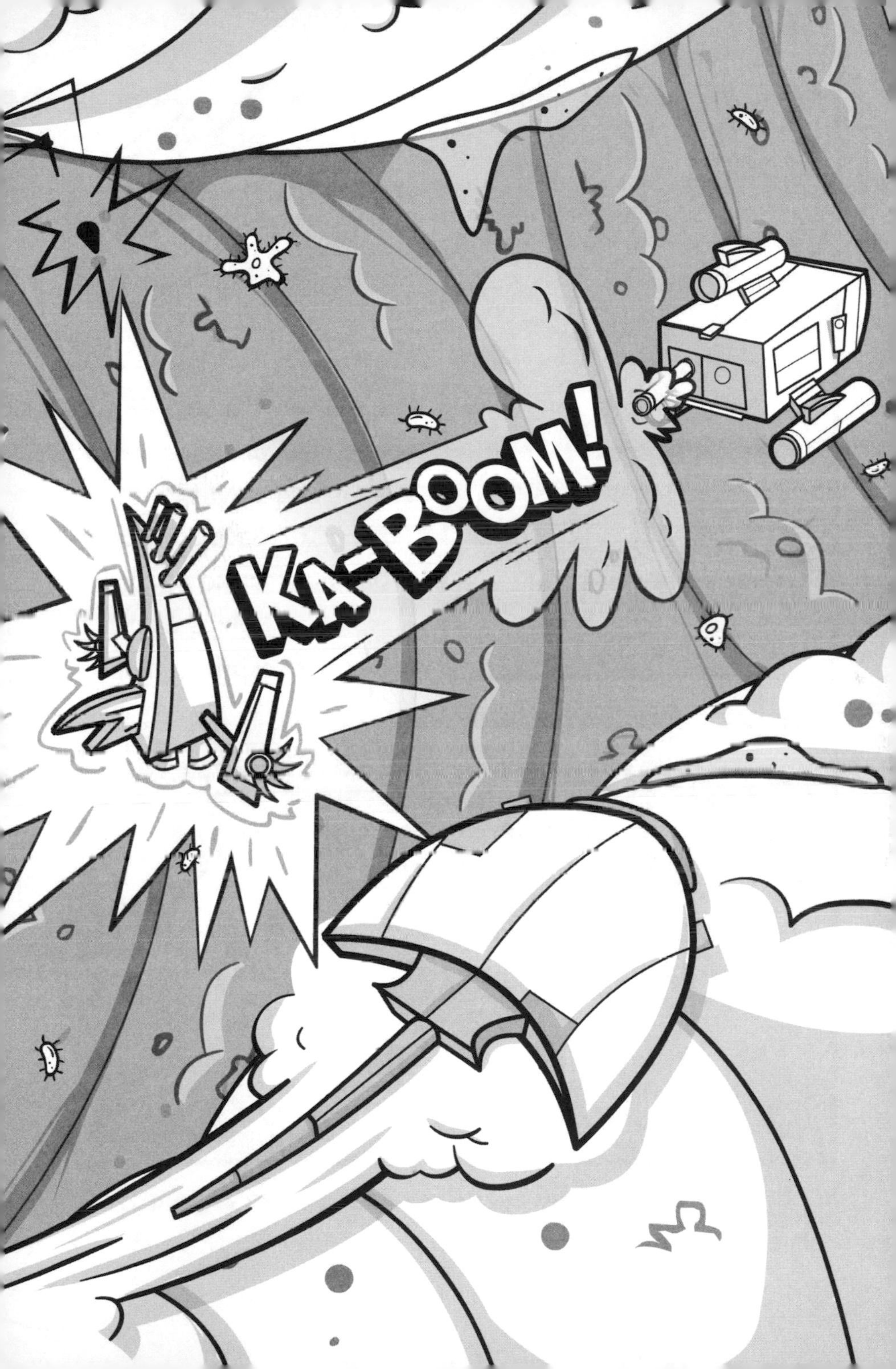
KA-BOOM!

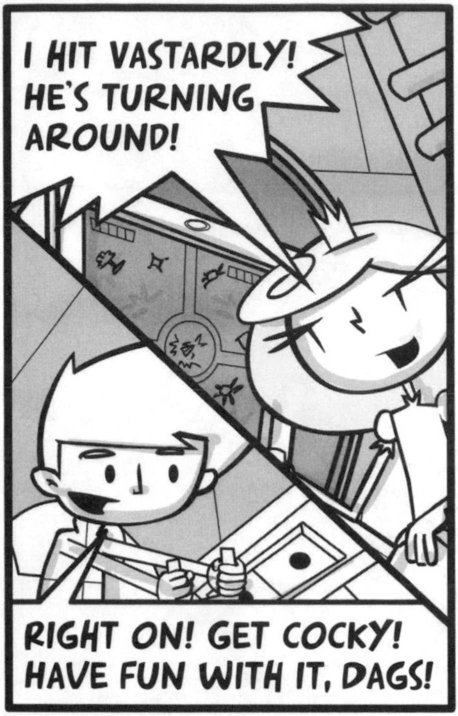
I HIT VASTARDLY! HE'S TURNING AROUND!
RIGHT ON! GET COCKY! HAVE FUN WITH IT, DAGS!

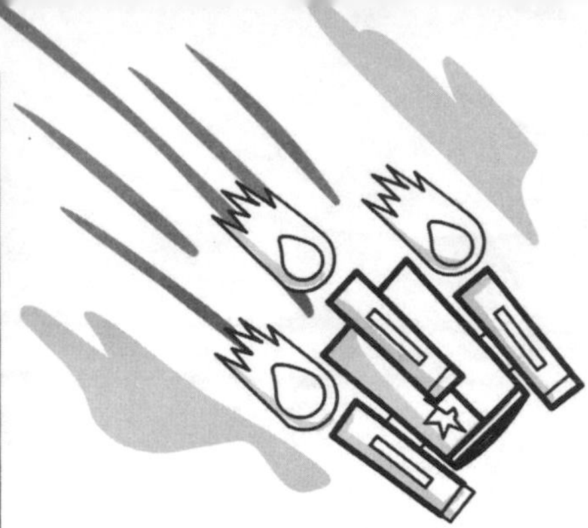

I'm pushing the ship at top speed past pumping blood vessels and valves. The *Wiener* is weaving around a swinging string of chest flesh when Humps charges into the cockpit.

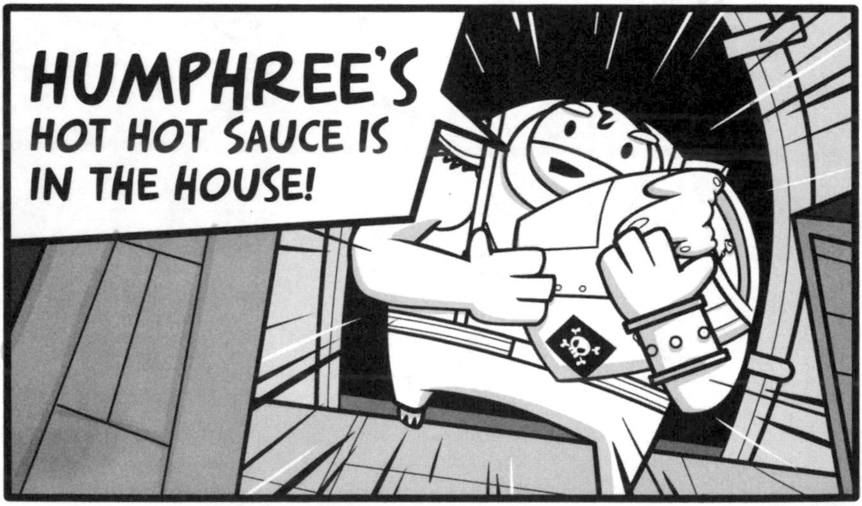
HUMPHREE'S HOT HOT SAUCE IS IN THE HOUSE!

"Good timing," I say, my eyes wide as we come around the corner. "Because there it is. The monster's heart."

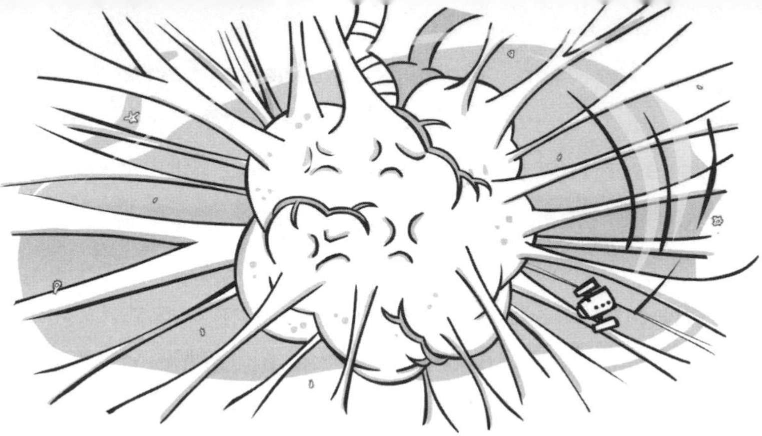

"Push the barrel into the air lock," I tell Humphree. "And get ready to kick it right into the monster's core. And then, hopefully, it makes a big boom . . ."

"I cleared out two more ships," Princess Dagger shouts over the radio, "but I can't find Krax!"

I shake my head. No matter about Krax. It's time. I bank the ship, bringing us as close as I can to the beast's beating blood pumper. Then I shout into the mic, "Go, Humps, go!"

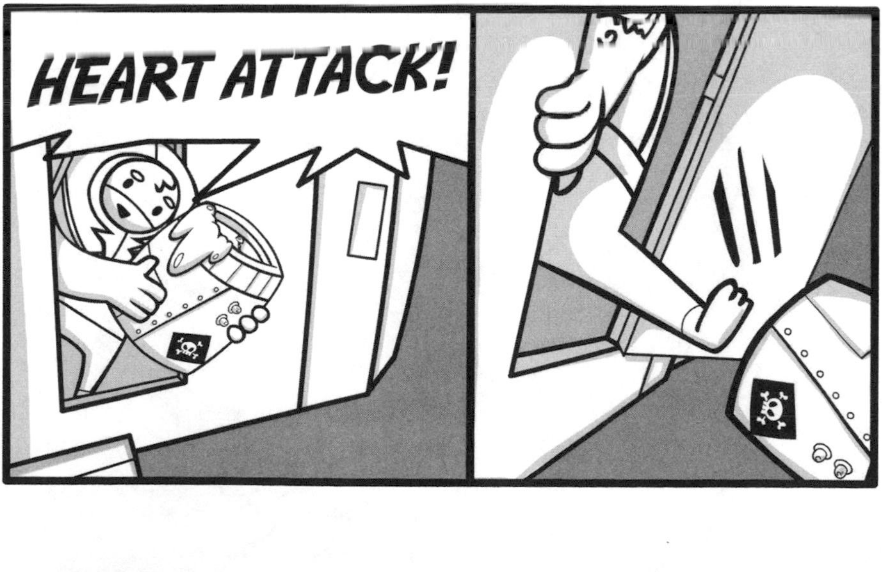
HEART ATTACK!

Looking out the port window, I see the big barrel tumbling, end over end, toward the heart. It seems to go down in slow motion as laser fire erupts around us and ships circle and the monster's heart has everything quaking.

At last, the barrel **SLAMS** into the heart and sticks into the side of the wet muscle. I hold my breath and grip the turbo-thrusters, ready to give us max speed for an escape.

But . . . nothing happens!

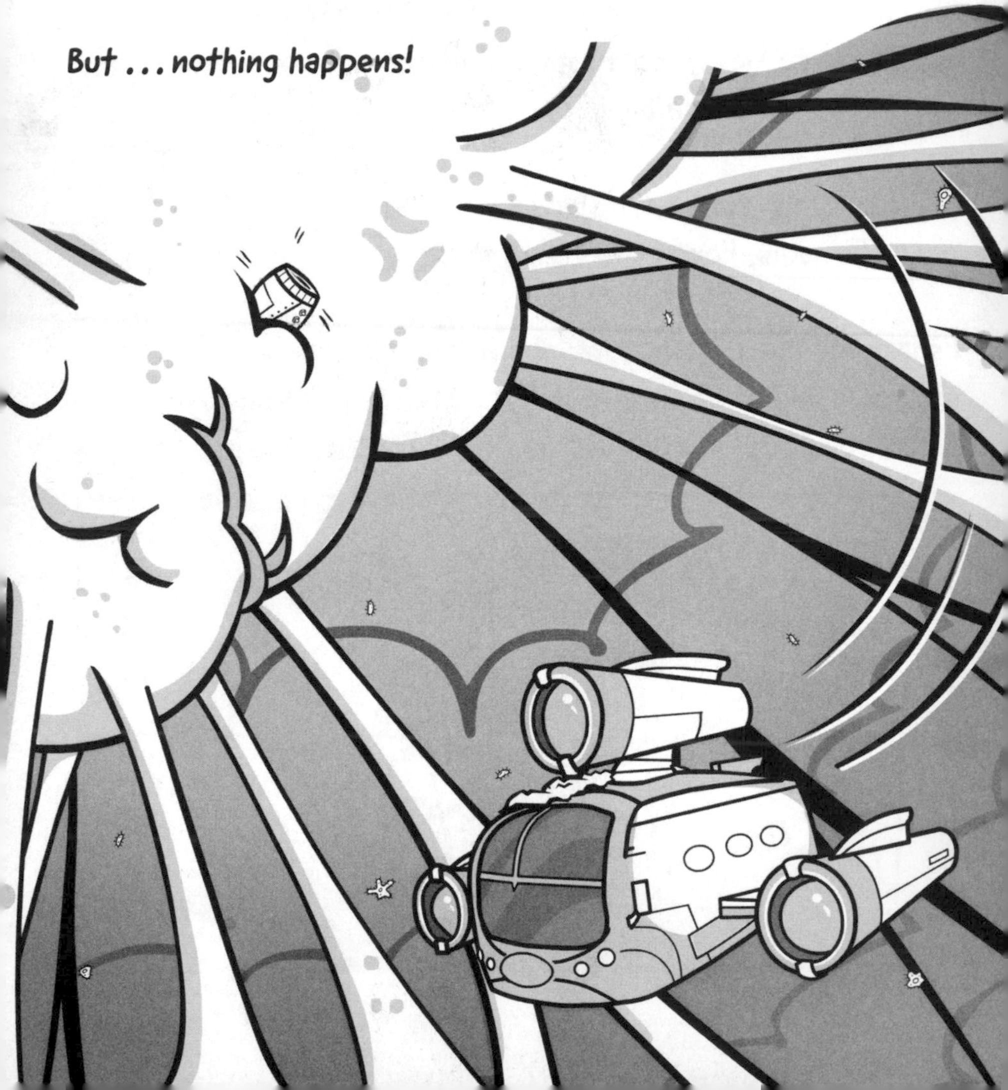

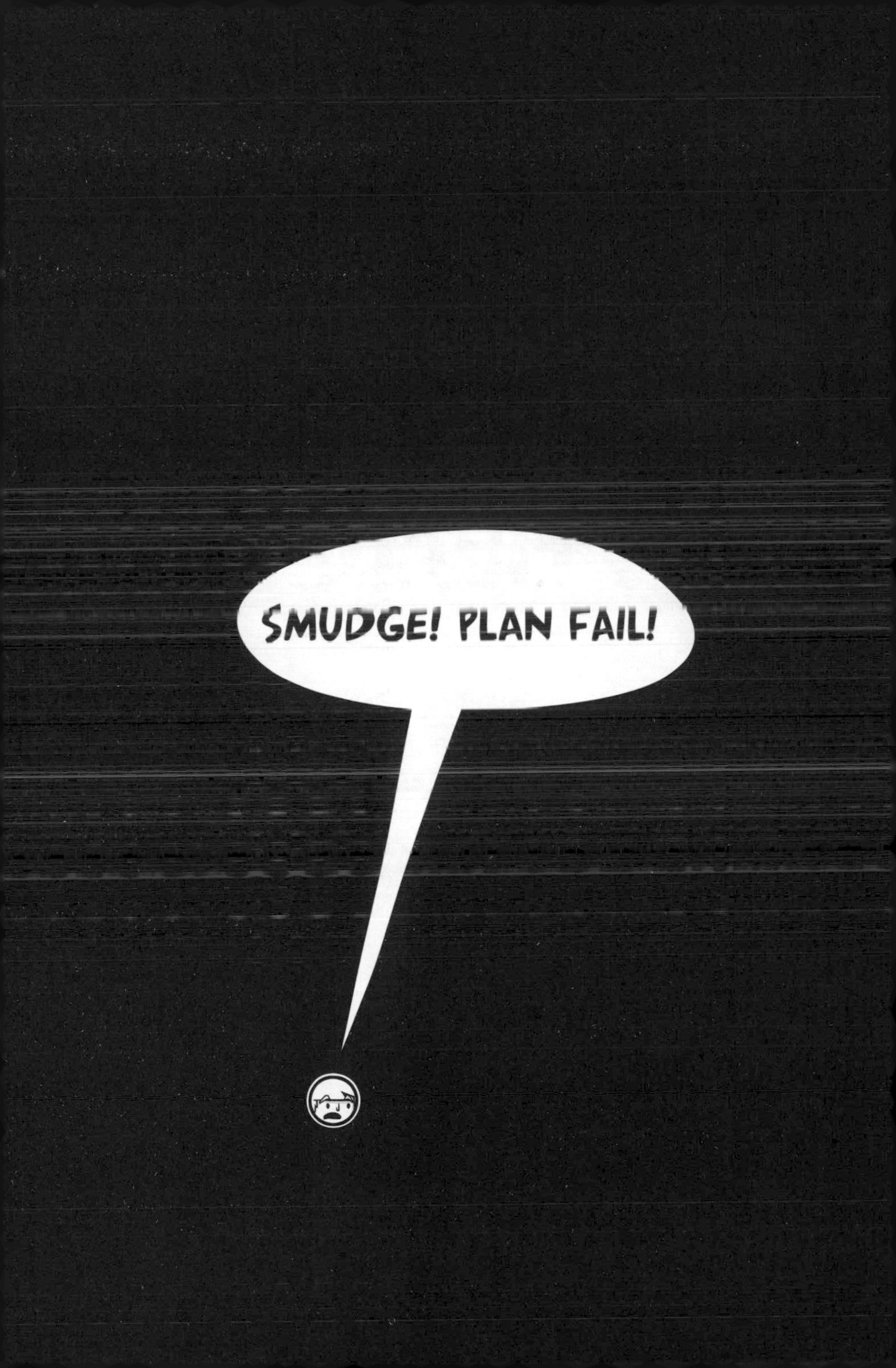
SMUDGE! PLAN FAIL!

OVER HERE, NUGGET HEAD!

25

The barrel didn't blow! I have to go out there. Two minutes later, Princess Dagger is helping me suit up while Humps works the wheel.

Time to head to the roof . . .

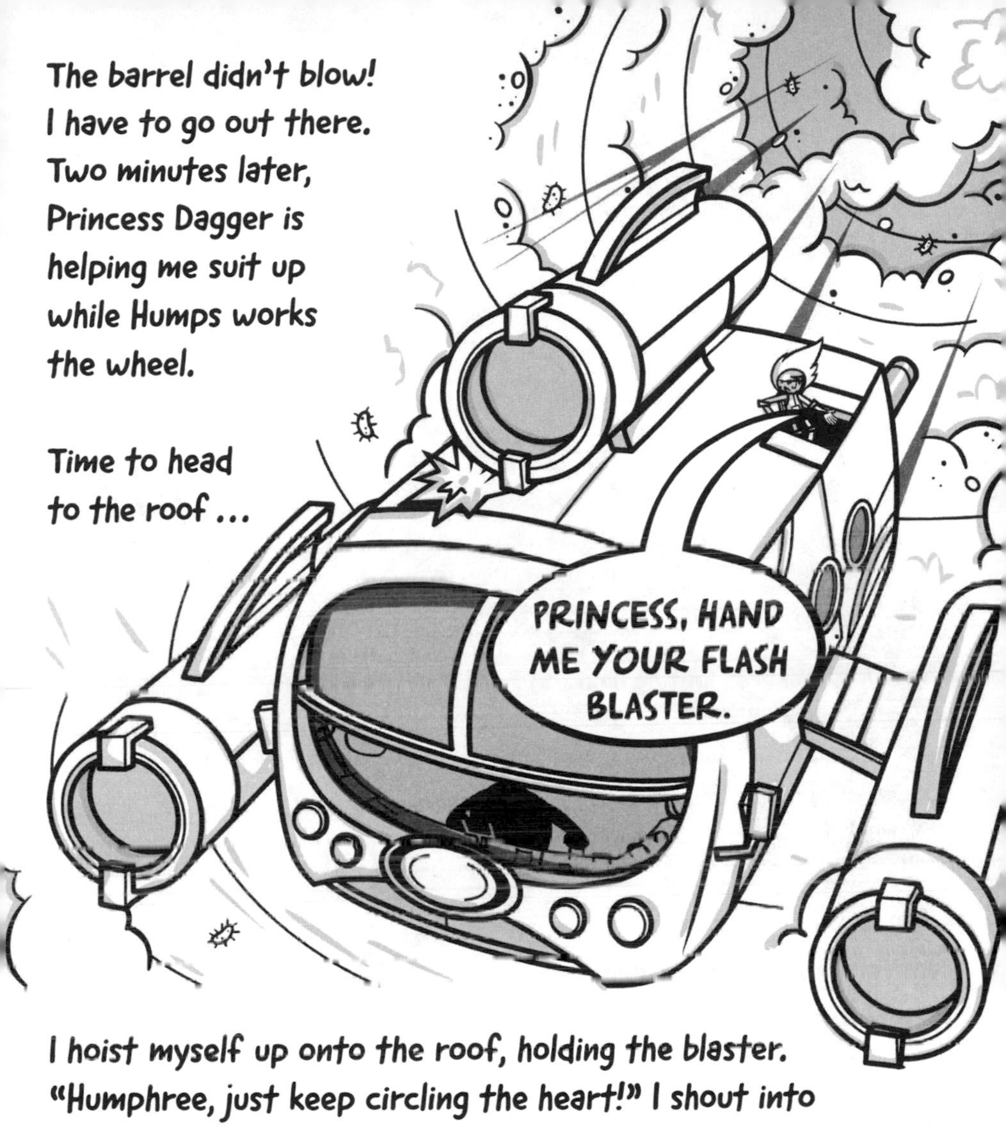
PRINCESS, HAND ME YOUR FLASH BLASTER.

I hoist myself up onto the roof, holding the blaster. "Humphree, just keep circling the heart!" I shout into the radio.

I grab the main jet and pull myself along the roof. Laser fire erupts all around me, and the airstream threatens to blow me off.

But that's nothing compared to—

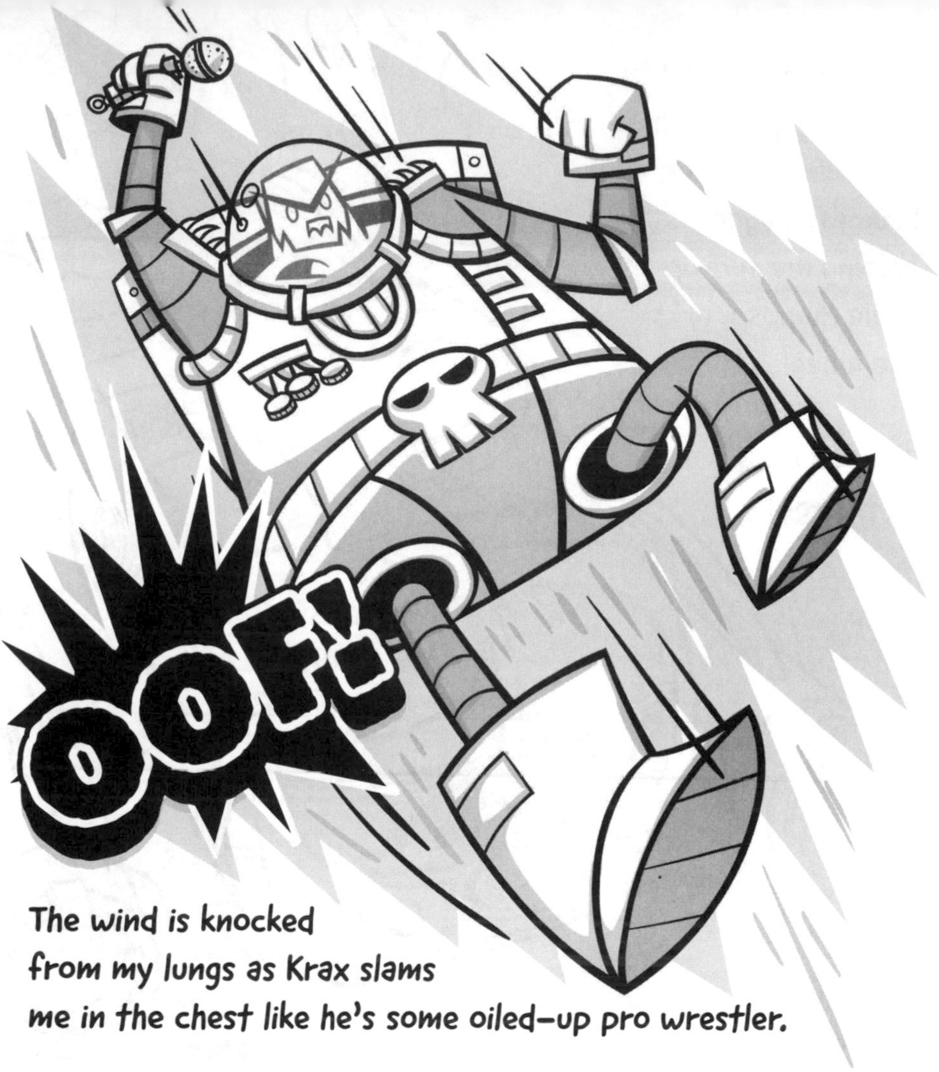
OOF!

The wind is knocked
from my lungs as Krax slams
me in the chest like he's some oiled-up pro wrestler.

Dagger's flash blaster slips from my hand and drops back down into the ship. I tumble end over end, back across the ship's roof. At the last nanosecond, I reach out, gripping the thruster!

"Krax, you dope!" I shout. "We don't have time for this! I'm trying to save everyone!"

Krax yanks his Micro-Blast Bat, and it extends to the full length of a sword with a *fa-shing!*

OK, I've had enough. There's no time for Krax's silliness . . .

"Goober, buddy!" I say, ***"LET'S WAX THIS KRAX!"***

But before I can do that, Krax roars and raises the Micro-Blast Bat. "Eat energy!"

Bolts of white-hot electricity shoot from the end of Krax's weapon, leaping into Goober. The little guy fries on my arm, all *sizzle, sizzle, sizzle!*

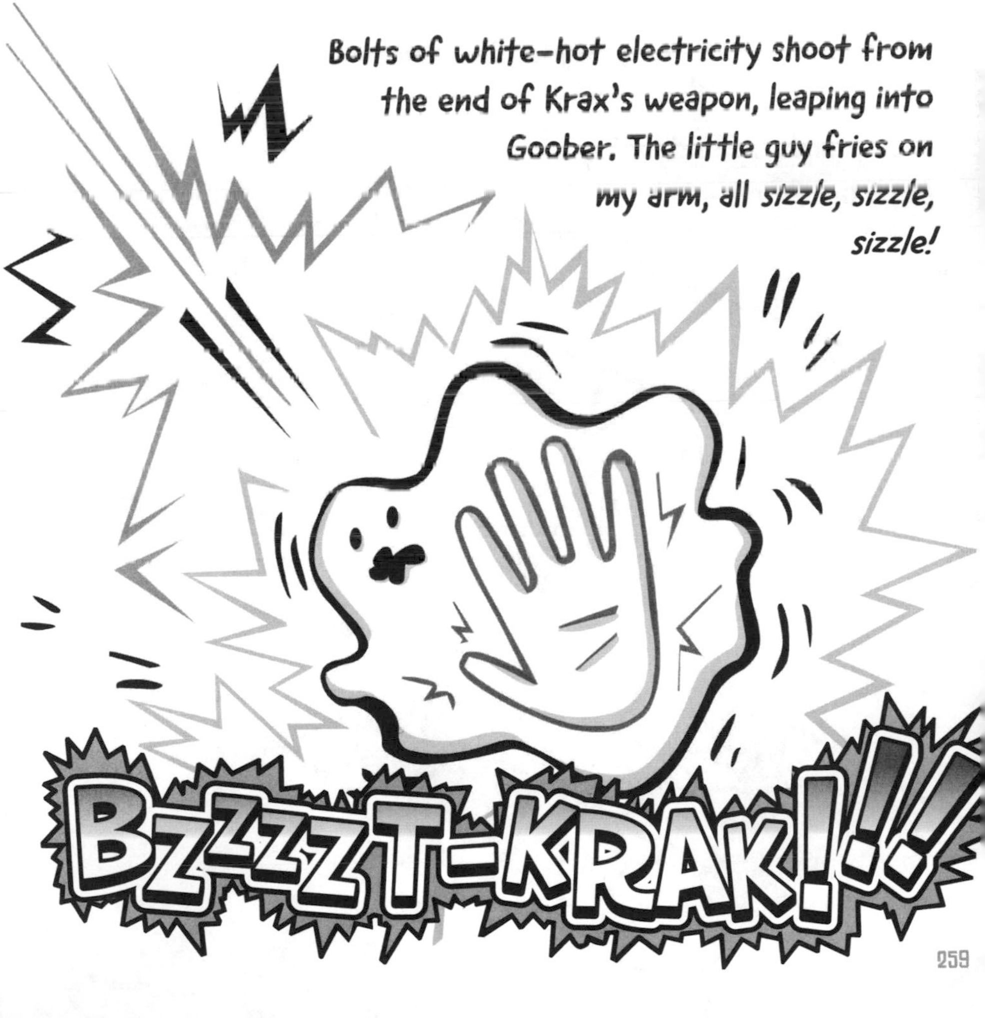
BZZZZT-KRAK!!!

"I will destroy this beast," Krax growls. "And I will be rich! Also, Evil Queen Dagger will love me and hug me. ***NOT YOU!***"

I sigh. "Dude, you are ***SO*** insecure. I don't care who gets the credit. I'm trying to **SAVE THE UNIVERSE** here! Big picture, Krax!"

Krax shakes his head and steps toward me, Micro-Blast Bat raised. I gulp. But then the voice of a friend—

"Hey, Krax! Over here, nugget head!"

Krax whirls around just as Dagger pops up, firing—

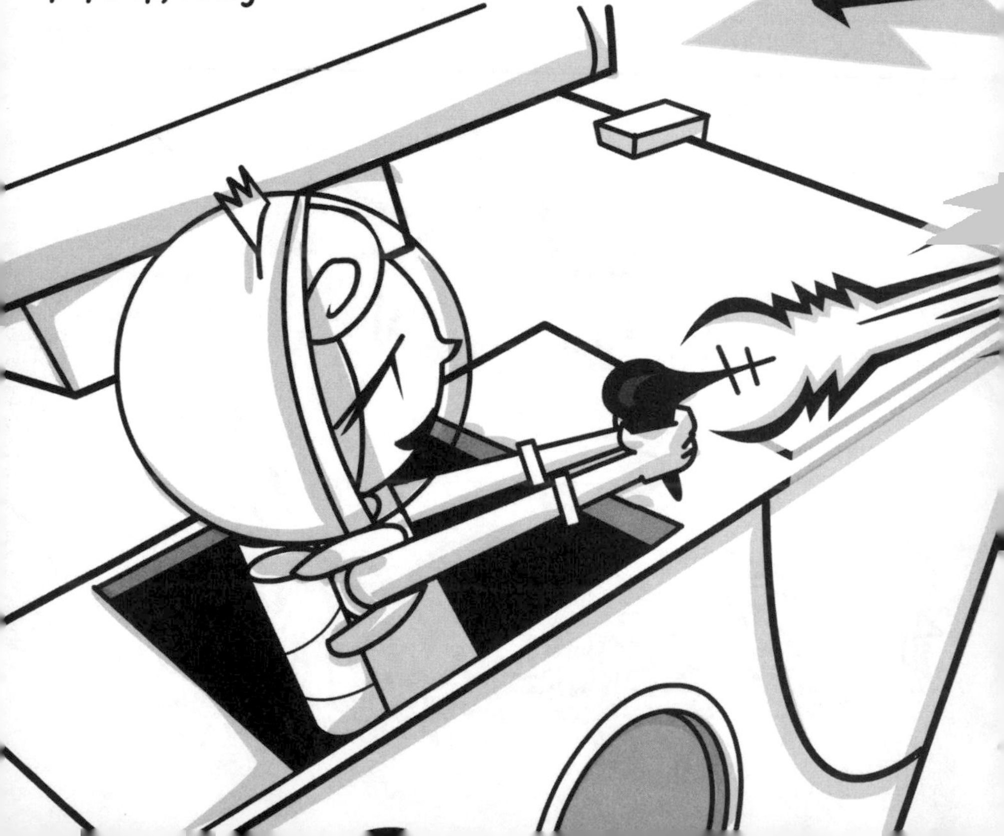

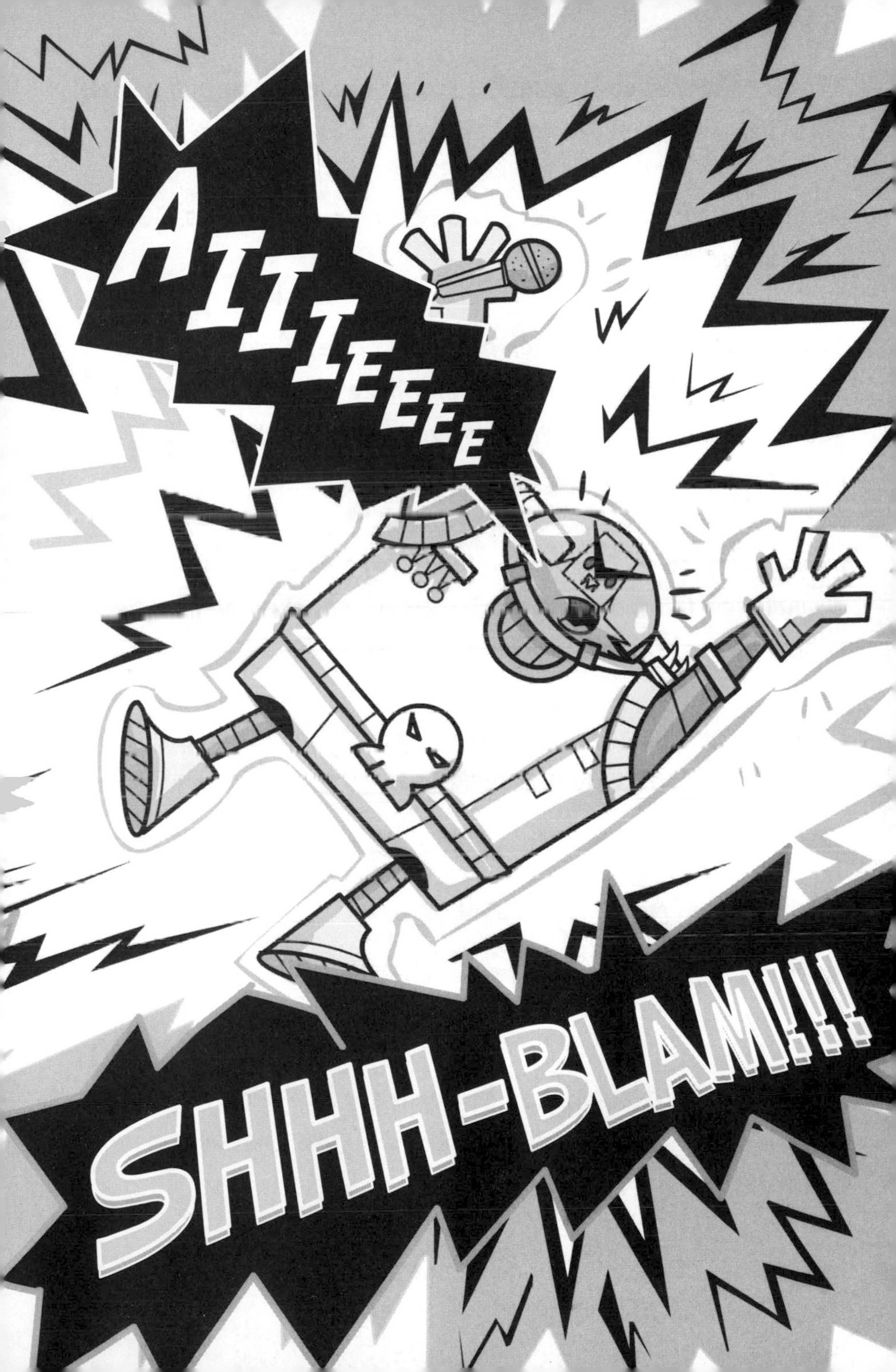
AIIIEEEEE
SHHH-BLAM!!!

"Thanks for the save, Dags!" I say as I manage to pull myself forward and get my feet back on solid *Wiener* roof.

Dagger tosses me the fiery flash blaster and shouts, "Go, Cosmoe, go!"

Gripping the blaster, I peer over the edge of the ship. Far below, I see the big barrel of Humphree's Original Hot Hot Sauce, resting against the massive heart. I just need one good shot . . .

I turn my gaze to Goober. He looks cute as ever but still a whole lot fried. Krax's electro-blast shocked him to his rubbery core. "Goober, you OK?" I ask.

Goober tightens around my wrist, gently squeezing me. Usually that's his way of saying yes.

USUALLY.

But right now it might just be some sort of electrical convulsion! And that would be bad. Because I'm counting on him for this—my big moment.

It's action-Cosmoe swan dive time . . .

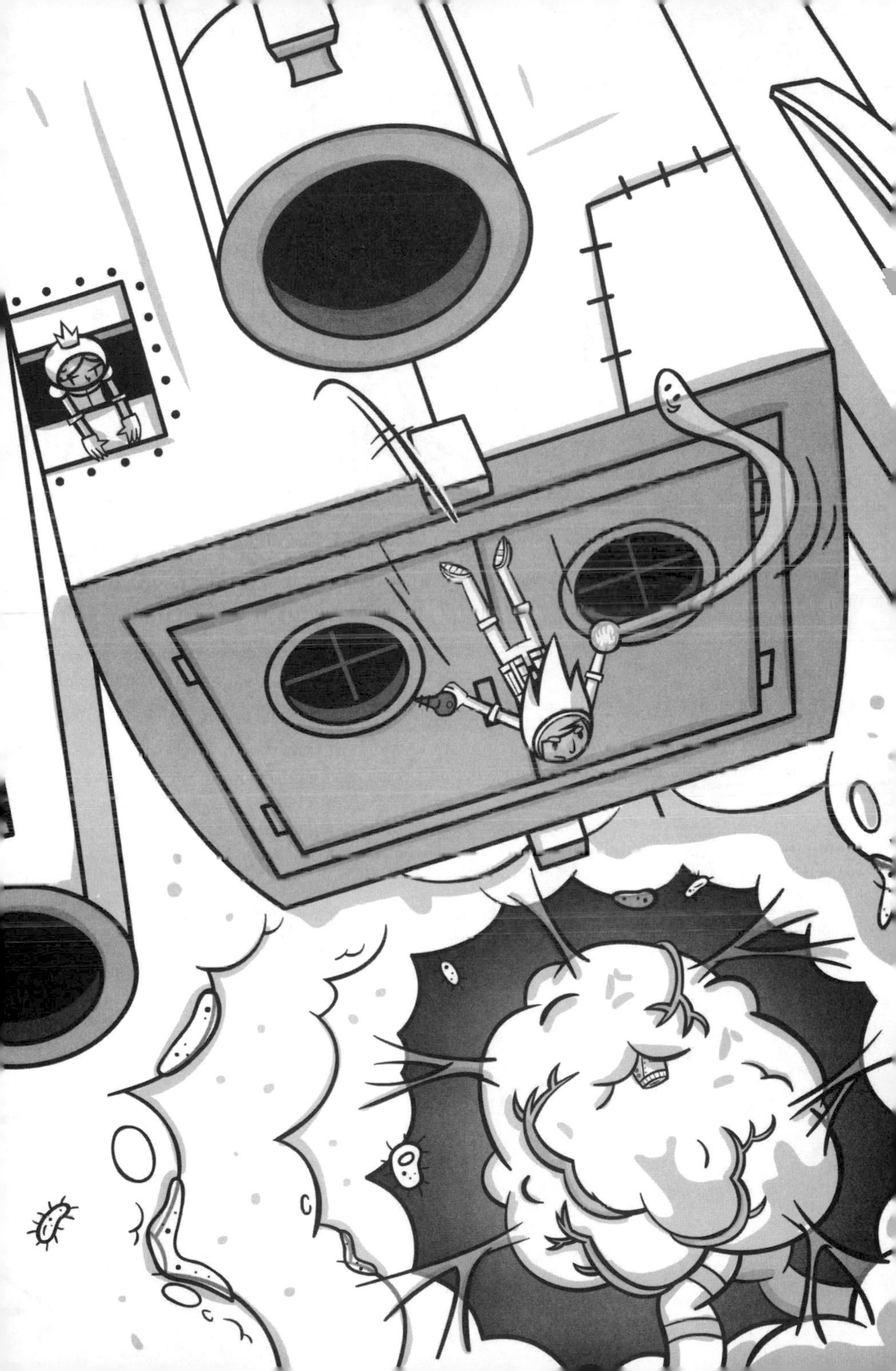

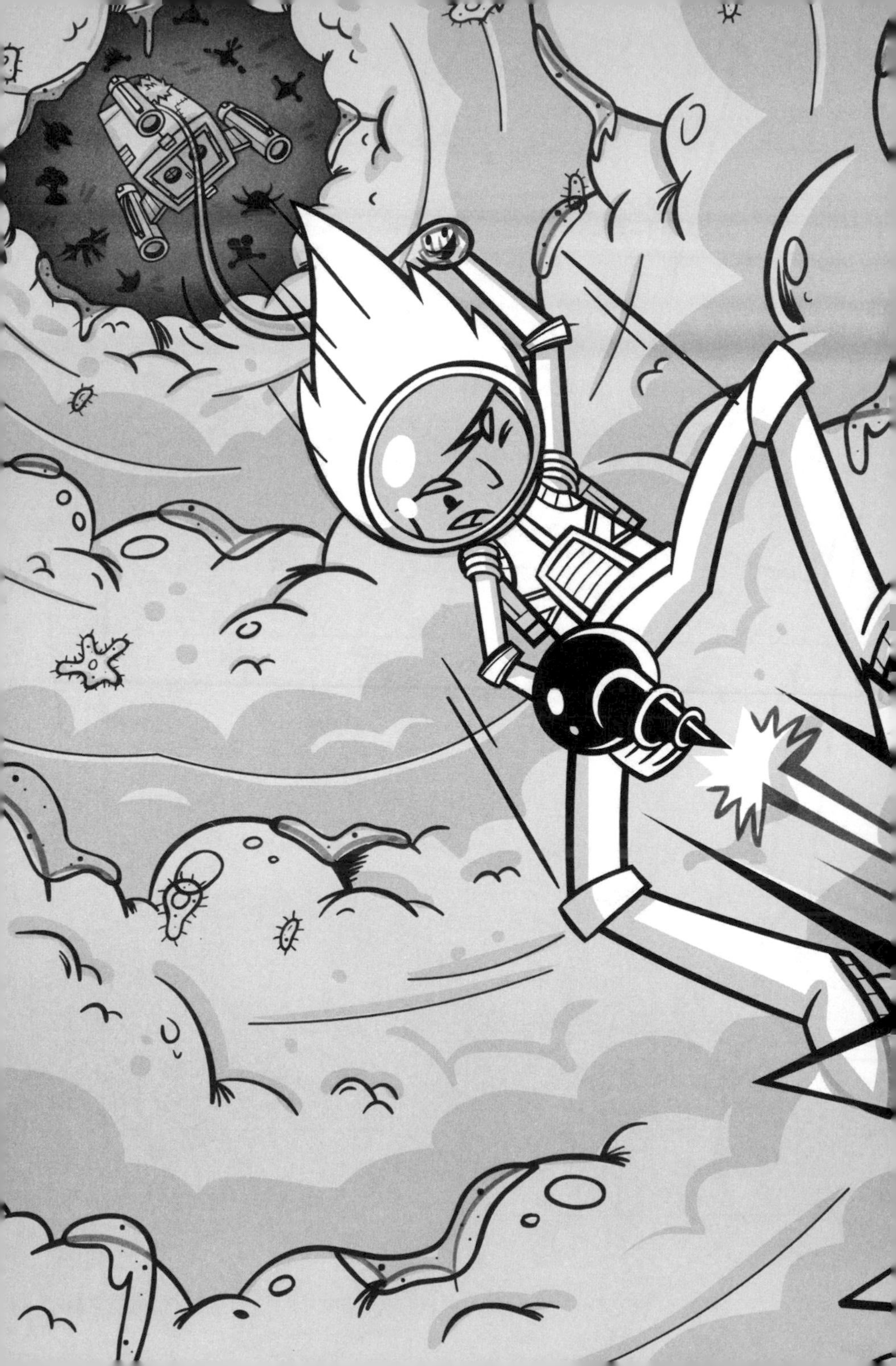

I'm being whipped around at about 1,000 klicks an hour. Above me, a very angry, very injured Krax is jetpacking back to his ship. Lasers are blasting. The beast is quaking.

But I focus.

I block out all the crazy space action madness.

And then time seems to slow down, like I'm in the zone, like it's all just a game, allowing me to close one eye and squeeze . . .

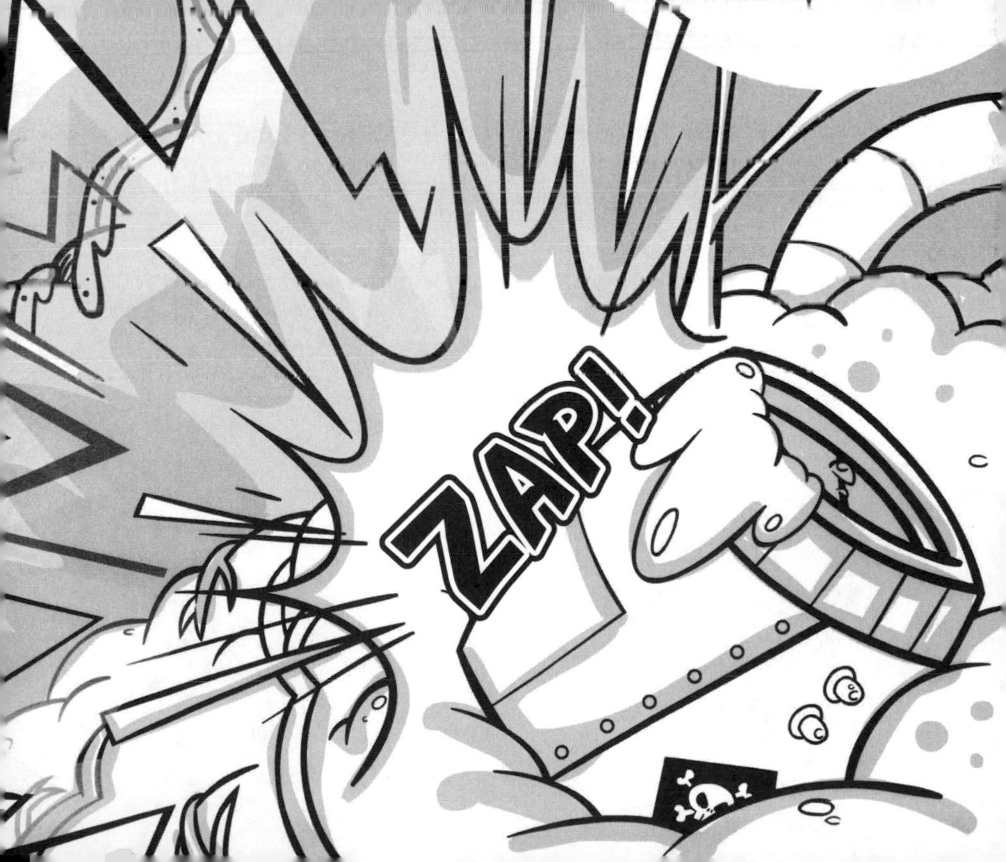
ZAP!

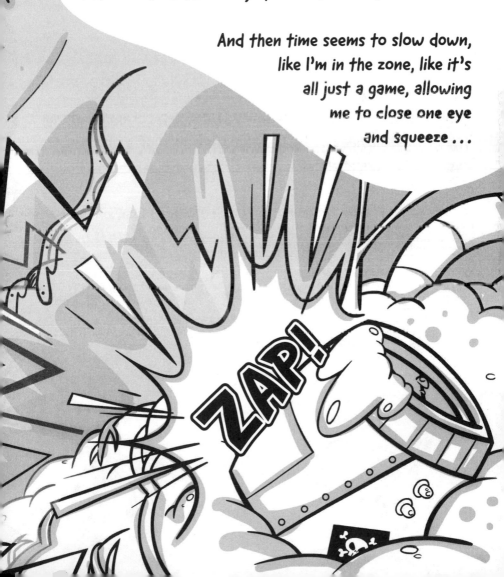

BADA-BOOM!

The explosion is immense and bright and powerful. I tumble back through the air. All I see is white-hot light. All I hear is a piercing ringing.

And suddenly, I'm being pulled away—dragged—as the *Neon Wiener* accelerates, racing to escape the flames.

Goober is stretched to his maximum length as Humphree maneuvers the *Wiener* though the twisting, turning body of the Ultimate Evil—chased by an explosion that's growing ever more immense!

As I'm pulled along, helpless, all I can think is, man oh man— HUMPHREE'S ORIGINAL HOT HOT SAUCE is *SERIOUS BUSINESS.*

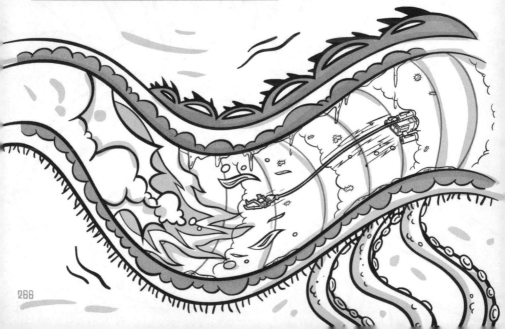

FLEEING, FIRE-STYLE!

LET'S FIND US SOME TROUBLE

26

The *Neon Wiener* bursts through the flames and out into open space, just as the hot, hot fire consumes the beast completely. Goober and I are pulled along like cosmic cargo.

I have a perfect view of the destruction: billions of fleshy pieces of evil exploding outward, detonated from the inside . . .

WE DID IT.
EVIL DEFEATED!

I'm about to start patting myself on the back for being a radical galaxy-saving hero, when I hear the howl of an engine.

Then I see him—General Krax von Grumble, closing in fast . . .

But before Krax can fire off a rocket and end us—

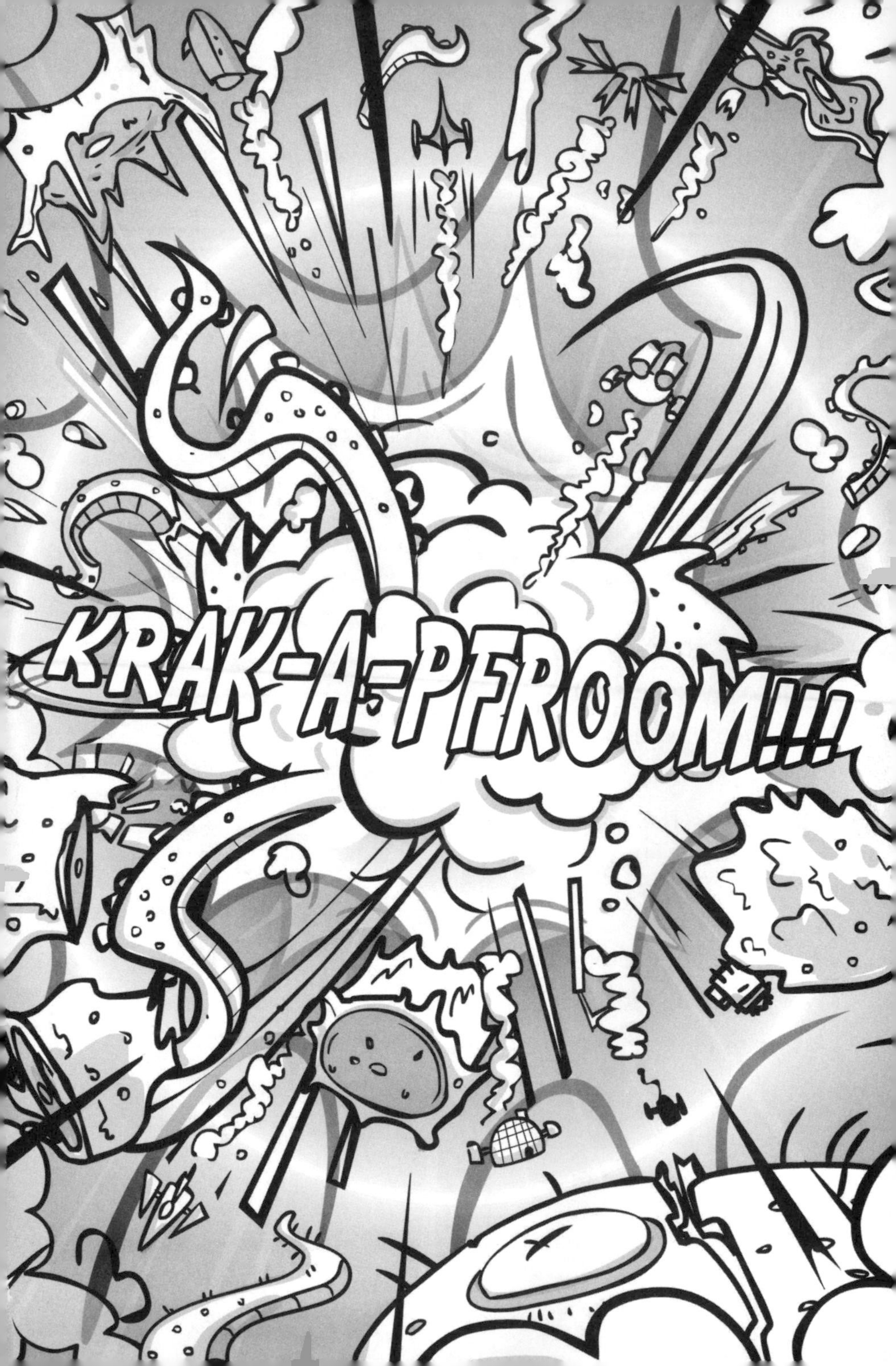
KRAK-A-PFROOM!!!

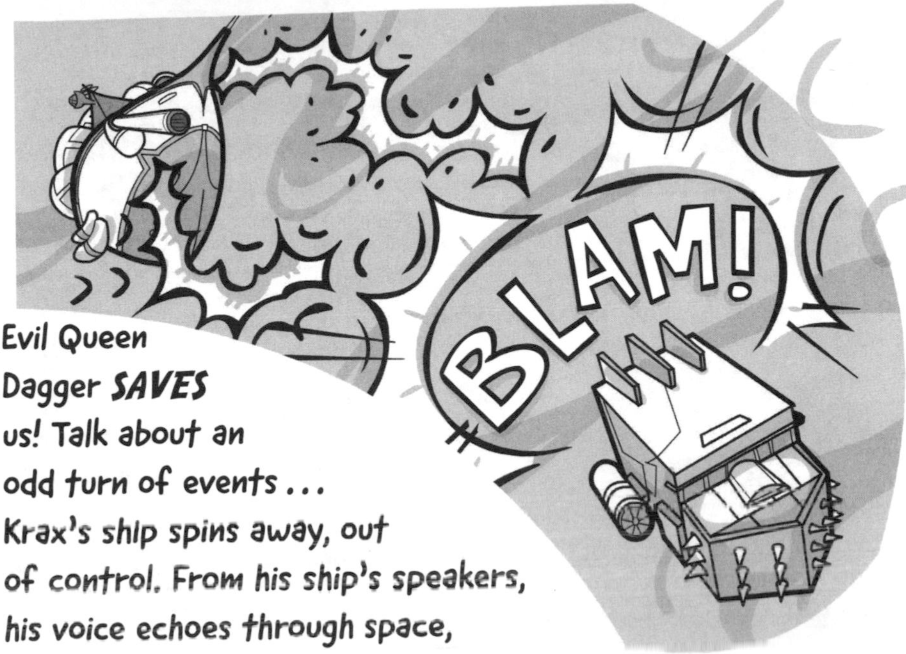
BLAM!

Evil Queen Dagger ***SAVES*** us! Talk about an odd turn of events . . . Krax's ship spins away, out of control. From his ship's speakers, his voice echoes through space,

"I'LL GET YOU, COSMOE THE EARTH-BOY!"

Maybe you will, Krax. Maybe you will. But not today . . .

Humphree buzzes in over my helmet-com. "You OK back there, short pants?"

"Just keep flying, Humps," I say, feeling nothing but pure relief.

"Just keep flying."

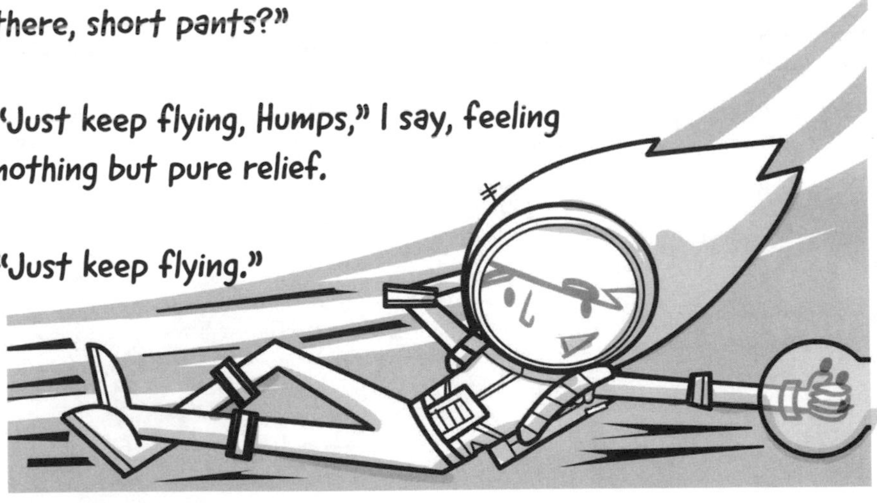

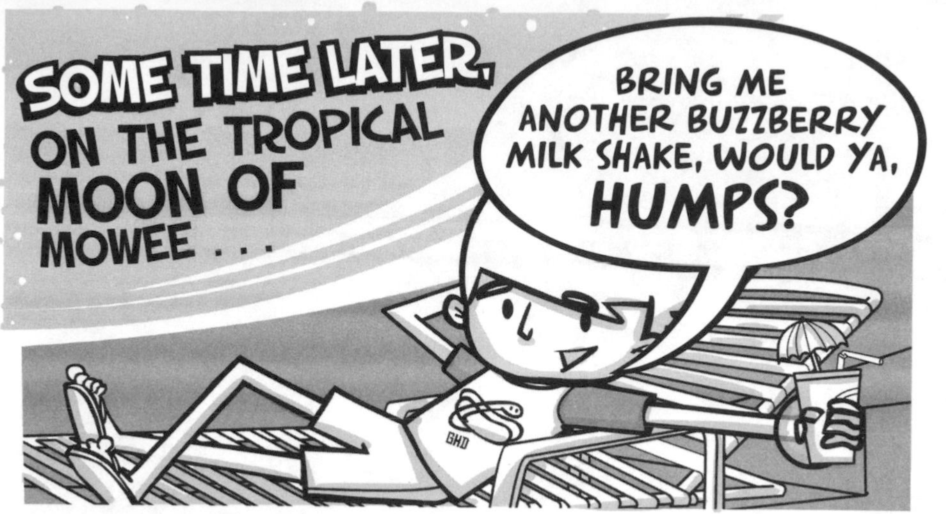
SOME TIME LATER, ON THE TROPICAL MOON OF MOWEE . . .
BRING ME ANOTHER BUZZBERRY MILK SHAKE, WOULD YA, HUMPS?
GHD

"No, Cosmoe!" Humphree barks. "I need you on mustard duty! We got customers lined up to the end of the beach!"

"Argh," I groan. "OK, OK, I'm coming . . ."

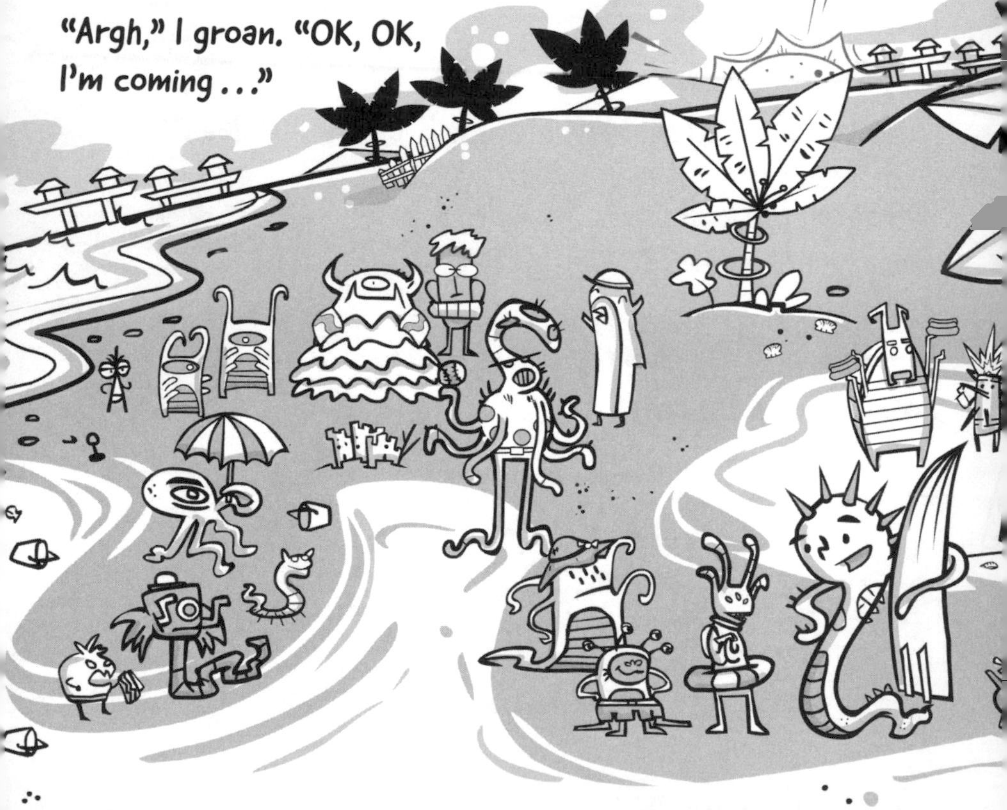

I get to my feet and trot across the hot sand. Humphree's a bit of a grump right now. He's annoyed the evil queen never gave us the reward **$$$.** But it's all good—word got around about our galaxy-saving adventure, and now business is booming!

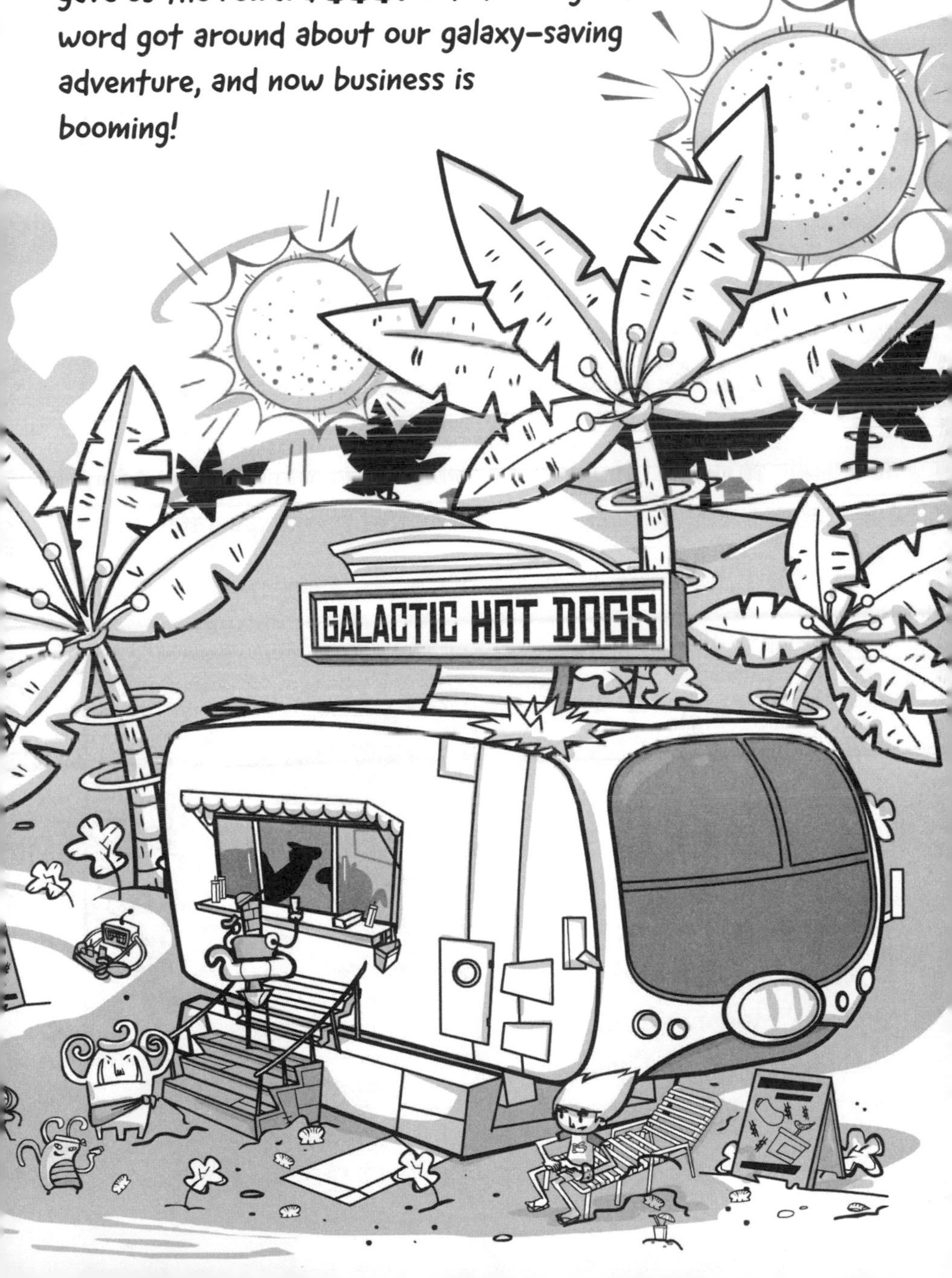
GALACTIC HOT DOGS

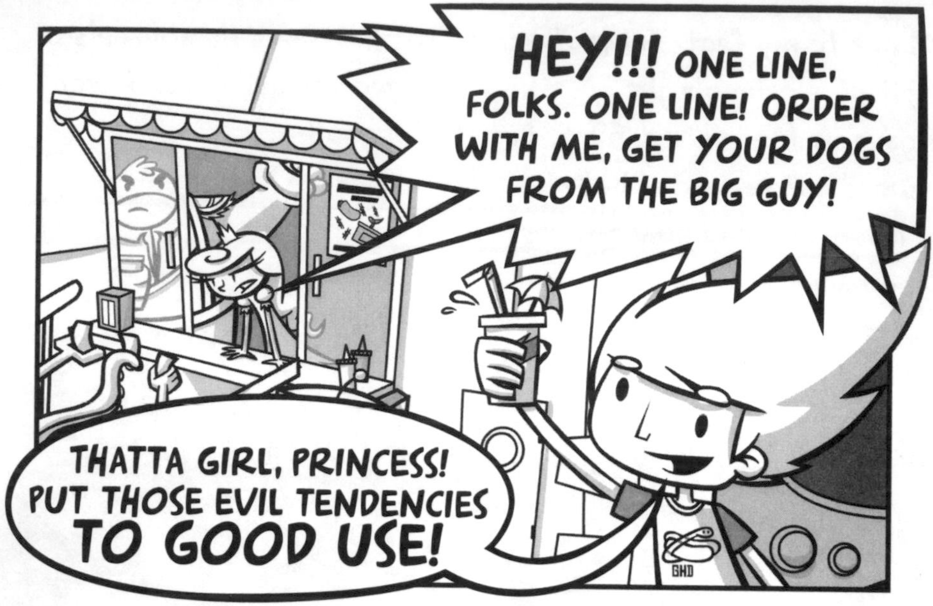
HEY!!! ONE LINE, FOLKS. ONE LINE! ORDER WITH ME, GET YOUR DOGS FROM THE BIG GUY!
THATTA GIRL, PRINCESS! PUT THOSE EVIL TENDENCIES TO GOOD USE!

Suddenly, there's a thunderous rumbling in the sky. A shadow falls over the bright pink ocean and the turquoise sand and, soon, over us.

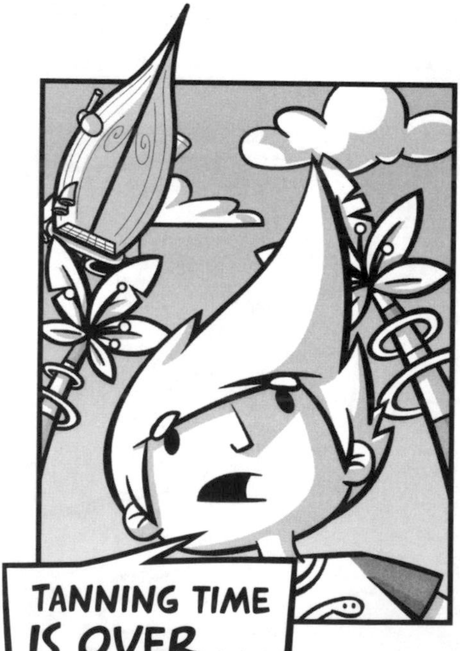
TANNING TIME IS OVER . . .

"It's her!" one tiny alien shouts, pointing to the sky. "Run!"

Just like that, our booming business is brought to a halt. A massive ship is descending, so large that it blocks all three of Mowee's suns. The rumbling turns to a heavy hiss as the ship begins to hover-dock.

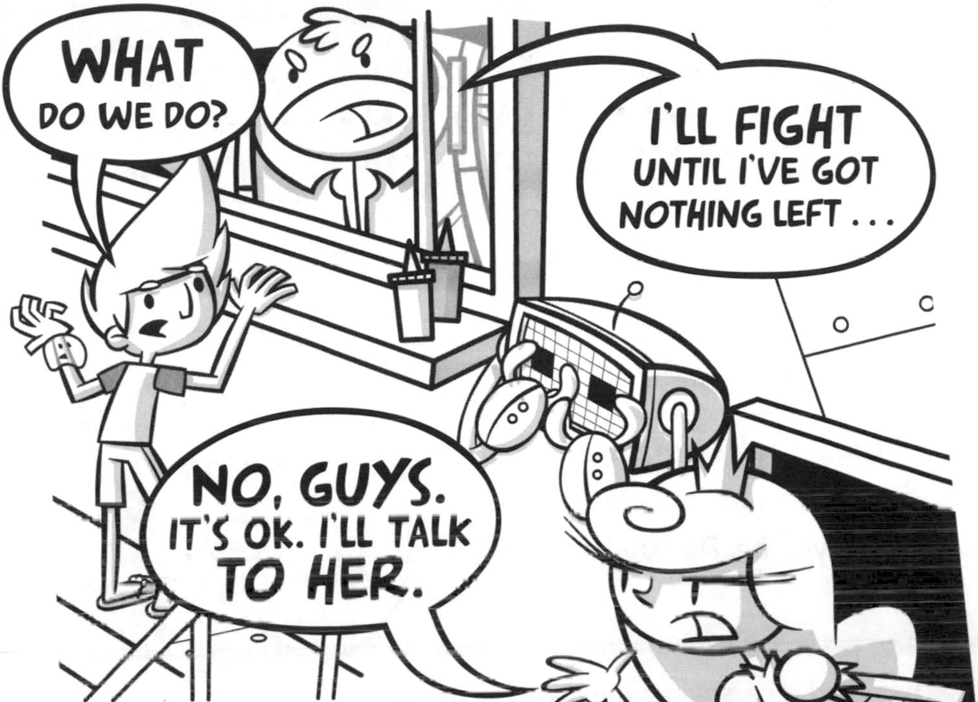
WHAT DO WE DO?
I'LL FIGHT UNTIL I'VE GOT NOTHING LEFT . . .
NO, GUYS. IT'S OK. I'LL TALK TO HER.

Humphree and I watch
Princess Dagger march bravely
across the sand, alone, to meet her mother.

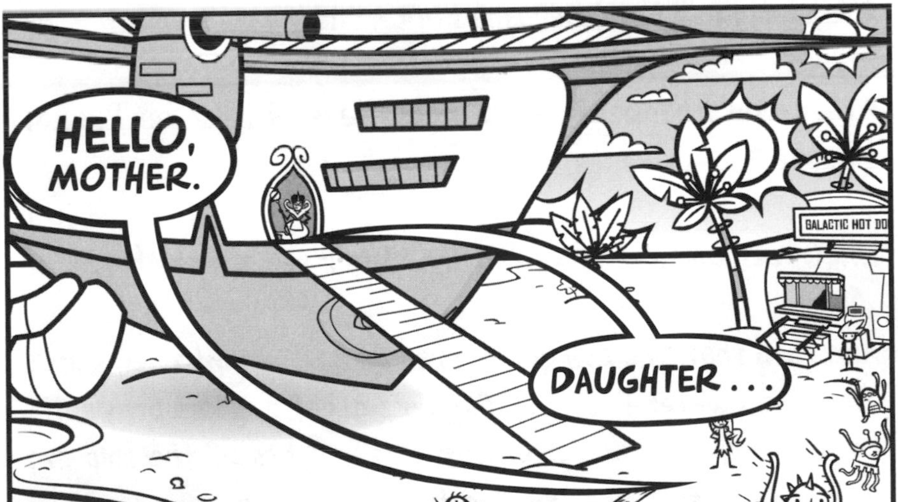
HELLO, MOTHER.
GALACTIC HOT DO
DAUGHTER . . .

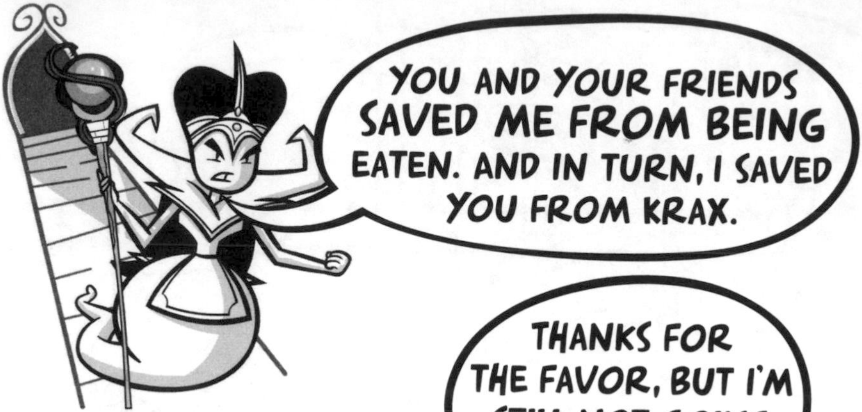
YOU AND YOUR FRIENDS SAVED ME FROM BEING EATEN. AND IN TURN, I SAVED YOU FROM KRAX.

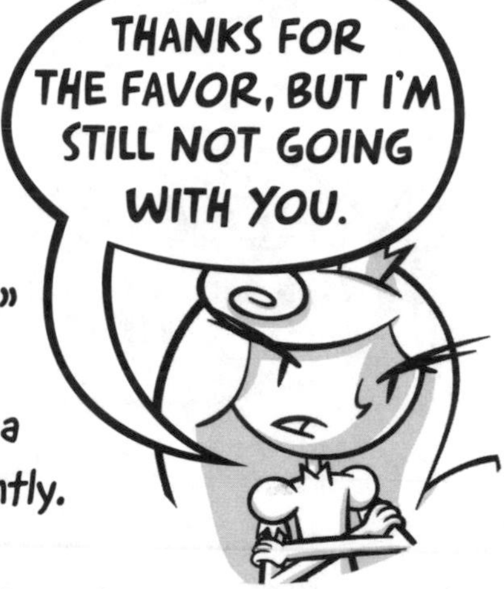
THANKS FOR THE FAVOR, BUT I'M STILL NOT GOING WITH YOU.

"I know you're not. I could force you, but I won't. I'm going to let you be. Do you know why?"

The princess says nothing. After a moment, she shakes her head tightly.

"Because I know, daughter, that deep down inside, you are pure evil. And that evil will bring you back to me. And oh my, the hurt you'll have unleashed upon the galaxy by then . . ."

"That won't happen," the princess says. "I told you, I'm not like you."

Evil Queen Dagger smiles cruelly. "We'll see about that."

And with that, the evil queen tramps back up into her ship. The ocean water foams as *Biggun*'s great engines propel it back into space. I watch until the rear lights of the ship are just faint dots in the sky, like two dark stars.

BOOM! FREEDOM! HOW YOU LIKE THAT?!? MY MOM'S NOT TAKING ME!

I smile. "I know.
We heard the whole thing."

"So now what?" Dagger says.

I look down the beach. "Your mom scared away all the customers, so I think we're done slinging wieners for the day."

The princess grins. "An adventure?"

Humphree looks like he's going to collapse. "We just saved the entire frappin' galaxy, mates! It's vacation time! I'm talking Grog Fizzies, blazer tag, picking our noses, being lazy!"

"Nah! I'm with the princess, Humps. Let's find us some trouble."

The princess looks at me and grins again. "But what if we can't find any?"

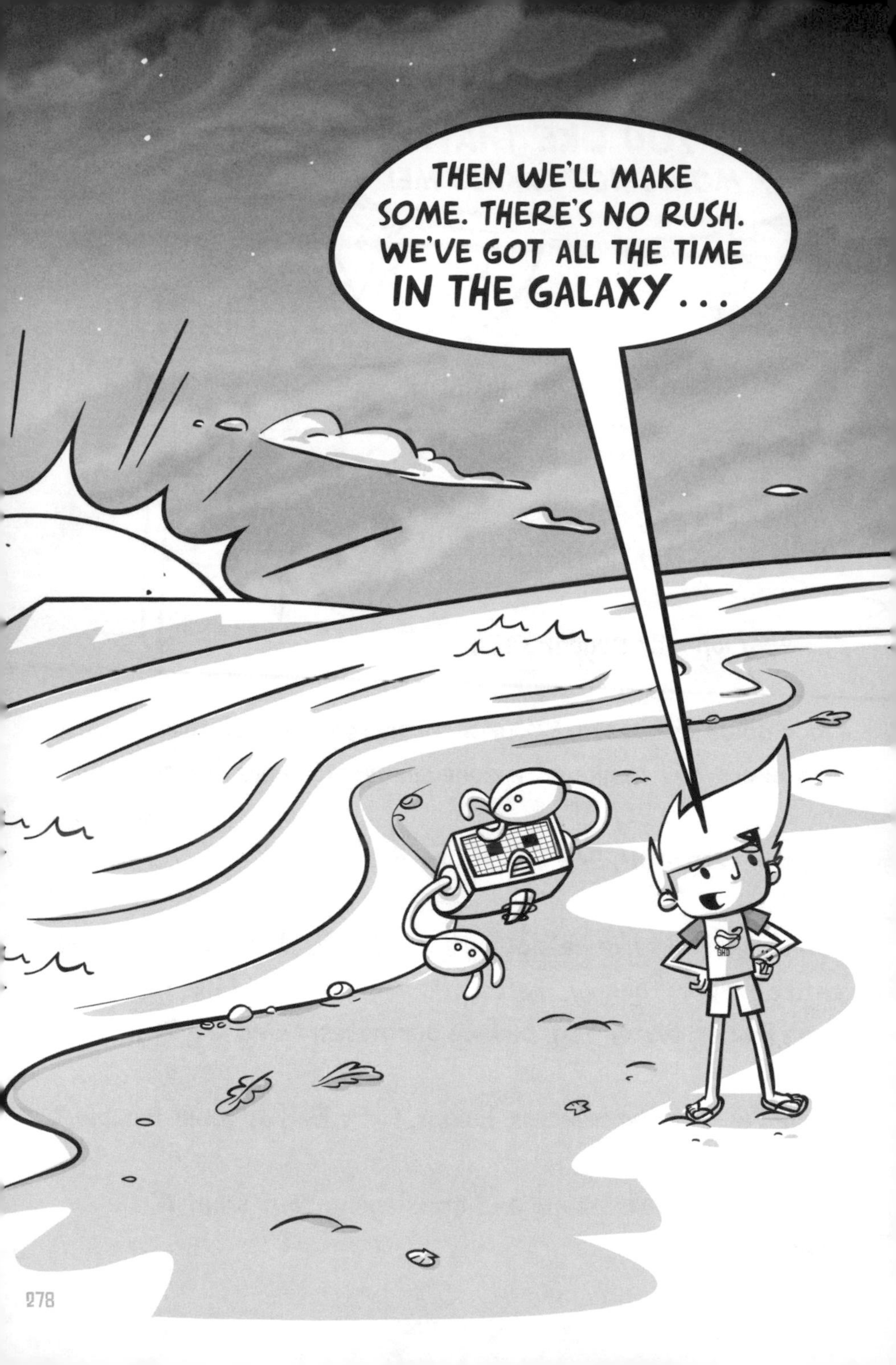
THEN WE'LL MAKE SOME. THERE'S NO RUSH. WE'VE GOT ALL THE TIME IN THE GALAXY . . .

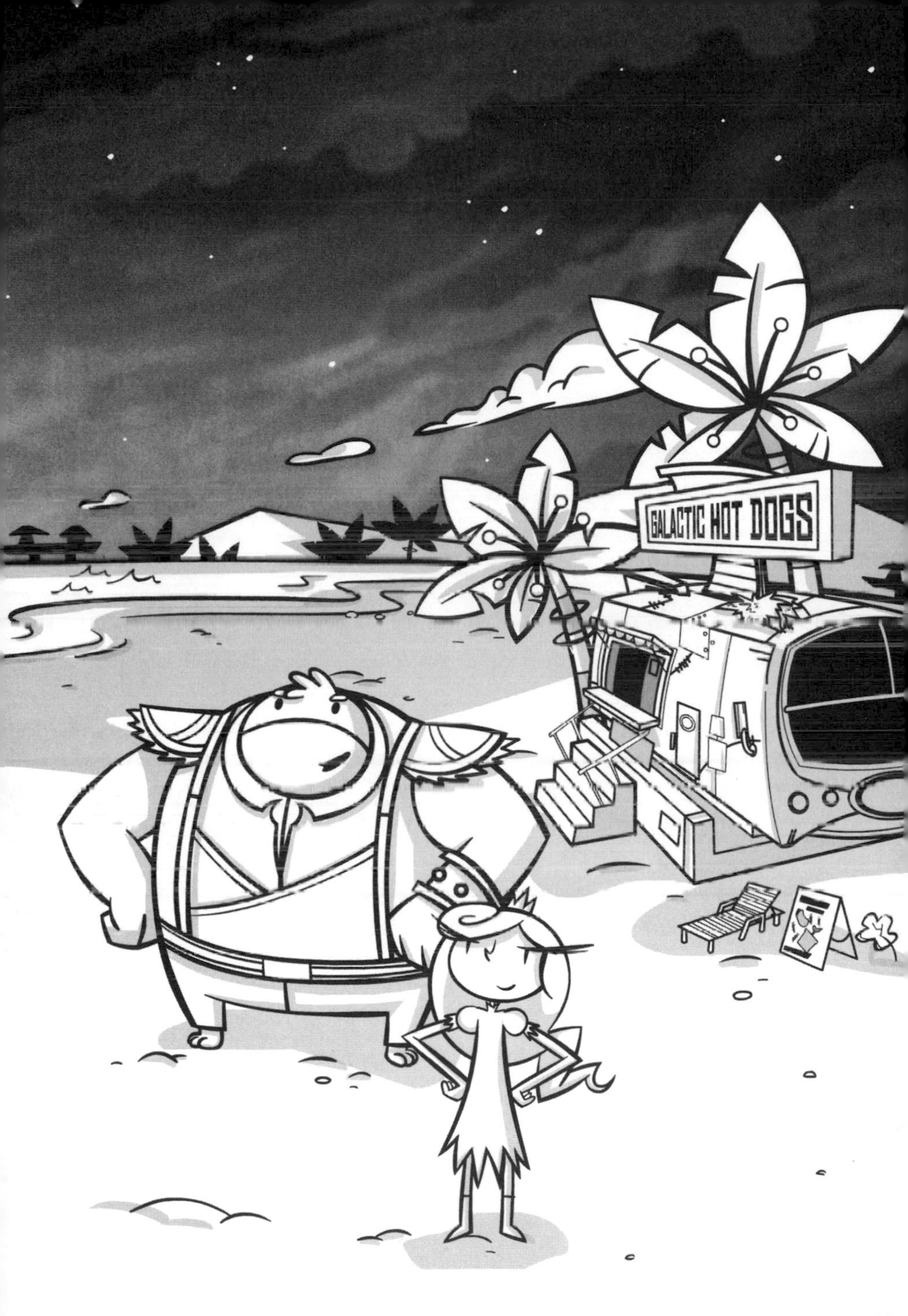
GALACTIC HOT DOGS

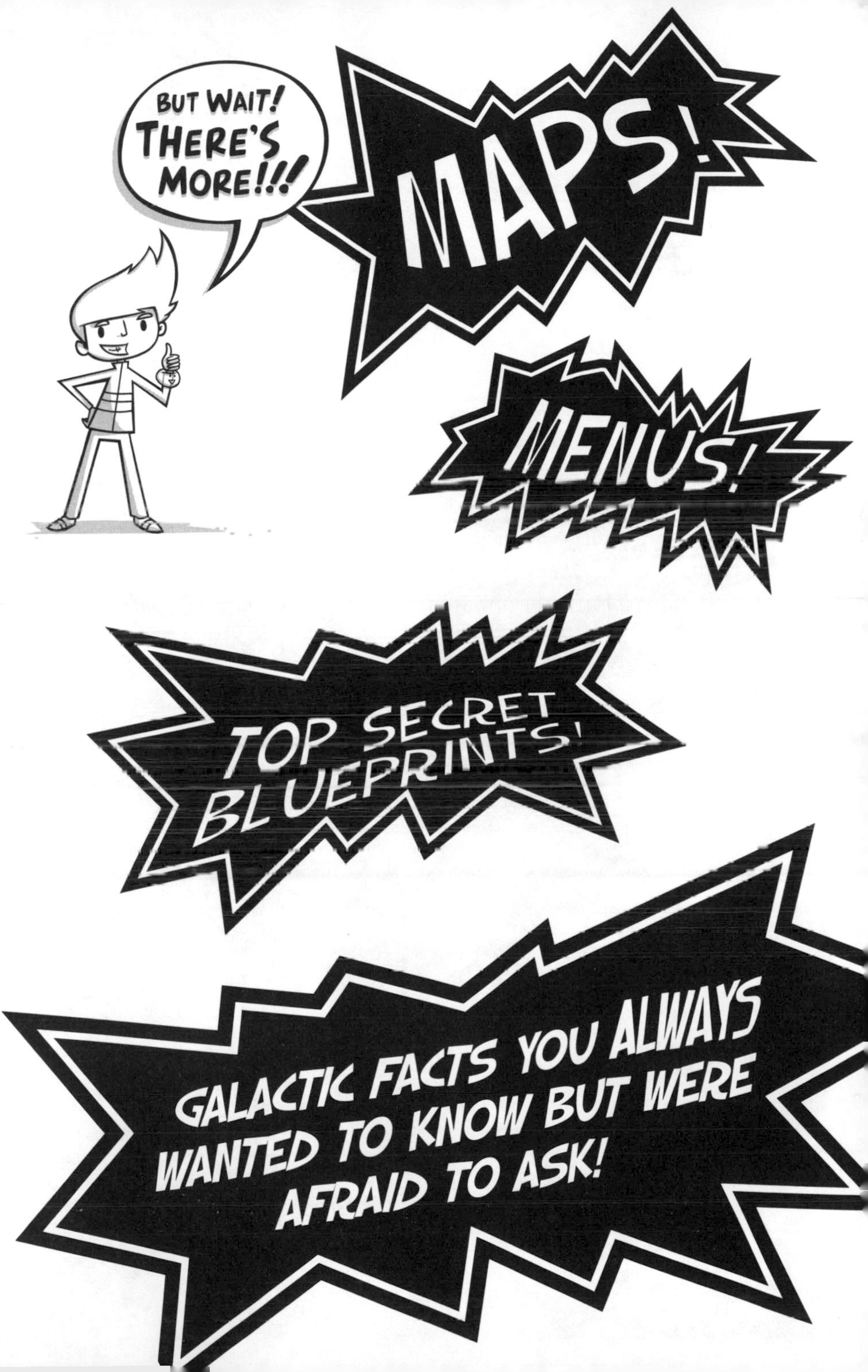
BUT WAIT! THERE'S MORE!!!
MAPS!
MENUS!
TOP SECRET BLUEPRINTS!
GALACTIC FACTS YOU ALWAYS WANTED TO KNOW BUT WERE AFRAID TO ASK!

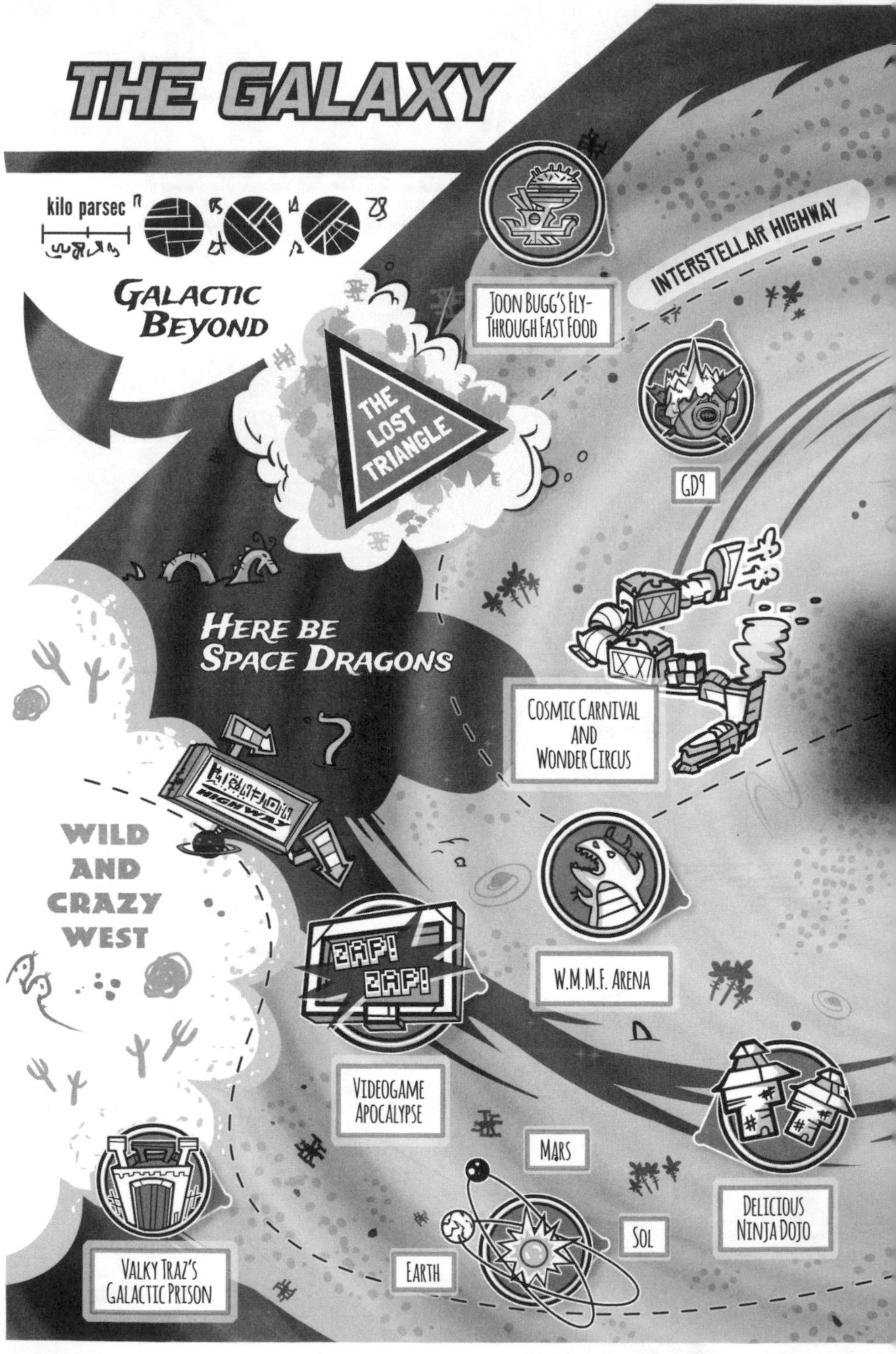
THE GALAXY
kilo parsec
GALACTIC BEYOND
INTERSTELLAR HIGHWAY
JOON BUGG'S FLY-THROUGH FAST FOOD
THE LOST TRIANGLE
GD9
HERE BE SPACE DRAGONS
COSMIC CARNIVAL AND WONDER CIRCUS
HIGHWAY
WILD AND CRAZY WEST
W.M.M.F. ARENA
ZAP! ZAP!
VIDEOGAME APOCALYPSE
MARS
DELICIOUS NINJA DOJO
SOL
EARTH
VALKY TRAZ'S GALACTIC PRISON

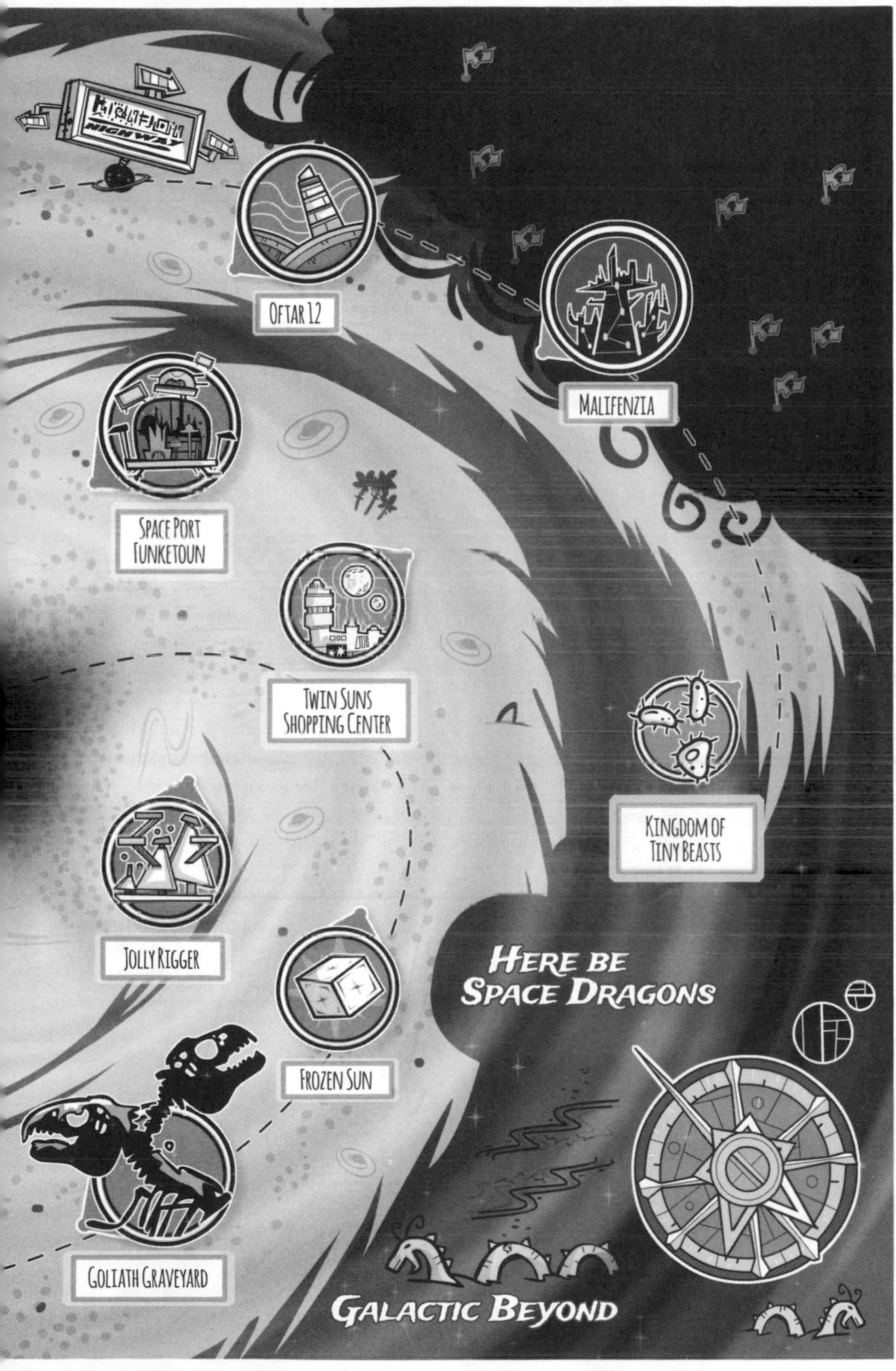
HIGHWAY
OFTAR 12
MALIFENZIA
SPACE PORT FUNKETOUN
TWIN SUNS SHOPPING CENTER
KINGDOM OF TINY BEASTS
JOLLY RIGGER
HERE BE SPACE DRAGONS
FROZEN SUN
GOLIATH GRAVEYARD
GALACTIC BEYOND

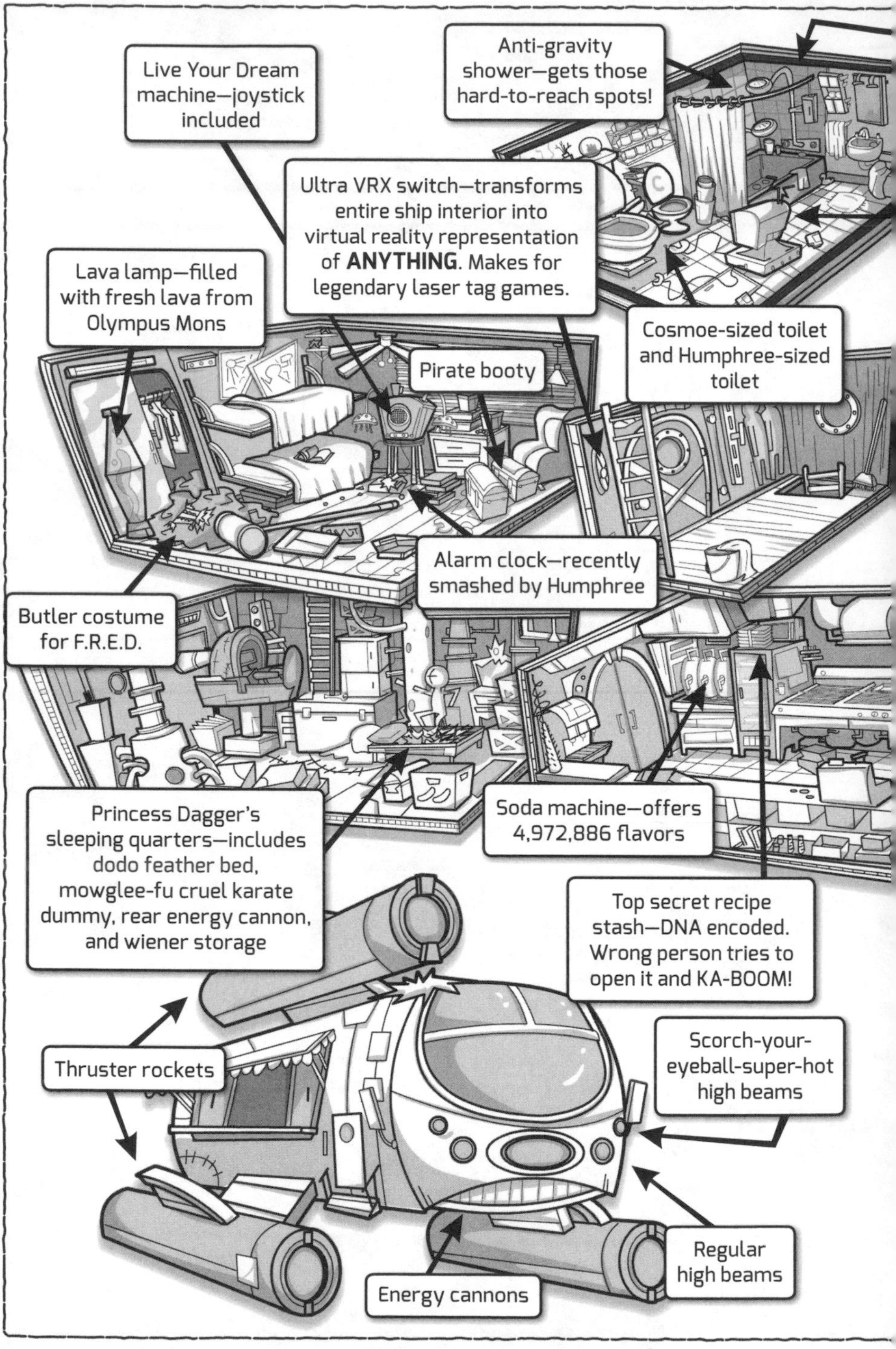
Live Your Dream machine—joystick included
Anti-gravity shower—gets those hard-to-reach spots!
Ultra VRX switch—transforms entire ship interior into virtual reality representation of **ANYTHING**. Makes for legendary laser tag games.
Lava lamp—filled with fresh lava from Olympus Mons
Pirate booty
Cosmoe-sized toilet and Humphree-sized toilet
Alarm clock—recently smashed by Humphree
Butler costume for F.R.E.D.
Princess Dagger's sleeping quarters—includes dodo feather bed, mowglee-fu cruel karate dummy, rear energy cannon, and wiener storage
Soda machine—offers 4,972,886 flavors
Top secret recipe stash—DNA encoded. Wrong person tries to open it and KA-BOOM!
Scorch-your-eyeball-super-hot high beams
Thruster rockets
Regular high beams
Energy cannons

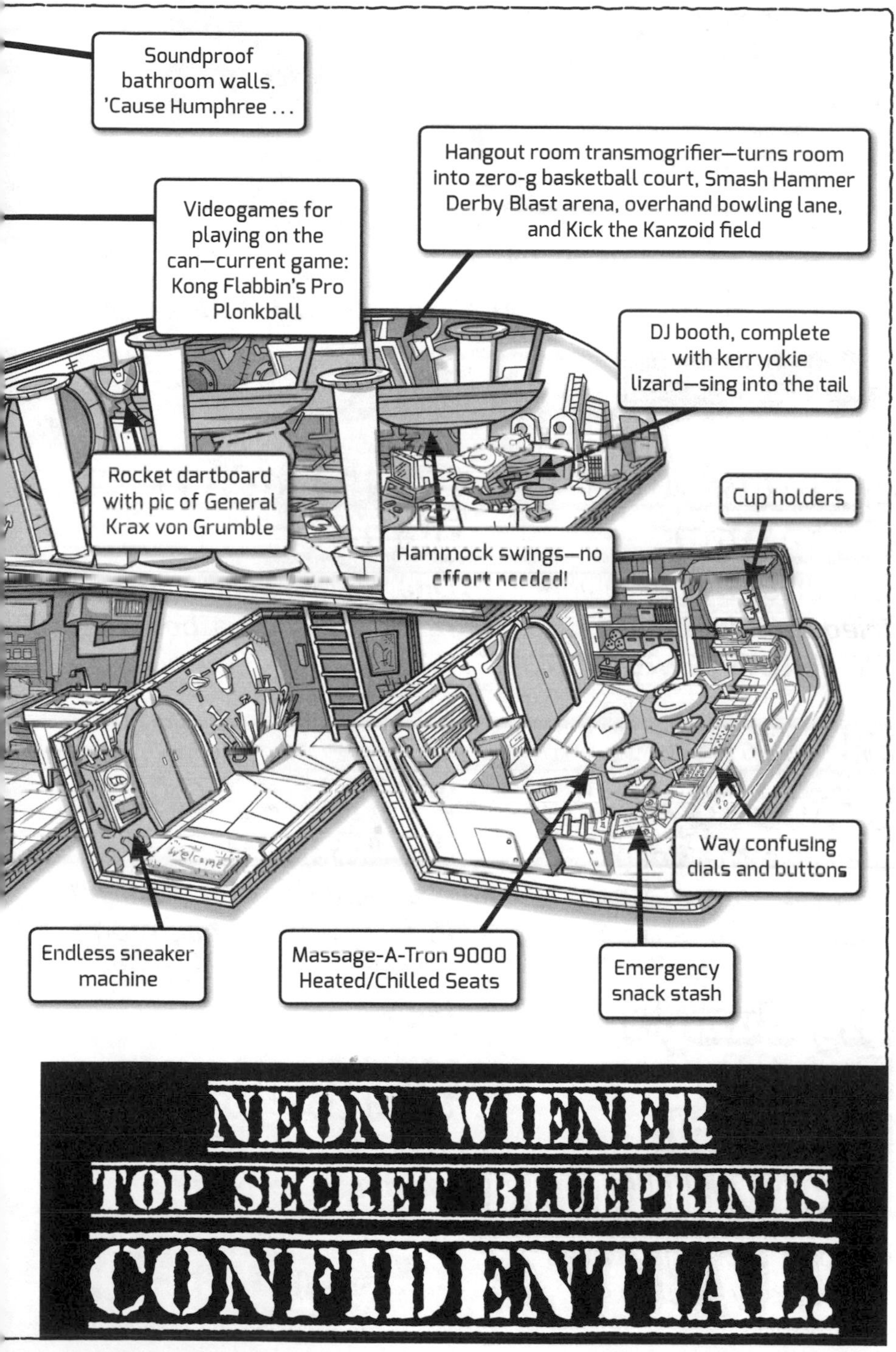
Soundproof bathroom walls. 'Cause Humphree . . .
Hangout room transmogrifier—turns room into zero-g basketball court, Smash Hammer Derby Blast arena, overhand bowling lane, and Kick the Kanzoid field
Videogames for playing on the can—current game: Kong Flabbin's Pro Plonkball
DJ booth, complete with kerryokie lizard—sing into the tail
Rocket dartboard with pic of General Krax von Grumble
Cup holders
Hammock swings—no effort needed!
Welcome
Way confusing dials and buttons
Endless sneaker machine
Massage-A-Tron 9000 Heated/Chilled Seats
Emergency snack stash

NEON WIENER
TOP SECRET BLUEPRINTS
CONFIDENTIAL!

GALACTIC HOT DOGS™

- SERVING UP ADVENTURE ... ON A BUN - **#5**

Official Galactic Hot Dogs T-shirts

WIENERS

Cosmoe's Classic Corn Dog

One classic dog, fusion-fried in cake batter.
NO NASTY SPACE BUGS!

The Double Whammy

Just like the Cosmoe Classic—but meteor! (Get it . . . meatier?!)

Big Hump's Knuckle Sandwich

Eight dogs jammed inside a fat loaf of dough. Topped with the works and crispy nuckto knuckles.

Dark Matter Doggie

One dog wrapped in fudge fur, served on a bonbon bun, topped with cocoa crawlzacs.

Deep Impact Chili Dog

A crispy fire dog covered in frozen lava chili, moon cheese, and bean slug-bugs.

The Mega-Dog

The legendry 498-pound wiener entered into the Intragalactic Food Truck Cook-Off

OUT OF STOCK

Prices may vary by star system.

TOPPINGS

Moon Rock Relish
Seyfert Sauerkraut

Raw Arakzid Legs
Lime Moon Cheese

NO LONGER ~~Humphrees' Hot Hot Sauce~~ HAD SOME
SERVED ↗ ISSUES ...

MILKY WAY SHAKES

Buzzberry Shake

Buzzberry ice cream, blotto berries, and Doug Adams' apples.

The Black Hole

Clandaapoo cocoa ice cream, chocolate creepy-crawlies, and nostromo nougat.

Blue and Cream

Inkskyn blue milk swirled with shaved Jeerjeer ice.

Princess Dagger's Royal Pain

Lavenberry ice cream whirled with Dark Kingdom kandy krystals

SNACKS and SWEET TREATS

Crater Tots
Bradbury Cream Egg
Onion Orbitals
Arthur C. Clarke Bar

F.R.E.D. FACT
Interstellar Highway

HIGHWAY
EXIT 2335,888
77
89
12
12

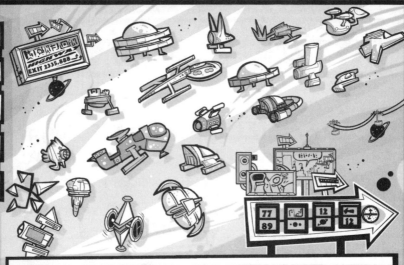

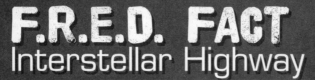

THE INTERSTELLAR HIGHWAY STRETCHES FROM ONE END OF THE GALAXY TO THE OTHER. AT ANY GIVEN MOMENT, THERE ARE ROUGHLY 6 BILLION SHIPS TRAVELING ITS LENGTHS. REST STOPS ALONG THE HIGHWAY ARE NOTORIOUSLY NASTY: FULL OF GREASY FOOD, BREATHING BATHROOMS, AND SHIP-DEVOURING TRAV-GRAB MONSTERS.

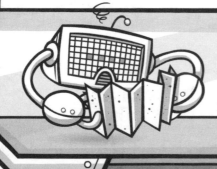

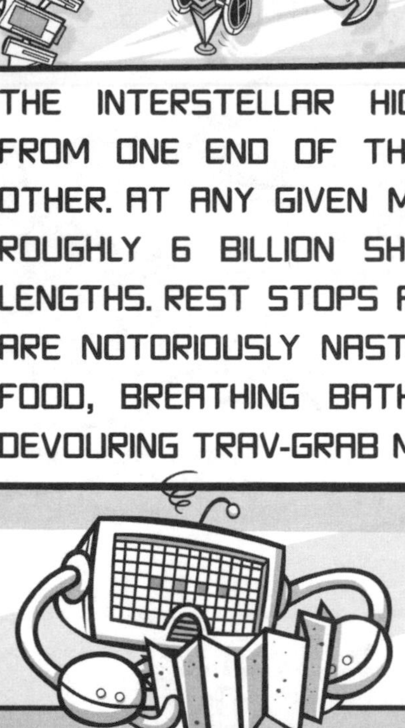

F.R.E.D. FACT
Jack Jet

THESE WICKED-FAST FIGHTER SHIPS MAKE UP THE EVIL QUEEN DAGGER'S ROYAL NAVY. PILOTED BY ROBOT SOLDIERS KNOWN AS JACKS AND ARMED WITH ENERGY CANNONS AND SUPER-FLAME ROCKETS, JACK JETS ARE BAD NEWS.

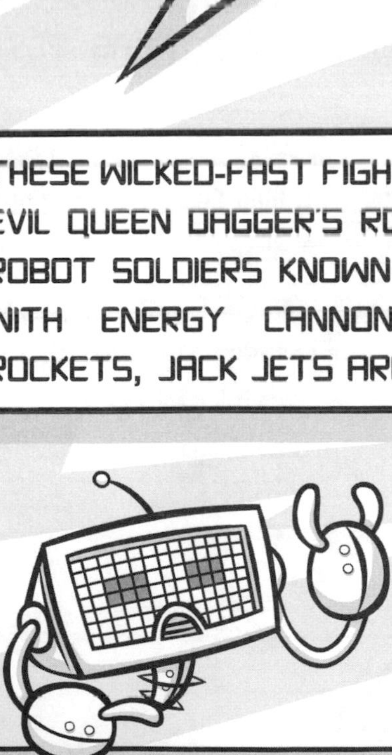

F.R.E.D. FACT
Space Treasure

THE MILKY WAY IS FULL OF LOST TREASURES, INCLUDING:

• THE LOST MOON OF XUMBOOR—400 YEARS AGO, IT SIMPLY VANISHED, ALONG WITH THE XUMBOORIANS WHO LIVED THERE.

• BRUUL'S EYEBALL COLLECTION—LEGEND SAYS THE MONSTER BRUUL PLUCKED AN EYEBALL FROM EVERY SPECIES IN THE GALAXY . . .

• MARTIAN BONES—HARD TO FIND!

F.R.E.D. FACT
Fire and Ice

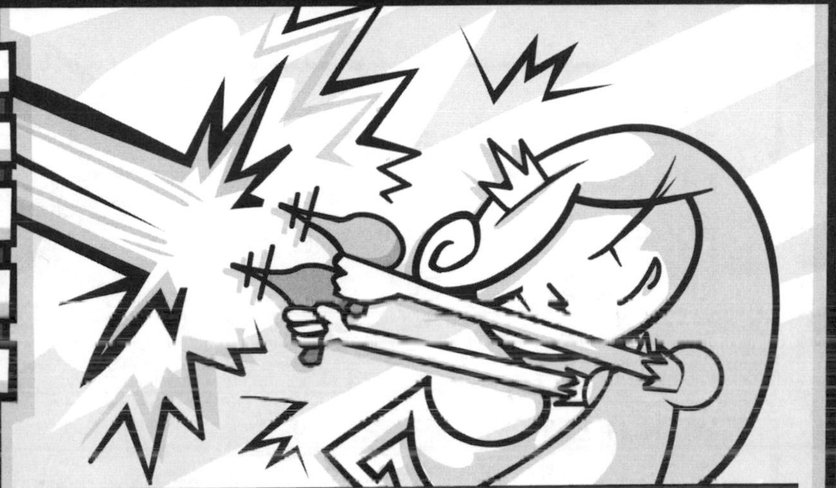

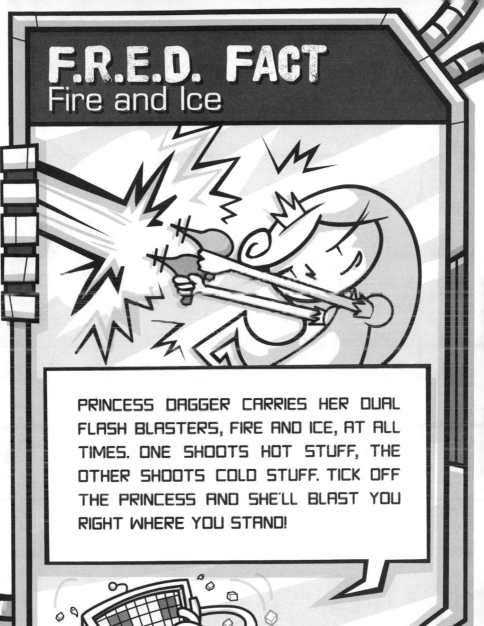

PRINCESS DAGGER CARRIES HER DUAL FLASH BLASTERS, FIRE AND ICE, AT ALL TIMES. ONE SHOOTS HOT STUFF, THE OTHER SHOOTS COLD STUFF. TICK OFF THE PRINCESS AND SHE'LL BLAST YOU RIGHT WHERE YOU STAND!

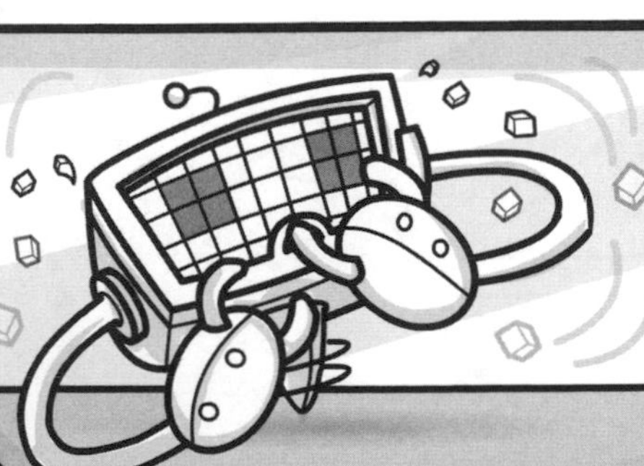

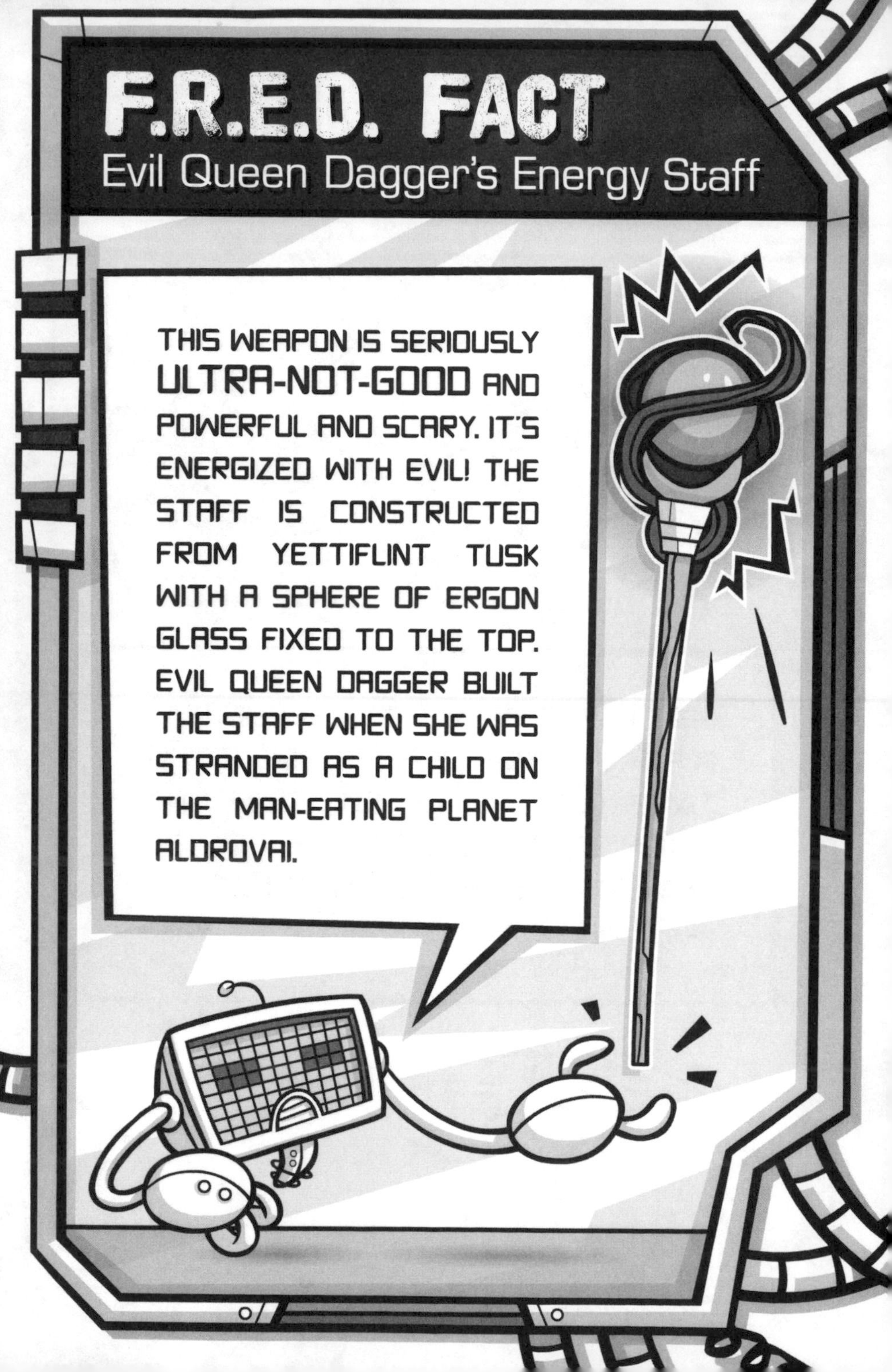
F.R.E.D. FACT
Evil Queen Dagger's Energy Staff
THIS WEAPON IS SERIOUSLY ULTRA-NOT-GOOD AND POWERFUL AND SCARY. IT'S ENERGIZED WITH EVIL! THE STAFF IS CONSTRUCTED FROM YETTIFLINT TUSK WITH A SPHERE OF ERGON GLASS FIXED TO THE TOP. EVIL QUEEN DAGGER BUILT THE STAFF WHEN SHE WAS STRANDED AS A CHILD ON THE MAN-EATING PLANET ALDROVAI.

F.R.E.D. FACT

Biggun

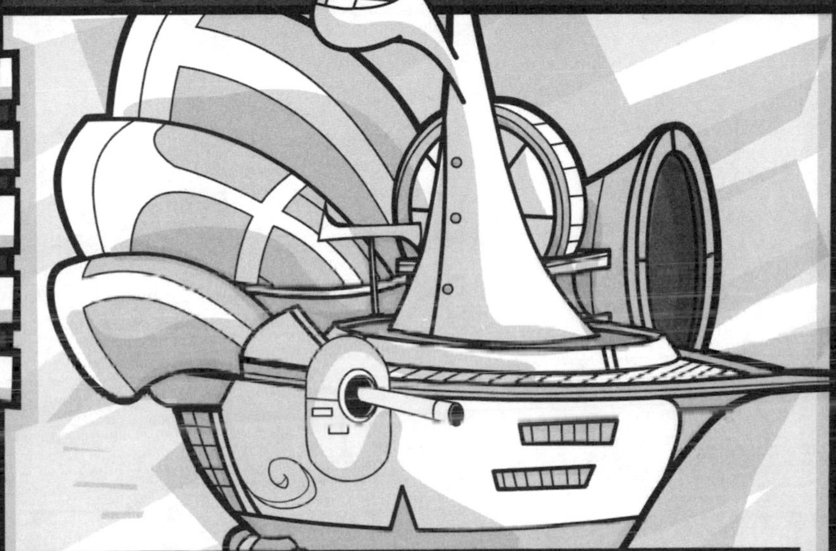

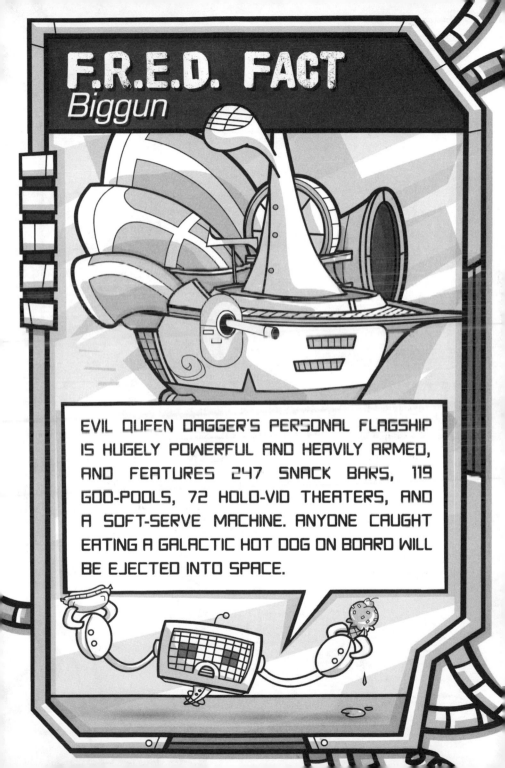

EVIL QUEEN DAGGER'S PERSONAL FLAGSHIP IS HUGELY POWERFUL AND HEAVILY ARMED, AND FEATURES 247 SNACK BARS, 119 GOO-POOLS, 72 HOLO-VID THEATERS, AND A SOFT-SERVE MACHINE. ANYONE CAUGHT EATING A GALACTIC HOT DOG ON BOARD WILL BE EJECTED INTO SPACE.

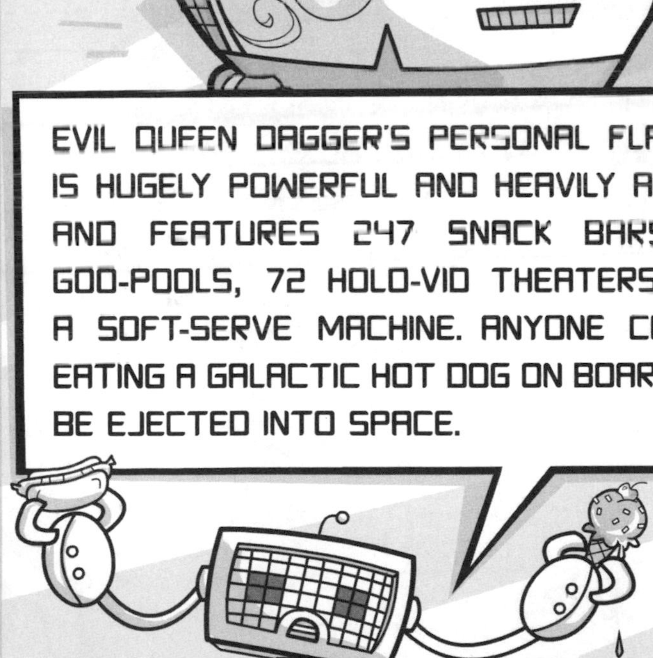

F.R.E.D. FACT
The Hefter

GENERAL KRAX VON GRUMBLE'S PERSONAL STARSHIP IS BULKY AND BOXY AND CLUMSY, JUST LIKE KRAX! IT'S CONSTRUCTED FROM JUNK FOUND ON KRAX'S HOME PLANET, AND THE INTERIOR IS DECORATED WITH PHOTOS OF KRAX POSING WITH GALACTIC CELEBRITIES. SERIOUSLY, HE'S SO VAIN!

F.R.E.D. FACT
Grumble's Rumblers

KRAX'S ROBOT MINIONS ARE BUILT FROM VARIOUS BITS OF TRASH AND SCRAP METAL, USING KRAX'S PATENTED JUNK-ROBO-ASSEMBLETRON 99. NO TWO RUMBLERS ARE THE SAME: SOME HAVE RUSTED DRILL-BIT HANDS, OTHERS HAVE TOASTER OVEN HEADS, AND SOME HAVE SODA CAN INTESTINES.

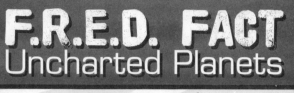

F.R.E.D. FACT
Uncharted Planets

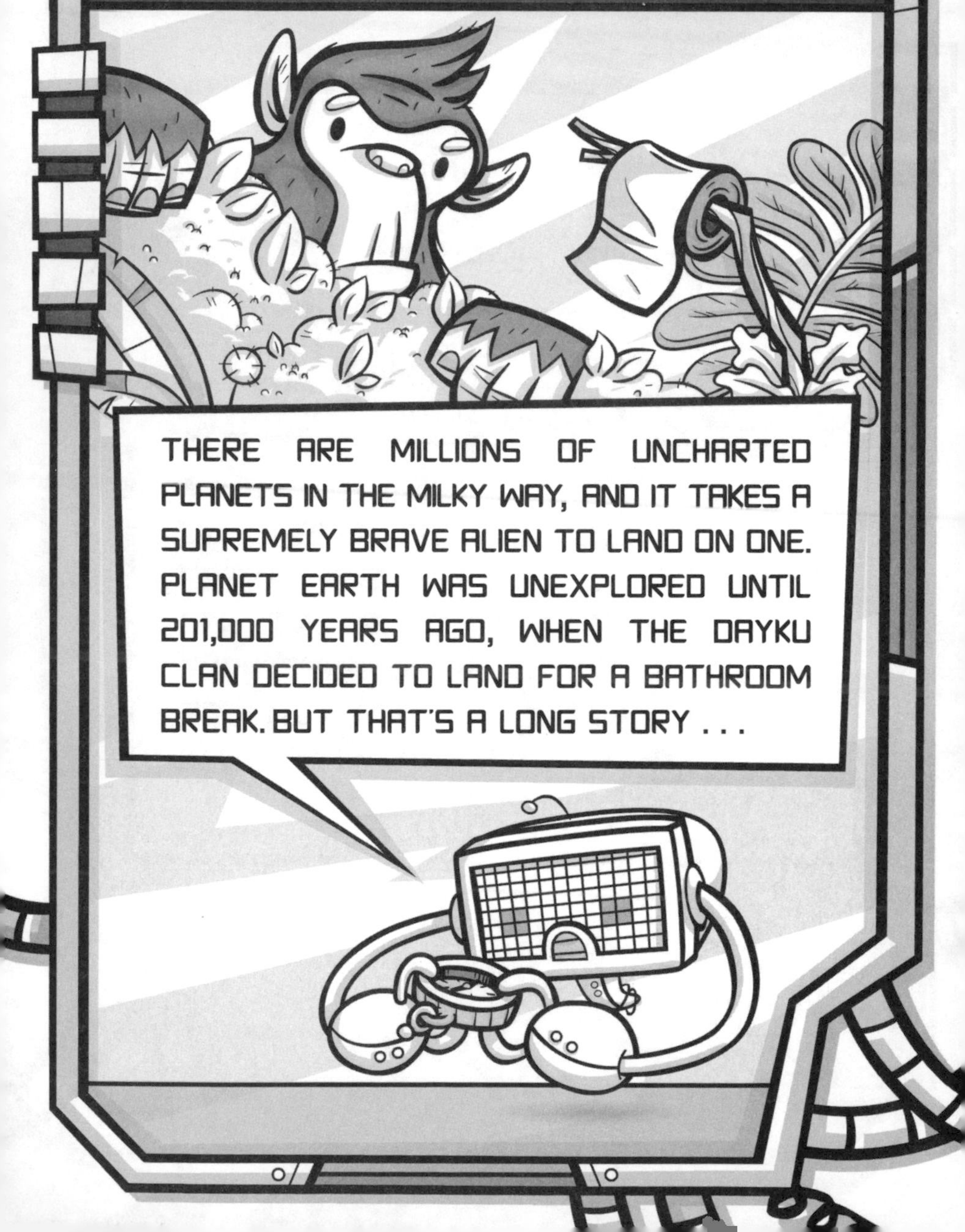
THERE ARE MILLIONS OF UNCHARTED PLANETS IN THE MILKY WAY, AND IT TAKES A SUPREMELY BRAVE ALIEN TO LAND ON ONE. PLANET EARTH WAS UNEXPLORED UNTIL 201,000 YEARS AGO, WHEN THE DAYKU CLAN DECIDED TO LAND FOR A BATHROOM BREAK. BUT THAT'S A LONG STORY . . .

F.R.E.D. FACT
Space Pirates

SPACE PIRATES CRUISE THE COSMOS, DOING ONE THING: STEALING! THEY COMMANDEER CRUISERS, THEY HIJACK HOTEL SHIPS, AND THEY RAID ROYAL ROTOR-SAILS. COSMOE MET HUMPHREE WHILE THE BIG GUY WAS FIRST MATE ON THE PIRATE SHIP *THE LOOTING STAR*—BUT THAT'S A STORY FOR ANOTHER TIME . . .

Acknowledgments

Rachel Maguire and Nichole Kelley for taking my goofy words and bringing them to life—I've never known anyone who worked harder, faster, longer, or better. Jeff "The Falcon" Faulconer for everything, big and small. Stephen Connolly and everyone at FunBrain for believing this thing could ever be an actual THING. Dan Lazar x100, Torie Doherty-Munro, Cecilia de la Campa and the entire Writers House crew for always pressing, never stressing. Liesa Abrams, basically the Bruce Wayne of book editors. Dan Potash, the man with the magic eyeballs (just made that up, but I like it!). Katherine Devendorf, Julie Doebler, Mara Anastas, Mary Marotta, Lucille Rettino, Christina Pecorale, Jennifer Romanello, Jodie Hockensmith, Michelle Leo, Carolyn Swerdloff, Emma Sector, Jon Anderson, and everyone else at Simon & Schuster for their constant confidence and enthusiasm. Bob Holmes, for his insight and guidance. Ruby, for never being helpful, not even once. Mom and Dad, for always being helpful, every time. And all my friends who chimed in with thoughts and opinions and high fives—THANK YOU!
—M. B.

The art for this illustrated novel came to exist on the shoulders of the following: Nichole Kelley, Jon Lay, Jeff Faulconer, Max Brallier, Becky my cat, the entire Maguire clan (Jess, Janet, Richard, Richie, Kelsey, Hannah, Grace), Karl Strange, Cara Finnegan, Jess Brallier, Paul Chapman, Shelli Paroline Lamb, Braden Lamb, Jeff Lay, Michael Jordan (the graphic designer, not the professional athlete), Rich Day, Dan Potash, Liesa Abrams, the folks at Simon & Schuster, and the folks at Pearson.

—R. M.

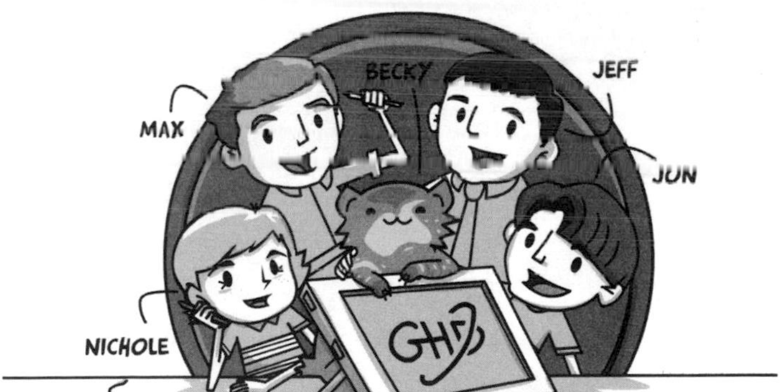
BECKY
JEFF
MAX
JON
NICHOLE

About the Author

Max Brallier is the author of more than twenty books for children and adults. He lives in New York City with his wife, Alyse, where he spends his time chasing fortune, glory, and the perfect hot dog.

About the Illustrator

In a realm south of Boston lives a humble artist armed with a whimsical drawing style and a Wacom pen. Companioned with a pirate cat and minstrel husband, she ambushes adventure, defeats daily obstructions, and quests for the unfolding unknown.